FLEETWOOD

FLEETWOOD:

OR, THE NEW MAN OF FEELING

William Godwin

edited by Gary Handwerk
& A. A. Markley

broadview literary texts

Canadian Cataloguing in Publication Data

Godwin, William, 1756-1836
    Fleetwood, or, The new man of feeling

(Broadview literary texts)
Includes bibliographical references.
ISBN 1-55111-232-9

I. Handwerk, Gary J., 1954- . II. Markley, A.A. (Arnold Albert), 1964- . III. Title. IV. Series.

PR4722.F5 2000   823'.6   C00-932113-6

Broadview Press Ltd., is an independent, international publishing house, incorporated in 1985.

North America:
P.O. Box 1243, Peterborough, Ontario, Canada K9J 7H5
3576 California Road, Orchard Park, NY 14127
TEL: (705) 743-8990; FAX: (705) 743-8353;
E-MAIL: customerservice@broadviewpress.com

United Kingdom:
Turpin Distribution Services Ltd.,
Blackhorse Rd., Letchworth, Hertfordshire SG6 1HN
TEL: (1462) 672555; FAX (1462) 480947; E-MAIL: turpin@rsc.org

Australia:
St. Clair Press, P.O. Box 287, Rozelle, NSW 2039
TEL: (02) 818-1942; FAX: (02) 418-1923

www.broadviewpress.com

Broadview Press gratefully acknowledges the financial support of the Book Publishing Industry Development Program, Ministry of Canadian Heritage, Government of Canada.

Broadview Press is grateful to Professor Eugene Benson for advice on editorial matters for the Broadview Literary Texts series.

Text design and composition by George Kirkpatrick

PRINTED IN CANADA

Contents

Acknowledgments

We would like to thank Shannon Kelley for her assistance in editing the text of the novel; and George Franz and Edward Tomezsko, Penn State University, Delaware County, who provided financial support for this aspect of the project. The Pforzheimer and Berg Collections at the New York Public Library allowed us access to the manuscript of *Fleetwood*, and to letters by Godwin relating to the novel's composition. Libby Chenault and the Rare Book Collection at the University of North Carolina at Chapel Hill provided the copy of the title page from the 1805 edition of the novel. Sandy Stelts and the Rare Book Collection at Pattee Library, Penn State University, made available their copy of the 1832 edition to serve as copy text. We are grateful to Grace Roosevelt, Robbie McClintock, and Frank A. Moretti of the Institute for Learning Technologies at Teachers College, Columbia University, for permission to reprint passages from Roosevelt's translation of Rousseau's *Émile* from their online database of documents pertaining to education. Pamela Clemit generously provided her expertise and encouragement; her earlier edition of the novel was of considerable use to us in preparing this edition. We would also like to thank David McCracken, Susan Ware, Sara Whildin, Jean Sphar, Jane Quinn, Jeanne Moskal, Lucy Morrison, and Brian J. Meyer.

Introduction

For William Godwin, the widely known author of *Political Justice* and *Caleb Williams*, the publication of *Fleetwood: or, The New Man of Feeling* in 1805 marked a new experiment in fiction. Six years after his previous novel, *St. Leon* (1799), Godwin returned to fiction and produced a work whose concerns typify the transition under way between Enlightenment and Romanticism, a novel that offers a probing view of British intellectual and social life in the immediately post-revolutionary period. In its shift away from the explicitly public and political concerns of the 1790s, and in its emphasis on the development of an individual mind, *Fleetwood* represents a significant stage both in the evolution of Godwin's personal philosophy and in the development of British fiction generally. The novel shows Godwin – who rose to fame as the reputed apostle of pure rationalism – increasingly recognizing that the perfectibility of human beings and of social institutions would depend not merely on a revolution of reason, but on a revaluation of imagination and emotion that would acknowledge their centrality in the development of the human mind. Very much like a case history in its probing of the psyche of a quite ordinary individual, *Fleetwood* embodies the analytical acuity of all of Godwin's later novels, novels that would make a profound contribution to the development of psychological realism in English fiction.

In developing the character of Casimir Fleetwood, Godwin drew on the popular contemporary genre of the novel of sensibility, celebrating the virtues of the intensely emotional heroes of such fiction, while critiquing their excesses. He joined the debate that the writings of Jean-Jacques Rousseau had engendered among British thinkers and writers such as William Wordsworth and Samuel Taylor Coleridge – writers concerned with exploring the influence of the natural world on human perception and behavior, and the degree to which that influence was to be considered beneficial. As he had in other writings in the years immediately preceding the composition of

Fleetwood, Godwin took up and critically responded to Rousseau's highly influential arguments concerning the uses of education for fostering the kind of sensibility and communal identification that Rousseau saw as essential both for the family and for political order.[1] At the same time, *Fleetwood* retains the spirit of social critique evident in Godwin's earlier radical fiction. It is perhaps the first British novel to expose the social injustices that occurred in the factory system during the initial stages of the Industrial Revolution, and thus helps prepare the way for the novels of social realism that predominated in Victorian fiction.

Political Philosophy, Personal Life: Godwin in the 1790s

It was during the 1790s, as the British people struggled to come to terms with the French Revolution and its implications for Britain, that William Godwin achieved widespread public fame as a political philosopher and novelist. His *Enquiry Concerning Political Justice and its Influence on General Virtue and Happiness*, published in February 1793, made him one of the most prominent voices in the debates that had flared up around such works as Edmund Burke's conservative *Reflections on the Revolution in France* (1790) and Thomas Paine's radical liberal statements in *Rights of Man* (1791, 1792). Despite its daunting size and cost, *Political Justice* went through three editions within five years and circulated even more widely in pamphlet and journal formats. Scores of radical thinkers who believed that the French Revolution offered Britain a model for political reform quoted Godwin's ideas at length, and Godwin himself intervened powerfully in ongoing political events such as the sedition trials in which radicals were put on trial for speaking out against the British government.

In *Political Justice*, Godwin combines many of the accepted principles of Enlightenment rationalism with his own distinctive utopian anarchism. At the core of the work lay a funda-

---

1   See, for example, his essays in *The Enquirer, Reflections on Education, Manners and Literature* (1797), and his *Memoirs of the Author of A Vindication of the Rights of Woman* (1798).

mentally deterministic principle – the belief shared by Lockean empiricists and the French materialist *philosophes* that the actions of human beings are caused by circumstances and events, and not by their innate dispositions. In Godwin's hands, this premise became the basis for a reformist and optimistic political agenda. Godwin argued that human circumstances are in some sense arbitrary and therefore variable, so that human beings are entirely susceptible to change and improvement. He strongly emphasized the foreseeable perfectibility of all individuals, both as ends in themselves and as a step toward the perfectibility of human society at large. Influenced by his strong background as a Dissenter, he felt that this improvement was to be achieved primarily by developing our capacity for rational judgment, which could guide our decision-making and instill in us a readiness to sacrifice self-interest to the impersonal dictates of reason.

Hoping to reach a wider audience for the arguments of *Political Justice*, Godwin followed the publication of his acclaimed political treatise with an experiment in fiction, the novel *Caleb Williams*. Along with a number of his fellow middle-class radicals, Godwin believed that fiction could be used effectively to expose social injustices and to hasten political reform. The political agenda of these writers caused them to be attacked as "Jacobin" writers, "Jacobin" being a term that British conservatives used to describe activities they wished to discredit by associating them with the most radical strand of French revolutionary politics. Godwin's *Things As They Are; or the Adventures of Caleb Williams* (1794) was destined to become the most successful and influential Jacobin narrative. It is a tale of "domestic despotism," where Godwin's first-person narrator recounts how his life has been destroyed by the capricious and tyrannical power that a former employer has over his reputation. The son of a farmer, Caleb takes employment as secretary to the wealthy squire, Ferdinando Falkland. Hearing the story of Falkland's troubled relationship with a tyrannical neighbor who had been mysteriously murdered years earlier, Caleb becomes determined to discover whether Falkland was the murderer. When Falkland suspects that Caleb has in fact uncovered his secret, he confesses his guilt, but then uses all the advantages of his aristocratic position to destroy Caleb's credibility – charging Caleb as a thief, and then having him discredited, thrown into jail, and harassed everywhere he tries to settle. Godwin demonstrates how easily Falkland can use the advantages of "things as they are" to silence Caleb's pleas for justice and crush his desire simply to be left alone, despite Caleb's innocence.

Already with this first novel, Godwin's move into fiction showed him making significant changes in the pure rationalism of his early political philosophy. As Godwin applied his theories to particular human lives, he came to acknowledge more fully the dependence of rational judgment upon other aspects of the human mind, such as emotion. Recognizing how hard it is for any individual to attain rational detachment, Godwin found himself needing to moderate his earlier emphasis on the singular importance of rational reflection in the improvement of individuals and society. In the revisions he made to *Political Justice* for its 1796 and 1798 editions and in his next novel, *St. Leon: A Tale of the Sixteenth Century* (1799), Godwin showed his increasing appreciation for the inevitable – and not wholly undesirable – impact that human feelings and relationships have upon our choices and our destinies.

Fleetwood is also testimony to the importance of biographical experience for intellectual transformation. It is a novel about human relationships that was itself deeply shaped by Godwin's own tumultuous personal life during the late 1790s and early 1800s. Particular people and incidents in Godwin's life during these years are reflected in the text of *Fleetwood*, none more important than Godwin's association with Mary Wollstonecraft. In early 1796, Godwin had renewed his acquaintance with this prominent feminist and social philosopher, and by the summer of that same year they had become lovers. Both Godwin and Wollstonecraft had a deep philosophical commitment to individual autonomy and their unusual relationship reflected these beliefs. They maintained separate households and social circles, and reserved a significant portion of every day for their independent literary endeavors. Yet once it became clear that Wollstonecraft was pregnant, the two decided to marry to spare their future child the stigma of an illegitimate birth. After they married in March, 1797, Godwin and Wollstonecraft were shocked to find themselves scorned and ostracized by some of their former friends and acquaintances. Both followers and critics of Godwin's political philosophy mocked him for marrying in spite of his professed belief in the destructiveness of marriage as a social institution. But Wollstonecraft's error was, by the social norms of the era, even more scandalous. While living in France in the early 1790s Wollstonecraft had identified herself as the wife of her American lover Gilbert Imlay in order to avoid imprisonment as a British citizen. Her marriage to Godwin made it clear that she had never actually been "Mrs. Imlay," despite the fact that she had publicly identified herself in this way and had given birth to a daughter by Imlay.

Wollstonecraft gave birth to her second daughter, the future Mary Wollstonecraft Shelley, in August of 1797, but died from complications of childbirth ten days later. Her death affected Godwin deeply, yet her loss intensified the powerfully transformative effect that her ideas and his personal relation with her had upon Godwin's vision of humanity and society. In the hope of memorializing her achievements, Godwin immediately set to work on gathering Wollstonecraft's *Posthumous Works* and on writing her biography, *Memoirs of the Author of a Vindication of the Rights of Woman*, both of which were published in January 1798.[1] Once again, he found himself the victim of public defamation, concentrated by his political enemies, but arising among some of his friends as well. Many objected to Godwin's decision to publish Wollstonecraft's letters to her former lover, Gilbert Imlay, among her *Posthumous Works*. They criticized Godwin's frank treatment of this relationship in his *Memoirs*, as well as his candid references to Wollstonecraft's attempts at suicide, and his unapologetic representation of his atheistic religious views in neglecting to summon a member of the clergy to Wollstonecraft's deathbed. Indeed, his reputation

---

1 A second, revised version of the *Memoirs* appeared in August 1798.

was so compromised that when he decided to try his hand at writing children's books in the early years of the nineteenth century, he felt obliged to do so under pseudonyms.

From working on the memoirs of Wollstonecraft, Godwin returned to his own fictional activity with the composition of *St. Leon* in 1798. For his second novel, Godwin chose a historical setting that would allow him to present political critique in a more indirect and allegorical way, thus continuing to engage in social criticism at a time when government repression was making such activities ever more dangerous. Yet his choice of fictional mode differed sharply from the realism of *Caleb Williams* and shows the impact of quite different literary influences upon his work, most notably the tales of the supernatural and the fantastic that were playing a seminal role in the emergence of Romantic literature. Godwin's narrative strategies in this novel show clear similarities to William Wordsworth's and Samuel Taylor Coleridge's *Lyrical Ballads* (1798), for instance, where poems such as Coleridge's "The Rime of the Ancient Mariner" sought to intensify their readers' reactions to poetic tales by depicting the most heightened emotions and by deploying supernatural elements.

In *St. Leon* Godwin began to use his fiction as a testing ground for familiar eighteenth-century Enlightenment principles in light of the new values of the emerging Romantic movement, a project he would continue in *Fleetwood*. One can productively read *St. Leon* as a political allegory of how established power can turn popular sentiment against the reformist projects of Enlightenment philosophy. But *St. Leon* is also a novel that concentrates a good deal more than *Caleb Williams* had upon domestic relationships and the importance of affective ties. Godwin's Reginald de St. Leon is a sixteenth-century French nobleman who becomes obsessed with two extraordinary gifts that he is given by a mysterious stranger: the philosopher's stone, which provides him with unbounded wealth, and the elixir of life, which renders him immortal. Obsessed by the potential power that these gifts offer him, St. Leon remains oblivious until far too late to their destructive impact upon his social and personal relations. Despite sharing certain traits with

Caleb, such as excessive curiosity, St. Leon is a far more sensitive and emotional character, a kindred figure to the "man of feeling" so prominent in the novels of sensibility that were enormously popular during this era. *St. Leon* is a striking portrait of a man caught between reason and feeling, between altruistic reformist impulses and personal ambition, between social duty and familial affection, indeed, between all that Enlightenment and Romanticism can be taken to represent. His tragedy arises from his own failure to recognize how these sides of himself fit together, for he proves unable to decipher the interplay of emotion and reason that motivates his own decisions, and consequently he fails to make productive use of the empathy he so deeply feels with his family and his fellow human beings.

Like *Fleetwood*, *St. Leon* testifies to the influence of Mary Wollstonecraft upon Godwin's thinking. Godwin paints a poignant image of Wollstonecraft in St. Leon's wise and saintly wife Marguerite, and many of Wollstonecraft's thoughts on the education of children are incorporated into the fabric of the novel. The measure of St. Leon's flaws as a human being can be seen in his incapacity to recognize and sufficiently value the domestic values that Marguerite embodies, or to see how they can be translated into politically effective terms.

Despite this burst of activity, Godwin remained deeply unsettled by the radical transformation of his life within a single year. Married at a fairly advanced age and then quickly widowed, he was now a single man once again, but with a household that included his own infant daughter, Mary, and Wollstonecraft's daughter, Fanny Imlay. In 1801, he married a neighbor, Mary Jane Clairmont, and the new Mrs. Godwin brought two more children, Charles and Jane ("Claire") Clairmont, into Godwin's home, and two years later gave birth to Godwin's son, William Godwin, Jr. Though several of Godwin's friends found Mary Jane Clairmont an unworthy successor to Godwin's first wife, the marriage was rooted in considerable mutual affection and lasted for more than thirty years. Mary Jane Godwin not only stabilized her husband's household, but proved to be a shrewd business partner in the effort that would occupy them (with uneven financial success) for a number of years, the "Juvenile Library" publishing house.

These changes in Godwin's personal life had a profound influence on his writings, and a reader familiar with the details of his life will find particular incidents often echoed in *Fleetwood*. The story that Godwin provides of Mrs. Macneil's past, her unfortunate early alliance, her abandonment, and her ensuing ostracism by British society, draws a good deal from Mary Wollstonecraft's experiences. Godwin drew freely from other lives around him as well, basing Mrs. Kenrick, the mother of Fleetwood's two nephews, on his friend and fellow writer, Mary Robinson, a woman who was also notorious for her personal history.[1] The romance between the young Kenrick and Louisa Scarborough may have been influenced by that between Godwin's pupil John Arnot and a servant in his household, Louisa Jones. Godwin's composition of *Fleetwood* shows how useful he found the lives around him to be for enriching his fiction, but its publication provided a reminder of the dangers of this process as well. One of Godwin's close friends, Thomas Holcroft, saw the figure of Mr. Scarborough as a critical portrait of himself and, in particular, of his troubled relationship with his own son, who died by suicide in 1789. Upon reading the novel, Holcroft wrote Godwin to announce that he considered their friendship at an end; and, despite Godwin's denial of having drawn material from Holcroft's life, the two friends were not to communicate again until shortly before Holcroft's death in 1809.[2]

The New Man of Feeling

By the last few years of the eighteenth century, the radicalism of the early 1790s had waned and a conservative backlash had grown increasingly powerful. The excesses of the Reign of

---

1 See Robert D. Bass, *The Green Dragoon: The Lives of Banastre Tarleton and Mary Robinson* (New York: Henry Holt, 1957) 397-98.

2 See Gary Kelly, *The English Jacobin Novel: 1780-1805* (Oxford, 1976) 259, and Peter Marshall, *William Godwin* (Yale, 1984) 260.

Terror in revolutionary France shocked many Britons, even those who had earlier praised the French for throwing off the burden of the *ancien régime*. The government proved largely successful in silencing for a time the voices of Jacobin dissent throughout Great Britain, and most of the radical groups that had worked for reform, such as the London Corresponding Society, had been forced to disband. A surge of nationalist patriotism became even more pronounced as war between France and the more conservative European political powers continued.

Influenced by these political events, but also by explicit criticisms of *Political Justice* and by the dramatic changes in his personal life, Godwin continued throughout these years to rethink his political philosophy in significant ways. The second and third editions of *Political Justice* (1796 and 1798) showed extensive revision of both its language and its ideas. While there is continued debate about the extent and meaning of these changes, it is clear that the failure of political reform led Godwin to revise, but not to renounce, his commitment to political anarchism.[1] In addition, his continued reflections on human psychology led him to give increasing weight to the power of sympathy and the role of feeling in shaping and sustaining our rational judgments. Even while working on these revisions, however, Godwin broadened his philosophical agenda into a number of new areas in a 1797 work entitled *The Enquirer, Reflections on Education, Manners and Literature*. Here Godwin took up in a series of essays a variety of practical philosophical issues, gauging the effects that particular social arrangements have upon the development of character. The essays in *The Enquirer* indicate Godwin's continuing interest in developmental psychology and his growing concern with the state of education in England. They acutely analyze, for instance, the role that literature can play in moral education. While the reception of *Political Justice* had been deeply divided along partisan political

---

1   The best overview of these debates is in Mark Philp's *Godwin's Political Justice* (Ithaca: Cornell UP, 1986), which argues persuasively that Godwin's fundamental beliefs in the primacy of individual judgment, the logic of human perfectibility, and the virtues of anarchism remain unchanged across the three editions of *Political Justice*.

lines, *The Enquirer* won much more uniform praise from critics, to Godwin's considerable pleasure.

At the same time, the conservative backlash meant that Godwin found himself the frequent target of satirical attacks in novels and in verse, and in scores of political lectures, sermons, and pamphlets.[1] In 1798, Thomas Malthus attacked Godwin's views on the accumulation and distribution of wealth in his influential *Essay on the Principle of Population*, which argued that the human population will perpetually tend to outstrip available resources. In 1800, Dr. Samuel Parr, a former friend of Godwin's, dedicated his annual *Spital Sermon* to a venomous attack on his general philosophical beliefs. Though Godwin had long kept silent in the face of such attacks, he decided the time had come to defend himself. Godwin used his *Thoughts Occasioned by the Perusal of Dr. Parr's Spital Sermon* (1801) to clarify aspects of his philosophy that had been misunderstood and distorted by his opponents.

Godwin's thinking and his writings continued to be controversial, yet his commitment to writing and to political reform was shaken neither by controversy nor criticism. He began close friendships with Samuel Taylor Coleridge and Charles Lamb, young Romantic writers who brought him the same sort of intellectual stimulation that he had earlier experienced as part of Jacobin circles. He continued to pursue his goal of attaining a wider public audience for his views as well, now turning to the medium of drama as the most promising outlet for his energies. Inspired in this endeavor by the success his fellow Jacobin novelists Elizabeth Inchbald and Thomas Holcroft had enjoyed as dramatists, Godwin spent several years working on his first tragedy, *Antonio; or, The Soldier's Return*. But the play's debut in December 1800 proved to be a complete disaster. Although he continued for a time to pursue several other ideas for dramatic works, he eventually concluded that his talents were not suited to the theater and he cast about for other outlets. He commenced work on his autobiography, but turned aside from that to devote himself to writing a biography of

---

1   See Peter Marshall, *William Godwin*, 211ff.

Geoffrey Chaucer, embarking upon a colossal program of historical research that led to the publication of his multi-volume *Life of Chaucer* in 1803. While ostensibly a biography, it includes detailed discussions of nearly every aspect of fourteenth-century English life and culture about which Godwin could uncover information, and indicates an important stage in Godwin's development as a writer. What began as a focused account of the development of the mind and sensibility of a single individual opens out into a widely ranging survey of British social history, where the role of the imagination and the power of literature and its depiction of emotions upon the general culture are given significant weight.[1]

Early in 1804, Godwin's interest in the emotional underpinnings of human thought and behavior led him back to the novel, and he began work on *Fleetwood*. As he explains in the Preface to the novel, Godwin wished in this new endeavor, "not to repeat myself," and thus chose to focus not on the uncommon events of *Caleb Williams* or the miraculous occurrences in *St. Leon*, but rather to tell a tale of events, "as for the most part have occurred to at least one half of the Englishmen now existing, who are of the same rank of life as my hero." As the subtitle of *Fleetwood* indicates, this time Godwin would focus specifically on the issue of sensibility and on the effects of this particular mode of feeling upon human relationships.

The novel of sensibility, or sentiment, was one of the most popular categories of fiction in the mid- to late-eighteenth century. By blending tales of the most affecting characters and incidents with highly moral outcomes and reflections, these novels succeeded in capturing their readers' interests while deflecting prevalent charges about the immorality of the fictional form. The form had its origins in such widely read epistolary novels as Samuel Richardson's *Pamela* (1740), *Clarissa* (1747-48), and *Sir Charles Grandison* (1753-54), all of which traced the power of sentiment to traverse the boundaries of class and gender. Johann Wolfgang von Goethe's *The Sorrows of Young Werther* (1774) and Rousseau's *Julie, ou La Nouvelle Héloïse*

---

1   See Marshall, *William Godwin*, 256ff.

(1761) were two of the most sensational publishing successes of the century, were both read widely throughout Europe and even led some readers to style their lives after the central characters in these texts. Rousseau's novel was of particular interest to Godwin for the manner in which it wove philosophical ideas into the story of the passionate love shared by the tutor St. Preux and his student Julie. Remarkably, their relationship persists even after Julie's arranged marriage to Baron Wolmar, as the three figures share a common life on the baron's estate.

In its supreme valuation of the emotional state of the individual character, the novel of sensibility was often identified with the liberal individualism of revolutionary politics. Nevertheless, few sentimental novelists other than Rousseau seem to have been dedicated to the idea of attacking social institutions, despite their emphasis on personal feeling over reason, and despite their exploration of the ways in which the free impulses of the individual mind are constrained by social institutions and conventions. The sentimental novel rarely challenges the status quo, and in most cases seems to have contributed to reinscribing social conventions rather than to challenging them.[1] Like Rousseau, however, Godwin recognized the latent potential of the genre for social criticism.

The novel of sensibility is perhaps best typified by Henry Mackenzie's extremely popular and frequently reprinted *The Man of Feeling* (1771), which the subtitle of *Fleetwood* directly evokes. Mackenzie presents his protagonist, Harley, in a variety of situations that illustrate his highly sensitive personality and the facility with which he can be moved to despondency and gushing tears. Harley is a simple and naïve young man who is distracted from his quest to establish a secure income of his own by a stream of needy characters whose lives he feels impelled to improve. Like Richardson's Pamela and Clarissa, whose heroic virtues defy pursuit by corrupt aristocrats, Mackenzie's noble (if ineffectual) Harley taught readers that

---

1   See G.A. Starr, "Sentimental Novels of the Later Eighteenth Century," *The Columbia History of the British Novel*. Ed. John Richetti (New York: Columbia UP, 1994) 191–93.

high sensibility provided one of the most secure foundations for moral excellence.

Among these novels of sentiment, Henry Mackenzie's *Julia de Roubigné* (1777) had the most clearly visible impact upon Godwin's *Fleetwood*. This novel was a quite explicit reworking of Rousseau's *La Nouvelle Héloïse*, centered on a love triangle much like that in Rousseau's 1761 text. The young Julia de Roubigné has loved her childhood companion Savillon all of her life, but she chooses to marry her father's friend Montauban when financial disaster makes it impossible for her father to continue to support himself or his family. Like Godwin's Fleetwood, Montauban begins to suspect his wife of an adulterous affair with her former companion. Godwin borrowed specific details from Mackenzie to depict his protagonist's growing distrust of his wife, such as Fleetwood's discovery of a miniature portrait of her putative lover among her possessions, which confirms for him his wife's infidelity.

Godwin's Casimir Fleetwood is, however, not just another version of the man of feeling, but – in a way typical of Godwin's fiction – an attempt to reflect critically upon the prevalent social assumptions that could lead to the creation and widespread popularity of such a figure. Godwin deepens the novel of sensibility in a number of ways, tracing the roots of such sensibility to his character's upbringing (in ways that anticipate the nineteenth-century novel of education, or *Bildungsroman*) and anatomizing the contours of sensibility in ways that refute its automatic alignment with virtuous behavior. Godwin thus participates in the important shift in which eighteenth-century sensibility became a constituent element in what would come to be called Romantic literature. Sparked by poets such as Wordsworth, Coleridge, Mary Robinson, Charlotte Smith, and Felicia Hemans, Romantic writers insisted upon the important role that nature played in nurturing human feeling, retaining sensibility's claim that feeling laid an essential foundation for ethical and social virture. Thus, Fleetwood begins his account of his life by describing the deep impressions he received from growing up in the wilds of Merionethshire, in Wales. His awareness of nature as a formative influence parallels the scenes from rural and ordinary life that constitute most of the background for Wordsworth's and Coleridge's *Lyrical Ballads*, the text frequently acknowledged as inaugurating British Romanticism. Like those Romantic writers, however, Godwin also showed a much deeper sensitivity to the complexity and ungovernability of feeling than was typical among his eighteenth-century predecessors.

Gary Kelly, for instance, has compared Fleetwood's personality to that of the speaker of Wordsworth's "Lines left upon a Seat in a Yew-tree."[1] That poem describes a man of unusual gifts, bred amid nature, whose pure spirit is crushed by the jealousy, hatred and neglect that he encounters in the world. Nature instills in the young Fleetwood a similar promise of heroic virtue, visible, for instance, in the episode where he saves a peasant from drowning. Yet his solitary upbringing in nature breeds in him a deeply egotistical streak as well, so that it is, from Godwin's perspective, entirely plausible that he should grow up to be a brooding misanthrope, deeply disappointed in all of his experiences within human communities by their failure to measure up to the moral sublimity of nature. Like Wordsworth's melancholic, Fleetwood neglects to master his sensibility and its errant influence upon his judgments until far too late. His failure to understand his own character, to appreciate the limits of his natural education, and to temper his high sensibility lead directly to the tragedies in his family life.

As *Fleetwood* makes clear, Godwin rejects the naïve confidence in nature as sole support of a virtuous education into which some of Wordsworth's poems, for instance, sometimes seem to lapse. For Godwin, true education cannot occur outside of community or apart from social relationships. To Wordsworth's expostulation, "quit your books," Godwin answers in the voice of Fleetwood's Swiss friend, Ruffigny. Like Wordsworth, Ruffigny extols the value of a life lived amid nature, but he immediately proclaims, "Let no man despise the oracle of books! ... Without books I should not understand the volume of nature" (p. 122). Ruffigny suggests that the voice of

---

1 Gary Kelly, *The English Jacobin Novel*, 241-42.

society represented in books must be seen as an essential commentary upon the text of nature, irreplaceable to us if we are to read its lessons rightly.

Godwin's next novel, *Mandeville* (1817), takes this critique even further. There, Godwin focuses on a character whose psyche proves unable to find in nature or society sufficient solace for a deeply traumatic childhood experience (he witnesses the brutality of the seventeenth-century religious wars in Ireland). Mandeville's increasing dementia makes him less and less able to function in the world; his intensity of feeling serves only to plague him and all around him. All of Godwin's later novels continued to explore the intricacies of human psychology, while offering a less explicit political agenda than Jacobin fiction seemed to provide. Yet one could as readily argue that Godwin's concerns remained much the same, and that *Fleetwood*, like all of his later texts, sought to explore ideology at its deepest levels, reflecting upon the complex ways in which socio-cultural factors – religion, politics, gender and class – become embedded within the psychic fabric of the individual mind and life.

The Influence of Rousseau

Although *Fleetwood*, like all of Godwin's novels, blends together a large number of influences, the figure that hovers most powerfully over this particular text is that of Jean-Jacques Rousseau (1712-78). As philosopher, novelist, and critic, Rousseau exerted an enormous influence upon contemporary European thought. Although he was a contemporary and even intermittently an associate of the French Enlightenment *philosophes*, such as Denis Diderot, Rousseau was much more a figure of the era to come. His work anticipated and in a significant degree helped to bring out about both the French Revolution and Romanticism. By the end of the eighteenth century, his life had become a legend, his gravesite a destination for devoted followers who wished to do honor to his name and his ideas.

Rousseau was a figure of particular interest to Godwin, and Godwin's active and ongoing struggle with and critique of

Rousseau's philosophy can be traced through all of his major works of the mid-1790s and early 1800s, as readily in *The Enquirer* and in his *Memoirs* of Wollstonecraft as in *Fleetwood*. For Godwin, Rousseau represented a predecessor whose work, like Godwin's own, straddled the border between Enlightenment rationalism and Romantic sensibility. In virtually every area of Godwin's intellectual activities, Rousseau was not simply a predecessor, but a rival – a political philosopher who had adopted the medium of fiction for better propagating his ideas, a theorist on education whose doctrines were among the most influential of his age. As his seminal impact upon Romanticism indicates, however, Rousseau was from the start a philosopher more wholly committed to the innate rightness of inner feeling as a guide for conduct than Godwin would ever be. Especially in his fiction, Godwin acknowledges the tremendous force of human passion, and thus also the pressing need to take it into account in our calculations of justice and virtue, but he remains deeply skeptical of its reliability as an exclusive guide for judgment. Godwin was also quite aware of Mary Wollstonecraft's scathing account in her *Vindication of the Rights of Woman* of how Rousseau's own biases against women irremediably marred his main treatise on education, *Émile* (1762).

Rousseau's work is altogether stunning in both its stylistic range and its intellectual scope, ranging from the closely reasoned arguments of texts like *The Social Contract* (1762) to the intense passion of novels like *Julie* and the meditative intensity of works like his *Rêveries of a Solitary Walker* (1782). In his fictional and autobiographical texts, he codified two fundamental dimensions of the Romantic sensibility. *Julie* displays, across its more than five hundred pages, the power of Romantic love to triumph over the social conventions that seem initially and inevitably to thwart it. The *Rêveries*, by contrast, show a Romantic sensibility battling its deep disenchantment with society and seeking instead to become attuned to generosity and tolerance by its solitary communion with nature. Yet Rousseau was also a theorist of education, extrapolating from his own relatively unstructured upbringing a pedagogical model whose main principle was that children should be left to follow their own aims and to pursue their own developmental course. He reshaped public debates about education by redefining its purposes as cultivating rather than disciplining the young mind, as nurturing its innate goodness amid nature rather than training it for social performance amid a deeply corrupt society. At the same time, Rousseau was in his political writings the foremost architect of the intellectual scaffolding for the French Revolution. He was raised by the revolutionary leaders to reverential status, his person offered as a symbol of what man could be, and his life displayed as an instance of how constrictive social and political relations could maim even the most benevolent of characters.

Fleetwood is on many levels an explicit dialogue with Rousseau, especially in the early parts that deal with the formation of Fleetwood's character. In true Rousseauvian fashion, Fleetwood is educated by nature, left free by his melancholic father largely to wander as he will and to develop his sensibility amid the wild Welsh landscape. As an adult, Fleetwood is deeply attracted by the life and ideas of Rousseau; his immediate impetus for getting to know the Macneil family, for instance, stems from the latter's reputedly close friendship with Rousseau. Macneil's brief portrait of Rousseau (p. 244) describes him as a man of "exquisite sensibility," a victim to the unfeeling and calculating nature of the social arrangements among which he was forced to live. Despite spending much of his life among "the French, that nation of egoists," Rousseau's life showed how the mind could use its sensibility for nature and for everyday life to rise above the petty rivalries of social existence.

The character of Ruffigny is quite explicitly Godwin's picture of a Rousseauvian sage, a figure whose lifestyle and moral character represent the attainable excellence of Rousseau's ideals under fortunate circumstances (and, it should be noted, when supported by a goodly measure of British business acumen). When Fleetwood visits this friend of his father's, he finds him living the modest lifestyle of an independent Swiss farmer, enjoying a tranquil and uninterrupted happiness that derives from his withdrawal into rural isolation. Ruffigny's ethical sensibility is nurtured by his innate sympathy with nature; his character absorbs the moral tenor of the sublime Swiss landscape where he was born. His liberal education in that setting had allowed him to survive and escape from his bondage as a child worker in the silk-mills of Lyon. And despite some early blows, his altruistic sensibility is reinforced by his experience of the goodness of his fellow human beings, most notably that of Fleetwood's grandfather and father, who take him in and treat him as one of their own family.

Fleetwood is himself a test case in many ways for the reliability of a liberated, Rousseauvian education amid nature. Yet he is at the same time a measure of the unresolved tension between self-reliance and sociability that exists at the heart of Rousseau's work. Fleetwood's deepest need, like that of Rousseau in his *Confessions* (1781-88), is for friendship, for the sympathy of a fellow human being in its most passionate and unintermitted intensity.

As its plot develops, *Fleetwood* more clearly becomes a critique of crucial assumptions in Rousseau's philosophical and pedagogical theories. Fleetwood's natural education fails to prepare him for life in society, for daily intercourse with individuals who do not measure up to the idealized vision he has of his father and Ruffigny. His education fosters his own egoism, his sense of his own superiority, and inclines him to an ineradicable misanthropy with a significant measure of contempt and intolerance for everyone he meets. So *Fleetwood* serves as a probing analysis of what might go wrong with such an education and thus with whether society would do well to adopt it on a wide scale.

The excesses that mark Fleetwood's adult behavior are traceable to both the substance and the method of his Rousseauvian upbringing. His father errs first in permitting arrangements that allow Fleetwood's sensibility to develop unchecked, so that his feelings are never brought under the control of reason, but routinely indulged for their own sake. He is never brought to recognize his dependence upon others or to acknowledge his inferiority to them in any respect; his relation with his tutor, for instance, serves largely to enhance his own self-esteem. He is, in short, never led to recognize that he is a social being. The consequence of this is that Fleetwood is wholly unprepared to preserve any moral balance when he finds himself in the twin pitfalls to moral sensibility – college and Paris.

The method used for Fleetwood's sentimental education is equally flawed, most visibly so in the scene on Lake Uri where Ruffigny announces to Fleetwood that his father has died. This scene is carefully crafted by Ruffigny for maximum impact, using the sublime natural setting and the tales of Swiss patriotic heroism to raise Fleetwood's own aspirations to a pitch. The news of his father's death is then meant to impress upon Fleetwood's mind his own lapse from these high ideals. This method does indeed cure Fleetwood's own tendencies toward dissipation, his active participation in the corruption of society. He relapses only once, and then briefly. But it succeeds at the price of a curious self-revulsion that manifests itself increasingly as an incorrigible misanthropy that works as the source of all of Fleetwood's tragedies. One might more precisely term this trait misogyny, for it is particularly toward women that Fleetwood directs the venom that he feels for human frailties. This aspect of Godwin's critique of Rousseau was already visible in his *Memoirs* of Wollstonecraft. There Godwin praised the value of Wollstonecraft's work and the importance of her public career – the sort of career that Rousseau's misogynistic philosophy would deny to all women. In *Fleetwood* Godwin extends this critique to the general place of women in society. Indeed *Fleetwood* is in many ways a continuation of Wollstonecraft's goal of exposing the exploitation of women in her unfinished novel *The Wrongs of Woman; Or, Maria* (1798); in effect, it is a rewriting of that novel from the unsettling perspective of the male perpetrator's mind rather than that of the female victim.

Godwin and the Institution of Marriage

What follows in the novel draws upon sources other than Rousseau – perhaps too heavily in some ways, for Godwin's love for Shakespearean plots comes through all too predictably in his deployment of *Othello* here. But the remainder of the novel also takes up a social theme that had considerable resonance in Jacobin literary circles and in Godwin's own earlier work — marriage. Godwin continued to read and to be influenced by the works of his fellow Jacobins, and one can see in *Fleetwood* some particularly striking connections to Elizabeth Inchbald's *A Simple Story* (1791). There Inchbald tells the story of the beautiful and coquettish Miss Milner, and her marriage to her dour guardian, Lord Elmwood. As a result of an adulterous affair, however, the heroine and her infant daughter Matilda are rejected by Elmwood, who refuses to see Matilda even after her mother's death. Matilda's thoughtful education at the hands of her father's chaplain is contrasted with that of her flighty mother, Inchbald's aim being to expose the importance of women's receiving what she refers to as "A Proper Education."[1]

Casimir Fleetwood's disastrous behavior as a husband and the sufferings of his wife Mary are very much like the marital tensions depicted in *A Simple Story*. Fleetwood's irrational response to his young wife Mary's desire to attend a neighborhood dance echoes a scene in Inchbald's novel in which Miss Milner and Elmwood argue over her desire to attend a masquerade. Yet while Miss Milner boldly decides to attend the function despite having been forbidden to go, Mary Fleetwood is placed in a situation in which she truly cannot win. Fleetwood becomes enraged when Mary expresses her wish to attend the party, and when she relents and chooses to stay home, he petulantly insists that she go. While Elmwood's brutal treatment of his daughter Matilda as a result of his wife's abuses clearly laid the groundwork for Fleetwood's own irresponsible and unloving behavior, Fleetwood's behavior seems from the start much less rational and consequently much more dangerous.

Thomas Holcroft's *Anna St. Ives* (1792) was equally important for Godwin as a meditation upon the contemporary meaning and purpose of the marriage bond. A beautiful aristo-

---

1   In composing *Fleetwood* Godwin was also influenced by Inchbald's 1787 play, *Such Things Are*. The manner in which Gifford encourages Kenrick to behave in particular ways that he knows Fleetwood will detest is drawn from the situation upon which Inchbald bases the comic aspects of her play.

cratic heiress, Anna St. Ives resists her own inclination to marry Frank Henley, son of her father's gardener, on the grounds that such a marriage would greatly fall short of her family's expectations. She chooses instead the rakish and dissolute Coke Clifton, presuming that she can convert him into an advocate for her reformist agenda. Holcroft's novel is far more overtly didactic than *Fleetwood*; many passages read as if they had been transferred from a treatise such as Godwin's *Political Justice*. But Clifton's distorted use of Holcroft's and Godwin's philosophical ideals in his attempt to seduce Anna shows how clearly Holcroft recognized the implicit dangers of their liberal ideas, while also believing firmly in the power of sincerity to triumph over pretense and hypocrisy.

Godwin's statements on marriage were among the ideas that most deeply infuriated his critics. His comments in *Political Justice*, though relatively brief, outraged the sensibilities of many in a society where divorce remained all but impossible for the mass of the population (see Appendix A). Godwin argued there that cohabitation was itself an evil because of the constraints it put upon the exercise of private judgment and personal behavior. In addition, the conditions under which most marriages occurred worsened the problem of incompatibility by yoking together for life two individuals whose romantic youthful inclinations could not necessarily be expected to persist. Worst of all, however, was the fact that "marriage, as now understood, is a monopoly, and the worst of monopolies" – a monopoly whose effects fell particularly heavily upon the women who were its commodities. Deprived in most instances of the power to make their own choices, women remained trapped in sexual bondage to their husbands or were tempted to transgress their marital bonds in "clandestine" and hypocritical ways, as Fleetwood's experience with the world amply confirms.

Having been scandalized by Godwin's condemnation of marriage in *Political Justice*, members of the Tory press reacted with sarcastic malice when word spread of his marriage to Mary Wollstonecraft. Conservative reviewers excoriated him for his treatment of his own marriage in his *Memoirs* of

Wollstonecraft and in *St. Leon*. Still smarting from these attacks, Godwin makes quite clear in the Preface to *Fleetwood* his confidence in the consistency of both his ideas and his behavior.

> Certain persons, who condescend to make my supposed inconsistencies the favourite object of their research, will perhaps remark with exultation on the respect expressed in this work for marriage; and exclaim, "It was not always thus!" referring to the pages in which this subject is treated in the Enquiry concerning Political Justice for the proof of their assertion. The answer to this remark is exceedingly simple. The production referred to in it, the first foundation of its author's claim to public distinction and favour, was a treatise, aiming to ascertain what new institutions in political society might be found more conducive to general happiness than those which at present prevail.... Can any thing be more distinct, than such a proposition on the one hand, and a recommendation on the other that each man for himself should supersede and trample upon the institutions of the country in which he lives?

In *Fleetwood*, the issue of marriage is a central concern, and Godwin's portrayal of the effects of a husband's bad behavior on his wife places it among important early texts that worked towards exposing the injustice that women suffered in contemporary Britain. In his sensitivity to the woman's point of view, Godwin was deeply influenced by his own relationship with Mary Wollstonecraft. He had sympathetically detailed the circumstances of her emotional relationships with other men in his account of her life in the *Memoirs*. Wollstonecraft's own *Vindication of the Rights of Woman* had sharply critiqued the institution of marriage as practiced in contemporary Britain for the insidious effects it had upon women's characters and intellects. In 1797, and with Godwin's strong support, she began work on a novel that would illustrate many of these beliefs in a fictional setting. Although she failed to complete the novel

prior to her death, *The Wrongs of Woman: Or, Maria* amply cata-
logues the mistreatment its title character suffers as the wife of
an abusive husband. Harassed by a husband who wishes to control her inheritance, Maria suffers the same injustice at the
hands of the legal system as Fleetwood's wife, Mary, does in
Godwin's novel. Fleetwood's abuse of his status and power to
legally prove his wife's alleged adultery and to arrange to
divorce her and to disinherit his child falls scarcely short of the
efforts of Maria's husband to have her imprisoned, which lead
Wollstonecraft's heroine to contemplate suicide. A cancelled
passage in the manuscript of the final chapter of *Fleetwood* indicates how closely the character of Mary Fleetwood parallels
that of Maria. Like Maria, Mary survives the trial that her husband imposes upon her only by dedicating herself to her child,
displaying an innately "feminine" empathy with her offspring
that her male counterparts seem not to possess.

> The only bond that yet held her to life was the thought
> of her child. Before he was born, she loved him. Now
> that she saw the poor helpless animal at her breast, she
> vowed that, if she could help it, he should never want a
> mother's care. For him she braved the pennyless condi-
> tion, to which I had condemned her; for him she braved
> the obloquy. In scorn of the world, which I too had
> brought upon her.[1]

This passionate concern with marriage and the status of
women was shared by other members of Jacobin circles such as
Godwin's friend and fellow novelist Mary Hays. In her highly
autobiographical *Memoirs of Emma Courtney* (1796), Hays boldly depicted the feelings of a young woman who defies convention in pursuing the man she falls in love with and in making
her powerful emotions quite clear. Hays's second novel, *The
Victim of Prejudice* (1799), follows Wollstonecraft's *The Wrongs of
Woman* (1798) in depicting the various ways in which women

---

1 The manuscript of *Fleetwood: or, The New Man of Feeling* by William Godwin, p.
   298. The manuscript is held by the Pforzheimer Collection, the New York Public
   Library.

were abused by the injustices of contemporary British society. Her narrator Mary tells of the disastrous turns that her life takes because, as the child of a fallen woman, she is dismissed and neglected by proper English society, forced to struggle to make an honest living, and left at the mercy of often unscrupulous men.

The Origins of *Fleetwood*: Other Literary Influences

Fleetwood is less overtly a political allegory than either of Godwin's previous novels, and yet its tale of domestic tyranny has obvious implications for social and political issues. It is telling in this regard that Godwin read a number of histories of Restoration England while preparing to write *Fleetwood*, a period he looked upon as generally corrupt and dissolute. Both the original title for the novel, "Lambert," and the name "Fleetwood" allude to generals who served under Oliver Cromwell, reflecting Godwin's fascination with the English Civil War, the Interregnum, and the restoration of the monarchy. As his essay "Of History and Romance" indicates, he was fascinated by the relationship between political history and individual character. For Godwin, Lambert and Fleetwood represented men who contributed towards a revolution and the establishment of a great Commonwealth in England, but who also outlived this new state only to witness a new age of vice and depravity when King Charles II was restored to the throne in 1660. In depicting Fleetwood's adventures as a young man Godwin studied such works as Marie-Catherine, comtesse d'Aulnoy's *Memoirs of the Court of England* (1707) and Anthony Hamilton's *Memoirs of the Life of the Comte de Gramont* (1713), and he was particularly influenced by Antoine-François, l'Abbé Prévost's French historical novel *The Life and Adventures of Mr. Cleveland, Natural Son of Oliver Cromwell* (1732-39), and Jean Baptiste Louvet de Couvray's *The Life and Adventures of the Chevalier de Faublas* (1789-90). Godwin drew in equally important ways upon Swiss political and social history as well in constructing the story of Ruffigny. Ruffigny himself recounts the history of the liberty of Switzerland, from the folklore surrounding the famous

William Tell to the "three immortal leaders" who brought their cantons into confederation in the "Eternal Union" of 1291.

Given the crucial relation between nature and moral sensibility in Rousseau, it is not surprising to see Godwin turning to another literary genre that was becoming particularly popular during the later decades of the eighteenth century, the travel literature in which leisure travelers began for the first time to share with their countrymen their impressions of foreign landscapes and peoples. The genre became all the more popular in the years during which England was at war with Napoleon, when all travel to the continent was prohibited. It became an important means by which the English preserved and underscored their own nationalistic identity in response to ongoing war with France in the early nineteenth century. To enhance the realism of Fleetwood's experiences in Switzerland, Godwin drew specifically from William Coxe's popular *Travels in Switzerland* (1789), a source as well for Wordsworth's *Descriptive Sketches* of 1793. The excerpt from Coxe in the appendix to this volume indicates how much Godwin borrowed in order to capture the scenic grandeur of the Swiss Alps.

One of the strongest literary influences on Godwin's work was that of Renaissance and seventeenth-century drama, which Godwin read voraciously during the years preceding his composition of *Fleetwood*. Always a great admirer of Shakespeare, Godwin had by the early 1800s also become a great enthusiast of the works of Beaumont and Fletcher. John Fletcher's 1624 *A Wife for a Moneth* (Month) plays a particularly important role in this novel. Fletcher's play tells of a cruel king, Frederick, who lusts for the beautiful Evanthe, despite Evanthe's love for Valerio. The king determines upon revenge, and agrees to allow Valerio to marry Evanthe, but only if he will submit to the condition that he face execution after a month of marriage. It says a good deal about Fleetwood's character that this is the play he chooses to read along with his wife as they attempt to settle into domestic harmony upon returning to his estate from their honeymoon. The title provides an ironic commentary upon the short term of happiness that will follow his own marriage, but a more significant parallel lies in the characters of

Fleetwood and Frederick. Although he is oblivious to any such connection, Fleetwood's irrational reaction when Mary interrupts their reading session to honor a prior commitment reflects all too closely the tyrannical behavior of the king in Fletcher's play.

Mary's passionate response to the situation of Frederick's neglected queen, Maria, is equally revealing about her character and fate. As Queen Maria helps Evanthe dress for her wedding, she offers Evanthe advice on how to maintain her dignity in the face of the king's unjust behavior. Though Mary could hardly realize this, the play closely foreshadows the situation of her own marriage, where Maria's advice will be equally apt in reference to Mary's own life. Godwin's use of literary allusion in this passage makes it one of the most powerful in the novel. The parallel from the past reminds us of how long such oppression of women has existed, and Fleetwood's reaction to Mary's departure, a maniacal waffling between love and rage, epitomizes the mental problem that cripples their marriage. As Fleetwood mournfully and self-indulgently concludes, "The reader who has had experience of the married life, will easily feel how many vexations a man stored up for himself, who felt so acutely these trivial thwartings and disappointments" (p. 303).

But the work that most pervasively shadows *Fleetwood* is Shakespeare's *Othello*, a favorite plot about the tragedy of conjugal jealousy that Godwin adopted not only here, but in his final novel, *Deloraine* (1833), as well. Godwin's characterization of Fleetwood's Iago-like nephew Gifford and his detailed account of Gifford's gradual corruption of Fleetwood's trust in Mary are heavily indebted to *Othello*, although the novel's eventual reconciliation between husband and wife against all odds recalls Shakespeare's less tragic exploration of the destructive behavior of a jealous tyrant in *The Winter's Tale*. Godwin was also familiar with a previous reworking of *Othello*, Thomas Otway's tragedy *Don Carlos* (1676). In this play, Philip II, King of Spain, impetuously decides to wed the young Elizabeth of Valois, the intended of Philip's son, Don Carlos. The evil Rui-Gomez and his wife, the Duchess of Eboli, plot to set themselves upon the Spanish throne by destroying the king and his family. Gradually, the two work together to convince the gullible king that his bride is carrying on an affair with his son, Don Carlos, with whom she had been in love.

Fleetwood: Reception and Influence

Fleetwood was, unsurprisingly, a difficult work for critics to absorb. Its mix of genres, its jarring shifts in tone, and, in particular, its depiction of Fleetwood's gradual slide into insanity made it an uncomfortable novel to read and a hard one to assess. Nearly every reviewer had trouble recognizing in Fleetwood the "new man of feeling," and the reviews overall suggest that Godwin failed to persuade readers that his rendering of the events of family life was either common or plausible. A reviewer in the moderately Whig *Critical Review* in April 1805 found the events of the novel all too ordinary, but a decided improvement over Godwin's earlier fiction in the sense that it was at least relatively "harmless" in its moral tendencies. The reviewer is simply perplexed by the idea that one might trace Fleetwood's extreme behavior to his sensibility and prefers to construe the novel as conveying a much narrower and more conventional moral about "the folly of ill-sorted marriages, in point of age." Yet even as the reviewer rebukes Godwin for creating "chief characters [who] are all metaphysicians; who are reasoning when they should be acting," he concedes that they "reason in so extraordinary a manner that they rivet our attention," and he notes the power of a number of specific scenes. In the same month Walter Scott (not yet a baronet, nor the renowned author of historical novels he was to become) reviewed the novel in the *Edinburgh Review*. Scott praised Godwin's earlier novels as of high interest, if not necessarily high morals, but objected to the "laboured extravagance of sentiment" attached to the most "ordinary occurrences" in the early parts of *Fleetwood*. Nor did what followed please him better. Scott shudders at the thought that sensibility might go as far astray as it does in Casimir Fleetwood's case, or that such aberrations might manifest themselves in everyday life, rather than being confined in a literal or literary madhouse. Sensibility, he asserts, is by definition "amiable" and altruistic.

The reviewer in the conservative *The Anti-Jacobin Review and Magazine: Or, Monthly Political and Literary Censor* starts from the same premise – that a man of feeling must necessarily exhibit a "warm and active benevolence" rather than the "disgusting" egoism displayed by Fleetwood. By violating this nearly "sacred" injunction upon writers, Godwin succeeded only in creating a text that was by turns mediocre and absurd. As the review goes on to demonstrate, however, there was a good deal more at stake for this reviewer than the value or interest of one particular novel. His review turns into a renewed attempt to bury Godwin's reputation, indulging in a lengthy, vitriolic attack upon Godwin's views toward marriage and his own marriage to Mary Wollstonecraft. The pro-government *British Critic* likewise finds the events that Godwin dramatized to be "incredible" and even "profane," and looks in vain for a conclusion that would punish all the wicked and reward the blameless. Taking solace from the belief that the novel held much less potential for immoral influence than Godwin's earlier novels, the reviewer concludes that "it is a work which we dare not wholly recommend, nor can severely censure."

By the time of the novel's reissue in Bentley's "Standard Novels" series in 1832, a reviewer in the *Examiner* can find other things to praise, welcoming the reissue of the novel and ranking it next to *Caleb Williams* among Godwin's fictions. His interest is drawn in particular to Godwin's attention to the issue of child labor in the story of Ruffigny, an instance of social realism which the critic can enthusiastically endorse. Speaking at the dawn of the Victorian age, when such social realism would reach its peak, the critic assures his readers that the spirit of Godwin's reflections on this issue would be felt in full force, "now that the attention of humanity is earnestly turned to the subject."

Indeed, the long section detailing the exploitation suffered by Ruffigny as a child worker in the French silk mills is an example of literary realism that is remarkable for its time. Just as Godwin had taken great pains to illustrate the reality of prison life in *Caleb Williams* to help bring about prison reform, he thoroughly familiarized himself with the effects of industry in preparing to write *Fleetwood*. He visited Etruria, the site of the Wedgwood family's pottery works in 1797; he toured the industrial regions of the English midlands in 1800 and 1803; and, while composing the novel, Godwin visited a silk mill in Spitalfields on July 12, 1804.[1] Three letters that Godwin exchanged with Sir Henry Ellis of the British Library indicate the lengths to which he went to determine that his use of factual information was accurate, from his references to the looms and "silk-throwing machines" at use in Lyon during the seventeenth century to his use of the French "Code Criminelle."[2] His treatment of child labor and the horrors of industry in the story of Ruffigny laid the foundation for subsequent treatments of this topic among such Victorian novelists as Elizabeth Gaskell and Charles Dickens. Ivanka Kovačević explores the novel's importance as the first prose attack on child labor and the factory system, and analyzes its specific influence on Dickens's *David Copperfield*. Similarly, Elizabeth Shore discusses *Fleetwood*'s importance as a source for George Meredith's novel, *The Amazing Marriage*, published in 1895.

As this survey makes clear, however, reviewers of the time were extremely puzzled and unsettled by a text that seemed to be by turns altogether ordinary and absolutely incredible, and by a character who could be at once warmly sentimental and perversely vindictive. They simply refused to accept, or even apparently to recognize, Godwin's claim that the pathways of sentiment could be so convoluted or the outcome of feeling so deeply problematic. Such linkages look far less alien to us two hundred years later, when the intricacy of emotional life and the reality of domestic violence have been more fully explored.

Unsurprisingly, those who responded most intensely and enthusiastically to *Fleetwood* included a number of figures in the second generation of Romantic writers. Like Godwin's earlier characters, Casimir Fleetwood made a great impression on

---

1   Gary Kelly, *The English Jacobin Novel*, 251.
2   These three unpublished letters are held by the Berg Collection, the New York Public Library.

Lord Byron, providing grist for the archetypal Byronic hero who resurfaces time and again in Byron's work, from *Childe Harold's Pilgrimage* (1812-18), *Manfred* (1817), and *Cain* (1821), to his Oriental Tales. As Gary Kelly has noted, the satirical elements of the novel can also be seen to prefigure Byron's mode of social satire in *Don Juan* (1819-24).[1]

Fleetwood, like Godwin's other novels, had a particularly strong and direct influence on the fiction of his daughter, Mary Wollstonecraft Shelley, whose novels often have at their center a melancholic, solipsistic hero of the Godwinian type. Like her father, Shelley typically uses the confessional form of a first-person narrator in several of her novels, lending to such works as *Frankenstein* (1818), *Mathilda* (1819-20), and *The Last Man* (1826) a distinctive emotional intensity. She, too, is deeply concerned with the destructive effects that irrational, irresponsible male behavior can have on the lives of women, as in both *St. Leon* and *Fleetwood*. And she displays a confidence acquired from her mother and father alike about the regenerative value of the domestic affections, not only in *Frankenstein*, but in nearly all of her other novels as well, particularly the very Godwinian *Falkner* (1837). A particularly subtle account of this father-daughter literary relation can be found in Tilottama Rajan's "Mary Shelley's *Mathilda*: Melancholy and the Political Economy of Romanticism," which explores the biographical resonance of *Fleetwood*. Rajan shows how Shelley's tragic novel of father-daughter incest, *Mathilda*, can be seen as a rewriting of *Fleetwood* "in which an incestuous patriarchy pays through death instead of being allowed the luxury of a Rousseauvian and self-vindicating confession" (52).

Although *Fleetwood* has yet to receive due acknowledgment from critics for its power as a novel or its importance during this transitional period of literary history, critics have in the last few decades begun to do fuller justice to its narrative interest and complexity. Gary Kelly discusses the novel at length in *The English Jacobin Novel, 1780-1805*, where he calls it the last of the

---

1 Kelly, *The English Jacobin Novel*, 252. For a more general study of Godwin's impact on Byron, see Peter Thorslev's *The Byronic Hero: Types and Prototypes* (Minneapolis: U Minnesota P, 1962).

Jacobin novels. He stresses its importance for illustrating the changes that Godwin's philosophy underwent as English Romanticism emerged and sees it as a movement away from political engagement and toward psychological interiority that typified all of English fiction in this period. B.J. Tysdahl focuses primarily upon *Fleetwood*'s place in the development of Godwin's literary style in *William Godwin as Novelist*.

Other studies have brought to light some of the considerable structural and generic complexity of the novel. In "The Study of Mind: The Later Novels of William Godwin," Mona Scheuermann discusses Godwin's manner of combining social, gothic, and psychological elements in depicting characters who are neither villainous nor benevolent, and who lack the self-awareness to know themselves despite their wish to do so. Scheuermann looks at *Fleetwood* and *Mandeville*, emphasizing the status of both as psychological studies where Godwin explores how the human mind can alienate individuals from their communities. In "William Godwin's *Fleetwood*: The Epistemology of the Tortured Body," Steven Bruhm attends particularly to Godwin's reworking of the theme of sensibility in the context of judicial enquiry, punishment, and torture. Bruhm focuses on some of the oddest moments in this text – the fascinating and disturbing effigy scenes of Withers's torture at Oxford by the puppet-judge and Fleetwood's demented destruction of the wax models of Kenrick and Mary.

What *Fleetwood* offers the modern reader is a probing portrait of gender relations in early nineteenth-century England. Godwin's Fleetwood is an absolutely memorable character, a figure of immense pathos who – despite considerable good will on his part – proves unable to extricate himself from the web of social circumstances and prejudices within which he was raised. Neither his sensitivity toward others nor his powers of logical judgment suffice to let him integrate himself within society; his actions remind us of the considerable risks in cultivating sensibility and of the potential for abuse latent in social institutions such as marriage. The road to reform, Godwin reminds us in this text, is likely to be a long one indeed.

William Godwin: A Brief Chronology

1756   Born on 3 March in Wisbech, North Cam-
bridgeshire, to Reverend John and Ann Hull Godwin, the seventh of thirteen children.

1767   Becomes pupil of Reverend Samuel Newton at
Norwich.

1773   Attends school at Hoxton Dissenting Academy.

1777   Begins work as a Dissenting minister.

1783   After dismissal from the pulpit over a theological
dispute, moves to London and begins a literary
career; publishes *Life of Chatham, Defence of the
Rockingham Party, An Account of the Seminary, The
Herald of Literature*, and *Sketches of History*.

1784   Publishes the political pamphlet *Instructions to a
Statesman* and two novels: *Damon and Delia* and *Italian Letters*. Works as a journalist for *The New Annual Register* and the *English Review*.

1785   Writes for the New Whig journal, *Political Herald
and Review*, and becomes its editor in August
(through 1787).

1787   Publishes *History of the Internal Affairs of the United
Provinces*.

1788   Begins keeping a daily journal.

1789   The Bastille is stormed on 14 July; the French Revolution begins.

1791   Meets Mary Wollstonecraft.

1792   Mary Wollstonecraft publishes *A Vindication of the
Rights of Woman*.

1793   Louis XVI of France is executed. Godwin publishes
Enquiry Concerning Political Justice and begins writing
Caleb Williams. Publishes the "Letters of Mucius" in
the *Morning Chronicle*.

1794   *Things As They Are; or, The Adventures of Caleb
Williams* is published. Godwin publishes *Cursory
Strictures* and contributes to the acquittal of twelve
British radicals being tried for treason. Mary Woll-

stonecraft gives birth to a daughter, Fanny, by her lover Gilbert Imlay.

1795   Publishes *Considerations on Lord Grenville's and Mr. Pitt's Bills.*

1796   Meets Mary Wollstonecraft again; they become lovers in August.

1797   Publishes *The Enquirer, Reflections on Education, Manners and Literature.* Marries Mary Wollstonecraft on 29 March. Wollstonecraft gives birth to Mary Wollstonecraft Godwin on 30 August, and dies of puerperal fever on 10 September.

1798   Publishes his *Memoirs* of Mary Wollstonecraft and her *Posthumous Works*, and is harshly abused in the press.

1799.   Publishes a second novel, *St. Leon: A Tale of the Sixteenth Century.*

1800   Godwin's tragedy *Antonio* is performed.

1801   Publishes *Thoughts occasioned by the Perusal of Dr. Parr's Spital Sermon*; Marries Mrs. Mary Jane Clairmont, who brings her daughter Jane (Claire) and son Charles into Godwin's home.

1803   William Godwin, Jr. is born on 28 March. Publishes *Life of Chaucer.*

1805   Publishes *Fleetwood: or, The New Man of Feeling* in February; With Mary Jane Godwin, establishes the Juvenile Library, a publishing house for children's literature. Begins to write children's books under the pseudonyms Edward Baldwin and Theophilus Marcliffe.

1806   Under his pseudonyms, publishes *Life of Lady Jane Grey, History of England,* and *The Pantheon.*

1807   Godwin's play, *Faulkner,* is performed.

1809   Publishes *Essay on Sepulchres,* and (as Baldwin) *History of Rome.*

1810   Publishes (as Baldwin) *Outlines of English Grammar.*

1812   Becomes acquainted with Percy Bysshe Shelley and his wife Harriet.

1814   Percy Bysshe Shelley elopes with Godwin's

daughter Mary, and stepdaughter Claire runs away with them to the Continent.

1815 Publishes *The Lives of Edward and John Philips* and *Letters of Verax*.

1816 Godwin travels to Edinburgh and meets Sir Walter Scott. Fanny Godwin commits suicide in October. Percy Bysshe Shelley marries Mary Godwin in December after the suicide of his wife Harriet.

1817 Publishes a novel, *Mandeville, A Tale of the Seventeenth Century in England*.

1818 Publishes *Letter of Advice to a Young American*. Mary Shelley's *Frankenstein* published.

1820 Publishes *Of Population*, a reply to David Malthus in the population controversy.

1821 Publishes (as Baldwin) *History of Greece*.

1822 Percy Bysshe Shelley drowns in the Bay of Spezia, Italy.

1823 Mary Shelley publishes her novel, *Valperga*, edited by Godwin; she and her son Percy Florence Shelley return to England.

1824 Begins publishing *History of the Commonwealth of England* (through 1828).

1825 Declared bankrupt.

1830 Publishes *Cloudesley: a novel*.

1831 Publishes essays, *Thoughts on Man*. *Caleb Williams* is republished in Bentley's Standard Novels Series.

1832 The Reform Bill is passed. William Godwin, Jr. dies of cholera in September. *Fleetwood* is republished in Bentley's Standard Novels Series.

1833 Publishes a final novel, *Deloraine*. Is offered a sinecure post of "Office Keeper and Yeoman Usher of the Exchequer" by the government.

1834 Publishes *Lives of the Necromancers*, and William Godwin, Jr.'s novel, *Transfusion*, with a memoir of his son.

1836 Dies in London on 7 April at the age of 80.

A Note on the Text

Fleetwood: or, The New Man of Feeling was first published by R. Phillips in three volumes in 1805. The present text is based upon the last edition that Godwin himself saw through the press: the one-volume edition published as part of Richard Bentley's "Standard Novels" series in 1832. Godwin's Preface to the original edition of the novel is reproduced in this volume. In the preface to the second edition, however, Godwin answered Bentley's request that he provide an account of the composition of his more famous novel, *Things As They Are; or, The Adventures of Caleb Williams* (1794), which Bentley had published in his series in 1831. The Preface to the second edition of *Fleetwood* is therefore included in the Broadview edition of *Caleb Williams* (2000), also edited by Gary Handwerk and A.A. Markley.

With the exception of a few silent corrections of obvious typesetter mistakes, the text has been left as close to its original state as possible. We have preserved peculiarities of punctuation, including Godwin's frequent use of dashes of varying lengths; as well as peculiarities of spelling, as in the case of such words as "visiter," and the division of such pronouns as "every one" and "any thing" as two words. Godwin's few annotations to the text, which he indicated with the use of an asterisk, are incorporated within the footnotes to the present edition. We have adhered to the same standards in editing the supplementary materials.

FLEETWOOD:

OR, THE

NEW MAN OF FEELING.

BY WILLIAM GODWIN.

IN THREE VOLUMES.

VOL. I.

LONDON:

PRINTED FOR RICHARD PHILLIPS,

NO. 6, BRIDGE-STREET, BLACKFRIARS.

1805.

PREFACE TO THE FIRST EDITION

February 14. 1805.

YET another novel from the same pen, which has twice before claimed the patience of the public in this form. The unequivocal indulgence which has been extended to my two former attempts, renders me doubly solicitous not to forfeit the kindness I have experienced.

One caution I have particularly sought to exercise: "not to repeat myself." Caleb Williams was a story of very surprising and uncommon events, but which were supposed to be entirely within the laws and established course of nature, as she operates in the planet we inhabit. The story of St. Leon is of the miraculous class; and its design, to "mix human feelings and passions with incredible situations, and thus render them impressive and interesting."

Some of those fastidious readers,—they may be classed among the best friends an author has, if their admonitions are judiciously considered,—who are willing to discover those faults which do not offer themselves to every eye, have remarked, that both these tales are in a vicious style of writing; that Horace has long ago decided,[1] that the story we cannot believe, we are by all the laws of criticism called upon to hate; and that even the adventures of the honest secretary, who was first heard of ten years ago, are so much out of the usual road, that not one reader in a million can ever fear they will happen to himself.

Gentlemen critics, I thank you. In the present volumes I have served you with a dish agreeable to your own receipt, though I cannot say with any sanguine hope of obtaining your approbation.

The following story consists of such adventures, as for the most part have occurred to at least one half of the Englishmen

---

[1] *Quodcunque ostendis mihi sic, incredulus odi* [Godwin's note]. Godwin quotes line 188 of the Roman poet Horace's *The Art of Poetry*, which is translated, "Whatever you show me in that way, unbelieving, I detest."

now existing, who are of the same rank of life as my hero. Most of them have been at college, and shared in college excesses: most of them have afterward run a certain gauntlet of dissipation; most have married; and, I am afraid, there are few of the married tribe who have not at some time or other had certain small misunderstandings with their wives:[1]—to be sure, they have not all of them felt and acted under these trite adventures as my hero does. In this little work the reader will scarcely find any thing to "elevate and surprise;" and, if it has any merit, it must consist in the liveliness with which it brings things home to the imagination, and the reality it gives to the scenes it pourtrays.

Yet, even in the present narrative, I have aimed at a certain kind of novelty; a novelty, which may be aptly expressed by a parody on a well known line of Pope; it relates—

"Things often done, but never yet described."[2]

In selecting among common and ordinary adventures, I have endeavoured to avoid such as a thousand novels before mine have undertaken to develop. Multitudes of readers have themselves passed through the very incidents I relate; but, for the most part, no work has hitherto recorded them. If I have told them truly, I have added somewhat to the stock of books which should enable a recluse, shut up in his closet, to form an idea of what is passing in the world. It is inconceivable meanwhile, how much, by this choice of subject, I increased the arduousness of my task. It is easy to do, a little better, or a little worse, what twenty authors have done before! If I had foreseen from the first all the difficulty of my project, my courage would have failed me to undertake the execution of it.

Certain persons, who condescend to make my supposed inconsistencies the favourite object of their research, will per-

---

1 I confess however the inability I found to weave a catastrophe, such as I desired, out of these ordinary incidents. What I have here said therefore must not be interpreted as applicable to the concluding sheets of my work. [Godwin's note]

2 Alexander Pope, *An Essay on Criticism* (1711), line 298: "What oft was thought, but ne'er so well expressed."

haps remark with exultation on the respect expressed in this work for marriage; and exclaim, "It was not always thus!" referring to the pages in which this subject is treated in the Enquiry concerning Political Justice for the proof of their assertion. The answer to this remark is exceedingly simple. The production referred to in it, the first foundation of its author's claim to public distinction and favour, was a treatise, aiming to ascertain what new institutions in political society might be found more conducive to general happiness than those which at present prevail. In the course of this disquisition it was enquired, whether marriage, as it stands described and supported in the laws of England, might not with advantage admit of certain modifications? Can any thing be more distinct, than such a proposition on the one hand, and a recommendation on the other that each man for himself should supersede and trample upon the institutions of the country in which he lives? A thousand things might be found excellent and salutary, if brought into general practice, which would in some cases appear ridiculous, and in others be attended with tragical consequences, if prematurely acted upon by a solitary individual. The author of Political Justice, as appears again and again in the pages of that work, is the last man in the world to recommend a pitiful attempt, by scattered examples to renovate the face of society, instead of endeavouring by discussion and reasoning, to effect a grand and comprehensive improvement in the sentiments of its members.

FLEETWOOD.

VOLUME THE FIRST.

CHAPTER I.

I was the only son of my father. I was very young at the period of the death of my mother, and have retained scarcely any recollection of her. My father was so much affected by the loss of the amiable and affectionate partner of his days, that he resolved to withdraw for ever from those scenes where every object he saw was associated with the ideas of her kindness, her accomplishments, and her virtues: and, being habitually a lover of the sublime and romantic features of nature, he fixed upon a spot in Merionethshire, near the foot of Cader Idris, for the habitation of his declining life.[1]

Here I was educated. And the settled melancholy of my father's mind, and the wild and magnificent scenery by which I was surrounded, had an eminent share in deciding upon the fortunes of my future life. My father loved me extremely; his actions toward me were tender and indulgent; he recognised in me all that remained of the individual he had loved more than all the other persons in the world. But he was also enamoured of solitude; he spent whole days and nights in study and contemplation. Even when he went into company, or received visiters in his own house, he judged too truly of the temper and propensities of boyish years, to put much restraint upon me, or to require that I should either render myself subservient to the habits of my elders, or, by a ridiculous exhibition of artificial talents, endeavour to extract from their politeness nourishment for his paternal vanity or pride.

I had few companions. The very situation which gave us a full enjoyment of the beauties of nature, inevitably narrowed both the extent and variety of our intercourse with our own species. My earliest years were spent among mountains and precipices, amidst the roaring of the ocean and the dashing of waterfalls. A constant familiarity with these objects gave a wildness to my ideas, and an uncommon seriousness to my temper. My curiosity was ardent, and my disposition persevering. Often have I climbed the misty mountain's top, to hail the

---

1   Cader Idris is a mountain in Gwynedd, North Wales.

first beams of the orb of day, or to watch his refulgent glories as he sunk beneath the western ocean. There was no neighbouring summit that I did not ascend, anxious to see what mountains, valleys, rivers, and cities were placed beyond. I gazed upon the populous haunts of men as objects that pleasingly diversified my landscape; but without the desire to behold them in nearer view. I had a presentiment that the crowded streets and the noisy mart contained larger materials for constituting my pain than pleasure. The jarring passions of men, their loud contentions, their gross pursuits, their crafty delusions, their boisterous mirth, were objects which, even in idea, my mind shrunk from with horror. I was a spoiled child. I had been little used to contradiction, and felt like a tender flower of the garden, which the blast of the east wind nips, and impresses with the tokens of a sure decay.

With such a tone of mind the great features of nature are particularly in accord. In her chosen retreat every thing is busy and alive; nothing is in full repose. All is diversity and change. The mysterious power of vegetation continually proceeds; the trees unfold their verdure, and the fields are clothed with grass and flowers. Life is every where around the solitary wanderer; all is health and bloom; the sap circulates, and the leaves expand. The stalk of the flower, the trunk of the tree, and the limbs of animals dilate, and assume larger dimensions. The cattle breathe, and the vegetable kingdom consumes the vital air; the herds resort to the flowing stream, and the grass drinks the moisture of the earth and the dew of heaven. Even the clouds, the winds, and the streams present us with the image of life, and talk to us of that venerable power which is operating every where, and never sleeps. But their speech is dumb; their eloquence is unobtrusive; if they tear us from ourselves, it is with a gentle and a kindly violence, which, while we submit to, we bless.

Here begins the contrast and disparity between youth and age. My father was a lover of nature; but he was not the companion of my studies in the scenes of nature. He viewed her from his window, or from the terrace of earth he had raised at the extremity of his garden; he mounted his horse for a tranquil excursion, and kept along the road which was sedulously formed for the use of travellers. His limbs were stiffened with age; and he was held in awe by the periodical intrusions of an unwelcome visitor, the gout. My limbs, on the contrary, were full of the springiness which characterises the morning of life. I bounded along the plains, and climbed the highest eminences; I descended the most frightful declivities, and often penetrated into recesses which had perhaps never before felt the presence of a human creature. I rivalled the goat, the native of the mountains, in agility and daring. My only companion was a dog, who by familiarity had acquired habits similar to mine. In our solitary rambles we seemed to have a certain sympathy with each other; and, when I rested occasionally from the weariness of my exertions, he came and lay down at my feet, and I often found relief in dalliance with this humble companion amidst the uninhabited wilds which received me. Sometimes, when I foresaw an excursion of more than usual daring, I confined him at home; but then he would generally break loose in my absence, seek me among the mountains, and frequently meet me in my return. Sometimes I would tie him to a tree or a shrub, and leave him for hours: in these cases he seemed to become a party in the implied compact between us, and waited in mute resignation till he saw me again.

Every thing, however, was not exertion in the rambles I describe. I loitered by the side of the river, and drank in at leisure the beauties that surrounded me. I sat for hours on the edge of a precipice, and considered in quiet the grand and savage objects around me, which seemed never to have changed their character from the foundation of the world. I listened in delightful idleness to the sound of the stones, which I gently let fall into the cavities of the rocks, or followed them with my eye as they bounded from protuberance to protuberance, till by distance they became invisible. I stretched myself at my length along the jutting precipice, while my head hung over the vast billows of the ocean, which seemed to gape and prepare themselves to receive me into their remorseless bosom for ever. Often I reposed by the side of a cataract, and was insensibly lulled into slumber by the monotony of its dashings.

While thus amused, I acquired a habit of being absent in mind from the scene which was before my senses. I devoured at first with greedy appetite the objects which presented themselves; but by perseverance they faded on my eye and my ear, and I sunk into a sweet insensibility to the impressions of external nature. The state thus produced was sometimes that which we perhaps most exactly understand by the term reverie, when the mind has neither action nor distinct ideas, but is swallowed up in a living death, which, at the same time that it is indolent and inert, is not destitute of a certain voluptuousness. At other seasons the abstraction of my mind was of a more busy and definite sort. I was engaged in imaginary scenes, constructed visionary plans, and found all nature subservient to my command. I had a wife or children, was the occupier of palaces, or the ruler of nations. There is this difference between the visions of the night, and the dreams, the waking dreams I mean, of the day: the former are often painful, the latter are perhaps always grateful and soothing. With the visions of the night there is ordinarily mixed a depressing sense of impotence; things without are too strong for us: in those of the day we are all-powerful; obstacles no sooner present themselves than they are conquered; or, if it is otherwise, we wilfully protract the struggle, that we may prolong our pleasure, and enhance our triumph. In the dream of the night, our powers are blunted, and we are but half ourselves: the day-dream on the contrary is the triumph of man; our invention is full, our complacency is pure; and, if there is any mixture of imbecility or folly in the fable, it is a mixture to which the dreamer at the moment scarcely adverts. The tendency, therefore, of this species of dreaming, when frequently indulged, is to inspire a certain propensity to despotism, and to render him who admits it impatient of opposition, and prepared to feel every cross accident, as a usurpation upon his rights, and a blot upon his greatness. This effect of my early habits I fully experienced, and it determined the colour of my riper years.

My youth, however, was not wholly spent in the idle and frivolous task of constructing castles in the air. The regard and affection my father felt for me, rendered him anxious that my education should not be neglected. He hired me a private tutor. I was perhaps sufficiently fortunate in the character of the person who was thus established in our house. He was not a clergyman. He did not shackle my mind with complex and unintelligible creeds, nor did he exhibit that monastic coldness and squareness of character which is too frequently the result of clerical celibacy. He was, however, a man of morals and of religion. But religion was distinguished in his mind more by sentiments than opinions. Whatever related to his conduct toward God or man was regulated principally by a desire to satisfy his conscience and obtain his own approbation, not to maintain a certain character and name in the world. He had been designed by his parents, who were poor, for the profession of the law; but he ultimately declined this pursuit, from an aversion, as he said, to disputes, and sophistry, and the deriving a subsistence from the misfortunes of others. He was one of those characters, so frequently found in civilised Europe, who imagine in themselves a vocation to the muses, and an interest in the temple of literary immortality, which all their efforts are unable to realise. He certainly was not a man of genius; and, though he had acquired a considerable facility in the art of rhyming, he was totally a stranger to those more essential qualities which constitute the soul of poetry. But he was that which is better than a mere poet; he was an honest man. His heart was guileless; his manners were simple; and, though he could never be cured of a lying estimation of his own greatness, this did not prevent him from feeling and discharging what was due to others. He also possessed those accomplishments, the reputation of which had principally recommended him to my father's choice; he had a very decent portion of learning, and understood the elements of Latin, Greek, French, and Italian, as well as possessed a smattering of astronomy, natural philosophy, mathematics, and history. But his favourite study was mythology; his select reading was in Plato, at least in his translators and commentators, which he incessantly perused, I am afraid without exactly understanding them. He had made great progress in what I may name a concordance of all religions. This was the second basis upon which, together with his poetical effusions, he proposed to erect the edifice of his fame. He alle-gorised whatever is fabulous or historical in the sacred books of all nations, and explained them all to signify a certain sublime metaphysics, the detail of which is to be found for the most part in the writings of Duns Scotus and Thomas Aquinas.[1]

This was exactly the sort of tutor adapted to my dispositions. I read with him occasionally the classics, and the elementary books of science, because I was unwilling to thwart or give any one pain, more especially my father, and because I was strongly impressed with a certain love for literature and science. But I studied for the most part when I pleased. My father was con-tented to discern in me a certain inclination to learning, and did not think of putting on me a task greater than I was willing to endure.

In the mean time there was this peculiarity in my tuition: though I learned from my preceptor almost every thing valu-able that he was able to teach, I never looked up to him. His foibles were obvious, and did not escape my observation. The understanding of my father was incomparably greater than that of this inmate of our family; nor did my father always refrain from ridiculing in his absence, and even sometimes alluding by a passing sarcasm in his presence, to my tutor's weakness. I secretly despised the good gentleman's sonnets and odes, and listened with an unattending ear to his mythological mysteries. I never dreamed for a moment that it could be less than sacri-lege to measure his understanding with my own. This system-atical persuasion of superiority occasionally broke out into little petulancies, which did not fail grievously to wound my kind friend's self-esteem. I was positive, assuming, and conceited. But the difference of our ages prevented these disputes from having any serious consequences. If I entertained little defer-ence for my tutor's talents, I was not insensible to that degree of consideration which is due to superior age, particularly when united with virtue; and my father, in his general demeanour, set

---

1   John Duns Scotus (c. 1266 or 1270-1308) was an Irish Franciscan philosopher, and St. Thomas Aquinas (1225-74) an Italian Dominican philosopher. Both were lead-ers of medieval Scholasticism, a theological movement which sought to reconcile Christian theology and Aristotelian philosophy.

me too excellent an example in this respect, for it to be possible for me not to profit by it. I might, perhaps, in my own nature have been sufficiently inclined to the impetuous and turbulent; if I had been one only of a class of pupils, it is probable enough that I should have joined in the conduct of unlucky tricks to be put upon my instructor: but I was alone; and therefore, however quick-sighted I might be to his weaknesses, they did not so expressly present themselves to my apprehension in the shape of ridicule.

CHAPTER II.

THE proper topic of the narrative I am writing is the record of my errors. To write it, is the act of my penitence and humiliation. I can expect, however, few persons to interest themselves respecting my errors, unless they are first informed what manner of man I am, what were my spontaneous and native dispositions, and whether I am such a one as that my errors are worthy of commiseration and pity. This must be my apology for the topic I am here to introduce,—a topic on which all ingenuous minds are disposed to be silent, and which shall in this place be passed over as slightly as possible,—my beneficence and charities.

I was fond of penetrating into the cottages of the poor. I should be greatly unjust to myself, if I suffered the reader to suppose that the wild elevation and intellectual luxuries I indulged, had the effect to render me insensible to the miseries of man. Nothing was squalid, loathsome, and disgusting in my eyes, where it was possible for me to be useful. I shrunk from the society of man in general; and foresaw, in the intercourse of my species, something for ever prepared to thwart my sensibility, and to jar against the unreal world in which I lived. But I never shrank from the presence of calamity. From the liberal allowance with which my father supplied me, I relieved its wants; I sheltered it from the menaces of a prison; and I even prevailed on myself to resort willingly to such towns as our vicinity afforded, to plead its cause, and parley with its oppressor.

No doubt, my pride did not come away ungratified from these enterprises. Far be it from me to assert, with certain morose and cold-blooded moralists, that our best actions are only more subtle methods by which self-love seeks its gratification. My own heart, in every act of benevolence I ever performed, gave the lie to this execrable doctrine. I felt that it was the love of another, and not of myself, that prompted my deed; I experienced a disinterested joy in human relief and human happiness, independently of the question whether I had been concerned in producing it; and, when the season of retrospect arrived, I exulted in my own benevolence, from the divine consciousness that, while I had been most busily engaged in the task, my own gratification was forgotten.

There is, however, as I have intimated, a very subtle and complicated association in human feelings. The generous sympathy which animated my charitable deeds was pure; it flowed from a celestial source, and maintained its crystal current, as unmingled with the vulgar stream of personal passions as the oil extracted from the most aromatic fruits flows separate, and unconfounded with the mire of the kennel on which it may have fallen. There is no doubt, however, that the honourable character I exhibited on these occasions prompted me the more joyfully to seek their repetition. Humanity and self-complacency were distinct causes of my beneficence; but the latter was not less powerful than the former in nourishing it into a habit. In other scenes of human intercourse, I played an equal and a doubtful part: the superior eloquence or information of my competitor might overwhelm me; he might have more passion to pursue his purpose, or more want of feeling to harden him against the obstacles that opposed: but in the cottage to which my benevolence led me, I appeared like a superior nature; I had here no opposition to contend with, no insult to awaken my irritability, and no superciliousness to check the operations of my sentiment. It was also fortunate for me, that the cases of distress which came before me in this remote part of the island were not numerous enough to distract my choice, or to render me callous by the too great frequency of their impressions.

One adventure of this sort interested me so much by the liveliness of its incidents, that I cannot refuse briefly to describe it in this place. The season had for many days been uncommonly wet. The waters were swelled with continual rains, and the low lands were almost inundated. It was July. After a series of heavy showers, one afternoon the sky brightened, the sun burst forth with redoubled splendour, and all nature smiled. This is a moment particularly dear to the lover of rural scenery. Dry weather tarnishes the face of nature, fades the lovely colours of hill and valley, and profanes and destroys those sweet odours which, more than any thing else, give the last finish to the charms of nature. I hastened to enjoy the golden opportunity. By long practice, I knew how to find the paths where mire and swamps would not occur to interrupt my pleasure. My way led me by a steep acclivity of the mountain, which overhangs the basin that forms the source of the Desunny.[1] I gained the eastern extremity of the ridge, that I might the more amply enjoy the beams of the setting sun as he sunk beneath the waves of the Irish Sea. It was the finest evening my eyes ever beheld. The resplendent colours of the clouds, the rich purple and burnished gold in various streaks fantastically formed and repeated, were beyond any imagination to conceive. The woods were vocal. The scents that surrounded me, the steaming earth, the fresh and invigorating air, the hay and the flowers, constituted, so to express myself, an olfactory concert, infinitely more ravishing than all the concords of harmonious sound that human art ever produced. This lovely moment combined in one impression the freshness of the finest morning, with all the rich and gorgeous effects peculiar to the close of a summer's day.

I stood, as I have said, on the edge of the precipice. I gazed for a long time upon the various charms that what we ordinarily, but improperly, call inanimate nature unfolded. I saw the rustic, as he retired from endeavouring to repair the injury his hay had sustained; and the flocks, as they passed slowly along to their evening's repose. Presently an individual object engrossed

---

1   The River "Dysynni" flows from Cader Idris into Cardigan Bay.

my attention. A young lamb had wandered by some accident to the middle of the precipice, and a peasant was pursuing it, and endeavouring to call it to his arms. I shuddered at the sight. The precipice was in some parts almost perpendicular. The rains had rendered the surface exceedingly slippery. The peasant caught at the shrubs and tufts of grass as he descended; and, with a skill peculiar to the inhabitants of the mountains, seemed to proceed securely in the most desperate places. The lamb, whether from heedlessness or wantonness, advanced further along the mountain-side, as the shepherd pursued.

While I was engaged in observing this little manoeuvre, I suddenly heard a scream. It came from a spot exceedingly near to me. Two boys sat in a nook where I had not perceived them, and cried out, "My brother! my brother!" A venerable grey-headed man was with them. He exclaimed, "My son! my William!" and prepared to plunge down the precipice. The scream I had heard was the effect of what at that moment happened before my eyes; yet such is the curious structure of the human senses, that what I heard seemed to be prior in time to what I saw. The peasant had almost overtaken his lamb. The lamb was on the point of escaping by a sudden leap; the peasant sprung upon him, and both were at the bottom of the precipice, and plunged in the basin, now swelled into a lake, with the rapidity of lightning. I flew to the group I have described; I laid hold of the old man at the moment of his purposed descent; I cried out, "Stay, poor man! what can you do? I will save your son!" I knew a path, more secure, yet scarcely more circuitous than that which the peasant had followed. I had the advantage over him, that I was not diverted from my course by any object whose deviations I pursued. For some time I went on safely; I saw the peasant rise to the surface of the water, and sink again; my impatience was too great to combine any longer with wariness; I lost my footing, and in an instant I also was in the lake.

My fall had been from a less terrible height than his, and I recovered myself. I swam toward the place where he had last sunk; he rose; I threw my arm round his neck, and supported him. The difficulty, however, which remained appeared insuperable; the shores on almost every side were shelving, and impossible to be scaled with the peasant in my arms, who was in a state of insensibility. As I was endeavouring to find the means of escaping from this difficulty, I saw a boat advancing toward us; it was rowed by a young woman; it approached; she was William's mistress, and the owner of the lamb for which he had ventured his life; we got him into the boat; he was more stunned with the fall, than injured by the water; he appeared to be gradually recovering; even the lamb was saved.

By the time we had reached the shore, the father and the two brothers were come round to our landing-place. All their attention was at first turned upon William; I was nothing to them: I retired to a little distance, and observed the group. The eldest boy supported William, as he sat; the blooming maid rubbed his temples; the father sat before him, and clasped his son's hands between his. It was an interesting spectacle; a painter might have sketched them as they sat. The eye of the boy glistened with eagerness; the girl hung over her lover, while her colour alternately changed from its natural ruddiness to a languid paleness; the hairs of the old man were as white as snow. Presently William uttered a profound sigh; it was a welcome sound to the whole assembly. The least boy was at first wrapped in silent attention; but presently began to play with Molly, the pet lamb, that frisked about him. In a short time the old man exclaimed, "Where is our deliverer?" It was now my turn; I was at a short distance; they were all tumultuous in their expressions of gratitude. The peasant-girl and myself supported William to his cottage; I offered my other arm to the father; the biggest boy led their favourite lamb by a string which hung from his neck; the youngest bore in triumph his father's stick, who, as he leaned on my arm, no longer needed its support.

Such was the commencement of my acquaintance with an honest family. The habitation of the girl was at a small distance from theirs; she was one of a numerous assemblage of sisters who lived with their mother. I found that the young persons had been lovers for more than a year, but had deferred their marriage for prudential reasons. The industry of William was the support of his own house; his father was past his labour;

they had resolved not to marry till the next brother should be able to take the place now filled by the eldest. The accident that had just occurred, in which the cottage-maid preserved the life of her lover, increased their affection, and doubled their impatience; an impatience, however, which they were resolute to subject to the most honourable considerations. I saw them often; I loved them much. William, was ingenuous and active; the maid added to a masculine intrepidity most of the more lovely graces of her own sex. The father often lamented, even with tears, that he was no longer capable of those exertions which might enable William freely to obey the dictates of his heart. The attachment which I felt to them was that of a patron and a preserver; when I observed the degree of content which prevailed among them, when I witnessed the effusions of their honest esteem and affection, my heart whispered me, "This would not have existed but for me!" I prevailed on my father to bestow a farm upon the lovers; I engaged, out of my own little stock, to hire a labourer for the old man; they married, and I had the satisfaction to convert one virtuous establishment into two.

Such were the principal occupations of my juvenile years. I loved the country, without feeling any partiality to what are called the sports of the country. My temper, as I have already said, was somewhat unsocial; and so far as related to the intercourse of my species, except when some strong stimulus of humanity called me into action, unenterprising. I was therefore no hunter. I was inaccessible to the pitiful ambition of showing, before a gang of rural squires, that I had a fine horse, and could manage him gracefully. I had not the motive, which ordinarily influences the inhabitants of the country to the cultivation of these sports,—the want of occupation. I was young: the world was new to me: I abounded with occupation. In the scenery of Merionethshire I found a source of inexhaustible amusement. Science, history, poetry, engaged me by turns, and into each of them my soul plunged itself with an ardour difficult to describe. In the train of these came my visions, my beloved and variegated inventions, the records, which to me appeared voluminous and momentous, of my past life, the plans of my future, the republics I formed, the seminaries of education for which I constructed laws, the figure I proposed hereafter to exhibit in the eyes of a wondering world. I had a still further and more direct reason for my rejection of the sports of the field. I could not with patience regard torture, anguish, and death, as sources of amusement. My natural temper, or my reflective and undebauched habits as a solitaire, prevented me from overlooking the brutality and cruelty of such pursuits. In very early youth I had been seduced, first by a footman of my father, and afterwards by my tutor, who was a great lover of the art, to join in an excursion of angling. But, after a short trial, I abjured the amusement for ever; and it was one among the causes of the small respect I entertained for my tutor, that he was devoted to so idle and unfeeling an avocation.

CHAPTER III.

At the usual age I entered myself of the university of Oxford. I felt no strong propensity to this change; but I submitted to it, as to a thing in the regular order of proceeding, and to which it would be useless to object. I was so much accustomed to self-conversation as to have little inclination to mix in the world; and was to such a degree satisfied with my abilities, and progress, and capacity of directing my own studies and conduct, as not to look with any eager craving for the advice and assistance of professors and doctors.

In setting out for the university, I was to part with my father and my preceptor. The first of these was a bitter pang to me: I had scarcely, from the earliest of my remembrance, ever been a week removed from the sight of the author of my being. He was the wisest and the best man I knew. He had all those advantages from nature, and from the external endowments of fortune, which were calculated to maintain my reverence. We had gradually become more qualified for each other's society and confidence. Our characters had many points of resemblance: we were both serious, both contemplative, both averse to the commerce of the world. My temper, as I have said, was to an uncommon degree impatient of contradiction; and a certain degree of heart-burning had not failed occasionally to invade my breast on this score, even toward this excellent parent. But my resentment and indignation in these instances had been short-lived. As the only representative of his person in existence, my father was ardently attached to me, and the occasions he administered to my impatience and displeasure were exceedingly few. On the other hand, whatever faults of character might justly be imputed to me, I had yet betrayed no tokens of an unmanageable boisterousness; my propensities were innocent; and my pursuits, most of them, such as seemed to conduce to the improvement of my understanding and my heart. In a word, my father and I, allowing for those failings which in some form or other are inseparable from the human character, were excellent friends; and it was not without many tears shed on both sides that we parted, when I mounted the chaise in which I set out for Oxford.

The separation between me and my tutor, which took place at the same time, was productive of a mixed sensation. I had long nourished in my mind a supercilious disregard of his mental discernment, and felt as if it were a degradation to me to listen to his instructions. The lessons he gave me appeared as a sort of shackles, the symbols of infantine imbecility. I was confident of my virtue and my perseverance, and longed to shake off these tokens of my nonage. But, besides these intellectual sources of weariness and impatience, there was an animal sensation, which made me regard the day of my separation from my tutor as the epoch of my liberty. His voice was sickly and unpleasing to my ear. He had cultivated the art of being amiable; and his cadences were formed by habit to a kind of tune of candour, and gentleness, and humanity. His gentleness was, unfortunately, twin-brother to the softness of his understanding, and expressed nothing so plainly as his ignorance of all the avenues of persuasion, and all the secret springs of hope, and fear, and passion, and will. In addition to this, the good gentleman loved to hear himself talk; and his explanations and exhortations were as long as the homilies of Archbishop Cranmer.[1] At my age,—the age of restlessness, and activity, and enterprise,—these discourses, unhappily, did not generate a propensity to sleep, and therefore produced in me an insupportable listlessness and *ennui.*

Yet I did not finally part with my old friend without pain. It was impossible a more innocent creature should live. If I did not highly respect him, I could not help approving and loving him. Had it been otherwise, there is something in the nature of habit which will for ever prevent us from parting with that to which we have been long accustomed, with indifference. I had been used to see my preceptor every morning. He was part of the furniture of our eating-room. As we had very unfrequent opportunities of various society, I often found relief in entering into conversation with him. If he could tell me nothing that appeared to me highly worthy of attention, in the way of fancy or deduction, he was at least well qualified to inform me of what he had read in books, relatively either to chronology, geography, or science. I am persuaded that if, when my tutor left me, I had remained among the same scenes, the crisis would have been a severe one. As it was, my understanding approved of the separation: I recollected that it was an event for which I had often and anxiously sighed; yet to part with a good man,—a man to whose cares and patience I owed much, who had bestowed on me a thousand benefits, and between whom and myself there had, from familiarity, grown up a considerable affection,—was no desirable task. I kissed his hand; I thanked · him a hundred times for his constant exertions; with bitter self-reproach, I entreated him to forgive every act of rudeness, impetuousness, and disrespect, I had been guilty of toward him: at this moment, these things struck upon my conscience like crimes.

My father was anxious that a decent provision should be made for his declining years. There was an ecclesiastical living of considerable value vacant in my father's gift, and he entreated my tutor to enter into holy orders, and accept of it; but this

---

1   Thomas Cranmer (1489-1556) was Archbishop of Canterbury from 1533 to 1555, a leader of the English Reformation, and a Protestant martyr.

my old friend strenuously declined. His creed did not exactly accord with the principles of orthodoxy contained in the code of the Church of England; and he disdained to compromise with his conscience.[1] Besides, regarding himself, as he undoubtedly did, as the first luminary of his age, he could not think with perfect temper of devoting the last maturity of his mind to the society of fox-hunting squires, and the reading prayers and sermons to rustics and old women. He retired, upon a small annuity which my father settled upon him, to a narrow lodging in an obscure street of the metropolis, and published from time to time pocket volumes of poetry, and sketches of a synopsis of his mythological discoveries, which some persons bought out of respect to the good qualities of their author, but which no person read.

A third separation which took place on this occasion, and which, I hope, the reader will not think it beneath the dignity of history to record, was between me and my dog. He was my old and affectionate friend, and the hours I had spent *tête-à-tête* in his society were scarcely less numerous than those I had spent with my tutor. He had often been the confidant of my sorrows; and I had not found it less natural to complain to him, than the heroines of fable or romance to the woods and the wilds, the rocks and the ocean, of the cruelties they experienced, or the calamities that weighed them down to the earth. One instance in particular I remember in very early youth, when my father had spoken to me with unusual sharpness about some fault that, in my eyes, by no means merited great severity of censure. I retired to the terrace in the garden which has already been mentioned, threw myself at my length upon the turf, and indulged a short fit of mutiny and misanthropy. As I lay, poor Chilo (that was the dog's name) discovered me, and leaped toward me with his usual demonstrations of joy.[2] I was in too ill a humour to notice him; and he, who seemed to have at least as much skill as my tutor in discerning what passed in my mind, crept along the turf toward the spot which supported my head, with pleading and most diffident advances. At length

---

1 Referring to the Elizabethan Thirty-nine Articles of 1563.
2 Chilo, or Chilon, of the sixth century BC, was one of the Seven Sages of Greece.

I suffered my eye to fall on him. This brought him close to me in a moment. He licked my hands and face, with every token of gratitude, affection, and delight. I threw my arms round him. "Fond fool!" said I, "every one else treats me with unkindness and injustice; but you will love me still!"

It was judged proper that this animal, who had passed the meridian of his life, should not accompany me in my entrance into the world, but should remain at home. I accordingly left him in Merionethshire. What was my surprise, then, one day, as I came down the steps of the chapel from morning prayers, after having been a week at Oxford, at meeting my dog! He fawned upon me, played a thousand extravagant antics, and was transported out of himself at the joy of finding me. I afterward learned that he had been at my rooms, had been repulsed there, and finally found his way to the chapel. By what sort of instinct an animal is thus enabled, for a distance of one hundred and seventy miles, to discover the trace of his master, I am unable to say. The thing itself, I am told, is not uncommon. But every ingenuous mind to whom such an incident has occurred, feels, no doubt, as I did, a most powerful impulse of affection toward the brute who has shown so distinguished an attachment.

What is the nature of this attachment? A dog, I believe, is not less attached to a fool than to a wise man, to a peasant than to a lord, to a beggar inhabiting the poorest hut, than to a prince swaying the sceptre of nations and dwelling in a palace. Ill usage scarcely makes a difference. At least, the most sparingly dealt kindness of the surliest groom affords a sufficient basis of attachment. The case is considerably parallel to that of a nobleman I have somewhere read of, who insisted that his mistress should not love him for his wealth nor his rank, the graces of his person nor the accomplishments of his mind; but *for himself*. I am inclined to blame the man who should thus subtly refine, and wantonly endeavour at a separation between him and all that is most truly his; but, where the course of nature produces this separation, there is a principle in the human mind which compels us to find gratification in this unmerited and metaphysical love.

At Oxford, the whole tone of my mind became speedily

changed. The situation was altogether new, and the effects produced were strikingly opposed to those which I had hitherto sustained. In Merionethshire, I had been a solitary savage. I had no companions, and I desired none. The commerce of my books and of my thoughts was enough for me. I lived in an ideal world of my own creation. The actual world beneath me I intuitively shunned. I felt that every man I should meet would be either too ignorant, too coarse, or too supercilious, to afford me pleasure. The strings of my mind, so to express it, were tuned to too delicate and sensitive a pitch: it was an Eolian harp, upon which the winds of heaven might "discourse excellent music"; but the touch of a human hand could draw from it nothing but discord and dissonance.[1]

At the university all that I experienced for some weeks was pain. Nature spoils us for relishing the beauties of nature. Formed as my mind had been, almost from infancy, to delight itself with the grand, the romantic, the pregnant, the surprising, and the stupendous, as they display themselves in North Wales, it is inconceivable with what contempt, what sensations of loathing, I looked upon the face of nature as it shows itself in Oxfordshire. All here was flat, and tame, and tedious. Wales was nature in the vigour and animation of youth: she sported in a thousand wild and admirable freaks; she displayed a masterhand; every stroke of her majestic pencil was clear, and bold, and free. But, in the country to which I had now removed, nature to my eyes seemed to be in her dotage; if she attempted any thing, it was the attempt of a driveller; she appeared like a toothless and palsied beldame, who calls upon her visiters to attend, who mumbles slowly a set of inarticulate and unintelligible sounds, and to whom it exceeds the force of human resolution to keep up the forms of civility. Why does the world we live in thus teach us to despise the world?

My father's house had been built in a style of antique magnificence. The apartments were spacious, the galleries long and wide, and the hall in which I was accustomed to walk in unfavourable weather was of ample dimensions. The rooms

---

1   An Aeolian harp is a stringed instrument constructed so as to produce music when exposed to a breeze. The quotation is adapted from *Hamlet*, III.ii.358.

appropriated to my use at Oxford appeared comparatively narrow, squalid, and unwholesome. My very soul was cabined in them. There were spacious buildings in Oxford; there were open and cheerful walks: but how contrasted with those to which I had been accustomed! There I expatiated free; I possessed them alone; Nature was my friend, and my soul familiarly discoursed with her, unbroken in upon by the intrusion of the vulgar and the profane. Here I had no green and heaven-formed retreat in which I could hide myself; my path was crossed by boys; I was elbowed by gownmen; their vulgar gabble and light laughter perpetually beset my ears, and waked up curses in my soul. I could pursue no train of thought; the cherished visions of my former years were broken and scattered in a thousand fragments. I know that there are men who could pursue an undivided occupation of thought amidst all the confusion of Babel; but my habits had not fitted me for this. I had had no difficulties to struggle with; and I was prepared to surmount none.

The morning of life is pliable and docile. I speedily adapted myself to my situation. As I could not escape from the coxcombs of the university, I surrendered myself with the best grace I could into their hands. It is the first step only that costs a struggle. At the commencement, the savage of Merionethshire made but an uncouth and ludicrous figure among the pert youngsters of Oxford. Their speech and gestures were new to me. I had hitherto spent more words, the repetition of lessons only excepted, in soliloquy than in conversation. My phrases were those of enthusiasm and the heart. They had the full and pregnant form which was given them by a mind crowded with ideas and impelled to unload itself, not the sharp, short, pointed turn of a speaker whose habitual object is a jest. My muscles were not formed to a smile; or, if at any time they had assumed that expression, it was the smile of elevated sentiment, not that of supercilious contempt, of petty triumph, or convivial jollity.

As soon, however, as I had chosen my part in the dilemma before me, I became instinct with a principle, from which the mind of ingenuous youth is never totally free,—the principle of curiosity. I was prompted to observe these animals, so different from any that had been before presented to my view, to study their motives, their propensities, and their tempers, the passions of their souls, and the occupations of their intellect. To do this effectually, it was necessary that I should become familiar with many, and intimate with a few. I entered myself an associate of their midnight orgies, and selected one young person for a friend, who kindly undertook my introduction into the world.

It happened in this, as in all cases of a similar nature, that familiarity annihilated wonder. As the hero is no hero to his *valet-de-chambre*, so the monster is no monster to his friend. Through all the varieties of the human race, however unlike in their prominent features, there are sufficient chords of sympathy, and evidences of a common nature, to enable us to understand each other, and find out the clue to every seeming irregularity. I soon felt that my new associates were of the same species as myself, and that the passions which stimulated them, had seeds of a responsive class, however hitherto unadverted to and undeveloped in my own bosom.

It is surprising how soon I became like to the persons I had so lately wondered at and despised. Nothing could be more opposite, in various leading respects, than the Fleetwood of Merionethshire and the Fleetwood of the university. The former had been silent and apparently sheepish, not, perhaps, more from awkwardness than pride. He was contemplative, absent, enthusiastical, a worshipper of nature. His thoughts were full of rapture, elevation, and poetry. His eyes now held commerce with the phenomena of the heavens, and now were bent to earth in silent contemplation and musing. There was nothing in them of the level and horizontal. His bosom beat with the flattering consciousness that he was of a class superior to the ordinary race of man. It was impossible to be of a purer nature, or to have a soul more free from every thing gross, sordid, and groveling. The Fleetwood of the university had lost much of this, and had exchanged the generous and unsullied pride of the wanderer, for a pride of a humbler cast. Once I feared not the eye of man, except as I was reluctant to give him pain; now

I was afraid of ridicule. This very fear made me impudent. I hid the qualms and apprehensiveness of my nature under "a swashing and a martial outside."[1] My jest was always ready. I willingly engaged in every scheme of a gay and an unlucky nature. I learned to swallow my glass freely, and to despise the character of a flincher. I carefully stored my memory with convivial and licentious songs, and learned to sing them in a manner that caused the walls of our supper-room to echo with thunders of applause. Here, as in Wales, I advanced toward the summit of the class of character to which I devoted my ambition, and was acknowledged by all my riotous companions for an accomplished pickle. In the contrast of the two personages I have described, I confess, my memory has no hesitation on which side to determine her preference. Oh, Cader Idris! oh, genius of the mountains! oh, divinity, that president over the constellations, the meteors, and the ocean! how was your pupil fallen! how the awestruck and ardent worshipper of the God who shrouds himself in darkness, changed into the drinker and debauchee, the manufacturer of "a fool-born jest," and the shameless roarer of a licentious catch![2]

I did not, however, entirely depart from the dispositions which had characterised me in Wales. My poetical and contemplative character was gone; all that refinement which distinguished me from the grosser sons of earth. My understanding was brutified; I no longer gave free scope to the workings of my own mind, but became an artificial personage, formed after a wretched and contemptible model. But my benevolence and humanity were still the same. Among the various feats of a college-buck I attempted, there was none in which I came off with so little brilliancy, as that of "quizzing a fresh-man," and making a fellow-creature miserable by a sportive and intemperate brutality. What scenes of this sort I have witnessed! There is no feature of man, by which our common nature is placed in so odious and despicable a light, as the propensity we feel to laugh at and accumulate the distresses of our fellow-creatures,

---

1   *As You Like It*, I.iii.118.
2   *Henry IV, Part II*, V.v.55; a "catch" is a round in which one singer catches at the word of another.

when those distresses display themselves with tokens of the ungainly and uncouth. I engaged in a project of this sort once or twice, and then abjured the ambition for ever. Thenceforward it was my practice to interfere in behalf of the sufferers by such hostilities; and my manner carried with it that air of decision, that, though the interference was unwelcome, it was successful; and the dogs of the caustic hunt let go their hold of the bleeding game. Another motive actuated me in this plan of proceeding. Though I had assumed an impudent and licentious character, I despised it; and I made conscience of debauching new converts into the inglorious school, which was usually the object and end of these brutal jests. I was contented to associate with those whose characters I judged to be finished already, and whom I persuaded myself my encouragement would not make worse; and thus with wretched sophistry I worked my mind into the belief that, while I yielded to a vicious course, I was doing no harm. In the midst of all this, my heart entered with prompt liberality into the difficulties and distresses of others; and as in Wales I was assiduous to relieve the wants of the industrious and the poor, so in Oxford, the embarrassments of those young men, whose funds derived from their families did not keep pace with the demands of their situation, excited in me particular sympathy, and received frequent and sometimes secret relief from the resources with which my father's bounty supplied me.

CHAPTER IV.

IN this place I feel inclined to relate one of those stories of ingenious intellectual victory, as they considered them, of dull and unfeeling brutality, as they really were, in which too many of my college contemporaries prided themselves. A young man, during my residence at the university, entered himself of our college, who was judged by the gayer Oxonians singularly well formed to be the butt of their ridicule. The dress in which he made his appearance among us was ungainly and ludicrous: the flaps of his waistcoat extended to his knees, and those of his coat almost to his heels: his black, coarse, shining hair, parted on the forehead, was every where of equal length, and entirely buried his ears beneath its impervious canopy. He had hitherto been brought up in solitude under the sole direction of his father, a country clergyman; but he was an excellent classic scholar and a mathematician, and his manners were the most innocent and unsuspecting that it is possible to imagine. In addition to these qualities, he had an exalted opinion of his own intellectual accomplishments; and he had brought with him, among his other treasures, the offspring of his stripling meditations, a tragedy founded on the story of the Fifth Labour of Hercules.[1]

In this performance the contents of the Augean stable were set out in great pomp of description; the ordure which had accumulated in thirty years from the digestion and dejection of three thousand oxen was amplified and spread out to the fancy; and Withers (this was the name of the poet) might be said, like Virgil, to "fling about his dung with an air of majesty."[2] The tragedy opened with a pathetic lamentation between the groom and the herdsman of the king, respecting the melancholy condition of the stable, and the difficulty of keeping the cattle which were so unroyally lodged in any creditable appearance. A herald then entered with a proclamation, declaring that three hundred of the king's oxen should be the prize of him who should restore the stable to a wholesome and becoming state. The chorus next sang an ode, in which they exposed the miseries of procrastination, and declared that none but a demigod could accomplish the task which had so long been postponed. In the second act Hercules appeared, and offered to undertake the arduous operation. He has an audience of the king, who dwells upon the greatness of the effort, and exposes, in a loftier style, what had already been described by his

---

1 For his fifth labor, Hercules was ordered to clean the notorious stables of Augeas, which had not been cleaned for years. Hercules managed the seemingly unmanageable task by diverting the river Alpheus so that it flowed through the stables.

2 Referring to the *Georgics* of the Roman poet Virgil (70–19 BC), poems on farming and rural industry. In "An Essay on the Georgics," appended to John Dryden's *The Works of Virgil in English* (1697), Joseph Addison wrote that "... he breaks the clods and tosses the dung about with an air of gracefulness."

..n familiar verse, the filth the hero would have to
..nter. Hercules answers modestly, and enters into the his-
..ory of the four labours he had already accomplished. The bar-
gain is struck; and the chorus admire the form and port of the
hero, and pray for his success. The third act begins with
expressing the general terror and astonishment. Hercules
removes the oxen from their stalls; and then a mighty rushing
sound is heard of the river leaving its ancient bounds, and
pouring its tide through the noisome and infectious walls. The
rest of the play consisted of the arguments on the part of the
king and of the hero, as to whether Hercules had fulfilled his
engagement; and the punishment of the tyrant. Here many
hints were borrowed from the contention of Ajax and Ulysses
in Ovid, respecting the preference of wisdom and ingenuity
over brute force: King Augeas insisting that the nuisance should
have been displaced with shovel and wheelbarrow; while Hercules with great eloquence maintained that to remove the
whole evil at once, by changing the course of a river, was a
more wonderful and meritorious achievement.[1]

This tragedy soon became a source of inexhaustible amusement to the wits and satirists of our college. One of the drollest
and demurest of the set had first wormed himself into the confidence of Withers, and extorted from him his secret, and then,
under the most solemn engagements not to name the matter to
a living creature, obtained the loan of this choice morsel of
scenic poetry. He had no sooner gained possession of it, than
he gave notice to four or five of his associates; and they assembled the same evening, to enjoy over a bottle the treasure they
had purloined. It must be owned that the subject of the drama
was particularly calculated to expose the effusions of its author
to their ridicule. The solemn phrases, and the lofty ornaments,
with which every thing was expressed, afforded a striking contrast to the filth and slime which constituted the foundation of
the piece. A topic of this sort, however slightly mentioned,

---

1   In Book XIII of the *Metamorphoses* of the Roman poet Ovid (43 BC-AD 17), a con-
    test was held after the death of Achilles in the Trojan War to determine who most
    deserved to be awarded the great warrior's armor. Ulysses, the cleverer speaker, eas-
    ily won over his compatriot Ajax.

must appear low and absurd; but, when the dung, accumulated in thirty years, by three thousand oxen, together with the solemn engagement between a demigod and a king for its removal, is set out in all the pomp of verse, the man must be more sad than Heraclitus, and more severe than Cato, who could resist the propensity to laughter at the hearing of such a tale.[1] In the present case, where every joyous companion was predetermined to find materials for merriment, the peals of laughter were obstreperous and innumerable; many passages were encored by the unanimous voice of the company; and, in conclusion, the scoffer, who had obtained for them their present amusement, was deputed to procure them the higher and more exquisite gratification of hearing the piece gravely declaimed to them by its author.

Accordingly, in a few days, he waited on Withers with a grave and melancholy face, manuscript in hand, and confessed, that by a very culpable neglect, he had fallen into a breach of the engagement he had made to the author on receiving it. He then named a young man of ingenuity and fancy in the same college, who had obtained considerable notoriety by several pieces of fugitive poetry, which were much admired at Oxford. Withers had heard of him, and felt that respect which might naturally be expected for a brother of his own vocation. Morrison, the jester, added, that this votary of the muses, and himself, were upon so intimate terms, that each had a key to the other's chamber; that he, not recollecting this at the moment, had left the manuscript, being called away by a particular occasion, open upon his desk, had locked the door, and departed; and that the poet, arriving soon after, had discovered, and seized with avidity, the Fifth Labour of Hercules.

Withers was greatly distressed at this tale. He had those feelings of modesty, which, under certain modifications, are most incident to such persons as are pervaded with an anticipation of their future eminence. He did not pretend, however, to blame his friend for a fault into which he seemed so innocently to have fallen, and which he so ingenuously confessed. On the

---

1   Heracleitus (540-480 BC), Greek philosopher and misanthrope; Cato "the Elder" (234-149 BC), Roman statesman who served as censor with notorious severity.

other hand, Morrison soothed the dramatist, by describing to him the transports of admiration with which the poet had been impressed in the perusal of this virgin tragedy.

While they were yet in conversation, the poet knocked at the chamber-door. The verses of this young man, Frewen by name, were not deficient in merit, or even in delicacy; but his features were harsh and his manners coarse. He began with saying, that he could by no means deny himself the pleasure of soliciting the acquaintance and friendship of a youth, to whose mind he had the vanity to believe his own was in so many respects congenial. He then launched out in rapturous praise of the Fifth Labour of Hercules. Seeing the manuscript on the table, he requested permission to open it, and point out to the author one or two places which had struck him as particularly excellent. He then read part of a speech from King Augeas's groom, and that with such emphasis of delivery, and seeming enthusiasm of intonation, as might have persuaded the most sceptical bystander that he was really smitten with approbation of the verses he pronounced. The eyes of Withers glistened with joy. His self-love had never experienced so rich a treat. Frewen then proceeded to descant, with great ingenuity, upon certain metaphors and ornaments of style interspersed through the composition; showing how happily they were chosen, how skilfully adapted, how vigorously expressed, and how original they were in the conception; and, though some of the clauses he fixed upon were to such a degree absurd, that the poet himself, when he heard them thus insulated from their connection, began to suspect that all was not right, yet the remarks of his panegyrist were so subtle, and above all, were delivered with an air of such perfect sincerity, that he finished with being completely the dupe his false friends had purposed to make him. In conclusion, Mr. Frewen observed that he had a select party of friends, whom he was accustomed to make judges of his own productions; and he earnestly entreated Withers that he would no longer conceal his talent, but would condescend to recite the tragedy he had written, to the same circle.

Withers unaffectedly shrunk back, with the diffidence of a young man, who had never yet, in so striking a manner, burst the bounds of modesty; but, urged alternately by the solicitations and the encomiums of his tempters, he suffered them to "wring from him his slow consent."[1] A day was then to be fixed. He refused to make it the same evening: he confessed to his visiters that it would be an unprecedented exertion to him, and that he must string up his mind to the task: it was ultimately fixed for the day following.

In the interval Withers had many qualms.

> "Between the acting of a dreadful thing,
> And the first motion, all the interim is
> Like a phantasma, or a hideous dream."[2]

He felt the sort of arrogance which was implied, in the seating himself in the chair of honour, fixing the eyes of different persons, strangers, upon him, and calling their attention to the effusions of his brain, as to something worthy of their astonishment. He recollected the faults of his poem, the places where he had himself doubted, whether he had not embraced a Sycorax instead of an angel.[3] He recollected his youth and inexperience, and the temerity of which he had in reality been guilty, in undertaking, in his first essay, to celebrate, perhaps, the most prodigious of the labours of the immortal Hercules. He remembered what he had somewhere heard, of the satirical and malicious turn of the elder Oxonians, and feared to become their butt. On the other hand, he called to mind the beauties of his poem, and was encouraged. Above all, he considered his character and fortitude as at stake, in the engagement he had contracted, and was determined, at every hazard, to complete it.

The evening arrived; the company assembled; the unhappy poet, the victim of their ridicule, was introduced. Mr. Frewen, at his entrance, took him by the hand, led him into the middle of the room, made a short oration in his praise, and, in the name of the company, thanked him for his condescension, in

---

1   *Hamlet*, I.ii.58-60 (adapted).
2   *Julius Caesar*, II.i.63-65.
3   Sycorax is referred to as a witch and as the mother of Caliban in Shakespeare's *The Tempest*.

admitting them to such a pleasure as they were about to receive. After a variety of grimaces on the part of the persons present, the manuscript was laid on the table. The poet took it up to read; but, in the first line, his voice failed him, he turned pale, and was obliged to desist. Morrison, his original seducer, and another, had so placed their chairs, that their countenances and action could not be perceived by the reader, they being partly behind him: they winked the eye, and pointed the finger to each other, and by various gestures endeavoured to heighten the entertainment of the party. The table was covered with bottles and glasses. Frewen, when he saw the unaffected marks of Withers's distress, began to feel an impulse of compunction; but he knew that such an impulse would render him for ever contemptible to the present society, and he suppressed it. He filled Withers a bumper, which he obliged him to take off; he snatched the play from his hand, and read with much gravity and articulation, the opening speech from the stable-keeper to the herdsman, in which the former bewails the miserable state of the stalls, and, not knowing what to quarrel with, shows himself ready to quarrel with his fellow-officer, laments that there are such animals as oxen, or that oxen cannot live but by food and digestion. This speech was received with bursts of applause, and Frewen particularly commended the "long majestic march and energy divine" of the concluding verse.[1] The poet was encouraged; he had had time to reason with himself, and recover his fortitude; Frewen restored to him his manuscript, filled him another bumper, and the scene commenced.

That my readers may more exactly understand the spirit of the transaction, I will insert here a part of the chorus at the end of the third act, with which the auditors pretended to be especially struck:—

I.

Illustrious hero, mighty Hercules!
Much hast thou done, and wondrously achieved!
Before thy strength

---

1   Alexander Pope, "First Epistle of the Second Book of Horace Imitated" (1737), l. 269.

The Nemæan lion fell subdued,
  Closed in a worse than Cornish hug!
The heads of Hydra, one by one, were crush'd
  Beneath thy club of brass:
While little Iolas, thy gentle squire,
  Stood by,
  With red-hot salamander prompt,
  And sear'd each streaming wound!
The stag so swift of Œnoe the fair
  Thou didst o'ertake,
  Or, if not overtake,
  Didst catch it in a trap!
How glared the eyes of Erymanthus' boar!
  How fierce his tusks!
  How terrible his claws!
His fire and fury calm thou didst survey,
And calm didst knock his brains out![1]

2.

  Oh! mighty man!
  Or rather shall I name thee god?
A different labour now demands thy care:
No fangs now menace, and no tongues now hiss,
No rage now roars, nor swiftness flies thy grasp;
  Terror no longer waits thee;
  But strength is here required;
Strength, patience, constancy, and endless resolution.

3.

Behold these mountains, how they rise!
The slow collections of three hundred moons;
  Nay almost four!
  Sleek were the oxen that produced them;
  And royally were fed!
  Canst thou abate the nuisance?

---

1 The first four labors of Hercules included his conquering of four infamous creatures: the Nemean lion; the Lernean Hydra, a poisonous and multiple-headed water
  monster; the elusive, golden-horned Cerynean stag; and the wild Erymanthean
  boar.

What gulf so wide that would receive its bulk!
     Much likelier might'st thou seek,
          With single strength,
To level Ossa, or to cast mount Athos
     Down to the vasty deep![1]

4.

Here too thou must encounter odours vile,
     And stand begrimed with muck:
          Thy cheeks besmear'd,
          Thy lineaments deform'd,
     Beneath the loathsome load:
A guise how much unworthy such a hero!
Ah, no! those godlike fingers ne'er were made
     To ply the nightman's trade![2]
          Ah, cruel fate!
     Ah, step-dame destiny!
     Inflicting such disgrace
Upon the last-born son of mighty Jove!

One apology may be made for the contrivers of this scene, that they by no means foresaw, in the outset, how far they should be drawn in to go, and the serious evils of which they might become authors. The purpose of the auditors was, under extravagant and tumultuous expressions of applause, to smother the indications of their ridicule and contempt. In this, however, they could not uniformly succeed. A phrase of a ludicrous nature in the piece, an abrupt fall from what was elevated to something meanly familiar or absurd, would some times unexpectedly occur, and produce a laughter that could not be restrained. Nor would the feelings allied to laughter always occur in the right place. Persons eager in search of the ludicrous, will often find it in an image, or mode of expression, which by others, not debauched with this prepossession, would be found fraught with pleasing illustration and natural sentiment. The circle, too, assembled on this occasion, acted by

---

1   Ossa is a mountain in Thessaly; Athos a mountain on the Chalcidian peninsula.
2   A nightman was an emptier of privies.

sympathy upon each other, and pointed many a joke, and gave vigour to many a burlesque idea, which perhaps, to any one of the associates, in his retirement, would have appeared unworthy to move a risible muscle.

For a short time the jesters, who had made Withers their prey, observed a certain degree of decorum. They bit their lips, affectedly raised their eyes, applied the finger to the mouth, the nose, or the forehead, and thus pacified and appeased their propensities to ridicule. One and another incessantly showed themselves lavish in commendation of the beauties of the poem; and with every compliment the glass of Withers was filled, and he was excited to drink. Presently the laugh, imperfectly suppressed, broke out in one solitary convulsion, and was then disguised in a cough, or an effort to sneeze. The dumb gestures of the auditors were unperceived by the reader, who for the most part kept his eyes on the paper, and but rarely ventured, when he came to some bolder flight, to look round him for applause. Then the countenances of the hearers suddenly fell, and their limbs were at once composed into serenity. This transition produced an effect singularly humorous, but which was wholly lost upon Withers, who had the misfortune to be purblind.

By and by an outrageous laugh burst forth at once from one of the audience. The poor novice, their victim, started, as if he had trod on a serpent. Frewen, making a motion to him to be tranquil, addressed the offender with much apparent gravity, and begged to know what he could find ludicrous in the passage which had just been read, at the same time repeating the two last lines with a full and lofty voice. The culprit, as soon as he could resume his seriousness, humbly sued for pardon, and declared that he laughed at nothing in the poem, of which no one could be a sincerer admirer, but that his fancy had been tickled at the sight of a corkscrew (picking it up), which had just dropped from Jack Jones's pocket. This apology was admitted. In a few minutes the same person broke out into an equally loud and clamorous fit of merriment, in which he was now joined by two or three others. Greater anger, as the tumult subsided, was expressed toward him; a more bungling and imperfect apology was tendered; and Frewen offered, if Mr. Withers required it, to turn the culprit out of the room. In one or two instances the poet was requested to read again some passage which the requester affected particularly to admire; and these repetitions were ever attended with additional merriment, sometimes suppressed, and sometimes ungovernable. In one or two of the choruses, several of the auditors repeated the concluding verses after the reader, sometimes as nearly as possible keeping pace with him, and at other times pursuing one another after the manner of a *fugue* in music; and, when the author expressed his surprise at this phenomenon, they defended it, first, from the enthusiastic admiration they felt, and next, from the nature of a chorus, which was designed to be sung, or chanted, and not spoken, and from their desire to enhance their pleasure, by bringing the tragedy they were hearing to as near a resemblance as they could, in this respect, to the state of actual exhibition.

By this time the mind of Withers was in a pitiable situation. That noviceship and total inexperience on his part, which made his torture, constituted the great pleasure of his remorseless tormentors. He was unaccustomed to wine; and they had made him extremely inebriated. He was unaccustomed to high commendations and vociferous applause; and they had raised his mind and purer feelings into a state of intoxication, little inferior to that of the more ponderous and corporeal particles of his nerves and brain. All was confusion and tempest within him. Upon this state of the man were superinduced the demonstrations of ridicule and laughter, which by degrees broke out in the audience. His brain was clouded; his understanding was in a maze; he apprehended nothing distinctly. Grave apologies were made to him; and he accepted them seriously; though, presently after, he was compelled to doubt whether they did not wholly originate in the grossest hypocrisy. Had he possessed the smallest portion of knowledge of the world, he could not have harboured a moment's uncertainty; but he was in all these respects a child. They nursed him, so to speak, in mistake, and rocked him in the cradle of delusion. By degrees they persuaded him to mount upon the table, that he might recite some of the most brilliant passages with greater effect. They crowned him with wreaths of parsley, which happened to be the vegetable at hand; they anointed him with libations of wine; and by this time his apprehension was so completely subverted, that he was unable to distinguish whether these things were done in mockery or honour, and willingly resigned himself to the more agreeable construction. At length the reading was finished; and the rioters (for all was now in a state of riot) burst open the door, placed the poet, crowned with parsley, and trickling with wine, in a chair, and carried him triumphantly through the streets to his apartment, with shouts, and vociferation, and uproar, enough to awake the dead.

The deluded rioters, for they laboured under a state of delusion not less complete than their victim, persuaded themselves to look back with complacency upon the diversion of the evening, and even agreed that they had not yet extracted amusement enough from so rich a subject as the unhappy Withers. The ringleaders, in their insatiate thirst after this species of gratification, planned a further scene to be grafted on what had passed in the evening of the reading.

Morrison accordingly waited on Withers the next morning, and found him a prey to a miserable headache. The poet was also, now that the fumes of wine were dissipated, full of melancholy reflections on the incidents of the day, and extremely apprehensive that in all that had passed he had been an object of mockery to the assembly. Morrison put the best gloss upon the whole, assured his dupe that all was done in sober sadness, apologised for the most extravagant particulars by observing that the whole party was nearly drunk, and declared on his honour that the manifestations, however uncouth, were those of genuine admiration; adding that, for the sake of their sincerity and good meaning, the poet ought certainly to excuse the rudeness and ungraciousness of the form they had assumed. During the harangue of this buffoon, the eyes of Withers once or twice flashed fire; they were turned upon the speaker with a searching penetration as if they would look him through; and the poet swore a great oath, that he believed he was deceived, and that, if it were so, he would die sooner than endure it.

This subject having been discussed, Morrison informed

Withers that he had a piece of bad news to communicate to him. The master of the college, he said, had got information of the riot of the preceding night, and the disorder they had committed in the streets, and had hinted that he was determined to make an example. While they were upon this painful topic, Frewen entered, and added to Morrison's intelligence, that by some unaccountable accident the master had got hold of the name of Withers, and that, as he had been carried in the chair, it was to be feared that he would be selected as the object of punishment. Withers was a young man of great intrinsic modesty and sensibility, and he felt the utmost distress at this information. While his hollow-hearted companions were pretending to console him, a young man, a stranger to Withers, entered in the character of a messenger from the master, and summoned the poet to make his appearance before his academical superior the same evening soon after sunset.

Machinery, such as the malicious and riotous genius of the young men concerned in the plot suggested to their thoughts, was prepared for the occasion. In a chair near the wall, at the upper end of a spacious room the use of which they procured, was seated a puppet, dressed up in a gown and wig similar to those of the master, which it was proposed to pass on the unfortunate Withers for the identical person of the superior whose reproof he dreaded. This image, by the ingenuity of some of the parties to the plot, was so contrived as to have its head and hands capable of being moved by one of the confederates, who unseen held the springs for that purpose. Morrison, so much admired by his fellow-collegians for wit and humour, had among other accomplishments the art, commonly called ventriloquism, of uttering articulate sounds without any visible motion of the lips, and of causing his voice to appear to come from whatever quarter he pleased; added to which he was an excellent mimic, and could copy the peculiarities of speech in almost any one he pleased, to a supreme degree. The fame of these qualities would no doubt in a short time have reached the ears of Withers; but he was newly come to the university, and had as yet no suspicion that Morrison was even considered as a wit.

In the evening, just after the shut of the day, Withers was introduced into the apartment which had previously been prepared. He was accompanied by Morrison, Frewen, and the other offenders; some having thrust themselves unauthorised into the list of offenders, that they might have an opportunity to be witnesses of the expected sport. The figure which stood for the master of the college then appeared to call over the names of the culprits; and a young person below him, who seemed to officiate as his secretary, answered to each of the names that the person called upon was present. The master began his harangue. He addressed himself first to Frewen, and after to Morrison; and each of these attempted a sort of excuse for the outrage, and professed great contrition. The address to Morrison was particularly diverting to the spectators, every one of whom, except Withers, well knew that it was Morrison in person who thus pronounced a severe and apparently angry censure upon himself.

The speech of the principal was then directed toward Withers, whom he declared he felt himself obliged to treat as the ringleader, as he had been the person elevated in the chair; he added, that certain privileges were by long practice conceded to the senior students in the university, but that it was intolerable for a young man, not many weeks entered in this seat of learning, to be seen drunk in the streets, and to be complained of for a riot.

Withers defended himself with more spirit than was expected. He protested that he was no drunkard, and was exceedingly chagrined that an unfortunate accident had exhibited him under that character. He added, that, so far from being the ringleader in the riot, he was made an unwilling tool in the hands of others.

"Name them!" replied the master, in a strong and imperious voice.

"Name them!" rejoined Withers: "no, I will not be an informer; consider me as the ringleader!"

He then proceeded to question the propriety of the rule just delivered, of punishing strictly in the juniors, what was winked at or slightly animadverted on in those of longer standing.

"Sir," interrupted the master, "you were not sent for to criti-
cise our rules, and to teach me how to conduct myself; and you
have just shown yourself refractory to the first principles of academical discipline by refusing to become what you call an
informer. What now remains is, that I should vindicate the
decorum of the college, by punishing you for the riot you have
committed; and I accordingly order you to strip off your gown
in my presence, and direct that you be excluded from all academical privileges for one month; at the end of which term, upon
your expressing a proper degree of sorrow and humiliation, you
may possibly be restored."

Withers felt indignant at this censure, and was going to
remonstrate; but was prevailed on by those who stood near him
to submit. He however threw his gown to the floor with some
resentment, and could not refrain expressing in three or four
words some contempt for such trappings, and the privileges
annexed to them. At this moment, to his utter astonishment
and confusion, the figure lifted up its hand, as if in the intention
of striking him. This indignity put Withers beyond all patience,
and worked him into a momentary insanity: he flew at the
master, and positively began to cuff the image with violence:
the machine was unable to resist this species of rudeness, and
actually fell in pieces about the ears of its assailant. The candles
were extinguished, and the room left in utter darkness; and at
the same moment a long, obstreperous, and deafening peal of
laughter burst out from every person in the assembly.

Thus ended the scene plotted and conducted by these ingenious gentlemen; but not thus ended the consequences which
resulted from it. The impression it made upon the mind of
Withers was indelible. He had given himself up passively from
the beginning to the ideas which his deluders wished to excite
in him; the last incident, therefore, of their comedy had taken
him at once, like a thunderbolt. He slunk away in confusion
and silence. His mind had been violently acted upon by the
events before him, while the whole appeared to him as serious.
He had been a stranger to any greater applause than that of
having construed well an ode in Horace;[1] and he now found

---

1   Horace (65-68 BC), Roman poet.

himself treated in one of our famous seats of learning as the foremost among the votaries of the muses. He had been a stranger to pointed rebuke under the indulgent discipline of his father; and he now found himself called before the dignified master of a college, and treated with injustice and contumely. He had been acting, as he imagined, a high and conspicuous part before his fellow-collegians, acquiring laurels in the temple of Apollo, and asserting the cause of justice against insolent and tyrannic authority. On a sudden all this was reversed; instead of honour, he encountered disgrace; he found he had been made a laughing-stock to all around him. The concluding moment of the business explained to him the whole; he saw that the applauses he had received were all ironical, that he had been invited to the reading his play only for contempt, that he had been treated as the weakest, the absurdest, and the most despicable of mankind. The scene of the master, the affected reprimand he had received, the stripping of his gown, the attempted blow, constituted a still deeper insult. It must be acknowledged that this was no flattering induction of an innocent and artless rustic into a great university. Withers lifted up his head no more. He could not bear to face any of his fellow-students; those who had not been actors in the plot against him were, he nothing doubted, well acquainted with all that had passed; he shut himself up, as much as possible, in his own apartment. After a brief interval it was sufficiently visible that his intellects were impaired; a keeper was planted over him. He raved against poets and poetry; he seized with avidity every scrap of written paper he could meet with, that he might commit it to the flames. These excesses, however, were rare; the greater part of his time was spent in dejection and silence. One morning he escaped from the man who was appointed to watch him, and was soon after found drowned in the Isis.[1] The cause of his unhappy catastrophe became public; the particulars were enquired into; and Frewen and Morrison were expelled from the university with a disgrace which pursued them for the rest of their lives.

This may serve as one specimen of the sort of grave-faced

---

1   The river Thames was also known as the "Isis," from its Latin name "Tamesis."

trick and delusion which the choice spirits among us delighted to put upon the more innocent and unsuspecting members of the university. The example here given was perhaps the most memorable, and attended with the most fatal effects, of any that occurred in my time. But all the tricks which were played were of the same class; all turned upon considering the simplicity displayed, and the anguish endured by the sufferer, as a source of merriment. For myself, as I have said, I had no relish for this amusement. Once or twice, inconsiderately and precipitately, I yielded to the importunity of my companions, and became entangled in such adventures; but I presently abjured every thing of the sort; and, having set my face against pleasures so criminal in their temper, was repeatedly successful in delivering the bleeding prey from the jaws of its devourers.

The adventure which I have here recorded may seem foreign to my object, of painting my own story: I know not where, however, I could have found a more apt illustration to set before my reader the character of the persons by whom I was now seduced, and with whom I at present associated. They were such youths as Frewen, Morrison, and the rest, whose applauses I sought, whose ridicule awed me, and whose judgment I looked to for the standard of my actions.

CHAPTER V.

It is not my purpose to convert these honest pages into a record of dissipations; far less, of the rude and unseemly dissipations of an overgrown boy. There are few characters more repulsive than that in which we find conjoined the fresh and ingenuous lineaments of a young man, in whom the down has scarcely yet shaded his prosperous cheek, with the impudence of a practised libertine. I look back upon it with horror. Youth, if once it has broken through the restraints of decorum, is the minister of cruelty. Even in me, whose disposition was naturally kind and humane, there was too much of this. It is suffering only that can inspire us with true sympathy, that can render us alive to those trifles which constitute so large a portion of earthly misery or happiness, that can give us a feeling of that anguish, which, sometimes in human beings, as most evidently in the brute creation, works inwardly, consuming the very principle of life, but has no tongue, not the smallest sound, to signify its excess and demand our pity. Over this, of which the soberest and most disciplined mind is scarcely prepared to make a true estimate, youth, when flushed with convivial gaiety and high spirits, tramples without remorse, and unhesitatingly assures itself that "All is well." Among the manifold objects which shock our imperfect reason, and make us wish that the constitution of things was in certain respects other than it is, I confess there is none which has at all times been more impressive with me than this, the vast variety of speechless misery which is every where to be found.

I passed through the usual period of education at the university, and then, by the liberality of my father, was sent to make a tour of other countries for my improvement. My father had, particularly, an old and much valued friend in Switzerland, whose kindness he wished me to cultivate, and whose affectionate and benevolent wisdom he thought would contribute much to the perfecting my character. To him I was furnished with a most exemplary letter of parental introduction, as well as with letters of the usual description to several distinguished and honourable individuals in the courts and principal cities of Europe.

The day on which I quitted the university was an important era in my life, and might have been expected to redeem me from the vices which I had there contracted. The necessities (such I was disposed to regard them) which had rendered me dissolute, were now removed. I had become vicious by the operation of a populous and crowded residence (from a contact with the members of which I found it impossible to escape) upon a young man, unwarned by experience against the rocks that awaited him, and stimulated to confidence and enterprise by the feeling that he was born to a considerable estate. When I quitted Oxford, I had once more the globe of earth to move in. I had elbow-room, and could expatiate as I pleased. I was no longer cooped and cabined in a sort of *menagerie*, in which I continually saw the same faces, knew the names and the little history of those I saw, and was conscious that I in my turn became the subject of their comment, of their contempt or their approbation. I now saw once again the fairest and most glorious of all visages, the face of nature. If I passed to the Continent, I should have the opportunity of viewing her in new aspects; and, if I hastened, as my father wished me to do, to Switzerland, I should be led to the contemplation of a more admirable scenery than my eyes had ever yet beheld. If I sojourned for a short time in cities, my situation there would be very different from what it had been at Oxford. There would be no particular set of men appearing under such circumstances as in a manner extorted my confidence, but I might associate indifferently with any, or with what persons I pleased.

Another cause was favourable to the melioration of my character. The great disadvantage to which young men in a populous place of education are exposed, is the freedom they enjoy from the established restraints of decorum and shame. They constitute a little empire of their own, and are governed by the laws of a morality of their own devising. They are sufficient to keep each other in countenance; and, if any one of them can preserve the good opinion and esteem of the rest of the body, it is all of which he feels that he stands in need. The principles by which he is regulated are voted by an assembly that is prompted by turbulence, high spirits, convivial good-humour, and a factitious sense of generosity and honour; and, provided these principles are obeyed, he looks down with contempt on the sense of mankind in general. Even the soberer laws which are promulgated by his academical superiors, are canvassed in a mutinous temper, and regarded as the decrees of froward age; obedience to them is sometimes contemplated as a dire necessity, and sometimes as a yoke which it is gallant and liberal to disdain.

But, when the same person goes out into the world, he becomes the member of a larger republic. He respects himself proportionably more, as he feels that he is acting his part upon a wider theatre. He grows a graver character, and is conscious that tumult and frolic are not the business of human life. He demands, not a boisterous approbation, but a sober deference and respect, from those with whom he has intercourse.

I grieve to say, that my character did not gain so much by this transplantation, as a person anxious for my reputation and welfare might have been willing to hope. It was at sixteen that I had repaired to the university, and I had resided there four years. These four years are the period of the developement of the passions. When I looked back from the close of this period, the years I had spent in Merionethshire appeared to me as a delightful dream, but only as a dream. It was a season of nonage, the infancy of man. It was visionary, and idle, and unsubstantial. I had now risen (thus I understood it) to the reality of life. The scenes I had passed through in Oxford were sensible, were palpable; those of my earlier and better years were the illusions as of a magic lanthorn.[1] I clung, at least on the threshold, and during the novelty of life, to the realities, and could not bear to exchange them for shadows. I felt as if I could not so exchange them if I would. I had leaped the gulf; I had passed the bourne, from which, as it seemed to me (in a different sense from that of Shakspeare) "no traveller returns."[2] Having once plunged into the billows, and among the tumult of the passions, I must go on. It was thus I reasoned, when the temptations, which presented themselves in the different stages of my travels, solicited my acceptance.

I would not, however, be understood for worse than I was. My life at Oxford was a life of dissipation; but it was not all dissipation. That curiosity, which had been one of my first seducers into vice, often assumed an ingenuous form. The various sciences which invited my attention at the university, did not always solicit in vain. My nature was not yet so brutified as to render me indifferent to the venerable achievements of human intellect in successive ages and in different countries. My mode of passing my days had too much in it of the life of a gamesome and inebriated savage; but all my days were not so passed. The same vanity that led me among the licentious to aspire to a

---

1 An optical instrument that projects upon a wall or screen a magnified image of a
   picture on glass.
2 *Hamlet*, III.i.81.

licentious character, gave me the ambition to show that I could be something more. I aspired to resemble the true Epicurean of ancient times, the more illustrious philosophers who had adorned that sect in Greece, or Horace, the graceful and accomplished ornament of the court of Augustus.[1] I had therefore my fits of study and severe application, as well as my seasons which were exclusively devoted to pleasure. And, when I once secluded myself from my riotous companions, I may, without vanity, affirm, that I effected more, and made a more full and pregnant improvement of knowledge in a week, than many of the mere bookworms of the university, and some too of no mean estimation among their fellows, did in months.

At Paris I met with Sir Charles Gleed, a young man who had been at Oxford at the same time that I was, and who had occasionally made one in the riotous and dissolute parties that I frequented. Sir Charles had appeared with no great brilliancy in Oxford. His mind was slow and indocile. He had a tutor, who took great pains with him, and who had occasionally persuaded Sir Charles to take pains too; but though the labour, and still more the apparatus and report had been great, the produce had been little. There was a bluntness and hebetude in poor Sir Charles's parts, that seemed to prove him adapted to an office like that of the horse in a mill, rather than of the race-horse or the hunter. When this operose and hard-working student descended from his closet, and gained a sort of tacit leave from his tutor to join in the circle of us gay and high-spirited fellows, the part he played was no more advantageous to him, than his former exhibition had been among the learned. He wished for the character of a wit, and had thought, that the ample estate attached to his birth would be a sufficient indorsement to the repartees which he uttered. But in this he was deceived. We were too thoughtless and frolic, perhaps I might say too liberal and independent of soul, to decide on the talent of our companions from the length of their purses. Sir Charles soon found that he was better qualified to be "the cause of wit in

---

1 An Epicurean was a follower of the hedonistic school founded by the Greek philosopher Epicurus (341-271 BC), which held pleasure to be equal with the good. Augustus (63 BC-AD 14) was Emperor of Rome from 27 BC until his death.

others," than to be a wit himself;[1] and the asperity and indignation with which he bore this, and the awkward attempts by
which he endeavoured to shake it off, fluctuating between
resentment and a suspicion that what he suffered was not a
fitting ground of resentment, only made the general effect
upon bystanders the more irresistibly ludicrous.

I observed, with surprise, that Sir Charles was received upon
a very different footing at Paris, from what he had been at
Oxford. Here he performed the part of an *elegant*, and was generally admitted as a man of breeding, amusement, and fashion.
No one laughed at, and almost every one courted him.

It has frequently occurred to me to see this metamorphosis,
and to remark persons, who in their boyish years had been
thought dull and poor fellows, afterward making a grave and no
dishonoured figure upon the theatre of life. At school, certainly, the number of dunces is much beyond its due proportion,
(particularly if we have regard to the higher classes of society),
to those who are ordinarily put down for such in maturer life.
Perhaps scarcely more than one boy in a hundred is clever; but,
when these boys grow up to be men, the dullard will frequently play his part to the great satisfaction of the spectators; and
not only outstrip his more ingenious competitor in the road of
fortune, but even be more highly esteemed, and more respect-
fully spoken of, by the majority of those who know him. I
have often been desirous to ascertain in what manner we are to
account for so curious a phenomenon; and I have found that
there are two ways in which it may happen.

First, the man who plays his part upon the theatre of life,
almost always maintains what may be called an artificial character. Gravity has been styled by the satirist, "a mysterious carriage of the body to conceal the defects of the mind"; and
young men educated together are scarcely ever grave.[2] They
appear in simple and unvarnished colours; theirs is not the age
of disguise; and, if they were to attempt it, the attempt, so far as
related to their colleagues, would be fruitless. The mind of a

---

1   *Henry IV, Part II*, I.ii.10 (adapted).
2   François de Marsillac, Duc de La Rochefoucauld (1613–80), *Réflexions ou sentences et
    maximes morales*, No. 257 (1665).

young man at college is tried in as many ways, and turned and essayed in as various attitudes, as the body of an unfortunate captive in the slave-market of Algiers. The captive might, with as much probability of success, endeavour to conceal his crooked back or misshapen leg, as the Oxonian or Cantab to hide his dulness, his ill-temper, or his cowardice.[1] But, when the same persons are brought out into the world, there are certain decorums, and restrictions from good manners, which operate most wonderfully to level the varying statures of mind: and (to pursue the idea suggested by the slave-market) the courtier, the professional man, or the fine lady, do not more abound in advantages for concealing their bodily deformities, than for keeping out of sight those mental imbecilities, which the lynx-eyed sagacity and frolic malice of schoolboy against schoolboy are sure to discover and expose.

Beside which, secondly, the part which a man has to play upon the theatre of life is usually of much easier performance than that of a stripling among his fellows. The stripling is treated with a want of ceremony, which deters him from properly displaying many of his powers. It has been remarked, that the severity of criticism in ages of refinement suppresses those happier and more daring fruits of genius, which the dawn of science and observation warmed into life; and in these respects the entrance of a young man into the world operates in a way something similar to the transportation of the poet to a period of primeval simplicity. He is no longer rudely stared out of countenance. To change the similitude, a college-life may be compared with a polar climate; fruits of a hardy vegetation only prosper in it, while those of a more delicate organisation wither and die. The young man, having attained the age of manhood, no longer suffers the liberties to which he was formerly subjected, and assumes confidence in himself. This confidence is in many ways favourable to his reputation and success. It grows into a habit; and every day the probationer is better enabled to act with propriety, to explain his meaning effectually, and to display that promptitude and firmness which may command

---

1 As the term "Oxonian" refers to a student at Oxford University, the term "Cantab," or "Cantabridgian" refers to a student at Cambridge University.

approbation. I should prefer, however, I must confess, the schoolboy hero to the plausible and well-seeming man of the world. Mistakes may occur, indeed, respecting the former as well as the latter. A false taste may lead his fellow-pupils to give the palm to a wild, adventurous, and boastful youth, over his more tranquil competitor, though the latter should be endowed with the most perspicuous intellect, the finest imagination, or the most generous temper. There is, too, a ready faculty of little depth, a rapid mimetic, superficial memory, which will some-times pass on inexperienced observers for a consummate genius. The judgment, however, which is formed on the phe-nomena of early youth, has two advantages: first, as this period of human life is free from deception and false colours; and, secondly, as qualities then discovered may be supposed more rooted and essential in the character, than such as discover themselves only in a season of maturity.

To return to Sir Charles Gleed. I found him, as I have said, established on an unequivocal and honourable footing at Paris. He was received with distinction by a minister of state, who invited him to his most select parties. He was a favoured guest in the coteries of ladies of fashion, and often spent his morn-ings in the *ruelle* of a duchess.[1] Sir Charles was certainly a man of displeasing physiognomy. It was a picture so rudely sketched, that the spectator could scarcely guess what was designed to be represented by it. The eyes were small and pinking; the nose colossal and gigantic, but ill-defined. The muscular parts were fleshy, substantial, and protuberant. His stature, however, was considerably above the middle size; and his form, at least to an ignorant observer, seemed expressive of animal force.

Sir Charles was perhaps sensible how little he was indebted to the bounty of nature; and he was careful to compensate his personal defects, by the most minute vigilance in conduct and demeanour. By some accident he had acquired, since he left the university, the happiest of all foundations for success in the world, a tranquil confidence in himself. His speech, his motions, were all slow; but, as no part was lost in false efforts, in

---

1 In eighteenth-century France, a lady's bedroom in which she might hold a morn-ing reception.

something done that was afterward to be done again, his slowness had, to a certain degree, the air and effect of haste. He
continually approached to the brink of enterprise, and was
never enterprising. He perpetually advanced to the verge of
wit and observation, and never said any thing that was absolutely the one or the other. The man however must, I believe, be
admitted to have had some portion of judgment and good
sense, who could so speciously imitate qualities, to the reality of
which he was a stranger. If he committed a blunder, the
bystander might look in his face, and would discern there such
an unsuspecting composure, as might lead him almost to doubt
his opinion, and believe that there was no blunder. With the
ladies he was attentive, officious, and useful, but never bustling
or ridiculous; by which means his services never lost their just
value. Nothing of a nature more weighty ever thrust the details
of a gallant demeanour out of his thoughts; and the sex was
flattered to see a man so ample in his dimensions, and therefore,
according to their reckoning, so manly, devoted to their
pleasure. For the rest, whatever they observed, which would
have been less acceptable in a Frenchman, was attributed to, and
forgiven in consideration of, his being a stranger to their
language, and having a disposition and bent of mind, appropriate, as they supposed, to the nation from which he came.

Such was the man who generously performed for me the
part of gentleman-usher, and introduced me to the society of
the courtiers and belles of France. Our characters were strikingly contrasted. He was set, disciplined, and regular; I was
quick, sensitive, and variable. He had speciousness; I sensibility.
He never did a foolish thing; I was incessantly active, and therefore, though frequently brilliant and earning applause, yet not
seldom falling into measures the most injurious to the purposes
I had in view. Naturally I was too tremblingly alive, to be well
adapted to the commerce of the world: I had worn off a part of
this at Oxford; I had gained a certain degree of self-possession
and assurance; yet was my sensibility too great, not frequently
to lead me into false steps, though I had afterward the fortitude
and presence of mind to repair them.

Sir Charles and I having every reason to be satisfied with our reception in this celebrated metropolis, engaged amicably in similar pursuits, and succeeded with persons of different predilections and tastes, without in the smallest degree interfering with each other. The court of Louis the Fifteenth, the then reigning sovereign, was licentious and profligate, without decency, decorum, and character; and the manners which prevailed within the walls of the palace, were greedily imitated by every one who laid claim to, or who aped, rank, refinement, or fashion.[1] It were superfluous for me here to describe, what the reader may find in so many volumes amply and ambitiously detailed, the contempt for the marriage bond, and the universal toleration then extended to adultery and debauchery, with the condition only that they should be covered with a thin and almost transparent veil, and not march entirely naked.

Prepared, as I had been, by my adventures at Oxford, I fell but too easily into the maxims and manners then in vogue in the court of France. Could I have been abruptly introduced to a scene like this, immediately after my departure from Merionethshire, I should have contemplated it with inexpressible horror. But my experience at the university had killed the purity and delicacy of my moral discrimination. In Wales, the end I proposed to myself in my actions was my own approbation; at Oxford, I had regulated my conduct by the sentiments of others, not those of my own heart. I had been a noisy and jovial companion; I had associated freely and cordially with characters of either sex, that my judgment did not approve. Friendships like these had indeed been of short duration; but they were of sufficient power to contaminate the mind and distort the rectitude of feeling and habit. From intimacies built on so slight and inadequate a basis, from a practical disregard of continence and modesty, the transition was easy to the toleration and abetting of the most shameless adultery.

At the university, I had been driven from a sort of necessity to live upon the applauses of others; and, the habit being once formed, I carried it along with me in my excursion to the

<hr />

1   Louis XV (1710–74) was King of France from 1715 to his death.

Continent. In the societies to which I was introduced, no man was considered as any thing, unless he were, what they styled, *un homme à bonnes fortunes*, that is, an individual devoted to the formation of intrigues, and a favourite with those ladies of honourable seeming, who held their virtue at a cheap rate. The men who were regarded in Paris as models of politeness, stimulated me to pursuits of this sort by the tenor of their conversation, while the women, from time to time, who boasted of rank, beauty, and elegant manners, invited me by their insinuations and carriage, and taught me to believe that I should not be unsuccessful in my enterprises. I was young and unguarded; I had no Mentor to set my follies before me in their true light; I had passed the Rubicon of vice, and therefore was deficient in the salutary checks of reflection.[1] My vanity was flattered by the overtures of the fair; my ambition was awakened by the example of the prosperous and the gay: I soon made my choice, and determined that I also would be *un homme à bonnes fortunes*.

CHAPTER VI.

THE first woman who in this career fixed my regard was a finished coquette, by which epithet I understand a woman whose ruling passion is her vanity, and whose invention is hourly on the rack for means of gratifying it. She was a lady of high rank, and married to a person of great figure at court. I first obtained her attention under favour of the epithet by which the Parisian belles thought proper to distinguish me, of *the handsome Englishman*. Sir Charles, my introducer, was certainly of more established vogue than myself, and in this respect might have seemed a conquest still more flattering to a person of her character. But the Marchioness easily discerned that he

---

1   Mentor was the loyal friend and adviser of Odysseus in Homer's *Odyssey*. Athena assumed Mentor's appearance in guiding Telemachus in search of his father. The Rubicon was the river which formed the boundary between Republican Rome and Cisalpine Gaul; by crossing it ahead of a legion in 49 BC in order to enforce certain demands, Julius Caesar initiated the first Roman civil war. "Passing the Rubicon" thus refers to making a decision that cannot be reversed.

would have afforded her less occupation and amusement. Sir Charles would perhaps have equalled me in constancy and perseverance; but he had a calmness of temper in affairs of this sort, which to her tastes would have been intolerable. Obedient, obsequious, patient of injuries, he would undoubtedly have shown himself; he was of a character unalterably obliging toward the fair; to violence he would have opposed no violence in return, but would have waited till the storm was dissipated, and then have sought to improve the lucky moment when the bird of peace brooded over the subsiding billows, and the tumult of the bosom was ended.

My character was of an opposite sort. Sir Charles appeared to the animated and restless spirit of the Marchioness more like a convenient instrument, or a respectable piece of furniture, than a living being whose passions were to mix, and shock, and contend, and combine, with her own. She would have preferred a lap-dog who, when she pinched or slapped him, would ruffle his hairs, and snarl and bark in return, to such a lover. To vex the temper and alarm the fears of her admirer was her delight. She would not have thought him worth her care, if she did not ten times in the day make him curse himself, his mistress, and all the world. She desired no sympathy and love that were not ushered in by a prelude of something like hate. In a word, she aspired to the character ascribed by Martial to one of his friends: "There was no living with him, nor without him."[1]

The singularities of this woman's temper particularly displayed themselves in the gradations she introduced into the favours by which my attachment was ultimately crowned. I might describe the transport of my soul, when I first became assured that there was no mark of her good will which she was inclined to withhold from me. I might delineate the ravishing sweetness of the weather on the day which first gave me possession of her person, the delightful excursion we made on the water, the elegantly furnished cottage that received us, the very room, with all its furniture, which witnessed the consumma-

---

1 Martial (c. AD 40-103), Roman poet known for his witty and often pointed epigrams.

tion of my joys. All these things live in my memory, and constitute a picture which will never be obliterated while this heart continues to beat. But I suppress these circumstances at the risk of rendering my narrative flat and repulsive by its generalities. I write no book that shall tend to nourish the pruriency of the debauched, or that shall excite one painful emotion, one instant of debate, in the bosom of the virtuous and the chaste.

The Marchioness tormented me with her flights and uncertainty, both before and after the completing my wishes. In the first of these periods I thought myself ten times at the summit of my desires, when again I was, in the most unexpected manner, baffled and thrown back by her caprices and frolics. Even after, as I have said, the first ceremonies were adjusted, and the treaty of offence was not only signed, but sealed,

> "Me of my yielded pleasure she beguiled,
> And taught me oft forbearance;"

though I cannot say, in the sense in which Shakspeare has imputed it to his heroine, that she did it, with

> "A pudency so rosy, the sweet look on't
> Might well have warm'd old Saturn; that I thought her
> As chaste as unsunn'd snow."[1]

It was in my nature to attach myself strongly, where I attached myself at all, and by parity of reason to be anxious concerning propriety of conduct, and the minutenesses of behaviour, in the person I loved. This was exceedingly unfortunate for me in my affair with the Marchioness. It was almost impossible to make her serious. At moments when all other human beings are grave, and even in allowing those freedoms which ought to be pledges of the soul, she could not put off an air of *badinage* and raillery. Her mind greatly resembled in its constitution the sleek and slippery form of the eel; it was never at rest, and, when I thought I possessed it most securely, it

---

1   *Cymbeline*, II.v.9-13 (adapted).

escaped me with the rapidity of lightning. No strength could detain it; no stratagem could hold it; no sobriety and seriousness of expostulation could fix it to any consistency of system.

Had this been the only characteristic of her mind, a person of my temper would soon have been worn out with the inexhaustibleness of her freaks and follies. But she had an ingenuousness of carriage by which I was for a long time deceived. She seemed, when I could gain her ear for a moment, to confess her faults and absurdities with a simplicity and unreserve that were inexpressibly charming: and she had in herself an equability of soul that nothing could destroy. Where other women would have been exasperated, she laughed; and when by her flightiness she had driven her lover to the extremity of human bearing, she mollified him in a moment by a gentleness and defencelessness of concession that there was no resisting. Yet it often happened that she had no sooner by this expedient won my forgiveness, than she flew off again with her customary wildness, and urged me almost to madness.

One passion which eminently distinguished the Marchioness, was the perpetual desire of doing something that should excite notice and astonishment. If in the privacy of the *tête-à-tête* she was not seldom in a singular degree provoking, in public and in society she was, if possible, still worse. The human being, who is perpetually stimulated with the wish to do what is extraordinary, will almost infallibly be often led into what is absurd, indelicate, and unbecoming. It is incredible what excesses of this sort the Marchioness committed. Her passion seemed particularly to prompt her to the bold, the intrepid, and the masculine. An impudent and Amazonian stare, a smack of the whip, a slap on the back, a loud and unexpected accost that made the hearer start again, were expedients frequently employed by her to excite the admiration of those with whom she associated. In the theatre she would talk louder than the performers; in a dance, by some ridiculous caprice, she would put out those with whom she was engaged; she was never satisfied unless the observation of all eyes were turned on her.

It might seem at first sight that a demeanour of this sort would excite general disapprobation, and make every one her enemy. On the contrary, the Marchioness was a universal favourite, at least with the male sex. Her countenance was exquisitely beautiful; in her eye was combined a feminine softness with vivacity and fire; her figure, which a little exceeded the middle size, seemed moulded by the Graces; and every thing she did was done with an ease and elegance that dazzled the beholders.[1] What would have been absurd and indecorous in most women, became pleasing and ornamental in her. Though the substance of the action was wrong, the manner seemed to change its nature, and render it brilliant and beautiful. She did impudent things without assumption and arrogance; and what in another would have been beyond endurance, seemed in her an emanation of the purest artlessness and innocence. Besides, that such was the rapidity and quickness of her nature, she did not allow to ordinary observers the time to disapprove. She never dwelt upon any thing; nothing was done with slowness and deliberation; and she passed so incessantly from one object of attention and mode of action to another, that every thing seemed obliterated as soon as seen, and nothing was left in the common mind but a general impression of wonder and delight.

This, however, was not the effect upon me. I often took upon myself to censure the improprieties of the Marchioness. My murmurs, as I have said, never put her out of temper. Sometimes she would rally me upon my severity, and vow that, instead of a young and agreeable lover, she had by some chance fallen upon a morose philosopher, who wanted nothing but a long gown and a beard to make him the worthy successor of Diogenes.[2] Sometimes she would play off her usual arts, and, by some agreeable tale, or amusing sally of wit, force my attention to another subject. At other times she would put the woman upon me, display her charms, assume the attitudes, the gestures,

---

1 The three Graces, Euphrosyne (Mirth), Aglaia (Brightness), and Thalia (Bloom), were the attendants of Aphrodite, goddess of love and beauty.

2 Diogenes (c. 400-325 BC) founded the philosophical school of the Cynics, who believed that self-sufficiency alone could bring contentment in life.

and expression of features, allied to voluptuousness, and make it impossible for a young and susceptible admirer as I was, to give breath to another word of harsh and ungentle signification. On a few occasions she would personate a seriousness, responsive to my seriousness, promise to be very good, and to conduct herself hereafter in a manner that should command my approbation. Her most ordinary method, however, was to ridicule my advices, and exasperate me by pertinacious and incorrigible folly; and it was never till she had exercised my patience to the utmost, that she condescended to soothe me with blandishments and promises of amendment.

Inconsistency was the very element in which she moved; and, accordingly, whatever was the penitence she displayed, and the amendment she promised, this one feature constantly attended her, that these little expiations never produced any effect on her conduct, and that the fault she professed most solemnly to abjure, was sure to be the fault she would be the earliest to commit.

The torment which this species of character in a mistress inflicted on me is undescribable. The pain I suffered from the excesses she fell into was vehement: when she frankly confessed how much she had been to blame, I became almost angry with myself for the gravity of my censure: and when again I saw her repeat the same unbecoming folly without reflection or hesitation, I was confounded at so unexpected an event, and cursed my own infatuation; at the same time that, in spite of myself, I could not help admiring the artless and simple grace, which even upon such occasions did not desert her. One thing that contributed, perhaps more than all the rest, to make this woman of so much importance to me, was the perpetual occupation she afforded to my thoughts. Abroad or at home, in company or alone, she for ever engaged my attention, and kept my soul in a tumult, sometimes, though rarely, of pleasure, frequently of apprehension, alarm, jealousy, displeasure, and condemnation.

One question continually haunted my thoughts. This woman, so frivolous, so fickle, so uncertain, could she love? If not, was it not beneath the character of a man to be so perpetually occupied about a person, whom I felt to be of so little genuine worth, and by whom I was continually deluded? These doubts, this self-questioning and compunction incessantly haunted me. Yet, in the midst of all my struggles, one inviting wave of her hand, one encouraging glance of her eye, brought me in a moment to her feet.

Never satisfied in this point, I, however, gratuitously ascribed to her a thousand virtues. Grace has something in it so nearly akin to moral rectitude and truth, that the unvitiated observer can scarcely disjoin them even in imagination, or persuade himself to believe that, where the former is, the latter is not. True, unaffected grace seems the very reflection of a candour and sincerity, which, knowing no wrong, has nothing to disguise. It is free from perplexity and effort; the heart appears to be on the lips, the soul to beam from the countenance. Was not so perfect an ingenuousness sufficient to atone for innumerable errors? I know not whether the rest of my species are framed to receive so pure a delight as I originally did from the very sight of a serene and composed human countenance. A thousand times, when my heart has burned with anger, the smile of him who has offended me, even though a common acquaintance, has disarmed me. I have said, "That calm expression, that unwrinkled physiognomy, that quiet, unruffled eye, can never be the cloke of a mind which deserves my hate; I feel in it, as it were, the precept of God speaking to *my* eye, and commanding me to cherish, assist, and love my fellow-man." When absent from him who had awakened my resentment, I could feel aversion, and recollect many severe and bitter remarks with which I was desirous to taunt him; when present, his voice, his countenance, changed the whole tenour of my thoughts, and tamed me in a moment. If this were the case in reference to one of my own sex, and an ordinary acquaintance, it may easily be supposed how I felt toward a mistress, who had excited in me, under some of its forms, the passion of love.

Our correspondence for some weeks was such, as, while it furnished an almost incessant occupation for my own thoughts, left me, I believed, little reason to apprehend that the Marchioness was less engrossed by me; but I was mistaken. I was at present wholly new to the world of gallantry. I had led a life of dissipation at Oxford; but, hardened and brutalised, as to a certain degree I was, by the associates of my excesses, and having never encountered in these pursuits a woman of distinction, of interesting story, or engaging manners, I had scarcely ever felt a single flutter of the heart in these idle and degrading engagements. It was far different now. My vanity was stimulated by a success so flattering as that of my amour with the Marchioness appeared in my eye. Often I trod in air; often I felt the quick pants of my bosom, and walked with head erect, as if respiring a sublimer element; even when in solitude I reflected on the homage which this proud beauty paid to the attractions of my person, and the persuasion of my tongue.

> "Of all the trophies which vain mortals boast,
>   By wit, by valour, or by wisdom won,
>   The first and fairest in a young man's eye
>   Is woman's captive heart."[1]

I was therefore in the wrong to measure the modes of thinking or of sensation in my mistress's bosom by my own. She had long been inured to those things which were new and interesting to me, and she felt them not less coldly than she expressed them. I was willing to impute a contrast between her language and her sentiments; but in this respect I did the Marchioness wrong; she was no hypocrite here.

At length Sir Charles Gleed removed the film which had grown over my eyes, and cured me of my infatuation. Sir Charles was a man who, in many points, observations of detail, saw the world more truly than I did. I have often remarked, though I will not affirm how far it is to be taken as a general rule, this difference between men of imagination, and those whom I will call men of simple perception. It is something like a poet and a cultivator of the soil, ascending one of the Welsh mountains, or tracing together the tracts of land, meadow by meadow, which might be discovered from the top of it. The

---

1   John Home (1722-1808), *Douglas* (1756), Act IV, lines 312-15.

farmer sees the nature of the fields, the character of their soil, and what species of vegetation is most adapted to grow in them. If he looks upward, he can tell the configuration of the clouds, the quarter from which the wind blows, and the prognostications of the weather. When he comes home, he can count up the plots of ground over which he has passed, the regions to the right and left, and enumerate the wheat, the barley, the oats, the rye, the clover, and the grass, which grew in each. The poet, during the progress we are supposing, saw much less, though his mind was more active and at work than that of the farmer. The farmer's were perceptions; his were feelings. He saw things in masses, not in detail. He annexed a little romance to each. In the clouds he discerned a passage, through which he passed, and beyond which he plunged in imagination into the world unknown. It was not green and blue, ripe and immature, fertile and barren, that he saw; it was beauty, and harmony, and life, accompanied with a silent eloquence which spoke to his soul. The universe was to him a living scene, animated by a mysterious power, whose operations he contemplated with admiration and reverence. To express the difference in one word: what the farmer saw was external and in the things themselves; what the poet saw was the growth and painting of his own mind.

The difference between Sir Charles Gleed and myself was parallel to this when we mingled in the scenes of human society. While he saw only those things in character and action which formed the substance of what was seen by every beholder, he was led astray by no prepossessions or partialities, and drew a great number of just conclusions from the indications before him. I, on the contrary, entered into every scene with certain expectations, and with a little system of my own forming ready digested in my mind. If I repaired to Nôtre Dame at Paris to assist at the celebration of the high mass solemnised on the eve of the Nativity, my thoughts were full of the wonderful efficacy which religion exercises over my species, and my memory stored with the sublime emotions which altars, and crucifixes, and tapers had excited in the souls of saints and martyrs. If I entered the walls of the British House of Commons, and waited to hear an important debate, the scenes of past ages revolved before the eyes of my fancy, and that parliament again filled the benches in which Pym and Hampden, and Falkland and Selden, and Cromwell and Vane, sat together, to decide, perhaps for ever, on the civil and intellectual liberties of my country.[1] These are only instances; but in reality scarcely any character of the smallest importance came before me, in whom, by retrospect or anticipation, by associations of pride, of instruction, or of honour, I did not make to myself a lively interest, and whom I did not involuntarily surround with an atmosphere of my own creating, which refracted the rays of light, and changed the appearances of the scene. These causes rendered me a less dispassionate, and therefore, in many, instances, a less exact, though a much more earnest observer than Sir Charles Gleed.

When Sir Charles told me what he had remarked, I was struck with inexpressible astonishment. I could not, at first, believe the report he made, and reproached him in my thoughts for that vulgarity of mind which made him always see in the actions of others something allied to his own. I asked him a thousand questions; I demanded from him a thousand proofs; and it was not till he had given me evidences amounting to demonstration, that I consented to part with a delusion which had been so delightful to my mind. That the Marchioness, whom I had so entirely loved, in whose partiality I had so much prided myself, whose smallest errors had afflicted me as spots upon the lustre of her qualities, should be a woman of abandoned character, disengaged from all restraints of decency and shame, that, when I thought I possessed her whole, I really divided her favours with every comer—a music-master—an artisan—a valet,—it is impossible to express how sudden and terrible a revolution this discovery produced within me!

---

1 Major figures in the English Civil War (1642-48) in which Charles I was over-thrown and beheaded in 1649. John Pym (1584?-1643), John Hampden (1594-1643), John Selden (1584-1654), and Sir Henry Vane (1613-62) were leading anti-royalists, while Lucius Cary, second Viscount Falkland (1610-43), was a well-known royalist. Oliver Cromwell (1599-1658) served as leading Puritan general of the parliamentary army and ruled England as Lord Protector from 1653 to 1658.

CHAPTER VII.

I was in Paris, and I did as people of fashion in Paris were accustomed to do. I consoled myself for the infidelity of one mistress by devoting my attentions to another. The qualities of the Countess de B——— were exceedingly unlike those of the Marchioness; perhaps, led by a sentiment to which I was unconscious, I selected her for that very reason. The Marchioness I have compared to the sleek and glossy coated eel: for ever restless, never contented with the thing or the circumstances under which she was, you could never hold her to one certain mode of proceeding. The only way in which for her lover to become satisfied with her, was to persuade himself that her external demeanour was merely a guise put on, which belied her heart, and that, when she seemed most impatient, capricious, and fantastical, her soul confessed none of these follies, but assumed them to veil the too great sensibility of her nature. The Countess, on the contrary, appeared to be wholly destitute of art. Though past the first season of youthful inexperience, she appeared to have acquired none of the lessons of prudery and factitious decorum. Her heart shone in her visage; the very tones of her voice were modulated to the expression of tenderness. Hers was "the sleepy eye, that spoke the melting soul."[1] Her cheek was full, her skin transparent; the least thought of pleasure or of passion suffused her countenance with a blush. The Countess had no atom of the restlessness of her rival; a sort of voluptuous indolence continually attended her; and the busy nothings of ordinary life seemed to be an insupportable burden to her. She appeared born only to feel; to reflect, to consider, to anticipate, to receive and concoct the elements of instruction, were offices in which she seemed incapable to exist. It was her habit, therefore, to resign herself wholly to her feelings, and to be in them undivided and entire. To judge from every exterior indication, it was impossible for a tenderer mistress to exist; she gave herself up to her lover, and treated him as if he were father, mother, fortune, reputation,

---

1 Alexander Pope, "First Epistle of the Second Book of Horace," l. 150.

and life to her, in one. She placed no restraint on herself, but appeared all anxiety, terror, apprehension, gratitude, enjoyment, as the occasions most obviously led to one or another of these emotions.

Yet this woman was capable of the more stormy impulses of resentment and jealousy, but only in such a way as best accorded with the sensibility and voluptuousness of her character. Her resentment was passive and desponding; when [it] wounded, it appeared incompatible with the purpose of wounding again; in the person against whom it was directed, it excited not sentiments of hostility, but of pity; and her tender bosom seemed to wait only the moment of passionate reconciliation. When her lover returned to her, or persuaded her of the sincerity of his affection, gratitude and delight possessed her wholly, and reproach died away upon her lips. The Countess, by her manners, reminded her admirer of the most delicate flower of the parterre, which the first attack of a rude and chilling blast immediately withers, but which, by the lustre of its tints, and the softness of its texture, seems to advance an irresistible claim to gentle protection and western breezes. Tears from her sparkling eyes broke forth almost at will; by a tear she expressed her sufferings, and by a tear her joy. This might, perhaps, have been grievous to her lover, had she had the smallest bias towards a querulous temper. But her character was a perpetual summer; her storms were only like the soft droppings of a sultry evening, and easily gave place to a fair sky and a radiant heaven.

The intellect of the Countess de B——— was of narrow dimensions. Her mind had never been turmoiled with the infusions of science; she scarcely knew that there were antipodes,[1] or that there had been ancients. She lived like those insects which the naturalists describe, generated on the surface of certain lakes, that are born only to hover along the superficies of the pellucid element, to enjoy, and to die.

What pity that the sentiments of such a person as the Countess de B——— were so little entitled to be depended

---

1 Opposite ends of the Earth.

upon! According to the ideas many men entertain of the fair sex, it was impossible for any one, in the particulars above described, to be more exactly qualified for a mistress or a wife, than this fascinating woman. There was no danger that she should become the rival of her lover in any man-like pursuits, or that with troublesome curiosity she should intrude herself into his occupations of learning, of gain, or of ambition. She had all the attributes that belong exclusively to the female sex, and as few as possible of those which are possessed by the whole species, male and female, in common. She was rather an Asiatic sultana, in her turn of mind, than a native of our western world. And her habits would have been equally accommodated to the man who, having serious pursuits for his graver hours, wished either not to impart or not to remember them in his hours of pleasure; and to the man who, being in the heyday of his youth, and favoured by nature and by fortune, desired to thrust the world aside, and take his swing of indulgence uninterrupted and unchecked. I belonged to this latter description.

Unfortunately, however, the Countess, though she seemed to feel with her soul, had the spring of her sentiments and actions in her eyes. Where she attached herself, it was with such a show of ardour, that the lover must have been captious and difficult indeed, who was not satisfied with the sincerity of passion she displayed toward him. Yet the passion of the Countess was rather an abstract propensity, than the preference of an individual. A given quantity of personal merit and accomplished manners was sure to charm her. A fresh and agreeable complexion, a sparkling eye, a well-turned leg, a grace in dancing, or in performing the manoeuvres of gallantry, were claims that the Countess de B——— was never known to resist. She appeared to administer her decisions upon these different pretensions with the most rigid equity; and they were sometimes very minute distinctions, scarcely discernible by the naked eye, that decided her hair-breadth preferences. Upon this rigid equity there was only one limitation; and this also was sufficiently in correspondence with the theory of the subject. Among the various sources of what are called the pleasures of the imagination, one, as learned doctors tell us, is novelty. To this the Countess de B—— paid the strictest attention; and, where there was any uncertainty in the comparison of personal advantages or polite accomplishments, the latest pretender was sure to carry the day. Amiable Countess! Like the wanton bee, which flits from flower to flower, equally enamoured with each in turn, and retaining no painful recollections of that which was last quitted, to render the qualities of the next offerer less agreeable and exquisite. I remember her even at this time with kindness. She seemed to skim the surface of life, and to taste of a continual succession of pleasures. It was, perhaps, unreasonable ever to be angry with her. She had almost too little reflection and concatenation of ideas, to make her a competent subject of moral jurisdiction. It was not, however, always thus with her; her career was short, and she expiated, by long and severe calamities, for her brief period of unchecked enjoyment. Whatever may be thought of her demerits, few persons ever drank more deeply of the cup of retribution. But this does not belong to my history.

It will easily be concluded from what I have stated, that the termination of my amour with the Countess de B—— was very similar to that with the Marchioness. I trusted; I was deceived; my eyes were opened; I suffered all the torments of disappointment and despair. A quick and living sensitiveness was one of the most obvious characteristics of my mind; and few men felt disappointment, of almost every kind, more deeply. When the breach took place between me and the Marchioness, I had been for some days like a man distracted. The Countess de B—— presented herself to my observation just at that critical moment; the more than feminine gentleness and softness of her nature, were exactly adapted to allure my attention in this period of anguish; and it was owing to this fortuitous concurrence, that I recovered my equilibrium, in a certain degree, much sooner than could reasonably have been expected. It has often been a matter of jest in the world, when a widower, who seemed to be inconsolable for the partner of his heart, suddenly marries again; and the inference usually drawn is, that his grief was pure mummery and representation. I grant that the man who thus conducts himself is guilty of a breach of decorum, and that his behaviour is rather calculated to excite our disesteem than our respect; but I affirm that it is sufficiently natural, and that there is no need of having recourse to the imputation of hypocrisy to account for it. There is a principle in man, impelling him to seek his own preservation, and pursue his own happiness; and this principle will frequently urge him, in proportion to the dreadful vacuity produced by the loss of that which no possibility can restore to him, to seek to replace it by somewhat of the same species, and to endeavour to relieve his disconsolate state by a companion, who may in like manner share his thoughts and engage his tenderness.

The loss of the Countess was much more terrible to me than that of her predecessor. The Marchioness had kept me in a state of perpetual agitation, a temper of mind not unallied to fortitude. The Countess de B——— had softened and relaxed my mind, and left in me a temper ill suited to the struggling with misfortune. The Marchioness was a woman that I loved and hated by turns; she was often too masculine and peremptory to be an object of tenderness; her character, adapted continually to produce wonder and astonishment, lost by just so much of the faculty to please. But the Countess was all sweetness. In the eyes of her lover she appeared like an angel. She rose upon him like the evening star, mild, radiant, tranquil, and soothing. In periods of the most entire communication and accord, she seemed to leave him nothing to wish, but appeared in his eyes the exact model of perfection. From the Marchioness you continually expected something extraordinary: her ambition was to shine; and that which is extraordinary must, of course, be sometimes good and sometimes ill. But the Countess de B——— was so simple, so intelligible, it seemed as if nothing could happen with her that might not exactly be foreseen; she was wholly engaged in the object of her selection, and appeared to live for that alone.

The distress I suffered from the inconstancy of the Countess de B——— was inexpressibly acute. It taught me to abhor and revile her sex. It inspired me with a contempt of human pleasures. I felt like the personage of a fairy tale I have somewhere read, who, after being delighted with the magnificence of a seeming palace, and the beauty of its fair inhabitants, suddenly sees the delusion vanish, the palace is converted into a charnel-house, and what he thought its beautiful tenants, are seen to be the most withered and loathsome hags that ever shocked the eyes of a mortal. My soul was in tumults. I loathed existence and the sight of day; and my self-love was inexpressibly shocked to think that I could have suffered so gross a delusion. I fled from Paris, and sought the craggy and inhospitable Alps; the most frightful scenes alone had power to please, and produced in me a kind of malicious and desperate sentiment of satisfaction.

Most earnestly do I entreat the reader to pardon me, for having thus much interspersed these pages with a tale of debaucheries. It is not, I solemnly assure him, that I have any pleasure in the recollection, or that I glory in my shame. Some men, I know, would palliate this narrative to themselves, by saying that the things here related belong to the country where my scene is placed, and that morals have no certain standard, but change their laws according to the climate in which they exist. From my soul do I abjure this apology. Without entering abstrusely into the general merits of the question, I intimately feel in myself, that I carry about me, wherever I go, the same criterion of approbation, which bends to no customs, and asks no support from the suffrage of others to make it what it is. At the time of which I have been speaking, I was young and wild; I had been much injured by the sort of company I frequented for some years before I left England; and I gave easily and without compunction into the dissipations of the metropolis of France. But I do not look back upon them without aversion. I have written the narrative of this period under impressions of deep pain, and every line has cost me a twinge of the sharpest remorse. There are some kinds of writing in which the mind willingly engages, in which, while we hold the pen in our hand, we seem to unburden the sentiments of our soul, and our habitual feelings cause us to pour out on the paper a prompt and unstudied eloquence. Here, on the contrary, I have held myself to my task with difficulty, and often with my utmost effort I have scarcely written down a page a day on the ungrateful subject.

Why have I introduced it then? Because it was necessary, to make my subsequent history understood. I have a train of follies, less loathsome, but more tragic, to unfold; which could not have been accounted for, unless it had been previously shown by what causes I, the author, and in some respects the principal sufferer, was rendered what I was. I was a misanthrope. Not a misanthrope of the sterner and more rugged class, who, while they condemn and despise every thing around them, have a perverted sort of pleasure in the office, whose brow for ever frowns, whose voice has the true cynical snarl, and who never feel so triumphant a complacency, as when they detect the worthlessness and baseness of whoever comes into contact with them. This sort of man, even in my unhappiest state of desolation, I could always look down upon with pity. My misanthropy was a conclusion, however erroneous, that I unwillingly entertained. I felt what I was, and I pined for the society of my like. It was with inexpressible sorrow that I believed I was alone in the world. My sensibility was not one atom diminished by my perpetual disappointments. I felt what man ought to be, and I could not prevent the model of what he ought to be from being for ever present to my mind.

CHAPTER VIII.

I HASTENED, as I have already said, from Paris, and plunged amidst the wild and desolate scenery of Mount Jura.[1] The next intended stage of my travels was Switzerland, and I pursued the road which led to that country. The first anxiety I felt was to escape from France. That kingdom had been the theatre of my sufferings and my disgrace. There first I had felt my mind agitated with those emotions which are destined to have so mighty an influence on the fate of man. But how agitated? I had loved. I had not loved innocence; I had not loved the

---

1 The mountain range along the border of France and Switzerland.

chaste simplicity of the female character: my affections had not gone forth toward any object, which might refine and elevate my soul, which might free me from the impurities I had contracted among the debauchees of the university, restore me to peace with myself, and prepare me to act an honourable part on the theatre of society. Unfortunately my initiation had been in the polluted tracts of adulterous commerce. My mind had been acted upon with vehemence, but not improved. What true sympathy and affection can arise between persons of opposite sexes, when the basis upon which their intimacy is founded is crime?—when all decorum and character are trampled under foot, and nothing is aimed at but licentious pleasure, at the expense of all our best duties, and all that is truly honourable in human life?

I had been interested in the Marchioness. She had originally been considered by me as the model of a spirited, frank, and ingenuous character. But the affections of my soul had been much more strongly excited by the Countess de B———. The Marchioness was, and had ultimately been set down by me for, a character merely artificial. But the Countess was a woman who appeared to set up no defences, and employ no stratagems; who surrendered herself fully, with all her faculties and all her soul, to her lover. In her I persuaded myself that I had found that true simplicity which is most worthy to engage the heart of every beholder. I did not perceive that she was in the worst sense of the word a sensualist, and that this was in a consummate degree a departure from the genuine female character; but unfortunately was induced to judge of the whole sex from the specimens which had thus been brought before me.

Amidst the mountains which separate Switzerland from France, the idea of the Countess was perpetually present to my thoughts. In Troyes and the other towns which lay in my route, along the populous roads, and by the side of navigable rivers, my thoughts were interrupted, if not amused: but the instant I plunged into solitude and the retreats of uncultivated nature, my reveries became endless and inexhaustible. When I turned round a point of the rock, when I gazed intently, yet with an absent mind, upon the deep shadows of the mountains, visto beyond visto, enveloped in clouds, lost in obscurity, and where no human form was to be discerned, there the figure of the Countess de B——— flitted before me. I heard her voice between the pauses of the echoes, and amidst the dashing of the cascades.

Why had I left her?—Had I left her?—Why had she proved herself dishonourable and unworthy?—Was she indeed unworthy?—I believed every thing, and I believed nothing. Ten times I was inclined again to turn my face toward Paris, and throw myself at her feet. She could not be guilty: that face was a pledge of her rectitude: depravity and inconstancy could not lurk behind the lovely expression of that angelic countenance!——What, turn back, and expose myself to the contempt of every one in Paris, and to her own? What, sue to her, that she would forgive to me the vices she had committed? Be a sharer of her caresses with———? There was no such woman! It was all a delusion! I might look for her through Paris, and through the world, but should never find her. The scales had dropped from my eyes, and I might pray in vain, if I could be worthless enough to pray, for the restoration of my former blindness.

I descended the Alps, and entered into Switzerland. It may be, the very air of this country,—the country of freedom, of independence, moderation, and good sense,—had a favourable effect on my temper. I began now to think of M. Ruffigny, to whose protection and counsels my father had so emphatically recommended me. Never did I hear the eulogium of one man pronounced by another with that energy and enthusiasm with which my father spoke of this venerable Swiss. He had told me once and again at our parting, and in the letters he addressed to me in my travels, that, if ever I became the ornament of my house, and the benefactor of my fellows, it was to the friendship, the instructions, and example of Ruffigny that he looked for that benefit. I had seen this friend of my father once only, when I was five years of age; and the vague and imperfect recollection which remained in my mind, gave a sort of sacredness to his figure, and made him appear in my thoughts like a visitor from the starry spheres.

As I approached nearer to the residence of this man, I began to examine whether I was prepared to appear in his presence. I painted to myself his habitation as the grotto of an aërial spirit, whither I was repairing to do homage, and to receive the communications of an all-penetrating wisdom. While I had been engaged at Paris in the giddy round of licentious pursuits, I had forgotten this incomparable friend; nothing that related to him sobered and awed me; but, now that I had set my foot upon his native soil, I already seemed to feel the contact of his mind and the emanation of his virtues.

M. Ruffigny lived in a neat house which he had built for himself in the valley of Urseren, near the foot of Mount St. Gothard, the tallest and most stupendous of the hills of his country.[1] It was a fine summer evening when I approached his residence. The beams of the setting sun illuminated the peaks of the mountain, and gave a divine tranquillity to the plains. I felt my heart relieved from the rude tempests and the flagging and noisome atmosphere which had oppressed it. The sun was declining, and the heat of the day was over, when I entered a wood of tall and venerable trees, through which the road lay that led to his habitation. Nothing could be more grateful than the fresh, cool air, which penetrated this wood. After having for some time pursued a serpentine path, I came within sight of the house, and perceived the old man in his garden, examining the processes of vegetation, and stretching forth his hand to relieve and to raise such of its productions as stood in need of his aid. I had no doubt it was M. Ruffigny. I leaped from my horse, and, delivering him to the care of my servant, hastened to join the friend of my father. A little wicket at one extremity of the front of the house admitted me into the *potagerie*.[2] The owner was tall, and of a venerable presence, with a little stoop in his carriage, his visage placid, his eye penetrating amidst the wrinkles of age, and his hair as white as snow. He was somewhat turned from me as I approached, but, hearing a quick step he lifted up his head and surveyed me.

---

1   Saint Gotthard is an Alpine mountain range between the cantons of Uri and Ticino.
2   A kitchen garden.

I was too much engaged in contemplating his interesting figure instantly to announce myself. He hesitated for a moment, and then spoke.

"Casimir Fleetwood!" said he.

"The same."—He pressed my hand with peculiar emotion.

"The very image of Ambrose Fleetwood, his grandfather! I have expected your visit some time. I have a thousand things to say to you, and a thousand enquiries to make. You look like an honest man, and an observing one. It does my old heart good to receive under my roof the last representative of the friends I have loved and honoured more than any others I ever had."

M. Ruffigny proceeded to question me respecting my travels. How long I had left England? Where I had been? What stay I had made in Paris? What society I had frequented? What connections I had formed? What remarks and conclusions I had drawn from what I saw? He addressed to me no interrogatories but such as a friendly anxiety for my welfare might naturally dictate; yet I could perceive that he endeavoured to draw from his enquiries materials for estimating my understanding and character. I acquitted myself in this experiment as I could, though I felt embarrassed with the recollection of affairs and transactions in Paris, which I was not at present disposed to confide to M. Ruffigny. My venerable host listened with attention to what I said, and sometimes interposed his commendation where he judged it deserved, but at no time did there drop from his lips a syllable of censure. He probably conceived that premature criticisms on what I thought proper to unfold, would check the spirit of communication, and lessen the opportunity to discover my character which he was desirous to obtain.

As we walked up and down in the garden, engaged in this sort of conversation, I turned my eye occasionally round, and examined the spot in which I was placed. It was a scene in which use seemed to take the precedence of ornament. Though roses, woodbines, lilacs, and laburnums, with such other flowering shrubs as require little aid from the hand of the cultivator, were interspersed, the plots into which the inclosure was divided were principally appropriated to pulse and other esculent vegetables, and were bordered with fruit-bearing plants and shrubs. On the lower side of the garden was seen the broad expanse of the Reuss, which, though a little further from its source it dashes over rude fragments of rock in a continual cataract, flows along the valley in a smooth and silent stream. The opposite side of the garden was skirted by the acclivity of the mountain, the surface of which to a considerable height was covered with the most luxuriant vines my eyes ever beheld.

After having walked for a considerable time, we went toward the house. Upon a smooth turf before the door was spread a table, with a few melons, grapes, and wall-fruit, a loaf of bread, and a flagon of weak but agreeably flavoured wine. "This is my supper," said M. Ruffigny. We sat down together. We talked of England, of France, and of the country, in which we then were, and I was charmed and instructed with the acute remarks delivered by my host upon the comparative manners of each. He spoke with enthusiasm of the scenery of his native country, of the enviable freedom enjoyed by its inhabitants, and the happy equality and competence in which they lived. "Here," said he, "you behold, in happy contrast, the simplicity of man, and the exuberance of nature. My countrymen appear in the plainness of what in England you would call a quaker-like habit and manners, while the region that sustains them is clothed in all the dyes of heaven, and wantons herself in more various forms of majesty and beauty than mere imagination could ever conceive. Hence I learn to venerate and respect the intelligible rectitude of the species to which I belong, and to adore with sacred awe the mysterious power which draws us into existence, and nurses our inexperience in its genial bosom."

The adventures through which I had passed, and the misanthropy I had contracted, did not allow me perfectly to accord with this sentiment of M. Ruffigny.

The next morning, my beneficent friend received me in his library. It was the only spacious apartment in his house, and was fitted up with peculiar neatness and convenience. I cast my eyes around upon the shelves, and perceived that they were principally furnished with the old poetical compositions of France, Germany, Italy and Switzerland, together with a very complete collection of botanical writers, particularly those which treated of the natural productions of Helvetia. One compartment of the library was devoted to English authors, principally from the age of Elizabeth to the Restoration.[1]

"I pass some hours of every day," said the old man, "in this apartment; but my life is principally in the open air: I think more than I read; and I am more attached to the great and living volume of nature, than to the cold, insensible, mechanically constructed pages and sheets that have been produced by my fellow-creatures. Let no man despise the oracles of books! A book is a dead man, a sort of mummy, embowelled and embalmed, but that once had flesh, and motion, and a boundless variety of determinations and actions. I am glad that I can, even upon these terms, converse with the dead, with the wise and the good of revolving centuries. Without books I should not understand the volume of nature; I should pass the scanty years of my existence a mere novice; the life of a single man is too short to enable him to penetrate beyond the surface of things. The furniture of these shelves constitutes an elaborate and invaluable commentary; but the objects beyond those windows, and the circles and communities of my contemporaries, are the text to which that commentary relates."

After breakfast, M. Ruffigny and myself walked out, and ascended one branch of the St. Gothard. I was surprised to observe with what agility and spirit the old man encountered this species of labour. "It is all use," said he. "Temperance and the habit of daily exercise have preserved, and probably long will preserve to me, these inexpensive and invaluable pleasures."

My host pointed out the various beauties of the successive landscapes which from the different points of the rock were presented to my view. It was a boundless magazine of the most ravishing objects. He directed my attention to the different towns, and villages like towns, which were discoverable from various distances, descanted on the ingenuity of manufactures,

---

1 Elizabeth I (1533-1603) ruled England from 1558 to her death; the Restoration of Charles II (1630-85) occurred in 1660.

and the vigilance and expedients of agriculture. "This whole territory," said he, "is one continued monument of the triumph of temperance, industry, and independence."

CHAPTER IX.

THE second day after my arrival, M. Ruffigny conducted me on a little tour to the lake of Uri.[1] "My country," said he, "makes but a petty figure in the map of the globe; and, perhaps, it may be a frivolous sort of pride in me, that makes me feel complacency in recollecting that I am a burgher of Uri. I do not merely exult that I am a Swiss, but I sometimes indulge myself in a fastidious comparison between my native canton and the more spacious and opulent republics of Zurich and Berne. The little state which I inhabit, is nearly one cluster of rugged and inhospitable mountains; yet this is the district in which the Swiss liberty was engendered; and from hence, as a centre, it spread on every side to the furthest boundaries of the union. I am myself descended from the patriots who secured independence to my native soil. As William Tell married the younger of the daughters of Walter Furst, one of the three immortal leaders, who in 1308 conspired for the deliverance of their country; so an ancestor of mine, in the direct line, married the elder.[2] I know that the pretension of an illustrious ancestry is too often a chimerical boast. I know that, wherever a pedigree is preserved, or a distinguishing compellation is conferred, it is in the nature of things almost impossible, that in a few generations a race should not degenerate, and that fools or villains should not corrupt the blood of the profoundest sages and the most disinterested citizens. I know that, wherever this is the case, wherever licentiousness or imbecility has crossed the glo-

---

1 Also known as the "Ürner See," the southern part of Lake Lucerne.

2 The peasants of Uri declared themselves independent upon the death of German Emperor Albert I of Hapsburg in 1308. William Tell is the legendary hero associated with the liberation of Switzerland; the "three immortal leaders" were Walter Furst of Uri, Arnold von Melchtal of Unterwalden, and Werner von Stauffacher of Schwyz. These three led their home cantons to establish with Lucerne an "Eternal Union" in 1291.

rious breed, every time such a descendant hears the repetition of his name, he hears a more deadly and outrageous satire, than the malice of his worst enemy could invent against him. Forgive me, my friend—I feel that this censure does not fasten on me. If I have not the public merits of a Furst and a Tell, I have their innocence of manners, and my life has been usefully and honourably spent.

"Zurich, and Basle, and some of our more opulent cantons, are full of manufactures and industry; they contain many citizens who are comparatively wealthy; and the style of living of several of these would not shame the capitals of Paris or London. My co-burghers are all feeders of flocks or cultivators of the earth; there are among them none who are opulent, and none who suffer the evils of poverty; and their tables are such as bring before us the uncorrupted plainness of patriarchal times. I have visited many countries of the globe; but this, instead of distasting me toward the simplicity of my early years, has made me relish it the more. Like a true Swiss of the earlier times, I have returned home, and bidden adieu, without a sigh, to the refinements and ostentation of other climates."

In the course of our excursion, M. Ruffigny pointed out to me the various spots still so dear to the genius of freedom: Gruti, the village where the three heroes of Switzerland planned their undertaking; Brunnen, where the fundamental league between their respective cantons was concluded; Kussnacht, the scene where an arrow from the bow of Tell reached the heart of Gesler, his own oppressor, and the oppressor of his country; and Morgarten and Sempach, the fields in which those celebrated combats were fought, that fixed the liberties of Switzerland on a basis which has endured the shock of ages.[1] All these places were within such a distance, that we either actually visited them in the course of the day, or discerned them, almost in full detail, from the tops of the neighbouring eminences.

---

[1] Gruti (Grütli, or Rütli) is the site where the three leaders swore their oath of confederacy. Küssnacht is the reputed site of Tell's shooting of the tyrant Herman Gessler after Gessler ordered Tell to shoot an apple from his own son's head. Morgarten and Sempach are the sites of Swiss victories over the Austrian Hapsburg army in 1315 and 1386, respectively.

After having sated my curiosity in the examination of these venerable scenes, we returned in the afternoon by the lake of Uri. It was along this lake that Tell is related to have been conveyed in fetters by Gesler, that he might be removed from his countrymen, and shut up in one of the dungeons reserved by the tyrant for the intrepid and the honest. As they rowed along a violent tempest arose. The shores on both sides are extremely craggy and dangerous; and the tyrant began to fear that his boat would be dashed to pieces against these insuperable precipices. Tell, perfect in the accomplishments of a Swiss peasant, and endowed with a firm and adventurous temper, surpassed his contemporaries in the art of navigating his native lakes. Gesler knew this, and, trembling for his coward life, ordered the fetters to be struck off from his prisoner, and the helm to be put into his hand. Tell used the opportunity which was given him. There are not above two or three points in the whole circumference of this lake, where it is practicable to land. Tell steered his boat toward the most rugged of these, leaped suddenly upon the rock, climbed with inconceivable adroitness up the precipice, and returned once more to his longing countrymen and confederates. A chapel, erected by admiring posterity on the spot, consecrates the memory of this magnanimous and important achievement.

One thing surprised me, upon reflection, in the conduct of M. Ruffigny. He had received me with particular kindness; yet he did not so much as mention to me the name of my father. I knew that the connection between them was of the most confidential nature, and included a variety of important obligations, though I was a stranger to the particulars. My host did not enquire when I had heard from my father. He might, indeed, have received letters as lately as I could have done. But he did not ask me respecting his health, his vigour, his sentiments, his habits, a thousand minutiae, to which ocular inspection alone can qualify a man to speak. It is so natural for a friend to be anxious about these, and to think he can never talk or hear enough upon these interesting topics!

After having busily employed ourselves in discovering and examining the various memorable objects which occurred in our route, we now passed quietly and silently along the lake. It was a deep and narrow water, about nine miles in length, and skirted on both sides with rocks uncommonly wild and romantic, some perpendicular, some stretching over our heads, and intercepting the view of the upper sky, and clothed for the most part with forests of beech and pine, that extended themselves down to the very edge of the water. The lake was as smooth as crystal, and the arching precipices that inclosed it gave a peculiar solemnity to the gloom. As we passed near the chapel of Tell, the bell happened to toll forth, as if for a funeral. The sound was full, the effect melancholy; each reverberation of the metal was prolonged among the echoes of the rocks. This continued for about fifteen minutes, and then ceased.

We were attended by only two rowers and a steersman, labourers in the corn-fields and garden of M. Ruffigny. Shortly after we had passed the chapel, the rowers suspended their labour, and we glided in silence over the water. We had been so busied in action and conversation during the whole morning, that the stillness which now succeeded seemed perfectly unforced and natural. I sunk into a deep reverie. I thought of William Tell, and the glorious founders of the Swiss liberty; I thought of the simple manners which still prevail in the primitive cantons; I felt as if I were in the wildest and most luxuriant of the uninhabited islands of the South Sea. I was lost in visions of paradise, of habitations and bowers among the celestial orbs, of things supernatural and remote, of the unincumbered spirits of the virtuous and the just, of the pure rewards and enjoyments of a happier state. I had forgotten Switzerland, and M. Ruffigny, and the world, and myself.

Accidentally I lifted my eye, and saw the countenance of my host fixed upon me with peculiar intentness; a tear moistened the furrows of his cheeks. This spectacle recalled me to the reality of things about me; but my heart was softened by the images which had passed through my thoughts, and I could not speak.

"I have not named your father to you," said M. Ruffigny.

My dear father!—His name, uttered at that moment, awakened the best feelings of my soul.

"Casimir! Casimir Fleetwood!" exclaimed my host, "where have you been?"

"In France:—at Paris."

"How have you been employed?"

"Not well.—My father sent me forth for improvement; but I have been employed in libertinism and dissipation."

"Fleetwood, I also am your father; and I will not be less indulgent, scarcely less anxious, than your natural parent. You know in gross, though you do not know in detail, the peculiar attachment I feel for every thing that bears the name of Fleetwood:—am I not your father?"

"This, sir, is the third day that I have ever seen you; I know little of you yet; the little I have observed has scarcely had time to strike its fibres deep in my bosom. But all that I do know, makes me presume that, were I worthy of the honour, you are the person of all mankind whom I should prefer for an adoptive parent."

"Casimir! my dear Casimir! let not your ears for ever abhor the sound of my voice; let not my form and my visage be for ever loathsome in your sight!—I cannot speak——"

"I understand you, sir,—my father is dead!"

Ruffigny held forward to me a letter; I took it from him; I gazed mechanically on the superscription, but could not make out a syllable. My friend drew nearer to me; he put his arm round me, as I sat; I rested my head on his shoulder, and burst into a flood of tears.

The communication of this melancholy intelligence no doubt affected me very differently from what it would otherwise have done, in consequence of the frame of mind, which this day's excursion, and the various objects I had beheld, produced in me. My sensibility was increased by the preparation, and the impression I received was by so much the deeper. I do not pretend to divine Ruffigny's motives for so contriving the scene. Perhaps he knew enough of human nature to believe that it rarely happened to a son in the bloom of life to break his heart for the loss of an aged parent. Perhaps he understood and disapproved of the train of life in which I had lately been engaged, and thought the thus softening my heart the most effectual way of recalling me to my better self.

"Why, sir," cried I mournfully, "did you suffer me to remain a moment in ignorance of this dreadful intelligence? Why all this pomp of preparation? What are scenery, and patriotism, and heroes, and the achievements of past ages to me? What have I to do with all this world?—My father! my only friend!—Where have I been?—Losing myself, while you stood in need of my consolation! Breaking through every plan that was arranged, loitering away my time among the frivolities and licentiousness of Paris, while you laid down an aching head in solitude, while your pulses failed, and your eyes were closed in darkness! Would to God it were in my power to recal a few past months!—No matter!—My prospects and my pleasures are finished; my life is tarnished; my—peace is destroyed:—I shall never again think of myself with approbation, or with patience!"

I did not say all this aloud, though a part of it I did. The short time I had passed with Ruffigny was yet long enough to make me feel no sort of constraint in his presence. On the present occasion he did not attempt to console me; he left my grief to its natural course: we finished our voyage in silence. By degrees, as I recovered the use of my reason, I felt myself grateful for his kindness, and respected his judgment in this forbearance.

The night of the day I have described did not pass in repose. Amidst short and disturbed slumbers I saw my father.—I heard his voice. I roused myself, and returned to recollection. "Dead?" said I.—"Impossible!"—Let the reader remember what I have already said of him; "He was the wisest and best man I knew. He had all those advantages from nature, and from the external endowments of fortune, which were calculated to maintain my reverence. We had gradually become more qualified for each other's society and confidence. Our characters had many points of resemblance: we were both serious, both contemplative, both averse to the commerce of the world."—This dear friend, this sharer in all my interests, should I never meet again? The well-known mansion in Merionethshire, in which I had passed all my boyish days, should I find it vacant of its respected inhabitant? That mild and affectionate countenance, which for many years I had beheld every day, almost at every hour, should I never again behold it? Sometimes he was my playfellow, and even shared in my childish amusements. The little implements and mechanical contrivances upon which my boyish thoughts were employed, and which my desires panted to realise, he would often lend me his hand to assist me to form. His lessons were so paternal, so indulgent, so considerate, so well adapted to my opening powers! The confidences he occasionally reposed in were so cordial! His descriptions and pictures of things to excite my curiosity and emulation were so admirable! I remembered how his manner successively adapted itself to my growing years and demands, from prattling infancy to the full stature of man. All these things rose at first confusedly to my mind, and jostled each other. Sometimes I endeavoured, with melancholy industry, to arrange them; at other times I threw the reins on the neck of my imagination, and resigned myself to the guidance of fortuitous associations. "My life," said I, "under the roof of my father, was the reality of life. The period I spent at Oxford and Paris was an interval of incoherence and inebriety; and this is all now ended! The reality of existence is for ever gone!"

Why is it that, from the hour I heard of my father's decease to the present distant period, the remembrance of that melancholy event has always become associated in my mind with the rocks of Switzerland and the lake of Uri? One of the most affecting of the catastrophes that beset this mortal existence, with what is most solemn and sublime in the aspect of the universe? Grief in all human minds soon assumes the character of a luxury to be indulged, as well as of a pain to be endured. The mourner recollects with complacency the tenderness of his heart and the purity of his feelings. The conscious recurrence of the scene in which my grief began, gave in my case to the grief itself a new merit at the tribunal of sentiment and taste. Honoured, beloved, ever-to-be-regretted author of my life! Never were the ashes of an Eastern monarch attended with so magnificent a funeral! The deep glen of the dark and tranquil lake of Uri was the cathedral in which the rites were solemnised! The chapel of the immortal Tell tolled out its bell to proclaim the ceremony! The patriots who, five centuries ago, established the independence of Switzerland, composed the procession that attended thee to the grave! All these images are for ever worked up together, and constitute in my memory one melancholy and indelible scene!

It was many days after the communication of this intelligence before my mind could recover any tolerable composure. How various circumstances combined to make this a terrible blow to me! I felt naked and unsheltered from the blasts of the world. I was like a vine that had long twined itself round the trunk of a sturdy oak, and from which at length the support and alliance of the oak is taken away. The shoots of my emulation and enterprise lay prostrate on the ground, and the fibres of my heart were torn and bleeding. If I had been present on this melancholy occasion, if I had heard from my father the accents of a last farewell, if it had been permitted me to soften the last pangs of expiring life, to say to myself, I now see the friend whom I shall see no more, to kiss his clay-cold forehead, to feel the affectionate pressure of his hand for the last time, my remorse would have been less. I remembered with insupportable anguish the manner in which my absence had been employed. Not in wholesome and salutary studies, not in useful and improving meditation, not in sound observations upon the varieties of man and the distinguishing features of nations; but in vice, in dissipation, in what I was sure my father would least of all have approved, in a timid and ignominious sacrifice to the licentious maxims of a nation among whom I was a sojourner.

The day after that of the lake of Uri, I did not come out of my chamber. I had no courage to lift up my head, and my passion once and again relieved itself by a flood of tears. I sat for hours immoveable, engrossed in dim and inexplicable reverie. This blunting of the senses was grateful and life-giving; the brief intervals in which I returned to myself were filled with intolerable anguish. "How happy was I yesterday!" exclaimed I to myself: "how desolate to-day!" Nevertheless, I was yesterday as fatherless as I am to-day; my dear parent for more than two months has been no more: but I did not know my misfortune! With what pleasure did I receive the kindness, observe the habits, and speculate upon the propensities, of my father's friend! With what interest did I set out yesterday morning upon the little excursion we had planned! How much did I enjoy the scenery, as it was formed by the all-directing hand of nature, and as it was modified by the recollection of the human acts which had there been performed! Cruel Ruffigny, how could you suffer me to live under this delusion! How could you look on, enjoying in malicious sport my blindness, and see me amuse myself with straws, while the rock, upon which my habitation had rested, was dissolved away beneath its foundations?—Yet, why, ah,—why has this delusion ever been taken away! Yesterday, and the day preceding, and the days before, I did not know my misfortune, and I was happy! Oh, that this dream could have lasted for ever!—I shall never again see my father,—never, never!—yet why might I not have been led on with the pleasing hope, and have said, "To-morrow, and to-morrow,—a short time yet,—and we shall meet!"[1] How happy, to have pursued an interminable route, and still have believed that I was almost at my journey's end! to have trusted for ever, and confided, as long as I continued to live!

My kind host sent me my morning's repast, but it stood by me untouched. Ever since I had received the news, I had a sensation within me that rejected food, as peremptorily as the glands of a person labouring under a hydrophobia throw back the water he might attempt to absorb. Dinner-time came; and hunger at length subdued the obstinacy of my grief. With bitter scorn of my own frailty, I swallowed a few morsels of the food which was set before me. In the evening, Ruffigny entered my chamber. He sat down, and for some minutes continued silent. At length he spoke. He did not ask me how I had rested, or how I felt myself. He began with words concerning my father; he made a calculation of their respective ages. I could not stand this: to myself I had repeated my father's name a hundred times; but I could not bear to hear it formed by the voice of another. Ruffigny desisted. A few minutes more, and he returned to the same topic with some variation. I now

---

1   Cf. *Macbeth*, V.v.19.

endured it better. He pronounced an eulogium of my father's virtues. This was not altogether without a soothing sensation; though from time to time I covered my face with my hands, struck my forehead with my clenched fist, and broke into other mechanical gestures of impatience. Ruffigny spoke of the years he had spent in society with my father. He recollected a variety of little incidents and adventures, which had served to display his judgment and humanity, the resources of his mind, and the generousness of his temper. If all this discourse had been artificial, if it had resembled the funeral encomium of a venal orator, it would only have irritated my impatience, and increased my sorrows. But Ruffigny loved my father only less than I loved him. The chief differences were, that he had not seen him for years, and this had served him for a weaning; and that the instinct of blood, or that prejudice and sentiment which amply supply the place of instinct, was in full ascendancy in me, and was wanting in him. We mingled our tears. His discourse was the overflowing of his heart,—a relief that was necessary to the anguish he felt, and to the restraint he had imposed upon himself in the two first days of my visit. His sorrow would have produced more injurious effects upon him, had it not been that he felt it as a duty incumbent upon him to console mine.

Ruffigny went on. "A most valuable life has been terminated, and you do well to weep. A great gap has been made in society; and, though you are the principal loser, yet all who knew your father, particularly all who were within reach of his wisdom or beneficence, are losers too. He has left a considerable estate, and there is need of some one to look into its condition and prosperity. He has left tenants, and they will miss his superintendence and indulgence. Because they have lost him, I hope that will not be a reason that they should lose you. Your father has perished from the face of the earth, but it is not your design that his memory should perish with him! Strangers, no doubt, have already given him a grave. But shall not his son enquire what they have done, and supply what they may have left deficient? Shall no stone mark the place where his ashes rest? Shall no filial curiosity demand, from those who were on the spot, the history of his last moments, the paroxysms he suffered, the consolations that relieved them, the last words which were breathed from his dying lips? Shall no one endeavour to draw out an image of his life, by enquiring into his injunctions, and perpetuating the execution of those plans upon which, it may be, his affections were bent? These are the duties of survivors; it is in this way that our offspring prove their attachment to those to whom they were bound in a thousand obligations."

The discourse of Ruffigny produced in me the revolution he meditated. "I will set out for England this moment!" cried I.

"Would it," answered Ruffigny, "be any increase to your satisfaction that I should accompany you?"

"Good Heaven! venerable old man," exclaimed I, "you cannot entertain the thought?"

"The wish to perform a pilgrimage to the tomb of my ancient friend is uppermost in my heart. Will you permit me to occupy a corner in the chaise that is to convey you to England?"

I threw myself into his arms; I burst into tears; I even sobbed upon his bosom. —"My father is not wholly dead! What must be my obligation to the friend, who at such a moment is willing to supply his place!"

When my first surprise at this generous proposal had subsided, I argued with Ruffigny: I objected his age and infirmities; I entreated him to consider well the extent of so unexampled a sacrifice. My arguments were not urged with all the force of which they were capable; my heart betrayed me; my very soul thrilled with pleasure, and yearned over the old man, who said, "Shall I not accompany you to England?"

My host concealed from me one part of the motive that induced him to this extraordinary resolution. My father, as I have said, had furnished me with a most exemplary letter of introduction to his Swiss friend, and had trusted much to his affectionate and benevolent wisdom for the perfecting my character. When I least suspected it, my deceased parent had obtained accurate accounts of my proceedings at Oxford and at Paris, and had transmitted a faithful abstract of these accounts to M. Ruffigny. He was exceedingly anxious for the future purity of my character and honour of my transactions, and was of opinion that a violent interference, and a rude check put upon my excesses, was by no means the most effectual method for my reformation. He therefore scarcely seemed to be aware of my errors, at the time that he was most exactly informed of, and most disapproved them. He believed that an unsuccessful attempt to place them before me in their full light, would be infinitely more injurious than if no attempt were made. His great dependence was upon my visit to Switzerland. He had the most exalted notion of the talents, the virtues, and the zeal of his friend in this corner of the world. He persuaded himself that the operation of novelty would be highly favourable to the accomplishment of his wishes, and that the unexpected meeting with a man so qualified, and the yet untried expedients which Ruffigny would employ for my improvement, would produce the happiest effects.

My father was now dead; and my host felt the task which had devolved upon him as of double obligation. I was a legacy which the friend most dear to him on earth had bequeathed to him, and a trust with which his last breath he had consigned to his care. As a legacy, the long attachment he had felt to the name of Fleetwood made him regard me as the most valuable estate that could have been conveyed to him; and as a trust, there was nothing for which he more desired to live, than the faithful discharge of what the person conferring that trust expected from him. When the choice of various means were in my late father's power, he had fixed upon the vigilance and discretion of Ruffigny, as that by which he desired to secure my improvement and happiness. Had fate not bereaved me thus untimely of a father's care, he would no doubt have employed various engines and instruments for the same end. While a parent's eye was upon me, however much he trusted to the discretion of this friend, Ruffigny would still have been a deputy, not a principal. Now the task became entirely his; and every engagement that he felt to the virtues and the memory of my father, called upon him, as the last tribute of friendship, to leave no effort unexerted for my welfare.

CHAPTER X.

DURING our journey, Ruffigny communicated to me at large the particulars of his connection with my family, of which I had before heard in general terms, but knew nothing distinctly.

"While I was yet a child," said my fellow-traveller, "I had the misfortune to lose both my parents. By this event I fell under the care of an uncle, a brother of my father. Hypocrisy and fraud are natives of every climate; and there are villains even in Switzerland. My uncle was copious in his professions of affection and fidelity during the last illness of my father, and protested a thousand times that he would in all respects treat me as if I had been sprung of his own loins. It was at about seven years of age that I was delivered to his guardianship. Unfortunately this uncle of mine had a numerous family, and had been unprosperous in several of his attempts for the improvement of his property. He was naturally of an impatient, discontented, and reserved disposition, yet with a considerable mixture of vanity. He had disbursed in several instances more money than he could well command. He had been restless, and eager to engage in various projects; and his projects had failed. My father, on the contrary, who was of an open and free disposition, cool in his temper, and sagacious in his determinations, had constantly prospered. Beside which, my father was greatly and universally beloved; every one consulted, every one distinguished him; he was courted by all his neighbours, made an umpire in every controversy, and on all hands admitted to be the most enlightened citizen in the canton of which he was a native. His brother, sullen in his disposition, perplexed and obscure in his intellect, and rude and unconciliating in his manners, was as generally avoided. The common observation respecting him among the candid and good-humoured Swiss was, 'Our dislike is more than we can give a reason for; we agree to look upon him as a bad man; but where is the guilt he has committed?'

"Such was the guardian, into whose family I was at this time removed. He saw me in the circle of his own children with a scowling eye. 'Why,' said he to himself, 'should this little vagabond be entitled to more property than all my children put together? He will come into possession of superfluity, while his cousins, not less worthy than he, will see their lives withered, by the scantiness of means which I have in vain exerted myself to increase.'

"The observations my uncle had occasion to make upon me in the sequel, did not by any means tend to tranquillise the storm already swelling in his bosom. His children inherited the same slowness and perplexity of intellect which characterised their father; I was remarked to have that facility of apprehension and quickness of parts which distinguished my deceased parent. Whatever we learned as pupils, we learned together; but I excelled them all. Whenever, which was not often, any visitor honoured our roof, we put ourselves forward with the easy frankness of Swiss manners, but I constantly bore away the prize. In the little exercises of the adjoining hamlet, in the questions proposed, and the remarks delivered, by the aged peasantry of the vicinage, the preference still fell to me.

"This was too much for my uncle's unquiet temper to endure.

"'Does the same fate,' murmured he in his meditations, 'still pursue me? As I was constantly eclipsed by this urchin's father, so shall my children be for ever surpassed by the son? Is there a fatality entailed upon our race? Surely from the womb there has been an antipathy between us; and, as long as the descendants of either exist, my progeny will for ever be made slaves to that of my brother!'

"About twelve months after the death of my father, my uncle had occasion to make a journey into France, and to my great surprise proposed to take me with him. My father had so disposed of his property, as to vest in his brother the full possession of the income during my minority, under the notion of a compensation for his expense and trouble in the care of my education. Other parents in other countries would have been anxious that the greater part of the income should accumulate, for the purpose of supplying me with a more ample fortune when I came of age. But this idea is foreign to the simplicity of the country in which I was born. The property of which my father died possessed was, without farther improvement, fully equal to any estate in the canton; and it would have been more agreeable to his modes of thinking, that I should, when arrived at years of discretion, come into possession of the very income that he had received, than of a larger.

"One evil, however, originated in this mode of settling his estate. My guardian found, immediately after the decease of my father, a considerable improvement to his own resources. The expenses which were in any way necessary to me at this tender age were extremely small, and my uncle had of consequence the whole present emolument of my property. This circumstance increased the strong dislike he entertained for me. His avaricious disposition caused him to look forward with horror to the time when it would be required of him to disburse large sums in the progress of my education, and with still greater horror to the period when it would be necessary to resign the whole.

"In our journey to France we were also accompanied by my eldest cousin, a youth of about seventeen years of age. This lad had always treated me with singular unkindness; and at his age he was less under restraint from the laws of decorum, and less capable of disguising his antipathies, than his father was. He never looked upon me but with a scowl of dislike; he never spoke to me but in a tone of severity and harshness. Some of his brothers were as young as myself, and to these he was a sour and unripened tyrant. Nevertheless, when it was my misfortune to have any difference with them (and indeed we never agreed), he was always, when appealed to, of the party against me, and his decisions were announced by cuffs and blows innumerable.

"When we arrived at Lyons, my uncle laid aside his proper name, and caused himself to be called M. Mouchard. Upon this occasion he called me in, and addressed me in a style of unusual seriousness. He had taken me round the town of Lyons, shown me the best buildings, and the handsomest of the suburbs, conducted me to the public gardens and the theatres, and endeavoured by every means to make it appear in my eyes an agreeable residence. It was indeed a perfect contrast to the wild and severe faces exhibited by the canton of Uri; and to my foolish and inexperienced heart, the populous streets, the thronged exchange, the crowded walks, and the illuminated theatres, appeared like fairy land.

"'When I return home,' said my uncle, 'it is my intention to leave you at Lyons.'

"My heart leaped within me at the intelligence, and I expressed my delight in unequivocal terms. Unfortunate as I was, I had no prepossessions to attach me to my native land. While my parents lived, I indeed loved it. All my hours had been winged with joy, and I experienced those pleasing emotions which arise in the human heart, when we perceive that we are looked on with partiality and affection by all around us. But the last of my parents had now been dead more than a year, and since that time the scene had been completely reversed. It was indeed an irksome and a melancholy year to me. Till then I had been a spoiled child; but in my new situation I was neglected and disliked by all. Wherever I was, I was one too much; whatever I did, my uncle and my cousins were sure to disapprove. I did not feel this so much at first; perhaps the unkindness I experienced was at first not so great as it afterwards became. I made those exertions I have already mentioned, and gained the applause of the neighbourhood and the envy of my cousins. But mine, perhaps, was not an age to struggle with discouragement; nor had the tenderness and indulgence of my first education prepared me for it. The volatility of youthful spirits in part supported me; but I had fits of melancholy and depression greater than might have been expected at so early a period of life. Gradually I came to hate the scenery about me, and to loath the routine of the passing day.

"'Your father,' continued my uncle, 'left you to my care, and many have been the anxious hours which this guardianship has cost me. My brother was a very foolish man, and has bred you in such a manner that you will be a great trouble to any one who has to do with you. If you had been brought up soberly and strictly, like your cousins, you would have been a very different sort of a boy; but that, poor child, is not your fault. I have tried to bring you into order; but I see it is necessary you should go out into the world. My brother, with all his mistakes, was my brother still; and you must needs think that I will do every thing in my power for the service of his child.

"'William, you must be aware that, if I had not a good opinion of your capacity, I should not talk thus to a child of your years. You certainly do not want for capacity, though you are a very perverse and wicked boy. I must own that I do not expect any good of you; but, if you come to harm, it shall not be through my fault. You will live, I hope, to thank me from the bottom of your heart for what I am now doing for you.

"'There is one thing more I have to say to you, a part of which you can understand, and a part you cannot. The part you can understand, I will explain to you; the part you cannot, you must trust for to my superior judgment, and to the paternal care I have ever shown for you.

"'You have observed, that, since I came to this city, I have called myself Mr. Mouchard. That is to be your name; you are to be called William Mouchard. You are a native of Bellinzone; that is the story I shall tell of you, and that you are to uphold.[1] There are many things that a child of your years cannot comprehend; you do not know what is good for you, and must trust to the better discernment of your elders. This I have to tell you; you must never on any account mention my real name or your own; you must never mention the canton of Uri, or any one of the mountains and valleys among which you have been brought up. You must never write to me or to any creature in Switzerland; you must never make any enquiries, or give the least sign that you are alive. I shall have my eyes upon you; I shall provide generously for your support; and, when I please, shall write to you, or come myself to see how you are going on. Upon this point, boy, I must deal plainly with you. All my attention is directed to your welfare, and I have only this injunction to give you. Upon your observance of it, depends every thing that is dear to you. The moment you break it

---

1 Bellinzona is a town in southern Switzerland, near the Italian border.

in the minutest particle, the most terrible misfortunes will instantly overwhelm you. I cannot tell you what they are; they are so great, that your understanding would be wholly unable to comprehend them. But be sure of this, all I do is for your advantage. When you least expect it, you will see that it is so. Remember and tremble! I put the happiness of your whole life into your own disposal.'

"It is inconceivable with what strange sensations I listened to this harangue. The phrases my uncle had employed, of the superior judgment of our elders, the incapacity and blindness of children, and every thing that older people do being calculated for our good, was the cant which I had incessantly heard during the last year; and, though these phrases certainly were never employed upon a more unworthy occasion, they excited in me a mysterious sensation of reverence and awe, which I felt incapable to shake off. A doubtful opinion,—Was this genuine kindness? Was it a masked hostility?—hung about me, and perplexed my resolutions. I was not, however, long in doubt. I was delighted with the city of Lyons; I could not endure the thought of returning to my uncle and his family. I looked upon my native home, now that my parents were removed from the stage of life, with horror; but I was in the morning of my days, and was inclined to regard every thing new, with hope, with exultation, and a bounding heart.

"One thing appeared to me singular. My uncle told me that Lyons was to be the place of my abode; but he mentioned nothing to me of the particular situation in which I was to be placed. Was I to be put *en pension* at a boarding school, or how? If I were, methought I should like to have seen beforehand the house in which I was to reside, the master who was to instruct me, the youths who were to be my companions. But I was totally destitute of every sort of knowledge of the world, and was in the hands of my envious and bad-hearted uncle to dispose of as he pleased. This might, for aught I knew, be the established mode of proceeding in all similar cases. It was perhaps one of those points, which were reserved for the wisdom of our elders to decide upon, and which the capacity of a child like me was held unable to comprehend.

"We had been now ten days at Lyons, and the next morning was fixed for my uncle and my cousin to set out upon their return. In the evening a M. Vaublanc visited us in our hotel.

"'This is the gentleman,' said my uncle, 'who is so obliging as to provide an apartment for you in his house.'

"I had never seen him before. He was a little man, with black, straight hair, his countenance clear and sensible, but with muscles that had not often been moulded into the expression of pity or tenderness. His dress was exceedingly plain; not without some appearances of negligence and dirt. My uncle and he talked a great deal about the silk manufacturers of Lyons; my guardian seeming to be desirous of information under this head, and the stranger well qualified to afford it. Neither of them took much notice of me, and at an early hour I was directed to go to bed.

"'My little man,' said the Lyonnese, taking me by the hand, but with no expression of kindness, 'you will be very comfortable at my house; I have two little boys just about your age, and you will be nice playmates together. Good night! I shall come for you in the morning.'

"I conceived no flattering augury in behalf of my new land-lord. What had pleased me in Lyons was the squares, the public gardens, and the theatres. These were exactly calculated to soothe my youthful curiosity. The plainness of the appearance of M. Vaublanc, and the dryness of his manners, were in perfect contrast with these. There was something in them which tended to chill the imagination, and inspire a dreary presentiment of the future.

"Yet I was willing to launch on this untried sea. I said, 'No, I will not go back with my uncle!'—The morning of our separation was heavy, and presently began to pour down torrents of rain. My uncle, at parting, put a louis d'or into my hand; I thought I never felt any thing so cold as his hand, when I touched it for the last time. My cousin presented me with a three livres piece.[1]

"You wonder, perhaps, at my recollecting so minutely a

---

1   The "Louis d'or" and the "livre" were French coins.

scene which passed at so early an age; but you will presently perceive what reasons there were that compelled me to recollect it. Accustoming myself to contain my recollections and ruminations in my own bosom, they took so much the deeper root.

"M. Vaublanc was punctual in meeting and receiving me, at the very instant that my uncle was stepping into the carriage which was to convey him to the foot of the mountains. I never saw or heard of my guardian from this moment.

"The wheels of the coach slowly rolled away, and my new landlord led me down another street. Our walk was not short, and we arrived at the meanest part of the city. M. Vaublanc led me up a narrow and silent alley. When we had passed through two thirds of it, 'This,' said he, 'is my house.'

"We entered, and were received by his wife, a woman plain and neat in her dress, and of a notable appearance. Presently came in the two boys he mentioned to me. They were clothed in remarkably coarse attire; and the rudeness of their countenances, and ungainliness of their carriage, well corresponded to their dress. All together,—the alley, the darkness of the apartments, the appearance of the family,—exceedingly displeased me. And this, thought I, is my residence in the magnificent city of Lyons! My youthful senses had been idly dazzled with the gaudiness of artificial life, as I had here first seen it. But I could not help saying to myself, 'How preferable are the mountains, and cascades, and cheerful cottages of the Swiss, to this miserable alley!'

"In one respect, however, my situation was better than I began to expect it would be. After two or three days I was conducted to one of the most respectable seminaries of education in the city of Lyons, such as young persons of the rank of the little Vaublancs never entered, where, under masters of great knowledge and humanity, I began to be initiated in every species of learning suitable to my age. What was my uncle's motive for taking this step, so little in consistency with those which afterward followed, I could never exactly conjecture. Perhaps he was desirous of letting me down by degrees, and had not the courage to drive me to despair at once, and risk the consequences which that state of mind might produce. Perhaps, wicked as he was, he could not himself form his resolutions immediately, and only by degrees worked up his mind to the plan which was intended to terminate in my ruin.

"Be this as it will, the studies and accomplishments, in the pursuit of which I was now engaged, afforded me much gratification. Though I had at first been dazzled with the splendours of Lyons, I knew that pleasure was not the business of life; and, regarding the acquisition of liberal knowledge as a badge of honour, I was willing to cultivate those improvements which might fit me to discharge with respectability the offices of a man. I recollected that in my native province I had always appeared to advantage in the field of emulation, and this naturally inspired me with an appetite for similar experiments. My parts were quick, my apprehension was clear, and I almost constantly obtained the praise and encouragement of the regents. The only mortification I suffered, during this period, was in going home every evening to M. Vaublanc's. There was such a contrast between his manners and those of my instructors! His children were so sordid and groveling in their habits, compared with the generous minds and spirited tempers of my schoolfellows, with whom I associated in the course of the day!

CHAPTER XI.

"I HAD for about three months frequented the lessons of my instructors, when one morning the elder of Vaublanc's sons came to my bed-side at about six o'clock, and bade me rise immediately, for his father wanted to speak to me. I obeyed.

"'My little lad,' said Vaublanc, 'you are not to go to school to-day.'

"'No, sir? What, is it red-letter day?'[1]

"'Your uncle has written to me to put you into a different berth.'

---

1 A saint's day or church festival day, indicated on the calendar by red letters.

"'Ah, I am very sorry! Ours is a sweet school, and I like the masters and every body that belongs to it.'

"'William Mouchard,' said my host, 'I know very little of you or your uncle either; but that is nothing to me. While he requires of me nothing that it is contrary to my notions, or out of my way to do, I intend to be his fair and punctual correspondent. All that he said to me, while he was at Lyons, was like an honest man. He said he had a numerous family of his own, and that he could not do much for you, an orphan cast upon his charity.'

"I stared. I remembered the severe injunctions of my guardian, and was silent.

"'It appears that he has had repeated misfortunes in the world, and that he can just make shift to bring up his children in a humble way. It cannot, therefore, be expected that he should do much for you. I can make his case my own, and I am sure I should look to my own flesh and blood. He has resolved to keep you from starving, and that is very generous of him. There is only one thing I cannot understand: why he sent you to this school at all. I think he was out in his judgment there.'

"This was the first time in my life that the ideas of subsistence and property had been plainly stated to me. My notions, like a child's, were very confused on the subject. But, I suppose, proceeding by a sort of implicit conclusion from the visible circumstances of my father, I had always considered myself as entitled to a full participation of those benefits and blessings which a child can enjoy. What Vaublanc said, however, convinced me that my uncle was deceiving him. I understood little of the descent of property, and whether, upon my father's death, it ought to devolve to his son or his brother; but I understood still less of the equity of just preserving from death by hunger the only son of a man who had possessed every luxury and indulgence that were in use in his country. In a word, the views now stated to me enlightened my understanding at once; and, when I found myself thus thrown upon the world, I apprehended, as it were by necessity, the laws and constitutions of human life.

"'What is to be done with me, sir?' said I.

"'You must do as I do,' replied Vaublanc. 'People who have

nobody else to maintain them, maintain themselves. You have seen shoemakers, and smiths, and joiners at their work?'

"'They get money by their work, and with that money they buy meat and drink. Does my uncle wish me to learn to be a smith or a joiner?'

"'No, no. Any body that taught you to be these trades would require to be paid for the trouble of teaching you, and you would get nothing by it these seven years. We have a trade in Lyons that we teach to younkers for nothing.'

"'And shall I get money by my work immediately?'

"'No, not for a month.'

"'What shall I get then?'

"'Twelve sous a week.'[1]

"'Will that be enough to save every body else the trouble of paying any thing for my food, and my lodging, and my clothes?'

"'That it will not. A sprig, like you, cannot do that; he must do what he can.'

"'And my uncle will pay the rest?'

"'He cannot help himself. You are willing, then, to do what I have been telling you?'

"'I must not say much about my willingness, M. Vaublanc. I never did any work in my life.'

"'The more is the pity! In Lyons we find work for children from four years old; sometimes sooner.'

"'And in—in—the country I come from, the children never do any work, till they are almost as tall as their fathers. They do little offices, indeed, to be useful sometimes; but nothing like what you call working for their living. I do not know which way is right; but I know which is agreeable. I should not so much matter a little hardship; but you say, I must go no more to school. I cannot think why, M. Vaublanc, you asked any thing about my willingness!' And saying this, a flood of tears burst from my eyes.

"'When a schoolboy,' continued I, 'is to be punished, the master never asks him whether he chooses it. M. Vaublanc,

---

1 Five-pence English. [Godwin's note]

I cannot help myself. I am in a strange country; and have neither father, nor mother, nor any body to care for me. Take me, and dispose of me as you please, and as you tell me my uncle directs. I dare say you are a just man, and will do me no harm. Wherever you put me, I will endeavour to be a good boy, and that nobody shall be angry with me. I will be attentive, and learn as well as I can, and work as hard as I can. But, pray, pray, M. Vaublanc, do not ask me another time, whether I am willing?'

"'That will do, boy,' said he, nodding his head. 'You will get better satisfied with your situation, as you grow used to it.'

"Saying this, he put on his hat, and bid me follow him. As we passed along,—

"'You know, I believe, what I am?'

"'I have heard: a manufacturer of silk.'

"'One part of this business is to prepare the silk, as it comes from the worm, for the sempstress and the weaver. This is done by means of mills. I have two or three large ones, and employ a great number of work-people in them. You had rather work for me, than for a master you did not know?'

"'That I had. The thing is frightful to me, because it is a thing I never thought of. But I should fear it more, if it placed me altogether among strangers.'

"'You cannot think,' pursued M. Vaublanc, 'what an advantage these mills are to the city of Lyons. In other places, children are a burthen to their poor parents; they have to support them, till they are twelve or fourteen years of age, before they can do the least thing for their own maintenance: here the case is entirely otherwise. In other places, they run ragged and wild about the streets: no such thing is to be seen at Lyons. In short, our town is a perfect paradise. We are able to take them at four years of age, and in some cases sooner. Their little fingers, as soon as they have well learned the use of them, are employed for the relief of their parents, who have brought them up from the breast. They learn no bad habits; but are quiet, and orderly, and attentive, and industrious. What a prospect for their future lives! God himself must approve and bless a race who are thus early prepared to be of use to themselves and others. Among us, it is scarcely possible there should be such a thing as poverty. We have no such thing as idleness, or lewdness, or riot, or drunkenness, or debauchery of any sort. Let the day of judgment come when it will, it will never surprise us in a situation in which we should be ashamed to be found.'

"I never heard M. Vaublanc so eloquent. Eloquence was not his characteristic; but he was now on his favourite topic,—a topic intimately connected with his fame, his country, and the patriotic services which he rendered her. He did not completely recollect, while he talked on so interesting a subject, that he was addressing himself to a child scarcely more than eight years of age. Some things that he said were not exactly in accord with the vivacity of my temper, and the present state of my feelings. But, on the whole, I was fixed and penetrated by the warm colouring he bestowed on his picture. I checked the rebelliousness of my heart, and said, 'Probably it is better for me that I should be admitted into so pure and exemplary a society.' I longed to set my foot upon the threshold of the terrestrial paradise he described.

"My impatience was speedily gratified. We entered a very spacious building, which was divided, however, no otherwise than into four rooms, floor above floor. The lower or underground apartment was occupied by the horse that gave motion to the mill, and he was relieved every hour. Two horses were the stock to each mill. Above stairs, the walls were lined on three sides with the reels, or, as the English manufacturers call them, swifts, which receive the silk as it is devolved from certain bobbins. Of these there were about eleven hundred in the first floor, as many in the second, and as many in the third; in all, between three and four thousand. It was curious to recollect that all these, by means of wheels and other contrivances in the machine, were kept in perpetual motion by a single quadruped. In each apartment I saw several men, more women, and a greater number of children, busily employed. M. Vaublanc was so obliging as to take me over the whole, before he assigned me my task.

"You will not suppose there was any thing very cheerful or exhilarating in the paradise we had entered. The idea of a mill is the antipathy of this. One perpetual, dull, flagging sound pervaded the whole. The walls were bare; the inhabitants were poor. The children in general earned little more than twelve sous in a week; most of the women, and even several of the men, but about one French crown.[1] We must correct our ideas, and imagine a very sober paradise, before we can think of applying the name to this mansion.

"I was most attentive to the employment of the children, who were a pretty equal number of both sexes. There were about twenty on each floor, sixty in all. Their chief business was to attend to the swifts; the usual number being fifty-six which was assigned to the care of each child. The threads, while the operation of winding was going on, were of course liable to break; and, the moment a thread was broken, the benefit of the swift to which it belonged was at a stand. The affair of the child was, by turning round the swift, to find the end, and then to join it to the corresponding end attached to the bobbin. The child was to superintend the progress of these fifty-six threads, to move backward and forward in his little tether of about ten feet, and, the moment any accident happened, to repair it. I need not tell you that I saw no great expressions of cheerfulness in either the elder or the younger inhabitants of these walls: their occupations were too anxious and monotonous—the poor should not be too much elevated, and incited to forget themselves. There was a kind of stupid and hopeless vacancy in every face: this proceeded from the same causes.

"Not one of the persons before me exhibited any signs of vigour and robust health. They were all sallow; their muscles flaccid, and their form emaciated. Several of the children appeared to me, judging from their size, to be under four years of age—I never saw such children. Some were not tall enough with their little arms to reach the swift; these had stools, which they carried in their hands, and mounted as occasion offered. A few, I observed, had a sort of iron buskins on which they were elevated; and, as the iron was worked thin, they were not

---

1   Two and sixpence English. [Godwin's note]

extremely unwieldy. Children, before they had learned that firm step with the sole of the natural foot, without which it is impossible ever to be a man, were thus disciplined to totter upon stilts. But this was a new invention, and not yet fully established.

"This, or nearly all this, I observed upon my first survey of M. Vaublanc's manufactory. In addition to this, I afterward found, what you will easily conceive, that it was not without much severity that the children were trained to the regularity I saw. Figure to yourself a child of three or four years of age. The mind of a child is essentially independent; he does not, till he has been formed to it by hard experience, frame to himself the ideas of authority and subjection. When he is rated by his nurse, he expresses his mutinous spirit by piercing cries; when he is first struck by her in anger, he is ready to fall into convulsions of rage: it almost never happens otherwise. It is a long while (unless he is unmercifully treated indeed) before a rebuke or a blow produces in him immediate symptoms of submission. Whether with the philosopher we choose to regard this as an evidence of our higher destination, or with the theologian cite it as an indication of our universal depravity, and a brand we bear of Adam's transgression, the fact is indisputable. Almost all that any parent requires of a child of three or four years of age consists in negatives: stand still: do not go there: do not touch that. He scarcely expects or desires to obtain from him any mechanical attention. Contrast this with the situation of the children I saw: brought to the mill at six in the morning; detained till six at night; and, with the exception of half an hour for breakfast, and an hour at dinner, kept incessantly watchful over the safety and regularity of fifty-six threads continually turning. By my soul, I am ashamed to tell you by what expedients they are brought to this unintermitted vigilance, this dead life, this inactive and torpid industry!

"Consider the subject in another light. Liberty is the school of understanding. This is not enough adverted to. Every boy learns more in his hours of play, than in his hours of labour. In school he lays in the materials of thinking; but in his sports he actually thinks: he whets his faculties, and he opens his eyes.

The child, from the moment of his birth, is an experimental philosopher: he essays his organs and his limbs, and learns the use of his muscles. Every one who will attentively observe him, will find that this is his perpetual employment. But the whole process depends upon liberty. Put him into a mill, and his understanding will improve no more than that of the horse which turns it. I know that it is said that the lower orders of the people have nothing to do with the cultivation of the understanding; though for my part I cannot see how they would be the worse for that growth of practical intellect, which should enable them to plan and provide, each one for himself, the increase of his conveniences and competence. But be it so! I know that the earth is the great Bridewell of the universe, where spirits descended from heaven are committed to drudgery and hard labour.[1] Yet I should be glad that our children, up to a certain age, were exempt; sufficient is the hardship and subjection of their whole future life; methinks, even Egyptian taskmasters would consent that they should grow up in peace, till they had acquired the strength necessary for substantial service.

"Liberty is the parent of strength. Nature teaches the child, by the play of the muscles, and pushing out his limbs in every direction, to give them scope to develope themselves. Hence it is that he is so fond of sports and tricks in the open air, and that these sports and tricks are so beneficial to him. He runs, he vaults, he climbs, he practises exactness of eye and sureness of aim. His limbs grow straight and taper, and his joints well knit and flexible. The mind of a child is no less vagrant than his steps; it pursues the gossamer, and flies from object to object, lawless and unconfined: and it is equally necessary to the developement of his frame, that his thoughts and his body should be free from fetters. But then he cannot earn twelve sous a week. These children were uncouth and ill-grown in every limb, and were stiff and decrepit in their carriage, so as to seem like old men. At four years of age they could earn salt to their bread; but at forty, if it were possible that they should live so long, they

---

1   English prisons, specifically houses of correction requiring forced labor, were often called "bridewells" for Bridewell Prison in London.

could not earn bread to their salt. They were made sacrifices, while yet tender; and, like the kid, spoken of by Moses, were seethed and prepared for the destroyer in their mother's milk. This is the case in no state of society, but in manufacturing towns. The children of gipsies and savages have ruddy cheeks and a sturdy form, can run like lapwings, and climb trees with the squirrel.

CHAPTER XII.

"You will readily imagine what a thunder-stroke it was to me, to be entered as one of the members in this vast machine. Up to the period of eight years of age I had been accustomed to walk upon the level plain of human society; I had submitted to my parents and instructors; but I had no idea that there was any class or cast of my fellow-creatures superior to that in which I was destined to move. This persuasion inspires into the heart, particularly the heart of the young, such gaiety of temper, and graceful confidence in action! Now I was cast down at once, to be the associate of the lowest class of mechanics, paupers, brutified in intellect, and squalid in attire.

"I had, however, the courage to make up my resolution at once to the calamities of my station. I saw what it was to which it would be necessary for me to submit; and I felt too proud, to allow myself to be driven by blows and hard usage to that from which I could not escape. I discharged with diligence the task assigned me, and wasted in torpid and melancholy labour the hours of the day.

"What may appear strange, this terrible reverse of fate by no means operated to stupify my intellect. I was like those victims of Circe that we read of in Homer, who, though they had lost the external symbols of a superior nature, retained the recollection of what they had been, and disgust at what they were.[1] You will perhaps scarcely suppose that my age was ripe enough for this. If I had been removed to a pleasing scene, if I had con-

---

1 In Book X of Homer's *Odyssey*, when Odysseus visits the sorceress Circe on the island of Aeaea, Circe turns his companions into swine and other beasts.

tinued a pupil in the schools of liberal education, the impressions of my early years would probably have faded by degrees from my mind. But in the dreary situation in which I was now placed, they were my favourite contemplation; I thought of them for ever. It was by remembering them only, that I felt the difference between myself and the squalid beings around me. When Adam and Eve were driven out of Paradise, and turned loose upon the dreary and inhospitable plains, how fondly did they recollect the bowers and lawns they had quitted, the luxuriant flowers and blushing fruits, and the light and soothing employments which had there been their pursuit!

"It was naturally to have been expected, that I should look back to my native country, and, finding myself thus cruelly and iniquitously treated, should seek among the scenes and the acquaintances of my infant years the redress of my grievances. If I had returned to the vale of Urseren, and the foot of the St. Gothard; nay, if I had whispered the particulars of my story in the ears of one man of eminence and respect within the circuit of Switzerland; it cannot be but that I should have found a friend, a protector, and a champion. But I dared not do this. The mysterious threatenings of my uncle still sounded in my ears. He had given me a new name; he had left me among new faces; he had entered me upon a new species of existence. He had expressly prohibited all reference and connection between my former and my present state. What did this mean? I had too little knowledge of the modes of human life to be able to appreciate his menaces. This was the second revolution in my fortune. By the death of my father I found myself placed in absolute dependence upon an uncle, who had before had no power over me. A child has no standard within himself for these things; he is sensible of his own weakness; he watches the carriage and demeanour of the persons about him, and from thence judges what he is, and what he can be.

"The injustice practised toward me by my uncle, rendered me from the period of my removal to Lyons a creature of soliloquy and reverie. Children, at the early age at which I then was, are usually all frankness and communication; they tell to their companions and playmates every thing they know, and every thing they conjecture. I had a secret that must never be uttered. Once or twice in the few months in which I frequented the school I have mentioned (for afterward my temptations grew less), I was on the point of disclosing my history to a youthful favourite. But, when I had half resolved to unload my bosom, such apprehension suddenly seized me, that my tongue faltered, and my heart beat with violence, as if it would choke me. At one time, walking with my youngster friend on a narrow bank, just as I had prepared myself to speak, my foot slipped, and I sprained my ankle, so as to occasion a considerable swelling. At another, by a strange coincidence, a terrible clap of thunder burst upon me, succeeded by uncommon lightning and rain, which of necessity forced the thoughts both of my companion and myself into a new channel. These accidents took a superstitious hold of my fancy, and made me more reluctant than before to break the injunctions which had been laid upon me.

"Had I dared to attempt to deliver myself from the cruel bondage into which I had been kidnapped, it would have been a very arduous task for a child of little more than eight years of age. I might have chosen for my confidant and preserver some creature of my uncle, and have thus rendered my situation more desperate. No indifferent man would have undertaken my cause and my rescue; he would have looked on my distress with a sense of momentary compassion, and then, like the Levite in the parable, have passed by on the other side.[1] It could be only a man of warm humanity, animated with a strong love of justice and hatred of oppression, that, for the sake of me, a friendless outcast and an exile, would have strung himself to the encounter of prosperous and successful vice. It would naturally have required on my part, that I should have digested a resolute plan, and have persisted in the execution in spite of every obstacle that might arise.

"But I had by no means the courage adequate to such an exploit. I felt like one of those unhappy beings we read of in books of supernatural adventures, who are placed in the hands

---

1 Referring to the parable of the Good Samaritan in Luke 10. Unlike the Samaritan, the Levite refused to stop to assist the man in need.

of some powerful genius invisible to mortal sight, who dare not move lest they should meet with his hand, nor speak lest they should offend an unknown and never-absent auditor. It was thus I feared the ascendancy of my uncle. If men of powerful and vigorous minds, a Rousseau and others, have surrendered themselves to the chimeras of a disturbed imagination, and have believed that they were every where at the disposal of some formidable and secret confederacy, what wonder that I, a boy of eight years old, should be subject to a similar alarm?[1] Childhood is the age of superstition. The more I indulged this fear, the more my terror grew; and, in a short time, I believe I could sooner have died, than have brought myself to divulge a secret, the publication of which so obviously led to my benefit. Thus, by the machinations of my cruel guardian, I was involved in a state of slavery, body and soul, such as has seldom been the lot of a human creature.

"I remained for a considerable time an inmate of my prison-house. M. Vaublanc found that a person, so mean in his destination as I was, was not entitled to the luxuries and refinements of his mansion and board, and placed me as a lodger with one of the labourers in his mill. At the same time he took from me the clothes which I had hitherto worn, and assigned me a garb similar to that of my fellow-slaves. Thus I became in all external respects like the companions with whom I was now associated; and, whatever I might feel within, could in no point be distinguished by the common observer from the miserable beings around me. I became familiar with objects of distress. The sort of training and drilling, necessary at first to preserve an infant during twelve hours together from the guilt of a distracted attention, was continually before my sight. The supervisor of the machine contracted, from necessity, a part of the rugged and ferocious character which belongs to a slave-driver in the West Indies. There was one phenomenon among us that might have surprised and misled an ordinary spectator. Our house of confinement often echoed with songs, and frequently

---

1   Jean-Jacques Rousseau (1712-78), Swiss philosopher, who in 1775-76 wrote three dialogues entitled *Rousseau juge de Jean-Jacques*, in which he described imaginary conspiracies being plotted against him.

an hundred voices from different parts of the machine joined in the same tune. Was not this a clear indication of gaiety and tranquillity of heart? I remembered one day, when I was in England, I had occasion to spend two hours in your prison of Newgate. The window of the apartment where I sat overlooked the press-yard, where a number of convicts were assembled, waiting the occasion of being transported to the other side of the globe.[1] They were employed in the manner I have mentioned, singing out in chorus some of the popular songs of their country. But, alas! there, as in the silk-mills of Lyons, it was a melancholy ditty. The tone was heavy, monotonous, and flat. There was the key and the note of gaiety, but the heart was wanting. It was like the spectacle of a fresh and well-grown human body placed erect against a wall, satisfactory in other respects,—but it was dead. They sung, bold and audacious in the face of despair, just as the fear-struck peasant sings along the churchyard at midnight, expecting every moment to see a ghost start up at his feet.

"On each returning Sunday the chains which confined my footsteps were suspended. This day I regularly devoted to solitude and reverie. It is not to be described what pleasure I derived from this resource. It was a new being that descended upon me. In the room of dead, naked, and discoloured walls, I beheld the canopy of heaven. In the room of the ever-turning swifts, which in multitudes surrounded me on every side, I beheld the trees and the fields, the fruits of rural industry, and the grand features of all-powerful nature. 'Oh, Switzerland!' I would have said, if I had dared trust my lips even in soliloquy with the enchanting sound,—'nurse of my cheerful infancy, in these beauteous retreats, methinks I see thee still!'— I scented the fragrant air, and I exchanged the flagging songs of my brother-slaves, for the joyous warbling of the vocal woods. The poorest slave that lives, when withdrawn into a solitude like this, is upon a level with the greatest lord. If he does not tread upon floors of porphyry, and is not canopied with roofs of granite, he, however, possesses himself in the

---

1 The yard of Newgate Prison in London where, originally, persons who refused to answer criminal charges were pressed to death.

midst of a palace more glorious than human fingers ever formed.

"You may think, perhaps, that my Sunday enjoyments, such as I describe, were of too grave and contemplative a character, to belong to such early years. I assure you, however, I do not describe them up to the height of what I then felt, and now remember them. In answer to your objection, I can only remark, that adversity, or rather the contrast between present adversity and past good fortune, tends beyond all other things to sharpen the apprehension. These scenes would have produced no such effect upon the other boys of the mill, because they had known no such contrast. They would not have afforded me the delight I describe, had I not been so much restrained from them, and restrained in so hateful a confinement. My heart felt no less unchained and free at these periods, than is the river, which had been locked up in frost, and at length by the influence of genial zephyrs is restored to her beloved murmurings and meanders.

"I firmly believe that, if there had been no Sundays and holidays, I should have remained many years the prisoner of M. Vaublanc. My days of labour were days of oblivion. It is impossible to describe to you the state of mind of a human creature, whose incessant office it is from morning to night to watch the evolution of fifty-six threads. The sensorium in man has in it something of the nature of a mill, but it is moved by very different laws from those of a mill contrived for the manufacture of silk threads. The wheels move in swifter rotation than those I was appointed to watch; and to keep this rotation constantly up to a certain pace is one of the great desiderata of human happiness. When the succession of ideas flags, or is violently restrained in its circumvolutions, this produces by degrees weariness, *ennui*, imbecility, and idiotism. Conceive how this progress is impeded by the task of continually watching fifty-six threads! The quantity of thought required in this office is nothing, and yet it shuts out, and embroils, and snaps in pieces, all other thoughts.

"Another law which governs the sensorium in man is the law of association. In contemplation and reverie, one thought introduces another perpetually; and it is by similarity, or the hooking of one upon the other, that the process of thinking is carried on. In books and in living discourse the case is the same; there is a constant connection and transition, leading on the chain of the argument. Try the experiment of reading for half an hour a parcel of words thrown together at random, which reflect no light on each other, and produce no combined meaning; and you will have some, though an inadequate, image of the sort of industry to which I was condemned. Numbness and vacancy of mind are the fruits of such an employment. It ultimately transforms the being who is subjected to it, into quite a different class or species of animal.

"My Sundays, as I have said, restored me to the sort of creature I had been. At first, the feeling of this was enough for me; I was too happy to be capable of much reflection. I leaped, and skipped, and ran, and played a thousand ridiculous antics, that I might convince myself that I was not wholly an automaton. In a few weeks, however, when the novelty of these periodical seasons of rest was somewhat worn off, I began to feel my pleasure tarnished by the recollection that, when Sunday was gone, Monday, and after that five other mortal days, would inevitably follow. The day of rest was so short!

CHAPTER XIII.

"By degrees I became more serious and meditating. I said to myself, 'What am I? and wherefore am I here?' The years of nonage in the human creature are many, partly because he is surrounded with parents, and kindred, and acquaintances, whose habit it is to take care of him, and to direct his steps. Perhaps the majority of human beings never think of standing by themselves, and choosing their own employments, till the sentence has been regularly promulgated to them,—It is time for you to take care of yourself. For my part, I found myself cast upon a new world, without relations, acquaintances, or friends, and this urged me on prematurely to acts of discretion. I could scarcely persuade myself that the life to which I was devoted, deserved the name of taking care of me, and therefore began to cast about in my own thoughts what I should do.

"I need not tell you that I detested the condition in which I found myself placed, and longed to escape from it, and seek my fortune. But whither direct my steps? I dared not think of Switzerland. There resided my uncle, that malignant demon, the recollection of whom haunted my thoughts, waking and sleeping. In all the rest of the world I knew not even the private and proper name of a human creature. I had listened, however, to the old songs of Switzerland, and had some acquaintance with the romances of the middle ages. Mine were the years of romance. Without knowledge enough of what was actually passing in the scenes of the universe, yet with a restless imagination, and a powerful motive urging me to consult it, I patched up as I could, from narratives of humble life, and tales of chivalry, what it was that I should have to encounter. I knew I must have bread, and that bread did not grow in every hedge. I concluded that I must find or make a friend, by whose assistance to support life, and, if possible, attain to something beyond bare subsistence.

"At first I was somewhat terrified with the project I had conceived. Again and again I sat down in despair, and said, 'I am too young; I must wait yet some years before I can launch upon so great an undertaking.' But my tasks would not wait: they beset me from morning till night, and, when I had once conceived the idea of flight, became continually more insupportable. From the extreme of despair, I passed to the extreme of sanguine expectation. I brooded over my plans, till all difficulties seemed to vanish before me; the scenes I anticipated at length became as familiar to me, as any thing which had absolutely passed in any former period of my life.

"You will smile when I tell you that my favourite scheme was to go to Versailles, and throw myself at the feet of the King of France. It was the project of a child, and will show you how ripe and unripe at once was the state of my intellect. The Gallic sovereign is, of all kings, the favourite of the people of Switzerland. I had listened to the songs and popular tales concerning Francis I. and Henry IV.; and a king of France appeared, in my eyes, the most gallant and generous of mortals.[1] I did not know exactly how much I proposed to tell the King; I scrupled the secret my uncle had so severely enjoined me to preserve; yet, if he should insist upon knowing the whole, surely he was able to protect me against the resentment of a burgher of Uri! However this point might be disposed of, I felt in myself a destination superior to that of a handicraft in the silk-mills of Lyons; I believed that I was capable of extraordinary things. What boy from the swifts, but myself, would have had the boldness to think of applying for redress to the King of France? I was persuaded that I could interest his Majesty in my case,—that I could induce him to judge me deserving of his protection. I would say to him, 'Sire, dispose of me as you please; make me one of your pages; you shall find me the most zealous and faithful of your servants!'

"Louis XIV. was at this time in the height of his glory.[2] Among the little topics, by my excellence in which I had distinguished myself in the halcyon days of my childhood, was history. It will easily be supposed that my knowledge amounted to scarcely more than a few names and dates; but I had heard certain familiar anecdotes of Henry IV. pleasing to my boyish imagination, and had long since made him my hero. I was told that Louis XIV. was the worthy grandson of this free-hearted prince. In one of my Sunday's excursions I fell in with an old French soldier. The military private is usually of a loquacious and communicative temper. I was eager to be acquainted with the character of his master; he was no less prompt to tell me all he knew. He spoke of the beauty of his figure, and the affability of his demeanour. He related the victories he had won, and described the palaces and public edifices which he had founded or adorned. He swore that he was the most generous, condescending, and tender-hearted of mankind; and he happened to have two or three instances, which he affirmed to have occurred under his own eye, not unhappily illustrative of this character. Every thing, as I thought, seemed to concur for the

---

1   Francis I (1494-1547) ruled France from 1515, Henry IV (1553-1610) from 1589.
2   Louis XIV, the "Sun King" (1638-1715), ruled France from 1643, and was known for the splendor of his court.

success of my design. The magnificence of Louis XIV. fascinated my imagination; the examples of his gentleness and humanity were so many omens assuring my good fortune. I bought a portrait of this monarch; it was almost the only extravagance of which I had been guilty since my last degradation. I carried it in my pocket. On Sundays, when I had wandered into the most obscure retreat I could find, I held it in my hand; I set it before me, I talked to it, and endeavoured to win the good-will of the King. Sometimes I worked myself into such a degree of fervour and enthusiasm, that I could scarcely believe but that the portrait smiled upon me, and, with a look of peculiar benignity, seemed to say, 'Come to Versailles, and I will make your fortune!'

"While I attended the lessons of the regents of the free-school of Lyons, I received the weekly stipend usually allotted to boys of my age. I had before, as I have mentioned, received a louis d'or and a three livres piece from my uncle and cousin at parting. Like a boy, I sometimes spent my money upon toys and *confitures*; but for the most part I reserved it, and suffered it to grow into a little stock. Young as I was, from the moment of parting with my uncle I could not conceal from myself that I was in an extraordinary situation. The secrecy that had been enjoined me weighed upon my mind. Compelled to deny my family, my friends, and my country, and suddenly dropped in a city where I was unacquainted with a single creature, I incessantly said, 'What is next to befal me? It is necessary for me to provide myself, and not to be wholly unprepared for events which it is not in my power to foresee.' Youth is, in some respects, the age of suspicion; at least it was so with me. Whenever a child of the age at which I was arrived, feels that he is thwarted and rigorously used, he half suspects some motive, obscure and unavowed, in the individual from whom his mortification is derived.

"The period I ultimately fixed for my flight was the week of Easter. At this time we were allowed at the mill two holidays, in addition to that of Sunday. I was perhaps partly influenced in choosing this season, by the idea that when I was not wanted at work, my presence or absence would be little taken notice of.

The people with whom I lived were too wretched, and too anxious about their own children, to feel much kindness for me; and I should not be reported to the overseer till Wednesday. But the principal consideration that guided me was the cheerfulness of the season; liberty was, to the whole lower class of the people, the order of the day. I had three days of freedom: why should I not make this the starting post of my eternal liberty?

"I will not trouble you with a detail of my smaller adventures on the road. Full of the anticipation of my grand undertaking, I had repeatedly turned my steps on my days of relaxation toward Paris, and made many enquiries respecting the way. I had learned the names of the principal towns. I set out with a beating heart; and, having walked gravely till I was out of the city, I then began to run. I did not, however, run far; my thoughts were too full of agitation to admit any regularity of motion. Sometimes I slackened my pace, because I feared I should be taken for a fugitive; and sometimes because I said to myself, 'I must manage my strength, if I expect it to carry me far.'

"Two hundred and fifty miles was a great undertaking for a boy under nine years of age. One advantage I possessed: I had money, more than I could prudently spend on the passage. My mind was too intently fixed upon the end of my journey, to be capable of much calculation respecting the obstacles I had to encounter. One resolution, however, I fixed, firm as the basis of my native mountains,—'No consideration on earth, no difficulties, no discouragements, shall ever carry me back!' A mechanic becomes a sort of machine; his limbs and articulations are converted, as it were, into wood and wires. Tamed, lowered, torpified into this character, he may be said, perhaps, to be content. It is well! It seems necessary that there should be such a class of animated machines in the world. It is probable, if I had continued much longer in the silk-mills of Lyons, I should have become such a being myself. But, with the conceptions and recollections which continually beset my imagination, it appeared the most horrible of all destinies. I, that dared, at nine years of age, launch myself in the world,—that dared, to a certain degree, to revolve the various chances of human affairs, and defy the worst,—that purposed to challenge the attention, the equity, and the compassion of the King of France, should I be thus neutralised? Why did I feel thus? Because my early education had not prepared me for my present lot. I understood why my companions of my own age were put into the silk-mill: their parents were engaged in employments equally deadening; their parents were unable by their labour to obtain bread for themselves and their offspring: but I did not understand why I was there. I felt such a loathing at this moment to the occupation which had engrossed me for months, that, if I could have been assured that such should be my occupation for as many months to come, I believe, child as I was, I should sooner have taken a knife and thrust it into my heart, than submit to it.

"In thinking over my situation as I passed along, I felt that the thing most immediately pressing upon me was to avoid exciting the curiosity and suspicion of the persons whose assistance might be necessary to me on the road. The production of a louis d'or, for example, might be fatal to a boy of my childish appearance and coarseness of attire. In my journey from Urseren to Lyons, I had learned something of the nature of inns; and I retained all these things as perfectly as if they had occurred only yesterday. I resolved to go only to the meanest inns, and ask for the plainest accommodations. On the second day I joined a wagoner, who was conducting his commodities to Dijon; and this considerably facilitated the first part of my journey. I began with asking him of my road to Mâcon, the first considerable place through which I was to pass. He was going through Mâcon.

"'How much further?'

"'To Dijon.'

"The meanness of my attire encouraged him to question me in his turn.

"'What had I to do at Mâcon?'

"'I was going to see the world,' I replied.

"'I perceive, my spark,' cried the wagoner, 'what you are. You belong to the silk-mills; you are a runaway, and I have a great mind to take you up, and send you back to your master.'

"I was surprised at his so instantly fixing on my true character; though, on reflection, it was by no means extraordinary that a person just come from Lyons should have made the conjecture; the costume was sufficiently peculiar.

"'I will never stay at the silk-mill,' said I; 'nobody has a right to confine me there.'

"'Nobody has a right, youngster? Not your parents? Your wildness, I dare say, will break their hearts.'

"'I have no parents.' - I confessed to him that I was determined to go to Paris.

"'And what will you do at Paris? You will be starved to death.'

"'Better be starved, than undergo such misery as I have suffered. But I will not starve!'

"The wagoner began to reflect, that, if I had no parents or kindred, nobody would be greatly injured by my elopement. He contented himself, therefore, with seriously expostulating with me on the folly of my project, and advising me to return. Finding his remonstrances of no avail, he agreed to take me under his protection as far as he was going on my way. Thus I conquered more than one third of the road.

CHAPTER XIV.

"Dijon was so capital a city, that I thought I might venture here to change my piece of gold, the parting present of my treacherous uncle. But I was mistaken. I hated the clothes I wore, since they had led the wagoner to discover the situation to which I belonged. I went into a clothier's shop with a determination to change them. Unfortunately I plunged headlong into the house of a man of rugged temper and a hard-favoured countenance. The moment I looked at him I trembled. But it was too late to draw back.

"'What is your pleasure, my lad?' said he.

"'I want some clothes.'

"'Where do you live? Who is to pay for them? Where shall I send them?'

"'I am a stranger in Dijon.'

"'Why does not your father or somebody come with you? How can such a child as you choose a suit of clothes?'

"'I am all alone.'

"'Alone! And how are you to pay for your clothes?'

"'Perhaps you would allow me something for the clothes I have got on. And I have a louis d'or,'—showing it.

"'A louis d'or!' said he, coming from the other side of the counter. 'Tell me, sirrah, where you got that louis d'or?'

"'My uncle gave it me.'

"'Who is your uncle? I shall send for him immediately, and find out the truth of this.'

"'I tell you, sir, he does not live here; I am a stranger in Dijon; never saw the city till last night. But you need not frighten me; if you do not choose to sell me any clothes, I will go away without them. I assure you, I am an honest boy, and my money is my own.'

"'We shall see that presently. You do not like to be frightened! But I shall frighten you, and most confoundedly too, before I have done with you. You must go with me to the mayor.'

"'I will go with you, where you please,' said I, believing it was impossible that any body should be more frightful to me than the honest slopman before me.[1] 'But I had rather go back to my inn.'

"The trader conducted me to the magistrate. I found myself right in my conjecture, that I should be better off in his hands than in those of the Argus who had first seized me.[2] The mayor was a sober, credible man, middle-aged, and inclined to corpulence, who made a point of faithfully discharging his duty, but who took no particular pleasure in frightening little boys. He was too much accustomed to office to feel any high

---

1 A merchant of ready-made, cheap clothing.
2 Argus was the hundred-eyed watchman of the goddess Hera, whose eyes were placed upon the peacock's tail after he was slain by Hermes.

gratification in its swagger and insolence. His passions were dead; he could scarcely be said to love or hate, to be gentle or furious; he was the law, and nothing but the law.

"As I and my conductor passed along the streets to this man's house, I fixed the plan of action that I would observe. I determined to take refuge in silence and reserve. I said to myself, 'They cannot find out that I have stolen my money, because I have not stolen it; and therefore, after having examined and tried me as much as they please, they must dismiss me. I will not betray my family story, and I will not furnish them with a clue by which they may send me back to Lyons.'

"The slopman led me into the justice-room, and told his tale. The magistrate listened, and made his observations. My adversary endeavoured in vain to inspire his own passions into the mayor; the clothier was earnest, abusive, and eloquent; the mayor was considerate and inquisitive. He asked me who I was, and I refused to tell.

"'Did I know what it was to be brought before a magistrate?'

"'Not very well,' I replied.

"'It would be worse for me, if I did not give a proper account of myself.'

"I answered that I could not satisfy his curiosity. I had been ill-used by cruel relations, but did not dare to complain. I had had a father, who was kind and rich; but my father was dead, and I was driven out from my country and friends.

"The magistrate employed every artifice to extort my story from me. He said, my secret should be safe with him, and my cruel relations should never know that I had disclosed it. He said, he would take me under his protection, and oblige them by the interposition of the law to do me justice. He then changed his tone, put on an angry brow, and told me, that he perceived that all I had related was a fiction, but that he would send me to prison, and have me punished, till I told the truth. He put a variety of subtle and artfully contrived questions to wrest my secret from me. I stuck to the same point, made two or three answers which I hoped would move him to favour me, and repeated them again and again in return to every interrogatory he uttered. He sent for the people of the inn, where I confessed to have slept the night before: luckily it was not the same inn the wagoner used, and they could discover nothing.

"The magistrate was as good as his word, and sent me to prison. At entering, it struck me, that the scene was not new to me, but that it was very like a silk-mill; the same meanness in the building, the same squalidness in the inhabitants, the same dejection in every countenance. Presently, however, I perceived a difference; the people there were employed, and here were idle; there were vacant and incurious, and here eagerly crowded about a new tenant of their wretched mansion.

"Thus I had twice in one day been introduced into situations calculated to impress a youthful mind with inexpressible horror. To be taken before a magistrate, to be thrust into a gaol, would to most children of my tender years have appeared no less terrible than death. But I had entered upon an extraordinary undertaking, and had worked myself up to an uncommon pitch of resolution. I knew that for such an urchin as I was, to undertake his own establishment in life was no holiday project. I knew that no small degree of courage and perseverance would be necessary to introduce me to the presence and speech of Louis XIV. It is inconceivable, at least judging from my own instance, of what an extent of exaltation and enthusiasm nine years of age are capable. Enthusiasm is often indebted for much of its fervour to a complete ignorance, and want of practice, in the ways of the world; and, as far as that constitutes a qualification, this immature period of life is of course admirably endowed. In this state of mind, I felt a contempt of difficulties, under which at any other time I should have sunk. I seemed to myself as if I were made of iron, and nothing hostile appeared to make any impression upon me. It was my business to proceed upon my high destination and my choice of life, and to suffer none of these things to interrupt me.

"The prisoners crowded about me, and were eager to learn for what crime such a child as I was, was brought into their society. It was presently rumoured, that it was upon suspicion of having stolen some money; that I had obstinately refused to tell the mayor how I came by it, and that I was committed for re-examination. The moment the word money was mentioned, two or three came about me at once, and told me that it was the universal practice for every newcomer to pay a certain sum by way of entrance-money, at the same time vociferously demanding from me the established fee. It fortunately happened that the magistrate had taken from me my whole stock, to be returned the next day, if no discoveries were made; otherwise it is highly probable these obliging comrades of mine would have stripped me of all that I had. After the first bustle of my introduction was over, a very grave-looking man of the set drew me into a corner, and told me I was the most promising boy of my age he ever saw. He said, he had conceived a particular liking to me; and greatly commended my firmness in refusing to tell the magistrate how I came by my money. That showed I was true game! He observed that he would, if I pleased, put me into a way by which I might make a man of myself for ever; and offered to become my instructor. He swore, that it would be a thousand pities that such talents as I had showed should be lost for want of encouragement.

"I made little answer to these compliments, though the person from whom they flowed certainly succeeded in exciting my curiosity, and I was desirous of hearing to what so extraordinary a preface would lead. Having intimated this, he entered into a very animated and earnest dissertation upon the different modes of committing theft without danger of detection. Observing, however, that I did not exactly enter into his feelings, he stopped short, and complained of my timidity. He soothed me in the gentlest, and, as he believed, the most flattering manner, and employed a hundred arts of rhetoric, worthy of a better cause. I told him, that he had mistaken my character, that I had stolen no money, and that what I had was honestly my own. On this he assumed a smile, expressive of grave and gentle derision, and replied, that that was all very well, but that it was not worth while to persist in declarations of innocence among friends. My mind was full of other projects, and therefore the representations of my sage Mentor had no effect upon me. This, however, was the sort of exhortation to which I was exposed; and, if I had been the kind of person the magistrate conceived me to be, this night's lodging would, too probably, have completed my character for ever.

"The next day I was brought again before the mayor, and persisted in my resolution to discover nothing. The interval which had passed during the silence of the night, enabled me to collect more firmness, and to express myself with greater coherence. I said, 'Sir, I am a friendless little boy, and you may do with me whatever you please. But I am not so much afraid of any body, as of my hard-hearted uncle. I am afraid, if I tell you who I am, you would send me back to him, or write a letter to him about me. You tell me you would not; but rich men think it a good action to deceive little boys: I am sure I have reason to know that. Oh, sir, do you think it was a small thing that determined me to run away, and go among strangers? I would sooner die than return!'

"You will easily imagine that what I said, did not in the smallest degree move the man to whom it was addressed, to compassion; the magistrate, who could consign such a child as I was, for one night, to the horrors and dangers of a prison, could be little accessible to the relentings of nature. This reflection is obvious enough to me now; but it was not so then. The actions of their elders are always mysteries to children; they do not see the springs of the machine; they wait with a sort of superstitious anticipation, to observe how their seniors will act upon every new event, and are surprised at nothing.

"But, though the magistrate was guilty of no meltings of compassion toward me, he was not inflexible. He saw not what he could do further with me; he had exhausted upon me every expedient he could devise to render me frank and communicative. At length he calculated within himself, as I suppose, the fruitlessness of detaining me: perhaps he was inclined to think me innocent, and to believe the story I told. If he detained me longer, it might be a trouble to him, and ultimately produce a burden to the corporation in which he presided. He dismissed me with a moderate portion of good advice; recommended to me not to become a vagrant, in consequence of which I should finally be made a scoundrel and a thief, if I were not so already; and, above all, warned me of the stubbornness of my temper.

He had never seen so stiff-necked a little villain; and he augured an untimely and a shameful death from such beginnings. I listened to his advice with passive attention; but, what I prized much beyond his advice, before he sent me from his presence he returned to me my money.

"I left Dijon with a beating heart. I was full of exultation at the thought of my liberty, once more restored to me. I foresaw every thing that was fortunate from the issue of my first adventures. The discovery of my class of life by the wagoner had been productive of no mischievous effects to me. The adventure of the shopman and the louis d'or had seemed to threaten the greatest dangers; but by my prudence and perseverance (for I was willing to take the whole praise to myself) I had been extricated from them all. All difficulties would vanish before my courage and abilities. I should infallibly become a page to the King of France. From this gaol my impetuous imagination took its flight. The marshal's truncheon and the ducal coronet danced before my charmed sight: I sighed for princesses, and the blood-royal was mixed in my offspring. Alnaschar in the Arabian Nights was but a driveller to me.[1]

CHAPTER XV.

"NOTHING further of material importance occurred, till I arrived at Fontainebleau. It is difficult to express the rapture I felt at entering this celebrated scene. Fontainebleau had been to the kings of France, what Versailles has become since. It had been particularly honoured by the residence of Henry IV.; and Louis XIII., his successor, was born here.[2] But, independently of this, here was a royal palace belonging to my intended patron,—the first I had ever seen. Having refreshed myself, and

---

1 Alnaschar was a dreamer who invested all of his money in a basket of glassware. Dreaming about how he might become rich enough to marry the daughter of the vizier, and then how he might quarrel with her, he kicked and broke all of his glassware; "The Tale of the Barber's Fifth Brother" in *The Arabian Nights Entertainments*, translated into English from Antoine Galland's French edition of 1736.
2 Louis XIII (1601-43) ruled France from 1610.

rested a short time, I found my way into the gardens, and viewed with enthusiasm the immenseness of the edifice. The fountains from which the place derives its name, the large and deep forests which on every side met my eye in the distance, all struck me with an idea of unbounded magnificence.

"'I wish the King was here!' exclaimed I. Presently, however, I thought again, 'Do I wish it? I must think a great deal of what I have to do, and what I have to say, before I meet him. No, I am not sorry I have a little further to go!' The idea of a king at a distance, is very different from what we feel when we come near him. The imagination never fences him round with so many obstacles, and enchanted circles, within which unhallowed feet may scarcely tread, as the reality presents. The very dinner which is set before him (to instance in a trite circumstance), no untutored fancy ever paints. We shape to ourselves what we have not seen, after the fashion of what we are accustomed to; and experience does not fail to surprise us with the immeasurable distance which refinement and art have placed between man and man. It would be an amusing picture, to set me on my wooden stool with my little dinner in an earthen pan, as I ate it at the silk-mill, beside even a *petit souper* of the King of France. I own that I felt certain qualms about my heart when I thought of my adventure, and looked round upon the splendours of Fontainebleau.

"As I was wandering about, full of these reflections, a grave-looking man came up and accosted me. He said, he saw I was a stranger, and offered to point out to me the curiosities of the place. It is singular, but I was struck with a certain resemblance between him and the man who had undertaken to be my tutor in the press-yard of Dijon. I was, however, now in a very different temper from that which inspired me then. Then I was under the pressure of a very dangerous embarrassment, and had determined to find my safety in the most inflexible reserve. Now my heart was open, and my spirits light; beside which, I was anxious for communication, and had a hundred enquiries which I wished to have resolved.

"I therefore willingly entered into conversation with this stranger. I asked him whether the King of France ever now came to Fontainebleau; I enquired of him concerning the structure and site of the palace of Versailles, how the King was attended, and where and in what manner he spent the different hours of the day. My communicative friend seemed to be well informed in all these particulars, and his intelligence was copious and interesting. In the mean time he observed me closely, and drew more sound and perfect conclusions respecting me and my fortunes than I was aware. At length he told me that he was going to set out the next morning for Versailles, and offered to become my guide. I willingly accepted his kind proposal.

VOLUME THE SECOND.

CHAPTER I.

"WE went together to Paris, and arrived about the close of the evening. Our conversation had been eager and animated, and my companion proposed our taking up our lodging at the same inn. I was a total stranger in this great metropolis, and willingly accepted his suggestion. The streets by which we entered the capital were by no means so sumptuous as the idea of so celebrated a city had given me to expect; but I presently observed that my conductor led me away from the principal streets, and that his route lay through many a dark passage and many an alley. The house of reception to which we repaired corresponded to the road by which we reached it. My fellow-traveller, however, appeared to be well known to its inhabitants, and I observed various significant winks and gestures that passed between him and the hostess. After a brief supper, we were shown to a room where there were two beds.

"The equivocal character of the inn in which I took up my night's repose did not disturb me. I sought for no present splendours, and my plan through my journey had been simplicity and economy. When the candle was put out, then the train of my splendours began. My heart bounded with joy, when I thought that I was thus far toward the end of my labours. I folded my arms about me with wanton triumph, as if I would bestow upon myself an embrace of congratulation. The turrets and the spires of Paris, I regarded as the emblems of my independence. In the midst of this mighty scene, the conviction came home to me with pleasure, that I belonged to no one; 'For, alas!' said I to myself, 'since the death of my father, I have not seen one human creature to whom I could wish to belong! I am set loose from all compulsory connections; but I will not long be alone!'

"This short meditation was to me the precursor of sleep; and my slumbers were sweet and balmy. I was fatigued with my long peregrinations, and the sun was high before I roused myself from repose. When I awoke, the first thing I observed was that my companion was gone. 'I wonder,' said I to myself, 'whether I shall see him again.' I thought that it would full as well content me that I should not. I determined to arrange the particulars of my plan in my own way; and the having such a companion as this would but have interrupted and embarrassed me.

"I began to dress myself. Through my whole journey, I had had the precaution to take my breeches, containing my little stock of cash, into my bed, and to place them near, or rather under, some part of my body. At first, I did not remark any difference from the morning before, and the usual appearance of things. Presently, however, a suspicion flashed across my mind; I passed my hand along the pocket; it went over smooth and without interruption. I felt within—there was nothing! I went to the other pocket; all was vacancy. I threw back the clothes of the bed, with a faint hope that my money was to be found there. I turned over and shook every thing: I felt in all my pockets a thousand times: I examined in the same manner the bed-clothes of my fellow-traveller: I searched impossible places.

"Pity me, my dear Fleetwood, pity me! Distant as is the period I am describing from the present, I can never think of this horrible event, without a twinge at the heart which I cannot describe. I was then a little, uninstructed boy, and now I am an old man, and my hairs are white; yet I cannot mention this adventure without feeling my throat dry, and my voice suffocated. Common robberies are committed upon a man, who goes home, opens his escritoire, and puts into his purse the exact sum of which he had been deprived. I had lost every thing I possessed in the world. I had just travelled two hundred and fifty miles, and was distant four hundred from the seat of my birth and my relations. All my visions, my golden dreams, my castles in the air, were demolished in a moment. What was I to do? My visions were not luxuries, were not changes of a worse state for a better; they stood between me and annihilation. I saw nothing that remained for me, but to be starved. For God's sake, turn to your Aesop; open at the fable of the Dairymaid and her Milking-pail; blot it out, and put my adventure in its stead![1]

---

1 Aesop (6th century BC) was credited with the authorship of a great number of fables, but this one is found in Jean de La Fontaine's *Fables* (1668-94). Like

"But this was not the principal aggravation of my case. Many men at many times have, no doubt, lost all that they had. But perhaps such an event never happened before to a child, entering for the first time a great metropolis, without a single friend, and four hundred miles removed from his home. Men have arms to work, and a head to contrive; they have experience, enabling them to foresee and calculate the results of a thousand schemes; and a tongue, to make good their story, to propose things which it shall be for the interest of the hearer to accept, to parley, and to demand, through that species of equality which no refinement can destroy, a fair hearing. I had nothing!

"I sat down, and found relief in a gush of tears. I wept, till I could weep no more, and felt myself stupified. By and by, a thought occurred, which roused me. If a man were in my place, what would he do? He would not sit still, and do nothing. I am alone in Paris; I must be my own man!

"I went down stairs, and saw my hostess. 'Where is the person,' said I, 'who came with me last night?'

"'Gone—he has been gone these two hours.'

"'Where is he gone?'

"'I do not know.'

"'When will he come back?'

"'I cannot tell. I never saw him in my life before.'

"To ask these questions I was obliged to follow the landlady from side to side in the great kitchen of the inn. She seemed to be exceedingly busy, and never stood still for a moment.

"'Madam,' said I, 'I have been robbed; this man has taken away all my money.'

"These words stopped her perpetual motion, and fixed her to the place where she stood.

"'Robbed!' said she; 'this is a fine story! No such word was ever heard in my house. What business, you little rascal, had you to come with a robber to my house? Robbed! He is a

---

Alnaschar, the dairy maid plans to sell milk until she has enough money to buy a calf. Imagining how the calf will skip, she skips herself, and spills her pail of milk. The story is also found in Godwin's pseudonymous *Fables Ancient and Modern. Adapted for the Use of Children from Three to Eight Years of Age*, by Edward Baldwin, Esq. (2 vols., 1805), I. 111-17.

highwayman, and you are his jackal. A pretty story, quotha, that you have been robbed! Such little villains as you always outwit themselves. Betty, look up the silver tea-spoons! Observe the brat! See what fine linsey-woolsey clothes he has got on! And pray, my little master, of what have you been robbed? Of a crooked copper, I warrant! Yes, I see, there are two of my silver tea-spoons gone. Step for an officer this moment! Search him! But that is in vain. The boy seizes the goods, and his companion neatly carries them off. You shall breakfast, my lad, in the *Conciergerie*, upon a salt eel! Why are not you gone, Betty?"[1]

"I own I was now terrified, in a very different style from any thing I had felt in the presence of the mayor of Dijon. I believed that the house I was in was appropriated to the consultations of robbers. I had observed the signals of intelligence which had passed on the preceding evening between my fellow-traveller and the hostess, and now she denied that she had ever before seen him in her life. I did not doubt that the story of the tea-spoons was a concerted fabrication, chosen as the most effectual means of quashing my complaint respecting the loss of my property. But what chance had I, an unprotected child, without a friend, and without a name, to be able to make good my own cause, and defeat the malicious accusation which was threatened against me! This was an intolerable addition to the shock I had just felt in finding myself unexpectedly left without a penny. The whole recurred to my mind at once, and, though already exhausted with weeping, I burst afresh into a flood of tears.

"Betty, a plump and fresh-coloured girl of nineteen, felt her bowels yearn with compassion for my case. 'Pray, madam,' said she, 'do not be too hard upon this little boy. I dare say he knows nothing of the tea-spoons.'

"'I dare say no such thing!' replied the mistress fiercely.

"'Upon my soul, madam, if you will send him to prison, you may go for an officer yourself. I will have nothing to do with

---

1 Linsey-woolsey is a fabric made from flax and wool; a crooked copper refers to a
· (worthless) bent penny; the Conciergerie was a prison in Paris; a "salt eel" refers to
   the end of a rope.

it. For my part, I wonder what your heart is made of, to think of such a thing.'

"'Go, you are a fool!—Well, let him get out of my house! Let him tramp, as fast as his ten toes can carry him! If ever I catch him again, I will have no more mercy upon him, than I would upon the claw of a lobster! Be gone, you gallows little rascal! Off with you!'

"I took advice of the relentings of the good woman, and decamped. I know not why, however, I was by no means eager to leave the street in which she lived. I felt as if in her house I had left behind me that property, which had been so essential to my projects. I began to suspect that, notwithstanding her loudness and apparent fury, the mention of the *Conciergerie* was a trick, and that all her aim had been to get me out of her territories. This, however, if true, would by no means mend the case: it was impossible that I should obtain redress.

"It was well for me that I lingered in my pace. I had not departed above two minutes, before I felt some one tap me upon the shoulder. It was my friend, Betty, the barmaid. She held in her hand a pretty substantial roll of bread ready buttered, which she presented to me. She chucked me under the chin; and, after an expressive God bless you, my brave lad! she tripped away by the path by which she came.

"The offerings of gold, frankincense, and myrrh, presented by the wise men of the East, were not more acceptable to the mother of Jesus, than this homely roll and butter were to me at this moment. Yet I was not hungry by sensation; my heart was too full of the crosses I had sustained: but I was hungry by reflection. This is a distinction that will be perfectly intelligible to every one, however heartfull, who shall suppose himself alone for the first time in an immense metropolis, without a morsel of bread, or the means of procuring it.

"Poor Betty's roll and butter proved to me nectar and ambrosia in one.[1] I did not eat it immediately; but, in proportion as I did, I felt my spirit revive within me. To have been left

---

1   Nectar and ambrosia are the drink and food of the Greek Gods.

without comfort and without food at this critical period might have been fatal to me. But the courage of a child, the sunshine of his soul, is easily called back; and, when the animal feeling of inanition was extinguished within me, something friendly seemed to whisper to me not to despair. I had conquered the greatest part of the distance; I was only twelve miles from Versailles. A walk of four hours would bring me to that place which I had regarded as the assured goal of my lasting prosperity.

CHAPTER II.

"No sooner did the thought occur to me, than I resolved to lose no time to realise it. I arrived at Versailles about the middle of a very hot day, broiling with the sun, and covered with dust. I immediately entered the park; and, having gained a favourable situation for viewing the palace, protected by the shadow of overhanging trees, I threw myself upon the grass. The first idea that struck me was, Versailles is infinitely grander and more magnificent than Fontainebleau. With my eye I measured the piles, surveyed the architecture, and remarked the moveable and immoveable objects around me.

"Shortly, however, I forgot myself, and fell asleep. Yes; arrived at my haven, and with every thing for which I had panted apparently within my ken, I fell asleep! Heat and fatigue contributed to this; but I apprehend I should not have been thus overtaken, if it had not been for the misfortunes which that morning had overtaken me. A mitigated and familiar sorrow blunts the faculties, and disposes to lethargy.

"I had not slept long before I was roused from my oblivion by the sound of a fife, and the passing along of a file of soldiers. This was to me a most agreeable moment. I shook myself, and gazed intently upon the men as they passed. I recognised in them, as I stood still to view, the physiognomy of my native country. While I lived at home, in the canton of Uri, I was unaware of the existence of this physiognomy; the particulars which distinguished the persons around me from each other, were more remarked by me than those in which they resembled. But my residence at Lyons had sharpened my perceptions in this respect. Every man loves his native soil; and the Swiss are said to have more of this sentiment than any other people. I had myself been in a state of banishment, and, as I may phrase it, a state of solitary imprisonment. Whenever I met a Swiss in the streets of Lyons, my little heart leaped within my bosom, and I could not help hailing him as a brother in the peculiar phraseology of my country. My salutation never failed to call forth a cheerful and affectionate response from the person to whom it was addressed. This was usually all that occurred: we mutually bade each other good day, and passed on. Yet this kind of encounter often furnished me with an intellectual feast for a whole day; it made the sun shine upon me through the opake windows of the silk-mill, and cheered my soul as I stood at the swifts. An accident of this nature did not fail to happen to me twenty times during my abode at Lyons, and, perhaps, with as many different persons.

"It had been one of the motives that secretly stimulated me in my project upon the King of France, that I knew that the favourite guards of his court were Swiss, and that, when I came there, I should feel so much the less a stranger, as I should be able to speak, and address my enquiries to my own countrymen. To a poor, destitute, and pennyless vagabond, it was at this moment like heaven, to gaze upon the countenance of a little cluster of my countrymen, at the same time that I recollected that I was four hundred miles distant from my native home. It was like Macbeth gazing upon the descendants of Banquo, except that, though the view in each instance was pregnant with emotion, my emotions were of a nature opposite to his: every countenance, as it passed in series and succession before me, gave new sting to my pleasure, and elevated my heart an inch the higher.[1] I said to myself, 'These men will surely be my friends; removed, as we are, from the spot where Nature produced us, they will feel that here I belong to them; they will

---

1   The allusion is to *Macbeth*, IV.i.112-25.

not leave a poor Swiss child to perish for hunger within their quarters.' It was a restoration from death to life.

"As they proceeded along in a sort of parade, I dared not, on this occasion, address them with my customary salutation, I resolved to wait till I could meet with one of them, not upon duty, and alone. It was not necessary for me to wait long. As I strayed about the park, I met with a respectable looking man, a private, with an infant in his arms. I saluted him, and we entered into conversation. He seemed surprised at seeing me there, and asked me whether I belonged to any of the companies on duty at Versailles. I told him nearly the same particulars of my story as I had communicated to the mayor of Dijon. I said I was the son of a Swiss, and that I was born at home. My parents had brought me up in ease and opulence; but they were now dead, and, having left me, their only child, to the care of an uncle, this treacherous guardian had turned me adrift upon the world. Agreeably to my former resolution, I did not mention Lyons, and I abstained from violating the secret which my uncle had so tremendously enjoined me. I concluded, however, with my adventure of that morning, and the loss of all that I had.

"The honest Swiss believed my story. He seated me by him on a bench, and put the child on his knee; and, in token of his sympathy with my adventures, took me affectionately by the hand when I had concluded my little narrative. He uttered several exclamations, and made several remarks upon the particulars as I related them; but, as his remarks were those of a common soldier, and his understanding, as I presently perceived, was in no respect superior to his station, they are not worth mentioning. He observed, that he was afraid I had not eaten that day.

"'Not a morsel, except the roll and butter given me by Betty, the bar-maid.'

"'God bless you, my boy!' exclaimed he, with some emotion, 'come home along with me, and you shall at least partake of the fare, such as it is, that I have provided for my wife and children.'

"I willingly accepted his invitation, and we went together. As we entered the little apartment of his family, 'My love,' said he, 'here is a poor Swiss boy, just come from his own country, and without a penny in his pocket: you must give him a little supper, and he shall stay with us to-night.' The wife was no less prompt in exercising this small hospitality than her husband. They had three sons, besides the infant; and we sat round a cheerful board together.

"I seized this opportunity of asking the soldier a variety of questions concerning the King, which he regarded, probably, as the mere curiosity of a stranger. He told me that the King was not at present at Versailles, but had been for some days at Marli, which place he principally frequented for the diversion of hunting.[1] I enquired into the situation of this place, and was pleased to find that it was only four or five miles from Versailles. I set off for Marli early the next morning.

"When I arrived, I found the King had gone forth already to his hunt, and, probably, would not return till the day was considerably advanced. A Swiss soldier gave me my breakfast at Marli, as the private at Versailles had entertained me the evening before. This man was a being of more reflection than the former; and, when I had owned that I was without money, pressed me to inform him what was my errand at Marli, and what prospects I had for the future. This generous anxiety and forecast warmed my heart: the deliberating benevolence of an ordinary soldier, however narrow may be his power, is not less interesting to the feelings than that of a lord. I begged him, however, to excuse me; I entreated him to give himself no concern about me; and assured him that, though I was destitute now, I had means of speedily putting an end to my distress.

"I broke away from this man as soon as I decently could, and wandered about the park and gardens. I saw him two or three times in the course of the day, and once passed so near a sentry-box where he was on duty, that he had an opportunity, in a low voice, to desire me to come again to his hut, when his business of the day should be over. At length I heard the sound of clarinets and horns, the signal of the return from hunting. I saw the hounds, and heard the trampling of horses; and presently the

---

1 Marly was a country-house of King Louis XIV, built between Versailles and Saint Germain.

cavalcade appeared. The sound and the sight were cheerful, and my bosom was in tumults. Suddenly I recollected myself, and started away for the door, of which I had previously gained information, where the King was to alight. Several attendants and lacqueys pressed to the same spot. I saw the persons on horseback alight; and, coming up to one of them, cried, with earnestness and enthusiasm, 'Sire, hear what I have to say, and listen to my prayer!' In the confusion of my mind, I had mistaken the individual, in spite of my precaution of the portrait: it was not the King. The nobleman to whom I spoke, exclaimed, 'What, what is all this?' The lacqueys hurried me out of the circle; the King alighted, and the scene was closed.

"I know not whether it will appear incredible that a child as I was should have been capable of this daring. It was in reality, perhaps, because I was a child, that I was capable of it. I understood very imperfectly the distinctions of rank in artificial society. I was wholly ignorant of the forms and fences which are set up to separate one man from the rest of his brethren. A king, to the imagination of a child, is but a man; and I was accustomed, as perhaps all boys are accustomed, to meet him in fancy in the fields and the highways, and to conceive him a guest in my father's house. The first time I ever beheld a peacock's feather, I found something royal in it; and a man wearing a peacock's feather upon his bosom would to me have been a king. Add to which, I had never disclosed my plan to a human creature. Timidity is the child of experience or of admonition. I was not without timidity in the present instance; I understood the degree of presumption there was in addressing a gentleman and a stranger; and I understood no more.

"If I set out in my project with these notions, my courage was considerably reinforced as I proceeded. I had meditated my project perpetually, till enthusiasm supplied the place of intrepidity. I had so often acted the scene over in my fancy, that the whole was become perfectly familiar: it was like some situations which perhaps every man has encountered in life, new and extraordinary in themselves, but which feel like recollections, and he exclaims, 'This is my dream!' Recollect, in addition to these things, the urgency of my condition, the desperateness of my fortune, my hatred to the silk-mills of Lyons, the long journey I had performed, the hard adventures I had encountered, the emptiness of my purse, the immediate cravings of nature. All these things goaded me forward, and made me look upon the ignominy of deliberation as the worst of evils.

"In the evening the King walked upon the terrace in the gardens. I informed myself exactly of his appearance and insignia, that I might make no second mistake. There was a flight of about fifty steps that led up to the terrace; and guards were placed upon a landing-place in the middle, and at the bottom. These guards were not Swiss, but French. I had reflected, and found this spot the most favourable in the world for the execution of my project. The King, I was told, usually walked here for an hour, and conversed familiarly with a variety of persons. I approached to ascend, but was stopped by the soldiers. My garb was mean, and they told me, a boy of my appearance could not go up there! I was filled with impatience. There was a similar flight of steps at the other end of the terrace; I burst away from these persons, and hastened to the second flight. Here I was stopped again. Repeated disappointments now made me desperate, and I struggled with the soldiers, in the vain hope to pass in spite of their efforts. An attendant who passed by, recognised me for the child who had endeavoured to speak with the King before dinner. This circumstance induced them to conduct me to the guard-house. A child, as I was, they took it for granted could not be a dangerous intruder; but it was their business to keep off impertinence, and prevent his Majesty from being disturbed. The soldier who took me under his care, asked me, with some degree of kindness, what I wanted, and what purpose I had in view in speaking to the King? But I was now grown sullen, and would only answer in gloomy monosyllables. After some time, I was conducted to the gate of the park, and thrust out into the high road. The soldiers left me, and I sat down upon a stone.

CHAPTER III.

£ my reflections were sufficiently melancholy. I would ⸗ returned, if I had been able, to the hut of the sentinel who ᴅd invited me; but that was unfortunately within the inclosure. What was I to do? I was by no means cured of my project of speaking to the King. How bitter were my rage and indignation against the villain who had stripped me of the trifling sum of money on which I had depended! I wanted, I thought, but a little time; but how was I to gain time, when I was without food? The objection I had heard made against me, was the meanness of my clothing: if my money had not been taken from me, I could have removed this objection. My ruminations were inexpressibly melancholy. As I sat, several gentlemen passed me, who had probably made part of the company in the royal promenade. I must endeavour to obtain from some one the means of appeasing the demands of hunger. Should I apply to these? There was nothing in their appearance that invited me. Moved by my experience of the past, I was inclined to wait till I could see a soldier and a fellow-countryman. Yet of what avail was the relief I could so obtain? I had not come hither to subsist upon the precarious charity of daily bread! Far different views had animated my steps in a course of three hundred miles! What was I to do to-morrow? At Marli, I should find myself marked, and watched, and thwarted in all my attempts. When would the King return to Versailles?

"Those of the persons who passed me and were on foot, passed me by twos and threes. Others went in carriages, and on horseback. At length one gentleman came alone. He looked at me, and advanced to the place where I sat.

"'My boy,' said he, 'are not you the little fellow that attempted to speak to the King?'

"I looked up at the gentleman. He was beyond the middle period of human life. I thought I had never seen so benign a countenance. Besides, there was something in him that struck me with a remarkable similarity to my own father.

"'I am, sir,' answered I with a sigh.

"'And what could you want to say to the King?'

"'I am friendless: I have nobody to take care of me: I wanted to tell him that.'

"'Was your father a military man? Did he wear the *croix de St. Louis?*'[1]

"'My father was no military man: he was never in France in his life.'

"'Good God!—And who told you to apply to the King?'

"'Nobody told me. The scheme is all my own. I have come three hundred miles to execute it.'

"The stranger became interested in my artless story.

"'Will you come to my lodgings to-morrow morning? I shall sleep at Marli.'—And he gave me his address.

"'I will, sir,' replied I. 'But—but—'

"'But what, my little man?'

"'I am very hungry!'

"Every new circumstance I mentioned astonished him the more. He perceived, as he afterwards told me, that I was by no means without education, and a certain refinement. To have formed such a project, to have come three hundred miles to complete it, and to be here without a penny!—He was determined to be more fully acquainted with so strange a story!— He took out his purse.

"'Do you know, my boy, how to procure yourself accommodations for the night?'

"'I have not travelled three hundred miles for nothing.'

"'Well, take care of yourself to-night, and come to me in the morning.'

"I looked at the address. The name on the card was Ambrose Fleetwood. The generous man who accosted me in my desolate condition was your grandfather. This was the first time I had ever seen the name of Fleetwood; and till this pulse ceases to throb, the occasion that brought us together will never be forgotten! This is the foundation of the friendly alliance of Fleetwood and Ruffigny.——Upon what a precipice was I then placed! Even at the distance of so many years, I cannot recollect it without feeling my head turn giddy. For what did

---

1 Referring to the insignia of the Order of St. Louis, instituted by Louis XIV to recognize military merit.

my destiny seem to reserve me? For beggary, for hunger,—to perish for want of food; or, if not, without guide or protector, and with no means of present subsistence, to become the associate of the worthless and the vile,—the only persons, probably speaking, who would court such an associate. Oh, how infinitely worse would this have been, than the most unpitied death! The King of France!—was ever poor wretch misled by such an *ignis fatuus*?[1] did ever condemned criminal brave the fury of the ocean in such a cockle-shell?

"I repaired at the appointed hour to the residence of my new protector. He asked me a number of questions; and I gave him the same answers, but with more of detail than I had given on previous occasions. He was urgent in his enquiries; he spoke to me in the most friendly and soothing manner; I was on the brink of discovering my secret; I entreated him, however, to spare me: I had been robbed by my uncle; but I did not dare to tell where and who he was. The generous Englishman perceived that I gasped and turned pale, as I touched on this tremendous subject. He became deeply interested in my behalf.

"'Will you go with me to my own country?' said he.

"'Oh, no, no! If you are so much my friend as to be willing to take me thither, then—pray, pray, sir!—do for me the thing I want; enable me to change these clothes for others more suitable to my projects.'

"I raved of the King of France. The scheme of applying to him had been my favourite contemplation for months. I had had his picture so often before me! The thought of him had soothed my weary steps, and comforted me under all my disasters. I could not give up my plan. I could not divest myself of the sort of robe of nobility with which my fancy had clothed me, and descend into the vale of ordinary life. I entreated my benefactor, with miraculous and unpacified importunity, that he would direct all his assistance to this end.

"Enthusiasm is always an interesting spectacle. When it expresses itself with an honest and artless eloquence, it is difficult to listen to it, and not in some degree to catch the flame.

---

1 "Will-o'-the-wisp"; light caused by the combustion of gases that is seen over marshes at night, and capable of leading travelers into danger.

Particularly at my age it was so extraordinary in itself, and so impetuous in its way of manifesting itself, that it was impossible to contemplate it without sympathy. There are so many ways in which the heart of man conceals itself from man! Beside the thousand motives which impel us to suppress one thing, and to be reserved respecting another, it is necessary that the human mind should be put into motion in order to its being seen. 'Speak, that I may see thee!'—said the ancient philosopher.[1] He might have added, 'Speak upon some subject, respecting which your feelings are spontaneous and strong.' The soul of man is one of those subtle and evanescent substances, that, as long as they remain still, the organ of sight does not remark; it must become agitated, to become visible. All together, Mr. Fleetwood grew exceedingly anxious respecting my welfare.

"On this account he condescended to a certain degree of artifice and temporising. He observed to me that I had ruined my own project at Marli, and that it would be ten days before the King removed to Versailles. He invited me to spend this time with him at Paris, during which I should be clothed and equipped more suitably to the great person I designed to address. He promised me that I should have the earliest intelligence of the removal of the court.

"In how new a situation was I now unexpectedly placed! I had not heard the accents of genuine kindness for almost two years; not since the calamitous moment, when my father uttered his expiring breath. Mr. Fleetwood, almost from the first, conceived for me the affection of a father. He did not treat me as a vagabond whom he had taken up out of charity, and kept at a distance from him. I saw him, morning, noon, and night. His accents were those of friendly solicitude; the looks I cast upon him were those of affection. My spirit was softened within me: my new situation took away from me the heart of stone, and gave me a heart of flesh.

"It was this heart of stone, if you will allow me so to express myself, that led me to the King of France. It was the sentiment

---

1 The reputed words of the Greek philosopher Socrates (469-399 BC) to a young man brought to be his student (referred to by Erasmus in his *Apophthegms*, in *Works* [1546]).

of despair: I had sent my enquiring glances round the world, and had not found a friend. Methodically and slowly I had worked myself up to the resolution I had adopted, and I could not immediately abandon it. It was a sort of frenzy; a high pitch of the soul, foreign to its natural temper. Kindness, the perpetual attention and interest of a real friend, in no long time brought me back to myself. It is impossible to express what comfort, what a delicious relaxation and repose of spirit, was produced by this revolution. Mr. Fleetwood gradually led me to consider the scheme I had formed, as wild, senseless, and impracticable. His expostulations were so gentle, benignant, and humane, that, while they confuted, they had not the effect of mortifying me. He took me with him to England.

"I have been thus minute in the description of my condition at Lyons, and of the manner of my deserting it, that I might the better demonstrate to you the infinite value of the kindness your grandfather bestowed on me. If I had not been the most unfortunate, the most abused, and the most deserted of my species, the favours I received would not have had a tithe of the value they actually possessed. I cannot recollect the situation I deserted, or that upon which I threw myself, without a horror bordering on despair. The generous and admirable mortal that then interposed for my relief, I must ever regard as my guardian genius, and my better angel. How distinctly have I passed over in my mind ten thousand times the stone upon which I sat at the gate of the park of Marli, and the gesture and countenance with which my preserver approached me! The day was declining, the landscape had assumed the grave and uniform hues of evening, and there was that sadness in the air which wakes up the tone of sensibility in the soul. The circumstances in which I was placed, sufficiently prepared me to be deeply affected. The first word that Ambrose Fleetwood uttered went to my heart. I had occasionally, perhaps, been treated during my journey with gentleness and civility; but it was the difference between the voice that tells you which turn you are to take in the road from Auxerre to Sens, and the voice that tells you by implication that the speaker is interested that you shall go right in the road of happiness and life. With what considerate wisdom did this noble Englishman soothe me in the midst of the exalted and enthusiastic fervour which had brought me to Versailles and Marli! How patiently did he wean me from the wild plan upon which my heart was bent! And all this to an unknown and pennyless vagabond! There is, perhaps, more merit in this temper, that listened to all my extravagancies without anger, and did not suffer itself to be discouraged by my tenaciousness and stubbornness, than in the gift of thousands.

"In our journey to England, I was so fortunate as continually to advance in your grandfather's good graces. He thought me, as he afterward told me, a youth of very extraordinary qualifications, and well deserving of his care. He sent me to proper schools, and had me taught every thing which he believed it would be important for me to know. He was an English merchant, and he determined to provide for me in some of those departments, in which commerce opens the road to competence and wealth.

"It was not till after a very long time that I could prevail upon myself to unfold my heart to my benefactor, respecting my extraction, and the way in which I had been driven to the deplorable situation in which he found me. Your grandfather often enquired of me what were the condition in which I was born, and the prospects which my birth had opened to me; but I manifested such a shrinking of the soul, such a convulsive kind of terror, whenever the subject was started, that for some time he forbore all mention of it. The alarm had been impressed on me early, and had taken deep root in my breast. While I was at Lyons, it formed the peculiarity of my situation, and I cherished it with a strange and mingled sentiment, something between horror and delight. Every human creature loves, perhaps, to think that there is something extraordinary about him, and dwells with complacency upon that which makes him different from all his race. I felt like an exiled sovereign, or a prince who roams about the world in disguise. I firmly believe that it was partly to both these notions, of self-complacency, and of terror, that I was indebted for the habit of regarding the names of my father and my uncle as the most inviolable of secrets.

"At length I became convinced, by the unaltered kindnesses of my benefactor, that my secret would be no less safely reposed in his keeping, than in the recesses of my own soul. I told him the whole. He was astonished at the terror with which I had looked forward to the disclosure, and proposed immediately to take such measures as should operate to compel my uncle to resign his ill-gotten wealth. I entreated him that he would engage in no proceedings of that sort; I reminded him of his promise that my secret should never be communicated to a third person without my consent. My uncle, however deeply he had injured me, was still the brother of my father, and in that quality I could not but feel reluctance at the idea of exposing him to public ignominy. The menaces with which he had so emphatically dismissed me, were impressed on my heart; they gave me a horrible anticipation of the event which would attend my hostile return to my native land; and I could not help apprehending that that event would be miserable to me, no less than to him. I implored your grandfather that he would suffer the question to remain unopened, at least till I had arrived at a mature age. He had often assured me that, having only one son, he did not regard the expenses I brought on him as a burden; but, if he did, I did not desire the situation he provided for me, or the advantages he bestowed; the tithe of his benefits would amply satisfy my ambition and my wishes. To occasion an entire revolution in the fortunes and situation of my family, was a very serious consideration; it might be the most important transaction of my life; and I earnestly entreated that in such a transaction I might be allowed to consult the ripest decisions of my own understanding. Your grandfather generously yielded to these representations.

"The principal friend I had in England, after my original benefactor, was your father. We were nearly of an age, and your grandfather brought us up together. I saw in him the image of the man who had rescued me from utter destruction, and loved him accordingly. Your father was acquainted with my situation, and knew that I had no claim either of blood or alliance upon my preserver: he saw me brought up with himself, and enjoying the same advantages; yet he never repined at the favour in which I was held. Not only while we were children together, he regarded me as a brother; but this sentiment never altered in him as he advanced in judgment and years. He never looked upon me as an intruder; never considered the large sums your grandfather laid out to procure me a respectable footing in life; nor even enquired whether, as I equally shared the bounties of my benefactor at present, he might not make a distribution of his property at death no less impartial. Could I help loving so disinterested and noble-minded a companion?

"Having been perfectly initiated in the principles of commerce in the country where they are best understood, it happened that, about the time when it was proper I should be launched in the world, a proposition was made to the elder Fleetwood, respecting a banking-house which it was in contemplation to set up at Lisbon. A countryman of my own was the principal in the project; but his capital was not sufficient for the undertaking as it had been chalked out, and he designed taking in one or two other persons as partners with him in the concern. Provided he could enter upon the affair in the way which had been delineated, he had the promise of being immediately installed as banker to the court of Portugal. Your grandfather was an opulent London merchant, and had no inclination to extend his concerns. His son he destined for his successor in the business in which he was himself engaged. Under these circumstances he thought of embracing the proposal in my behalf.

"I was never more surprised than when the idea was suggested to me. The money necessary to be advanced, was more than three times the amount which my father's property would have produced, if it had been all sold immediately on the event of his death. I was suffocated with the thought of so incredible a generosity exercised toward me. I told my benefactor that I was as far from the expectation as the wish of becoming opulent; and that, independently of a secret feeling which led me to the hope of one day settling in my native fields, I could be contented to remain for ever the first clerk in my preserver's counting-house.

"Your grandfather answered me, that he much disapproved of a character deficient in enterprise; and asked, how the humility of the views I at present professed, accorded with the ardour which had formerly led me to throw myself at the feet of the sovereign of France? He said, I had with my own consent passed through all the stages of a commercial education, and that therefore it seemed but reasonable, that whatever enterprise I possessed, should be directed into that channel. He expatiated upon the uses of wealth; and observed that, however limited might be my desire of indulgences for myself, I ought by no means to forget the great public works which an opulent man might forward for the benefit of his species, or how extensive was his power of relieving distress, of exciting industry, of developing talents, of supplying the means of improvement to those who panted for, but could not obtain them, and of removing the innumerable difficulties which often surrounded the virtuous and the admirable, that impeded their progress, and struck despair into their hearts.

"My benefactor recommended to me to make myself perfectly easy, as to the money necessary to be advanced, to launch me in the undertaking proposed. He could spare it without the smallest inconvenience. If my views in life were unsuccessful it should never be repaid, and he should then have the satisfaction of having exerted himself liberally to establish in life a youth, whom he loved no less than his own son. But he had no doubt that the undertaking would be prosperous; and then he consented, if that would be any gratification to me, that I should repay the present loan, only upon one condition, that the first instalment of the repayment should not commence till that day seven years, counting from the day of my landing in Lisbon: young men, who entered upon business with a borrowed capital, had often received a fatal check in the midst of the fairest prospects, by a premature repayment of the loan which had originally set them afloat on the ocean of life.

"'Ruffigny,' continued your grandfather, 'what miserably narrow notions are these which you seem to have fostered in your bosom! Are all the kindnesses of the human heart to be shut up within the paltry limits of consanguinity? My son will have enough; and I am sure he will not repine, that you should be made a partaker of the opulence with which Providence has blessed me. If you will, we will ask him, and I will do nothing for you that has not his entire and undissembled approbation. Why should I not set up two persons in the world, instead of one? Thirty-six princes, we are told, erected each of them a pillar in the temple of Diana at Ephesus: why should I not erect two pillars in the edifice of human happiness, and prepare two persons, instead of one, to be benefactors of their species?[1] You are my son, a son whom the concourse of sublunary events has given me, no less dear to me than the heir of my body. I found in you various estimable qualities, which won my attachment in the first hour I saw you; and, I trust, those qualities have lost nothing in the cultivation I have given them. You belonged to me, because you belonged to no one else. This is the great distribution of human society; every one who stands in need of assistance appertains to some one individual, upon whom he has a stronger claim than upon any other of his fellow-creatures. My son belongs to me, because I was the occasion of his coming into existence; you belong to me, because you were hungry and I fed you, because you wanted education and a protector, and have found them in me. You are now arrived at man's estate, and I regard you as the creature of my vigilance and of my cares. Will you not acknowledge me for a father?'

"I was convinced by the arguments of my preserver; I was moved by the feelings he expressed: my beloved companion, the brother of my heart, declared most warmly his consent to the arrangement. I resided twenty-one years at Lisbon; and in that time, by honourable and just traffic, made a fortune infinitely beyond the most sanguine of my wishes. I faithfully repaid to my benefactor, at the time he had himself limited, the capital he advanced to me. During the period of my residence at Lisbon, I several times came over to England, and visited the two persons whom I reasonably regarded as the most generous of mortals; and in one of these visits, after I had been ten years engaged as a principal in my commercial undertaking, I witnessed the expiring breath of my original benefactor. Never, perhaps, did I love a human creature, as I loved that man. My father, good, and kind, and affectionate as he had been, was, to

---

1   One of the seven wonders of the ancient world, this massive temple had a roof supported by 127 columns.

my mind, a sort of air-drawn vision, the recollection, as it were, of a pre-existent state. My youthful companion and sworn confidant, no less generous than my preserver, was inexpressibly dear to me; but the sentiment I felt for him was altogether different. Nature has formed us to the love of the venerable. Filial affection is an instinct twined with the very fibres of our heart. For the grey hairs of your grandfather, I had a mystical and religious awe; and age had softened his features into an expression of such calm benignity, that, if I were an adherent of the sect of the anthropomorphites, I should take from his countenance my idea of the object of my worship.[1]

CHAPTER IV.

"I should have told you, that about the time of my original departure for Lisbon, your grandfather settled with my consent a correspondence with a citizen of Zurich, upon whose integrity and discretion he could perfectly rely: he observed, that whatever forbearance I might think proper to exercise toward my uncle and his family, it was but reasonable that I should obtain, from time to time, information of his affairs, and learn which of the family were living and dead. I have already said that my uncle had been unprosperous in all his undertakings: the estate of my father, which he so wickedly seized, by no means introduced a better fortune into his affairs. One by one his children died; he survived them, but survived not long; and the estate fell, in the twentieth year of my residence at Lisbon (for it was understood that I was dead, and my uncle procured vouchers to establish the fact) to a distant branch of my father's family.

"Circumstances were now sufficiently favourable to the project upon which my wishes were bent, of returning to my native country, and spending the remainder of my days in the valley which had given me birth. I communicated my purpose to my correspondent at Zurich; but I was somewhat divided

---

1 A religious sect of fourth century BC Egypt whose followers conceived of God as having a human form.

in my mind, whether I should purchase my paternal estate, and live upon it as a stranger, or should openly claim it as my rightful inheritance. What inclined me to the former, was, that by this expedient I should avoid casting any slur upon the memory of my false guardian. Our family had always ranked among the most patriotic families of the Union, and had never sustained any dishonour, except in the person of my uncle. On the other hand, I could not bear the idea of appearing as a foreigner in my own country: this was but a half restoration. Why did I love my country? Not merely for that its scenes had been familiar to my infancy; but that the human mind irresistibly wishes to connect itself with something. I had ancestors, the ornaments of the people among whom they were born. These ancestors had married and given in marriage, had received and conferred obligations and benefits, and their memory was in odour and in favour through the neighbouring districts. I wished to adorn my ancestors, and to be adorned by them. This is the genuine idea of going to one's home.

"I was averse, however, to the idea of appearing in my own country in the character of a litigant, an individual unexpectedly calling his neighbour into contest about a property of which he believed himself to be lawfully possessed. I therefore instructed my correspondent to bring this question to a full decision, before I should take my departure. My resolution was formed, as soon as I received intelligence of the death of my uncle. I immediately transmitted documents to Zurich, proving my parentage and identity, and directed my correspondent to serve the new claimant with a notice, that the true heir, who was supposed to be dead, was still living. He was exceedingly surprised, and somewhat chagrined with the intelligence, as he was a poor man, and burthened with a numerous family. He consented, however, after the manner of the country, to go before the chief court of the canton, for the decision of the question. After a full and minute investigation of the evidences, my claim was ultimately established. This point being gained, I despatched to Zurich an instrument settling on the losing party in the contest, an annuity to one half of the value of the property of which he was dispossessed, accompanied with bills of exchange destined to repurchase the lands which my uncle had sold, and to redeem them from the burthens he had laid upon them.[1] These objects were, in most instances, happily accomplished.

"While my affairs were going on thus auspiciously in Switzerland, I employed the time necessary for maturing them, in adjusting and transferring in the most advantageous manner the commercial undertakings, in which more than twenty years of my life had been consumed, in Portugal. When every concern of this sort was now completed, and all things prepared for my reception in my native canton, I bade farewell to Lisbon, and prepared to return to Switzerland by way of London.

"My business in England was to visit your father. I found him the same in tastes, in moral dispositions, and in affection, as his father's death had left him. In many respects he was different. Ten years of added life had brought him to a nearer resemblance of my original preserver; and, as I remarked in him the tokens of advancing age, I felt the agreeable sentiment of contemplating my venerable benefactor and my schoolboy associate blending themselves, as it were, in one person. Your father had also married since I was in England, and yourself was born. I think I never saw so affectionate a husband and a father. In domestic life it was impossible to be more fortunate than I found my beloved friend.

"He was not equally fortunate in every thing. He had experienced two or three severe miscarriages in his commercial concerns; and this, so far as I could understand, without the smallest fault on his part. In one instance he had connected himself with, and given large credit to, a house, where all appearances were fair, but where extravagance and secret gaming brought about a ruin, the most sudden and unforeseen. In another instance, a war had broken out at a time when he apprehended no such thing; his transactions were multiplied in the country which was now declared an enemy; and all his

---

1   An instrument is a formal legal document.

investments failed. At a different time, bankruptcy upon an extensive scale took place in Holland, one great house drawing on the ruin of another, till half the most opulent merchants of the republic were destroyed: your father suffered deeply in this calamity.[1]

"I soon discovered a cast of melancholy in the demeanour of my quondam playmate, and that there was something which hung painfully on his mind. In truth, I had somewhat suspected his real situation before I left Lisbon, and this contributed, with other circumstances, to hasten my conclusion of my affairs in that city. With difficulty and effort I wrung from your father a full confession of his misfortune.

"'Ruffigny,' said he, 'I am a beggar. You and I set out together in life, but under different auspices.'—He paused.

"'No matter,' added he. 'I hope I shall be able to discharge all my debts to the uttermost. A trifle will remain to me from the wreck. I will venture no more upon the treacherous sea of commerce. What is the value of riches? I shall still have enough left to retire with to some remote corner of the island, and cultivate a small farm in tranquillity. My dear wife will be perfectly contented with the exchange. She will give up her equipage and her liveries without a murmur. She will not sigh for the amusements of the court and the metropolis; and she will look more beautiful in my eyes, clad in the plain attire of a rural housewife, than hung round, as I have seen her, with diamonds and rubies. My son shall be a peasant swain, not ignorant, not ambitious, viewing the storms of life from a distance, and fearless of bankruptcies, shipwrecks, and war. Is not this happiness?'

"Your father never dropped a syllable which should sound toward the asking me to assist him in his adversity. He knew my ability in this respect, and the prosperous event which had crowned my efforts. Perhaps he would have been willing to have made another experiment in the affairs of commerce, and not to have quitted the world a bankrupt, had he known where to have raised a sum adequate to his purpose, and upon terms sufficiently eligible. But all that I had derived from the bounty

---

1 The Dutch economy suffered a great crash in April 1672 as a result of war with Louis XIV.

of your grandfather, and this consideration sealed up his lips toward me.

"One morning I came to him early, and requested him to assist me in casting up the profits of my commerce, and the amount of my fortune. He turned upon me a wistful eye, as I stated my proposal. At first sight it seemed to imply an insulting comparison between my success and his. On the other hand, he, perhaps, half suspected the true meaning of my visit.

"'Come, my dear Fleetwood,' said I; 'my affairs are in good order, and the task will not occasion you much trouble.'

"Saying this, I opened again the door by which I had entered, and called to my servant to come in. He brought with him three or four pocket-books and a box. He put them down, and departed.

"'Let us sit down!'

"I opened the pocket-books, and examined their contents. Some were bills of exchange; some were warrants of capital in the English and Dutch stocks; and some securities of various sorts. I explained to my friend the nature of the commerce in which I had been engaged, the profits from year to year, and the particulars of one or two fortunate speculations. I took pen and ink, and summed together the amount of my bills, warrants, and securities.

"I then pushed aside the pocket-books, and drew toward me the black box.

"'This,' said I, 'I regard as peculiarly my own.' It contained the evidences of my birth and identity, the sentence of the judge who had awarded to me my estate, the ejectment of the late possessor, and the titles of the landed property which my agent had purchased for me in Switzerland.

"'As I have now quitted trade,' resumed I, 'and am going to retire from the world, I have been trying to make my will. Here it is,' pulling a pretty large parcel from my pocket: 'I will leave it with you, Fleetwood; peruse it at your leisure. One thing only I have to say; I do not show it you to consult you upon it; I am peremptory in its contents, and will not alter a letter; but, between such old friends as we are, I think it right you should be acquainted with my thoughts.'

"'Is it your will?' said your father.

"'Pooh!' said I, smiling, 'do not let us deal in quibbles and disputes about a word! If, however, I must come to definitions, I will tell you, that by a will I understand a paper or parchment, containing my final and irrevocable disposition of that property over which the municipal laws of Europe give me an empire; and to tell you the truth, I hold a man's making his will and the different provisions it contains, to be one of the most sacred and indispensable duties he can perform, and one of those circumstances which may best serve as a criterion to distinguish the honest man and the knave, the man of narrow, and the man of capacious and liberal, views.'

"The parcel I tendered to your father contained a regular and formal transfer to him of all the property which I had just put upon his table, with the exception of the contents of the black box.

"'It is not your will,' said Fleetwood: 'I will not touch a farthing of your property.'

"'You shall not. My property is contained in this black box. The rest is a debt I am come to you to pay. Why will you make many words in a case which common sense decides in a moment?'

"'It is yours. The small germ from which it sprung was the gift of my father. The rest is the accumulation of your industry, the fruits of twenty years' occupation and labour. I insist upon it that you take it away.'

"'Fleetwood, if I must speak on such a subject, hear me! Good God, it is the plainest question in the world! I have been your father's steward, and bring back the fruits of my stewardship to his son. I have abstracted from it a considerable sum, which was necessary to my eligible settlement in my own country. I had always determined to settle exactly in the way I am now executing. You have not disturbed my projects a jot. If I had retained the property which is now yours, I never would have spent an atom of it upon myself or any of my relations. I should have been a trustee for others, and a very laborious office I should have had. As it is, the whole is yours. I have calculated the matter with great niceness, and I find that you will this day be placed exactly where your father left you. We shall neither of us be the better or the worse for each other, except, as I hope, we shall be both gainers in the possession of each other's friendship and affections. Did I say that we shall neither of us be the better or the worse? Alas! how grievous an error did I commit! I am still indebted to your father and you, for my life, my education, my estimation in the world, the years of respectability and peace I have enjoyed, and the power I have at last exerted to recover the property of my ancestors. When I owe you so vast a debt that I can never repay, how can you be so ungenerous as to endeavour to prevent me from reimbursing this insignificant portion of the obligation I owe you?'

"I was peremptory, and your father was obliged to submit. We had each our place, assigned us by the destiny under which we were born; and the arrangement I now made was restoration to us both. I wanted to end my life like my father, a citizen of Uri; it was proper that my friend should live like his ancestors, a great English merchant, and, when he retired from active life, an opulent English country gentleman. What had I, a republican of the old model, to do with bonds, warrants, and securities? To me they were an insupportable incumbrance; to your father they were necessary. You perceive with me, my dear Casimir, that all the obligation was on one side. Your father and grandfather had done every thing for me; I did nothing for them. They had taken me in an outcast; they had made me one of their family equal with themselves; they had given me my education, and by consequence every quality that made me respectable in the eyes of my fellow beings; I had lived upon them for twenty years in the style of a German sovereign. If the venerable Ambrose Fleetwood had been more actively my friend, I always considered the part your father acted as not a whit less honourable. Human beings are in all cases so fond of their creatures! In the objects of their generosity they behold the mirror of their own virtues, and are satisfied. Your grandfather made me his child, and doted on me as such. But your father, without the smallest pretence to this original merit, without any stimulus in the gratification of his own complacence, entered into the sentiment of my preserver, never uttered a murmur, never felt a compunction, but fully approved of the lavish bounty which stripped him of so considerable a portion of his fortune. It was this feeling of his heart which made us brothers, brothers by a dearer bond than that of nature, by a more sacred tie than that of a common descent. My soul has always panted for an occasion of showing myself worthy of such a friend, of repaying some small part of the obligation I owe to the name of Fleetwood; but I shall go down to the grave ungratified in this first wish of my heart."

CHAPTER V.

IN such talk I and my friend spent the chief part of our journey to England. We reached Merionethshire, and found a desolated mansion, and a tenanted grave. In the one, and over the other, we united our tears. "My friend! my father! most generous of men!" were the epithets with which a thousand times we saluted the shade of the departed.

And here I beg leave to protest against the doctrine too commonly promulgated in the world, that we ought to call off our thoughts, as speedily as possible, from the recollection of our deceased friends, and not waste our spirits in lamentation for irremediable losses. The persons from whom I have oftenest heard this lesson, have been of the class of the hard-hearted, who have sought in such "counsels of prudence" an apology for their own unfeeling serenity. He was a wiser man than they, who said, "It is good to dwell in the house of mourning; for by the sadness of the countenance the heart is made better."[1] Certainly I found a salutary and purifying effect, in talking to the spirit of my father when I was alone, and in discoursing of his good deeds and his virtues when I came into society. I cannot accuse these habits of having generated in me an inclination to indolence and inactivity; or, if they introduced a short interval of that sort, it was a heaven-born inactivity, by which my whole character was improved. Woe to the man who is always busy,—hurried in a turmoil of engagements, from occupation to occupation, and with no seasons interposed, of recollection,

---

1 Ecclesiastes 7:2-3 (adapted).

contemplation, and repose! Such a man must inevitably be gross and vulgar, and hard and indelicate,—the sort of man with whom no generous spirit would desire to hold intercourse.

After having spent about two months with me in Merionethshire, M. Ruffigny consented to accompany me in an excursion, rendered necessary by particular business, to London. I was not at first exactly aware of the motive of my venerable monitor to this new compliance. In the sequel it became sufficiently evident.

This was the first considerable visit I ever paid to the metropolis of England. Beside the change of scene, I had a new character to sustain. I had travelled in France a young heir, and in a certain sense under a state of pupilage. In London I was obliged to regard myself as the head of a family, and, in point of fortune, one of the most eminent country gentlemen of that part of the island where my estates lay. This was calculated in its first impression to inspire me with a certain seriousness. But, beside this, I felt, by the death of my father, and the society of my father's friend, purified from the dissipations which had too long engrossed me. I swore, in the views which I meditated for my future life, that I would never again yield to the degrading follies which had already cost me so bitter a pang.

For some time I kept this resolution. By the persuasions of Ruffigny I frequented, in a moderate degree, the society of my equals; but the very mourning I wore for my deceased parent served as a memento, keeping alive in my heart the recollection of my duties.

In one unfortunate moment I felt my good resolutions thawing before the flame of beauty. A friend, who had made one with me in a rather numerous party at dinner, persuaded me, when the company broke up, to accompany him to a *petit souper* at the lodgings of his mistress. Wine is a most eloquent advocate—the Burgundy and Champagne had been pushed about somewhat briskly at our dinner, and I suffered myself to be persuaded in the gaiety of the moment. I said, no ill consequence can result from this deviation—I am fortified by a thousand arguments against a relapse into my former errors— why should I deny myself the sight of beauty?

My inviter, Sir George Bradshaw by name, had boasted of the charms of his mistress; but there happened to be present, as the friend of the lady of the house, a female whose pretensions, at least in my eyes, outshone those which I had heard so vaunted in an unspeakable degree. I will not allow myself to dwell upon her features or her figure; suffice it to say, that her motions were lighter and more graceful than those of a fawn, that the playfulness of her manner and the sports of her fancy were inexhaustible, that her voice was more rich and harmonious than the lute of Apollo, and she sung twenty frolicsome and humorous songs in the course of the evening with an inexpressible charm. The lady was called Mrs. Comorin—she had lately cohabited with Lord Mandeville, but she had quarrelled with her admirer, and her heart and her person were now vacant.

By what infatuation was it that I instantly felt myself attracted toward her? Surely, when nature kneaded my frame, she cast in a double portion of her most combustible materials! Deep scars were left in my heart by my Parisian amours, and I believed it impossible that any of the sex could again possess herself of my inmost affections. I had argued myself into a contempt of their character; an opinion that to be a woman, was the same thing as to be heartless, artificial, and perfidious. But what a delightful plaything, what an inexhaustible amusement, should I find in the bewitching Mrs. Comorin! This was the most dangerous stage of my character. The heart cannot be used for ever; after a certain number of experiments it becomes obdurate and insensible; but, if I fell, as I now seemed on the point to do, into the mire of sensuality, I should become a gross and impudent libertine for the term of my life, and remain a hoary and despicable lecher to the brink of the grave.

I saw this alluring woman again and again, and every time I saw her I was more pleased than before. She was made up of pride of heart, ease of manners, and an inexhaustible flow of spirits,—of sentiment and real attachment she was wholly incapable. I saw her for such as she was; but, such as she was, she won my partiality; and, perhaps, owing to the dear-bought experience, which I could not yet recollect without agony, I liked her the better, for her want of those qualities which had so fatally stung my tranquillity.

I had strange qualms in my bosom, when the recollection of my inconsistency recurred to my thoughts. I, that had felt with such bitter remorse my debaucheries at Paris, and the shameful way in which I had wasted my time when my father lay on his death-bed, to be so soon caught in the same toils!—Yet, what, alas! is the firmness of twenty-one? Five years of licentiousness had laid the foundation in me, deep and broad, for a dissolute character. In my adventures in Paris I had lost all that ingenuous and decent shame, which so often and so happily stops a young man on the brink of the precipice. Even the original sensitiveness and delicacy of my character rendered me but the more tremblingly audacious in certain situations.

I was beyond all things alarmed that the caprice which had thus seized me, should remain unknown to M. Ruffigny. His thoughts on the other hand were continually alive to watch. I had been in the habit, while I had nothing to conceal, of mentioning to this aged friend, the persons I saw and the places I visited, whenever we were separated from each other. A practice of this sort, once begun, cannot, without awkwardness and exciting suspicion, be broken off; circumstanced, therefore, as I now was, I named to my monitor Sir George Bradshaw, and the other young men of fashion with whom I associated, but observed an inviolable silence as to the female members of our parties. Ruffigny's suspicions were probably excited. Sir George Bradshaw was by no means the ally he would have chosen for me. Once or twice he expostulated with me upon the new intimacies I seemed to be contracting. I assured him that they were matters of convenience or accident merely, and that I felt no such partiality to the Baronet, as a mere change of place would not immediately break off.

One evening that I had left M. Ruffigny to his solitary avocations, the fancy took him to beguile a few hours at the opera. As he had no acquaintance among the audience, he sat in the pit. I was with Sir George Bradshaw, Mrs. Comorin, and her friend, in the Baronet's box. Ruffigny perceived me, long before I had an idea that I was become a spectacle to him. The publicity of the situation restrained my familiarities with this new mistress of my affections within certain bounds; but Ruffigny saw enough, to leave no doubt in his mind as to the true explanation of the scene. My fair friend was of too vivacious a temperament, not to play a hundred whimsical tricks in the course of an hour; I caught the tone from her, and made myself no less ridiculous. In the heyday of youthful blood, I was capable of little restraint; and my infant passion inspired me with unwonted eagerness and activity. In one of my idlest and most forward sallies I caught the eye of Ruffigny; my face instantly became as red as scarlet.

The next morning at breakfast we met. Ruffigny charged me seriously with what he had discovered, with the disgrace I was bringing on my father's name, and the weakness and frailty of the resolutions I had solemnly made. The infatuation under which I laboured, stung me to a defence of the situation in which I had been found. I more than half suspected that I was wrong; and this rendered me tenfold the more peremptory and earnest in my vindication.

"Could I," asked Ruffigny, "apologise for this recent misconduct, when I had expressed such bitter compunction for the errors I had fallen into at Paris?"

"Very easily, and very consistently," I replied. "Those errors I should ever regret, and regarded now with as much abhorrence as ever. With whom were they committed? With women having husbands and children, and occupying a respectable situation in society. I could conceive nothing, which would be pronounced more atrocious by an uncorrupted mind. If the crimes, thus committed under a decent veil, and which, like the thefts of the Spartan youth, were commended as long as they were carried on with a dexterous obscurity, came to be detected, what misery and confusion would they produce in families?[1] But, detected or not detected, they poisoned every thing that was valuable in social ties. They depended for their perpetration upon one eternal scene of hypocrisy and dissimulation.

---

1 Referring to a tradition of military training in ancient Sparta in which young boys were put on a restrictive diet and encouraged to steal food so as to develop skills of resourcefulness needed in times of war.

The guilty female, instead of being that exemplary character which her situation called upon her to fill, was devoted to licentious thoughts, and must in her cooler moments be the object of her own contempt. The children she brought into the world she could not love, and the husband she received with personated caresses was the individual in the world she was conscious of most deeply injuring. Where such a state of society prevailed, every lover must regard his mistress with moral disapprobation, and every husband suspect that by the partner of his bosom his confidence was betrayed.

"But in the acquaintance I contracted with this English lady, I injured no one. No delusion was practised by any of the parties. She would not be made worse by any thing into which she was induced by me; and neither I nor any one else understood her but for what she was. Unfortunately my adventures in Paris had led me to form such an idea of the sex, that I could never be reconciled to the thoughts of marriage: must I on that account remain as solitary and continent as a priest?"

The conversation between me and Ruffigny gradually became warmer; but I was like Telemachus in the island of Calypso, so inflamed by the wiles of the God of Love, so enamoured with the graces and witchcraft of my Eucharis, that all remonstrances were vain.[1] In vain were the reasonings of honour and truth; in vain the voice of my venerable instructor, to which I had vowed everlasting attention. I parted from him with peevishness and ill humour.

"Is it possible," said I, as I sallied into the street, "to conceive any thing so unreasonable as Ruffigny? There are two principal crimes which, in the code of just morality, respect the relations of the sexes,—adultery and seduction. I know that puritans and monks have added a third to the class, and have inveighed indiscriminately against all incontinence. I do not decide whether their censure is wholly destitute of foundation. But was ever any one so absurd, as to place simple incontinence upon a level

---

1 An allusion to François de Salignac de la Mothe Fénelon's *Télémaque* (1699), in which Telemachus, like his father Odysseus, travels to the island of the goddess Calypso. Although Calpyso falls in love with Telemachus, Telemachus is driven mad by Cupid for the nymph Eucharis, despite the protestations of his advisor Athena (disguised as Mentor).

with incontinence attended by one or the other of these aggravations? And yet this obstinate old Swiss will not be beaten out of it!"

This argument, no doubt, was exceedingly demonstrative and satisfactory; but, as I passed and repassed it in my mind, I did not altogether like it. I hastened to dine with Sir George Bradshaw, and to visit Mrs. Comorin. I believed I should derive better lights on the subject from the brilliancy of her eyes, than from Burgersdicius or Condillac.[1]

My sensations of this day were in a high degree painful and perturbed. I confess that at moments Mrs. Comorin never appeared to me so beautiful as now. I gazed on her with ecstasy; but that very ecstasy was tempestuous, and interrupted with visions of my father and my father's friend. Nothing was clear and perspicuous in my mind. I suspected that my present passion was a vapour only, was lighter than vanity; my thoughts whispered me, that all I had seen most worthy and excellent on earth, was my deceased parent and Ruffigny. My soul was chaos.

A certain sentiment of remorse led me, sooner than usual, to quit the company and hasten home. I tasked my thoughts as I went,—"Shall I be distant and cold to Ruffigny? Shall I endeavour to soothe him, and appease his anger? or, shall I sacrifice every thing at once to his invaluable friendship?" I enquired of my servant as I entered,—Where is M. Ruffigny?"

"Gone."

"Gone? Whither?"

"Into the country. He has been employed all day in preparations, and set out in a post-chaise about half an hour ago."

"Impossible! Gone into the country, and say nothing to me of the matter!"

"He has left a letter for you."

I was impatient to peruse this letter. Yet, even while I opened it, a thousand contending thoughts were embattled in my mind. I felt that his going was intimately connected with our dissension of that morning. I vehemently accused myself

---

1 Francis Burgersdyck (1590-1629), Dutch professor of logic; Etienne, l'abbé de Condillac (1715-80), French philosopher.

for having so far offended the good old man. I was full of resentment against him for having, at this first difference, conceived a mortal offence. It was not till after repeated efforts, that I found myself in a state sufficiently calm to read the letter.

"CASIMIR FLEETWOOD,

"The fact is at length ascertained. I have travelled from Switzerland to Britain, and my dear friend, your late father, has died,—in vain.

"Is it possible? Shall this be so? Casimir Fleetwood, you are called on to decide!

"I cannot descend to altercation. It is not seemly, that tried and hoary integrity should come into the lists, to chop logic with petulant and hot-blooded vice. If events, such as have lately been brought to strike upon your heart, will not waken you, in vain might a stronger impulse be sought in the deductions of Zeno, and the homilies of Epictetus.[1] Remember what I am, and how related to your family; remember your late father; remember the day of the lake of Uri!

"On that day you said, 'Would to God it were in my power to recal a few past months! My prospects and my pleasures are finished; my life is tarnished; my peace is destroyed; I shall never again think of myself with approbation, or with patience!'— And you are now returned to the course of life which you then censured with so much bitterness. Was it you that said it?

"One of the worst symptoms on the present occasion, is the sophistry with which you defend your error. A beginning sinner offends, and accuses himself while he offends; a veteran in wrong has still some flimsy, miserable dissertation, by which he proves that wrong is not wrong.

"Another symptom which almost bids me despair, is the recent date of your conversion and good resolutions. The evening before we set out from Merionethshire, we wept together at your father's grave. The monitor whom you consented, at seventy years of age, to withdraw from his native valley, and to bring along through various climes and states, has

---

1 Zeno (c. 333-262 BC) and Epictetus (c. AD 60-140), Greek Stoic philosophers.

not yet quitted you. If you relapse, while all these things are green and fresh before you, what shall be predicted of the actions and pursuits in which you will be engaged a few years hence?

"Shame, my dear Fleetwood, shame is ever the handmaid of vice. What is the language you have held to me for the last three weeks? What shall I name you? Mean prevaricator! You pretended to inform me who were the persons with whom you associated. You mentioned all the men of your society; you did not hint at a single woman. You said, you felt no such partiality *to Sir George Bradshaw*, as a mere change of place would not immediately break off.—Do you think, that there is no vice in the conduct, which led you thus pitifully to juggle with your friend? Do you think that such a juggler is worthy the name of Fleetwood, or worthy the name of man?

"You say that, in attaching yourself to the mistress of Lord Mandeville, you neither seduce innocence, nor make yourself responsible for the violation of solemn vows. Be it so. A sound mind would prompt you, not to describe your conduct by negatives, but to enquire, what it is that you do? You sacrifice the serenity of an honourable mind to the tumult of the lowest passions in man. It is as true of the connection you now propose, as of any of the past, that you cannot esteem the person with whom you form this warm and entire intimacy. Every creature that lives, derives some of the colour of his being from the objects which are continually and familiarly around him.

"You have heard it said, that no man can be a great poet, or an elevated and generous writer, who is not first a good man. Goodness is the corner-stone of all true excellence. You cannot be blind enough to believe, that the course to which you are returning, is consistent with goodness. Many of your most familiar thoughts will be sensual and grovelling; not of the class of impulses of sense which are purified by the most sacred charities of our nature; but of those which lead us to associate with the debauched, and to have our favourite resort in the haunts of profligacy. You will have a succession of mistresses; there will not be one vestige of the refined and the ideal, what is noblest in taste and most exquisite in moral feeling, left within you. By gross and vulgar souls you will be admitted for respectable; the men who do honour to the species to which they belong, with one consent will pity and will shun you.

"Fleetwood, you must now decide—now, and for ever.

"Casimir, my heart bleeds for you. Think what my feelings are; the feelings of Ruffigny, to whom the name of Fleetwood is a name for every thing sacred, who cannot be content that one spot should stain the lustre of its white, who lives only in the hope to discharge a small part of his obligations to your father and grandfather, and whose aged heart will burst, the moment he is convinced the son is fixed to disgrace the virtues of his ancestors!——

"You will recollect that I had a business which made it desirable for me to make an excursion into Devonshire, previously to my return to my native country. I have seized this occasion for that purpose. I shall be absent a fortnight. Casimir, I cannot parley with you. I leave you to your reflections. When I return, I shall know, whether Ruffigny is to live or die.

"Yours, more than his own,
"J. F. R."

Before I had half read this letter I rung the bell, and ordered myself a post-chaise. I felt that I could suffer a thousand deaths sooner than pass this fortnight in separation, or suffer my friend to remain a moment in doubt of my good resolutions, when I had formed them. I travelled all night, and overtook Ruffigny at Basingstoke. I rushed into his arms; I could not utter a word; I sobbed on his bosom. When I could speak, I was endless in my professions of gratitude, and in protestations of a future innocent and honourable life. I spoke of the recent delusion into which I had fallen with accents of horror, self-detestation, and despair. Ruffigny was deeply affected.

"This prompt and decisive return to reason and virtue inspires me with the most sanguine hope," said he.

CHAPTER VI.

M. RUFFIGNY continued with me several months; and during the remainder of his life, which was about six years, I generally made a visit once a year to the canton of Uri. The relation which existed between his family and mine was of the most interesting sort. Never in any age or country were two parties bound together by ties so noble. I looked in his face, and saw the features of the venerable Ambrose Fleetwood, and of my beloved father. What I remarked was not the thing we denominate family likeness,—the sort of cast of countenance by which descents and pedigrees, whether wise men or fools, whether knaves or honest, are, like the individuals of different nations, identified all over the world. The resemblance I perceived, though less glaring at first sight, extended its root infinitely deeper. It was that their hearts had been cast in the same mould. He must have been a very slight observer of men, who is not aware that two human creatures, equally good, that love each other, and have during long periods associated together, unavoidably contract a similarity of sentiments, of demeanour, and of physiognomonical expression. But, beside this resemblance of Ruffigny to my parents, which some will regard as fantastical, the countenance of the venerable Swiss was a book where I could trace the history of my ancestors. It was like the book of the records of King Ahasuerus in the Bible, in which the good deeds and deserts of the virtuous were written, that they might not perish from the memories of those who were indebted to them, unhonoured and forgotten.[1]

The benefits my father proposed for me from the counsels and intercourse of Ruffigny I extensively obtained. From this period I became an altered man. The ebriety and extravagance of youth were at an end with me. The sobriety, the delicacy, the sentimental fastidiousness of my childish days, revived in my bosom; and I looked back with astonishment at my adolescence, that I could ever have departed so widely from my genuine character.

---

1 An allusion to Esther 10.

The means employed for my conversion were indeed amply commensurate to the end proposed. There was something so venerable in the figure and appearance of Ruffigny, and primitive and patriarchal in his manners and modes of thinking, that it was perhaps impossible to converse intimately with him, and yet continue whelmed in the mire of licentiousness. But, beside his general qualifications for the office, he came recommended to me by considerations so sacred, as to render his expostulations, his persuasives, and his alarms to my virtue and honour, irresistible. What an unexampled friendship was that which bound together the names of Fleetwood and Ruffigny! Could I listen, otherwise than as to the admonitions of a God, to the discourses of a man who had generously, in his lifetime, and in the full vigour of his age, surrendered to my family a fortune almost princely, and tranquilly retired to the simplicity of his ancestors? In every word he spoke, I felt this circumstance enforcing his remarks. The misery of admonition in general, is that it is so difficult for the person whose benefit it professes, to be convinced of the disinterestedness of his monitor. Some suspicion of selfishness, of ostentation, of vanity, of false colours, and the disingenuousness of a pleader, lurks within, and poisons every clause. Could I suspect any thing of that kind, in this living Curius, who had come from his Sabine farm, the voluntary obscurity to which he had withdrawn his age, purposely to fulfil the last injunctions of my father, and to provide for the tranquillity and virtue of the son?[1] While I listened to his voice, my conscience whispered me,—It is the voice of him, but for whose absolute self-denial and heroic friendship, my father would have been bankrupt of comforts and fortune, and myself a beggar.

By degrees—let me venture to say—I became assimilated, however imperfectly, to my admirable monitor. I whispered to my swelling heart, "Never, no, never will I belong to such men as these, and not make it the first object of my solicitude to

---

1   Manius Curius Dentatus (third century BC), considered a model of Roman virtue and frugality, served as consul in 290, 275 and 274, and led Rome to a victory against the Samnites. Rejecting the booty that was his due, he retired to the modest life of a farmer.

become like them. Let other men talk of their heroic blo
and swear they will not blot a long line of princes from wh
they may be descended! Here is my patent of nobility,[1] t
which I defy all the monarchs of the earth to show a brighter;
not sealed by the ruin of provinces and empires, but by the
purest and most godlike contempt of all selfish views that ever
was exhibited. In me the race of the Fleetwoods shall survive; I
will become heir to the integrity and personal honour of the
virtuous Ruffigny."

Why do I write down these elevated vows, which, alas! I
have never redeemed? I but the more sincerely subscribe to my
own condemnation. My history, as I early remarked, is a register of errors, the final record of my penitence and humiliation.

From this period, however, I ceased to practise the vices of a
libertine. The faults I have further to confess are of a different
nature. My heart was henceforward pure, my moral tastes
revived in their genuine clearness, and the errors I committed
were no longer those of a profligate. Thus far I became
unequivocally a gainer by this great event of my life.

CHAPTER VII.

MY education and travels had left me a confirmed mis-
anthropist. This is easily accounted for. I had seen nothing of
the world but its most unfavourable specimens. What can be
less amiable, than the broad, rude, unfeeling, and insolent
debaucheries of a circle of young men, who have just begun to
assume the privileges of man, without having yet learned his
engagements and his duties? What can be more ignoble and
depraved, than the manners of a court and a metropolis, especially of such a court and metropolis as those of the last years of
Louis XV.? My constitutional temper was saturnine and sensitive. This character of mind had been much heightened in me
in my early solitude in Wales. I came into the world prepared
to be a severe and an unsparing judge. For a time I did violence

---

1   The conferring of noble rank by "letters patent," a document issued by the
    monarch.

to myself, and mingled in the vices I witnessed. But this had not the effect of making me less, but more intolerant. When I came to myself, the spots I observed upon the vesture of my innocence, made me feel a still deeper loathing for the foul and miry roads through which I had journeyed. It has often been said that there is no sharper Argus or severer judge, than a superannuated debauchee. I know not how generally this is the case; but it may easily be supposed that there is much truth in the maxim, where the mind was originally virtuous, and was endowed with a taste vivid and thoroughly alive to the difference of beauty and deformity, whether intellectual or moral. I loved and inexpressibly honoured the characters of Ruffigny and my own immediate ancestors; but this only whetted my disapprobation of the rest of my species. They were so totally unlike every other person with whom I had familiarly associated, that they struck me like luminaries sent into the world to expose the opacity and disgraces of the rest of its inhabitants. Perhaps that is the most incorrigible species of misanthropy, which, as Swift expresses it, loves John, and Matthew, and Alexander, but hates mankind.[1]

Here then begins the moral of my tale:—I "repented", but I was not "made whole." My entire future life was devoted to the expiation of five years of youthful folly and forgetfulness. If I had retained the simplicity and guilelessness of my Merionethshire character, it is impossible but I should have been happy. As it was,

> "——All the voyage of my life
> Was bound in shallows and in miseries."[2]

I had contracted a contamination, which could never be extirpated. Innocence is philanthropical and confiding, "believeth all things, and hopeth all things."[3] I looked upon

---

1 In reference to his *Gulliver's Travels* (1726), Jonathan Swift (1667-1745) wrote to Alexander Pope on 29 September 1725, "I hate and detest that animal called man, although I hartily love John, Peter, Thomas and so forth."
2 *Julius Caesar*, IV.iii.218-19 (adapted).
3 I Corinthians 13:7.

every thing with an eye of jealousy and incredulity. The universe had lost to me that sunshine, which it derives from the reflection of an unspotted mind. All was dark, and dreary, and sable around me. I wandered in pathless wilds, unable to arrive but at regions of barren rock and immeasurable sands. Innocence is a sort of magnetism by which one good heart understands another. It is peaceful when alone; and, when it comes out into the world, it meets with individual after individual whom it confesses for brothers. I had lost this touchstone. In solitude I was disconsolate; and, if I mixed in the haunts of men, I understood them not; in no one did I find a companion; and in the most populous resorts and crowded assemblies, I was perfectly and consummately alone.

I returned to my solitude in Wales with an arrow in my heart. What did I want? I knew not. Yet I was not happy. I regarded my own life with no complacency or approbation. Oh, Cader Idris! Oh, beloved banks of the Desunny! Glorious men once trod your shades, my father, and my father's friend. How can I compare with these? Their lives were generous, and marked with the most disinterested sacrifices; but what have I done? If my days had been spent in innocence, that were much. I passed but a short period in the tumult of society; but in that period how many blots did I contract! These blots make all my history.

There are but two principal sources of happiness to the man who lives in solitude: memory, and imagination. The recollections which offered themselves to my memory gave me no pleasure. That period of my life which was most fraught with impressions, and which, therefore, made the principal stock of my memory, was hateful to me. Imagination in the days of my youth had been the main fountain of my delight. The materials of my imagination had been childish impressions, eked out with the books of children, with pastoral ideas, and fairies, and magic, and processions, and palaces. But, when we have mixed in real scenes, the materials furnished by books shrink into insignificance. The actual affairs into which the passions of man have obtruded themselves, ambition, and vanity, and shame, and love, and jealousy, and despair, take so much faster hold of the mind, that even when we would expatiate in worlds of fancy, these affairs will push forward, and in spite of us make a part of the landscape we delineate.

I know that most men would have been happy in my place; at least, much happier than I was. The transactions of my early years have nothing singular in them, except as they were made so by my turn of mind, and the strong and subtle passions which were thus called forth in me. A dissipated and riotous life at the university, and a succession of mistresses at first introduction into the world, compose the history of most young men, born to the inheritance of a considerable fortune, and whose education has been conducted in a style of liberal expense. Such young men are usually found to retire contented after the effervescence of youth is over, and unreluctantly to exchange the drawing-rooms of foreign courts, and the contemplation of foreign manners, for the country club and the bowling-green. They lay aside their satin suits, and take up their pipes, and become as complete rustics, as if they had never wandered beyond the smoke of their own chimneys.

Such was not the case in my instance. At no time of my life did I ever delight in such "worshipful society;" and I retained too deep an impression of the scenes of courtly refinement I had witnessed, to be capable of dwindling into a mere justice of the peace. I sought consolation in the exercise of my beneficence; and, though I never entered the halls of the wealthy, I often penetrated into the cottages of the poor: and I found what I expected. But, though I found the consolation I looked for, I did not find it in the degree I looked for. I had recourse to the amusements of literature: I formed projects,—sometimes of investigating the progress or decay of national genius and taste, and sometimes of following through its minutest ramifications a certain memorable period of history,—projects which led me from author to author in wide succession, and took away the oppressive feelings of passiveness which frequently pursue us, when we resign ourselves to the simple and direct reading of a single work.

But neither beneficence nor study afforded me sufficient occupation. The relieving the wants of our neighbour is a pursuit which can only employ us at intervals, and can never form the leading and regular business of our lives. Reading has its periods of satiety. I fell sometimes, for want of an object sufficiently to exercise the passions, into long fits of languor and depression, which were inconceivably wearisome. Exercise and the scenes of nature no longer relieved me. The inactivity which came over me made it very difficult for me to summon the resolution to go out of doors in search of variety. But, when that difficulty was conquered, variety itself afforded me no pleasure. The landscape was as if it had lost the prismatic illusion, which clothes it to the sense of sight in such beautiful colours. The fields were no longer green, nor the skies blue; or at least they afforded no more pleasure to my eyes, than they would have done if the grass had been withered, and the heavens shrouded in pestilence and death. The beautiful and the bold forms of valley and mountain, which had frequently delighted me, seemed to my eye loathsome, and tame, and monotonous. The refreshing breeze, which gives new life even to the wearied patient perishing with a fever, played in vain upon my countenance and among the locks of my hair.

CHAPTER VIII.

TIRED of the country, I repaired to London. To be presented at court, and occasionally to make one in the rout, the ball, or the *festino* of a lady of quality, were rather necessities I submitted to, than pleasures I sought. One advantage which I knew I should find in the metropolis, was an opportunity of frequenting the society of men of genius. I heard of a club of authors, several of whose works I had read with pleasure, and I obtained the favour of being admitted an honorary member. The society had assumed to itself a Greek name, as if by way of hint to the ignorant and the illiterate to keep their distance.

I did not, however, find in this society the pleasure I had anticipated. Undoubtedly, in the conversations they held I heard many profound remarks, many original conceptions, many pointed repartees, many admirable turns of humour and wit. I impute it to the fastidiousness of my own temper, bred in solitude, and disgusted with the world, that I so soon grew weary of this classic circle. I saw better men than myself, men of elevated rank and refined breeding, as well as of accomplished minds, who derived from the dinners and suppers of this club, and still more from the separate society and acquaintance of its members, an enjoyment upon which they set a high value. As far as my observation of the world extended, it was always the more valuable individuals in the class of men of quality and fortune, it was such as possessed the most generous minds and the most comprehensive views, who delighted most in the intercourse of men of literature. They were the fools, the envious, and the selfish, who shunned such intimates, because they could not bear to be outdone by persons poorer than themselves, and because they felt the terrifying apprehension of being reduced by them into ciphers. I saw also, contrary to the received opinion, that the men of real genius, and who were genuine ornaments of the republic of letters, were always men of liberal tempers, of a certain nobility and disinterestedness of sentiment, and anxious for the promotion of individual and general advantage, however they might sometimes be involved in petty and degrading altercations and disputes.

On the other hand, I must do myself the justice to say, that I discovered many real blemishes and errors in these conversations. The literary men whose acquaintance I could boast, were frequently as jealous of their fame and superiority, as the opulent men, their neighbours, were of the preservation and improvement of their estates. This indeed is but natural: every man who is in any way distinguished from the herd of his species, will of course set no small value upon the thing, whatever it is, to which he is indebted for his distinction. No one who has tasted of honour, would willingly be thrust out among the ignoble vulgar. The only thing which can defend a man against this pitiful jealousy and diseased vigilance, is a generous confidence in his own worth, teaching him that it will find its place without any dishonest and clandestine exertion on his part. The individual who is continually blowing the fire of his own brilliancy, who asserts and denies, is direct or artificial, serious or jocose, not attending to the inspirations of truth and simplicity of heart, but as he thinks may best contribute to advance his reputation, if he can at all be acknowledged for a pleasant companion and associate, is so at least with a very powerful drawback. Such men form to themselves an art in conversation by which they may best maintain the rank in intellect they have acquired. They think little of the eliciting truth, or a conformity to the just laws of equal society, but have trained themselves to a trick, either by an artful interruption, a brutal retort, a pompous, full sounding, and well pronounced censure, or an ingeniously supported exhibition of sarcastic mockery, to crush in the outset the appearance of rivalship, and to turn the admiration of bystanders entirely upon themselves.

This is altogether a pitiful policy. True literary reputation does not depend upon a man's maintaining a shining figure in the conversations in which he mixes. If an individual has no nobler ambition than to be the chairman of his own club, why does he commit his thoughts to paper, or send them through the medium of the press into the world? The moment he has done this, he ought to consider himself as having pronounced his disdain of the fugitive character of a conversation wit or a conversation bully. I am inclined to believe that no one ever uniformly maintained, in various companies, the first place in subtlety and wit, who has not cultivated this character with dishonest art, and admitted many unmanly and disingenuous subterfuges into the plan by which he pursued it. If so, the shining man of a company is to be put down in the lowest class of persons of intellect. If men entitled to a higher place have too often submitted to this, it is that they have inflicted on themselves a voluntary degradation.—One exception only can I devise to this disingenuousness, which is, where a man has the absolute *cacoëthes loquendi*,[1] and where his thoughts are so brilliant and elevated, that all other men will be eager to listen to them.

The man of genius, who has delivered the fruit of his meditations and invention to the public, has nothing naturally to do

---

1 Disease of speaking. [Godwin's note]

with this inglorious struggle. He converses that he may inform and be informed. He wishes to study the humours, the manners, and the opinions of mankind. He is not unwilling to take his share in conversation, because he has nothing to conceal, and because he would contribute, as far as with modesty and propriety he can, to the amusement and instruction of others. But his favourite place is that of a spectator. He is more eager to add to his own stock of observation and knowledge, than to that of his neighbours. This is natural and just: since he knows better his own wants, than he can know the wants of any other man; and since he is more sure of the uses that will be made of the acquisitions he shall himself obtain.

Among the literary men I saw in this club, or with whom I in some way became acquainted in consequence of being a member of it, I found one or two exceptions such as I have last described; but the rest were stimulated by the love of praise in society, as much as they had been in their writings; and the traps they laid for applause were no less gross and palpable, than those employed by a favourite actor, or the author of a modern comedy.

Even such members of the club as did not sacrifice all truth and justice at the shrine of a sordid vanity, had the habit, as I heard it once expressed by a captious visiter at his return from one of their meetings, of speaking as if they talked out of a book. I admit that this is a fastidious objection. He who spends his life among books, must be expected to contract something of the manner of his constant companions. He who would disentangle a knotty point, or elucidate a grave question of taste, morals, or politics, must discourse to some degree in the way of dissertation, or he would discourse in vain; and if, like a dissertation for popular readers, he takes care to relieve his style with something pointed and epigrammatic, paints his thoughts, as he goes on, to the imagination of his hearers, interrupts himself gracefully, and is on his guard not to say a word too much, he may be allowed to have played his part commendably. If by talking as out of a book, is meant no more than that a man speaks correctly, with well chosen words, in a perspicuous style, and with phrases neatly turned, the objection is eminently unreasonable. Such is the true and sound view of the subject; but it was in vain to argue the point; so I was made, and so I found myself affected.

I was the spoiled child of the great parent, Nature. I delighted only in the bold and the free, in what was at one and the same time beautiful and lawless. What aspired to please me, must be as wild as the artless warblings of the choristers of the woods. Its graces must be unexpected, and were endeared so much the more to me as they showed themselves in the midst of irregularity. What spoke to my heart must be a full, mellow, and protracted note, or a bewitching vibration of sound, which seemed to come on purpose to reward me for listening, for a time, to what gave no express promise of so pure a delight.

But, had it been otherwise, an attendance once a week, during the season, at a club of authors, and the occasional society of its members in the intervals, would have afforded but slender materials for happiness. It might have answered to the confections which amuse the palate at the end of a feast, but it could never appease the appetite of him, who feels an uneasy and aching void within, and is in hot chase for the boon of content.

CHAPTER IX.

AMONG the members of our club who were not themselves authors, there were a few who were among the most distinguished ornaments of the English senate. The intercourse of these men was particularly delightful to me. Their manners were more urbane, attentive, flattering, and uniform, than those of the professional authors. They were gentlemen by birth and by education; and, as they had not the same goad urging them along in the pursuit of praise as those who embraced literature as a profession, their passions, at least as seen within these walls, were less restless, their views more enlarged, and their souls possessed of more calm and repose.—In this comparison, be it remembered, I speak only of the majority of the authors who were members of this club. Among them I knew some illustrious exceptions; and I should think myself highly censurable in deciding, from those I saw, upon the merits of others whom I never knew.

The pleasure, however, I felt in the intercourse of such of our members as were senators, and the admiration with which I was impressed of their manners and temper, inspired me with the desire of becoming myself a representative in the English parliament. It will readily be perceived how ill my temper was suited to the office of courting suffrages and soliciting votes. In this one instance I conquered my temper. I promised myself that it should be but for once. I blamed myself for being so unbending to the manners of the world. I saw that the task I was undertaking, would afford me a copious opportunity of studying the humours and predilections of the middling and lower classes of the community: why should I quit the stage of human life without having obtained such an opportunity? I made myself popular, and I resolved to do so. I gave entertainments, and I delivered speeches. I laughed at the rude jokes of handicraftsmen, and I cracked my jokes in return. I smoked my pipe, and toasted Church and King, and the wooden walls of old England.[1] I saw that, in complying with the plain, coarse manners of my constituents, I ran no such risk as I had done in my former compliances with the manners of the Oxonians and the Parisians; and, instead of despising myself for what I did, I esteemed myself the more, in proportion as I found that I possessed one faculty which I had not before suspected, and as I was able thus stoically to adapt myself to a certain object, and pursue it to the end. I was elected by a considerable majority of votes; and those who had supported me with their suffrages, or who had vociferated and huzzaed in my behalf, were satisfied that they had gained a more important Cause, than could have been secured by the deliverance of an oppressed country, or the emancipation of one quarter of the world.

I entered with awe the walls of the British parliament. I recollected the illustrious men of past ages who had figured upon that scene. I recollected the glorious struggles of our ancestors which had there been made, and by means of which greater

---

1　An expression referring to the British navy.

privileges and liberties had been secured to the people ͼ
land, than any of the neighbouring countries could ⁄
looked round with complacence upon the accomplishͼͼ
acters who now filled some of the most conspicuous seats on
those benches. I eagerly courted the acquaintance of these
leaders. I was desirous to understand their views, and enter into
their projects.

There is always something more interesting to a young and
uncorrupted mind, in the cause of opposition, than in the cause
of administration. The topics on which they have to expatiate
are of a more animated and liberal cast: rhetoric ever finds a
more congenial and less thorny field, in the office of attack,
than in that of defence. Liberty is the theme of their declamation; and their bosoms beat with the thought that they are
pleading the cause of the great mass of their countrymen, who
are denied the advantage of being able to plead for themselves.
Beside which, modern governments always must, or at least
always do, have recourse to various modes of proceeding not
exactly in accord with pure notions of integrity: a statesman in
place cannot, but in a very limited sense of the word, be an
honest man. I therefore enlisted myself in the ranks of opposition.

But, in proportion as I became more familiarly acquainted
with the maxims and views of opposition, I felt my satisfaction
in them diminished. I saw that their aim was to thrust the ministers in possession out of office, that they might take their
places. I became aware that they objected to many things, not
because they were bad, but because their defects, real or apparent, afforded plausible topics of declamation. I perceived that
the spirit of censuring the measures of government grew too
much into a habit, and was directed too much by the intention
of bringing the immediate conductors of public affairs into discredit and contempt. I acquitted the most considerable of the
leaders from the consciousness of pursuing so pitiful a plan.
Men of generous minds will always dwell upon that view of
the business in which they are engaged, which is most congenial to their natural tempers. But, beside every other disadvantage attending them in this situation, persons of merit, engaged

in a party, must accommodate themselves to the views of the dullest and meanest of their adherents,—to their impatience, their perverseness, and their acrimony; they must employ a thousand arts to soothe their prejudices and keep them in temper; and as, in every party that ever existed, the fools greatly outnumber the men of understanding, so in matters of party it will infallibly happen that the honourable and the sage must, on a thousand occasions, be made the tools and dupes of the vilest of the herd. A parliamentary leader scarcely appeared to me the same man in a political consultation, that he had done in a literary club. In his club he was free, ingenuous, and gay; in his political character he was vigilant and uneasy, calculating with restless anxiety upon appearances and results, and still burning with ever-new disappointments.

I saw that the public character of England, as it exists in the best pages of our history, was gone. I perceived that we were grown a commercial and arithmetical nation; and that, as we extended the superficies of our empire, we lost its moral sinews and its strength. The added numbers which have been engrafted upon both houses of parliament have destroyed the health and independence of its legislature; the wealth of either India has been poured upon us, to smother that free spirit which can never be preserved but in a moderate fortune. Contractors, directors, and upstarts,—men fattened on the vitals of their fellow-citizens,—have taken the place which was once filled by the Wentworths, the Seldens, and the Pyms.[1] By the mere project,—the most detestable and fatal that ever was devised,—of England borrowing of the individuals who constitute England, and accumulating what is called a national debt, she has mortgaged her sons to an interminable slavery.

I did not, however, immediately see things in this point of view. I regarded my entrance into the station of an English senator as a memorable epoch in my life. I said, "I have been too long a mere spectator of the scene of existence; it is owing to this, that I have felt such a constant corroding and dissatisfaction. I will now take an active part. In the measures which are

---

1 Sir Thomas Wentworth, first Earl of Strafford (1593–1641), chief adviser to Charles I from 1639. For Pym and Selden, see note on page 109.

adopted I will have a voice; I will contribute by my advice to their improvement or their overthrow; I will study the principles of legislation; I will detect bad laws, and procure their abrogation; I will bring forward such regulations as the present state of manners and policy demands; I will from time to time urge and unfold, in a greater or a smaller circle, as occasion may offer, such maxims as may insensibly tend to the correction and elevation of the character of my country."

I know not whether it was owing to any radical vice in my disposition, but I did not long persist in these gallant resolutions. The difficulties were much greater than at a distance I had imagined. The contrast, which gradually obtruded upon me, between England as I found her in the volumes of her history, and England as she now was, and had insensibly become for more than a hundred years, damped the ardour of my enthusiasm.

Once or twice, indeed, I felt that animation which raised my soul to such a pitch, that I was conscious I had nothing left, for the moment, to desire. Some measures in which I had a part, were of immediate importance to the welfare of thousands. Some struggles in which I had joined were arduous; some victories, in which I was one among the conquerors, carried transport to my heart. I witnessed situations like that which Burke describes upon the repeal of the American Stamp Act,—"When at length, after the suitors most interested respecting the issue had waited with a trembling and anxious expectation, almost to a winter's return of light, the doors of the house were thrown open, and showed them the figure of their deliverer in the moment of his well-earned triumph; when they jumped upon him like children on a long-absent father, and clung about him as captives about their redeemer."[1] But these occasions were of rare occurrence; we soon fell back into the shopkeeping and traffic-trained character I deplored; and even to these triumphs themselves, so beautiful to the eye, it was often found that treachery, calculation, and cabal had contributed their polluted aid.

---

[1] Referring to the "Speech on American Taxation, 19 April 1774" (adapted) of Edmund Burke (1729-97), influential British statesman and political writer.

CHAPTER X.

DISPLEASED with the phenomena which I observed in the seat of empire, and satiated with the beauties of my paternal estate, I resolved once more to pass over to the Continent; and to seek, in the spectacle of different countries, and the investigation of dissimilar manners, relief from the *ennui* which devoured me.

This expedient seemed at first to answer my purpose. Novelty and change have a sovereign power over the human mind.

But the efficacy of this remedy did not last long. Wherever I went, I carried a secret uneasiness along with me. When I left Paris for Vienna, or Vienna for Madrid, I journeyed a solitary individual along the tedious road; and, when I entered my inn, the same solitude and uncomfortable sensation entered along with me.

I turned aside to examine remarkable objects, the fame of which had reached me; I visited some celebrated convent of monks; I took the freedom to introduce myself to some elaborate collector of curiosities—to some statesman or general retired from the busy scene—to some philosopher or poet whose lucubrations had delighted the world. I was generally fortunate enough to make my visit agreeable to the host I selected: I flattered his tastes; I expressed, in the honest language of truth and feeling, the sense I entertained of his character and merits. This sort of avocation afforded me a temporary pleasure; but it often left me in a state of more painful sensation than it found me, and impressed upon me the melancholy conviction of the unsubstantial nature of all human enjoyments.

Sometimes I joined company with a fellow-traveller, whom chance directed to the same point, or whom I was able, by some allurement of pleasure or advantage, to prevail upon to pursue my route. In some cases I was disappointed in my companion; found him totally different from what, on a slight observation, I had conceived him to be; and either separated from him before half our journey was completed, or cursed a hundred times the obligation I had contracted, which, perhaps, for twenty days successively, rendered me the slave of a frigid civility. At other times, it may be, the conversation of my fellow-traveller afforded me an unfeigned delight; and then I bitterly regretted the fugitive nature of our intercourse. The sensation I felt was such as has been experienced by passengers in a stage-coach, who have just had time to contract a liking for each other—who have whispered to themselves, "How agreeable, how animated, how well-informed, or how facetious, is this stranger!"—who have met in a domestic way at breakfast, at dinner, and at supper—who have wished each other good night at the close of the day, and met with salutations in the morning; when suddenly the vehicle whirls them into some vast city—the step of the carriage is let down—one passes one way, and another another—one calls for a chaise to convey him up the country, and another hastens with his baggage to the port, being engaged in some distant voyage.

Frequently I sojourned for two, three, or four months in some polite or learned residence: and, when I had just had time to familiarise myself with its most valuable inhabitants, was impelled to call to mind that this was not my home, and that it was time to withdraw. Why should I stay? The language, the manners, and the scene were not native to me; and it was nothing but the necessity of departing that made me regret a place, which, if I had been compelled to take up my abode in it, would speedily have lost its illusion.

CHAPTER XI.

I SAW that I was alone, and I desired to have a friend. Friends, in the ordinary sense of the word, and that by no means a contemptible sense, I had many; friends who found pleasure in my conversation, who were convinced of the integrity of my principles of conduct, and who would have trusted me in the most important concerns. But what sort of a friend is it whose kindness shall produce a conviction in my mind that I do not stand alone in the world? This must be a friend, who is to me as another self, who joys in all my joys, and grieves in all my sorrows, not with a joy or grief that looks like compliment, not with a sympathy that changes into smiles when I am no longer present, though my head continues bent to the earth with anguish.—I do not condemn the man, upon whom a wound through my vitals acts but as a scratch; I know that his feelings are natural; I admit him for just, honest, and humane—a valuable member of society. But he is not the brother of my heart. I will not suffer myself to be beguiled, and to fall into so wretched an error as to mistake the friendship of good-humour, or even of esteem, for the friendship which can best console a man in calamity and wretchedness, whether of mind or external circumstances. I walk among these men as in an agreeable promenade; I speak to one and another, and am cheered with the sight of their honest countenances; but they are nothing to me: I know that when death removes me from the scene for ever, their countenances will the next day be neither less honest nor less cheerful. Friendship, in the sense in which I felt the want of it, has been truly said to be a sentiment that can grasp but one individual in its embrace. The person who entertains this sentiment must see in his friend a creature of a species by itself, must respect and be attached to him above all the world, and be deeply convinced that the loss of him would be a calamity which nothing earthly could repair. By long habit, he must have made his friend a part of himself; must be incapable of any pleasure in public, in reading, in travelling, of which he does not make his friend, at least in idea, a partaker, or of passing a day or an hour in the conceptions of which the thought of his friend does not mingle itself.

How many disappointments did I sustain in the search after a friend! How often this treasure appeared as it were within my grasp, and then glided away from my eager embrace! The desire to possess it, was one of the earliest passions of my life, and, though eternally baffled, perpetually returned to the assault. I met with men, who seemed willing to bestow their friendship upon me; but their temper, their manners, and their habits, were so discordant from mine, that it was impossible the flame should be lighted in my breast. I met with men, to whom I could willingly have sworn an eternal partnership of soul; but they thought of me with no corresponding sentiment; they were engaged in other pursuits, they were occupied with other views, and had not leisure to distinguish and to love me.

Some one, perhaps, will ask me, Why are qualities of this nature necessary in a friend? If I die, why should I wish my friend to bear about him a heart transfixed with anguish for my loss? Is not this wish miserably ungenerous and selfish?—God knows, in that sense I do not entertain the wish: I wish my friend to possess every possible enjoyment, and to be exempted from every human suffering. But let us consider the meaning of this. I require that my friend should be poignantly affected by my death, as I require that he should be affected if I am calumniated, shipwrecked, imprisoned, robbed of my competence or my peace. Not that I have any pleasure in his distress, simply considered; but that I know that this is the very heart and essence of an ardent friendship. I cannot be silly enough to believe that the man who looks on, at my calamity or my death, without any striking interruption of his tranquillity, has a vehement affection for me. He may be considerate and kind; he may watch by my bed-side with an enlightened and active benevolence; he may even be zealous to procure every alleviation of my pains, and every aid for restoring me to enjoyment and health: but this is not love. No; if he can close my eyes, and then return with a free and unembarrassed mind to his ordinary business and avocations, this is not love.

I know not how other men are constituted; but something of this sort seemed essential to my happiness. It is not wonderful, perhaps, that I, who had been so circumstanced from my infancy, as to accustom me to apprehend every discord to my feelings and tastes as mortal to the serenity of my mind, should have had so impatient a thirst for friendship. The principle of the sentiment may be explained mechanically, and is, perhaps, to a considerable degree, mechanical in its operation. The circumstances, whether allied to pleasure or pain, in which I am placed, strike upon my mind, and produce a given sensation. I do not wish to stand alone, but to consider myself as part only of a whole. If that which produces sensation in me, produces sensation no where else, I am substantially alone. If the lash inflicted on me will, being inflicted on another, be attended with a similar effect, I then know that there is a being of the same species or genus with myself. Still we are, each of us, substantive and independent. But, if there is a being who feels the blow under which I flinch, in whom my sensations are by a kind of necessity echoed and repeated, that being is a part of myself. Every reasoning and sensitive creature seems intuitively to require, to his perfectly just and proper state, this sort of sympathy. It is inconceivable how great an alleviation is in this way afforded, how it mitigates the agony of every kind of distress. It is inconceivable in how deep and insurmountable a solitude that creature is involved, who looks every where around for sympathy, but looks in vain. Society, an active and a crowded scene, is the furthest in the world from relieving the sensation of this solitude. The more moving and variegated is the assembly in which I am present, the more full is my conviction that I am alone. I should find as much consolation and rest among what the satirist calls the vitrified inhabitants of the planet Mercury, as here.

The operation, as I have said, is in one view of it mechanical; in another it is purely intellectual and moral. To the happiness of every human creature, at least in a civilised state, it is perhaps necessary that he should esteem himself, that he should regard himself as an object of complacency and honour: but in this, as well as every other species of creed, it should seem almost impossible for any one to be a firm believer, if there are no other persons in the world of the same sect as himself. However worthy and valuable he may endeavour to consider himself, his persuasion will be attended with little confidence and solidity, if it does not find support in the judgments of other men. The martyr, or the champion of popular pretensions, cheerfully encounters the terrors of a public execution, provided the theatre on which he is to die is filled with his approvers. And, in this respect, the strength of attachment and approbation in a few, or in one, will sometimes compensate the less conspicuous complacence of thousands. I remember to have heard a very vain man say, "I have a hundred friends, any one of whom would willingly die, if it were required for my preservation or welfare:" no wonder that such a man should be continually buoyed up with high spirits, and enjoy the most enviable sensations. Alas! what this man was able to persuade himself he possessed in so wild an exuberance, I sought for through life, and found in no single instance!

Thus I spent more than twenty years of my life, continually in search of contentment, which as invariably eluded my pursuit. My disposition was always saturnine. I wanted something, I knew not what. I sought it in solitude and in crowds, in travel and at home, in ambition and in independence. My ideas moved slow; I was prone to *ennui*. I wandered among mountains and rivers, through verdant plains, and over immense precipices; but nature had no beauties. I plunged into the society of the rich, the gay, the witty, and the eloquent; but I sighed; disquisition did not rouse me to animation; laughter was death to my flagging spirits.

This disease, which afflicted me at first but in a moderate degree, grew upon me perpetually from year to year. As I advanced in life, my prospects became less gilded with the sunshine of hope; and, as the illusion of the scenes of which I was successively a spectator wore out, I felt with deeper dejection that I was alone in the world.

It will readily be supposed, that in these twenty years of my life I met with many adventures; and that, if I were so inclined, I might, instead of confining myself as I have done to generals, have related a variety of minute circumstances, sometimes calculated to amuse the fancy, and sometimes to agitate the sympathetic and generous feelings, of every reader. I might have described many pleasing and many pathetic incidents in Merionethshire: I might have enlarged upon my club of authors, and thus, in place of making my volumes a moral tale, have converted them into a vehicle for personal satire: I might have expanded the story of my political life, and presented the reader with many anecdotes of celebrated characters, that the world has little dreamed of: I might have described the casualties of my travels, and the heart-breaking delusions and disappointments of a pretended friendship. It is by no means for want of materials, that I have touched with so light a hand upon this last portion of my life. But I willingly sacrifice these topics. I hasten to the events which have pressed with so terrible a weight on my heart, and have formed my principal motive to become my own historian.

CHAPTER XII.

I was now nearly forty-five years of age. Travelling on some factitious occasion near the lakes of Westmorland and Cumberland, and listening, as my custom was, after whatever was extraordinary and interesting (I listened, as the reader has by this time perceived, with vain hope; what was called extraordinary, had scarcely the power to excite my attention; what interested others, moved not me),—I was told of a gentleman, by name Macneil, that had resided much in foreign countries, and was supposed particularly to have possessed the confidence of the celebrated Jean Jacques Rousseau, who had been some years an inhabitant of the banks of the Windermere.[1] He had a family of daughters, to the forming whose manners and mind he and his wife had devoted themselves; so that this man, who had travelled so much, and whose understanding was so highly cultivated and refined, seemed to have no further business remaining in life, except to provide the children, the offspring of his marriage, with the motives and means of a virtuous and happy existence.

The history of his wife was somewhat uncommon. She had been born on English ground, but he met with her in the Ecclesiastical Territory in Italy.[2] She had eloped to her present consort, not from her parents, but from a man calling himself her husband. This man, an Italian by birth, had been her instructor in music; he was old, deformed, avaricious, and profligate. The father of the lady had considered his exterior as a sufficient security against any injury to which his daughter might be exposed, and, pleased with his visiter's conversation

---

1 Lake in England's "Lake District," bordering Cumbria (Westmorland) and Lancashire.
2 The Papal States.

and professional talents, had, without scruple, invited him to spend month after month under his roof. This repulsive baboon, however, soon conceived the plan of robbing his benefactor of his only child; and he succeeded in the attempt. He talked the language of love to a blooming and inexperienced girl, to whom that language had never before been addressed; his voice was harmony, and his manners specious, gentle, and insinuating. He won her regard, and, before she had completed her sixteenth year, prevailed on her to desert her paternal roof.

No sooner had he conveyed her to his native country, than he threw off the mask toward her. Her fortune was entirely dependent on her father, except a small portion, which was disputed with the worthy bridegroom in the English courts, and which he soon found reason to believe he should never obtain. He made her a prisoner in a dismantled and unwholesome castle which he had inherited from his father, and set over her his sister, as ugly as himself, but who, having obtained no advantages either from education or example, was in a singular degree vulgar, insolent, and brutal.

In this situation she lived when, about twelve months after the period in which she left her father's house, Mr. Macneil, on his travels, heard something of her story, and, like a true knight errant, was prompted to besiege her castle. He had seen her twice under her father's roof; he had lamented, like every other friend of the family, the vile artifices by which she had been trepanned; and, being now informed that she was shut up as a prisoner, and kept from the sight of every human being, except her betrayer, and the hag, his sister, he determined to offer her deliverance. By means of a bribe to one of the servants, he contrived to have a letter conveyed to her hands. The young lady had had leisure to repent of her rashness, and to recollect with infinite remorse the endearments of her natal roof. To receive a line from her countryman, a gentleman whom she remembered to have seen at her father's table, afforded her indescribable pleasure. She knew that the character of Mr. Macneil had always been spoken of as the model of integrity and honour. In her perilous situation, which she regarded with infinite loathing, she judged that some risk was indispensable. She wrote an answer, enquiring respecting her father; mother she had none in existence. Being informed that he still lived, but was inconsolable for her loss, she became not less earnest than her correspondent, that he should provide the means of her escape. She trembled to think whether her father would receive her: sometimes she represented him to herself as a stern judge, refusing her entreaties; at others, as the victim of offended love, reproaching her with eyes of death and despair: she desired, however, to cast herself at his feet, though that moment were to be her last.

Mr. Macneil concerted every thing with the utmost delicacy and honour. He provided an Italian, a woman of character, and of some rank, to be the companion of his *protégé* in her journey; he himself observed the strictest ceremony toward them, and attended them no more than was necessary for safety and indispensable accommodation; and he had the satisfaction to deliver this interesting female into the hands of her aged parent.

The reconciliation was easily made, and was scarcely more affecting to the parties themselves, than to the person who had been the happy means of their restoration to each other. Mr. Macneil became the declared lover of the lady he had rescued from slavery. Her marriage with her Italian seducer was speedily dissolved; and, fortunately, no child had been the issue of this ill-omened connection. Still, however, there was a difficulty. The beautiful penitent dwelt, with all the bitterness of remorse, upon her youthful offence, and a thousand times protested that, as she had rendered herself unworthy, she would never consent to become the wife of an honourable man. Beside which, she continually recollected with agony the cruel manner in which she had fled from an indulgent father, and almost broken his heart; and vowed that, so long as he lived, she would never again quit the paternal roof. These objections, the impassioned dictates of a well-constituted mind dwelling with exquisiteness upon an offence so early committed, and so exemplarily atoned, were at length got over; and, after eighteen months of struggle and sorrow, she gave her hand in second and happy marriage to the man of her father's choice, as well as of her own.

I know not whether this story will be found so striking in the repetition, as it was to me when I first heard it. But I felt an uncommon desire to visit the family which I heard thus described. My desire was increased by a conversation respecting the character of Mrs. Macneil, between two ladies, within the walls of one of the most elegant mansions on the lakes, at which I happened to be present. One of them was her opponent, and the other her admirer. The latter spoke, in terms of the highest applause, of the qualifications and accomplishments of the young ladies, her daughters.

This drew from the gentlewoman of severer temper a pathetic lamentation over their unfortunate situation. "No woman," she said, "who respected her own character, could afford them countenance; no man, who was not dead to all the decencies of human life, could offer them his hand in marriage. They were devoted to misery and dishonour by the very circumstance of their birth; and she held the father no less culpable in marrying a woman under Mrs. Macneil's unfortunate predicament, and making her the mother of his children, than if he had married a person on whom was entailed the most loathsome hereditary disease. What could be thought, as a matron, of a girl who at sixteen had run away with an Italian fiddler? How many clandestine provocatives to depravity must she have listened to from him, before she could have been prevailed upon to take so outrageous a step? When he had conveyed her into Italy, he introduced her to his own friends, and no doubt her principal associates *for two or three years* had been sharpers and prostitutes. The consequence was, that she impudently eloped with a stranger from the husband of her choice, as she had before eloped from her misguided father. Poor, wretched Miss Macneils, sealed to perdition! What lessons could they receive from such a mother, but lessons of debauchery! So impure a mind could not instil into them sentiments of virtue, if she would; and would not, if she could. She remembered," the gentlewoman added, "to have seen the young ladies at Kendal theatre: they were fine girls; the more was the pity!"[1]

---

1 Kendal is a town in Cumbria (formerly Westmorland).

The partisan of Mrs. Macneil put no less warmth into her reply, than her adversary had given to her invective. "She knew little of the lady herself, in consequence of the rules of society, by which she was excluded from the visiting circles of the neighbourhood. Once, however, she had chanced to be her fellow-traveller in a public vehicle from York to London; and she had heard much more of her, than she had then had an opportunity to observe. From every thing she had seen, and every thing she could collect, she was persuaded it was impossible for any thing in the form of a woman to exceed the present correctness of Mrs. Macneil's conversation and conduct. Why should it be supposed that an error committed before the age of sixteen could never be atoned? How much was a young person, at so immature an age, exposed to the stratagems and wiles of an experienced seducer! A better judge of morals than she could pretend to be, had pronounced, that deep and exemplary penitence for an unwary fault was a fuller security for rectitude than innocence itself.[1] Mrs. Macneil," her advocate added, "had been distinguished, when a child, for the strength of her judgment and the delicacy of her sentiments; once she had fallen; but she had speedily recovered; and malice itself could not discover a blemish in her since that period. Might she not, if her present character was such as it was represented, be a more perfect monitor for the young, in proportion as she understood more of the evils against which she warned them, and had felt the calamity?" The lady who maintained this side of the argument said, that she did not pretend to dispute the propriety of the rule by which Mrs. Macneil was given up almost exclusively to the society of the other sex, but added, that a humane judge would often drop a tear of pity over the severity of the sentence he was compelled to pronounce. Why, though Mrs. Macneil could never atone to the rules of established decorum, should we refuse to believe that she had atoned to God, and to the principles of rectitude? Why, though she was forbidden the society of her sex, should the same prohibition be extended to her daughters? Indeed, most of the ladies in the neighbourhood

---

1   Luke, chap. xv. ver. 7. [Godwin's note]

of the lakes had felt the propriety of the distinction, and had been eager to afford them every countenance in their power. She understood, from the most undoubted authority, that they were brought up with a refinement and rigidness of sentiment, in every point with which modesty was concerned, beyond what was furnished by any other living example of female education. Their father was the most faultless and unexceptionable in his habits, of any gentleman in all the northern counties; and, if propriety of character in young women could be secured by the diligence, discernment, and rectitude of both their parents, there were no persons of their age who bid fairer to be an ornament to their sex than the Miss Macneils.

All that I heard of Mr. Macneil and his family inspired in me the wish not to quit Westmorland till I had seen them. The father of the family was represented as extremely attached to his wife; and, as her unfortunate history rendered her liable to little slights and affronts, he shrunk from all intercourse with his provincial neighbours. He would not accept any privilege from the males of a house, which might only serve to remind him of the severe law dealt out to the partner of his life. He felt too intimately for her honour, her pleasures, and her pains, to be capable of being persuaded of the justice of the treatment she received. In truth, as I understood from the most exact information, it was no great sacrifice he made in giving up the conversation of his rural neighbours. He had resources enough in himself and the inmates of his own roof. They were far the most polished and elegant family, if politeness consists in intellectual refinement, in the circuit of the lakes. He had accumulated from the living society of men of genius, the materials and the principles of thinking. The young ladies excelled in the arts of music and design. The mother had paid dear for her progress in the former of these; but her progress was conspicuous. They frequently made little concerts under their own roof. They read together, and compared the impressions they received from, and the judgments they formed upon, what they read. They spent solitary hours enough in the sobriety of the morning, to inspire them with a zest for each other's society in the latter part of the day. Mr. Macneil, as I have said, had no object which he had at present so earnestly at heart as his children's improvement. He shut up, therefore, no knowledge, no tasteful feeling, no moral sentiment, no speculation or deduction which his sagacity inspired, in his own bosom. All his treasures of this sort were brought into the common stock. In this happy family there were no discordant opinions, no one ready to say, "This is rash; that is singular; this is contrary to the judgment of the world; you must learn to think like others, or you must expect to be disliked"; and thus to chill the opening blossoms of reflection and of mind. They needed not to be told, that he who is afraid to think unlike others, will soon learn, in every honourable sense of the word, not to think at all.

Mr. Macneil, after he had withdrawn from the conversation of the gentlemen of the neighbourhood, had found himself intruded upon by stragglers, whom the fashion of an excursion to the lakes had brought to his door. Some came with letters of recommendation, and some without. Some were induced by curiosity to see the friend of Jean Jacques Rousseau; and some to see the lady who had two husbands, both of them living. With the improper conduct and indelicacy of one or two of these wanderers, Mr. Macneil had been highly displeased. He had desired his friends to yield no more letters of introduction to the mere importunities of the idle. He saw no reason why he should suffer his time to be intruded upon, and his serenity to be ruffled, by the curiosity of indolent travellers who did not know how to dispose of themselves. The lady, the advocate of Mrs. Macneil, to whom I communicated my wish, did not fail therefore to assure me, that I should not gain entrance over the threshold of their house. This unfavourable prediction, perhaps, piqued me the more; and I sat down, and addressed the following letter to the gentleman whose acquaintance I was so desirous to obtain:—

"Sir,
"I have heard your character described in a way so peculiarly conformable to my notions and predilections, that I am desirous to be indulged with an hour of your conversation.
"You have been intruded upon, I am told, by the idle and

the frivolous; you are a lover of solitude; you are happy in the bosom of your family: these are the reasons which have been alleged to me, why I ought not to expect to obtain the favour I solicit. I shall at least weaken the objections which have been urged, if I can satisfy you that I am not of the class of the persons who have occasioned your displeasure.

"I am no curious man: what have I to be curious about? I am nearly forty-five years of age. I have seen the world, through all its gradations, and in most of the countries of Europe. In my youth I was a wild roe among the mountains of Wales: as I grew up, I entered upon the scenes of active life, foolishly, not criminally. I contracted an early distaste for the practices and the society of the world. I have lived much alone—I have not been happy. When I have gone into company, mere acquaintance have not interested me; a friend (a friend, in the perhaps romantic sense of the word) I never found. I am, no doubt, a very weak creature; I am not like Solomon's good man, 'satisfied from myself.'[1] Such is my history; am I one of those persons whose intrusion you would wish to forbid?

"Why am I desirous to pay one visit to the roof of Mr. Macneil? I know not whether the answer I can give to this question, will be or ought to be satisfactory. I am not idle enough to imagine that our interview will improve into acquaintance, far less into friendship. We dwell in different and remote parts of the island; we cannot be acquaintance. My habits and temper (it is a million chances to one) will not suit you; in those indescribable minutiae which do not affect the essentials of a character, but which make each man an individual by himself, and which divide you from the rest of your species, you will probably not be approved by me: we cannot be friends. What then? You are, I believe, a good and a wise man (two qualities much more inseparable than the world is willing to allow): I have found so few of these, as sometimes to be almost tempted to think that the race is growing extinct; and I would not willingly miss an opportunity of seeing so extraordinary a creature.

---

1 Perhaps alluding to Proverbs 14.

Your family is happy—(Oh, happiness! thou perpetual object of pursuit! always showing thyself in prospect! always cut off from our attainment by insurmountable precipices and impassable torrents!)—do not refuse me the sight of a happy family! I ask only for a transient and momentary pleasure! I ask only for something to stock my memory with—the recollection of which I may call up from time to time, and with the image of which I may gild my solitude!

"I am, Sir,

"Your very humble servant,

"Lowood Inn,   "CASIMIR FLEETWOOD
Ambleside."[1]   of Merionethshire."

CHAPTER XIII.

MY application had the desired issue. A polite answer was returned, expressing that Mr. Macneil would be happy to be favoured with my visit. I was the more flattered with this, as the lady to whom I had mentioned my desire, a woman of no common sagacity, had predicted a different event.

I hastened to make use of the privilege I had obtained. I found the house of Mr. Macneil uncommonly plain in its style, yet replete with every temperate convenience. The father of the family seemed to be upward of fifty years of age, and was tall, robust, and manly in his appearance. His hair was brown, short, and unpowdered; his ruddy cheek confessed that he was not negligent of the care of his fields, and that he had received in his constitution the reward of his care.[2] Mr. Macneil was a Scotchman. The brogue of every country is, perhaps, pleasing to the ear of sensibility, especially when it falls from the lips of a man of cultivation; it seems to assure us that simplicity and the native features of mind have not been eradicated. With me the Scottish dialect is somewhat a favourite; it softens and mellows

---

1 Town in Cumbria.
2 Following the example of the revolutionaries in France, British radicals wore their hair unpowdered to distinguish themselves from the aristocracy.

the sound of our island tongue; and the gravity which accompanies it, gives an air of sobriety and reflection to the speaker, which are particularly in accord with my serious disposition. It reminds us of the fields, and not of cities.

"I thank you for your visit," said Mr. Macneil, taking me by the hand. "Your letter is a masterly picture of your character. I know not what you have heard of me that made you desirous of seeing me; but I suspect that I, rather than you, shall be the gainer by the intercourse. I am no humourist, nor misanthrope, though circumstances have obliged me to be a little abrupt with some of the persons I have seen since I took up my residence here. I am a very plain man, and if you expect any thing else you will be disappointed."

I did not find Mr. Macneil what I should have called a very plain man, yet I do not blame him for his assertion. It would be best of all, if every man knew himself exactly for what he was, and announced himself accordingly. But this, alas! is impossible. Every one who does not think too humbly of his qualities, sets too high a value upon them. And how ridiculous a thing is self-importance—a fancied sovereign demanding a tax from his imaginary subjects, which they will never pay! False humility is, indeed, if not a more ridiculous, yet a more degrading error than arrogance. But every man who is aware of all the artifices of self-delusion, will rather set his demands below, than above, the true rate.

Among other subjects, we talked of the character of Rousseau. Mr. Macneil expressed himself with a veneration and a tenderness toward this extraordinary man, which I suppose were universally felt by all who approached him, except those who, thinking less of his weaknesses, and the indulgence they demanded, than of their own offended pride, finished by quarrelling with him.

"I saw much of Rousseau," said my host. "He reposed many confidences in me. He often told me that he felt less suspicious and embarrassed with me, than with almost any man he ever knew; and he asserted that the reason was, that I thought more of the subject discussed, and the scene before me, and less of how they would affect my own tranquillity and importance. I could see that one of his great misfortunes had been, that almost all his intimates were chosen from among the French, that nation of egotists! Rousseau was a man of exquisite sensibility, and that sensibility had been insulted and trifled with in innumerable instances, sometimes by the intolerance of priestcraft and power, sometimes by the wanton and ungenerous sports of men of letters. He lived, however, toward the close of his life in a world of his own, and saw nothing as it really was; nor were his mistakes less gross, than if he had asserted that his little cottage was menaced by a besieging army, and assailed with a battery of cannon. Whether from the displeasing events that had befallen him, or from any seeds of disease kneaded up in his original constitution, I was convinced, from a multitude of indications, that Rousseau was not in his sober mind. How much are those persons mistaken, who imagine that a madman is necessarily incapable of composing orations as ardent as those of Demosthenes, and odes as sublime as those of Pindar![1] How small a portion of the persons who, upon some topic or other, are unhinged in their intellectual comprehension, is it necessary to place under corporeal restraint! Yet I was often led to doubt whether Rousseau, spite of the disease under which he laboured, deserved, upon the whole, to be termed unfortunate. When he was induced to dwell for a time upon the universal combination which he believed to be formed against him, he then undoubtedly suffered. But he had such resources in his own mind! He could so wholly abstract himself from this painful contemplation; his vein of enthusiasm was so sublime; there was such a childlike simplicity often uppermost in his carriage; his gaiety upon certain occasions was so good-humoured, sportive, and unbroken! It was difficult for me to persuade myself that the person I saw at such times, was the same as at others was beset with such horrible visions." Mr. Macneil related to me several curious anecdotes in support of these observations.

The wife of my new acquaintance was one of the most accomplished and prepossessing women I ever beheld. I have

---

1 Demosthenes (383-322 BC), Greek orator and prose writer; Pindar (c. 522-440 BC), Greek lyric poet.

often remarked that this mixture and result of the manners and habits of different countries, particularly in the female sex, presents something exquisitely fascinating and delightful. She was never embarrassed, and never appeared to meditate how a thing was to be done, but did it with an ease, a simplicity, an unpretendingness, which threw every studied grace into contempt in the comparison. She had been humbled by the miscarriage of her early youth. But for this, her person and her accomplishments, the acknowledged sweetness of her temper and clearness of her understanding, might, perhaps, have made her proud, and thus have tarnished the genuine lustre of her excellencies. The modesty with which she presented herself was inexpressibly engaging. There was a cast of the Magdalene in all she did; not of the desponding, not of a temper deserting its duties, unconscious of recovered worth, or that invited insolence or contempt.[1] It was a manner that had something in it of timidity, yet could scarcely be said to amount to self-reproach; a manner, indeed, that, by the way in which it confessed her frailty, made reproach, either by look or gesture, from any other impossible. Her failings had chastised in her the pride of birth, and the assurance that superior attainments are apt to inspire, and had generated that temperance, moderation, and gentle firmness, which, wherever they are found, are the brightest ornaments of human nature.

The young ladies, whose merits I had heard so highly extolled, were three. Each of these had principally devoted herself to some particular accomplishment, in which, though not unskilled in other pursuits, she had made extraordinary progress. The eldest applied to the art of design; she drew, and even painted in oil; and her landscapes in particular had an excellence which, to speak moderately of them, reminded the beholder of the style of Claude Lorraine.[2] The principal apartment of the house was hung round with a series of the most striking scenes in the environs of the lakes, delineated by her

---

1 Referring to Mary Magdalene, the repentant prostitute who became a devoted disciple of Christ.
2 Claude Lorraine, originally Claude Gellée (1600-82), influential French landscape painter.

pencil. The second daughter had chosen music for her favourite pursuit; and her execution, both on the piano forte and in singing, was not inferior to that which her eldest sister had attained on canvass. The youngest was a gardener and botanist. She had laid out her father's grounds, and the style in which they were disposed did the highest credit to her imagination. One side of the family sitting-parlour was skirted with a greenhouse, of the same length as the room, and which seemed to make a part of it. This apartment was furnished with nearly every variety which Flora had ever produced in our island, or which curiosity has imported, and were entirely cultivated by her hand.[1] In her prosecution of the science of botany, she had also resorted to the use of colours; and, though the employment she made of them was inferior in kind to the studies of the eldest, it is almost impossible to conceive any thing superior to what she had reached, either in faithfulness of delineation, or brilliancy of tints.

The names of these young ladies were Amelia, Barbara, and Mary. The eldest had no pretensions to beauty, though there was an uncommon appearance of quick conception and penetrating judgment in the various turns of her countenance. Barbara was a brunette: her features were regular, her mouth was alluring, and her dark eyes flashed with meaning, and melted with tenderness. Mary had a complexion which, in point of fairness and transparency, could not be excelled: her blood absolutely spoke in her cheeks; the soft white of her hands and neck looked as if they would have melted away beneath your touch; her eyes were so animated, and her whole physiognomy so sensitive, that it was scarcely possible to believe that a thought could pass in her heart, which might not be read in her face.

I never saw a family that excited in me so much approbation. Individuals I had encountered of great worth and extraordinary qualifications; but here was a whole circle of persons, such as a man would wish to spend his life with: so much concord of affection without any jarring passions; so much harmo-

---

1 Flora was the Roman goddess of flowers and gardens.

ny of interests, yet each member of the family having a different pursuit. To me, who was prone to regard the whole world with an eye of censoriousness and displeasure, and who, having conceived this propensity, but too easily found materials to foster and nourish it, this was a ravishing spectacle. The father so well informed; the mother so interesting; the daughters so accomplished and so lovely! Mr. Macneil seemed to feel a kindness for me, proportioned to the gratification I experienced in my visit; and, after having pressed me to partake of their family fare, proposed a ride along the shores of the Windermere the next morning. The day following was occupied in a party on the lake; and thus, by insensible degrees, I became for a time almost an inmate in the family. I was so far advanced in life, as to preclude any idea of indecorum in my visits; and I addressed myself to the different members of the little commonwealth, as if I had been a brother to the master of the house, and an uncle to the daughters. I sat sometimes for hours by Amelia as she painted; I listened with unwearied attention to the lessons executed by Barbara: but my chief pleasure was in attending the gentle and engaging Mary, in her morning visits to her flowers, and in her walks among the avenues which had been constructed, and the bowers which had been planted under her direction.

CHAPTER XIV.

MR. Macneil was a man of the warmest philanthropy, and by degrees I reposed in him a confidence, to which I had seldom felt excited toward any other man. After a time, I hired apartments in the house of a substantial farmer in his neighbourhood, that I might the more freely enjoy his conversation and acquaintance, without being an interruption to the domestic economy of his family. I laid before him the secret grief that preyed upon my heart. I described the sickly sensibility of my temper, the early disgust I had taken at the world, and the miserable sense of desolation which preyed upon my life, in my detached and unconnected situation.

"Come," replied my friend, in that vein of playful good-humour which he delighted to indulge, "whether you consult me, as a good Catholic does his priest, for the salvation of his soul, or as an invalid does his physician, for the restoration of his health, let us try if we cannot make a conversion or a cure of it!"

Many were the debates that passed between me and my host respecting the true estimate of the human species. We differed, I suppose, first, because we had seen them under unlike circumstances, and in unlike aspects. We differed, secondly, because we compared them with different ideal standards. I thought, so to express myself, too highly of the human mind in the abstract, to be able to consider with patience man as he is. I dwelt upon the capacities of our nature, the researches of a Newton, the elevation of a Milton, and the virtues of an Alfred; and, having filled my mind with these, I contemplated even with horror, the ignorance, the brutality, the stupidity, the selfishness, and, as it appeared to me, the venality and profligacy, in which millions and millions of my fellow-creatures are involved.[1] I estimated mankind, with an eye to the goal which it is ardently to be desired they might reach; Mr. Macneil estimated them, with an eye to the starting-post from which they commenced their career.

"In every man that lives," he stoutly affirmed, "there is much to commend. Every man has in him the seeds of a good husband, a good father, and a sincere friend. You will say, perhaps, these are not sublime and magnificent virtues; yet, if each man were enabled to discharge these, the world upon the whole would afford a ravishing spectacle. What a spirit of forbearance, of gentle attentions, of anxiety to maintain the cheerfulness and peace of his female companion, inhabits every human breast! Scarcely do we hear of the monster in whom this spirit is ever extinguished. It accompanies almost all men, with whatever unhappy interruptions, from maturity to the grave. Look upon the poorest clown in the midst of his children; what a heavenly

---

1 Sir Isaac Newton (1642-1727), English philosopher, mathematician and astronomer; John Milton (1608-74), English poet; Alfred "the Great" (848?-899), King of the West Saxons from 871.

picture! How do his eyes glisten at their little pleasures, their sallies of penetration and vivacity! How disinterested a sentiment burns in his heart! Yes, disinterested: for I know you will laugh at the silly sophism which, when it regards the immense sacrifices that every father is ready to make for his child, calls the impulse from which they spring a selfish one. I acknowledge, I am weak enough to be as much delighted with the spectacle of the lively and ardent affection of an Englishman to his son, as if it were directed toward the child of a Japanese. It is equally affection, and equally beneficent. How much good neighbourhood there is in the world! what readiness in every man to assist every stranger that comes in his way, if his carriage is broken down, if his horse has run from and left him, or almost whatever is his distress! how cheerfully does he give his day's labour, or the produce of his day's labour, to his friend, till that friend, by injustice, has proved himself unworthy of the kindness! For my part, instead of joining in the prevailing cry of the selfishness, the wickedness, the original sin, or the subsequent depravity of mankind, I feel my heart swell within me, when I recollect that I belong to a species, almost every individual of which is endowed with angelic virtues. I am a philanthropist, in the plain sense of the word. Whenever I see a man I see something to love,—not with a love of compassion, but a love of approbation. I need not put the question to him—I know without asking, that he is fully prepared and eager to do a thousand virtuous acts, the moment the occasion is afforded him.

"I have sometimes had the thought," continued Mr. Macneil, "of composing a little novel or tale in illustration of my position. I would take such a man, as my friend Fleetwood, for example, who looks with a disdainful eye upon his species, and has scarcely the patience to enter into discourse and intercourse with any one he meets: I would put him on board a ship; he will, of course, be sufficiently disgusted with every one of his companions: all of a sudden I would raise a most furious tempest: I would cause him to be shipwrecked on a desert island, with no companion but one man, the most gross, perverse, and stupid of the crew: all the rest—the captain who, though sagacious, was positive, the surgeon who, though skilful, was tiresome by his pedantry—I would without mercy send to the bottom. What do you think I would represent as the natural result of this situation? My fastidious misanthrope would no longer have a world or a nation, from which to choose his companion, and, after trying all, to reject all: he would be wholly deprived of the power of choice. Here, sir, I would show how by degrees he would find a thousand resources in this despised sailor. He would find him active, spirited, and alert. Where before he believed, without examination, that all was stupefaction, he would find, by a variety of tokens, good sense and sagacity. How these two companions would love one another! How they would occasionally spend the livelong night in delightful chat! How they would study each other's virtues and attainments—even each other's foibles! With what eager anxiety, when any necessary occasion separated them, would they look for each other's return! With what daring and superhuman courage would they defend each other from danger! ——And do not be perverse enough to believe that all this anxiety would be the fruit of selfishness! They would have discovered in each other inestimable qualities, a large stock of sound judgment and excellent sense, and an inexhaustible fund of kind and benevolent propensities. After some years I would bring back my misanthrope to England. Sir, he would never be able to part with his companion in the desert island. He would believe that there was not a creature in the world, take him for all in all, so valuable. Yet observe, he would only entertain this opinion of him, because he knew him more thoroughly than any of the rest of his species. I took my sailor merely as a specimen of human nature, and of human nature in one of its most unfavourable forms."

I hope my reader will be convinced by the arguments of Mr. Macneil. What a blessed state of mind was that, to which he appears to have attained! Yet, for myself, I acknowledge, either because truth was on my side, or, it may be, merely from the excessive susceptibleness of my nature, or the accidents of my life, I remained unaltered by his discourses, and, though I wished to be a philanthropist, was a misanthrope still.

CHAPTER XV.

"WHAT I have been yet saying," continued Macneil, "is speculation; let us now come to the most important part of my function, which is practice. Fleetwood, you are too much alone. I hear people talk of the raptures of solitude; and with what tenderness of affection they can love a tree, a rivulet, or a mountain. Believe me, they are pretenders; they deceive themselves, or they seek, with their eyes open, to impose upon others. In addition to their trees and their mountains, I will give them the whole brute creation; still it will not do. There is a principle in the heart of man which demands the society of his like. He that has no such society, is in a state but one degree removed from insanity. He pines for an ear into which he might pour the story of his thoughts, for an eye that shall flash upon him with responsive intelligence, for a face the lines of which shall talk to him in dumb but eloquent discourse, for a heart that shall beat in unison with his own. If there is any thing in human form that does not feel these wants, that thing is not to be counted in the file for a man: the form it bears is a deception; and the legend, Man, which you read in its front, is a lie. Talk to me of rivers and mountains! I venerate the grand and beautiful exhibitions and shapes of nature, no man more; I delight in solitude; I could shut myself up in it for successive days. But I know that Christ did not with more alacrity come out of the wilderness after his forty days' sequestration, than every man, at the end of a course of this sort, will seek for the interchange of sentiments and language.[1] The magnificence of nature, after a time, will produce much the same effect upon him, as if I were to set down a hungry man to a sumptuous service of plate, where all that presented itself on every side was massy silver and burnished gold, but there was no food.

"He is a wise physician, that knows how to prescribe for his own malady. Were the case you have described to me, the case of a bystander, you would immediately see into its merits as clearly as I do. You have no certain and regular pursuit; you

---

1 See Matthew 4:2 and Luke 4:2.

have no equal alliances and connections. The miracle would be, if it were possible for you to be happy. You are too rich to be able to engage with sincere eagerness in any undertaking or employment. The remedy, therefore, in your case must be derived from the other quarter. Marry! Beget yourself a family of children! You are somewhat advanced in life; time must elapse before your children will be at an age to occupy much of your cares; if you feel any vacuity in the interval, call about you your distant relations! Sit down every day at table with a circle of five or six persons, constituting your own domestic group. Enquire out the young men on the threshold of life, who, from the regulations of society, have the best claim upon your assistance. Call them round you; contribute to their means; contribute to their improvement; consult with them as to the most promising adventure in which they can launch themselves on the ocean of life. Depend upon it, you will not then feel a vacuity; your mind will no longer prey upon itself."

I was some time before I could believe that my friend was in earnest.—"I, to entangle myself with a numerous family, whose temper was so fastidious and sensitive that I could scarcely choose a companion for a day that did not become in twenty ways disgusting and insupportable to me before the close of the day!

"I, to marry! Had I not now passed the flower of my days in a state of celibacy? Whom was I to marry? I was near forty-five years of age. Was I to make what is called a suitable match; that is, marry a woman of the same age as myself? Beside that there would then be small chance of offspring, I could not say I felt in myself much propensity to fall in love with a lady of this staid and matronly age.

"Add to all this, I am impressed with no favourable prepossessions toward the female sex. I cannot be blind enough to credit what some have maintained, probably more from the love of paradox than any other cause, that there is any parity between the sexes. Till the softer sex has produced a Bacon, a Newton, a Homer, or a Shakspeare, I never will believe it.[1]

---

1 Francis Bacon (1561-1626), English statesman and philosopher.

Who does not see that the quickness and vivacity of their temper sets them at an immense distance from profound sense, sublime feeling, and that grand species of adventure, which engrosses, from puberty to the grave, the whole energies of the human soul? But, beside this, I think ill of their dispositions. The impressions of my adventures of gallantry in France I cannot overcome. Perhaps, in the tranquillity of sober discussion, you might bring me to confess that these impressions are unjust; but there they are; such are the associations of my mind; I never can think seriously of a woman, still less propose her to myself as a companion, without calling to mind the Marchioness de L—— and the Countess of B——.

"I have another disqualification for marriage worse even than this. I am grown old in the habits of a bachelor. I can bear no restraint. You, sir, happy as you are in your family, must be fully aware that it is impossible for two persons to associate for a day without some clash of their different inclinations. It is like hounds in a leash; the chain is upon their necks, and not upon their wills. But we bear this wonderfully well for a time, because we see where it will end; most men bear it better than I do. But let the chain be such, the padlock of which cannot be unloosened but by the death of one party or the other; Gods, how galling does it become! In an 'agreeable companion in a post-chaise,' in the guest that visits, or the host that receives me for a day, though his desires are absurd, though his manner be abrupt, and his sentiments dissimilar to my own, I am too proud to suffer my temper to be much ruffled by so fugitive an inconvenience.[1] But how trifles swell into importance when the individual whose temper jars with mine is to live with me for ever! Whatever offends me I feel as in the utmost degree grave; every accidental difference preys upon my heart, and corrodes my vitals."

Mr. Macneil laughed at the vehemence of my satire against marriage. "No," said he, "I do not absolutely insist that you shall

---

1 According to James Boswell in his *Life of Johnson* (1791), Samuel Johnson said, "If I had no duties, and no reference to futurity, I would spend my life in driving briskly in a post-chaise with a pretty woman; but she should be one who could understand me, and would add something to the conversation" (19 September 1777).

fix upon a lady of forty-five years of age, or that you shall estimate her fitness to become your wife by the wrinkles in her brow. The man may love the wife at forty-five, whom, twenty years before, he received a blushing virgin to his bed; habit may do much for him; a friendship has gradually sprung up between them, which death only is powerful enough to dissolve; but this is not exactly the period at which the familiarity should commence. No; if you marry, Fleetwood, choose a girl whom no disappointments have soured, and no misfortunes have bent to the earth; let her be lively, gay as the morning, and smiling as the day. If your habits are somewhat rooted and obstinate, take care that there is no responsive stiffness in her to jar and shock with. Let her be all pliancy, accommodation, and good humour. Form her to your mind; educate her yourself. By thus grafting a young shoot upon your venerable trunk, you will obtain, as it were, a new hold upon life. You will be another creature; new views, new desires, new thoughts, will rise within you. While you are anxious to please and sympathise with your beauteous bride, you will feel as alert as a boy, and as free and rapid in your conceptions as a stripling.

"You will tell me, perhaps, that you could not make such a young creature happy. I differ from you in that. Women are not like us in their tastes. A lady, as you say, past the meridian of life, will seldom be courted for a bride, unless with some sinister view; but at least half the young girls you meet with would be well contented with a husband considerably older than themselves. Man marries because he desires a lovely and soothing companion for his vacant hours; woman marries, because she feels the want of a protector, a guardian, a guide, and an oracle, some one to look up to with respect, and in whose judgment and direction she may securely confide. Besides, Fleetwood, you mistake yourself if you think you are old. Your visage is not wrinkled, and your hair is not grey. The activity of your temper, the many plans of life you have tried, your perpetual change of place, have effectually preserved you from that running down of the wheels of fancy, that decay of the principle of life, which should render you an unfit companion for a blooming bride.

"You allege, that your temper, which is so fastidious and sensitive, that you can seldom support the companion of a day, is a cause that would reduce you to make an ill figure, in a domestic circle, with five or six individuals who sat down with you every day to table. Alas! Fleetwood, this is the very thing you want, the cause why your temper is so blameably fastidious. The horse, however generous his blood, and graceful his limbs, who has never learned certain paces, and had his temper subdued to the intimations of the bridle, will never be victor in the race. Subject yourself to the law of associating with your fellow-men, place yourself in the situation to be the guardian and benefactor of your consort and kindred, and you will soon feel and bend to the necessity of consulting their predilections as well as your own. You will be a million times the better and the happier for it.

"But the main error into which you have fallen, is to suppose that the way of living between a man and his wife, bears any resemblance to that with a chance companion in a post-chaise, or between an ordinary host and his guest. The first principle of society in this relation, if it is actuated with any spirit of kindness, is the desire each party feels to be the sacrifice of the other. Instead of regretting the unavoidable differences of inclination, they become, where the topics to which they relate are not fundamental, an additional source of pleasure. Each party is eager to anticipate the desires of the other, to smooth the way to their gratification, to provide for their happiness. If, between a pair thus kind and thus wise, any little debates chance to arise, this, too, adds to their enjoyment. You know the proverb which says, 'The falling out of lovers is the renewal of love.' Between man and man differences are gravely discussed and argumentatively settled. Each revises the imaginary brief of his own cause, and becomes confirmed in his private view of the question at issue. But, between man and woman, the smile which unexpectedly displaces the clouded brow, is the symbol of peace. Arguments are thrust away by hundreds, like beggars from the façade of a palace. The party most in the right mourns over this degrading advantage. The party most in the wrong confesses the error incurred with so ingenuous a grace, as to make error look as if it gave new improvement and finishing to a character.—Marry, Fleetwood! If you live, marry! You know nothing of happiness if you do not! You are as ignorant of the true zest of human life, as the oak which at this moment over-canopies us with its branches!"

Such were the advices of the intelligent and kind-hearted friend I had thus accidentally acquired. They made a strong impression upon me. I know not whether the impression would have been so forcible, had the circumstances under which the advice was given been different. But the reader must recollect that it was addressed to me in the midst of an amiable family, the children of which were daughters. While Macneil was earnest in describing the sort of wife he would recommend to me, I thought of these accomplished young women: when we returned home from the walk or ride which these discussions had occupied, I looked round upon the circle, with different emotions from those which had previously accompanied the spectacle: could it be otherwise? I have already said that the junior of the three particularly engaged my attention: I now caught myself repeatedly in my solitude uttering the involuntary exclamation, "Mary, if ever I marry, it is thou that shalt be my bride!"

The conversations between me and my host, the sense of which I have thus compressed, occupied many successive excursions. One day, when Macneil was most deeply engaged in the argument, I turned suddenly upon him, and cried out somewhat gaily, "Now, my friend, shall I try whether you are in earnest in all this declamation? If such a marriage as you describe is desirable for me, it will be no less desirable for the woman I shall choose; one of the parties in wedlock cannot be happy alone. You say, I should choose a young person, a person of pleasing manners, and a cultivated mind: where can I verify this description so truly as by your fire-side? Will you give me one of your daughters?"

My friend paused. "A question like this compels one to be serious indeed.—But——you have no grave meaning in proposing the interrogatory?"

"I cannot tell. Your arguments have made me think: I do not say they have converted me. Macneil, I do not wish to trifle with you: if my question touches you too nearly, I dispense you from a reply."

"No; the question has been asked, and it shall be answered. Only, as I by no means wish to restrain you, by treating your question as a proposal, so I must request you in return to consider my answer, as belonging merely to an abstract illustration, as a logical experiment to try the soundness of my recommendation. I should be as much to blame in violating the modesty and maiden dignity of my children, as in imposing fetters of any sort on the freedom of your deliberations."

"Agreed! Nothing can be more reasonable."

"Well, then; I have no objection to your person, your family, your fortune, your understanding, your accomplishments, not even to your age. But then as to your temper——"

"Ay, there is the point!"

"What a strange thing is advice! How difficult is it to put one's self exactly in the place of another? How hard, to be sure that the advice we give, is exactly that which we should think reasonable, could we change persons with the man upon whom we are so ready to obtrude it? Fleetwood, I swear that I am your friend: I swear that the project I urged upon you, was urged in the sincerity of my heart."

"*Io, triumphe!*[1] I see, I shall die a bachelor!"——Shall I confess my secret weakness? My *Io, triumphe*, was uttered with a heavy heart. The lovely Mary had gained a station in my bosom, from which I felt I could with difficulty dislodge her.

"I love my children; you, all the world, would despise me if I did not. It is so difficult to judge for a child, conscious of unripened discernment, and relying on my superior penetration and experience, or by whom, if this reliance is not placed, it clearly ought to be! I could cheerfully commit my own happiness to the lottery of human affairs, but thus to dispose of the little all of one's daughter, is a fearful responsibility!

---

1 The traditional cry of Roman soldiers when they followed a victorious general in the public celebration of his triumph.

"Yet, after all, this responsibility I must encounter. If my daughter marries a wise man or a fool, a prodigal or an economist, an honest man or a knave, and it is done with my approbation, it must alike happen that I may consider myself as the author of her happiness or her misery.

"Well then, Fleetwood, I confess, that the woman who marries you, will engage in a considerable risk. But, God knows, all marriage is a risk—is the deepest game that can be played in this sublunary scene. You say true, that your risk will not be less, than that of the dame who accepts your hand. Yet I adhere to my advice, 'Marry!' or, which is, indeed, merely dressing that advice in another guise, 'Fleetwood, take the child of my bosom! win her partiality and kindness; my approbation waits on her preference!'

"By this question, however, which, as I said, I have answered merely under the notion of a logical experiment, you have brought to my recollection a part of the subject, which, before, I ought not to have forgotten; and I thank you for it. If you should ever feel seriously disposed to adopt my recommendation, let it not be done lightly and unadvisedly. Consider it as the most important transaction of your life. Consider that not merely your own happiness, but that of the woman who has consented to embark hers under your protection, the virtue and respectability of your possible offspring, and the peace of the venerable parents who have resigned her to your discretion, are at stake upon the due regulation of your temper. Here, indeed, lies the great difference between your present condition, and that which I have been chalking out for you. Independent and sole as you now stand, you find yourself answerable to none: you can discard your servants when you please; you can break off with your acquaintance; and you need scarcely deign to ask yourself, 'Was I in fault?' But you cannot so break off from the ties of affinity and blood. Believe me, too much independence is not good for man. It conduces neither to his virtue, nor his happiness. The discipline which arises out of the domestic charities, has an admirable tendency to make man, individually considered, what man ought to be. I do not think you, Fleetwood, worse than your neighbours. You are an honest and a just man, with sense enough to discern the right, and courage enough to pursue it. If you are now wayward, and peevish, and indolent, and hypochondriacal, it is because you weakly hover on the outside of the pale of human society, instead of gallantly entering yourself in the ranks, and becoming one of the great congregation of man."

It was in such conversation that Macneil and I passed our time in our excursions on the banks of the Windermere. With what delight did I recollect this happy interval of my life! Ruffigny and Macneil were the only two men I ever knew, the clearness of whose thinking was an ever fresh source of delight; and the generosity of whose souls, enlightening their discourse, made their face occasionally look as if it had been the face of an angel. But in the society of Macneil my happiness was even purer than in that of my father's friend. Ruffigny, gallant, noble-hearted mortal as he was, stood alone; my intercourse with him was a perpetual *tête-à-tête*, and had too much of monotony and uniformity for the unsatisfied cravings of the human mind; but to return home with Macneil, after a morning's temperate and sober discussion, and to see him surrounded with his blameless wife and accomplished daughters, what could the heart of man look for more? Add to which, I was occupied with the new sensations which agitated my bosom for the charming Mary. While I talked with her, I forgot my prejudices against her sex; the Marchioness de L——— and the Countess of B——— seemed daily more and more to become the shadow of a dream; her conversation was so inexpressibly ingenuous, and her sallies so artless, that, in spite of my preconceptions, she stole away my heart. Her delight was in flowers; and she seemed like one of the beauties of her own parterre, soft, and smooth, and brilliant, and fragrant, and unsullied.

CHAPTER XVI.

WHY did these days of yet unexperienced delight pass so quickly away? Mr. Macneil, before I knew him, had determined to pass over with his family to Italy, with the intention of spending the remainder of his days there. He had a friend in the Milanese with whom he had contracted the strictest bonds of intimacy, and who had often pressed him to take up his residence in his neighbourhood; he was promised that circle of female associates and acquaintance, which was denied to Mrs. Macneil in England; and this, though the admirable matron could have dispensed with it for herself without repining, he judged to be an advantage of the first importance to his daughters. Having formed a project of this sort, he had proceeded so far as to have settled to dispose of all his property in England, and to vest his fortune in lands to be purchased on the spot of his destined abode. The affairs which related to this intended transplantation had already detained the family in England longer than they wished; and I agreed to purchase the Westmorland estate, rather to facilitate the projects of my friend, than with any intention to take up my residence in this part of the island. The property was transmitted, and lodged in the hands of a banker at Genoa; and Mr. Macneil determined to take his passage by sea, from Falmouth, for that city. The adventurers in this voyage were Mr. Macneil, his wife, and his two eldest daughters; the youngest was to remain, at least till the next season, upon a visit to a family, who, in the winter, resided in London, and during the summer, upon their estate in Gloucestershire.

Every thing being prepared for the journey, the whole establishment removed from the Windermere, and set out for Falmouth; I myself, as well as the charming cadette,[1] making part of the escort. I shall not dwell upon the particulars of a tour, stretching almost from one extremity of the kingdom to another; we reached the celebrated and commodious port from which my friends were to take their passage. Here we spent a period of seven or eight days, which was rendered so much the more interesting to me, as I knew not whether I should ever meet this amiable family again, and as it seemed to be at the mercy of the winds whether almost every hour of our intercourse should be the last.

---

1   The youngest daughter.

The day after our arrival, Macneil and myself took an excursion on the sea coast and among the cliffs, to explore the beauties of this delicious country. Previously to our quitting the borders of the lakes, I had come to a more precise explanation with my friend, of the thoughts I entertained respecting his youngest daughter. The removal, which was impending, had brought on somewhat the more hastily the communication of my views. I fairly confessed that the married life was now much in my thoughts; and I owned that the eyes of Mary had, perhaps, contributed more to my conversion, than the arguments of her father. My friend asked me, if I had ever opened myself to her on the subject, or was informed of the state of her inclination toward me?

I owned I had not. The subject was in itself so interesting, and was so new to my thoughts, that, whenever the impulse of confessing my partiality had presented itself to me, it had always brought with it such a palpitation of the heart, and tremulousness of voice, as had compelled me for the time to desist from my purpose. Nor could there ever, in my mind, be sufficient reason for an early declaration, except where the parties were so circumstanced, that they could not otherwise have the opportunity of a protracted intercourse, and a more minute acquaintance with each other's qualifications and temper. Was it not much more gratifying to a delicate mind, by silent attentions to steal away the soul, and to observe the gradual demonstrations of kindness in a mistress, growing up unconsciously to herself, than by an abrupt question to compel her to check or to anticipate the progress of sentiment?

Should I own the truth? Whenever I meditated the proposing of the question, I was immediately beset in two ways with the passion of fear. I feared to be refused: else why did I put the question? I also feared to be accepted: perhaps no ingenuous mind, not yet lost to a serious anticipation of the future, could be free from that fear. It was a question of so deep a stake, to both the parties to whom it related! The man who was about to form it, could scarcely help recollecting on the verge, "Now I am free; I am master of my own actions and of my plans of life: before the clock shall strike again, it may be I shall be bound by the sacred ties of honour, and the fate of my future life will be at the disposal of another!" The season of courtship is, at least to the man who has outlived the first heyday of his boiling blood, a season of probation; it is the business of either party to study the other, and in each interview distinctly to enquire, "Is this the person with whom I ought to embark in the voyage of life?" Every species of promise, express or implicit, ought to be kept back, that he may preserve, as long as possible, the healthful and genuine character of the scene in which he is engaged.

"Farewell," said Macneil, in the close of the interesting conversation in which we were engaged. "I leave my daughter behind me; and I may say, I leave her in your protection. The family with which she is to spend the winter are very good sort of people; but they are people of fashion, and without hearts. No man knows any thing amiss of them; they are correct in their methods of acting, and punctual in their payments; I feel satisfied that nothing amiss can happen to my daughter while she is an inmate of their house. But it is to your sentiments, as a man of worth and honour, that I confide her. I believe she approves of you; I think she will accept of your tender, if you shall judge proper to make it. In this, it is of course as much your desire, as it is mine, that she should be free. Fleetwood, it is a very deep and solemn confidence that I repose in you. If you marry my daughter, you must be to her, father, and mother, and sisters, and all the world in one. If you are unjust to her, she will have no one to whom to appeal. If you are capricious, and rigorous, and unreasonable, she will be your prisoner!"

This pathetic appeal from the father of her I loved, suddenly filled my eyes with a gush of tears. I eagerly pressed his hand. "Macneil," said I, "I will never be unjust to your daughter; she shall never find me capricious, or rigorous, or unreasonable. I swear to you, that I will be such a husband as the most tender of fathers would choose for his daughter!"—It will be seen how I kept my oath.

After the interval of a few days we parted. I will not repeat here what Mrs. Macneil said to me concerning her child, as that would be to go over again in substance what had been already said by the father. This accomplished woman never appeared so amiable to me as during our short residence at Falmouth. She had as much right, perhaps more, than her husband, to urge upon me the justice I should owe to the lovely Mary. Never had any mother more affectionately or more diligently discharged the duties of a parent; never was mother more amply qualified to discharge them.

I, and Mary, and one of the daughters of the family with whom Mary was invited to visit, attended the rest of the party in a boat, to the side of the vessel in which they embarked for Genoa. We went with them on board the ship, and spent still two hours more in their company. Never was a family so equally or so strongly inspired with love for each other, as the group before me.

"Why am I not going with you?" said Mary.

"Do not talk of that," replied the mother; "we shall else never be able to leave you behind."

CHAPTER XVII.

I ATTENDED on horseback the chaise which conveyed Mary, and the young lady, her companion, to London. Having fixed her there, I was obliged to set out on an excursion of a few weeks into Wales, to inspect some affairs which required my presence. It was on the twentieth of September that the Macneils sailed from England; and the weather had proved squally and uncertain almost from the hour we parted. On that day week from the time we quitted Falmouth, I slept at Shrewsbury and never in my life do I recollect a night so tremendously stormy. My thoughts were of course wholly on the Romney, the vessel on board which these dear friends were embarked. I could not refrain from anticipating every thing dreadful. How curiously is the human mind affected by circumstances! I have often listened to a storm, without almost recollecting that the globe of earth contained the element of water within its frame; I have felt entranced with the hollow sound, and the furious blasts, that sung round and shook the roof that sheltered me; I have got astride in imagination upon the horses of the element, and plunged with fearful delight into the vast abyss. Now every blast of wind went to my soul. Every thought was crowded with dismal images of piercing shrieks, of cracking masts, of the last despair, of dying clasps, and a watery grave. It is in vain to endeavour to give an idea of what, this night, I endured. It was not fancy or loose conjecture; it was firm persuasion; I saw my friends perish; when the morning dawned, I rose with a perfect conviction that they were no more.

So deep was the suffering I endured, that I had not spirit the next morning to leave Shrewsbury, and proceed on my destined journey. I could think of nothing but the sad fate of Macneil, and affairs of business appeared wholly unworthy of attention. What a long and melancholy day did it seem! A calm had succeeded; the sun shone, and nature was cheerful; to what purpose? The sun no longer shone on Macneil!—By the evening, however, the monotony of rest became more intolerable to me than travelling; I ordered a chaise; I drove all night; and in the morning arrived at my paternal abode.

The day after my arrival I received a letter from my adored Mary. The sole topic of the letter was the storm of the twenty-seventh. She wrote in broken sentences, with grief, with terror, with distraction. "My all," said she, "is embarked in one adventure! father, mother, sisters! What infatuation prevailed upon me to separate myself from them? It is a crime no less deep and terrible than parricide! What shall I do alone in the world? Ye wild and raging winds! Ye merciless and all-devouring waves! Ye have made me tenfold a vagabond and a beggar upon the earth! The remembrance of last Saturday is distraction to me! Would that total distraction, would come and drive all remembrance from my brain for ever!" She continued in a style no less incoherent, and seemed to be as fully impressed as myself, with the conviction that the late storm had proved fatal to her whole family.

I no sooner read the letter of Mary, than I lost no time in setting out for London, that I might afford her every consolation in my power. It was particularly since this fatal prognostic had struck her, that she felt how forlorn was her situation in the family where she resided.

She had met one of the daughters upon a visit in Stafford-shire; they two had been the only individuals of the party, who had not reached a demure and sober age; and for a month they had been sole companions to each other. They had sung and danced to each other; they had strolled through the meadows and reclined in the shade together; Mary had instructed her friend in botany, and her friend had been eager to learn, because she was told that botany was a fashionable accomplish-ment; she had, in return, been copious and animated in her description of the town amusements. All this ended in the two young ladies, with that ardour and levity which is perhaps inseparable from youth, swearing to each other an everlasting friendship. Mary was a total stranger to every member of the family, except this young lady; and the seniors complied in this point with their daughter's wishes, in inviting the youngest Miss Macneil to pass the winter with them. Mr. Macneil wished, for my sake, to leave Mary in England, and easily turned the balance of her mind toward accepting the invita-tion.

For the first two or three days Mary had been delighted with the metropolis; and, no doubt, would have continued to be delighted for as many months, had not anxiety for the safety of her family gradually driven all other thoughts out of her mind.

At first she had conceived of a voyage by sea no otherwise than of a journey by land: her father had been a great traveller; her mother had been in Italy; yet tempests and shipwrecks had made no part of the little histories she had heard them relate of their past adventures. The ocean occupied no distinct region of her fancy: she had devoted no part of her thoughts to meditate the natural history of the world of waters. In the past years of her life she had had no interest, giving to her ideas that particu-lar direction; she had committed no rich freightage to the mercy of the unfaithful element. Now the case was altered. She had parted with her friends in a gentle and prosperous gale; but the late squally weather had given being and substance in her mind to the phenomena of the sea. What occupied her thoughts became the theme of her tongue; but she soon found that her fashionable friend lent an idle ear to the monotonous topic. Miss Matilda Rancliffe was what is well expressed by the phrase, a fair-weather friend; she loved no dismals; her step was airy; the tone of her voice was frolic and cheerful; and she owned that her sensibilities were so overpowering, as to make the impulse in her to fly from the presence of distress irresistible.

The servant at Mr. Rancliffe's showed me into the drawing-room, where the whole family, with one or two visiters, was assembled. Every one was cheerful and amused; the young ladies were busy talking of a party of pleasure, and anticipating the happiness they should reap from it. I looked round the circle and could not at first discover the object of my search. The poor Mary had withdrawn into a corner, neglecting all, and by all neglected. Her cheeks were pale; her eyes were sunk; her attitude was the attitude of despair. As soon as she saw me, she hastened to me, and led me into another room.

"Oh, sir," said she, "tell me all that you know, and all that you can guess respecting my poor father and mother. You, Mr. Fleetwood, are acquainted with these things; you, no doubt, have witnessed storms at sea, and know the different coasts near which they were to pass in their voyage. Are there any hopes? Whereabout was the vessel likely to be when the storm came on? Was there ever so dreadful a tempest?" I endeavoured to encourage the unhappy orphan; I sought to inspire courage, with as much skill as it could be communicated by one who had not a spark of hope existing in his mind.

"And how, Mary," said I, "do you find yourself situated in this worthy family?" "Ah, Mr. Fleetwood," replied she, with a desponding voice, "this is a sad place for me! As long as I was gay, and could join in their amusements, we went on well enough; I was a sort of favourite. But now that my heart sinks within me, nobody cares for me; they are glad to pass me by, and crowd together in a laughing knot, at the most distant part of the room. This whole family,—father, mother, brothers, sisters,—seem to live only for amusement. What a situation for me, who have spent my whole life in a family of love?—a family, where no individual could suffer, without exciting the liveliest anxieties, and the tenderest attentions, in all the rest?"

A month longer elapsed, before we had any intelligence of the fate of the Romney. During this period, my visits to the amiable forlorn were unintermitted. If Mary had before conceived a nascent partiality to me, it now became much stronger. The sight of me was the only pleasure the day afforded. The contrast between my sympathy and affection, and the indifference of the Rancliffes was extreme. Into my bosom only could she pour her sorrows; in my eye alone did she meet the expression of humanity. On my part, the situation was no less favourable to the growth of attachment. The sweet and affectionate disposition of Mary was conspicuous. Her desolate situation rendered her tenfold more interesting. I now felt, for the first time in my life, how delightful a task it is to console distress, when the sufferer is a woman, beautiful and young. At the proper hour I always flew to the presence of my charming ward with the most eager impatience. In general, when the mind is engaged in the performance of virtuous actions, one of the sentiments which most palpably offers itself is an honest pride. It was not pride that I felt on the present occasion. My mind was too much softened to be able to entertain so erect and prosperous a passion. There was something deliciously languid in the tone of my spirits; it was sadness, but a sadness not without its gratifications. Sorrow brings two generous hearts nearer to each other than joy. I was astonished, when I reflected on the ignorance in which I had lived of the most delicious emotions of the human breast, and how near I had been to going to the grave without once participating what is most precious and excellent in the life of man.

The melancholy news at length reached us, which with so pure a foresight we had anticipated. The vessel in which the family of my beloved had embarked, was tossed several days in the Bay of Biscay, and at length dashed to pieces near Cape Finisterre, upon the iron-fronted coast of the province of Galicia.[1] The captain only, and a few of the officers and sailors, were saved in the long-boat. They had proffered to receive two of the passengers into the boat. But this kindred of love refused to

---

1 Cape Finisterre is found at the tip of the most western peninsula in France; Galicia is a former kingdom in northwest Spain.

be separated; they could not endure to cast lots upon their lives; and, rather than submit to so dire an extremity, father, mother, and daughters preferred to perish together. How painfully are we apt to reflect afterward upon a project such as this of the voyage to Italy, as partaking of the nature of suicide! If the Macneils had been content to live in England, they might have enjoyed many years of pleasure, and have been long an ornament and advantage to their species. I never from this hour recollected the scene of their embarkation, without figuring them to myself as so many victims, robed in white, and crowned with chaplets, marching along the beach, as to be sacrificed.

When the melancholy event was ascertained, it was no longer possible for Mary to continue in the family of the Rancliffes. She hired a lodging to which she retired, with only one humble female friend to accompany her. The family, who politely dismissed her, condoled with her upon her misfortune. It is impossible to conceive any thing more hard and unfeeling, than the condolences which politeness extorts on so terrible an occasion. If a man could observe, from a place of safety, the roarings of a tiger, as he tore the palpitating limbs of his own brother, they would scarcely jar more painfully on the sense. The adieux of the Rancliffes said but too plainly, "As soon as we have shut the door on you and your woes, we purpose to forget that there is any such being in the world."

CHAPTER XVIII.

I was now poor Mary's only visiter. I shall not undertake to detail the progress of our amour under these tragical circumstances. For a long time, though our courtship substantially proceeded, no word of love, or hope, or of prospect to the future, fell from my lips. If I had attempted to utter such a word, I should have felt it like sacrilege; and I am sure the pure and affectionate heart of Mary would have sustained such a shock as must ultimately have proved a bar to our union for ever. No; she regarded me merely as a zealous guardian, and a faithful protector. She saw in me her father's friend; and, as I seemed busy in performing the functions of that friend to his surviving representative, she honoured me for my fidelity, she felt toward me an increasing reverence, and had no thought nearer her heart than the gratifying my wishes, and anticipating my requests. The passion of the sexes will, perhaps, infallibly grow up between male and female, wherever they are much together, and feel much mutual approbation, provided they are impressed with no adverse prepossessions, and there is nothing in the discipline and decorums of society that forbids and sets a brand on its completion. The melancholy, too, that hung over our interviews, softened our minds, and prepared them for tender and passionate feelings.

One further misfortune impended over my ward; for such by the most sacred obligations she was now become. Her father, as I have said, had converted his whole property into money, which he lodged, previously to his embarkation, in a banking-house in Genoa. He, of course, received, in the due forms practised on such occasions, two complete duplicates of the titles or instruments by which he, or his representative, might claim the property at Genoa, on producing the said titles or instruments. These duplicates were enclosed in two boxes of ebony, in figure and appearance perfectly similar. One of them Mr. Macneil designed to take with him on board the Romney, that he might employ his fortune in the purchases he meditated, with the least possible delay; the other was to be left in my hands, with a view to any possible accident or miscarriage. I was present with my friend when he closed and sealed his different packages, the last day but two before he left the Windermere. We read over on that occasion the papers received from the Genoese banker. The room in which we sat was crowded with trunks and boxes, some already locked, others waiting for their last complement. In the middle of the room was a large table, covered with valuable trinkets, banknotes, money, books of accounts, and packets of papers of a thousand denominations. Suddenly Macneil was summoned out of the room, to speak to a land-bailiff, or tradesman of some sort, who had come for the second time upon some trifling and vexatious question. Before he left the room, my friend hastened to put away his most important papers. He closed the two boxes of ebony, and carefully placed some other papers in a trunk which was near him. His seal lay on the table; and, taking it in his hand, he requested me to affix it where it was wanting. In all this he seemed to proceed so cautiously, as to leave my mind entirely free from suspicion; while, at the same time, his attention was really engaged by another subject. This is the only account I can give of the affair. The trunks were opened no more. One of the ebony boxes, together with the rest of the packages, was finally conveyed on board the Romney: the other, as was previously determined, remained in my possession. When, in consequence of the shipwreck in which Macneil perished (for he had placed a will he had lately made in my hands, and had appointed me, in conjunction with an eminent barrister-at-law, his executor), I broke the seal, and opened the box which was supposed to contain the title and instruments of his fortune, now become the fortune of his sur- viving child, I found it entirely empty.

I was thunderstruck with this circumstance. I entered into a correspondence with the banker at Genoa; I afterward com- menced a lawsuit against him. His answers to my letters were cautiously and artfully expressed; they avoided saying any thing directly respecting the sum of sixty thousand pounds sterling which I stated Mr. Macneil to have remitted; the writer entrenched himself in the forms and language of business; he said that he should be glad to see the titles and instruments on which I founded so considerable a claim; but, till he saw them, he could deliver no opinion on the matter. As this detestable correspondence proceeded, and in proportion as he felt himself more secure of his ground, he assumed a loftier and more inso- lent tone. He was astonished that I should trouble him with repeated applications in an affair which he knew nothing of, and required that I should desist from such extraordinary and discreditable importunities. This may well appear to the reader somewhat wonderful: the banker who committed this enor- mous fraud had hitherto borne an unimpeachable character: all I can say is, that the temptation was probably too large for his sentiments of integrity. I may be permitted, as a misanthrope, to remark, that the integrity of too many men has its limits, and that it is to be feared there have been bankers, even in England, who would have sold themselves to the devil for sixty thousand pounds.—The fact is, however, in a word, that the property of the Macneils was never recovered. I have often thought it was fortunate for me, that I and my good friend, the Genoese banker, were not inhabitants of the same country. It was certainly in some measure an issue of character that was tried between us. I do believe that, if the Genoese had not entertained the hope of keeping his reputation as well as the money, he would have paid Mary her fortune. What applause would he have obtained, if he had disbursed out of his coffers sixty thousand pounds, which, as every one who repeated the story would have been forward to remark, he was not obliged to pay! On the other hand, what a villain was I, if, on false or uncertain grounds, I charged him with fraudulently detaining so enormous a sum! "I must take care," as he observed to me in some of his letters, "how I advanced an accusation against him, tending to subvert the whole basis of his transactions, without having in my possession documents by which it could be supported." The good Genoese, as I afterward learned, made out a plausible and even pathetic story, to his acquaintance and friends, of the injury he sustained. "It might," he said, "have been the intention of the unhappy gentleman who was lost at sea, to have vested this property in his hands; the more was his misfortune that he never received it! Sixty thousand pounds, however, was a large sum; he had never in the whole course of his business held cash to that amount, at one time, for any one individual; and he took upon him to doubt, from every thing he had heard, whether the deceased had ever been worth half the sum. It was a hard thing, indeed, to be made accountable for money he never saw, and to be called a cheat and a villain unless he would give away half his estate; and, though he trusted in the equity of the laws of Genoa to protect his fortune, and in the candour of his countrymen to vindicate his character, yet the uneasiness which the rashness of this Englishman, to say the least of it, had given his mind, was such as no vindication could ever compensate."—I am not sure, if I had gone at this time to Genoa, whether I should not have been publicly hooted, as I passed along the streets.

Yet, in reality, spite of the loss of these important instruments, I had documents left, sufficient to justify me in the mind of every impartial observer. The amount of Mr. Macneil's fortune was, of course, a matter that had been sufficiently obvious to many. This fortune could not suddenly be annihilated. The Milanese friend of Macneil was ready to attest that it had been his purpose to lodge his property in this house, and that he certainly believed he had done so. He produced a letter in which the fact was strongly implied, though it was not affirmed in words that admitted not of debate. In his will my friend described the receipt of the sum as being acknowledged by the banker, and entered into some detail as to the number and titles of the instruments under which he claimed.

But all this was not sufficient to procure a decree in my favour before the Genoese magistrates. The Italian lawyers observed, that a description of property in a man's will was the most unlike thing in the world to a title to an estate; and that, if such a doctrine, as this claim turned on, were admitted, which they well knew the equity of the bench before which they pleaded would reject with indignation, every man who pleased, in every country of Europe, might bequeath his daughter sixty thousand pounds, not only from their client, but from every banking, and every considerable mercantile, house within the limits of the republic. They dwelt at great length upon the high character for integrity, which had ever been preserved by the commercial class of the citizens of Genoa,—a class which was well known to consist principally of the most ancient and honourable nobility in the world; they expatiated pathetically upon the virtues, the charities, the religious observances, and the unblemished life of their client, and the agonies his pure and uncorrupted mind had suffered from so foul an imputation; and they earnestly called on the court by their present decree to vindicate, not the defendant only, whose character in this case had been grievously aspersed, but the whole state, from the suspicion that such a crime could have been so much as conceived by one of her citizens. Their exertions and eloquence were crowned with the most entire success.

I hesitated long to disclose to the unfortunate Mary the new calamity which hung over her. One consideration at length decided me to make her of council in the controversy that was going on. I found her mind dwelling with incessant anguish on the image of her departed kindred. She refused all amusement and avocations. The employments which had lately been so dear were now loathsome to her. The fields and the garden had no charms. Her spirits and her appetite deserted her. I saw that there was no chance of recalling her to life, but by giving her some object to which she could not refuse to attend. I believe the loss of her fortune of sixty thousand pounds was the direct means by which she was preserved from the grave.

At first she declared in the most peremptory manner that she would listen to nothing that related to the goods of life. What were the means of life to her when she was already bereaved of every thing that made life worth having! It was a pleasure to her to conceive, that, when she lost parents and sisters, she had nothing left! There was something soothing in the idea that the same billows which had devoured her dearest relatives, had swallowed up their wealth, and left her a helpless beggar in the world!

By degrees I recalled her to a sounder mind. I represented to her the importance of wealth, and the duty which prescribed the preservation and right disposition of it. With the fortune which had thus devolved to her, how respectable might she become! She might maintain a household of temperate and happy individuals. She might relieve the wants of multitudes, might unfold talent, encourage industry, and multiply around her the class of sober and honourable citizens in the state. Even the inherent qualities which she or any other individual possessed, were illustrated, when they appeared in conjunction with the goods of fortune. The merits of the poor man were always clouded, undervalued, and baffled of their utility; while those of the rich were illuminated with the beams of applause, and enabled to appear with tenfold effect upon the theatre of society. I further reminded her of the guilt she would incur, if, instead of endeavouring to make a proper use of the wealth which had devolved to her, she suffered it, by any negligence of hers, to become the prize of profligacy and fraud, and to be administered in the depraved manner which such dispositions would dictate.

I prevailed on the sorrowing maid to suffer me to bring to her the barrister, who was the joint executor of her father's will. We read together, in her presence, the letters which had relation to the subject. We canvassed the evidence, nuncupatory and scriptory,[1] which might be made useful in the cause. We brought together in her apartments a consultation of English lawyers, with whom we thought it necessary to advise as to the measures to be pursued. Add to this, that the letters which from time to time reached us from the Genoese banker, and from the lawyers it was necessary for us to retain in that city, both when they were expected, and when they arrived, kept alive our interest, and furnished topics for our conversation. A lawsuit is like an adventure in a gaming transaction; the mind is continually upon the stretch—the affair which day to day assumes a new face—hope and fear dance an alternate measure before the eyes, and we are now sanguine with expectation, and now speechless and dejected with intolerable despair. How many waking and anxious nights may he expect to pass, who, from choice or necessity, is obliged to commit his property to the discussions of the wrangling bar! The degree of uneasiness which is inseparable from an affair of this sort, was, as I have already said, salutary to Mary, and served by imperceptible degrees to bring her back to the considerations of the world.

Here, then, was a strange series of vicissitudes in the pecuniary fortune of my destined bride. When I had first contemplated marriage with her, she was one of three coheiresses merely of a man of a given fortune, who might expect on the day of her marriage to receive a certain portion, and, after the death of her parents, to divide in equal allotments the property which they possessed. In the few days that elapsed between the melancholy intelligence of the loss of her family, and the period when it became necessary to look into the affairs of my deceased friend, she stood forth the undoubted successor to his ample property. I never had been, in any occurrence of my life,

---

1   Oral and written.

a mercenary character; and I doubt whether, in any moment of these few days, the idea of Mary's accession of property offered itself to my thoughts; certainly it was very far from being among the early suggestions inspired by this melancholy catastrophe. But, after this, there was a long time, nearly a year, before the question was finally set at rest (the action, indeed, was not dismissed by the Italian courts under two years; but I had, before that, resolutely driven the expectation of my advantage to result from my thoughts); and during this period, amidst the various fluctuations of our cause, and the sanguine hopes which were occasionally held out to me, the successive images of my mistress as the possessor of an ample property, and a beggar, could not but forcibly present themselves to my apprehension.

What a strange thing is the human mind! Of what consequence was it to me, whether the amiable and accomplished woman I married were, or were not, amply endowed with the goods of fortune? I had already enough for every honest and honourable purpose in life. Fortune could not make her more amiable and accomplished than she was: adversity could take nothing from her. I can safely declare that I never repined for a moment that she gave me her hand without bringing me a shilling. Yet I am formed like all other corporeal essences, and am affected by the adventitious and unmeriting circumstances of rank or riches with which my fellow-being is surrounded. Had Mary entered into my alliance a distinguished heiress, this, in spite of my philosophy, would have commanded from me a certain deference and homage. As she was pennyless, a mere pensionary on my bounty,—I swear I did not value her less,— I felt more tenderness, more humanity, a more religious kind of forbearance toward her. But the sentiment was of a different sort; her first claim was upon my pity. I experienced this a hundred times, when I hastened to pay her my customary visit. When I waited upon her as an heiress, I approached with a certain submission; I looked at her as an independent being; my thoughts moved slow, and my tongue was apt to falter, if I suggested to her any idea of a freer and more unceremonious sort. When I visited her portionless, my mind moved freer; I breathed a thinner and more elastic atmosphere; my tongue assumed a tone of greater confidence; and, at the same time that I felt for her the deepest compassion and the most entire sympathy, my speech became more eloquent, and I caught myself talking with the condescension of a superior—superior in the possession of that sordid dirt which the system of human things much oftener bestows upon a driveller or a knave than upon a being of genuine excellence and worth.

Another idea of a subtler nature offered itself to my thoughts, which I will state here, as calculated to illustrate the whimsical composition of the human mind. I felt that, in consequence of the heavy calamity which had overtaken this beautiful orphan, it was become doubly incumbent on me that I should marry her. She was left, by a deplorable and astonishing event, desolate upon the stage of the world; and she was in all moral and religious obligation entitled to the full benefit of my fortune. But this is not exactly the idea to which I refer. An ample property of sixty thousand pounds had unaccountably disappeared. What was become of it? I charged the malversation on the Genoese banker: he denied the charge. The question was at issue before the laws and lawyers of his country: it was probable that the accused would ultimately be acquitted. He would be acquitted, because I had no sufficient evidence to exhibit, to substantiate the assertion. Well, then; here was a horrible fraud which had been perpetrated. As I charged it on the banker, might not another charge it on me? I had been trusted by Macneil in all his affairs; there was no apparent individual to whom the guilt could belong, but the Genoese or myself. He had no more visible temptation than I. His opulence was not less; and, like me, he was childless and a bachelor; it was generally believed that, when he died, he would bequeath his property to the church. But, if the fraud were mine, how much more complicated would be my guilt! I was the friend of the deceased, the Genoese a stranger; I had been fixed on by Macneil, as the select depositary of his interests. Then imagine for a moment, how inexpressible must be the height of my profligacy, if, conscious to myself that I alone was guilty of the embezzlement, I deliberately charged it upon another, and solemnly prosecuted the charge! Imagine what the guilt must be, of stripping a wealthy orphan, left in my guardianship, of her property, at the same moment that fate had robbed her of her natural protectors, and of thus turning her forth pennyless, to seek the means of a wretched subsistence!

These, it will be said, are but wild and air-drawn pictures. I had passed through the world with an unimpeached reputation: the integrity and liberality of my transactions were known to every one that had heard of my name; no creature would ever dream of suspecting me of so flagitious an action. Be it so. A man is diversely viewed by the variously circumstanced inhabitants of the globe. Milton is known to one man merely as the Latin translator to a secretary of state; and the nurse of La Fontaine interrupted his confessor, who was setting before him on his death-bed the terrors of another world, with the exclamation, "For Christ's sake, do not disturb the poor wretch; he is less knave than fool; God can never have the heart to damn him."[1] Such was my temper, that I could not sleep tranquilly upon my pillow, while I thought it possible that a native of Genoa or Peru should regard me as a villain, pampering my own follies and depraved propensities with the purloined property of another.

CHAPTER XIX.

LET me not be misunderstood. Let it not be supposed that the passion and determination of my mind in favour of this charming girl were less fervent than they ever had been. On the contrary, she became every hour more interesting to me. While she sat like Niobe,[2] her whole soul dissolved in tears for the untimely destruction of her family, it was impossible not to feel

---

1 John Milton served as Secretary for the Foreign Tongues to the republican Council of State from 1641 to 1660. Jean de La Fontaine (1621-95), French poet; this incident is recounted in *Fables and Tales from La Fontaine in French and English. Now first translated. To which is prefix'd. The Author's Life* (1734), p. xxiv.

2 In Greek mythology, Niobe bragged that her 7 sons and 7 daughters surpassed Apollo and Artemis in their accomplishments; when the two angered gods slew her children in revenge, Niobe wept until she turned to stone.

in its utmost energy the wish, Might I be your comforter! In proportion as she gained the power of attending in some degree to the objects before her, her intercourse gave me nameless emotions. There was a gentle sweetness in her manner, that I never saw in any other human creature. I remembered her gay, and active, and spirited; it was now a faint and undefined image of these qualities that presented itself—a sun that yielded an uncertain beam, amidst the mass of clouds that sought to overwhelm it. That transparent complexion, that countenance in which, like a book, the spectator might read every emotion and temporary impulse of the soul, rendered every state of mind of the angelic creature to whom it belonged interesting. When the first faint smile, after the death of her father, illumined her features, it struck me like a resurrection from the dead: my sensations were such as those which Admetus must have felt, when Hercules brought back to him his heroic consort from the regions of Pluto.[1] There was something too aërial, too subtle, too heavenly in her countenance, to be properly the attribute of a terrestrial being. The glories of Elysium seemed to hang round her.[2] Poor Mary had nothing on earth left her to love, but me; and she felt toward me as toward father, mother, sisters, in one. Nothing could be so delicate and flattering to me as the whole of her demeanour; and every demonstration of this sort had a double price, as it appeared a gentle, and voluntary, and cheerful restraint upon the state of her mind; so much taken away from the dead to give to the living.

Thus we passed the winter. The cheerful blaze of our quiet hearth compensated for the driving hail and snow which raged without. Gradually I endeavoured to engage the attention of my charmer with indifferent objects. I adorned her apartments with the most beautiful products of the gardener's care I was able to procure. I obtained some for her which she had never

---

1 In Greek mythology, King Admetus was fated to die unless another person agreed to die in his place; ultimately, his noble wife Alcestis consented to do so. When the hero Heracles heard of this, he fought Hades for Alcestis's soul, and brought her back from the dead. The story was dramatized by Euripides in his *Alcestis*.
2 Elysium, or the Elysian fields, was the region of the Greek underworld reserved for heroes and the blessed.

seen before. She instructed me in botany; she brought forth her portfolios, and showed me her charming drawings. I called her attention to the beauties of the English writers from Queen Elizabeth to the Civil War,—writers who had always appeared to me to surpass those of any other age or country.[1] It was one of the agreeable attributes of this winter, that our interviews were never broken in upon by any accidental interloper. One peaceful hour of animated disquisition, or soothing remission, passed away after another, unmarked. When I saw my adorable ward, if not happy, at least peaceful and pleased, my heart beat with honest exultation, and I said, "This is my work!" She was willing to yield equal credit to my exertions. It was the work of nature! Time, youth, and health, inevitably did so much for my patient, that there was little left for me, her soul's physician, to effect. If the intercourse and position I have described would have been delightful to any one with the soul of a man, imagine what they were to me, who, from the hour of my birth till now, had never experienced the sweets of honourable love.

A brilliant and genial spring succeeded the winter. I had never felt this interesting period of the awakening of the universe from its torpor, so deeply as now. Nature became restored to life and the pulses of life, and my charmer sympathised with the general tone of created things. During the winter I had never ventured to propose to her a visit to any of the scenes of public amusement which the metropolis affords; no one could have looked in her face, and started the proposition; it would have been treason to the majesty of her grief; it would have been sacrilege, to bring forward the dejected mourner amidst the hardened gaiety and indifference of an assembly, or the unhallowed jests and obstreperous mirth of a theatre. An excursion into the country is an amusement of a different sort. Nature in her gayest scenes is never drunken and tumultuous. A cheerful sobriety is their characteristic. When I escape from the multitude, and hasten to her retreats, I am never incommoded with obtrusive and discordant sounds; all around me is silent; or, if any thing is heard, it is the rustling of the wind, or

---

1 See note regarding Ruffigny's library on page 122. The English Civil War took place between 1642 and 1648.

the uncouth warblings of the feathered tribe; even the lowing of the herds is sweet; and if I were placed amidst a forest of wild beasts, I should find, could I divest myself of the terror they excite, that the mighty Master had tempered their roarings, till they afforded a sublime mellowness, not unpleasing to the ear.—I invited Mary to join with me in a short excursion.

The soft tints of the morning had a staid liveliness in them, which led my poor Mary out of herself, ere she was aware. The air had a sweet alacrity which she could not resist.

"Mr. Fleetwood," said she, "your attentions are a thousand times greater than I deserve. Had they a character of obtrusiveness and command, I should know what part to take: but I can discover nothing in them which betrays that you think of gratification to yourself; you appear to be the soul of humanity and tenderness. I should be the most ungrateful creature in the world, if I did not accept your solicitudes for my health and invitations to the air, or if I refused to smile, when nature and Fleetwood summon me to smile."

We made a tour in succession to almost all the environs of the metropolis. If one is content to give up the demand for the wild, the majestic, and awful in scenery, I know of no city, the neighbourhood of which affords a greater variety of rich, and beautiful, and animated spots, than London. The Thames is the great wealth of this vicinity. What can be more striking than the crowd of masts and vessels of various sizes, as discovered from Greenwich, or the frolic meanderings of this rural stream, as it shows itself at Richmond? What objects can be more unlike than these two? If you recede from the river, Sydenham, and Epsom, and Esher, and Hampstead, and Hendon, and twenty other delightful scenes, are ready to advance their several claims for the prize of beauty. Let not my readers wonder at this enumeration, which to some of them may perhaps appear trite. Let them recollect that with every one of these places I associate some interesting scene of courtship, which renders the remembrance dear to me. Let them be thankful that I dismiss this part of my narrative so lightly. If I were to enlarge upon the history of this beautiful spring, and relate at length the pleasing incidents which occurred, particularly at Epsom and Richmond, instead of consecrating a page to this topic, I should fill volumes.

In the month of July I became a husband. When a sufficient period had elapsed to make my poor Mary feel that she belonged in some measure to the world, she was too ingenuous not to disdain the forms and semblances of grief. As she had scarcely any visitor beside myself, it became proper that we should, as soon as might be, put an end to this equivocal situation, upon which the good-natured world is always eager to interpose its constructions.—"My beloved Fleetwood," said Mary, "I feel that I love you to the full as much, I believe more, than I could love a man of my own age. The sentiment that I feel for you has a sort of religion in it, which renders it a thousand times sweeter and more soothing to my heart. I reverence, at the same time that I love you. I shall be infinitely more reluctant to wound you, and more solicitous for your peace, than I should be, if you were a youth in the full revelry and exuberance of the morning of life. In all partnership engagements, there must be a subordination. If I had a young husband, I might, perhaps, sometimes be presumptuous enough to estimate his discernment at no higher a rate than my own; but the case is otherwise now. Mistake me not, my dear Fleetwood. I am not idle and thoughtless enough, to promise to sink my being and individuality in yours. I shall have my distinct propensities and preferences. Nature has moulded my mind in a particular way; and I have, of course, my tastes, my pleasures, and my wishes, more or less different from those of every other human being. I hope you will not require me to disclaim them. In me you will have a wife, and not a passive machine; but, whenever a question occurs of reflection, of experience, of judgment, or of prudential consideration, I shall always listen to your wisdom with undissembled deference. In every thing indifferent, or that can be made so, I shall obey you with pleasure. And, in return, I am sure you will consider me as a being to be won with kindness, and not dictated to with the laconic phrase of authority.

"Yet I am sorry, my dear love, that you should marry a woman who has suffered so cruelly as I have done. My father's advice to you was, 'Fleetwood, if you marry, choose a girl whom no disappointments have soured, and no misfortunes have bent to the earth.' Fleetwood, be assured, that I shall often recollect, and recollect with agony, that my father, mother, and sisters, all perished together by an untimely and tragical fate! Peaceful and serene as I may appear to you, I bear a wound in my breast, which may be skinned over, and seem as if it were cured, but which will occasionally break out afresh, and produce symptoms of fever, impatience, and despair. How exquisite are the various charities of human life! From the most venerable of these,—those which are entailed upon us without asking our leave, and are stamped with the highest sanctity,—I am cut off for ever. I am like a being who, by some severe ordination of Providence, is destined to stand alone, to know no kindred, to have no alliance or connection, but what my own election and voluntary engagement may eventually supply. If you should fail me, Fleetwood!——I have faults; you unquestionably have faults too. You are difficult to be pleased; I see it; my father told me so; my powers of pleasing, perhaps my inclination to please, have their limits. If you should fail me, I have no one to fly to; I shall remain a solitary monument of despair! These thoughts will sometimes intrude, and make me sad. Other persons lose their relations one by one; they are gradually broken into their forlorn situation. I was overwhelmed at once: and never, so long as I shall continue to exist, shall I recover this terrible stroke.

"But why do I thus cheat my sorrows, by dwelling in general propositions! If my lost relatives had been otherwise than they were, I could have borne it, I ought to have borne it. Fleetwood, you knew them! No, never was there such a father, such a mother, such sisters. How we loved each other! How happy we made each other, and what powers we had of contributing to each other's happiness!—Barbara! Amelia! my father! my mother! If I dwell upon the horrible theme I shall go distracted!—Fleetwood, how I wish that I too could commit myself to the mercy of the ocean! When the thought of my own death rises to my mind, it never comes in so soothing a form, as if I imagine it to happen by drowning. Believe me, there is nothing I so earnestly pray for, as that this may be the means by which I may cease to exist. I should not feel it as death; it would be a reunion to all I love!

> "'Life is the desert; life the solitude,
>   This mingles me with all my soul has loved;
> 'Tis to be borne to sisters and to parents;
> 'Tis to rejoin the stock from which I sprung,
> And be again in nature.'"[1]

CHAPTER XX.

FROM the church of St. George's, Hanover Square, where the marriage ceremony was performed, we set out for the baths of Matlock in Derbyshire, where we stayed an entire month.[2] This was the happiest month of my life. My dear Mary became placid and cheerful; without forgetting the terrible calamity which the last autumn had brought upon her, she opened her heart to the gratifications which were before her; she felt that, in the solemn contract she had formed, she had undertaken in some degree for my satisfaction and tranquillity, and she determined to watch over her trust. Nor will I be guilty of the false modesty to insinuate, that she did this merely as the discharge of a duty; on the contrary, I was so fortunate as to interest and please her. This she manifested by a thousand flattering symptoms, attentions which can flow only from the heart, and which the head can never supply. Nor let it be forgotten that, though I was now somewhat beyond the meridian of life, I was not destitute of many advantages, calculated to recommend me to a delicate and refined female companion. My person was pleasing, and my demeanour graceful; circumstances which had acquired me in Paris the appellation of *the handsome Englishman*. That very sensibility which constituted the torment of my

---

1 See Edward Young, *The Revenge* (1721), Act IV: "Life is the desert; life the solitude, / Death joins us to the great majority. / 'Tis to be borne to Platos, and to Caesars; / 'Tis to be great for ever."

2 Town on the river Derwent visited for its therapeutic water treatments.

life, gave a feeling sweetness to the tones of my voice, and a gentleness to my attentions, such as are found peculiarly acceptable to the better order of females.

If Mary was cheerful and pleased, the happiness I felt is such as cannot be described. What a contrast did there exist between the tumultuous scenes of my Parisian amours, and my relative situation with the accomplished female whom I had now made my wife! The women I had loved, furiously and distractedly loved, in the early period of my life, I had never esteemed. How could I? They had each a husband; they had each children. How can a woman discharge the duties of these sacred relations at the same time that she is amusing herself with the wishes, or gratifying the appetites, of a lover? The idea is too shocking to be dwelt upon! She puts off the matron to play the wild and loose-hearted coquette. She presents to her husband the offspring of her criminal amours, and calls it his. All her life is a cheat, one uninterrupted tissue of falsehoods and hypocrisy. Can she tell her thoughts? She who has not a single thought which, though it may be tolerated in silence, would not, if uttered in appropriate language, make every one of her acquaintance turn to marble at the sound. Esteem her! She is not worthy to live; or, if to live, to be confined in some cloister of penitents, where rigid discipline, and coarse attire, and scanty fare, might at length purge her of that ferment in her blood, or that giddy intoxication of thought, which at present renders her the blot of her sex, and the disgrace of the marriage tie!

There are persons who sport the opinion, that the pleasure which is gained by stealth, is the genuine pleasure; and that the prohibition which waits upon the indulgence, gives it its highest zest. It is not so! This opinion is not more pernicious in its tendency than it is ridiculous in the grounds upon which it rests. What, is it the consciousness of crime that makes our pleasure? the fear which continually haunts us with a presentiment that we shall be detected? the cowardice that forces our countenance to fall in the presence of our fellow-men, and makes a hundred accidental and harmless remarks in conversation or in public, enter like a sword into our vitals? the fearful struggle for ever repeated within us, which leads us to do the thing we condemn, and repine over our weakness that we do it?

No; it is innocence that is the soul of pleasure, with which the sentiment of shame is incompatible. The truly happy man lifts up his face with serenity, and challenges the eyes of all the world. Without frankness, without a conscience void of offence, without a feeling that the being I love is of a worthy nature, and that no one can stand up and say, "In consulting your own inclination you have done me unmanly wrong," there cannot be "the sunshine of the soul". Most especially in the connection of sex with sex, it is necessary to substantial enjoyment, that virtue should spread the couch, and that honour and peace of mind should close the curtains. The kiss of honest love, how rapturous! But the true ingredients in this rapture are, a heart-felt esteem of each other's character; a perception that, while the eye we see sparkles, and the cheek glows, with affection, the glow is guiltless of any unhallowed and licentious propensity; in fine, the soothing state of mind which tells us that, while we freely indulge the impulses of our heart, we are not disgracing, but honouring, the mighty power by which we exist. To recollect that neither my own character, nor that of the partner of my joys, is injured, but improved, by the scope of our mutual partialities, is the crown of social pleasure. To persons thus attached, thus bound in honourable connection, each day may be expected to add to their enjoyment, and increase the kindness and esteem with which they regard each other.

To me the situation was new, was such as I had not anticipated, and was so much the more enchanting to me. I had lived long in the world, and I had lived alone. My soul panted for a friend, and I had never found such a friend as it demanded,—a friend "who should be to me as another self, who should joy in all my joys, and grieve in all my sorrows, and whose sympathy should be incapable of being changed by absence into smiles, while my head continued bent to the earth with anguish." I had not been aware that nature has provided a substitute in the marriage-tie, for this romantic, if not impossible friendship. The love which Pythias is said to have borne for Damon, or

Theseus for Pirithous, many a married pair have borne for each other.[1] The difference of sex powerfully assists the intimacy; similarity of character can never unite two parties so closely, as the contrast of masculine enterprise in one, and a defenceless tenderness in the other. Man and wife, if they love, must love each other vehemently. Their interests are in almost all cases united. If they have children, these children form a new bond, either party pursues the same end, and has its affections directed toward the same object. Independently of this, whatever contributes to the welfare of the one is advantageous to the other; and the calamity or death of either is a kind of destruction which overtakes the by-stander. Habit assists the mutual dependence; and very often it happens that, when a wedded pair has lived for a long series of years together, the death of the feebler of the two is only a signal calling on the other to be gone, that he survives but a few days, and they are deposited at the same moment in a common grave.

Thus does the system of things of which we are a part supply our inherent deficiencies; and conscious, as it were, in how small a degree we are adapted for sublime virtues, assists, by a sort of mechanical link, in the construction of that vivid and unremitting attachment which the human heart demands.

To me, who had been accustomed to live alone with dependants, with acquaintance, and with servants, how delicious were the attentions of a beautiful and accomplished woman, whose interests were for ever united with my own! A servant dares not, and an acquaintance but coldly performs the ordinary duty of enquiring after your health, and sending you forth to the occupations of the day crowned with their good wishes. How pleasing to be an object of interest and concern to the person whom I deeply esteem and fervently love! How delicious the eye that glistens with pleasure to hail my return, and the cheek

---

1 When Damon was condemned to death by Dionysius I of Syracuse, his friend Pythias agreed to take his place in prison while Damon arranged his affairs. Dionysius was so affected by this display of trust that he remanded the punishment and asked to be admitted into the men's friendship. Mythological figures Theseus, King of Athens, and Pirithous, King of the Lapiths, were famous friends who engaged in numerous adventures together.

that reddens with kindness! It is this which constitutes the unspeakable charm of home. My home is not a fabric of walls which shelters me; is not even the windows, the furniture, the elbow-chair, and the mute fireside, which habit has endeared and hung round with a thousand pleasing associations; it is that there I find the countenance that gladdens at my approach, and the heart that welcomes me. The affection of Mary I felt as a charm reconciling me to life; it gave me value in my own eyes, to observe her beautiful and well-proportioned presence, her speaking eye, her lucid complexion, and to say, "To the soul that inhabits there I am of importance; she is cheerful, because I am happy and well; if I perished, she would feel she had lost every thing!" How flattering to the human heart, that there is a being, and a noble one whom with one accent of my voice I can delight, with one glance of my eye I can fill with sweet content! My tenants loved me, because I had power; my acquaintance, because I could contribute to their entertain- ment; the poor who dwelt near my mansion, for my wealth; but my wife would love me in sickness or in health, in poverty, in calamity, in total desolation!

While we resided at Matlock, we visited the beauties and romantic scenery of Derbyshire. I was familiarly acquainted with the whole before, and I now performed the office of cicerone[1] and interpreter to Mary. But how different were the sensations with which I now visited each charming, or each wonderful scene! Even a bright and spirit-stirring morn did not now stir in me a contemplative and solitary spirit; it turned my eye on my companion, it awakened us to the interchange of cheerful and affectionate looks, it tipped our tongues with many a pleasant sally, and many a tender and sympathetic expression. When we looked down upon the rich and fertile plains, when we hung over the jutting and tremendous precipice, I perceived, with inexpressible pleasure, that mine was no longer a morose and unparticipated sensation, but that another human creature, capable of feeling all my feelings, rejoiced and trembled along with me. When I retired to my

---

1 A guide.

inn after the fatigues and dangers of the day, I did not retire to a peevish and froward meal among drawers and venal attendants; I sat down with the companion of my heart, and shared the pleasures of idleness, as we had before shared the pleasures of activity. How many agreeable topics of conversation did the rivers and the mountains suggest! how many occasions of mutual endearment did they afford! It seemed that the spirit of kindness still gained new strength, as the scene was perpetually shifted before our eyes, and as we breathed an atmosphere for ever new.

VOLUME THE THIRD.

CHAPTER I.

AFTER having resided at Matlock somewhat more than a month, we set out for Merionethshire. Mary had never before entered my paternal mansion; she had never been in Wales; and she expressed herself extremely pleased with all she saw. The vast and uncouth forms of the neighbouring mountains were exceedingly striking. The mansion itself was built in a style of antique magnificence; it had been erected by one of the leaders in the commonwealth of Cromwell;[1] and, to an admirer of whatever is venerable for age, the shining and polished floors, the huge and misshapen tapestry figures in some of the apart-ments, and the dark-coloured wainscot with its diminutive panels which adorned the rest, were infinitely more gratifying than all the sumptuousness of modern prodigality. The win-dows, as well as the halls and galleries, were large, and almost collegiate.

The day on which we entered the house in Merionethshire may be considered, in some sense, as the first of our marriage. Here we were to make our establishment, and set up our taber-nacle; at Matlock and other places we shifted as we could. Here then was a rock upon which we were in danger to be destroyed. They were no trifling and fugitive discussions we had to adjust; I, on my part, had formed habits, of which it would be difficult for me to divest myself.

We arrived in the evening, and were in want of repose. We sat down to the fire-side where I had sat with my father a thousand times; we ate a delicious meal, while Mary listened with attention to many little anecdotes I related of the deceased, and stories of my boyish exploits and sorrows.

The next morning we walked round the apartments. There was a handsome, retired closet, opening into the principal drawing-room and at a short distance from my bed-chamber, the window of which commanded the most admirable prospect we had. The steeple and roofs of a beautiful village were distinctly visible; the river, beset with willows, meandered

---

1   The Commonwealth lasted from 1649 to 1660.

below; a venerable wood of everlasting oaks grew on one side, beyond which was discovered the silver main; while the other side was skirted by the crags of the gigantic mountain, that from my infancy I almost adored. This closet was my favourite retreat. Here I had been permitted to con my lessons while I was yet of schoolboy age; and here it had ever since been my custom to retire with some favourite author, when I wished to feel my mind in its most happy state. In this closet I meditated, I composed, I wrote. If I wanted an ampler space to move in, I had but to open the door, and the largest drawing-room in the house offered itself for my promenade. By the side of the closet was a private staircase, which led me, by a short cut, to the river, the wood, and the mountain. I preferred this sequestered nook to all the rest of the mansion taken together. I entered it now, after a twelvemonth's absence, with a full recollection of all the castles which I had sat there and builded in the air, the odes, the tragedies, and heroic poems which, in the days of visionary childhood, upon that spot I had sketched and imagined. I turned to Mary, with the purpose of telling her the many ravishing associations which this closet presented to my mind.

"This is an enchanting closet!" said she.

"It is."—My heart knocked at my bosom, my very soul was full of its little history, as I spoke.

"Do you know, Fleetwood, I shall take this closet for mine? I will have all my drawings brought here, and arrange my favourite flowers in the window. Will you give it me?"

"Surely, my love! I am glad it pleases you so much."

My sensations at this moment were of a singular and complicated nature. I had been on the point of employing all my eloquence to describe to Mary how I loved this closet—how unalterably it had fixed its hold upon me as my favourite retreat. For this purpose I had recollected in rapid succession all the endearments that made it mine, all the delights which, almost from prattling infancy, it had afforded me. In an unlucky moment my wife pronounced the decree, "It shall never be yours again!" The decision was unexpected, and my animal spirits were suddenly driven back upon my heart.

Yet I call Heaven to witness, it was only the suddenness of the blow, and not any intimation of selfishness, that produced this effect. On the contrary, the moment I had had time to recover myself, my sentiment was,—"Mary, it is for ever yours! Dear, angelic sweetness, I shall be too happy, to witness your gratification! Shall I think this too great a sacrifice, who would offer up my life for you? It is no sacrifice! I have more joy in considering the things I love as yours, than in regarding them as my own."

Presently the bell was rung; and the flower-stage,[1] the portfolios, and the drawings, one after another, made their appearance. In the midst of the confusion, I withdrew to have some necessary consultations with my steward.

After an absence of three hours, I returned, and visited Mary in her retreat. By this time all her little sources of occupation and amusement were in order. I observed with delight the arrangements she had made. I gazed on the features of her charming face; she never looked more beautiful, than thus surrounded with the emblems of the innocence of her mind and the elegance of her taste. My heart exulted in beholding these human graces, associated and set off with a back-ground of my favourite steeple, mountain, and prospect to the neighbouring main. I fed my eyes with the pleasing scene. I sat down by her side, viewed her drawings, and admired the delicate forms and brilliant colouring of the flowers she loved. I turned to the prospect from the window, with the purpose of pointing out to her in detail the objects of which it consisted.

What a fool is man! My own folly, however much I may feel ashamed of it, I have sat down with the purpose to relate. The next morning, and the morning after, I missed my favourite, my old, my long-accustomed retreat, and sought in vain for a substitute for it. My library was in the other wing of the house, and answered to the drawing-room I have mentioned. It had a closet in it, built in the fashion of that which had caught Mary's fancy, with no other difference than that the prospect from the window, though for the most part the same, was in two or three

---

1 A standing-place or tier of shelves for flowers.

points essentially inferior. I repaired to this closet; I took two or three books from the library, one after another; I tried to compose myself. It would not do. This, in the days of my boyhood, had been my father's privacy; and, when by his death the use of the whole mansion devolved to me, I felt the closet which Mary had chosen as already mine, the scene of a thousand remembered pleasures, the object of my love.

Discontented here, I resolved to seek the garden. Immediately I missed my private staircase. I had no resource, but in the public staircase of the whole house. I could not get to that part of the garden which led to the river and the mountain, but by a formidable circuit. If I might not resort to my favourite haunts at perfect liberty, if I could not reach them unseen by any human eye, they were nothing to me. My domestics knew my customary seasons of taking the air; they watched the variations of my temper; and, when I was pensive and melancholy, were careful that the shadow of no one of them should obtrude in my path.

I will go, and tell Mary what she has done. I will confess to her all my weakness. Nothing could be further from her thought than to occasion me this disturbance, and it will afford her the purest pleasure to repair it.

May I perish, if ever I breathe a syllable on the subject! What, shall I paint me thus pitiful and despicable in her eyes? Shall I tell her, that I love nobody but myself, and regard her gratifications with indifference? I will not tell her so! I will act so, that, if any one else should affirm it, he shall affirm the most impudent falsehood.

She will never know that I have made this sacrifice at the shrine of love. So much the better. I shall know it. It shall be to my own heart a testimony of my affection. I do love her: Heaven only knows how much. I love her for her misfortunes and her desolate condition; I love her for the charms of her person, and her unrivalled virtues. The smallest indulgence to her, is dearer to me than ten thousand gratifications to myself.

The generous exultation with which I surrendered my own accommodation in silence was temporary; the want of that accommodation which I had so long enjoyed, daily and hourly recurred. There is something wonderfully subtle in the operations of the human mind. Do I differ with another, in project for the future, or judgment on our past conduct? I immediately begin to find a hundred arguments to prove, how absurd and unreasonable he is, how just am I. No man can completely put himself in the place of another, and conceive how he would feel, were the circumstances of that other his own: few can do it even in a superficial degree. We are so familiar with our own trains of thinking: we revolve them with such complacency: it appears to us, that there is so astonishing a perverseness in not seeing things as we see them! The step is short and inevitable from complacency in our own views, to disapprobation and distaste toward the views of him by whom we are thwarted.

"Mary, Mary," said I sometimes to myself, as I recurred to the circumstance, "I am afraid you are selfish! and what character can be less promising in social life, than hers who thinks of no one's gratification but her own?" It was true, I could not tell her, "This, which you so inconsiderately desire me to give up, is my favourite apartment." But she should have enquired of my servants. The housekeeper or the steward could have informed her. She should have considered, that a man, at my time of life, must have fallen upon many methods of proceeding from which he cannot easily be weaned.

The thing of which I could reasonably accuse her, was, at worst, a rapidity of decision incident to her early years. Could she suspect that my practice was, to leave the closet adjoining to the library, and carry my books to the other end of the house? I was incapable, however, of passing a just judgment in the case, and the transaction had an unfavourable effect upon my mind.

CHAPTER II.

SUCH was the incident of the first morning of our arrival in Merionethshire. Another question arose. Mary had heard of several respectable families in our neighbourhood, particularly the Philipses and the Morgans, the female members of which she understood to be agreeable and entertaining; and she was desirous to have intercourse with them. For this purpose it was necessary to go in form to our village church, and to have it given out that there were certain days on which Mrs. Fleetwood would sit to receive company. In the evening of our first day in Merionethshire, my wife entered on the subject.

To a person of habits different from mine, this circumstance would have been trivial. To me the idea came with many a painful twinge. I had all my life shrunk from this mummery, this unmeaning intercourse. I had travelled from one side of Europe to the other, in search of persons whose conversation should be tolerable to me. Mary saw with how ill a grace I received the proposition.

"My love," said she, "act in this matter as you please. Whatever shall be your determination, I promise to be satisfied. I will just mention what occurs to me concerning it, and will then be silent for ever. We are sitting down in Merionethshire, perhaps for life. Whatever we decide, cannot be reversed; we cannot repel our neighbours in the present instance, and call them about us again hereafter. Recollect, then, my dear Fleetwood, the disadvantages under which I have hitherto laboured. My dear mother, the best of mothers, and most admirable of women,"—and at this recollection she burst into an agony of tears.

"My dearest creature," interposed I, "do not distress yourself with the melancholy recollection! Mary, I love you. There is no honest gratification, no gratification which you can desire, that I will not be zealous to procure you."

"Hear me, Fleetwood!" said she. "Consult the merits of the case, and not the ardour of your kindness. We had no lady visiters. I have had no female acquaintance. Shall it be always thus? The manners of my sex are different from yours; what is graceful in a man, would be shocking in a woman; and what would be becoming in a woman, is effeminate and reproachful in the stronger sex. I am afraid I can never learn, and improve myself in the genuine female character, without the observation of my own sex. 'The eye sees not itself, but by reflection from some other thing.'[1] Let me say, too, that the society of her own sex is one of the natural consolations of a woman. I can feel a strong and entire affection for a man; I acknowledge it for you. But there is a certain repose and unbending in the occasional familiarity of woman with woman, of the softer and more fragile nature with its like, that powerfully conduces to the healthful and contented condition of the mind. Fleetwood, I have the greatest reluctance to thwart you in any thing. Choose for me. Determine as you will, I swear you shall never find in me, either by word or look, the hint of a reproach."

Our discussion terminated in the formal churching, and the commencement of a tremendous series of wedding visits. Artful hussy! In the way she put it to me, could I refuse? Could I refuse a thing upon which, in this mild and specious temper of mind, her heart appeared to be set?——I wrong her. There was no art in what she did; it was all the most adorable ingenuousness and sincerity. Or, if I may venture, by a bold allowance of speech, to call it art, it was that art, with which nature adorns her lovely sex more richly than with all the mines of Golconda,[2]—the art of persuasion, compelling us to feel the impossibility of resisting their honourable desires, and cheerfully to resign the compass of domestic affairs into their hands, to set us to what point they please.

On the first two mornings of our residence in Wales, I made a pleasant excursion, by way of exhibiting to Mary the beauties of the country. In the former I showed my wife the precipice from which, at the age of fourteen, I had fallen into the basin, then swelled by continual rains into a lake, which forms the source of the Desunny. She would climb the acclivity along with me. She made me point out to her the inequalities of the almost perpendicular rock along which the lamb had frisked, while William pursued. She particularly noted the place from which the peasant and the lamb had been precipitated together. We fancied, as we viewed it, that we could see the mark among the tufts of grass, where my foot had slipped thirty years before.

1   *Julius Caesar*, I.ii.52-53 (adapted).
2   An ancient city in India famous for its diamonds.

After having remained a long time on the spot, we took occasion, by Mary's desire, to make our way home by the cottage of William and the heroic girl, who had come in her boat to save him. The father had long since been dead; William and his wife had the appearance, by means of perpetual labour and frequent exposition to the air in all weathers, of an old man and woman. They had had a large family of children; but these were all grown up, the girls gone to service, and the boys to sea; only their youngest child, a robust lad of fifteen, was at home with them.

In our mountainous country the use of a carriage is exceedingly limited, and three fourths of the most exquisite points of view in my neighbourhood would have been lost to my wife, if she had not been an excellent walker. It was with pleasure that I perceived I could take her a walk of ten or twelve miles in extent, or invite her to climb the highest precipices, without her sustaining the smallest injury. When a woman is so unfortunately delicate, or has been so injudiciously brought up, as to be unable to walk more than a mile at a time, this effects a sort of divorce, deciding at once that, in many of the pleasures most gratifying to her husband's feelings and taste, she can be no partaker.

Our excursion of the second day was less adventurous than that of the first, and we were able to make more use of the carriage. After dinner I proposed reading with Mary a play of my favourite Fletcher. The piece was that admirable one of a Wife for a Month.[1] Mary seemed to enter strongly into the feelings of the poet; we admired equally the high and generous sentiments of the tragedy, and the glorious imagery with which those sentiments are adorned. The character of Valerio particularly riveted her attention.[2] She agreed with me that no poet of ancient or modern times, as far as her acquaintance with them extended, was able, like the writer before us, to paint

---

1 John Fletcher (1579–1625), English dramatist; his play *A Wife for a Moneth* was first performed in 1624.
2 The play's hero, Valerio, is permitted by Frederick, the usurping ruler of Naples, to marry the heroine Evanthe, but only if he agrees to submit to execution at the end of one month of marriage.

with all that body and retinue of circumstances which give life to a picture, a free, heroic, and gallant spirit. We especially commended his style, and coincided in opinion with Dryden, who confesses himself "apt to believe, that the English language in this author arrived to its highest perfection; what words have since been taken in being rather superfluous than ornamental."[1] Mary was roused in an extraordinary degree with the exhortations addressed by the queen to the heroine in the second act, stimulating her to the contempt of tyranny and death, and persuading her, that by such contempt she will even subdue the tyrant, and compel him to repent his ungenerous purpose. I read the sentiments of the royal speaker, as they occurred, in the animated eye and glowing cheek of the charmer who sat beside me. She could scarcely help starting from her chair.

I was delighted with the effect of my experiment. How exquisite a pleasure may thus be derived from reading with a woman of refined understanding so noble a composition as that which engaged us! It is a pleasure that should be husbanded. I have demonstrated to me, at once the acuteness of her taste, and her aptness to conceive and participate the most virtuous sentiments. I almost adore her for these high and excellent qualities. At the same time we are like instruments tuned to a correspondent pitch, and the accord that is produced is of the most delightful nature! We communicate with instantaneous flashes, in one glance of the eye, and have no need of words. When we have recourse to their aid, I instruct at once, and am instructed. I see how my companion feels the passages as they succeed; I learn new decrees of taste, and am confirmed in the old. Male and female taste are in some respects of different natures; and no decision upon a work of art can be consummate, till it has been pronounced on by both. Besides, that in such discussions we intermix

---

1 John Dryden (1631-1700), English poet who discussed the works of Fletcher and his frequent collaborator Francis Beaumont (1584-1616) in his *An Essay of Dramatic Poesy* (1668).

> "Grateful digressions, and solve high dispute
> With conjugal caresses: from my lips
> Not words alone please her."[1]

We proceeded, and came to the scene so wonderfully imagined, in which Valerio is seen dressing on the morning for church, and scorning with inimitable grandeur and ease the sentence of the tyrant, who had pronounced, that at the expiration of the first month of his married life he should lose his head. I had just read those words of his—

> "*Thou*, that hast been a soldier, Menalo,
> A noble soldier, and defied all danger—
> Wouldst *thou* live so long, till thy strength forsook thee;
> Till thou grew'st only a long, tedious story
> Of what thou hadst been; till thy sword hung up,
> And lazy spiders fill'd the hilt with cobwebs?"[2]

when the door opened, and the servant announced a visiter to my wife. It was the boy of fifteen, the son of William the peasant, whom we had seen in the cottage of his father the day before. I asked the servant somewhat angrily, why he entered, disturbing our afternoon's tranquillity, to announce a visiter of this class?

"The boy had come down," he replied, "by the appointment of his lady, who had fixed that hour for his attendance."

"Bless me!" replied Mary, "and so I did: I had entirely forgotten it. Do you know, my dear, in our stroll along the side of Idris yesterday, I observed two or three plants of a very rare species, and I thought I would return to them to-day, and take this boy for my guide? I would not trouble you yesterday to collect them, for I know you do not like such interruptions." It was true, I had received with pleasure the early lessons of Mary in botany, aided by the beautiful drawings with which she had illustrated them, and relieved with all the piquancy of

---

1 Milton, *Paradise Lost* (1667), VIII.54-57 (adapted).
2 *A Wife for a Moneth*, II.v.34-40 (omitting line 36: "Adopted thy brave arm the heir to victory").

courtship; but, by some fatality, I could never shape my mind to the office of herborisation: it appeared too pinched and minute an object for the tastes I had formed.

"I must go: I cannot send the boy away: we will finish with your beloved Fletcher after supper."—And away she tripped.

"Good bye! *Au revoir*, Fleetwood! you shall see me again by dusk."

All this passed in a minute. Valerio and Evanthe, their perilous situation, and the deep interest my wife seemed to take in their adventures, were instantaneously banished, as if by the touch of a magic wand. I was too proud to struggle with this unsteadiness, even if there had been a probability that my struggle would have been successful; that is, that my wife would have sat down again to our reading with an unconstrained and genuine preference.

Before I had time for recollection, I found myself alone, with no object to remind me of what had passed, except the volume of Fletcher which lay open upon the table. The reader must recollect my character, as an old bachelor, as a man endowed with the most irritable structure of nerves, and who from infancy had always felt contradiction with inexpressible bitterness, to conceive how much I was disturbed with this pelting and pitiful incident.

"Is this the woman," said I, "whom I have taken as the partner of my life, who is more interested in two or three blades of grass, or a wretched specimen of mosses, than in the most pathetic tale or the noblest sentiments? If she has no respect for the illustrious dead, who cannot feel her contempt, methinks she might have had some for me, whose heart still beats, and whose blood continues to flow. Oh, it is plain she cares only for herself, and is prepared to tread, as on an insect, upon every one who stands in the way of her present caprice! A curse on all mosses and botanical specimens!"

This was the first sentiment I conceived. Presently however, love, almighty love, returned, and I said, "God bless you, dear empress of my bosom! Can any taste be more pure than that which delights in the beauties of nature? How have I sat by her a thousand times, and admired, even in picture, the flowing and graceful forms, the soft and delicate surfaces, and the brilliant tints, of the vegetable tribe! What an honest and sincere mind is hers, that soars to admire the tremendous precipice and the gathering tempest, and can then descend to the frailest and minutest herb which clothes the face of our mother-earth! They are all alike the productions of that mysterious Power, which is every where at work, and every where engenders the patterns of grandeur, of majesty, and of grace. Would I destroy in Mary this noble relish, this generous affection, that embraces all the creatures of God?——God bless her, even in her caprices! They prove the youth and elasticity of her mind; they mark the morning of life; they are symbols of that truly feminine character, which so delightfully contrasts with my own sex, and constitutes the crown and essence of the life of man. I will turn botanist myself!"

While these reflections passed in my mind, I was almost tempted to pursue Mary, and join her in her herborising excursion.—"I know the place to which they are gone; I shall easily find them. How beautiful will the carnation of her cheeks, and the lilies of her soft fingers, the fairest blossoms creation ever saw, appear amidst the parterre of wild flowers that skirts the ridge of Mount Idris! I think I see her now, as she stoops to cull them. I will tell her that I will never have a taste, a pursuit, a gratification, but what is hers." Saying this, I put on my hat, I walked out at the hall door, and hurried along the avenue.

"No, I will not go to her! She has used me ill. She has wounded me in a point, where I am most alive. Fletcher, my old friend, friend of my boyish days, whose flights I have taught the echoes of the mountains to repeat, whose pages I have meditated in my favourite closet,——she has affronted me in thee, Fletcher; and for thee, if not for myself, I will resent it.

"No, this will not do. I will not be an uxorious, tame, wife-ridden husband. Has she shown any disposition to comply with me?

"If I begin, I can never continue to sustain this part. In all my life I have been unused to brook control. The sensitiveness of my temper will never allow me to bear to be thwarted, crossed, the chain of my sensations snapped and crumbled to pieces at every moment, with impunity. There is no reciprocity in this commerce. I could be content to yield much to her. ——Ay, again I say, God bless her in her caprices!——But I cannot be content to be reduced to nothing. I must have an existence, a pursuit, a system of my own; and not be a mere puppy, dangling at her heels, and taught to fetch and carry, as she gives the word."

As time glided on, these meditations became less pleasant: they burned at my heart, and were bitter in my mouth. Tediously and heavily dragged along the two hours of her absence: I could fix on no plan, I could form no conjecture for the future. I could sit down to no occupation or pursuit. I paced the hall and the avenue with impatient strides. Tired with this exertion, I threw myself indolently in a chair, and reclined my head on my hands upon the table.

At the end of two hours, Mary tripped with light and elastic step into the parlour.

"I have had a delightful walk!" cried she.

"Have you?" answered I, with a drooping and heavy voice, my powers blunted by the exhausting effects of all I had done and thought.

"Bless me, Fleetwood! you are not ill?"—And, saying this, she kissed my hand, drew a chair by my side, and soothed me with irresistible blandishments.

What a state was mine! If she had not been thus consummately lovely, if she had not mollified me with so divine a grace, I should have known how to have determined.

The reader who has had experience of the married life, will easily feel how many vexations a man stored up for himself, who felt so acutely these trivial thwartings and disappointments. Human beings, who enter into the engagements of domestic life, should remember, that however man and wife may in interests and affections be one, yet no interests and affections can prevent them from being in many respects distinct. No creature that lives can be always the same. Accidents of body or mind will frequently subvert the equilibrium of the system. Domestic avocations and cares will often call away the mind; and my wife will be thinking of the family linen or plate,

when I want her to be thinking of the caverns of Pandemonium, or the retreats of the blessed.[1] Even those observances of
ceremonious life, which induce us to listen to the story of a
stranger with appearances of interest greater than the reality, or
which stimulate us to actual attention, cannot always be preserved between persons who live together in a style of equality.
He who flies from all contradiction, must dwell alone, or dwell
with those to whom he never opens his soul. He who would
reap the unspeakable joys of a social existence, must set his
account with a life of accommodation, in which both parties
will have many things to sacrifice, many things to forgive, many
things that will be sure to keep their equanimity and good temper in exercise.—I can reason well upon these things now; but I
bought my power of doing so at a very high price.

CHAPTER III.

AT the close of a visiting-day, when we had had a full circle of
the neighbouring gentry, Mary informed me, that she had been
invited by the Miss Philipses to join them to a dance, which
was to take place at Barmouth the day after tomorrow.[2]

"And you have accepted the invitation?"

"Laetitia offered me tickets, and I have taken two. You will
go with me, will not you?"

"What time do you suppose you shall return home?"

"About three or four in the morning. The moon will serve,
and it will be a pleasant ride."

"Mary, did I never tell you my age?"

"And what of that? You are not too old, I hope, for amusement, or for happiness?"

"My dear love, I have formed inveterate habits, and outlived
the age of experiments. I can neither figure in a country assembly, nor sit up with impunity till four in the morning."

"Then, Fleetwood, if you will not go, neither will I. I desire

---

1   In Milton's *Paradise Lost*, Pandemonium is presented as the capital of Hell.
2   Coastal town in Gwynedd (formerly in Merionethshire).

no pleasures of which you are not a partaker. I will send John to-morrow morning, to carry back the tickets."

"Oh, Mary," cried I, "I see more and more that our tastes are different. It is very natural; you are young; you ought to have married a man nearer your own age. Do not let me stand in the way of your amusements!"

I had suffered much during the visit which was just concluded. My patience had been played upon beyond the extent of my bearing. I was impressed with a sentiment approaching to despair. Mary did not at this moment comprehend the feelings which agitated me.

"If it will be more pleasing to you," resumed she, "I will go by myself."

"And, who, do you expect, will be your partner in the dance?"

"Laetitia has promised to get me a partner. There is the handsome Mr. Matthews. As a new-comer, she told me, she dared say I might have him."

"Very well! very well!"

"My dear love, what is it you would have?"

"I wish you were married to Mr. Matthews!"

"Good God, Fleetwood, what have I done to deserve this unkindness?" And she burst into tears.

I took her hand.—"Do not weep, Mary! I beg your pardon. I am to blame."

"I try every way to please you, but in vain. I ask you for your company; you refuse it. I offer to stay at home; you reproach me with my youth. In the innocence of my heart I name to you a gentleman as my partner, and you insult me. My dear parents! Is my happiness for ever sunk with you in the caverns of the ocean?"

As she spoke thus, I felt the bitterest self-reproach for what I had done. Yet she had touched me in a very tender point. Loving her as I did, I felt that she must be every thing, or nothing, to me. I could not bear that my wife should have amusements for which I felt no partiality; least of all, amusements of dissipation. I particularly felt an antipathy to this of dancing. I had not joined in recreation of that kind since my juvenile residence in France. And there, at least in the instances of which I had been a sharer, it seemed to me incompatible with decorum or modesty. The eyes sparkled, the performers handled each other in a way that fired the blood, the wholesome restraints of sobriety were banished, a species of electricity flowed from the joining fingers and meeting frames, and every thing seemed to beat an alarm to the ruder passions.

I found in Mary a considerable degree of resentment, or, to speak more properly, a strong impression of sadness, ensuing on this little conversation. The next morning at breakfast she rung the bell, and ordered that John should get ready to go with a message to Mr. Philips's. The moment the servant had left the room, I went up to her, and said,—

"My love, I cannot bear to see you sad. Pray, oblige me, and go with the ladies to their assembly."

"Fleetwood," said she, "do you think I regret the assembly? What have you ever seen in me so frivolous, as to justify the imputation? No; it is not the trip to Barmouth, it is the unkind way in which you expressed yourself to me, that I regret. I chose you from all the world. If you prove austere and unkind, what will become of me? You said, you wished me married to another: how many harsh and unfriendly thoughts are implied in that wish!"

"I am hasty; I am irritable: you know my foibles. My dear girl will have many things to forgive in me; but I hope my errors, thus acknowledged, will only draw us together the closer."

"Then do not, Fleetwood, let many of them be of this kind! Have pity on the poor orphan, who has no shelter but in you!"

"I will be careful. But do not, Mary, lay any stress on such speeches as that of which you complain! The thought of not being yours never seriously entered my mind. You are every thing to me. For your sake I am reconciled to the world. In you, for the first time, I feel that I belong to the great family of man, and experience those delicious sensations which grow out of the charities we form for ourselves."

"Thank you, Fleetwood! And now who shall say, we are not happy?"

"But, Mary,—but—there is one favour you must grant me."

"Name it! What can I refuse you?"

"You must go to the assembly."

"Never. I see you have a strong objection to it, and that is enough. I wonder what possessed me, to think of it. It well suits a poor orphan as I am, to make one in a dance."

"Fie, Mary! I shall never think you regard me as your whole family in one, if you always refuse to be gay. I am very angry with what I said to you about it last night. It was harsh; it was cruel; it was wicked. I shall not believe that you have forgiven me, unless you execute your original intention."

We argued the point for some time; but at length I triumphed. In a high spirit of romance I determined to go with her, and even insisted that she should dance with the young and handsome Mr. Matthews, as Miss Philips had proposed.

Yet my objection to the recreation of dancing remained as strong in my breast as before. I thought that no modest single woman should dance with any partner but her brother, or matron but with her husband. To witness this petty prostitution of my wife, was a penance I enjoined myself, for having so undeservedly mortified and insulted her.

One thought which occurred to my mind, between the arrangement of this plan and its execution, I will mention, to show how unreasonable and unjust I was prepared to be.—"How came it," said I to myself, "that Mary rung the bell in the breakfasting-room, to give her orders for John to carry back the tickets? Might she not have done this in some way when I was not present? Does it not look, as if she designed that the giving these orders should produce a scene? If there was art in this, how deep and odious must be her art, and how egregiously am I her dupe?"

We went to Barmouth. It was impossible for man to entertain a greater detestation for the mummeries of a country assembly than I did. How much had I already suffered from the youthful and heedless disposition of my wife! I had lost the use of my own house, in the way I liked. I had attempted to call her attention to the noblest objects of literature and refinement, and the attempt had only ended in my mortification. I was involved in an endless series of visits with fox-hunting squires, and fat justices of the peace, their wives and daughters. Though I abhorred this sort of company, I had not equanimity to retire to some obscure corner of the house, and pursue my own occupations, while they acted over their etiquettes and decorums: nor, indeed, was this compatible with the complaisance I wished to show for my beloved.—But the worst was to come.

I soon distinguished among the beaux of Merionethshire the handsome Mr. Matthews. He was a man of family, had been well educated, and possessed an advantageous air. He displayed, like some young noblemen I have seen, an easy assurance, which seems designed to put every one, less eminent in rank, or less captivating than themselves, out of countenance. He was soon introduced to my wife, according to the arrangement which had been settled. I stood at a little distance, and observed his *début*. Mary was the most beautiful woman in the assembly, and accordingly Mr. Matthews appeared highly satisfied with his fortune. As they passed me, my wife slightly named me to her partner, who bowed; but I thought I could discover a smothered contempt in his air. When they had gone a little way, he looked back at me; I persuaded myself that he was saying to her, "Is it possible such an old fellow as that, should be husband to so fine a young creature as you are?"

I could not avoid watching Mary and her partner during the dance. I observed that he was infinitely gallant and attentive to her. To my thought his countenance proved that he was exceedingly struck with her figure and beauty. He omitted no exertion to appear amiable in her eyes. They were the most graceful dancers, as well as the handsomest couple, in the room; and both entered with no little spirit into the amusement. I never saw Mary so conspicuously alive; Matthews's demeanour, I believe, never absolutely overstepped the bounds of propriety; he was certainly exceedingly well-bred; yet many of his actions were strikingly free. They escaped being vulgar or offensive, by the airy and flying manner in which they were performed; so that, if a woman, situated as Mary was, might in some instances have been startled, and felt prompted to complain, she would probably have been convinced by the little stress which was laid on such advances, that all was meant in innocence. Matthews talked to her incessantly in every interval of the dance, and Mary seemed sufficiently ready to sustain her part in the conversation.

I was consummately miserable. Whenever they talked with more then usual earnestness, I could not help believing that Matthews was exciting her to lament her condition, in being married to a man of more than twice her own age. Every free and familiar action, every attention that this coxcomb paid to my wife, was a dagger to my heart. "How beautiful," exclaimed I to myself, "were the manners, in this particular, of the ancient Greeks and Romans! How charming does Lucretia appear, spinning at midnight in the midst of her maids, and Cornelia, surrounded with her children![1] Surely no wife ought to endeavour to make herself amiable and engaging in the eyes of any other man than her husband! When a marriageable girl allows herself, without fixed purpose, in sportive intercourse with a youth of her own age, we call her a coquette; what epithet, does the mistress of a family deserve, who acts in a similar manner?"

I felt all the torments of jealousy. How new to me were the sensations I experienced! I was in this sense a happy fellow, when I had no one's conduct to attend to but my own; and, being a bachelor, was not called upon to be minutely scrupulous in that. Now my reputation—no, that was not the first object of my care; reputation was not the bread of my life,—my peace of mind depended on the conduct of another. How wretched is the state of that man who is deceived in so material a point, who presses to his heart the wanton partner of his bed, and believes her innocent; nay, who, perhaps, is habitually engaged in acts of civility to the coxcomb-serpent that stings

---

1   Roman women famous for their virtue. Lucretia (fifth century BC) was seen sharing the work of her maids by a group of young men. One of the men, Sextus, son of Tarquinius Superbus, later raped Lucretia. Rather than live with such dishonor, Lucretia committed suicide. Cornelia (second century BC) was famous for taking upon herself the education of her twelve children upon the death of her husband Tiberius Sempronius Gracchus.

him in the tenderest point! But, short of this, I could not bear that Mary should be weaned from me in any respect, or find amusement in the conversation of any man but myself. Perhaps this might lead her by no slow progress to regret that we were ever united. I depended now for all that was dear to me upon the disposition of one who was young, gay, versatile, and a woman. I watched over her, with the same sleepless anxiety with which a miser watches over his treasure: less happy in this, that his vigilance may be expected to be effectual to his purposes, while the vigilance of a suspicious husband is essentially powerless, and often contributes to give existence to the evil, alienation of mind or perpetrated infidelity, which he fears.

I had prided myself in the generosity of my conduct, in having insisted that Mary should go to the assembly, that she should dance, that I would myself be her escort, and that Matthews should be her partner. If I had yielded one of these points, it was by no means necessary that I should concede them all. There was heroism in my determination; but it was a heroism beyond the mettle of my spirit, and I ought not to have attempted it.

At length this eternal evening drew to a conclusion. From the day of my birth to the present moment, I had never suffered so many hours of slavery. When we got into the carriage to return, I felt irresistibly prompted to avenge my sorrows by inveighing against the neighbourbood, the evening, and the gay elegant dancer who had almost uninterruptedly engaged the attention of my wife. Poor Mary was in high spirits, and pleaded the cause adverse to mine in each of these points. I must confess that I to a certain degree inveigled her into this hostility. I asked her opinion of every thing that had passed, and was tardy in giving my own. She therefore frankly declared, that she was enchanted with our neighbours, who she thought were most amiable people, that Barmouth assembly was a ravishing scene, and that she had never met a more agreeable and well-behaved young man than Mr. Matthews.

When she had finished her panegyric, I echoed it with a deep groan. Mary started. My spirits had too long been pent up, and I now gave a loose to my speech. I cursed the neighbourhood, and declared that country assemblies were a device of the devil. I said that such young men as Mr. Matthews answered no mortal purpose but to disturb the peace of families. The conversation they held was seduction, their attentions were lime-twigs[1] to entrap the unwary, and their touch was contamination.

"Oh, Mary," cried I, in a tone of heartfelt anguish, "did I ever think it would come to this? Ought you not well to have reflected, before you accepted the hand of Fleetwood, whether your taste led you, in preference to the sobriety of a domestic fire-side, to dances and assemblies, the society of giggling girls, and the gallantries of a coxcomb? What prospect can we have of peace and felicity, when you have now declared your partiality for those things, which are equally abhorrent to my personal habits, and irreconcileable to my period of life?"

Mary burst into tears.

"My dear love," said she, "you, in this instance, and not Mr. Matthews, are my seducer. Did not I at the first word give up my engagement; and did not you insist that I should adhere to it at all points? When you obliged me to go to this assembly, and to dance with the young gentleman who has been my partner, you, in all reason, engaged that you would not put yourself in ill humour with that which your own decree imposed upon me."

"This is evasion, Mary. When I insisted that you should go, I did not include in my demand that your partner should be so insidious and persevering in his siege, that you should encourage him to still greater boldness, or that you should afterward become his advocate and eulogist. If your sentiments had been pure, instead of the delight you take in the bare recollection of Matthews, you would not endure so much as to hear him named."

---

1   Twigs smeared with sticky bird-lime; used for catching birds.

CHAPTER IV.

CONVERSATION like this occupied us during a part of our ride home, which afterward subsided into a somewhat sullen silence. The next morning at breakfast I revived the subject.

"Mary," said I, "have you thought of the incidents of yester-evening? My heart bleeds while I recollect it. It has been the incessant occupation of my thoughts."

"Fleetwood, we might be happy, if you were consistent. Tell me the habits of life you wish me to pursue, and I will exert my utmost efforts to conform to your will."

"Mary, we might be happy, if you were consistent. I do not desire you to conform to any system of my prescribing. I want the heart, and not an exterior pliableness."

"Alas! my love, let me assure you that you do not know what you want. I am young. Fleetwood, you might have married an old woman if you had pleased. I have somewhat, yet I think no inordinate share of the gaiety and spirits incident to youth. Yet I am very sure that my sallies are perfectly innocent."

"Oh, yes, madam; exceedingly innocent to encourage such an enterprising young fellow as Matthews, and to find an ecstasy of delight in that scene which was tearing your poor husband's heart into a thousand pieces!"

"Fleetwood, you oblige me to tell you that I have very little encouragement to become a dutiful and attentive wife, when, with the unreserved conformity I use, I find it impossible to please you."

"Very well, madam! very well!"—And I left the room.

My character by this time is sufficiently manifest; I was to the last degree impatient of contradiction. Mary had shown herself an exemplary wife; if there was any sharpness in what she said, it was no more than is inseparable from the clear and open temper of an honourable mind. She was conscious of the entireness of her duty, and the disinterested sentiment which animated her; and it is no wonder that she felt some indignation at the ungracious way in which all this was received. There is not a word that she uttered, which now, as I write it down, I do not approve. She might have courted me more, and have abstained from every thing that could increase the exacerbation of my spirit. But, if she had, she would not have been more successful.

Every thing I saw and felt at this time was so new to me! I had scarcely ever been checked by my tutor or by my father. Since I grew up to man's estate, the system of my domestic life had been with servants only, where every thing was done in uncontending obedience. The acuteness of my feelings had prevented me from being tyrannical and severe to my dependants; but, if my government was mild, it was not the less absolute. Now I lived for the first time familiarly, every day, and all day long, with a person claiming to have a will of her own; with one, who, in every thing she was expected to do, had a right to have her feelings consulted, and was surrounded with privileges of a very different stamp from those of a servant; and, which is perhaps of more importance, with one whose feelings made the principal part of the question, and respecting whom it was of less moment what she did than with what temper every thing she did or suffered, was sustained.

Unused, as I have said, to encounter the smallest obstacle to my will, or to have any of my decisions replied to, I felt the utmost impatience at those gentle manifestations of independence, which, to a man inured to better habits, would have made the person in whom they appeared a thousand times more lovely. The irritation I expressed was softness and conciliation to what I felt. The words I uttered were nerveless, compared with the tone in which they were spoken, and the gestures that accompanied them. My eyes flashed fire: my teeth ground against each other. When I burst out of the room thus abruptly, chains of steel and rocks of adamant could scarcely have withheld me.

The scene I have related was hardly over, when Mr. Matthews rode up to my door, to pay his respects to his partner of the preceding evening. This circumstance had not been expected; and, in the remote situation in which we lived, strict regulations are not enforced, as in the metropolis, respecting what visitors are to be let in, and what to be excluded. Mr. Matthews was shown into a parlour; the servant went to seek my wife. It so happened that Mary, who had been in the garden to visit the favourites of her care, entered the parlour by another door, before she was informed that Mr. Matthews was there: otherwise, after what had just passed between us, she would most assuredly have excused herself from seeing him. She was going to retire, but she felt that that was impossible; and therefore, with much uneasiness and perplexity, entered into conversation with him.

When I had left my wife, I strayed into a well-known path which led toward the sea-side. At first I felt in the highest degree irritated against her behaviour. "What chance," said I, "have we for happiness, if, supposing me to be in the wrong,— it is impossible I should be wrong!—she, instead of soothing my weakness, thus answers me with taunting and retort?"

Soon, however, I came to see the subject in a different light. "Fleetwood! Fleetwood!" said I, striking my forehead with my hand, "what is it you are doing? I have entered upon a serious and weighty task, the guardianship of the felicity of a young woman, who, without reserve, or defence, or refuge against me, has thrown herself into my power. What engagements did I form to her father! with how solemn protestations did I undertake to remove all uncertainty from his mind! Macneil! death has given to these engagements an added sacredness: thy ghost shall be appeased!—Look upon this young creature! Soft, and tender, and winning as she is, shall I be her destroyer? Do I doubt her innocence? Truth and honour are written in her front, in characters which folly itself cannot mistake. Was ever conduct more exemplary? Was ever temper more generous and obliging? What a brute then am I, to misuse, and give uneasiness to so much excellence! I will throw myself at her feet, and with tears of anguish confess to her my fault."

Full of these sentiments of remorse, I hastened back by the way I came, and entered the house. As I approached the parlour, and had my hand on the lock of the door, suddenly my ears were saluted from within with a burst of idle and obstreperous laughter. I was in the highest degree astonished. I instantly turned back, and enquired of the servants into the cause of this phenomenon. I no sooner heard from whom it proceeded, than all my good resolutions vanished in a moment. In the disturbed state of my thoughts, it seemed to me that the visit of Matthews was an express declaration of war against me; and, unacquainted as I was with the circumstances which had betrayed Mary into the admission of his visit, I regarded the scene now going on, after what had just passed, as the most atrocious of crimes. I wished that my wife had embarked with the rest of her family, And were sunk in the caverns of the ocean. I wished that her name might never again be pronounced in my ears. I ordered my horse to be instantly prepared.

Whither was I going? I could not tell. For how long a time did I purpose to be absent? I knew not. I only knew that all places were paradise compared with that in which I was, and all modes of thinking heaven compared with the reflection that Matthews was at this moment alone with my wife.

Before my horse was brought to the door, I began, however, to ask myself, whether it became me thus to go away, and leave my wife in undisturbed conversation with her paramour. Incensed with this idea, I suddenly altered my plan, and burst into the parlour. Both my step and my countenance were extremely discomposed.

My wife, conscious how strange an appearance this visit would have, was greatly embarrassed. Matthews remarked the fierceness of my demeanour, and distinctly read what was passing in my mind; but, like a man who knew the world, he assumed a more courtly and ingenuous air, in proportion as he saw I was enraged against him. He was aware that, if he gave the least encouragement to my passions, they would produce a scene. But this neither suited him, as a gentleman, nor as a man of the world. His character for insinuation and good breeding was at stake, that he should appease the vehemence of my feelings, without seeming to notice them. He played his part in a masterly manner. At first my answers were short, and sullen, and in a style approaching to defiance. He was upon the alert to avoid every topic, which could, by any chance direction, strike a spark into the train that was ready laid in my bosom. He praised my house, and the prospect it commanded. He observed, that he had heard I was a great traveller: he had himself lately returned from Paris; and he described the barriers which had been erected, with some other alterations which had recently been made there. By degrees I recovered my self-possession. Mr. Matthews delivered about a dozen remarks of nearly the same degree of importance, but uttered with spriteliness and grace, and then took his leave.

As soon as he was gone, Mary informed me, in the simplest and most ingenuous terms, how she had been betrayed into the receiving his visit. The story was so natural; her countenance, as she spoke, was so sweet and engaging; she was evidently so much distressed at the effect she feared this *mal-encontre*[1] would produce upon me; I could not altogether resist the force of these demonstrations. I said little; but I withdrew, that I might seriously take myself to task for the weakness into which I saw I was falling.

"Fleetwood," said I, "is it possible thou shouldst commit such egregious folly? What ground hast thou for this outrageous and frantic jealousy? What has passed, what can have passed, between Matthews and thy wife? Is she not the most innocent and affectionate of her sex?—I am myself the most fortunate of men. After having trifled away the flower of my age, and conceived so strong an antipathy to the sex, have I not met with the best of wives,—a creature who, for beauty, for accomplishments, for gentleness and tenderness, has not her equal on the face of the earth? I am old: what matters that? She does not see it; she does not impute to me an imperfection. Flower of creation, most angelic, noblest of mortals, thou shalt be rewarded! Yes, if it is in my power, thou shalt be rewarded!"

Would to God, I had always continued in this temper! But I was subject to perpetual relapses. Every thing that thwarted and crossed me, still produced in me new displeasure against this charming woman. She was like the angel appointed by Heaven to defend my steps; and whatever circumstance of a painful nature occurred to me, still seemed to be chargeable upon some neglect of hers. I suffered from visits and visitors; I felt

---

1 An unfortunate event.

myself restrained in going out and coming in; the liveliness of Mary's temper, and the quickness of her perceptions, made her, in spite of her gentleness, unfit for the curb; a thousand times, when I wished to fix her attention to a particular point, and when I had worked up my whole soul with the imagination of it, she was drawn aside by some new phantasy, and left abruptly the pursuit, the lecture, and the professor: all these evils came to me from my wife.

It is human nature, that a man should retain some resentment against the instrument that has often wounded him, however valuable the instrument may be, and however innocent of any purpose to harm. The man, who has repeatedly crossed me in my desires, and has constantly stepped before me in the objects of life, it is morally impossible I should not come to consider as a bad man. It was thus with Mary. Every time she did any thing that jarred with my propensities,—and by some accident or other no day passed without something, greater or smaller, of this kind,—my favourite theory about the female sex revived; I recurred to the bitter experience of my youth; and swore that, however it might in certain instances be glossed over, all women were in the main alike, selfish, frivolous, inconstant, and deceitful.

It was a strange war that was continually going on in my bosom. I doted on my wife to distraction; I felt that I could not exist without her; I saw that she was every thing that was lovely; her tones penetrated my soul; her smiles drew me from my most steadfast purposes, and made me as ductile as wax to the aims she proposed. Yet I taught myself gradually to curse this as weakness, and to regard it as a slavery which some devilish witchcraft had fastened on my heart. I murmured at my way of life; I roared like a lion in the toils. My whole existence was tempestuous. At certain moments, when Mary directed against me all her powers of fascination, I felt the joys of heaven; at other times, and these were of longer duration, I suffered the torments of the damned.

CHAPTER V.

THE month of September came, and with September that variable weather, which ordinarily marks the period of the equinox. At this time a sensible change discovered itself in the health of my wife. Her appetite left her; her nights were sleepless; she became languid and meagre. I was deeply affected with the alteration I perceived; I was beset with the fear that my unkindness was the occasion of what I saw.

"Alas! Mary," said I, "you wanted a very different treatment from that which you have received from me! All tender and gentle you are in your own nature; all tenderness and gentleness ought to have been the behaviour that was addressed to you. With mildness and benignity were you brought up by the best of fathers and of mothers; I myself have witnessed their affection; often have I heard you describe it. It was not fit you should fall from the hands of these kind guardians, into those of a husband, harsh, severe, and capricious as I have been." She has suffered the most terrible of all losses; she thought to find a refuge from calamity, and a compensation for her sufferings in me; was it right that I should have been the person to aggravate her woes? She cheerfully resigned the prerogative and the preference of her sex and age, the marrying a young man, in the bloom of life, with the wholesome hue of youth in his cheeks, with a smooth and unfurrowed brow, not yet enslaved to peculiar and unaccommodating habits, with a warm imagination, and a fresh and unsated relish of the various pleasures of existence. Ought I not to have done every thing that my mature period of life would admit, to lessen to her the sacrifice she had made?

Mary saw the anxiety and remorse under which I laboured. She exerted herself, to the utmost of her power, to relieve them. She dressed her pallid countenance in smiles; they were the smiles of a winter's day, when the sun sends forth a sickly beam, amidst watery and congregated clouds. She protested she was happy; she solemnly assured me that she thought my conduct toward her immaculate. I caught her repeatedly in tears. I endeavoured to tempt her with parties of pleasure. With very different feelings from those I have formerly described, I called the Philipses and the Morgans around me. She refused these avocations as often as she could. When compelled to accept them, she sat passive and joyless amidst the youthful circle, except at moments when she perceived my eye turned inquisitively upon her, and then she forced an artificial animation, which quickly again subsided into cureless dejection. I enquired after another country assembly; I wished for Mr. Matthews again to waken her into enjoyment. When I proposed tickets to her, she smiled significantly in my face; but added, that it would not do.

"What a life is this?" said I. "What a life for me, who had ever led my days free from dependence or restraint? Am I converted into a *garde-malade*,[1] having for my constant occupation to watch the symptoms of another? Are my sensations, to which I have so long been a slave, to pass unheeded, and as nothing? Is all my happiness, my peace of mind, through every successive moment, to depend, not merely on the good pleasure and complacence of another, but on the state of that person's pulse, or the clouds which may accidentally hover over her diseased fancy?"

Yet I call Heaven to witness that, however I occasionally murmured under a system of life so opposite to that to which I had been accustomed, my love for my wife was no wise diminished. The more she wanted my aid, the more eager I was to afford it. The more she fell away from the healthful sleekness of a beautiful woman, the more she appeared to me like an angel. If it was but seldom that she could rouse herself to an entire interchange of affectionate thoughts, these intervals became as transporting as they were rare. I could patiently watch through a month of eclipse, to be rewarded at last with a sight of the God of my idolatry. The mother who rears a sickly and perishing child, is always found to love that child better than her robust and comely one; her own labour has become kneaded up in the little being before her; he seems the creation of her hands, continually dependent for his existence on her breath. It

---

1 A nurse.

was thus I felt toward Mary. She in return became more affectionate than ever; she was sensible of my cares, and eager to acknowledge them.

I firmly believe that I am the most capricious and wayward being that ever existed. I never remained permanently in one state of mind. After fits of fondness, anxiety, and disinterestedness inexpressible, my mind, exhausted with cares, would sometimes recoil on itself; and I pretended, in the bitterness of my heart, to cast up my gains. "It is true," said I, "I love Mary; I cannot help it; this love is the star of my ascendant for the rest of my days. But what am I the better for it? What are her merits? What have I ever experienced from her but thwarting and disappointment? I feel that I have lost the freedom which was once my portion; and without freedom what is life?"

Mary, as I have said, was exceedingly anxious to conceal from me the uneasiness under which she laboured. Symptoms occasionally appeared in her which alarmed me, and which seemed to partake of an alienation of the understanding. Though generally comfortless and sad, she would now and then break into an opposite tone of mind, and be seized with fits of merriment and laughter. I can conceive nothing more horrible then this laughter; it expressed misery more strikingly than all the sighs, and tears, and groans in the world could have done.

My wife slept little; and her short and unfrequent slumbers were exceedingly disturbed. She talked in her sleep; her words were murmuring, indistinct, and incoherent; but they referred to her family; particularly to her mother.

"Mary," said I, "you will break my heart. What can I do to comfort you? Your mother I cannot restore to you; I cannot compel the ocean to give back her dead. But all that I can, I will do. I will in all things study your inclinations; I will never thwart and oppose you, as I have done; I will bestow all my thoughts in the effort to relieve you; I will seek for still new pleasures, till I find some that shall be cordial to your bosom."

"My dear Fleetwood," she replied, "never mind me. Do not give yourself this uneasiness about me. All will be well. I feel a weight just here (clapping her hand to her head); but it is only a cloud, that will blow away, and the sun will shine again. I will talk to myself, and bring my temper into better order. I am ashamed, that I should thus torment you, who ought to be your comfort and your helper. It shall not be thus long."

At other times I talked to her in a style partaking of reproach.—"Would to God, Mary, you loved me as I love you! Your thoughts would not then be all upon the things you have lost and cannot regain. You would sometimes think of me, and be happy. To me you are every thing; I think of you as an angel, and think of nothing else; having you, I want nothing; friends, fortune, country, all the gratifications of life, I should never regret, if blessed with your affection. Hard is the fate of him, whose passion is unreturned by the object of his love; or who, when his bosom burns with all the ardour of attachment, obtains nothing but a moderate and glimmering kindness, insufficient to awake contentment in the mistress of his heart!"

There were occasions when I talked to her in a stronger style. I told her, that the weakness she indulged was unworthy of her education and her powers. I described it as the characteristic of a feeble mind and a vacant understanding, to dwell thus obstinately upon what was now placed beyond the reach of fate. I exhorted her peremptorily to oppose the foe that had invaded her peace. I told her, that human creatures had a being and duties of their own; and that it became every one who would escape the contempt of his fellow-men, to rouse himself to the consideration of them.

One further circumstance occurred in the progress of Mary's distemper. She would steal from her bed in the middle of the night, when no one perceived it, and make her escape out of the house. The first time this accident occurred, I was exceedingly alarmed. I awoke, and found that the beloved of my soul was gone. I sought her in her closet, in the parlour, and in the library. I then called up the servants. The night was dark and tempestuous; the wind blew a hollow blast; and the surges roared and stormed as they buffeted against the hurricane. A sort of sleet blew sharp in our faces when we opened the door of the house. I went myself in one direction, and despatched the servants in others, to call and search for their mistress. After two hours she was brought back by one of my people, who, having sought in vain at a distance, had discovered her on his return, not far from the house. Her hair was dishevelled; her countenance as white as death; her limbs cold; she was languid and speechless. We got her, as quickly as we could, to bed.

This happened a second time. At length I extorted her secret from her. She had been to the beach of the sea to seek the bodies of her parents. On the sea-shore she seemed to converse with their spirits. She owned, she had been tempted to plunge herself into the waves to meet them. She heard their voices speaking to her in the hollow wind, and saw their faces riding on the top of the waves, by the light of the moon, as it peeped precariously through the storm. They called to her, and bid her come along, and chid her for her delay. The words at first sounded softly, so that it seemed difficult to hear them, but afterward changed to the most dolorous and piercing shrieks. In the last instance a figure had approached her, and, seizing her garment, detained her, just as she was going to launch herself into the element. The servants talked something of a gentleman, who had quitted Mary, precisely as they came up to conduct her home.

She confessed that, whenever the equinoctial wind sounded in her ears, it gave a sudden turn to her blood and spirits. As she listened alone to the roaring of the ocean, her parents and her sisters immediately stood before her. More than once she had been awaked at midnight by the well-known sound; and, looking out of bed, she saw their bodies strewed on the floor, distended with the element that filled them, and their features distorted with death. This spectacle she could not endure; she had crept silently out of bed, and, drawing a few clothes about her, had found her way into the air. She felt nothing of the storm; and, led on by an impulse she could not resist, had turned her steps toward the sea.

This was a terrible story. I saw that some immediate and decisive remedy was indispensable. I saw that the state of mind she was in, if not effectually changed, led in direct course to one of two issues,—derangement of intellect, or suicide. Poor Mary! How deep an impression the fatal catastrophe of her family had made upon her mind! I was of all men most inexcusable in having forgotten this. I had seen the whole progress of the impression, and with what difficulty she had been recalled to the world at first. If, in the warm affection she had conceived for me, in her marriage and subsequent prospects with the man of her choice, she had in some degree risen from the tomb, and come away from the recent graves of those she loved, did that form an excuse for me? On the contrary, it laid me under the highest and most indelible obligation. What a proof of love! Did ever wife give to her husband, or mistress to the most devoted of her admirers, a more incontrovertible evidence of attachment? And I, in my ingratitude and insensibility, had shut my eyes upon the true merit of this conduct, and treated with rudeness and asperity the amiable devotee!

CHAPTER VI.

CHANGE of scene was a medicine which the case obviously required. She must not be within reach of the sea. She must be, where it was impossible for the ear to catch the roaring of the waters. I further conceived that it was desirable to convey her to some place, where variety of amusement should draw off her attention from the horrible imaginings with which she had lately been haunted. Mary was young; and there is something in the spring and first unfolding of life, which seems particularly to demand the interposition of diversified objects and vivacious entertainment. In the present case, nature herself appeared to point out the remedy. Mary had shown a decisive partiality for visits, and assemblies, and crowds. I now believed that it was an indistinct consciousness that she could not support herself without these aids, that had directed her choice. I fixed upon a removal to Bath.

My wife derived great and evident benefit from this transplanting. Some languor remained for a few days; but it speedily disappeared.

It is impossible to conceive with what joy I hailed her return to health. I had had the most horrible prospect before me. I had seen the wife of my bosom given up to the agonies of a distracted spirit. I had felt a remorse and oppression of mind, to which, till that hour I had been a stranger. I accused myself as the author of her calamity. The tenderest flower in nature's garden had been committed to my care, and I was deeply responsible for the manner in which I had treated it. If she seemed to have forgotten the premature destruction of her family, I ought not to have forgotten it. I ought to have considered her as a convalescent, that required every art to defend from a relapse, and to lure away from the action of those causes which had produced her disease.

For many days I fed upon the pleasure which her recovery afforded me. I saw, with ecstasies of delight, the roses once more unfolding their bloom upon those cheeks, late so livid and so pale. For several weeks before we left Merionethshire, Mary had gradually become more and more dejected; and, if at any time she smiled, her smiles, as I have said, had in them something more sad and terrible to my heart, than tears in any other case would have suggested. Now I saw in them, once again, the honest expression of a mind accessible to amusement and pleasure. I saw those gathering clouds, which had been felt by me like the end of the world, dispersed and clearing away, as if they had never been. I thanked her a thousand times; I kissed the new-blown roses; I clasped her in my transported arms.

"Mary," said I, "you have brought me back from the very dens of despair. Oh, Mary, what alarms have I felt! It is indeed an awful thing to be in love! Poor creature, how much must you have suffered! Do you remember when you sallied forth on that terrible night? Do you remember, when, as you said, some friendly, unknown hand snatched you back, just as you were going to be swallowed up by the billows?——No, I will mention the subject no more. I will be the most cautious and attentive of husbands. Brute that I was, I had not considered how much delicacy and forbearance your sweet frame demanded. You are an angel, and I treated you like a mortal. Will you forgive me?"

I wish this recovery had taken place less rapidly. Mary passed from one extreme to the other, without almost an interval between. She made acquaintances, she resorted to all public places; she was involved in a perpetual round of engagements; she laughed, and talked, and danced, and sung, for ever; at least so it appeared to my sickly apprehension. Yet I was upon my guard, not to check, or seem to disapprove, as I had formerly done, the avocations she chose. Sometimes, indeed, with ever-subtle anxiety, I was alarmed for the sanity of her intellect. Once or twice I hinted to my charmer, in an obscure and distant way, that she was over-acting her part. On these occasions she looked at me with a wistful and wintry smile, that brought back to my recollection all the horrible apprehensions I had lately entertained. I kissed her, and told her, I saw she was right.

Here then I was, torn, not now from my closet and my private staircase, but from my paternal mansion, and the haunts, where once my careless childhood strayed. Lately the most independent man alive, I was become a mere appendage to that tender and charming trifle, a pretty woman. I adored my wife; but I had cultivated high ideas of the prerogatives of my sex, and I did not altogether relish the being thus reduced to a cipher. My geographical situation was now the offspring of necessity, not of choice. I felt like the persons I have somewhere read of, acted upon by a magnetic influence, who wore no chains or fetters, and yet were prisoners, struggling, perhaps, to advance in an opposite direction, but always compelled to follow the steps of him who exerted this ascendancy over them.

Bath, of all places on earth, I detested. I had some unpleasing associations respecting it, arising from certain trivial adventures, which I have not thought it necessary to record in this history. But, independently of these, I had been, through life, with very few interruptions, a lover of nature, of her romantic and magnificent scenery, of her simple and unvitiated manners. Bath appeared to me the very focus of artificial society; of every thing that was frivolous, affected, impertinent, overreaching, and licentious.

Deeply in love as I was, I could not help speculating, with no agreeable reflections, from the new lights I had derived on the character of my wife. Fickle and capricious I judged her;

and, thus judging, I could not avoid sometimes viewing her under the notion of a beautiful toy, a plume of costly feathers, or a copious train of thinnest gauze, which nods gracefully, or floats in a thousand pleasing folds, but which is destitute of substance, firmness, or utility. There must be something, I thought, radically defective in so fluctuating a character. She acted (thus I construed her demeanour) inconsiderately and idly; she could be induced to no fixed spirit of attention; she was at one moment sunk in the lowest depths of misery, and at another wild with extravagant gaiety, with no interval to qualify the transition, with no self-government to give propriety or moderation to either. A being acting thus, was it entitled to be ranked in the scale of moral existences? What dependence could be placed upon the consistency of any thing so versatile? What principles could dwell in the bosom of so mere a woman?—All these reasonings brought back to my mind Mrs. Comorin, the Marchioness de L———, and the Countess of B———; and I reverted to my long established sentiment, that the sex were all alike. What a fool was I, ever to have doubted it!

Indulging this ill-humoured and inequitable estimate of my wife, it was natural that I should be displeased with the figure I made on the present occasion. "Once," said I to myself, "I was a man! Ambition had its dwelling-place in this bosom. How many thoughts, and projects, and inventions, for fame and for usefulness, have passed through my mind?" In reality, it was this ardent desire to be something, to record myself on the rolls of my species for some praiseworthy deed, that had haunted me for ever, and poisoned my tranquillity in every stage. My father and my grandfather were admirable men. What matters it, that they were merely opulent English merchants? Not to introduce here many other anecdotes scarcely less honourable to their characters, the senior, who took up the little vagrant Ruffigny and made him his son, and the junior, who willingly yielded that this vagrant should enter into the joint possession of his inheritance, were no ordinary men. Ruffigny himself and Macneil, the two most distinguished of my friends, were of that stamp, who did nothing for fame, but every thing for utility, for venerable simplicity, and for virtue. It was not the loud blast of applause that I demanded; it was, that I might look on myself with a satisfied mind; and those who knew me most, might love me, and who could judge me best, might say, "He has not lived in vain!"

And were all my projects, and was the never-resting anxiety of my bosom, reduced to this? Formerly I said, "I am nothing;" because no achievement I ever performed came up to my own ideas of what became me. Now I might say, "I am nothing;" because, with regard to any such ideas, I was literally palsied. I was a lover! Alas! I was past the age, when a man can rest satisfied with this one frivolous passion, and see in the world only his Julia! Love is a passion in which soul and body hold divided empire. The meaner half of our nature is essential to its support. It is sex, it is "a set of features and complexion, the tincture of a skin," that constitutes its origin and principle.[1] Considered in this light, it is, all through, a selfish sentiment, the pampering of a weakness, a delicious scheme for beguiling the hours and weeks of our existence. Certainly man, particularly the man whom Heaven has endowed with inventive faculties and a comprehensive intellect, was made for something better than this. I was now engrossed by a single individual; I was playing a subservient and humble part in her train; and even the character and attributes of this individual did not at all times command my approbation. Assuredly I did not always look back upon this with complacence, or with patience.

CHAPTER VII.

It was at Bath that I first reduced to practice the other part of the advice of my deceased Mentor,—the calling about me my distant relations, young men who, from the regulations of society, had the best claim upon my assistance.

I had had a kinswoman, descended from a sister of my grandfather, with whom we had preserved little intercourse,

---

1   Joseph Addison, *Cato* (1713), I.iv.143-44.

because we had always considered her character as by no means calculated to do credit to any one who should be connected with her. The woman was now dead; but, while living, she had run a singular career. She had been given in first marriage to a wealthy esquire of Wales, of the name of Gifford. This man she had led for several years a weary life. She was of exquisite beauty, tall, graceful, and captivating. Her tastes were expensive, and her manners gay. Her demeanour was spirited and impressive, her passions volatile, and her temper violent. With all this, she was by no means destitute of capacity. She was eloquent, witty, and sarcastic; exhibiting, when she pleased, the highest breeding, and delivering her remarks with inexpressible vivacity and grace. Thus endowed, she was surrounded, wherever she appeared, with a little army of suitors. Every youth of fashion, who had the courage to look up to her, became her professed admirer; and, among these admirers, it was pretty universally believed that all had not offered up their incense in vain. At length, impunity made her heedless; she was caught in a situation with a young officer, a West Indian of colour, which admitted of no ambiguity; her husband could no longer overlook her offence; and a divorce was the result. Her character being thus blasted, she gave full scope to her appetite for pleasure; she retreated to London, and occupied a very elegant mansion, which was for some time a favourite haunt for the most dissipated of our young nobility. While the divorce was depending, she was allowed, by the ecclesiastical court, a tolerably handsome income out of her husband's estates; and, when this ceased, the defect was understood to be supplied by the more opulent of her guests.

This prosperity, however, did not last for ever. Mrs. Gifford's charms, by the effect of late hours and incessant dissipation, rapidly subsided. She was no longer a novelty. She had had many fortunate lovers; but she had not been lucky enough to secure one, who, by the entanglement of habit or otherwise, should be inclined to preserve the autumn of her days from indigence. She retired, with a dejected heart, and an empty purse, into Wales, and took up her residence in a market-town, in the very next county to that where my father lived. But, though Mrs. Gifford was no longer handsome enough for Rotten Row or Pall Mall,[1] she made a great figure in the remote quarter of the world which now received her. Her recommendations, as I have already said, were not merely those of person; she possessed understanding, animation, and taste. She had seen much of the high world, and she had eminently the talent of giving poignancy to her anecdotes and remarks.

In the town where she dwelt, lived also a Mr. Kenrick, a surgeon, of great skill and ability in his profession. This man was beloved by all the country round, not only on account of his art, and the humane and liberal style in which he dispensed its benefits, but for his manners, which were in the most striking form of artlessness and simplicity. With an uncommon fund of good sense and profound sagacity, he was, as to all the affairs of the living world, a child. He was imposed upon by every artful story, and his purse was open alike to relieve distress and gratify imposture. He could not find in his heart to be severe to any one; and the wretch who had ten times deceived him, was sure, if detected, to be dismissed, at worst, with nothing harder than a patriarchal rebuke. Add to this, he was subject to the strangest fits of absence, which often involved him in incredible mistakes and absurdities; though, as if by the interposition of a good genius for ever watchful over the steps of this admirable creature, his distractions had never been known to produce a pernicious effect in the exercise of his profession.

My worthy kinswoman saw at once into the value of this memorable person. She thought him as exactly fitted to become her second husband, as if he had been made for the purpose. Poor fellow! he had, perhaps, never in his life bestowed a single thought upon love and marriage. But Mrs. Gifford knew, that the man who cannot be brought to enact the personage of a suitor, may, by a dexterous change of the character of the sexes, be an admirable subject for a clever

---

1 Places where the fashionable could be seen in eighteenth-century London: "Rotten Row" was a road in Hyde Park where Londoners made outings in carriages. Pall Mall is a road through St. James's Park.

woman, who should think proper to pay her addresses to him. The ladies of Llanvelling refused to admit the visits of this interesting Magdalene, and therefore she had no chance to meet the doctor at a third place; but that obstacle was immediately removed, when Mrs. Gifford opportunely fell ill of a languishing distemper.[1] She had great address in conducting the symptoms of her indisposition, as she had address in every thing she seriously undertook; poor Kenrick could not tell what to make of it. One thing, however, he better understood,—the charms of her conversation: she exerted all her talents to fix herself in his good opinion; and never, perhaps, in her life had she failed in an attempt of that sort. She did not choose to have a tedious illness; for it was not to her purpose that he should regard her as a decided invalid. She was ill long enough, however, to secure poor Kenrick's partiality. He had never before experienced, in any eminent degree, the pleasures of female society; the Welsh ladies were not calculated to afford them to a man of science. Mrs. Gifford's fire-side was a most delightful retreat to the rural surgeon, after the labours of the day; if he was not there every evening, he every evening wished to be there. The lady, on the other hand, took every precaution to remove his diffidence; she showed him, not so much by words, as by affectionate expressions, and a seeming overflowing of the soul in his company, that he could not visit her too often. Kenrick had been a total stranger to this species of flattery, not because his neighbours did not honour his merit, but because they wanted the skill to honour it in this way; and he was so much the more passive and defenceless to its operations.

All this coquetry terminated in marriage; but the man of medicine found Mrs. Kenrick a very different sort of woman from what Mrs. Gifford had appeared. The bent of his mind rendered him incapable of the habits of accumulation; but the income of his professional labours was far from despicable. When Mrs. Gifford had come down into Wales, fifty pounds constituted the whole fortune, principal and interest, that she possessed. So circumstanced, it was impossible for any woman

---

1 Llanfyllin is a town in Powys (formerly Montgomeryshire).

to have more unexpensive tastes, or a more decisive relish for rural retirement. No sooner, however, had fortune changed, than she resumed her former propensities. She began with adding an elegant saloon to her husband's house, and decorating his little grounds in a sort of Versailles style. It was in vain for Kenrick to remonstrate; she was dashing and peremptory; he gentle, forbearing, and unqualified to contend. She soon grew tired of the delights of Montgomeryshire. One morning she read in the papers of the death of a surgeon of the first eminence at Bath; she found that this afforded an opening of the most auspicious nature for her husband, and insisted upon his removing thither. Kenrick's talents and knowledge of his profession would have made their way any where; but his wife was a clog hung about his neck that made it impossible for him to rise. She filled his house with assemblies of demireps[1] and debauchees; desperate as to the recovery of any character in the world, she resolved to make that figure by dissoluteness and effrontery, which, if she had set out right in life, she might have made by elegance, accomplishments, and virtue. Kenrick lost his courage, his activity, and his employers. Death came at a convenient moment, and, by means of the disease, usually styled a broken heart, rescued him from the horrors of poverty. His wife had taken no care in the seasons of her prosperity to provide for an evil day. She sunk into obscurity, by all neglected and by all despised; and, after several years of wretchedness, terminated her existence in a parish workhouse.

This woman had two sons. The fate of both was singular. Born, the eldest under the roofs of magnificence, and the second in the mansion of competence and plenty, they were reduced at an early age to absolute want. The former bore the name of Gifford. After several years of marriage without the least promise of offspring, his mother had at length presented this son to her first husband. But, in the ecclesiastical proceedings which took place soon after his birth, it was proved to the satisfaction of the court that he was illegitimate, and he was cut off by act of parliament from the large inheritance to which he

---

1 From the French "demi-reputable"; women of poor reputation.

seemed to have been born. Her second son was the offspring of the excellent and guileless Kenrick; and he was ruined, equally with his elder brother, by the unhappy issue of his father's professional life.

Between these two youths there had been an antipathy from the earliest period of the existence of the latter: at least, it was deeply felt by Gifford for his unwelcome cadet. Gifford was a youth of a dark complexion, and elegant figure, sagacious, shrewd, supple, and insinuating. He had been only seven years of age at the period of his mother's second marriage. She had never loved her son; for she beheld him as the innocent instrument of her disgrace. He harboured in his childish bosom a secret abhorrence of his mother. The extraordinary change which had taken place in his fortunes in infancy had probably, when he came to know it, served in a wonderful degree to sharpen his faculties. His nurses and attendants did not fail to tell him that he had, during the early months of his existence, been looked upon as the heir to twenty thousand a year. The eternal recollection that the open misconduct of his mother had been the cause of his losing this, made him look upon her with the sentiments of a demon. Extraordinary as it may seem, long before he was seven years of age, he understood all he had suffered, or at least felt it as deeply as a man of forty might have done. This boyish impression of dislike to her on whom he solely depended, taught him early habits of hypocrisy. Two or three times, in the beginning, his feelings of antipathy had broken out; but the haughty and imperious temper of his mother had crushed them with such terrors as no schoolboy courage could withstand. From this time he learned the tones of submission, and even of reverence; and, being of a remarkably quick capacity, no Roscius or Richard could have played the character he assumed more consummately.[1] Even the penetrating observation of Mrs. Gifford was deceived, and she was persuaded that this viper doted on her to distraction. Love, in an infinite majority of cases, begets love. Perceiving how much the boy seemed attached to her, and remorseful perhaps for the

---

1 Quintus Roscius Gallus (c. 126-62 BC), a famous Roman actor; "Richard" probably alludes to the Richard of Shakespeare's *Richard III*.

great injury he had suffered from her licentiousness, she became tolerant and even kind to him. His figure was graceful and prepossessing; his capacity was every where remarked with sentiments of astonishment; the mother gradually became proud of her son.

She introduced him into the family of the mild Kenrick, and caused him to be treated as the proper heir of all he saw. The age at which Mrs. Gifford had arrived, rendered it somewhat improbable that she should have any child by her second marriage; the habits of her past life seemed to have increased this improbability. The boy, of course, did not exactly understand the state of his step-father's fortune. He saw every thing in plenty about him; and meditated in his youthful heart to give himself full scope in enjoying all at present, and to possess the same means, sole and uncontrolled, when the present proprietors were gone off the stage. It was therefore with a sort of despair that he found that his mother became pregnant in the second year of her marriage. A thousand plans for removing this infant rival, whom he regarded as destined by law the proprietor of those funds which he had so lately counted for his own, suggested themselves to his working brain. Again and again he had thoughts of removing him by poison; Gifford was no coward; but he was also too good a calculator not to give due weight to the chances that this action might conduct him to the gallows. While these sentiments were ever uppermost in his mind, he carried every thing with an external smoothness; and often nursed, and seemed to fondle the child whom he wished to strangle.

The mother of these youths was five summers the wife of Kenrick; when the honest surgeon died, the dreams of wealth immediately vanished which had for years occasioned the little Gifford so many heart-burnings. He saw that his poor half brother was no better off than himself: there was no dispute about the succession, for there was nothing to inherit. Young Kenrick, however, was taken home by his father's relations in the neighbourhood of Llanvelling; they were in narrow circumstances, but exceedingly honest. Gifford was owned by nobody; unhappy in the incident of his birth, he was akin to no living creature but his profligate mother. Once, in the decline of her life, I made enquiry into her situation, and sent her a handsome present: afterward I lost sight of her. It has been seen, how wandering and uncertain a life I led; add to which, she had relations by the father's side, nearer to her than myself, and fully, or nearly, equal to me in point of fortune. They neglected her; they pretended to feel paroxysms of wrath at the very mention of her name; they would extend no indulgence or assistance to the progeny of her adulterous amours. When this wretched woman was taken to the parish workhouse, it was proposed by the churchwardens to bind her son apprentice, as it was called, to a neighbouring farmer; that is, to sell him for a term of years to perform the most oppressive and brutish offices of rural drudgery. A neighbouring clergyman, of considerable learning and a liberal mind, had seen the boy occasionally, and observed in him the tokens of a superior understanding. He took him from the situation to which he was condemned, received him into his house, and determined by his own exertions to cultivate and improve the faculties he discerned.

The mind of Gifford had been deeply affected by every successive revolution in his circumstances. He had written, with his mother's connivance, divers very supple and insinuating letters to her relations by the father's side: without her consent, and in defiance of her prohibition (for in her deepest distress, she still felt an ingenuous pride, which forbade her offering any supplications in this quarter), he wrote to his nominal father. In all things the boy discovered a sagacity beyond his years. As long as there was a hope of obtaining any thing from his mother's relations, he was, in appearance, filial and dutiful to her. When every prospect of that kind was at an end, and he seemed condemned to obscurity and misery for ever, the bitterness of his nature broke out. He reviled her in language so harsh and horrible, that it appeared wonderful where he had acquired his fecundity of invective. In cursing to her face the mother who bore him, he seemed to find ease for the disappointments and adversity he endured. A part of every day he devoted to this gratification; and the once proud and haughty Mrs. Gifford, now reduced by misery and hunger, had not spirits to stand up against this unnatural usage. It was universally believed by those who witnessed the scenes, that the son had thus succeeded to shorten the life of his parent.

When young Gifford was admitted under the roof of the benevolent clergyman who seemed to intend to adopt him for his own, he may be considered as already consummate in every vicious disposition. He had not, however, lost his talent for hypocrisy; and, as the world now began to smile upon him, he became more smooth and insinuating than ever. During his residence in this house, his patron was seized with a dangerous fit of sickness, and with great difficulty recovered. A short time after, the clergyman discovered, by an extraordinary train of accidents, that little Gifford had entered into a plot with a knavish attorney, if he had died when it was expected he would, to rob the wife and only daughter of his patron, of all they should possess. This discovery cured Mr. Parkhurst of his fondness for this extraordinary inmate. He sent him to sea, where Gifford speedily acquired the favour of his superior; and, at the age of twenty-eight, at which I invited him to my house in Bath, he had passed through a series of adventures, scarcely less diversified than those of Gil Blas or Gusman d'Alfarache.[1] His evil genius meanwhile still pursued him; and, however deep were the schemes he had laid, he had not made that progress in life, which assuredly his talents would have obtained, could he have confined himself to the character of an honest man. One, however, of the circumstances, not the least extraordinary, that attended him, was, that he was still followed by the good word of at least half the persons with whom he connected himself. It was not till a considerable time after, that I learned the particulars concerning him which I have here related.

---

1   The heroes of two very popular picaresque novels. Gil Blas was the hero of Alain René Lesage's *L'Histoire de Gil Blas de Santillane* (1715-35), translated into English by Tobias Smollett in 1749. Guzmán was the hero of Mateo Alemán's *Guzmán de Alfarache* (1599, 1602), translated into English by James Mabbe as *The Rogue* in 1622, and into French by Lesage as *Don Guzman d'Alfarache* in 1732.

CHAPTER VIII.

ᴊᴇɴᴄᴇᴅ, as I have said, by what I may call the testamentary advice of the generous Macneil, and desirous of calling about me my nearest existing relations, my mind immediately recurred to the two sons of my frail kinswoman. Previously to this time I had not been wholly inattentive to their interests. Gifford, whose life was wandering and unsettled, I had never seen; but the little Kenrick, who dwelt with his relatives not more than twenty miles from my residence, had often drawn from me the marks of my personal attention. He was a florid and beautiful boy, alert and nimble in his motions, and singularly open and ingenuous in his demeanour. A school-fellow of his, a favourite companion, had been destined by his parents for the army; in their youthful frolics they had played at soldiers; and little Kenrick had often, in his artless prattle, and looking at me with one of his innocent looks, entreated me to let him be a general. I indulged his youthful preference, and at the proper period bought him a pair of colours.[1] A more gallant and kind-hearted soldier the world never saw. There was a brilliancy in his eye, a modest blush in his cheek, and a sensibility in his accent, that, all together, constituted one of the most interesting objects that can be imagined.

These two young men, I, at one and the same time, invited to come to me at Bath. Gifford was at present out of employment, and to be provided for. The profession in which he was most exercised, though he had left it for considerable periods and returned to it again, was that of the sea; and, if I thought proper to push him forward in the path of independence, I might, in no long time, be able to make him a captain in the navy. Kenrick was engaged; he was recently entered in the army; and, at my invitation, obtained a leave of absence for two months, to visit his wealthy kinsman.

Though born of the same mother, it was impossible for two human beings to exhibit a stronger contrast to each other. When Kenrick appeared before me for the first time at Bath,

---

1 An ensign's commission.

dressed in the uniform of his regiment, and glowing with all the bloom of eighteen, I thought I had never beheld so prepossessing a creature. His address was irresistible; his words seemed the image of his heart; and the tone of his voice, when he accosted me, implicitly told the love, gratitude, and respect he entertained for me. The entrance of Gifford, whom I now saw for the first time, by no means impressed me in the same way. His dark complexion, approaching to the mulatto, was no agreeable portent. There was a roving in his eye, which seemed to warn me to put myself upon my guard against him. His general physiognomy conveyed the idea of something obscure and problematical, which I was at a loss to expound. He was ten years older than Kenrick; and, if his understanding, even in infancy, had been premature, it may well be supposed that he had by this time lost all vestige of juvenile simplicity. I did not like him. I said to myself, "Gifford, you shall not stay a week under the roof of your patron."

These were first impressions. As I observed more of these young men, my feelings toward them became essentially altered. Kenrick was full of gay and volatile spirits, which, though qualified with the best heart in the world, rather shocked with the gravity of my age, and the saturnine turn of my disposition. As a boy, I felt kindly toward him; but I soon found that he was by no means fitted to be my companion. Gifford, on the contrary, was serious and of wide information; had read much, and thought more; his researches, especially into the human heart, were profound. He talked like an oracle; and I soon learned to place a great dependence upon his judgment. His sentiments in many respects had a striking similarity to my own. But what was most material he flattered me in my notions and weaknesses, with the greatest imaginable address. It had so happened, that I hitherto had little experience of this sort of flattery. I had been too singular and solitary in my habits, and too frequent in my changes of abode, to have been exposed to this kind of attack so much as men of my fortune usually are. Before many days had elapsed, my two kinsmen fell naturally into their places. Kenrick, who had no secret ends in pursuit, desired nothing on his part but to preserve a complying and respectful carriage toward me. Gifford purposed, from the moment he entered my house, to possess me entirely to himself, and proceeded accordingly. That insinuating voice and dexterous artifice I have before described in him, he now employed with unwearied diligence. It is surprising how soon I lost sight of those prepossessions against him, which his first appearance had inspired. I no longer perceived the portentous roving of his eye, or the mysterious significations of his brow; and the graces of his figure, and the admirable subtlety of his understanding, pleaded strongly with me in his favour.

He no sooner crossed my threshold, than, agreeably to the uniform tenour of his life, he looked round upon all the individuals who dwelt there, for the purpose of discovering where, and toward whom, the craftiness of his nature might be directed to the greatest advantage. A visit paid to a man so rich as I was, and who had no nearer relation than himself, except so far as depended upon my recent marriage, was an epoch in his life. The first question he asked himself, as he set his foot beneath my roof, was, "How can I make myself, by succession or otherwise, the possessor of the estate of my kinsman?"

The persons principally entitled to his attention, when he sat down to the solution of this question, were myself, my wife, and the thoughtless but amiable Kenrick. The latter he scarcely deigned to think of as a rival, but rather as an instrument by which his plots might be forwarded. He felt his genius soar above the opposition of such a minor. Mary was at this time with child. She was little advanced in her pregnancy; and I can scarcely think that Gifford, when he first entered my house, was aware of her condition. As soon as he was so, his machinations became principally directed against his unborn adversary. He felt, I believe, an unreal and anticipated resemblance between the circumstances of this creature beginning to exist, and those under which he had himself been born: and he resolved that, as he, in the early months of his infancy, had been cut off from an inheritance of twenty thousand a year, so should this child be disinherited and abandoned to the world, before it became acquainted with the first elements of speech or of reason.

One of the main artifices of Gifford through life was, if he felt animosity toward any one, to personate a more than usual affection and kindness to that individual. By this method he gained possession of that person's secrets, and insinuated himself into his confidence; while at the same time his ostentatious show of regard gave treble weight to the tales, which the hypocrite seemed reluctantly to utter against his ally. I have already said, that Gifford nourished an inextinguishable antipathy to Kenrick. For this very reason, he assumed the appearance, from the hour they met, of attaching himself to his interests; and the demonstrations of that attachment were constantly accompanied with notoriety and eclat. Kenrick had a certain tone of levity and giddiness about him, though the goodness of his heart prevented him from falling into the excesses to which such dispositions too frequently lead; and Gifford voluntarily undertook to be his monitor. The ingenuous and upright character of Kenrick made him receive these offices with the utmost gratitude; while I myself could not help being edified with this disinterested conduct in the elder brother, where an ungenerous mind would rather have felt envy and a sentiment of competition.

Gifford early remarked the grave turn of my disposition, as well as the volatility of that of his brother; and he resolved to improve and heighten these hints of contrast. He accordingly insinuated such remarks as the following, into the ear of Kenrick:—"Do not think, because you observe our cousin to be of a serious temper, that it is necessary you should suppress before him the gay impulses of your mind. If you do, instead of gaining, you will ruin yourself in his esteem. He told me the other day, as we were walking together, that he had always been accustomed to prognosticate ill, of a solemn, sober-sided boy. 'Youth,' said he, 'is the season of cheerfulness; and it is in this way that the faculties and force of the mind, if any exist, display themselves in early life.' Besides, Mr. Fleetwood has the most ungovernable dislike to what he calls hypocrisy; and he carries this principle so far, that whoever, in his sight, puts any constraint upon his natural bent, he sets down for a hypocrite.

Remember too, that a grave man is a man devoured with *ennui*, and, however contrary to his temper it may seem, that he feels toward no person so sincere a gratitude, as toward him who convulses him with laughter, and distracts his melancholy with sallies of extravagance. I know, my dear Kenrick, that you are too high-souled a lad, to do any thing for the express purpose of insinuating yourself into an old man's testament. But that same temper of yours ought to prevent you from mortifying yourself, and giving pain to your protector, to no manner of purpose. Show yourself to him nakedly as you are: he will honour you the more, and like you the better for it. Kenrick, you are a spirited fellow; but you have not the heedlessness and obstinacy, which make many young men of your stamp disdain advice. Yours is the season to lay hold of fortune's plough, and turn up her treasures; it would not be amiss, as graver years advance, to find that you had a comfortable annuity on Mr. Fleetwood's estate. He must be an ass, and not a man of spirit, who never thinks beforehand of a rainy day. For my part, I should have no enjoyment of any legacy our cousin bequeathed to me, if my dear brother, my brother, whom I received in these arms almost on the day of his birth, whom I have dandled on my knees, and toward whom my affection has grown with added years, were not at least equally a gainer with myself." The consequence of all this sage and generous advice was, that I was perpetually tormented with the buffooneries, the boy's tricks, and the unlucky scrapes, of the handsome young soldier. To many men, no doubt, they would have been exquisitely delightful; the cheerful and light-hearted tone of voice with which they were accompanied, often spoke to the soul; and the honest hilarity of countenance that adorned them, a painter would gladly have stolen, when he was delineating the figure of a youthful Apollo. Still they were too much for the habits of my mind, and the restless anxieties that haunted me. Mary, all lovely and bewitching as she was, frequently vexed me with her over-much liveliness and gaiety; and I could ill brook to have this stimulated and doubled upon me, by the presence of a young man of her own temper and age.

Gifford speedily discerned the feelings I nourished toward my wife, and planned his operations accordingly. "Allow me," said he to the young ensign, "to explain to you another feature of our patron's character. He has passed the better days of his life a bachelor. Just at the period of existence, when the most uxorious man alive begins to detach himself from the vehemence of passion, he married. You may easily conceive what a ridiculous blunder he committed. He was not long before he detected his folly. This is the very reason that has led him to call his relations about him, and endeavour to relieve his domestic scene by the presence of strangers. He wishes to lead a creditable life with his wife; but he finds himself disqualified to become her esquire and associate. He is desirous of resuming, as far as possible, the independence of a single state, and of having as little familiarity with his wife as decorum will allow of. It is in your power to amuse him; it is in mine to beguile his hours with serious discourse; these benefits he expects from us. But the man who would do him the most precious service, is he who would relieve him from the duty of constant attendance upon the skittish, capricious, kind-hearted, excellent creature, to whom he finds himself unfortunately linked."

It is no wonder that Kenrick became the dupe of these representations. I was the furthest in the world from a hypocrite; and it was easy to see, ten times a day, how much I vexed myself at sight of the *étourderies*[1] of Mary. Thus all the weaknesses of the Ensign's character were carefully fed and expanded by his treacherous adviser. He was lively, restless, and turbulent; Gifford stimulated him to become more so. At his age, and in the very dawn of puberty, his eye was prompt to the notice of female attraction; there was nothing to which he was more prone, than to those little frolics and sports, in which the young of either sex indulge themselves reciprocally with the utmost innocence of thought and intention: Gifford prompted him to turn this foible upon my wife, and to ascribe to himself a merit, while he obeyed the impulses of his nature.

---

1   Silly actions.

I have already said, that I had no sooner removed my wife to Bath, than she emerged from the melancholy and dejection which had overwhelmed her at the equinox, and rose to an extravagant degree of vivacity and spirits. She made acquaintances; she resorted to public places; she laughed, and talked, and danced, and sung, for ever. It will easily be imagined how this disorder was heightened, now that I had an inmate under my roof, no less wild, remiss, and rambling than herself. I did not know my own house. A hurricane would have been a mansion of peace to that in which I lived. Consider then the grave cast of my spirits, the trembling sensibility of my nerves; and imagine what I must have suffered in a scene so new, where my nerves were not only shaken, but my ears sometimes deafened, by the obstreperous mirth of Mary, Kenrick, and their train of visiters. Yet I saw occasionally, in the countenance of my beloved wife, some of those wild and terrible expressions which had driven us from Merionethshire; and I dared not remonstrate. Frequently I took refuge from the tumult in the separate society and conversation of Gifford: this was what the villain intended; he was secure that he should gain more perfect possession of me, in proportion as our conferences became more repeated. Sometimes I desired him to speak to Kenrick about the excess of his riots: he did speak to him; and the style in which he spoke has already been detailed.

Thus becoming daily more confidential with the elder of my two kinsmen, I could not refrain from sometimes opening my soul to him on the most sacred of all subjects, my sentiments respecting my wife. This I did without premeditation or design: it was the genuine overflow of a mind, sometimes irritated, sometimes stung, sometimes swelled almost to bursting. Gifford was the only person on the face of the earth, with whom I now discoursed familiarly: who, in my place, could have been uniformly silent upon the subjects always uppermost in his thoughts? No man: at least no man subject to be so deeply impressed and agitated as I was. None but the worst of villains could have made an ill use of such disclosures. He saw how my bosom was wrung, how my heart was torn in a thousand pieces. Was I a husband, indifferent to the affections of his wife? Was I a man, to whom *the kindest service would be to relieve him from the uniformity of attendance* upon the partner of his bosom? Did I desire, to have *as little familiarity of intercourse with her as the laws of decorum would allow?*—No, no, no! Tortured as I was with her instability, I loved her beyond all names of love: to see her happy, was the utmost aim of my ambition: to be gratified with her compliances, the indirect, silent evidences of her regard, elevated me to an enjoyment that kings might envy. But I complained—fool that I was, I complained, and dreamed that I received the retribution of sympathy!—This was enough for Gifford; this he accepted as the fulcrum of his engines.

Enamoured of Mary, I also affected, with a love equally sincere, though not equally ardent, the engaging Kenrick. His countenance was so honest; his manners so affectionate! Though occasionally boisterous in his demeanour, he would not intentionally have hurt a fly. Like the elephant, he might have trod down armies in his mood; but, if a blind puppy lay in his path, and he was aware of it, he would carefully have removed it from harm. His manly heart was subdued, and his eyes suffused with the precious drops of pity, if he heard a tale of woe. He was unwearied and unconquerable in his efforts to relieve distress: nor merely that; but every opportunity, however trivial in name, to do an act of kindness, and give vent to the goodness of heart with which his bosom laboured, was sure to be embraced by him. The accents of generosity which this temper supplied to him, thrilled through the frame of every hearer. He was active, impetuous, and ungovernable; but how unlike was the impetuosity of his character, to that of Morrison, Frewen, and the other untamed barbarians, with whom it had been my unhappy lot to be associated at the university! One strange thought I could not sometimes defend myself from, when Kenrick and Mary chanced to sit next each other at the breakfast-table, or on other occasions: they were the loveliest couple that Europe perhaps could have supplied; both so animated and so accomplished; both having that uncommon class of countenance, in which, as it appears, the thoughts may be read. A painter, who wished to represent Romeo and Juliet, as they offered themselves before Friar Lawrence to be joined in bands of holy wedlock, would have been too happy if he could have obtained Kenrick and Mary for his models.[1]

CHAPTER IX.

THE young Ensign, governed, as I have said, by the admonitions of his elder brother, was eager in his attentions and services to my wife. His honest heart, that witnessed the rectitude of his views, prevented him from suspecting that any one could put a wrong construction on his conduct. One evening, as I returned home at about eleven o'clock from a party in which I had been engaged by the importunities of Gifford, who seemed always anxious to invent means for diverting my melancholy, I was accosted by a woman, well dressed, and, as far as I could distinguish, of a noble air, in the streets. The night was exceedingly dark; but the air was balmy and refreshing. The incident occurred near the door of the Upper Rooms,[2] and took place just at the time the assembly was breaking up. Gifford had left me for an instant to speak to an acquaintance who passed us. Several of the ladies went home in chairs;[3] others, invited perhaps by the softness of the air, and considering the small distance they had to go, preferred walking. The woman I have mentioned was arm in arm with another lady; but she let go her hold as I approached, and addressed me. Her face was covered with a veil; so that, particularly in the glimmer and obscurity of the night, I could make no judgment of her features.

"Your name, I believe, sir, is Fleetwood?"

"It is."

"Excuse my speaking to you in this strange manner. I cannot stay a moment. Perhaps I ought not to say a word. But meeting you thus in the instant, my feelings will not be suppressed. Do not make yourself uneasy; I dare say, there is no cause; I only wish to warn you."

---

1 See *Romeo and Juliet*, II.iv.
2 A popular gathering place in eighteenth-century Bath; called the "Upper Rooms" because of its having been built on high ground in the upper part of the city.
3 Sedan chairs.

"For God's sake, what do you mean? What is it has happened?"

"Only, sir, I do not like the behaviour of Mrs. Fleetwood and the young Ensign, her kinsman, to each other. They were at the Rooms to-night. Really, sir, their manner of proceeding is quite shocking. I cannot tell you the particulars. I know that the Ensign is wholly dependent on your bounty. Upon my word, their indecorums will become the talk of every mouth. I cannot bear to see so good a man as, I am told, you are, so grossly abused. Look to yourself!"

And with these words the unknown broke from me, joined her companion, and in a moment was lost in the train of persons that poured out of the Rooms. I was too much taken by surprise, to have the thought of following her. Besides, of what use was it that I should know my informer? She was acquainted with nothing but circumstances that might furnish ground for suspicion, not that afforded foundation for certainty.

I might have asked of other persons who were present the same evening. I had no familiar acquaintance there. I could not endure to address such a question to any living creature. What husband, not lost to feeling as well as decency, could frame his lips to ask, "Did you observe any undue levity in the carriage of my wife? Did you see any thing that might lead you to suppose she was, unfaithful, dishonest to my bed?"

I ought to have despised the tale of this anonymous informer. I could not drive it from my mind. Kenrick and my wife (thought I) must have gone far indeed, if they no longer scruple to expose their familiarities before the whole city. I recollected the scene at Barmouth, and how much I had been tortured by the gallantries of the fluttering Matthews. The idea pursued me to my pillow: all night in my slumbers I imagined myself in the Rooms, and saw the indecorums and guilty intelligence of Kenrick and Mary. The pulses of my head beat violently: my whole frame was in the paroxysm of a fever. I exclaimed, "Shall all Bath see these things, and I alone be ignorant and secure?"

As the dawn advanced, my disorder in a great degree subsided. At breakfast I saw the parties against whom these suspicions had been insinuated. I searched for guilt in their faces. I never saw a more charming and heartfelt serenity. The brightness of heaven was in their features. I looked round the room. I involuntarily said to myself [it was the contrast only that struck me; I was far from entertaining a suspicion against my confidential friend], "Under the olive-tinctured skin of Gifford, beneath his scowling brow, and among the lines which time and climate have indented there, hypocrisy might hide herself; but, in the other two, there is no opacity or discoloration to intercept the passage of a thought, there is not a furrow in their cheeks for treachery to lurk in. Mary, Heaven has moulded its own image in thy features: if thou art false, oh, then Heaven mocks itself!"

To the mind already indisposed to a liberal construction, every indifferent circumstance is food for jealousy.—Had Mary left any thing behind, in removing from one room to another? Kenrick was sure to be on the alert to present it to her. Did Mary prepare for a walk in the Circus,[1] or the adjoining fields? Kenrick's gloves and hat were immediately forthcoming. Kenrick had a fine voice and an admirable taste in singing; Mary had never, till now, discovered any vehement propensity that way; but now she was for ever requesting him to teach her his songs, and practising them with him without end. They danced together at every interval of leisure; or rather rehearsed particular movements, in which one or the other did not think they had arrived at sufficient ease or grace; while either, as chance directed, hummed the tune to the other's steps. In this system of conduct Gifford was for ever urging them to persevere. If at any time they observed the deep melancholy that seemed to come over me, he assured them that nothing could operate upon me as a restorative, more than the appearance of gaiety and good spirits in my wife. If I left the apartment in displeasure, he warned them against taking the least notice, or suffering the smallest change in what they did. On the other hand, he was so frequently alone with me, that they placed the most implicit confidence in his information as to the state of my

---

1 A circular row of houses in Bath.

thoughts and my wishes. In short, he appeared to each party the good genius of the household, so benevolent, so attentive, so perpetually on the watch to prevent mistakes, and to provide for the tranquillity and advantage of all.

I had already, previously to the horrible idea which had now been intruded upon me, and which perpetually disturbed my mind, been incautious and wicked enough to complain to Gifford of the fickle temper of my wife. It is the first word, in cases of this sort, that rends in pieces the veil, as sacred as that which modesty draws over the female form, by the intervention of which, slight misapprehensions are enabled to digest and disperse themselves in silence. Having proceeded thus far, I could not help naming to him the thoughts that beset me about Kenrick. Gifford appeared to be astonished at the bare suggestion.

He would stake his life upon the integrity of the Ensign. Honesty flowed in the very blood of the Kenricks. Could I be so inattentive as not to see, how a self-acquitting conscience brightened in the countenance of his brother, and gave liberty to all his motions? He must be free enough to put me upon my guard against the vice of my disposition, and to warn me not, by ill construction, to poison what in itself was as guileless as infancy. Poor Kenrick! Was he to be the victim of my groundless guesses? He was glad I had named the matter to him, as it was of infinite consequence to check a habit of this sort in the beginning. I had married a beautiful and excellent wife, through whose means he doubted not I should be blessed with a numerous progeny. What infinite gratifications were in store for me! But all these would be forfeited, if I did not repose in her the confidence she so justly demanded. The plagues that haunted a suspicious husband, were not less numerous than the joys which waited upon a generous one; he saw in his wife the instrument of his dishonour, his bosom-serpent. He could not toy with, and open the flood-gates of affection to, his children, without fearing that a bystander, who saw what passed behind the curtain, should deride him as the most miserable of gulls.

I named to him the woman, who had given me the mysteri-

ous hint at the door of the Upper Rooms. On this intelligence
he appeared to ruminate.

"Did I know her?"

"No."

"Had I the smallest guess who she could be?"

"None upon earth."

"It was strange! very strange! It was not easy to imagine
what end she could have in view. An unknown could not have
planned to begin with a step of this sort, to alienate my affections from my wife, that she might afterward fix them upon
herself? What enemies could Mrs. Fleetwood, or could
Kenrick, have at Bath, where nobody knew them, and where,
in every respect, their appearance was such as to engage all
hearts in their favour?"

"Be silent! Gifford!" interposed I. "I cannot bear this
methodical and cold-blooded reasoning! I am sure my wife is
innocent! Are you going to turn the enemy of her good name,
and of my peace, at once?"

"You are right, sir, quite right, in the confidence you thus
generously repose. It does my heart good to see you take the
thing so wisely!"

"Who was this woman? Her warning voice pursues me for
ever."

"Never mind who she was. There are people in the world,
whose grand pleasure is malignity; whose delight it is to disturb
the peace of families; who never witness a scene of happiness,
without a wish to crush it. This anonymous accuser is one of
them. Let not your noble mind be disturbed by such hateful
trash!"

"Oh, Gifford, what a life is mine! Why did I marry? I
know,—I think, I ought to mistrust nothing between your
brother and Mrs. Fleetwood. Yet my sick imagination is for
ever busy, shaping the attitudes and gestures which this monitor
of mine saw, or pretends to have seen. Was it with hands, with
eyes, or with lips, that they communicated their souls? Was the
fire of lust in their glances? or did their smiles betray a conscious guilt? Did he thrust his arm about her waist, or with sac-
rilegious fingers invade the transparency of her bosom?—Pity

me, Gifford! pity me! It is not enough that the act of lewdness has not been perpetrated; if Mary has for one instant wished that the tie which makes her mine had never been, the warrant of our divorce is gone forth in the tribunal of souls. Why are she and the Ensign so continually together? why so familiar, so mutually pleased with each other?"

"It is the proof of their innocence! Guilt is ever on the alarm!"

"Is there no such thing as brazen, unfeeling guilt?"

"Be tranquil, sir! I will speak to my brother. You shall not hereafter be offended in the same way."

"What will you say to him? Will you bid him pursue a guilty purpose with more prudence and caution? No; let me at least see their proceedings genuine and unforced! Otherwise I shall never be able to form a just conclusion, and shall be secretly more tormented than ever."

What Gifford did in the affair I know not; but the evil grew worse, as I now perceive was always the case, when this pernicious confidant undertook for the cure. I must, however, be ingenuous enough to confess, that it would not have been easy for the young people so to have acted, as to have given me tranquillity. If they were familiar and sportive, I was distracted. Did they at any time appear more grave and less confidential? It was still worse. I believed they discerned the state of my mind, and were only playing a more treacherous game.

About a week after, the question again arose of their going to the Rooms. As soon as I was aware of this, my mind was distracted by a variety of plans. Should I forbid the scheme? Should I go myself, and watch their behaviour? How should I act? I had recourse to my oracle.

Gifford said, "By all means give way to their purpose. If you interpose, you will occasion much disturbance, and a discovery of your jealous thoughts. If you cannot dismiss these thoughts, go yourself, and watch their actions. If, on the other hand, you can adopt the generous confidence you so lately professed, this is the favourable moment to resume yourself, and discard such pernicious cares."

"I will go myself!"

"There is, however, a difficulty in that. How can you be sure that their conduct will not be quite different, when they see that your eye is upon them?"

"Gifford, you are my friend. Undertake this office for me. You may even witness their behaviour, at the same time that they shall not be aware of your presence."

"I, sir! I be a spy upon them! I play the eaves-dropper, and watch for intelligence from eyes! I enter into a plot against my brother! Where did you ever perceive in me the qualifications fitting me for so base a part?"

"I thank you, Gifford! You have now told me all. I perceive plain enough that you know a great deal more than you have confessed. It is very well! I have no friend! I am the veriest wretch on earth!——If you did not believe them guilty, would you not eagerly embrace this opportunity for their vindication, which would afford you a prospect, if your opinion corresponded with your professions, of becoming the ambassador of peace to all?"

"By my soul, I believe them innocent! I never will harbour a thought to the contrary. And, to convince you of my sincerity, I will undertake the office you propose!"

The party took place in the manner which was thus previously settled. I waited with impatience for the breaking up of the assembly. When they came home, I hurried Gifford to my private apartment. This was a thing that happened so frequently, as to have no tendency to excite notice.

We drew near to the table, and I looked in his face. I never saw dejection so powerfully expressed. His visage was colourless; his eyes averted with a mournful air; his hands hung down, as languid and incapable of motion.

"What have you seen? What have you observed?"

He spoke not.

"I need not ask you; I read it all in your countenance."

"No, nothing. Let us talk of it to-morrow morning."

"This hour! this instant! This is the moment of my fate. Gifford, by your eternal salvation I adjure you, do not trifle with me!"

He then proceeded to relate a most artful tale. It contained most of those particulars which my diseased imagination had before presented to my thoughts. It contained every thing of impropriety that could be supposed to pass before a public assembly. When Kenrick and Mary caught his eye, and perceived for the first time that he was in the Rooms, he owned that their faces were immediately overspread with the deepest crimson. Yet every circumstance seemed to come from the relater with unwillingness, and to be softened and qualified by the guardedness of his manner. From time to time he interposed that this was nothing, that it was mere giddiness and want of reflection, that all was meant in innocence. He concluded in a more earnest and impassioned tone:—

"And now I have discharged the most painful office of my life. Your character, my dear sir, engages all my partialities; I feel the warmest gratitude to you as my benefactor. But never, never will I be put upon such a task again. What had I to do, to turn spy and accuser upon my brother? For God's sake, sir, let my name never be mentioned in this business! I shall never forgive myself for this act of undue complaisance."

By all these expressions he contrived to fix upon my mind the serious nature of the discoveries he had made. He proceeded:—

"Forget for ever the conversation of this evening! It ought never to have existed. You have obliged me to repeat trifles the most frivolous and contemptible. I have sacrificed every thing to the faithful performance of my task. Yet, in spite of all the pains I have taken to bring these trifles down to their true level, I can see that you misconstrue every thing. Things make so different a figure, when brought regularly together in a narrative, from what they made as they actually passed. If you had yourself been present, you would have thought nothing of them. You are greatly moved. Do nothing rashly! Give the whole a dispassionate examination! If you make any conclusions to the disadvantage of my brother or Mrs. Fleetwood, it is your own fault! Such conclusions have no support from me, I will stake my soul on their innocence!"

Ten times during the narrative of Gifford I felt impelled to seek the criminals, believing that such impudent neglect of all decorum could lead to nothing less than the immediate perpetration of guilt. Once he withheld me by force, and succeeded in soothing my tumultuous passions. A second time, when I had almost reached the parlour-door, I was called back by my own reflections, and said to myself, "Whatever is done in a case of this sort, must be done with deliberation and solemnity." Afterward, I met Mrs. Fleetwood's woman in the gallery, who appeased my passions by informing me, in answer to my enquiries, that her lady was gone up to her chamber, and that the Ensign was alone in the supper-room.

I saw Mary no more that night. When I came to the chamber in which we rested, she was already asleep. I went softly and drew back her curtains. There was a sweet tranquillity in her countenance; her head reposed gracefully upon her snow-white arm. She looked, as one might conceive the archetype of her sex to have looked, before guilt or fear found entrance into the world.[1]

I threw myself into an easy chair, and sat for some time in horrible musings. My mind vibrated between discordant and opposite judgments. Sometimes I said, "No, Mary, thou canst not be guilty! Guilt cannot incorporate with a demeanour like thine. Was ever any thing so artless, so simple, so heartfelt, as all thy accents? The very playfulness of thy temper is the pledge of thy integrity. Can guilt be so sweetly frolic? Can guilt smile so like an angel?"

Again, my ideas took an opposite beat. "Yes," said I, "this is the very character of the world in which I live. Storms, and tempests, and volcanoes are all beautiful or majestic. Destruction smiles on us from every side. Nature herself is the great parent-hypocrite, deluding us onward from the cradle to the grave. Her daughters do but inherit the same treacherous smiles, and tempt us to damnation!"—Furious with these imaginations, I burst away from the bedchamber, and returned

---

1   The "archetype of her sex" refers to Eve.

to the apartment where I had listened to the conversation of Gifford.

"I will not injure," thought I, "the ill-starred daughter of Macneil, unless I had proofs that rose to demonstration. Why do I inherit the guardianship of this desolate orphan?—Yes, Mary, I feel that my fate is for ever involved with thine! The sacred rite that joined us at the altar was a decree upon my life. Without thee, without thy affection, I must cease to be.—Then I am dead already!

"One thing, however, I can do. I can separate thee, and this youth, the disturber of my peace. It is madness to keep him here. As long as he remains, his most innocent actions—God grant they indeed be innocent!—will fill my brain with images of frenzy. Would he were removed to the furthest island of the Indian sea! Would he were merged in the caverns of the ocean!—When he is gone, my respiration will no longer be choked. My judgment will be sound and free; and I shall make a true estimate of the past."

CHAPTER X.

I INVENTED an errand for the Ensign to the estate of Macneil in Westmorland. I had received proposals for the purchase of it; and, not being myself inclined to the journey, I requested Kenrick to take the business on himself. I further stated it as my pleasure, that he should set out by one or two o'clock of this very day.

I communicated my plan to the Ensign as soon as he rose. He listened to it with that deference and desire to oblige, which characterised all his actions; but I could see that he was not delighted with the expedition.

"And shall I return to Bath, my dear sir, when I have finished the business in Westmorland?"

"No: after that, I have some employment for you in Merionethshire. By that time your leave of absence will have expired."

I watched the countenances of Mary and Kenrick at the breakfast-table. I could see that he had informed her of my plan. All parties were unusually blank.

"And so, my love," said she, after some minutes' general silence, "we are going to lose my cousin?"

"It is necessary, my dear. A business has occurred in which he can be of great use to me."

"I am sorry, methinks," resumed Mary, "that it is so sudden. I had counted upon a visit of two months. Edward (that was his name), I hope you will not forget us!"

"Never will I forget the pleasure I have experienced at Bath, or this dear fire-side, while I have life!"

In conversation like this, frankly demonstrating the sincere regard they entertained for each other, passed the time of breakfast. I withdrew early, and desired Kenrick to hold himself in readiness. When I called him in, and had given him the necessary directions, I held out my hand to him (though with an ill grace), because nothing had passed between us that entitled me to part with him in anger. He took it with both his.

"My dear uncle,"—thus he delighted to call me: in his playful and familiar moments he gave my wife the appellation of aunt; a circumstance, trifling in itself, yet strongly indicative of the innocence of his thoughts,—"My dear uncle, it breaks my heart to leave you thus. I can see I have offended you; all your motions prove it. What a foolish, hair-brained fellow am I! I wonder when I shall grow discreet and sober like my brother. I have done something heedless and disrespectful, or I have said something that I ought to cut out my tongue for. I am always getting into scrapes, and displeasing my best friends. If you could see my heart, I am sure you would not be angry with me. That has always acknowledged you for the best of men; nothing disobedient or unfaithful has ever harboured there. Dear uncle, forgive me! Now I am going away, I cannot offend you. I only wish to carry your love with me. I only wish you to say one word, to enable me to forgive myself."

My heart melted over the boy. My bosom swelled, as if it could no longer contain its fraught. I looked at him with eyes of affection. I sobbed out, "God bless you! God bless you! God bless you!"—and burst out of the room.

The moment I was alone, I cried, "This is the triumph of innocence! No; it is impossible such expressions, such accents, could be forced from a guilty bosom!"—I was beside myself with joy.—"Happy, happy Fleetwood!" said I: "I will make ample amends to both these injured angels, for my misconstruction!" I wished to revoke the orders I had given for the journey of the Ensign. But no; part of the amends I owed, was to bury for ever so dishonourable a suspicion in my own breast. I returned to Kenrick. I poured out to him the torrent of my feelings.

"Go, my sweet lad," said I, "object of my dearest love! Wherever you are, my heart goes with you. You are the honestest fellow that ever wore the human form. There is no resisting the eloquence of your emotions. Depend upon it, from me, you never shall experience anything but kindness!"

"Thank you, thank you, uncle! You have taken a thousand weight from my breast. But, uncle, you were angry with me?"

"Do not talk of it! It is all a mistake. God bless you! Farewell!"—We parted.

Kenrick took a most affectionate leave of his brother. "This is the first time," said he, "we have ever been together, since I was quite a child. Do not think, however, I have forgotten your kindness to me then! You have borne me in your arms a thousand times! You brought me apples and dainties; and defended me against playmates who wished to injure me. But now, Gifford, we know each other. I do not now like you, because you have procured me pleasure, but because I read your brotherly heart. I shall never, I am afraid, be so sagacious and clearsighted as you are; but I shall always remember how anxious you have been to employ those talents for my benefit. Let us now exchange the engagements of an everlasting friendship! I can never be of the use to you, that you always have been, and ever will be, to me. Never mind that! My heart will beat as warmly to you, as heart of brother ever did; and I know your good-nature will accept that as frankly, as if it brought the Indies along with it. My interests will be safe in your protection; and you will never allow me to lose ground in the affections of my kind uncle in absence."

Gifford was not behind his brother in protestations of attachment; and solemnly prayed that he might so prosper in the journey of life, as he should prove, on every momentous occasion, the vindicator and advocate of his friend. Tears embellished the instant of their separation.

Kenrick had but one spare hour. That hour Mary and he spent in a sociable walk. I felt no displeasure that they did so. No; I had sworn that suspicion should never again pollute my bosom. I, however, thought it somewhat remarkable; and with an unspotted curiosity determined to watch their steps. They went toward the Abbey churchyard. There a plain slab was affixed against the wall, to mark the place where the ashes of the elder Kenrick reposed. They approached it together. Satisfied as I was, that there could be nothing very private in such a conference, I made a small circuit, and joined them as if by accident.

"Uncle," said Kenrick, "I am glad you are come. Many a pilgrimage have I made to this unornamented spot; and my aunt insisted that, before I left Bath, I should lead her to my father's grave. Look at that stone! The name and surname inscribed there, and the register of birth and death, are to me the most eloquent epicedium that ever was penned. I do not know whether I at all remember my father; the images I have of him are mixed up with the descriptions I have heard from his kindred; I was only three years old when he died. Nobody speaks of him in Montgomeryshire without enthusiasm; the moment they mention his name, the guardian genius of the departed seems to descend upon them, and to utter the words of saintlike praise by their humble organs. They never speak of him, but their eyes emit sparkles of fire. Never man, according to them, was so consummate in a knowledge and skill, almost supernatural. His flesh was macerated, and his complexion blanched, with indefatigable research; and he never came forth from his retreat, but to dispense health and scatter benefits all around him. But what they speak of with most admiration, is his temper, so innocent, so sweet, so affectionate; his mild eye, beaming with goodness to the whole world. The tongue of my father never held acquaintance with a falsehood; duplicity and artifice never coloured an action of his life. You cannot think, aunt, you cannot think, uncle, what good it does me to remember my father! I never hear the honest people talk about him, but I feel his blood stirring in my veins. Yes; I may do a thousand imprudent and foolish deeds; but the son of Kenrick can never commit an act of lying or treachery."

The honest eulogium of the poor Ensign drew tears from both his auditors. I was astonished at myself that I could have distrusted so gallant and single-minded a youth. I resolved that this should be a lesson to me, how I ever again admitted suspicion into my bosom. Yet there lay, in apparent repose, the embers of jealousy, the communications of my unknown informer, and the remarks of Gifford upon what he had seen at the Rooms; liable to be called up into a blaze, whenever new fuel should be brought to the spark within me. The whole family attended Kenrick as he mounted his horse; in going through the passage, he pressed the hand of Mary to his lips, and said, "Remember!" He was out of sight in a moment.

The temper by which I was actuated, and which made me all my life no less eager and exemplary to repair wrong, than I was sometimes rash to commit it, directed me on this occasion. I could not bear to think that I had misconstrued the guileless and generous heart of my military cousin. I could not sleep in my bed, till I had atoned to the extent of my power for the injury I had done him. I procured for him an exchange of his colours for a lieutenancy, and added to it the lucrative appointment of paymaster to his regiment. I enclosed this double commission in the following letter:

"DEAR EDWARD,

"You thought I parted from you in anger. You must not think so. Perhaps you are too flighty and full of spirits for such a grave fellow as I am. But, if I ever felt that, it was my infirmity, and not yours, that I accused of unreasonableness. I know your heart, and I would trust my life and all that is dear to me, to its integrity. Go on as you have done: you cannot alter, but for the worse. Your light and lively carriage adorns the rectitude of your sentiments, often makes you amusing, and never leads you to any thing vicious. I enclose you a little Christmas remembrance. Be assured of the unalterable affection of your faithful friend,

"CASIMIR FLEETWOOD."

To this letter I received an answer, full of gratitude and the ingenuous phrases of regard.

The same turn of thought which rendered me thus friendly to Kenrick, inspired me with a more than usual degree of kindness to my wife. Though she was unacquainted with the wrong I had done her, it did not the less haunt my remembrance: and, as is perhaps always the case with a generous spirit, the innocent person whom I had injuriously treated, appeared more lovely, and worthy of esteem in my eyes, than ever. The departure of Kenrick gave a little more sedateness to our domestic economy. Mary seemed to have got the better, both of the alarming depression she had suffered at the equinox, and the hardly less alarming levity which had succeeded. She appeared to me scarcely to have a fault. We had never been so happy. I was all solicitude for the gratification of her desires and inclinations. I anticipated her wishes; I attended her, wherever she went. But, what was most pleasing to her, I sympathised in all her feelings, and was cheerful or serious, as her countenance gave me the signal to be one or the other. While I procured the advancement of Kenrick, I was also employed in negotiating an appointment for Gifford. At no time of my life had I been so perfectly in good humour with my own thoughts. I could at least congratulate myself on being instrumental to the advantage and happiness of every member of my family. I said, "Macneil, you were in the right; you are no less infallible than the oracles of antiquity were fabled to be; your advices deserve to be written in letters of gold, and placed on the front of the Pantheon of the human race!"[1]

Gifford congratulated me upon the satisfaction I had

---

1 A famous temple in Rome that was dedicated to all the gods.

obtained to all my doubts. He reminded me, how constantly ... had been on the side which I had now happily embraced; how, under every unfavourable appearance, he had pledged himself for the innocence of both the suspected parties.

In reality, he witnessed the triumph of truth on this occasion, with the sentiments of a demon. Deep as he thought himself in plotting, and consummate in the arts of hypocrisy, he saw all his webs swept away in a moment, merely through the frank and ingenuous carriage of his destined prey. The innuendoes and subornation of a whole month were destroyed. His own practices were turned against him. Kenrick stood higher in my favour than ever; my wife was restored to my confidence; and, for aught that appeared, my unborn heir might make his entrance into the world, without having the circumstances of his birth tarnished with the blasts of suspicion and calumny.

Shortly after the time when the honest Ensign took his leave of us, I hired for myself a convenient residence near the town of Newbury in Berkshire. I have already mentioned that I had a particular antipathy to the city of Bath. I thought myself fortunate, in being able to impute the uneasiness and ill-humour I had sometimes betrayed while I suffered under the practices of Gifford, to this antipathy. Mary was now become the pattern of reason and accommodation; our harmony was unmingled and entire; she cheerfully concurred in, and even promoted, my removal, though it was yet the depth of winter; being desirous, as she said, to make some compensation for the repeated causes of uneasiness she had administered to me. One other circumstance made this change of scene not ungratifying to her. Mr. Scarborough, the father of a young lady for whom my wife had conceived a strong affection at Bath, had a seat within two short miles of the house I had fixed upon; and he, about this time, summoned his daughter to quit Bath, and return home. Mr. Scarborough himself was disliked by his neighbours, and many calumnious stories were propagated to his disadvantage; but his daughter was every where regarded with affection.

Poets have been most ambitious to describe the beauties of nature, as they are seen in the freshness of spring or the luxuri-

ımn. I know not whether it was any depravity of
that I viewed her with almost equal pleasure in the
of winter. Strange sensations of grandeur are always
n my heart, when I behold the leafless trees, and hear
:ing of the north wind. At times when the whole
th land and water, is bound up in iron, and every
branch and shoot are fringed with the congealed moisture
which the frost expels from them, I am filled with admiration
at the extraordinary scene, so unlike that universal pregnancy
and growth which form our most familiar idea of the globe we
inhabit. What can be more magnificent than a snow-storm,
when ten thousand flakes are whirled in circling eddies, and
drifts are formed, that might almost bury an army in their capacious bosom? The sad-moving cattle, which just serve to spot
the unbounded scene, make me feel that the world is not yet
robbed of all living inhabitants, and remind me that there is still
a Power which cares for the creatures it has made. When the
whole heavens are blackened with congregated clouds, I have
the sublime sensations of a friendless and deserted adventurer
cast alone upon an unknown shore, without the terrible anticipations which fill his heart with anguish: and if at any time, in
the midst of this ungenial season, the sun bursts forth with tenfold glory, and seems to diffuse a more resplendent beam than
autumn ever knew, I feel that the human species has one friend
left—a friend that may gladden the heart, and animate the
countenance, of all sadness but despair.

CHAPTER XI.

WE had not been long in Berkshire, before Gifford set his
machinations fresh at work. Ignorant as I was of my true
interest, of who loved and who hated me, I could not easily
command the resolution to part with his society. I carried on
certain negotiations for obtaining him an advantageous situation in the navy. In this pursuit repeated difficulties started up,
that procrastinated our success. To say the truth, Gifford himself
did not appear anxious about the prosperity of my application.

He had projects, in the event of which his guileful heart was more interested, that required his presence at home.

It was on the day preceding the festival of Christmas, that I happened to pass through my wife's dressing-room, about half an hour after she had set out in the carriage upon a morning visit to the friend and neighbour I have mentioned. By seeming accident, the corner of a letter caught my eye, which jetted out from one of the toilet-boxes that formed a portion of the furniture of this apartment. The first undesigning glance I caught of it, suggested to me the idea, It is the hand-writing of Kenrick. I could not refrain from examining the superscription. Beyond a doubt it was the pen of the Ensign that had written it. It was directed to my wife. I started at the circumstance.

"This is not well," cried I. "I am satisfied of the innocence of your sentiments: yet why correspond? why carry on a clandestine correspondence, of which I have never received the least intimation?"

Most assuredly this discovery would not have made the smallest unfavourable impression upon me but for the incidents and insinuations which had been thrust on my notice at Bath. What if my wife corresponded with my kinsman? What harm was there in that? What if these letters had never been communicated to me? Did I demand that Mary should give me an account of all her steps? There is no true generosity in such a demand. There can be no genuine love, love that derives its nurture from the plenteous storehouse of esteem, where a large reliance is not placed on the discretion of the person loved. A thousand actions, not modelled by the laws of hoary-headed vigilance, here are graceful. "Where virtue is, these are most virtuous."[1]

How was I to conduct myself? Was I to pass on, and not deign to notice what I saw? Was I to say, I will give an attentive heed to events as they rise, but I never will be indebted for knowledge, either of a gratifying or distressing nature, to any indirect proceeding? This mode of acting was most agreeable

---

1 *Othello*, III.iii.200 (adapted).

to what was moral and decorous; but I had not fortitude enough for this.

Should I determine to gratify my curiosity by the most generous means? Should I avow to Mary the fact, that I had met with the superscription of the letter by accident, and request her to acquaint me with its contents, and the circumstances that had given birth to it? Neither was my fortitude equal to this. By applying to Mary in person, I put myself in the power of the offender. I should be exciting, almost compelling her, if guilty, to invent a plausible story, by which my understanding might be duped.

All these views of the subject passed through my mind with the utmost perturbation, and I snatched up the letter, resolved not to defer a moment longer the satisfaction of my doubts. I tore it open. I glanced my eyes over the contents. The first words that presented themselves were those of love, "impatience of absence," and amorous complaints that the writer's "ardour had not obtained a like return." The paper dropped from my hand.

"It is all over," I said; "and I am a wretch for ever!"

This was indeed a thunderstroke to me. The reports of what passed at the rooms at Bath depended for their meaning upon the fidelity of the reporter, and at worst were ambiguous, admitting of a variety of interpretations. Here was the handwriting of one of the parties, witnessing to the offences of both.

Was it the hand-writing of Kenrick? It would be idiotism to doubt it! The conviction that it was, did not rest upon my infirmity of temper. I had perceived it at once, when I was far from being aware of the guilty contents of the writing within.

"No, no; never again will I confide in the integrity of a human creature! Kenrick, did your countenance and tones cure me of all my doubts? That countenance was the steadiness of a villain; those tones were the glossiness of a hypocrite. How unheard-of a wretch! I threw myself into his arms; that did not move him. I wrote him a letter burning with words of affection; I told him I would trust my life in his hands. He returned me an answer, echoing and mimicking back to me the emotions of my heart. That did not disturb him; he did not suspend for a moment his traitor machinations. He put the certificate containing my liberal benefactions into his writing box; he took out at the same instant the sheet of paper which he has scrabbled over with stimulants of lust and adultery to my wife!

I took it up to examine it more minutely. "Such a paper," said I, "may be conclusive against the writer; does it with the same certainty involve the condemnation of the receiver? Kenrick, thou art a villian! Thou hast subscribed thyself such! Half my confidence in the human species is subverted for ever. But what mean thy complaints? What means the expression of an 'ardour that is not returned with a correspondent ardour?'"

"Miserable wretch! what straws are these at which I catch to preserve myself from despair! The natural sense of the phrase is, 'You love me little; you burn for me with a fervour not altogether equal to that which pervades my bosom.' Would he have written of love, would he have avowed a lover's impatience of absence, to one who had never heard and acquiesced in a similar language from his lips? Where is the profligate so hardened, that would dare to insult a matron's purity with such an address? And what did she, when she received the villainous billet? Did she communicate to me the insult which had been put upon her, and expose the natural viper in the manner he deserved? Did she at least send back the envenomed scrowl to him from whom it came, and by her noble indignation convince him how much she disdained his criminal suggestions? No, no; none of these. She receives it in all tranquillity, as a matter of course, as a matter well corresponding with the temper of her mind, and at which she conceives neither surprise nor resentment. She thrusts it carelessly into an open casket, so little does her heart regard it as the horrible thing which it is.

"Gracious God, to what a height of impudence and remorseless crime must this woman have attained! It is the concluding stage of guilt, that takes no precautions against discovery. She who offends for the first time against the laws of chastity and God, with how confused and fearful a mind does she do it! How does she dread the encounter of every eye! In what tenfold misery does she envelope this deed of darkness!

And Mary scatters about her at random, and without adver-
tence, the evidences of her guilt!"

In this terrible state of my thoughts, I sought relief in the
conversation of Gifford. I put into his hands the letter I had
found. I fixed my eyes upon his countenance as he read it. He
betrayed successive tokens of the deepest consternation. He
folded it up, with a slow and dejected motion. "It is all over!"
said he.

"She shall not sleep another night under my roof!" I cried,
with a voice frantic with rage and despair.

Gifford started.——"What do you mean?"

"Mean?" said I. "Do you think I will bear the presence of an
adultress? Do you think I will not make them both an example,
for terror to all future offenders?"

"Take care, sir, take care! This is evidence only against one of
the parties."

"One! Did she not receive it? Did she not receive it in
silence? Has she not kept it in her possession, instead of returning it to the accursed writer?"

"It is too true! I can no longer attempt to vindicate either.
How much has your worthy and noble nature been abused!
Wretched brother! No, no longer my brother!—Yet still, sir,
this is not evidence, either for a court of justice, or for an
unmoved and cold-blooded bystander. If you proceed against
Mrs. Fleetwood on no stronger grounds, the world will condemn you."

"What care I for the world?"

"Dear sir, in so solemn a transaction, let me entreat you to
go on the surest proofs. You may wish you had done so, when
it is too late. I would have evidences, that none could refute or
question, that should shut up the mouths of the transgressors
themselves, that should entitle you, if you think proper, to strip
her of the name she had dishonoured, by due process of law. A
letter! a mere love-letter, written at random, that may have
been a pure experiment, that may be pretended to have been
designed for another, that was never answered, so far as we can
tell, that was never acted upon! Fie, sir, fie! These are not things

to annihilate the peace of families, and to dissolve the most sacred ties religion itself can frame!"

"What would you have me do?"

"Return the letter to the very place in which you found it."

"Well!"

"Hold yourself upon the alert! A short time will, no doubt, produce further proofs."

"A short time! Perhaps not! Time may weaken, instead of corroborate, the proof in my hand. And what shall I do with this short time? Unhappily, alas! Mary and I have been for some weeks on better and more affectionate terms than ever. Barbarous, remorseless crocodile!—Shall I, for this short time, personate the fond lover, the confident, secure, and transported husband? Yes! and, if no new proofs arise, I suppose I am to set all my fears at rest, and confess that this is exemplarily virtuous!"

"This letter is, probably, not the only one that has passed between them. There may be others in her possession, which speak of the sort of answers she has returned to her correspondent."

"That shall be known! I will break open, and search every repository she has!"

"And suppose you find nothing? May there not be a quieter and less violent way of proceeding?"

"I will steal her keys from her to-night, as she sleeps."

Thus we concerted every thing, with a view to the completely confounding the guilty parties. I resolved not to see Mary, again, till I completed the search I designed. I took horse, and rode over into Hampshire, leaving word at home, that I should not return till late. This was unusual; the days were short; Mary was alarmed. She and Gifford dined together. The remarks of this conspirator did not tend to calm her spirits. He told her I had gone out, apparently in much disturbance. She enquired of the servants: no letter or message had been brought me, to account for this. All this struck her as of evil augury. She recollected the impatience and unreasonableness of my temper, and was appalled. Gifford artfully turned the conversation upon the dark imaginations of jealous husbands, and the sufferings of the innocent victims of their suspicion. He left her early, and left her in tears.

Gifford took his leave of my wife, under the pretence of retiring to his chamber to look over some accounts which I had desired him to inspect; but, in reality, to meet me according to appointment, at a small inn in the neighbourhood. I had passed a joyless and oppressive day. Winter no longer conveyed to me, as it did on my first arrival in Berkshire, sensations of delight. The weather was flagging, sombrous, and melancholy. It mutually gave colour to, and received it from, what passed within me. I dismissed my servant, after a few miles' riding, and bade him return home. I could not bear to be subjected to the observation of a human creature. I did not flatter myself with the hope that my wife was innocent. I have, before this, called myself a misanthrope; but I never felt the bitterness of misanthropy invade, and lord it triumphant over my breast, till now. I saw Kenrick, as he stood at the tomb of his father, and in his parting embrace; I recollected his letter of thanks on his late promotion, the devotedness of heart that breathed in every line of it. No; I defy the whole world to draw a picture of hypocrisy, to be compared with that which my recent discovery had brought home to my mind!

When I thought of my wife, the case was still worse. Till this hour, I never knew how much I had loved her. The passion I had felt for the ladies of quality who had been my mistresses in France, young as I then was, and full of the ardour and enthusiasm of beginning life, was nothing. I had entertained for her so perfect an esteem! My passion, beginning in the instinct of the sexes, had been consecrated by sentiments so generous, so elevated, so spiritual! We had lived together. He that has never experienced, can form no idea of the effects of sitting together continually at the same hearth on terms of entire equality and cordiality. It had made the partner of my roof flesh of my flesh, and bone of my bone. Recent as our union had been, I could no more form a distinct idea of living without her, than without any of those vital parts, which were born with me, and which together made me man. The very infirmities of her delicate frame had rendered her dearer to me; I was her shelter, her bed-side watch, the physician of her soul. I wanted such an object to engage my care; she stood in need of such a guardian.

My last Parisian mistress had driven me out among the wilds of Mount Jura, more a maniac than a man. What was I now? I had pistols with me! As I strayed without a path on one of the heaths of Hampshire, I grasped them in my hand. I applied one of them to my head. I dashed it upon the ground. I whirled the other with the whole force of my arm to a distance from me. "Vengeance! vengeance!" I cried. "I will not die like a dog; I will have vengeance!" I dismounted from my horse; the bridle dropped from my hand. The beast stood pensive and faithful beside me. I threw myself on the ground. I wallowed and roared aloud, as I measured my length on the earth. Let my fellow-being look upon me in this abject condition, and despise me! He that despises me is no man!

"How ridiculous are all other stories of adultery compared to mine! The adulterer is no Kenrick! The accursed minion is not the surviving daughter of Macneil! They are not two persons, selected out of all countries and ages of the earth, to laugh at future professions of sincerity, to make it impossible that the word Honesty should ever again be pronounced among the children of men. One sees how they came together. One sees their despicable politics and manoeuvres, with what shallow gestures they pretended to be sober, with what flimsy outsides they veiled their pollution. One of the parties is practised in guilt; the other is of so idiot and imbecile a character, as to seem to have waited only for the occurrence of temptation. They are not, like my betrayers, in the full bloom of innocence, with every virtuous sentiment, and every just principle beaming from their eyes. If ever angels fell from the majestic purity of heaven, this at least was the first time that such a scene had been realised on earth."

CHAPTER XII.

I RETURNED toward my own house in a delightful mood for the investigation of matron innocence. I met Gifford. He told me how my wife had conducted herself; that, on the mere intelligence of my absence, she had been greatly alarmed, that she had passed the evening in tears, and that, fatigued with the anxiety of her thoughts, she had retired early to bed.

I grasped his hand.—"I cannot bear her tears."

"Are they not the witnesses of her guilt? Who told her you suspected her? What is it that has thus whispered her to anticipate accusation?"

"Gifford, you are my friend! You do not attempt to excuse her. I may pity her; my friend cannot."

We entered the house with cautious and wary steps. We stole along softly to my apartment. I felt that we trod the galleries carefully, like conspirators going to commit murder.

We had come home late. I said, "I can have patience no longer. No doubt, Mrs. Fleetwood is asleep. Sit you here, while I go and fetch the keys, and make the search I have resolved on."

I entered the bed-chamber. I hastily drew back one of the curtains. She was in a sweet sleep; I saw no mark of the grief and uneasiness she had endured. There she lay, all unsuspecting of the mischief that impended over her! In my agitation I threw down a candlestick. She moved. She murmured something indistinctly with her lips. I stooped down that I might catch the words. "Fleetwood, my love!" she said.

"Good God! is her hypocrisy perfect even while she sleeps? She thinks I hear her!—No, it is impossible! For one moment, perhaps for the last moment so long as we both shall live, I will believe her innocent!"

I stole a balmy kiss from the ripest lips that nature ever formed. She stretched out her arms toward me. I kissed her again. I felt one flash of the joys of heaven, on the verge of the abyss. I drank in madness as I stood.

I drew back precipitately; I found the keys, and hastened to my wife's dressing-room.

A variety of drawers and boxes engaged my attention. I found no letter from Kenrick, no fresh evidence of their familiarity, in any one of them. At first, this circumstance, which ought to have given me pleasure, was felt by me like a calamity. I said, "They are eluding my search; their wary guilt will come off with impunity!"——By degrees my ideas took another turn. I forgot the letter which had first inflamed me. I said, "Here is nothing! There is no guilt! If there were, they must have written. If there were letters, they could not escape me.——I turned to the toilet; I looked at the toilet-box, which had contained the first evidence of their perfidy, and to which, by the advice of Gifford, I had carefully restored it; the letter was no longer there!

Nothing remained to be examined, but a small casket, in which Mary kept her most valuable trinkets. I no sooner opened this, than the first thing which met my eye was the miniature of Kenrick. I looked steadfastly at it: I burst into an idiot laugh. I examined it again. "What lovely features; what an air of integrity!" said I.——"No, it is not so! Do not you see those lines of dissimulation and craft? Now I consider it more attentively, I mark the devil peeping out from behind the beauteous mask, and laughing in my face!"

I carried the picture to Gifford. I threw it upon the table before him, and then rushed to a sofa on the further side of the room. I buried my face in darkness.

"Ha! ha!" said Gifford. "Where did you find this?"

I answered him with a groan.

"Where are the letters?"

"There are no letters."

"I am sorry for that!—What will you do with the picture?"

I was silent.

"Strike it," said Gifford.

"Strike it! What do you mean?"

"Break the glass!"

"What then?"

"Break the glass, and return it to the place in which you found it! This will be a means to ascertain the guilt or innocence of the possessor. If she is innocent, she will enquire how it came by this accident; she will express her anger against the carelessness of her maid. If she is guilty, and retains this portrait to foster her guilt, she will not utter a word.

"This picture," pursued my adviser, "is a circumstance that may well prove distressing to your mind. But it does not carry you forward in the design in which you were engaged. It is no evidence. A married woman may possess the portrait of her young kinsman; may, even in such a place as Bath, have caused it to be painted, unknown to her husband, in perfect innocence."

"What shall I do? Advise me to no delay! Do not bid me wait the progress of events! I cannot bear it."

"Dispose of the picture as I told you. If Mrs. Fleetwood says not a word on the subject, that will be something. But, if you are impatient to bring the affair to an immediate conclusion, I could advise a measure——I do not like the office. What have I to do, to destroy Mrs. Fleetwood and my brother?"

"Gifford, when you see me in this terrible situation, if you refuse me your aid, you are not my friend!"

"I am conquered!——Let Kenrick be invited here into Berkshire. When I was a schoolboy, I had a particular facility in the imitation of hands. I am sure I could imitate Mrs. Fleetwood's with the utmost nicety. If you approve of it, I will write a letter, in her name, to my brother. It shall speak, unequivocally, the language of a mistress to a favoured lover; it shall entreat him, for private reasons, to come down *incognito* into Berkshire, and grant her an interview. If he comes, this will be to you the most incontestible evidence of their mutual crime; and the interview, of the very day and hour of which you will be apprised, and can provide yourself witnesses of it accordingly, will, probably, produce something that will at once place the criminals under the lash of the law."

I consented to this perfidious measure. My mind was in a state of too violent ferment, to perceive all the marks of a degraded and dangerous character, which this proposal betrayed.

Gifford artfully led to another part of the subject.——
"Mary was with child. From what time did she date the commencement of her pregnancy?"

"From October."

"Full three months after your marriage! It was before you removed to Bath?"

"It was."

"I do not know whether you recollect,——I am not sure, indeed, that you observed,—when Mrs. Fleetwood and Kenrick met at Bath, that they did not meet like persons who saw each other for the first time?"

"I did observe it. I saw it with surprise, and, to confess the truth, not without perturbation."

"Well! Did they ever account to you for this?"

"My wife told me she had seen him in Merionethshire. She reminded me of the person, whom she had spoken of as rescuing her from the waves, when she laboured under that terrible alienation of mind at the period of the equinox."

"From that period their intercourse commenced. It was kept a secret from you, till you invited Kenrick to come and reside under your roof. Perhaps, indeed, you were never told how frequently they met."

Thus did this damnable calumniator lead me on, with half words, with broken sentences, and "ambiguous givings-out," to the most horrible conclusions.[1] All the while, he interspersed his innuendoes with the remark, that this was nothing, that these were particulars which had no necessary connection, and adjured me to draw no inferences which might disturb my future peace, or urge me to any unjust proceeding. These cautions of Gifford persuaded me, that he was a conscientious and scrupulous observer, that I might trust all my interests to his hands, and that he "saw, and knew more, much more, than he unfolded."[2]

Only this aggravation could have been added to my calamity. With what feelings had I gazed on my wife in a state of pregnancy! I had anticipated a successor to the Macneils and the Fleetwoods, with emotions of ecstasy. If I looked upon my individual existence with little complacency, and regarded myself as a degenerate shoot, I was determined that my child

---

1   *Hamlet*, I.v.187 (adapted).
2   *Othello*, III.iii.259 (adapted).

should not be so. He should be a genuine representative of the benefactors of the citizen of Uri. The lowest wretch that lives, the offender who is just going to expiate his crime at the gallows, yet loves his offspring, and rejoices that he shall thus survive himself in an innocent infant. To be cheated here was the cruelest of all impostures. To strain to one's bosom the thing that we hold as our own flesh and blood, while that thing is, in reality, the impure brood of unhallowed lust, the enduring monument of the worst of crimes! Already I had begun to conceive that, if Mary proved unworthy, and were cast out, I might find some small refuge from despair in this child, who, in spite of her degeneracy, I judged was truly mine. This, I believed, would be an unadulterate Macneil, the substance in which the innocent Mary, the wife I had so fervently loved, would survive her fall. That last consolation Gifford tore from me. I could never again return to serenity and fearless confidence. I, who had been so wretchedly deceived in one point nearest my heart, had a right to believe all the rest: it was the proper and legitimate second part to the imposition that had been acted.

All was done as Gifford had projected. The picture, with its glass broken, was restored to Mary's casket. The letter, to invite Kenrick to a secret interview, was written. I never saw so exquisite a forgery. You might have taken a letter of Mary's, and placed it by the side of the counterfeit, without discovering a single character that, by the imperfectness of imitation, could have led to a suspicion. This letter was never sent.

Our consultations and proceedings took up the greater part of the night. Toward morning I threw myself upon my bed. To sleep I had not the smallest inclination. My eyelids were weighed down with the anguish of my tortured heart; but they shut out, instead of receiving within their folds, the balm of repose. Every articulation of my frame seemed to beat with a separate pulse; I was in a high fever. I tossed and turned from side to side; my eagerness to make an end of the scene which engaged my thoughts was inexpressible.

Mary rose with the dawn of the morning. She was invigorated with repose; she had an animation and alacrity, the symbols of conscious innocence. She approached my bed; in the gentlest and sweetest voice that ever came from a human organ, she pronounced my name. I feigned sleep. She stole out of the room, and shut the door softly after her.

No sooner was she gone, than I started from my bed. I paced the room with strides of rage and despair. The breakfast-parlour, to which my wife had bent her steps, was in a distant part of the house.

In about an hour Mary came to see me again. I could no longer persuade myself to play the farce of sleep. I looked at her with eyes that glared. She spoke in the most soothing and affectionate accents. She enquired for my health, whither I had gone yester-evening, and at what hour I had returned. She tried by smiles and little sallies of cheerfulness to excite me. I muttered between my teeth, "Hypocrite! monster! devil! woman!" but I retained sufficient command of my passions not to break out into open extravagance. I answered with coldness and indifference. I regarded what she did as a perfect scene. The manner was like that which had subdued me, on the evening of the day when we read Fletcher's "Wife for a Month." But the present case was out of the reach of such remedies. It was thus that Cleopatra inveigled Mark Antony to his ruin, when she had determined to play him false with his confidant Dolabella.[1] As my wife left the room, I saw her apply her handkerchief to her eyes, for anguish that she could not please me, and conscious that it was some unjust displeasure against her that was at the bottom of my conduct. I steeled my heart against her sorrow: I said, "She must perceive that I am animated with some resentment; and were she not cowed with guilt, she would certainly demand an explanation."

The next time she approached me, she said, "My love, I am sure all this disturbance proceeds from some groundless resent-ment you have conceived against me. Acquaint me with the cause, and I have no doubt I shall be able to satisfy you."—This I found I could bear least of all. It seemed to me the most incredible degree of effrontery, to challenge a discussion. The proofs of her crime were too certain. The very child that exist-

---

1   In John Dryden's *All for Love: or, The World Well Lost* (1678), IV.i, Cleopatra pretends to love Dolabella in order to make Antony jealous.

ed in her womb witnessed that she was unfaithful. In spite, however, of the tortures I suffered I constrained myself to play the dissembler. I told her, "No, it was nothing; I was perfectly satisfied; I had no complaint to make." I then kissed her. Oh, such a kiss was transport, was frenzy! My lips seemed to feel again the Mary that I had adored. I then recollected, that Kenrick had planted a thousand miscreant kisses upon that very spot. I wished that my lips could have made a brand upon her cheek, as broad, as deep, as horrid and distempered, as her guilt. I added with a sepulchral voice, that she should be informed what it was that had weighed upon my mind.

I waited all the morning for the event of Gifford's stratagem of the picture. Mary spent a full hour in her dressing-room. This apartment had a glass door with a curtain. Gifford assured me, that, passing accidentally by this door, and the curtain being displaced about a quarter of an inch at the bottom, he had seen Mary open the casket with some caution, examine the glass of the picture with marks of surprise, and then return it to its place. Certain it is, she made no enquiries or remarks upon the subject of the accident.

We made a silent dinner; and soon after it was over, I walked into the garden. The weather was bleak and severe; but I felt it not. A sharp north wind blew in my face; it only seemed to increase the heat within me. By and by I saw Mary come down the avenue. The day was so exceedingly disagreeable, that there could be no question her sole errand was to seek me; I turned into another walk to avoid her. I thought she was gone in. Presently, having taken a small circuit, she was close upon me before I was aware.

"My dear Fleetwood," she said, "you are not well. Why do you expose yourself to the weather on such a day?"

"Mary, take care of yourself. You are tender and open to impression. It will do me no harm."

She took hold of my hand.—"Bless me, how cold you are! Come in, my love!"

"Mary, I cannot go in. Leave me."

"You do not love me!"

"Love you!—Why do you talk thus?——By God, I love you to madness. Those eyes, those lips, these arms, why were they formed so beautiful? I feel you through my soul; and your idea lives in every fibre of my heart."

"If you loved me, you would not make me a stranger to your thoughts."

"I have told you, you shall know them. You will know them too soon."

"And in the mean time I see you pale, indisposed, and uneasy in mind! Fleetwood, I am your wife. What did you mean when you made me so? I have a right to know your thoughts, and share your sorrows. Think how we stand toward each other, if you deny me this!"

"You claim, then, justice and your rights? Have a care!"

"I will claim nothing. I will accept every thing as favour and indulgence. Fleetwood, my life, do not distract me with uncertainty and fears! If you have any compassion for me, tell me what it is that distresses you! Open your bosom to your faithful wife, and let me soothe your sorrows! I will smooth your pillow, and cover you with my arms; I will take care, by my assiduities, to deserve your confidence."

I turned upon her, enraged at her duplicity.—"Be gone! How dare you torment me thus! I intended to have been gentle and forbearing with you, but you compel me to be severe. Learn not to intrude upon my privacy, when I choose to be alone! By the eternal God, you shall repent your officiousness!"

Mary heard me with astonishment, and burst into tears.— "Fleetwood—is it come to this?—This is too much—too much!"

I listened to her with an unmoved heart. I said to myself, "These tears are Kenrick's!"

She took hold of my arm.—"If ever you had compassion on the wife of your bosom——!"

I shook her from me. I said, "Will you not leave me?" She trembled, and fell with one knee and one hand upon the ground. I hurried to another part of the garden. When I was got to a distance, I could not help looking back after her. I saw her return with staggering steps to the house. I said to myself, "I did not wish for this. No, though I will be severely just, I would not be a brute!"—I recollected she was with child.

Demons of hell! why was I reserved to this? What an insupportable, what a damnable situation!—Why was she formed so beautiful? Why are innocence and truth written on her front? How like a saint, how like the purest of all mortal creatures, she talked!—With child! the child is Kenrick's!—Grant, all-merciful Heaven, that it may never see the light! Would God, it could be intercepted in its entrance into existence!—Why did I marry? I, that had already passed the middle stage of life? I, that knew the sex so well, that had gained my knowledge by such bitter experience?—What shall I do? How shall I signalise the terribleness of my justice? And in what dungeon shall I afterward hide myself?

Mary did not yet suspect any connection between the disorder in which she saw me, and the accident of the picture. Her innocent heart failed to suggest to her that I could be jealous of my kinsman.

CHAPTER XIII.

I SPENT this night from home, at an obscure inn, where I was entirely unknown, and returned in the morning. About two o'clock I walked out with Gifford. He was my confidant; and I consulted him a little respecting the past, and talked somewhat by broken sentences in gloomy anticipations of the future. But my heart was too heavy to allow me to say much. My steps were those of despair; my frame was worn out with watching and perturbation. Gifford led me unawares toward a little remote public house.

"Come in here," he said. "It may be worth your while."

I followed mechanically. I paid no heed to what he said; I scarcely heard it. I was totally indifferent whither he led me.

He conducted me to a room on the first floor. Beneath the window there was a double row of elms with a smooth and regular turf between them. The afternoon was fine. It was a clear, frosty day; and the sun, as it now approached to the west, painted the clouds with brilliant colours. These things I scarcely perceived at the time; but I have recollected them since.

After a time I heard the sound of voices at a little distance from the window. It was not natural that in my state of mind I should have paid attention to this; but, though the voices were low, there was something in the accents that arrested my soul. After a minute's earnest and impatient listening, I rushed to the window. I saw the speakers. They were Kenrick and my wife! Astonishing, soul-blasting sight! They appeared to be in the act of parting.

I rushed down stairs in a state of frenzy. Before I could get round to the spot, they were at some distance from each other. I pursued the villain. I called to him to stop. He stood still, but did not advance toward me. As I came up to him, he seemed to be in great confusion.

"My uncle!"

"Kenrick, how came you here?"

"I beg your pardon, sir. You shall know all. Indeed you shall."

"Know all?—Am I of so little consequence to you? Have not you received the commissions I sent you? Did not you protest that your life would be too little to show your devotedness? Ungrateful villain!"

"I am afraid I have been wrong. Do not be angry with me!"

"Be gone, sir!—I shall find a time for you!"

"Only one word, uncle. Do not betray me! Do not tell any one that you saw me! It may do me the greatest injury in the world."

"Scornful boy! insolent wretch! I command you to leave me. I only wanted to be sure it was you. Go; I will be obeyed!"

Kenrick was aghast at the vehemence of my manner. He would have expostulated. But I would not hear him. I even raved at so shameless a persistence, till at length he became convinced that this was no time for conference, and departed.

I was alone. Gifford presently came and joined me.—"Oh, God! oh, God!" I cried; "could I have believed it? It was but yesterday that I discovered the last proof of her falsehood! It was but yesterday that I confounded her with the bitterness of my reproaches upon her guilt! And to-day she meets him here! How came he here? What is the meaning——? Gifford, leave me! For a moment, leave me!"

"I dare not. In the state of mind in which I see you, I am afraid lest you should do some act of desperation upon yourself!"

"Upon myself!—Ha! ha, ha! I value them not a straw. I have no love for my wife; I never did love her! I hold myself at a price greater than ten thousand such strumpets and profligates! They have no power to ruffle my thoughts. I am calm! Perfectly calm! They thought to sting me! I never possessed my soul in more entire tranquillity than at this moment!——Go into the house; I will join you instantly."——Gifford left me.

"Shall I go to my wife, and confront her with this new evidence of her guilt?—No, I will never speak with her, never see her more. It is a condescension unworthy of an injured husband, ever to admit his prostituted consort into his presence! It is as if God should go down and visit Satan in his polluted, sulphureous abodes!—How from my inmost soul I abhor her! How I will hold her up to the abhorrence of the world! How I should like to see her torn with red-hot pincers!—To what a height I have loved her! No, no, no, no, no——never!"

Presently the words which Kenrick had uttered came back to my ears. What did he mean, by asking me not to betray him, not to let any one know I had seen him? Was he mad? Are these the words of a dependent, who has wronged his patron in his bed?

"If they were but innocent!—if they were!—I will go this moment to my wife!"

I left Gifford waiting for me in the public house: I entirely forgot him.

As I passed along, I endeavoured to collect my thoughts. I determined to exercise the utmost degree of subtlety and craft in exploring the truth. I found Mary in her dressing-room.

I said to her, "Have you seen my shirt-pin?[1]—I have lost one

---

1 A piece of jewelry used to fasten the shirt at the collar.

of my tan-coloured gloves.—I think it is a long time since we heard from Kenrick."

The words seemed to stick in my throat, as I endeavoured to speak them. When I uttered the name of my kinsman, I fixed my eyes upon her countenance. I saw she was much disordered.

"It is a long while."

"How long?"

"It must be almost a month."

"You have not heard from him?"

Her lips formed themselves to say the word, "No."

"You have not seen him to-day?"

"To-day?—How should I?—Is not he at his quarters at Beverley?"[1]

I grasped her by the arm.—"Did not you see him to-day, in the elm-walk behind the alehouse of the Spotted Dog?"

"Unhand me, sir!—Mr. Fleetwood, this is not the tone in which I am to be interrogated!"

"Cunning witch! artful hypocrite! What matters it whether the questions are asked in polished words and a gallant tone? They must be answered!—How came Kenrick in Berkshire?"

"That is a question I am not at liberty to resolve. And, whatever may be the consequence to myself, I will not reply to it!"

"Not at liberty to answer! And all the confusion you betrayed at the mention of his name, your prevarication, your circumlocution, the guilty stops in your voice, these you disdain to account for!"

"Fleetwood, you will repent this violence! Yesterday in the garden, for no cause whatever, you used me like a brute."

"Pooh, pooh!—Answer to the purpose, and leave these subterfuges!—When were you first acquainted with this wretch? How frequent were your interviews in Merionethshire? You are with child! Mary, fall upon your knees, and answer me, by the great God, who made heaven and earth, whose child is that in your womb?"

"Almighty God! and is it I, of whom such a question is

---

1   A town in East Yorkshire.

asked?—Lightnings blast me! God, in thy mercy strike me dead!—Fleetwood, if I were to live to the ages of eternity, never from this hour would I hold intercourse with you!"

I was moved at the earnestness, the dignity, that appeared in her rage. "Mary, I entreat you; by every thing sacred, by all the endearments that have passed between us, answer my questions, and resolve my doubts! Oh, if you could but take away the horror that overwhelms my soul, worlds could not buy the happiness!"

I thought she hesitated for a moment.—"Fleetwood, it is too late! I have been an exemplary wife to you; from the hour of our marriage I have studied your happiness in every thing; my tenderness and forbearance have only served to render you more unjust. I am an altered woman since yesterday. And the man who has uttered against me such brutal reproaches as you have now done, is no husband of mine!"

"Very well, madam, very well! I was a fool to ask you a single question. I had evidences enough before. But the despicable subterfuges to which you have now resorted, one after another, are equal to a thousand witnesses."

She cast up her eyes with wildness, yet with a concentred spirit.—"My dear father! my angel mother! you are my only refuge! Come, and let your spirits rest upon my bosom! Come, and console your brutally treated, unsheltered daughter."[1]

This was the tenderest argument upon which she could have touched. It ought to have won my protection and forgiveness, even to an adulteress. It struck upon a wrong string. Bursting as I was with rage and agony, I could not bear any thing that was calculated to excite an opposite passion. It created confusion in my mind; it made me half fear I was doing wrong: and to conquer this fear, I became ten times more furious and peremptory than ever.

"Be gone from my presence. For the last time, be gone!—Horrible wretch, do you think to disarm my justice by naming your parents! How dare you take their pure and sacred name into your lips!"

---

1 Compare *The Winter's Tale*, III.2.120f.

She proceeded a few steps; she moved with all the pride of innocence.—She recollected herself, and turned again.—"Hear me, miserable, deluded Fleetwood, a word!"

One expiring sentiment of nature stirred in my breast. In a dead and scarcely audible voice I said, "Speak!"

"I have no wishes for myself. I scorn to defend my actions. You are nothing to me.—But Kenrick, poor Kenrick,—it is my last request—do not let him suffer for any misconstruction on my conduct!—You will soon be undecei——."

At the name of Kenrick thus falling from her lips, my heart swelled as if it would have leaped from my bosom.—"Impudent harlot! Do you come back for this?——Yes, I will fondle and caress him!—I wish I had him now writhing at my feet!——Kenrick!——Ha, ha, ha!"

CHAPTER XIV.

I BURST out of the room. As I went, I met Gifford. I caught hold of his arm. "Lead me, lead me any whither from this hated house!"—We passed along. We came near the great road. A chaise (how it came there I knew not; I did not once think of so unimportant a question; I scarcely considered any thing I did) was standing near a stile. We got into it. It proceeded toward Newbury.

"I will set out for the Continent this night!"

Gifford expostulated with me on this sudden resolution. His objections were for the most part trivial and insignificant, when weighed with the terrible situation in which I stood. Slight opposition, as he well foresaw, only served to make me more determined. If he suggested any difficulty which seemed of more serious import, he took care himself to supply me with the arguments that might invalidate it.

We went across the country to Brighthelmstone, whence I immediately took passage for Dieppe.[1] From the former of these places I despatched a letter to my principal *homme*

---

1   Brighthelmstone is an earlier name for the coastal town of Brighton in Southern England, on the English Channel; Dieppe is a city in northern France.

d'affaires, acquainting him of my intention of instantly proceeding for the Continent, where I might perhaps remain for years, and directing him how to conduct himself with regard to the remittances to be forwarded to me. But the main purport of my letter was concerning my wife. I gave the most peremptory orders, that she should not remain another night under my roof, that she should be suffered to take away with her nothing but what strictly belonged to her person, and that she should, on no pretext whatever, receive a farthing out of the produce of my estate.—I delighted myself with the hope that she would perish in abject misery.—This letter was in the hand-writing of Gifford, and I annexed to it my signature.—From Dieppe I and my fellow-traveller proceeded to Paris.

It is impossible for words to express any thing so wretched as the state of my mind during the whole of this journey. Sometimes I was turbulent and ungovernable; I was little less than raving mad. At other times I was silent, and seemed wholly bereft of sensation. For days I did not utter a single word; I could scarcely be prevailed on to take a particle of sustenance. Sleep was wholly a stranger to my eyes; for fourteen days and nights neither I nor my companion was aware that I slept for a moment. Nothing could be more exemplary than the attention I received from Gifford during the whole of this period. He never left me; he never ceased from studying the means of restoring me; the meanest offices were not repulsive to his kindness and zeal. I am certain that, in this extremity, I owed the preservation of my life to his care.

Yet I did not thank him for all his assiduities. Life was the subject of my hatred. Often did I meditate the means of self-destruction. Ten times did he prevent the accomplishment of my purpose, by the indefatigable way in which he watched the turn of my eye, and the movement of my limbs, and by constantly removing from me the instruments of death I had fixed upon. He talked to me in tones of the sweetest humanity. He contrived a thousand ingenious methods of diverting me from the griefs that absorbed my mind. Frequently I fell into paroxysms of rage against him. I loaded him with every opprobrious term that frenzy could invent. I would not suffer him to sit down at table with me. I obliged him to squeeze himself into the remotest corner of our travelling carriage, and raved with resentment and fury, if he happened to touch me. He bore all with unconquerable patience. At times I became sensible of his merit in this. I thanked him for his distasteful attentions, and begged his pardon for all my violence and unreasonableness. I owned (and then a burst of tears gushed into my eyes) that I had no friend in the world but him, and entreated that he would never desert me. He readily promised that he would stick to me for life.

In the bitterness of my soul I imprecated the most horrible curses that imagination could devise, upon the memory of the excellent Macneil. But for him I should have exhausted the miserable dregs of my existence in quiet. I had fallen into a sort of lethargy compared with what I now felt, in which, if I was wretched and forlorn, habit had taught me not to writhe under my misery. Every one of his advices had fallen out unhappily to me. He had recommended to me a wife, the society of my kindred, and that I should cherish the fond anticipation of offspring. Each of these pretended sources of happiness had proved a scorpion, stinging my before palsied senses into a capacity of the acutest torments. Had Mary and Kenrick been really as guilty as I believed them to be, if they had seen the condition to which I was reduced, they would have pitied me; and guilt itself would have generously wished to impart its privileges to my insupportable innocence. There was but one man, who, whatever fair appearances he might put on, never pitied me for a moment.

Every time a packet of letters reached me from England, strange as it may seem, I tore them open with furious impatience, in hope of finding one line from Kenrick or Mary. I had built my conclusions upon such strong circumstances, that scarcely a husband in existence would have resisted their evidence. Yet a sentiment still lingered in the corner of my heart, that whispered me at times the possibility of their innocence. I therefore suffered a continually renewed anguish in the still repeated disappointments I experienced. In my frenzy I had written letters to both to Mary and the adulterer, full of the sharpest reproaches, curses, expostulations, stained with blots, and in every other respect expressive of the disorder of my mind. These Gifford, with apparent propriety, confessed he had intercepted. When I had outlived the most terrible distemper of my mind, I wrote to my wife a sedate, heart-breaking letter, in which I rebuked her conduct, described with what vehemence I had loved her, and informed her that I had ordered my steward to supply to her one thousand pounds per *annum* in quarterly payments. Could any thing but self-convicted guilt have persisted in so ill-boding a silence?

Gifford hurried me from place to place, through France, Germany, and the north of Italy. He had acquired an ascendancy over me during my frenzy, which afterward I could not easily shake off. I did not fully understand the reason of these frequent removals, but I regarded them with an eye of passiveness and indifference. Gifford's general pretence was the benefit which my health would derive from travelling and change of air.

At length the time came, when it was necessary that I should think of the law-proceedings, if they were to be entered upon, for a divorce and the illegitimating my unborn child. Gifford often reminded me of these things, yet contrived to present the subject under such faces, as could least suggest the idea of his being animated by any views of personal interest. I on my part willingly entertained the project. It well suited the gloomy conceptions in my mind, of the justice I was bound to execute upon my guilty wife; nor could I endure to think that the child of her polluted embraces should inherit any part of my estate. I had also for some time cherished the plan of making my faithful and entire friend heir to the gross of my fortunes, and this I could not do without thus cutting off the descent of my land. When every thing was ready, I requested Gifford to proceed to England for the management of my cause. My presence was judged not to be indispensable, and I gladly excused myself from the journey. We parted at Marseilles. There I met with an English lawyer of some eminence, with whom I advised on the subject; for I was peremptory that I would not separate myself from this only friend I possessed, till I had executed an instrument, by which I should make him, to the utmost of my power, in the event of my decease, the successsor to all my estates. Among other provisions of this my last will and testament, I stated that it was my intention, in case, which I had every reason to expect, the proceedings now depending should terminate in rendering my marriage null, and declaring the child with which my wife was great a bastard, that my kinsman and fellow-traveller should be deemed to be as fully and entirely the successor to my property, as if he had been my only son. Gifford seemed earnestly to oppose the execution of this testament. He represented such a measure, particularly under the present uncertainty of my affairs, as in a high degree indecorous and premature. The more he resisted my pleasure in this article, the more obstinately I became bent upon it. The will was drawn out in complete form; I delivered it into his hands, and insisted upon it, as he valued my future favour or peace, that he should never suffer it to go out of his possession.

The proceedings upon my complaint were complicated and tedious. I know not whether my mode of existence during this suspense and desertion, does not deserve to be styled more deplorable, than under all the agony and delirium of the first detection. My mind was then hurried with never-ceasing vehemence from thought to thought. Even when I appeared, to the eye of the bystander, bereft of all sensation, and was wholly without motion or notice to indicate that there was a soul shut up within my corporal bulk, my brain was for ever busy, and I might fitly be compared to an immense pile of mechanism, the furniture of a dead and windowless structure, on surveying the walls of which you perceive no signs of activity, though a thousand cogs and ten thousand wheels are for ever working within. The distempered activity under which I then suffered, was now gone. I became jaundiced, body and soul. My blood loiteringly crept through palsied veins. I was like one of the metamorphoses of the Grecian fables, rooted to a spot, and cursed with the ineffective wish to move.[1] How slowly did the never-ending days and nights revolve over my

---

1 An allusion to the *Metamorphoses* of the Roman poet Ovid (43 BC-AD 18). This fifteen-book poem is a compilation of Greek myths, each of which involves a transformation on the part of the character(s).

head! How deep was the despair that embraced and struck its fangs into my soul! Hope, under no one of the varied forms in which she ever showed herself to mortal eye, came near me! My great constant sensation was a sickness of heart, nauseating existence, and all that existence brings along with it. With vacant eye I observed every thing that moved around me, and said, "Would to God it were all still!" What a relief would death, or the resolution to die, have been from this insupportable burden!

CHAPTER XV.

JULY came, and brought along with it the anniversary of my marriage. It was July, too, that was to give birth to the child, to whom I had once looked forward with raptures, on whom I now thought with sensations little less than infernal. I resolved to solemnise a strange and frantic festival on my wedding-day. I wrote to Gifford to procure me, by some means, a complete suit of my wife's clothes, together with a lieutenant's uniform, made to pattern, according to the mode of the regiment to which Kenrick belonged. I assured him that my life depended upon the fulfilling my present demand. Ever faithful to gratify my slightest request, he punctually sent me the articles I desired. I had in my possession a miniature of my wife. I went to a celebrated modeller in wax, in the city of Florence, where I now was, and caused him to make a likeness, as exact as he could, of the size of life. I was myself not without some skill in modelling, and I directed and assisted him. For the wearer of the regimentals, I fixed upon a terrible and monstrous figure of a fiend, which I found in the magazine of my artist. I ordered a barrel-organ to be made for the same occasion. I recollected the tunes which Mary and Kenrick had sung together when at Bath, and I caused my instrument to be made to play those tunes. I bought a cradle, and a chest of child-bed linen. It is inconceivable what a tormenting pleasure I took in all these preparations. They employed me day after day, and week after week.

When at length the fifteenth of July came, I caused a supper of cold meats to be prepared, and spread in an apartment of my hotel. All the materials which I had procured with so much care and expense, were shut up in the closets of this apartment. I locked myself in, and drew them forth one after another. At each interval of the ceremony, I seated myself in a chair, my arms folded, my eyes fixed, and gazed on the object before me in all the luxury of despair. When the whole was arranged, I returned to my seat, and continued there a long time. I then had recourse to my organ, and played the different tunes it was formed to repeat. Never had madness, in any age or country, so voluptuous a banquet.

I have a very imperfect recollection of the conclusion of this scene. For a long time I was slow and deliberate in my operations. Suddenly my temper changed. While I was playing on my organ one of the tunes of Kenrick and Mary, it was a duet of love; the mistress, in a languishing and tender style, charged her lover with indifference, the lover threw himself at her feet, and poured out his soul in terms of adoration,—my mind underwent a strange revolution. I no longer distinctly knew where I was, or could distinguish fiction from reality. I looked wildly, and with glassy eyes, all round the room; I gazed at the figure of Mary; I thought it was, and it was not, Mary. With mad and idle action, I put some provisions on her plate; I bowed to her in mockery, and invited her to eat. Then again I grew serious and vehement; I addressed her with inward and convulsive accents, in the language of reproach; I declaimed, with uncommon flow of words, upon her abandoned and infernal deceit; all the tropes that imagination ever supplied to the tongue of man, seemed to be at my command. I know not whether this speech was to be considered as earnest, or as the sardonic and bitter jest of a maniac. But, while I was still speaking, I saw her move—if I live, I saw it. She turned her eyes this way and that; she grinned and chattered at me. I looked from her to the other figure; that grinned and chattered too. Instantly a full and proper madness seized me; I grinned and chattered, in turn, to the figures before me. It was not words that I heard or uttered; it was murmurs, and hissings, and lowings, and howls. I became furious. I dashed the organ into a thousand fragments. I rent the child-bed linen, and tore it with my teeth. I dragged the clothes which Mary had worn, from off the figure that represented her, and rent them into long strips and shreds. I struck the figures vehemently with the chairs and other furniture of the room, till they were broken to pieces. I threw at them, in despite, the plates and other brittle implements of the supper-table. I raved and roared with all the power of my voice. I must have made a noise like hell broke loose; but I had given my valet a charge that I should not be intruded upon, and he, who was one of the tallest and strongest of men, and who ever executed his orders literally, obstinately defended the door of my chamber against all inquisitiveness. At the time, this behaviour of his I regarded as fidelity; it will be accounted for hereafter. He was the tool of Gifford; he had orders that I should not be disturbed; it was hoped that this scene would be the conclusion of my existence. I am firmly persuaded that, in the last hour or two, I suffered tortures, not inferior to those which the North American savages inflict on their victims; and, like those victims, when the apparatus of torture was suspended, I sunk into immediate insensibility. In this state I was found, with all the lights of the apartment extinguished, when, at last, the seemingly stupid exactness of my valet gave way to the impatience of others, and they broke open the door.

The ceremonies of this evening had a terrible effect upon me. For fifteen days I never left my bed. For the most part of the time I was really insane, but I was too weak to break out into the paroxysms of insanity, and those about me were scarcely aware of the degree of my derangement. From the moment the physicians were called in, they pronounced that it was impossible I should recover. I gradually wasted away, till I seemed to be arrived at the last gasp. They were mistaken, however; I was reserved for more sufferings, and for stranger adventures. A favourable crisis took place in my disease, and I became slowly and tediously convalescent.

Gifford wrote to me regularly during the whole period of his absence. I always opened his letters with vehement emotion; a strange expectation still lingered about me, that I should find the accused parties innocent. Nothing in Gifford's communications encouraged this idea; the delays that the cause suffered, appeared to be no more than is always incident to such prosecutions. He wrote me word, that he had procured witnesses of the criminal conversation of my wife and her paramour, in Merionethshire; he had even been so fortunate as to meet with an evidence, to whom Mary had expressly confessed, that the child with which she was great, was the child of Kenrick. The lieutenant had quitted England; heavy damages were awarded against him in the Court of King's Bench. A decree of divorce was obtained from the ecclesiastical judges. At length my correspondent informed me, that an act of parliament, completing my objects, had gone through nearly all the forms, but the last; and he desired me to meet him on a certain day at Paris, where he assured me he should arrive, bringing over with him the full and consummate fruit of his labours. I had already crossed the Alps, and come as far as Montpelier for that purpose.[1]

Gifford had received but an imperfect information of the state of my health during the latter part of July. As soon as I became capable of reflection, I was alarmed, lest the accounts he received from my valet should have the effect of making him desert the business in which he was engaged, and come over instantly to Florence to attend me. Gifford was in no danger to be misled by any such sentiments as I imputed to him. All the world could not have induced him to such an act. He had my testament in his possession; and the cause was by this time in such forwardness, that the news of my death could not arrive in time to suspend the conclusion. Besides, he had given the necessary directions for making my death, if it took place, a secret, till he should give the signal for its publication. I went at Florence by a false name. Previously to his departure for England, he had watched over me with more anxiety, with more demonstrations of affection and concern, than a mother over her firstborn son. Now he did not care, if I died. He had punctually supplied me with all the particulars I required, for the solemnity of the fifteenth of July, in the hope of such a conse-

---

1   A city in southern France.

quence as resulted, and that that consequence would have led to a more perfect termination.

How perverse was the constitution of my mind! The act of parliament, dissolving my union with my wife, and disinheriting my only child, was an object I had sought for with the greatest ardour. When Gifford and I parted at Marseilles, I thought the only chance I had for ever enjoying a peaceful moment rested in the success of his expedition. What could be more natural? Who would not wish to be disjoined for ever from a perfidious and abandoned consort, and to prevent all possibility that the offspring of her guilty amours should succeed to the inheritance of his ancestors? Yet, as I have said before, it was Gifford that kept alive this object in my mind. When he had left me, my contemplation took a different turn. If I thought of Mary as guilty, still I remembered how I had loved her, I regarded her as a consecrated piece of earth, never to be violated by any irreverence or levity of mine; if I beheld her covered with the deformities and leprosy of her fall, I did not also fail to recollect how white, and smooth, and rich in lustre, that figure had once appeared to me. I never repeated her name in soliloquy, in my sober moments, without that awe, and suspension of voice, with which a pious man speaks of his God. But I did not always think of her as guilty: I had visions of her restoration to character and honour. These sentiments, and the feelings with which I was accustomed to open his letters, sometimes obtruded into my replies to Gifford, and made him comprehend that I was not a man to be depended upon. In my earliest letters after the event of July, I spoke of my determination to see Mary once again, and to extort from her own lips an explanation of her perfidy.

It was the end of August. I was no longer subject to the transports of passion from which I had already suffered so much. My frame was feeble and languid. I was wasted almost to a skeleton. My face was thin, and wan, and colourless. I seemed to be overtaken with a premature old age. My hair was almost changed to grey. Yet, as I have said, I was convalescent. My eyes were brighter than they had been, and my countenance, though exceedingly pale, was of a less leaden and death-like hue. It seemed probable that I was reserved for years more of existence. My constitution had been originally robust; I had been all my life accustomed to travelling and exercise; and these favourable circumstances now began to show on which side the victory would be—for life, or death.

CHAPTER XVI.

I APPROACHED Paris. The day and hour had been fixed between Gifford and me, at which I should arrive. About six miles from the capital we had to pass through a wood, celebrated for the robberies and murders that had been committed in it. I thought not of this, and paid little attention to any of the objects in the road. As we entered the wood, my mind was absent and dreaming; I was like a man asleep, but my eyes were open. I was in my travelling chariot, with my valet sitting beside me. Suddenly I heard a voice, which called to the carriage to stop. It stopped. Three men in masks came up to the door, opened it, and laid violent hands upon me. Mechanically I had had recourse to my pocket, and drawn out my purse, which I proffered to the assailants. They took no notice of this action, but proceeded to endeavour to force me from the chariot. Alarmed at this, I struggled with the ruffians, and called out to my valet, and to my servants who were in sight, to assist me. No one assisted me; and, as I was dragged from my seat, I felt my valet give me a push from behind. In all the confusion and violence of the scene, this action forcibly struck me. It gave a sort of convulsive shock to my mind, and made me view all that was passing in a very different light. Is it one of the effects of wealth, that with it we enlist men into our service to murder us? The feeling of my situation made me desperate, and I struggled more violently than my feeble condition could have given reason to expect. I wished for my pistols; it was too late; they were left in the carriage. I saw that it was impossible to escape, and that I had but a few minutes to live.

Two men who had hold of me, dragged me a considerable way from the chariot; a third stayed with the carriage; my own servants remained behind. At the fatal moment, four horsemen advanced at full speed in the opposite direction. As they came near, the assassin who had hold of me on the right side, presented his pistol at my head. It missed fire. Goaded with desperation, he struck me a furious blow with the butt end of it just above the ear, which brought me senseless to the ground. Instantly the ruffians left me, and ran as fast as they could. One of the horsemen remained with me; the other three pursued the fugitives. The assassins endeavoured to make their way into the thickets: one of them was shot dead by the pursuers; the other two escaped.

The horseman who had remained to take care of me, had endeavoured to raise me from the ground; the others now assisted him, and conveyed me to my chariot. I was stunned with the blow I had received, and continued speechless. My conductors, therefore, did not convey me to the hotel in Paris where I was to have met Gifford, but to another of their own choosing. They put me to bed, and sent for an eminent surgeon, who took from me a considerable quantity of blood, and then left me, with directions that I should be kept as quiet as possible.

In the course of the night I perfectly recovered my recollection. I saw myself in a strange chamber, with a taper glimmering in the chimney, and an old woman sitting at some distance from the bed, to watch by me. I said, "Where is my friend, my only friend?—where is he?"

"Who, sir?"

"Mr. Gifford."

"I never heard of him."

"Where is my valet?"

"I do not know. You are a stranger to me."

"In what place am I? Whose are these apartments?"

"I am ordered not to answer questions. You are in very good hands. Keep yourself quiet. Suspend your curiosity till the morning."

Here our dialogue ended. After a minute's silence, I heard the door of my chamber softly open; and the nurse went toward it, and she, and the man who opened it, spoke two or three times alternately. What was said was uttered in a whisper; yet I thought the voice of the unseen was like some voice with which my ear was acquainted. I could not solve the mystery. The door was then shut again with equal caution. I obeyed the injunction of the nurse, and was silent.

The woman who had watched in my chamber during the night, was French. In the morning, when the surgeons attended me, a second female of menial rank entered the apartment. There was something about her that caught my attention, and made me inquisitive. I was sure I had seen her before, and that feelings of warmth and interest had been connected with her person in my mind. This was my first impression. After a few minutes of doubt and perplexity, I perceived who it was. It was Martha, the wife of William, the Merionethshire peasant, whose life I had contributed to save, while yet a boy with my father. "Bless me, Martha," said I, "is it you?" When the surgeons had finish their visit, she was going out of the room with them. I said softly, "I want to speak with you." She promised to return, and was not long in keeping her word.

"My dear master," said she, "the doctors say you are better, and have given me leave to speak to you, so it be only for five minutes. I did not understand their jabber, but my master's gentleman told me that was the meaning of it."

"Who is your master? How came you in France?"

"Ah, sir! that is a long story. You shall know all by and by."

"Whose apartments are these? They are not the same I tenanted before."

"They are Mr. Scarborough's."

"Of Berkshire?"

"Yes, sir."

"How came I here? Where is Mr. Gifford?"

Martha shook her head.—"You will not see him, I believe, of one while."

"What misfortune has happened to my friend? Is he not in Paris?"

"That he is!"

"Why is he not with me? Why am I separated from the only man that for long time I have dared to trust? I insist upon his being sent for immediately. Go, Martha, and tell Mr. Scarborough I am dying to see him."

"Mr. Gifford is in prison; the Bastille, or the *Con—* *Concier——*, I do not know what name they call it."[1]

"In prison? my friend in prison? I will rise this moment, and procure his freedom! What is he in prison for?"

"Why, sir, it is a queer kind of a story. I do not exactly understand it. It is something about your valet, that ran away from you yesterday. They are both in prison. Captain —— Lord bless me, I had like to have let it all out!—the gentleman, you know, sir, that delivered you from the robbers yesterday——"

"That gentleman was not Mr. Scarborough?"

"No, sir, no, but I am bid not tell his name. Well, sir, he went to a place they call the Police. Those people of the Police are as quick as lightning. The first inkling we had of the matter was from the valet's running away. Captain —— the gentleman, I mean——told them no more than that; and what did they do, but caught Gifford last night, and this morning early they sent word they had caught the valet too."

Saying this, she left me; and in about an hour returned.— "Well, sir," said she, "it is all out. Gifford is the great rascal of the whole gang, and he will be hanged."

"Martha, be silent. I always had a respect for your qualities, and I cannot bear to hear from your mouth, whatever I might from others, these scurrilities against the only honourable man I have lately found in the world.—Where is Mr. Gifford? what has happened to him?"

"We all saw from the first, sir, that it could be no common robbery. Why did your valet take to his heels, and leave you?"

"Martha, I am thoroughly convinced in that point. He was an accomplice with the villains who attacked me."

"Ah, sir, but that is not all. If he had been only their accomplice, he would have been only a robber. What have you lost? You must have been some time in the hands of the rogues, and yet your watch, your purse, your rings, your pocket-book, every

---

1 The Bastille and the Conciergerie were prisons in Paris.

thing is safe. They meant to murder you, sir, to murder you, not for what you had about you, but for your estate!"

"Martha, leave me! I shall for ever abhor the sight of you, if you talk thus. It has been my fault to be too mistrustful———"

"That it has, sir!"

"I cling to Mr. Gifford as my last hold upon human nature. If I could think him base, I would fly the face of man, and herd with wolves and tigers. Thank God, there is no danger of that! He has done me such services, as scarcely ever one man did for another. He unmasked all my treacherous friends."

"He *put on* a mask yesterday."

"When their perfidy had reduced me to the brink of the grave, when it had unseated my reason, and made me a maniac, he only comforted me; he watched by me day and night; his services and attention were inexhaustible; he has saved my life over and over. He conspire my death!—Pooh, pooh, Martha, if you would deceive me, let it be with things possible, and not with such absurd romances as children would laugh at."

"What signifies talking, sir?—They have given the valet the boots,[1] they call it a contrivance the French have to squeeze the truth out of a man—and he has confessed that Gifford was at the bottom of all."

"I am more grieved than I can express, at what you tell me, Martha. But that accounts for all. Diabolical contrivance!— Oh, England! beloved country, that gave me birth! nurse of liberty, virtue, and good sense! never shall thy gallant name be deformed with this sabaoth of demons!—Now, Martha, learn from me, and blush for what you have said![2] Can you, a Briton, believe, that torture makes a man speak the truth? that, when he writhes with agony, and feels himself debased below a brute, his words are to be regarded as oracles? Would not a man then say any thing, to put an end to what he suffers? I would not hang a dog on such evidence! What sort of creature should I be, if I could give up my friend, my tried friend, a man unequalled in fidelity of spirit and honourable sentiment, for the random accusations of a thief on the rack?"

---

1   An instrument of torture.
2   "Sabaoth," army or host.

"There may be something in that, sir. But *we* knew Mr. Gifford before. The valet can tell nothing of him too bad for what he has done already.—However, they will give *him* the boots, and we shall then hear what *he* will say!"

"God of heaven!—Gifford!—God, that we were escaped from this den of barbarians!—Call Mr. Scarborough! Say, I must speak to him immediately!"

"I will, sir. All, I see plain, will soon come out."

"I understand you, Martha. You have been cheated with the story of those domestic pests of mine, whom Gifford's generous exertions have succeeded to rid me of for ever. Every unhappy transgressor against virtue and integrity has a plausible story of his own to tell; and does not fail to boil with indignation against some one of those by whom he is detected and punished. I did intend to give a fresh hearing to the cause of my unhappy, pernicious wife——"

"God bless you! I am very glad of that!"

"But I have no leisure for this now. Gifford is to me father, brother, wife, and children, all in one!"

Mr. Scarborough came in. I had seen him casually in Berkshire, but I had never carefully observed his figure till now. There was something almost awful in it, and that even to me, who could have no extrinsic occasion to stand in awe of my country neighbour. He was tall, and of a carriage bold and graceful. His hairs were of a pure brown, uncontaminated with art. There was good sense and penetration, mixed with an uncommon air of severity, in his countenance. He seemed born to command. When he spoke, there was no spark of self-diffidence or embarrassment. He appeared always to see the right method of proceeding, to confide in his own judgment, and to be firm. Had I beheld such a figure placed on a bench of justice, I should have said, "There sits one of the judges of the patriarchal world, invested with native rank and conscious discernment, not one of the modern race, who place their hopes to awe us in accoutrements of velvet and ermine!"

"Mr. Scarborough," said I, "I know not exactly how I came here, but I have first to thank you for your hospitality."

He bowed.

"Having acknowledged this favour, I have another still greater to demand. My friend and kinsman, Mr. Gifford, is in prison. Martha, your servant, tells me he is in a very distressing situation. I am not in a fit condition to go and solicit his liberation myself——"

"Mr. Gifford is a villain!"

"For God's sake, Mr. Scarborough!—This is no time to discuss his merits. You are, I am sure, too generous and too just to defame the absent."

"I wish Mr. Gifford had been so. My friend, lieutenant Kenrick——"

"Kenrick! is he in Paris?"

"He is under this roof."

"Oh! then I see how it is! You are deceived, Mr. Scarborough. You are the dupe of unfortunate criminals that hope, by means of your character and authority, to destroy the honest man whose integrity they fear."

"*You* are deceived, Mr. Fleetwood. *You* are the dupe of a criminal, a wretch whom I will not condescend to grace with the term unfortunate. *I* am not used to be deluded, sir, nor does this case admit of ambiguity. Mr. Kenrick, the best man on earth, and who loves you the most devotedly,—it was he who rescued you last night from the assassins who were on the point to murder you——"

"Kenrick!"

"—Went instantly, when he had conducted you hither, to the Police. He had no information to give, but that of the disappearance of your valet, and that he saw a figure among the ruffians greatly resembling that of Gifford."

"Accursed calumniator!"

"On these grounds Monsieur the *lieutenant criminel* proceeded. He caused both the persons informed against to be apprehended. Though the valet had taken refuge in a remote part of the city, he easily succeeded to discover his retreat. Gifford appeared boldly at his own lodgings. When told, however, that the valet was in custody, he dropped something of his assurance. The wretched hireling, being put to the torture, laid open a long train of villainy, and pointed out his accomplices; they are all now in custody."

"Mr. Scarborough, I will not stay a moment longer in this house. Procure me a litter, a *fiacre*,[1] any thing! I fly to the vindication of my friend."

"Of the man who waylaid you yesterday? Who, with his own hand, presented a pistol to your head?"

"It is waste of words for us to talk longer. You lend your ear to the wretched, the unnatural Kenrick, the Cain who is at this moment pursuing the destruction of his virtuous brother.[2] Do you, as you please! I, for my part, listened to and believed him too long."

"If you wish to see the *lieutenant criminel*, he will in two hours transport himself hither to complete his examinations. I cannot consent to your removal, which, in your present situation, might be fatal. If you wish to serve Gifford, you cannot do it more speedily, than by waiting the arrival of the magistrate.— In the mean time, suffer me to instruct you in some particulars. It will bring the matter to a more ready conclusion. I wish to satisfy you of the innocence of Kenrick and your wife."

"Mr. Scarborough, it is absurd for us to talk on that head. *I* did not proceed but upon the most demonstrative evidence. The case has been tried by the criminal courts of my country; the wariness of justice has been satisfied; Kenrick has been declared guilty, my wife an adulteress, and her child illegitimate. Why should you open afresh wounds in my soul, to which the blow I received yesterday is the stroke of a feather, and which will assuredly bring me to the grave?"

"Mr. Fleetwood, ask yourself! Would it afford you no pleasure to find, that your wife is the most innocent of mortals, that Kenrick's heart is as honest and generous as his countenance, and that the lovely boy which Mrs. Fleetwood has brought into the world, is your true and proper offspring?"

"No pleasure! It would make me young again! It would translate me to Elysium! I should feel as the founder of the

---

1   A small carriage.
2   Alluding to the story of the brothers Cain and Abel in Genesis 4.

human race felt, before guilt and treachery got footing in the world!"

"And is not the chance of this worth one hour's enquiry?"

"The very thought transports me! Go on!"

"Be patient then, and strict, and impartially severe. What evidence had you of Mrs. Fleetwood's guilt?"

"A love-letter of Kenrick, which I took on her dressing-table."

"That letter was not written to her."

"For whom was it intended?"

"For my daughter.—What else?"

"The miniature of Kenrick, which I found locked up in her casket."

"That, too, was for my daughter.—Proceed!"

"An interview which I witnessed between her and her paramour in the elm-walk, on the right bank of the Kennet.[1] My perfidious kinsman came from Beverley to Berkshire for the express purpose of this interview."

"That also had relation to my daughter."

"My wife, when challenged by me respecting this interview, prevaricated, pretended to know nothing of the matter, and asked whether Kenrick was not at his quarters in Yorkshire."

"That I can explain."

"These were the circumstances on which I acted personally. But the whole has since been cleared up by the laws of my country. Witnesses have proved the criminal conversation in Merionethshire, as well as Mary's confession, that the child was the child of Kenrick."

"These witnesses were suborned. They are now under prosecution for perjury."

"Why did my wife refuse to justify herself, when, for the last time before I left England, I reproached her with her guilt, and called upon her to answer?"

"Fleetwood, you then said to her,—you adjured her by the great God, who made heaven and earth, to tell you, whose child was that she bore in her womb?—Could a woman,

---

1 A river in Berkshire.

shocked with such a question, a woman who knew the integrity of all her actions, the purity of all her thoughts, the devotion
with which she had ever watched and served her lord, answer
the deluded insolent that proposed such an interrogatory?
Then may virtue stoop to vice, then may heaven and hell mix
in eternal confusion, and honour and nobleness of soul no
longer have a name in the universe!

"As you put it, it was an insufferable question, and such as
conscious rectitude might well disdain to answer. Yet surely,
after the first shock had subsided, the interests of herself and her
unborn child, the happiness and reputation of all parties, which
were so intimately concerned, might have induced the most
innocent and proudest woman on earth to descend to explanation!

"It was exactly thus that Mrs. Fleetwood conducted herself.
She transmitted you, three days after, when, to my knowledge,
you were still at Brighthelmstone, a detailed explanation of the
whole affair. Why did you take no notice of that letter?"

"I received no such letter."

"Received!—I am not surprised. The master-villain, whose
task it has been to paint every thing in false colours, and to
obstruct all the glimpses of truth and virtue, has then intercepted it. Other letters were written by your kinsman, and by me;
did you receive none of these?"

"None. You express your surprise, Mr. Scarborough, at my
not answering letters. I was not less surprised at Mary's returning no answer to the letter, in which I informed her that,
notwithstanding all I had suffered from her perfidy, I had spon-
taneously settled upon her an annuity of one thousand pounds.
Guilt itself, I thought, would have expressed some gratitude for
my generosity. Innocence!—it was impossible that innocence
should at such a moment have sat down in silence!"

"Seeing the case as you saw it, this was a generous determination, Mr. Fleetwood, and proves to me that you are the good
and honourable man I ever believed you to be.—No such letter
as you describe, no letter of any kind, was ever received from
you by Mrs. Fleetwood. I see plainly that, from the moment
you left Berkshire, you have been a close prisoner in the keep-

ing of the villain, who was proceeding with rapid, yet deliberate steps, to thrust you out from the scene of the world, and to reap the inheritance of your estates. But it is time, my dear sir, that you should be somewhat acquainted with the affairs of myself and my daughter, which have so intimate a relation to Mrs. Fleetwood's unfortunate story."

"Proceed, sir! You have created in me a desire, at least to hear what can be suggested in behalf of my wife, and of the man you call your friend. You have made bold assertions; I do not see how they can be supported. If they can, I have been the most unfortunate, the most unjust of mankind."

CHAPTER XVII.

"I HAVE been many years a widower," resumed Mr. Scarborough. "When my wife died, she left to me the care of two infants, a son and a daughter. The birth of my daughter, my Louisa, who is now with me, preceded by only two years the death of her mother. The charge which thus devolved upon me, weighed heavy upon my mind, and it is with unintermitted anxiety that I have sought to perform it.

"I brought into the world with me the seeds of a stern and severe disposition; this has been the source of all my misfortunes. My temper is firm; my judgment, perhaps, is clear; and I have ever been somewhat too peremptory in enforcing it. My ordinary speech—whatever (added he, smiling) you may have found it on the present occasion—is pithy and sententious. I have been prone to lay down the law, and too impatient of the perverseness, real or imaginary, that demurred to my dictates. I have always seen these faults of my character, though never so clearly as now, and have endeavoured to correct them. But either they were so twisted with my nature, that they could not be separated and discarded, or I have found myself weak, and insufficient to the office.

"I wished to inspire attachment and confidence into my wife; but I could never succeed. She was a gentle and amiable creature, beautiful as the day, and of manners inexpressibly enchanting. She confessed, that she feared, as much as she loved me; I thought that the former was the predominant passion. The perception of this, instead of correcting me, rendered me more gloomy, and increased my original defects. I saw that I was poisoning the existence of her I loved. I believe that, when she came to die, she was the more reconciled to her fate, because, while living, she was a stranger to the enjoyments of life. Oh, Mr. Fleetwood, you called yourself the most unfortunate of mankind! You have never known, like me, the misery of not being able to excite love in any of the persons most dear to you! Men style me honest, and honourable, and worthy; I am alone in the world, surrounded with a magic circle, that no man oversteps, and no man is daring enough to touch me! This is called Respect—its genuine name is Misery!"

As Mr. Scarborough spoke thus, I saw his lips quivering, and he wiped the moisture from his eyes, and from his brow. After a pause he resumed:—

"My son was the loveliest boy that ever was beheld. His temper was gentle, his heart was affectionate, his understanding was clear, and his views were noble. I was the father of this boy—it was I that killed him! You will not suppose that I did not love him; I loved him to the utmost excess of paternal attachment. But this very excess rendered me restless, impatient, and exacting. I was never satisfied with any thing short of perfection. I crossed him in all his humours; I never allowed him a moment of freedom. Task still succeeded to task, and in none of them could he obtain my applause. He was often very earnest in his exertions; but earnestness gradually gave place to despair. With what severity I have rebuked him! With what contumely and contempt I have treated him! It is one of the infirmities of our nature, that the very sound of the voice of him who reproves, warms the speaker into higher passion and more terrifying fury. The very dissatisfaction that we feel with ourselves, the consciousness that all is not right in this mode of proceeding, increases our ill-humour, and impels us to plunge into greater excess, in the hope that we may drown our remorse. The spirit of my son was broken. Finding himself habitually treated with contempt, he began also to despise himself. He became negligent of his person and his health; and, bereft of hope, he was incapable of exertion. As he grew taller, he felt more deeply the misery of his situation, and at the age of thirteen literally fell a victim to my ill-placed severity.

"He sunk into a deep decline. Too late I became sensible of my injustice. How many bitter tears I have shed over him! They were almost as plentiful, as those which my cruelty so often caused to trickle down his innocent, beautiful cheeks. He told me that he pardoned me with all his heart, that he was conscious that all I did had been designed for his advantage. I sought to recover him to cheerfulness and health; I promised that I would never again utter a harsh word, or entertain a harsh thought toward him. It was too late. With his dying lips he kissed the lips that had so often reviled, and the hand that had smitten him.

"You would think, Mr. Fleetwood, that two such terrible events as the deaths of my wife and son would have been sufficient to correct in me this odious propensity. It did for a while. I made a thousand good resolutions. It was impossible to feel with more horror than I did, that I was the murderer of my only son, and deserved the gallows more than all the highwaymen and housebreakers that are brought thither. But the habit was rooted within me, and, though repeatedly pared away to the quick, it shot up again with as vigorous and rank a vegetation as ever. You only, by the entanglement of your affairs with mine, have led me to reflect decisively on the enormity of my crime, and inspired me with the resolution to banish it for ever.

"You have seen my daughter. I need not tell you that she is beautiful, or that she is the most gay and animated creature in the world. These last advantages she has owed to my happy providence, in taking care that she should be seldom, and only for short intervals, at home. If she had resided with me, I should have rendered her as gloomy as myself; I should have sown in her infant constitution the seeds of destruction. But I determined, that a man, living alone, was by no means the proper person to form the mind and manners of a daughter. I resigned the care of her to her mother's relations. They were of the same soft and gentle mould with my deceased wife. If I

may presume to judge, in a point where I have myself so greatly erred, they rather exceeded on the side of indulgence.

"She was at Bath with one of her aunts, when she first
formed an acquaintance with Mrs. Fleetwood and lieutenant
Kenrick. With the former she exchanged the vows of an eternal friendship. She was delighted with both; and it was, perhaps, the circumstance of seeing her chosen female friend and
the amiable young soldier continually together, that made her
with girlish heedlessness conceive a passion for the latter. The
sentiment was mutual; and Kenrick, infinitely superior to all
interested views, became enamoured unawares of the opulent
heiress. From the moment they were lovers, they grew sensible
of the necessity of secrecy. I cultivated with great assiduity
ambitious projects for my daughter, and resolved not to marry
her below the peerage. I also prescribed it as an indispensable
condition, that her husband should lay aside the name of his
own family, and assume that of mine. With both these resolutions Louisa was acquainted; but, alas! she did not love me. She
lived much with her mother's relations, and little with me; the
austerity of my manners, though I endeavoured to tame and
assuage it, repelled her, and she was influenced by what had
been told her of the unhappy fate of her mother and brother.
She felt, therefore, in a very small degree the inclination to
oblige me; and, perhaps, you will think they were no trivial
compliances that I required of her.

"This situation was the first cause of the equivocal appearances you observed at Bath. Kenrick and Louisa contrived to
be as much together as possible; but my daughter prescribed it
as an indispensable condition to this, that they should avoid all
public manifestations of the understanding which subsisted
between them. Mrs. Fleetwood was attached to both; the kindness of her nature rendered the idea of thwarting their desires
alien to her thoughts; she lent herself willingly to the prosecution of their plans. It was concerted that, whenever they walked
together, Kenrick should give his hand to your wife, while my
daughter should accept the civilities of any chance comer.
They seldom or ever sat together; they scarcely spoke. Mrs.
Fleetwood was the interpreter of their mutual passion. She

received and conveyed from one to the other the protestations of eternal love; she stood the proxy of each, listening to the effusions of sincere affection, till a bystander might have imagined that Louisa mistook her for a lover, and that Kenrick was employing every detestable art to seduce her from her wedded faith. This situation undoubtedly led to extreme familiarity between Mrs. Fleetwood and your kinsman; but, if Kenrick had not been secured against a guilty flame by his admirable principles and the integrity of his nature, he would at this time have been triply armed by his passion for my daughter, which, the more it was restrained, the more it grew. Louisa, perpetually terrified with visions of a haughty and inexorable father was unintermitted in her injunctions of secrecy, and above all insisted that you should on no condition be admitted to a knowledge of the affair.

"At length I completed the preliminaries of the business I had most at heart, the splendid marriage of my daughter. I negotiated a union for her with the eldest son of Lord Lindsey, whose estate was in a ruinous situation, and who therefore willingly agreed to all my conditions. The affair was already in great forwardness, when I summoned my daughter from Bath, without informing her of the purpose I had in view. She came to me with a presentiment of evil, and certainly not with a mind prepared for compliance. I presented the young gentleman. I will now confess, that his most striking characteristics are ugliness, imbecility, and effeminacy. But, infatuated with the grandeur of his alliance, I did not at that time notice these disadvantages. The proposition of marriage had been agitated between me and Lord Lindsey, before I saw the young gentleman; and, when he was introduced, I turned my attention to the father, who was handsome, sagacious, and accomplished, and, in the pleasure of his conversation, found reason to approve my choice.

"Louisa, if she had not been already prepossessed in favour of another, would most likely have shrunk from the marmot I presented to her.[1] Her character on this occasion exhibited a

---

1 A marmot is a rodent similar to a woodchuck.

singular mixture of *naïveté*, rashness, and fear. I could discern a wanton air of contempt and ridicule in her glance, whenever she looked at her noble admirer; it sometimes expressed itself in little sarcastic sallies, and smothered bursts of laughter. When she caught the flash of my eye her countenance instantly fell. She would often, if I were absent, or if she thought I did not observe her, amuse herself with leading him a fool's dance, and humorously praising his wit, his accomplishments, or his beauty, till the poor gentleman was completely in a labyrinth, and looked with a whimsical perplexity, not knowing whether to laugh or cry. Whenever I remarked these things, I sternly discountenanced them. I endeavoured to convince her of the advantages of the proposed marriage. I talked much of parental authority and the duty of a child. I even condescended to entreat her to yield to a plan upon which my heart was entirely bent. She tried at first to rally me out of my purpose. She painted her suitor in ludicrous colours. She repeated his foolish sayings, and mimicked his gestures. But she soon found that this was a style in which her father would not endure to be treated. She then, in the most pathetic manner, besought me, that I would not sacrifice the whole happiness of her life, and solemnly protested that she should never know a tranquil moment, if united to the son of Lord Lindsey. But neither of these modes of attack succeeded with me. I was unalterably fixed upon my project. Thus situated, my native character came over me. I exclaimed that I was the most abused of fathers. I burst into paroxysms of rage. Often in her absence, sometimes in her presence, I cursed her for her unnatural obstinacy, and swore that I would rather follow her to her grave, than not see her united to the husband I had chosen.

"The only confidant my daughter and Kenrick had in the whole of this business, except Mrs. Fleetwood, was Gifford. He was his brother's friend, as your wife was the friend of Louisa. Various advantages seemed to spring to the enamoured pair from this arrangement. Gifford and Mrs. Fleetwood consulted together for their benefit; and, though nothing could exceed the zeal of your wife, she was by no means a match for Gifford in policy and expedients. Beside this, I looked upon the friendship Louisa had formed with a jealous eye; I naturally judged that woman would be apt to be the abettor of woman in rebellion against the stronger sex. But I had met with and conceived an immediate kindness for Gifford. His serious and contemplative nature seemed easily to assort with the sternness of mine. I had an entire confidence in his prudence. I laid before him all the arrangements I had made for the marriage of my daughter, and described its various recommendations. As I saw Louisa paid him a particular attention, I requested him to endeavour to subdue her repugnance, which he readily promised to do.

"To the young lovers he appeared as anxious for the accomplishment of their views, as in conversation with me he showed himself favourable to mine. At first, indeed, when Kenrick communicated to him at Bath the secret of his passion, he set himself in opposition to it, and urged to his brother the many misfortunes and adversities he saw likely to grow upon it. But, as he perceived his remonstrances were fruitless, he changed his tone, yielding rather to the vehemence of Kenrick's importunity, than to the propriety of the pursuit. He swore he would move heaven and earth, rather than not conquer every obstacle to his brother's wishes. He encouraged him to go on, and often told him that all difficulties yielded to perseverance. He, however, recommended, as earnestly as my daughter had done, that you should be kept in entire ignorance of the affair. He said, that your prudence would make you insist that Kenrick should renounce the pursuit, and that you would consider yourself as for ever disgraced at your unportioned kinsman's clandestinely aspiring to the hand of an heiress. He was consulted in every thing. Not a letter was written on either side that did not pass through his hands. In short, he appeared so actively engaged in the interests of the lovers, that the further interference of Mrs. Fleetwood would have been unnecessary, were it not that she had been originally in the affair, that her attachment for the parties was vehement, and that Louisa, though always respectful and grateful to Mr. Gifford, felt a repugnance to him.

"If you found a letter of Kenrick thrown carelessly into one of the toilet-boxes in Mrs. Fleetwood's dressing-room, I now entertain no doubt that it was placed there by Gifford. Mrs.

Fleetwood was too careful of the secret of her friend, ever to have been guilty of such negligence. As to the letter itself, the address was the address of your wife, which for the sake of precaution, it was agreed should always be used; but the person to whose acceptance every line of the contents referred was my daughter. Gifford knew of the miniature, which had the same destination, and could have referred you at once to the very spot where it was found.

"Thus, Mr. Fleetwood, were you, and I, and indeed all the parties in this unhappy business, made the dupes and puppets of a single villain. Louisa, who till now had seen but little of me, though she had always heard my name with a certain degree of dread, had by no means at first that terror of my anger and inflexibility which she afterward conceived. She believed that I could not be inexorable to the tears of my only child; and in this vain hope had indulged with less apprehension the passion of her virgin heart. She longed to tell me that her affections were engaged, and that, if the son of Lord Lindsey had not been in all respects so repulsive as he was, she could never, without a certain kind of prostitution, have become his wife. But the more carefully she watched for an opportunity, the more clearly did she perceive that an opportunity, attended with the smallest degree of auspicious appearance, would never arrive. I in the mean time continued to act the part of a despotic father, and pursued my schemes unintermittingly, in the opinion that the caprices of Louisa would at length yield to my enlightened firmness. Driven to extremity, she came into the plan of an elopement to the north.

"Gifford was a party to every thing that was settled, but he secretly resolved that the marriage should never take place. It was part of his project, that Kenrick should be reduced to beggary. Gifford really stood in awe of his honest and single-hearted brother, and never thought he should be entirely safe, till Kenrick was brought to a state of impotence and desolation. The first great mortification he suffered from the hour that he became an inmate of your family was on the day that Kenrick set out for Westmorland from Bath. That day, to his astonishment, a reconciliation took place between you and your younger kinsman. The consequence was, your procuring for Kenrick a lieutenancy and adjutantship, and thus raising him at once into the receipt of a plentiful income. Gifford's measures, for months after, were directed to the repairing this miscarriage; and his inward animosity to his brother was heightened by the recollection that, while he was pursuing his ruin, he had unwittingly rendered him an important service. His present plan was, by infusions of jealousy to ruin Kenrick for ever in your esteem, at the same time that he should give me timely notice of the projected elopement, and, by the representations he should induce me to make to the lieutenant's superiors, deprive him at once of his military appointments.

"Gifford was acquainted with the day and hour of Kenrick's arrival from Yorkshire, and himself contrived the interview between him and Mrs. Fleetwood in the elm-walk on the right bank of the Kennet. He took care to prepare you with proper views of the affair, and to induce you to believe that the lieutenant came, by Mrs. Fleetwood's invitation, for the basest and most unnatural purposes. The rest you know.

"An anonymous letter was brought to me at this time, informing me that my daughter was on the point of eloping to Scotland with lieutenant Kenrick, a kinsman and dependant of my nearest neighbour. This letter was the contrivance of Gifford; it could come from no other quarter. I never felt so terrible an access of rage as at that moment. I sought Louisa, my child, in the spirit of a murderer. It was, perhaps, happy for us both that she had already disappeared. The letter by some accident had been brought too late. I ordered post-horses without a moment's delay, and set off in pursuit of the fugitives. I took the noble youth, my intended son-in-law, in the chaise with me. My daughter being no where to be found, left no doubt on my mind as to the authenticity of the intelligence I had received; and, though I could gain no intelligence of her at Newbury, I easily conceived that the ravisher might have procured the means of her flight from some other quarter.

"I pursued the route of Scotland for upward of one hundred miles. But, though I was incessant in my enquiries, I could learn no tidings of the persons I sought, at any one of the stages. I then began to believe that it was to no purpose to go in this direction any further. With a heavy heart I turned my face toward home. By this time we happened to be near one of Lord Lindsey's country seats, and I gladly dropped my travelling companion. I was too disturbed in mind for society. Now, for the first time, I felt toward my daughter like a father. If I had overtaken her on the road, nothing would have exceeded my fury. It would then have been a question of rebellion to have been quelled, and guilt to have been prevented. I now felt as if I had lost her for ever, and anger died away in my breast. To be thus left totally alone, wife, son, and daughter, to be successively lost, and all by my own fault,—it was too much!

CHAPTER XVIII.

"WHEN I returned to my own house, I enquired eagerly from every one of Louisa: they had no intelligence to give. I had not been at home half an hour, when lieutenant Kenrick was announced. At the mention of that name all my blood boiled up at once; my rage returned in full force; the paternal feelings, which had begun to sway me, instantly vanished. He entered. His looks were expressive only of the deepest distress and anguish.

"'Villain,' I cried, 'what have you done with my daughter?'

"'I appear before you,' answered the graceful youth, 'a criminal. But I repent of my fault; I will restore to you your daughter, pure and uncontaminated as she came into my hands. But, sir, I also come as a supplicant. You, and you only, can repair a thousand mischiefs, which I have undesigningly perpetrated.'

"He then told me all that had passed at your house; that by equivocal appearances you had been induced to believe the existence of a criminal familiarity between him and your wife; that you had insulted her in the most opprobrious terms; that even in such a moment she had heroically refused to betray the secret of her friend; that you had quitted your house with a determination not to return for years, and gone nobody knew whither; and that you had since written to your steward, ordering that Mrs. Fleetwood should instantly be expelled from your home.

"'Do you think, sir,' added my visitor, 'that on such an occasion, when I have been the cause of so vast a series of calamities, I can aim at any gratification to myself? Do you think, that while my patron and his amiable wife are plunged in the depths of distress, I can engage in the festivities of marriage? No; take back your daughter! I love her with an imperishable affection. But I have no heart, even for Louisa, while I witness this desolation of all that ought to be most dear to me. I never till in this instance engaged in a plan of dissimulation; and see to what it has led me! Do you believe I will ever repeat it? No; I will never wed your daughter, unless it pleases Heaven that I shall wed her in the face of day.'

"My soul yearned toward the boy. There is a contagion in virtue and ingenuousness, that not the hardest heart in nature, not even my heart, can resist. The paternal feelings, which had so auspiciously begun to influence me in my journey home, revived as he spoke. I said to myself, 'This is the husband for my daughter!'—I was never mercenary. I had always been an admirer of virtue, though, alas! from a distance. My stubborn nature bowed before the integrity of Kenrick. I locked his hand in mine. I said, 'You are an honest fellow! I forgive you the past; I will find a time to settle accounts with you. I will be the protector of Mrs. Fleetwood; I will not rest, till I have cleared the misunderstanding between her and her husband.'

"'Let us then,' said Kenrick, 'set out hand in hand on this pious expedition! I have no fears for our success, if I am supported by a man of Mr. Scarborough's fortune and consequence.'

"I took Mrs. Fleetwood into my own house——"

I interrupted my neighbour in his narration.—"Into your own house! Oh, if I had known that single circumstance, how much anguish should I have been saved! I should instantly have commenced a new and temperate investigation of the whole affair."

Mr. Scarborough resumed.—"That and every other particular were solicitously concealed from you by the villain who held you his prisoner. It is his characteristic, wherever he goes, to scatter darkness around him, and every man who comes within his circle, is smitten with blindness.

"I left Mrs. Fleetwood and Louisa together, and proceeded with Kenrick to Brighthelmstone. You were gone. We crossed to Dieppe, and went on to Paris. You were not to be found. I employed my agents in England to discover the place of your abode; but to no purpose. Sometimes I imagined I had gained a clue; I pursued it; always without success. I have now no doubt that these false intimations were supplied to my people by Gifford. At length I learned, by letters from home, that a prosecution for adultery and divorce was commenced on your part against your wife. When we received this information, we were already in Poland, lured on by the false intelligence that had been supplied to us. We instantly set out for England; we met with some unavoidable delays; and, when arrived, we found that the trial had been pushed on with extraordinary exertions; that a solemn adjudication had been pronounced at midnight, just seven hours before we reached London; and a verdict, with ten thousand pounds damages, had been given against your kinsman.

"For our regale at our first breakfast in the metropolis, the newspaper was brought to us, seven columns of which were filled with the trial for criminal conversation, Fleetwood *versus* Kenrick.

"It is impossible to conceive the astonishment with which we perused it. First came the speech of an eloquent counsellor, who detailed the case with all its aggravations before the court. He said, that so strong and complicated a charge had never been submitted to that bench. That the defendant, a mere pauper, a very distant relation, had been taken up by the plaintiff out of charity. That, while he had been receiving hourly benefits from your hands, he had gone on for months polluting the wife of your bosom under the roof of his benefactor. He mentioned the evidences he had of the criminal conversation in Merionethshire, who would state such particulars, as would leave no doubt in the minds of any of his hearers. He added, that he could further establish the charge, by a witness, a discarded servant, who had heard the confession of the illegitimacy of the child just born, from the mouth of the adulteress."

"'The counsellor is mad,' said I. 'What does he mean?'

"'These allegations,' he proceeded, 'are all in my instructions.'

"I looked on to the report of the evidence: they stated and swore specifically to every thing the pleader had described. The paper dropped from my hand.

"'Kenrick!'

"The lieutenant fell upon his knees. 'By the great God that made me,' he said, 'all this is utterly false!'

"For a moment, prepared as I was with a knowledge of the truth, I believed the examinations on the trial. Kenrick at length succeeded—what is impossible to ingenuousness like his?—in restoring himself to my good opinion. If you had witnessed his earnestness, his agitation, his vehemence, his broken exclamations of surprise, and his tears, you would have been convinced, as rapidly as I was.

"I sent instantly for the lawyers whom I had retained for the defence, and we settled measures for the prosecution of the perjurers. Kenrick knew them all, and was able to supply such a clue for their detection, as bore with it every promise of success. If we had arrived in London a week sooner, my lawyers assured me the cause would have taken a very different turn.

"Having occasion to go out about some business in the evening, I saw from the window of my coach the figure of Gifford gliding along by the light of the lamps. I had now no doubt that he was the secret spring of all these machinations. I stopped the carriage. I was in the street in a moment. I no longer saw him. I glanced a figure that seemed to be his. At the corner of a street I lost it. Of two directions I did not know which the person had taken. I suppose I took the wrong first; but I saw him no more.

"The next morning, as Kenrick and I sat at breakfast, to our exceeding surprise, Mr. Gifford was announced. We consulted for a moment. I said, 'Kenrick, he is come with a warrant to arrest you for the damages awarded; you had better withdraw.' This seemed infinitely improbable; Kenrick could not resist the desire he felt to face his brother; he was admitted.

"This accomplished hyprocrite succeeded in convincing us, that he had no concern in the plot, which had advanced thus far triumphantly against us. He owned that he had almost constantly attended upon you; but he protested that his motive had been the desire to mitigate your resentment against Mrs. Fleetwood and his brother. He said, that after encountering much resistance and obstinacy, he had in a great degree subdued you, and had come over for the express purpose of postponing the trial. But, unfortunately, he had come too late; the diligence of the lawyers had outstripped his. He called Kenrick aside; he enquired particularly into the situation of Mrs. Fleetwood, and gave him a draft of two hundred pounds for her use. He furnished us with the address of the place where he said you at present were, and advised Kenrick by all means to repair to you, and to improve upon the measures of reconciliation which he had so happily begun.

"At the city in Italy which Gifford pointed out to us, we learned that you had lately been there, but were gone, and had left no clue by which we could pursue you. We made an appointment, on our return, to meet Mrs. Fleetwood and Louisa at Paris, whither a relation of Mrs. Fleetwood's mother, whom I had waited upon when, a few months before, I came to that metropolis, and to whom I had explained the unhappy situation of her kinswoman, invited her, to come and lie in. This seems to be the only circumstance that escaped the vigilance of Gifford. He had improved the period of our absence to complete the ecclesiastical proceedings, and the act of divorce. He contrived, at the same time, to put off the trials for perjury. Reviewing the whole affair, I have now no doubt that he succeeded in corrupting our lawyers, the solicitors, if not the pleaders, as well as made use of extraordinary applications to accelerate his own.

"At Paris we received an account of the conclusion of the whole proceedings, and certainly now saw the conduct of Gifford in a very different light, from that in which he had persuaded us to view it in London. It would have been madness any longer to doubt. The veil which hid from us the truth was demolished, even beyond the skill of that arch-deceiver to repair it. Not the generous confidence and fraternal sentiments of Kenrick himself could delude him. Gifford, in the mean time, came over to Paris, pursuant to his appointment with you. We were once more within the walls of the same city.

"Two days since, Kenrick and Gifford met each other in the Palais Royal. They were mutually surprised, neither having the least idea that the other was in Paris. The behaviour of Gifford, on this occasion, was very different from what it had been a few months before in London. Kenrick went up to him with a fixed brow, and said,—

"'Whence do you come, sir? Who is it that has been so diligent in procuring the decree of the ecclesiastical court, and the act of parliament, against my aunt? Appearances are grievously against you!'

"'Have a care, my friend!' retorted Gifford. 'I will not be suspected for nothing!'

"'Gifford, Gifford, if in reality you have been playing a traitor's part, it is time you should drop the mask!'

"'You discredit, then, the professions I have made you? Every thing that I have done to save you from ruin you regard with a malignant eye? Another time you shall know whether I am your friend! The next service I render you, be sure of it, shall have your thanks!'

"'Where is my uncle? is he in Paris?'

"'Your uncle and your aunt! Lay aside these fopperies, which so ill become you. Talk, if you can, like a man! If Mr. Fleetwood persists in believing you perfidious, am I to blame? If he is able to prove it to the satisfaction of the whole world, whose fault, pray, is that?'

"'Where is Mr. Fleetwood?'

"'He is not in Paris.—I will answer no more questions.— Kenrick, I do not understand the tone you assume. I have stuck by you too long. Henceforth be no brother of mine!'

"'Then as enemies!'

"'Then as enemies!'

"'In that character I shall find a time, and shall call you to account!'

"'When you please. I am to be found.'

"Gifford, it appears, was now so near the accomplishment of all his objects, that he thought it unnecessary to practise disguise any further. The devil himself sometimes grows tired of the character of a deceiver, and appears in his true colours. In imagination already the possessor of all your estates, Gifford was in haste to shake off his brother as an useless incumbrance.

"He had, in reality, no time to lose. You had expressed repeatedly a desire to elucidate the truth in person, and by a temperate discussion with the parties themselves. Gifford found that we were in Paris; and, perhaps, suspected that Mrs. Fleetwood might be so too. One unlucky hour might overturn the fabric which he had erected at the expense of such a world of guilt. He touched the goal.

"Kenrick had the next day, yesterday, an engagement with a young French nobleman to proceed to Fontainebleau. They were attended each with a servant. They met you on the road. You know the rest."

CHAPTER XIX.

I LISTENED to the narrative of Mr. Scarborough, with emotions of shame and horror against myself. It was a wonderful story; but I was convinced.

I had scarcely had time to utter a few incoherent exclamations it drew from me, when Kenrick burst into the room. It was he I had heard in the night conferring with my nurse. He had constantly kept watch at my chamber-door; but he had not ventured to intrude, till Mr. Scarborough had prepared the way by a full explanation.

He flew to my knees! "Uncle, uncle," said he, "will you forgive? It was all my fault. How could I dare to deceive, to have a secret from, a benefactor I so loved?"

"This is too much!" I exclaimed; and fell back upon my pillow. I thought that, if Mary and Kenrick were proved innocent, it would be all joy. It is the reverse. It is a feeling without a name. It is worse than remorse; it is hell. "Kenrick, I dare not look upon you. Kill me, my friends, in pity kill me! I am unworthy to live."

Kenrick exerted himself to soothe me; and never did male of the human species enjoy so great powers for the purpose. Martha understood what was going on, and would come in. She had a child in her arms.

"Oh, sir, you asked me whose servant I was, and I would not tell you. I am my mistress's, your lady's, servant. She brought me over to France. She would have me to be with her in her lying-in. And there is her child, the dear boy, that so much harm has been brewed about. Look at him! He has exactly your mouth; nothing can be more like than his brow; I will take my death, that he is as like you, as if you had spit him out of your mouth. Oh, my dear master, my benefactor, will you acknowledge him? Kiss him! I die to see you kiss him."

I took the child in my arms. I willingly believed all that Martha said of him; my eyes were too much dimmed with tears to see any thing distinctly. I pressed him to my bosom. I felt that he was the pledge of the most injured of women. I experienced a hundred times the joy that the tenderest-hearted man in the world ever felt, when his first-born son was presented to him; because I had believed—what had not infernal villainy induced me to believe?

Mary, my wife, the mother of my child, only was absent. I enquired for her with a faltering tongue.

"Ah, sir! she lives," said Martha.

"Do not think I enquire for her, as wishing to see her! Dear, injured saint! I could not look at her. What had I to do to marry? to choose the most accomplished and admirable of her sex? I, that had done wrong, and miscarried, in every station and stage of my life! Would God my eyes were closed for ever! that recollection were at an end in my mind! that mountains pressed down in peace this hand that has acted, and these lips that have spoken, so much evil!—Yet tell me, I entreat you, Martha, how your mistress is?"

"It will do you little good, sir, to hear of that!"

"Dear uncle," interrupted Kenrick, "compose yourself! You appear scarcely glad to have all your suspicions removed. That which should elevate you with the highest pleasure, seems only to torment you."

"True, true, Kenrick! Can I do otherwise than lament, that the woman I have lost for ever is so excellent,—would have made me inexpressibly happy, had I not been the wickedest of men? She can never approach me, never condescend to speak to me, more. Have not you heard her say so?"

They were silent.

The period at which I quitted her, had been to Mary a terrible crisis. What I did appeared to my own mind sufficiently justified, for I regarded her as guilty of the most enormous of all social crimes, a complicated, a studious, a shameless delusion put upon the husband of her bosom, an elaborate pretence to the purest faith, when all was false and hollow. But as it appeared to her,—let me speak plainly,—as it was in itself, as it appeared in the eyes of heaven and earth,—my conduct was the most cruel and atrocious that ever was perpetrated.

Poor Mary! her heart, that heart which had "grown with her growth, and strengthened with her strength," was buried in the caverns of the ocean.[1] Fifteen months before the period at which I deserted her, she no longer held to the great mass of living existences but by a single thread. For my sake, with great difficulty and anguish, she had formed to herself a new scheme of being, and had come back into the world from which she was broken off. And now I, the man for whom she had done this, left her without a home, without reputation, without bread. "I had delighted myself with the hope that she would perish in misery."

How had all this happened? Mary had never, till within a few minutes of our final parting, heard her name coupled disreputably with that of Kenrick. Kenrick, half an hour before, when I flew toward him, bursting with abhorrence and revenge, did not understand me, was unable to conceive the slightest idea of what it was that had roused me to this tumult.

---

1   Alexander Pope, *An Essay on Man* (1733-34), ii.135-36.

However strong were the grounds that I thought I had for condemning my kinsman and my wife, she could discern none; to her it must appear the most infamous caprice that the heart of man ever harboured.

Mary was turned out, like Lear in the old chronicles, to the fury of the elements.[1] Had not Mr. Scarborough taken the generous resolution to shelter her, she must have died. At the time when she found herself treated with this inconceivable barbarity, was that a moment when she could devise schemes to support existence? She would not have had the spirits to ask one human creature for a morsel of bread. Speechless she would have sunk into the arms of death. And she was several months gone with child!

Louisa did every thing in her power to support her languishing friend. Alas; poor Mary abhorred the light of heaven! She detested the idea of taking nutriment within her lips. Her state of pregnancy co-operated with the disorder of her mind. For the first two days she was almost continually in fainting fits. Her life was not expected. It seemed scarcely less than a miracle, that her condition did not at least produce a miscarriage.

Indignation, I believe, in this situation served her for her daily bread. Though her nature was gentle, and her manners bland and unassuming, she had pride at the bottom of her heart, a pride that perhaps towered the higher, in proportion as it was slow to be awaked. She remembered the scene in the garden when I had so brutally insulted her; she remembered the dialogue in which I had interrogated her, "Who was the father of the child she bore in her womb?" She sat down under this treatment without any manifestations of violence and rage. But she said to herself, "The daughter of Macneil shall never forgive this!" She reflected, as was but natural, upon the desolate condition in which her family misfortunes had left her, and she regarded these as so many aggravations of the cruelty she had experienced. "Fleetwood, if I had had patrons and protectors still living, if I had not come dowerless to your bed, you could not have used me thus ungenerously. No; I could live at a

---

1   A reference to *King Lear*, II.iv (the incident is not in Shakespeare's sources for the play).

distance from the abodes of my species on the fruits of the earth; I could labour among peasants for my bread; this I should not feel as humiliation; but I cannot stoop ever again to hold intercourse with the husband that has wronged me."

If Mary recollected these aggravations of my offence, they did not present themselves with less bitterness to my mind. I dwelt upon her innocence, her merits, her defenceless situation, her extinguished race, her embezzled fortune. It seemed as if, now that what the vulgar mind would call the obstacles to our re-union were removed, we were more certainly divided than ever. While charges, and accusations, and historical details, were the mountains that separated us, the case was not altogether hopeless. These might be cleared away and refuted. Now we were separated by sentiments, that must for ever twine themselves with the vitals of every honourable individual, and that can only be exterminated by the blow which lays the head that has conceived them in the dust.

Once, as we have seen, Mary so far mastered her feelings as to write me a letter. The purport of that letter was to reinstate the injured Kenrick in my good opinion, and to claim my justice for the child, my own child, which was shortly to be born: even in that letter she recited the decree that she had herself pronounced between us, that we were never to see, that we were mutually to be dead to each other. When she saw that letter producing no effect, the horror she had conceived against me changed, from a passion, into a habit of her soul. She never thought of me, but as of a man resolutely unjust, to whom the most earnest appeals of eternal truth might be addressed with as much hope as to the Great Wall of China.

Kenrick and Scarborough were indefatigable in their endeavours to restore me to her good opinion and favour. They assured her that the letter upon which she laid so much stress had never reached me: they described to her the complicated machinations of the villain Gifford, which might have succeeded with the most clear-sighted and cold-blooded husband in the world. She listened to all this with an unattending ear. "Very well!" said she. "Do not you perceive, that one dispassionate question, one five minutes of tranquil investigation, would have brushed away in a moment the cobweb intrenchments of Gifford? Did I deserve no more than this?"

Kenrick was now become my confidant. I related to him all that had happened from the evening that I burst away from him on the banks of the Kennet. These things he faithfully repeated to my wife. He described to her my sufferings, my insanity, my despair. He spoke of the supper I had celebrated on the fifteenth of July. On this she seemed to ponder. "Poor Fleetwood!" she said.

My wife and I had now been four weeks in Paris, with only the length of a street between us. I thought of her continually; but I knew the integrity and elevation of her sentiments; and I felt as if I should die, if I met her even by chance.

One evening I sat alone in my hotel. I had had a long and affecting conversation with Kenrick. I had settled the arrangements of my future existence, and had been acquainting him with the particulars. I was resolved to retire to a strange, wild, despairing situation, which had formerly left a deep impression upon me, in the midst of the Pyrenees. I found that this little estate was to be sold. I reserved to myself an annuity of four hundred pounds a year upon my property in England. The rest of my possessions I made over in full to my wife and child, except one agreeable manor, worth about eighteen thousand pounds, which I settled on Kenrick; a testimony that, of all the men living on the face of the earth, he was the one that most deserved my love. I demanded of him that he should visit me in my retreat once in two years, bringing my child with him, and should remain each time a few weeks under my roof.

It was dusk. Miss Scarborough and another lady entered the room where I sat. The apartment was large; they withdrew to a distant corner of it; and, upon the terms on which we lived, it was not necessary for me to derange myself. If it were a Frenchwoman of fashion and high spirits, she would be told, it was only the melancholy Englishman; and that would be deemed a sufficient apology. I was buried in my own thoughts. They seated themselves, and continued in a dead silence. I know not how it was, but this silence disturbed me. It was so unlike what I had been accustomed to expect. I looked toward them. Just at this moment lights were brought in, and placed silently upon the table. The strange lady was clad in black, and a veil covered her face. It struck me that her figure was the most beautiful that was ever seen. Her attitude was expressive of dejection and melancholy. She seemed, so far as I could judge, again and again to glance at me, and then turn away. I felt my heart thump at my bosom, and my sight grew dizzy.— She wrung her hands, and put them to her head. She rose as if to go, and leaned on Miss Scarborough. Her legs tottered, and she sat down again upon another chair. "Fleetwood!" said she.—Oh, that voice! Contending emotions, hope, fear, transport, and shame, held me motionless.

She threw back her veil, and I saw the godlike irradiations of innocence: pale she was, and emaciated with all she had suffered. She looked the less like an inhabitant of this terrestrial globe.

"Take my hand!" she said; and stretched it out. "Take my heart." She fell into my arms. "You shall not make your next wedding supper like the last!"

It is impossible for any one to imagine what I felt at that moment. Whenever I recollect it, I am astonished that I did not expire on the spot. Remorse, while the party against whom we have offended still retains its resentment, and regards us with disdain, scarcely rases the outermost cuticle of the heart. It is from the hour in which we are forgiven, that the true remorse commences. That I could ever have acted thus toward the angelic creature who condescends to pardon me for what I acted,—this is the sensation that is sharper than all the pains of hell!

Another feeling succeeded. Mary never looked half so beautiful, half so radiant, as now. Innocence is nothing, if it is merely innocence. It is guileless nature, when impleaded at a stern and inhuman bar, when dragged out to contumely and punishment, when lifting up its head in conscious honour, when Heaven itself seems to interpose to confound the malice of men, and declares, "This is the virtue that I approve!" there, there is presented to us the most ravishing spectacle that earth can boast. I never till now was sensible of half the merits of my wife.

Gifford died by the hands of the public executioner. The ministers of law who pronounced upon him, knew little of the series of his crimes; but it was proved that he had assailed me on the highway, and purposed to assassinate me that he might possess my estate; and he was adjudged to die.

I shed no tear upon the bier of Gifford. I reviewed the whole series of his life from the cradle to the scaffold. I have always regarded with horror those sanguinary laws which, under the name of justice, strike at the life of man. For his sake I was willing to admit of one exception. His whole existence had been a series of the most monstrous and unnatural crimes. For what society, or plantation of men, in the remotest corner of the globe, was he fitted? What discipline, or penitentiary confinement, could rationally be expected to inspire him with one touch of human nature? Die then, poor wretch, and let the earth, which labours with thy depravity, be relieved!

On the seventh day from that in which Mary and I met in the manner I have described, Kenrick and his Louisa were united: and Mr. Scarborough, who had shown himself so harsh and austere as a parent, became the most indulgent of grand-sires.

THE END.

Appendix A: Foundations of the Novel

1. Selections from William Godwin, *Enquiry Concerning Political Justice and its Influence on Morals and Happiness* (1798).

i. From Book V, Chap XV, "Of Political Imposture"

> "*Pour qu'un peuple naissant pût gouter les saines maximes de la politique & suivre les regles fondamentales de la raison de l'état, il faudroit que l'effet pût devenir la cause, que l'esprit social, qui doit être l'ouvrage de l'institution, présidât à l'institution même, & que les hommes fussent avant les lois ce quils doivent devenir par elles. Ainsi donc le législateur ne pouvant employer ni la force ni le raisonnement; c'est une nécessité qu'il recoure à une autorité d'un autre ordre, qui puisse entrainer sans violence, & persuader sans convaincre.*"[1] *Du Contrat Social, Liv. II. Chap. vii.*

Having frequently quoted Rousseau in the course of this work, it may be allowable to say one word of his general merits, as a moral and political writer. He has been subjected to continual ridicule, for the extravagance of the proposition with which he began his literary carreer; that the savage state, was the genuine and proper condition of man. It was however by a very slight mistake, that he missed the opposite opinion which it is the business of the present enquiry to establish. He only substituted, as the topic of his eulogium, the period that preceded government and laws, instead of the period that may possibly follow upon their abolition. It is sufficiently observable that, where he describes the enthusiastic influx of truth, that first

---

1 "In order that a people at its birth can taste the healthy maxims of politics and follow the fundamental rules of reason of the state, it is necessary that the effect could become the cause, that the social spirit, which ought to be the work of the institution, would preside at the moment of institution itself, and that people would already, prior to the laws, be what they are supposed to become as a result of them. With the legislator thus unable to employ either force or reason, it is a necessity that he have recourse to an authority of another order, one which can impel without violence and persuade without convincing."

made him a moral and political writer [in his second letter to Malesherbes], he does not so much as mention his fundamental error, but only the just principles which led him into it. He was the first to teach, that the imperfections of government were the only perennial source of the vices of mankind; and this principle was adopted from him by Helvetius and others. But he saw further than this, that government, however reformed, was little capable of affording solid benefit to mankind, which they did not. This principle has since (probably without being suggested by the writings of Rousseau) been expressed with great perspicuity and energy, but not developed, by Thomas Paine, in the first page of his Common Sense.

Rousseau, not withstanding his great genius, was full of weakness and prejudice. His *Emile* deserves perhaps, upon the whole, to be regarded as one of the principal reservoirs of philosophical truth, as yet existing in the world; though with a perpetual mixture of absurdity and mistake. In his writings expressly political, *Du Contrat Social* and *Considérations sur la Pologne*, the superiority of his genius seems to desert him.[1] To his merits as an investigator, we should not forget to add, that the term eloquence, is perhaps more precisely descriptive of his mode of composition, than of that of any other writer that ever existed.

ii. From Book VIII, Chapter VIII, Appendix, "Of Cooperation, Cohabitation, and Marriage"

From these principles it appears, that every thing that is usually understood by the term cooperation, is, in some degree, an evil. A man in solitude, is obliged to sacrifice or postpone the execution of his best thoughts, in compliance with his necessities, or his frailties. How many admirable designs have perished in the conception, by means of this circumstance? It is still worse, when a man is also obliged to consult the convenience of others. If I be expected to eat or to work in conjunction with my neighbour, it must either be at a time most convenient to me,

---

1 *Considérations sur le gouvernement de Pologne* was published in manuscript in 1771.

or to him, or to neither of us. We cannot be reduced to a clock-work uniformity....

Another article which belongs to the subject of cooperation, is cohabitation. The evils attendant on this practice, are obvious. In order to the human understanding's being successfully cultivated, it is necessary, that the intellectual operations of men should be independent of each other. We should avoid such practices as are calculated to melt our opinions into a common mould. Cohabitation is also hostile to that fortitude, which should accustom a man, in his actions, as well as in his opinions, to judge for himself, and feel competent to the discharge of his own duties. Add to this, that it is absurd to expect the inclinations and wishes of two human beings to coincide, through any long period of time. To oblige them to act and to live together, is to subject them to some inevitable portion of thwarting, bickering and unhappiness. This cannot be otherwise, so long as men shall continue to vary in their habits, their preferences and their views. No man is always chearful and kind; and it is better that his fits of irritation should subside of themselves, since the mischief in that case is more limited, and since the jarring of opposite tempers, and the suggestions of a wounded pride, tend inexpressibly to increase the irritation. When I seek to correct the defects of a stranger, it is with urbanity and good humour. I have no idea of convincing him through the medium of surliness and invective. But something of this kind inevitably obtains, where the intercourse is too unremitted.

The subject of cohabitation is particularly interesting, as it includes in it the subject of marriage. It will therefore be proper to pursue the enquiry in greater detail. The evil of marriage, as it is practised in European countries, extends further than we have yet described. The method is, for a thoughtless and romantic youth of each sex, to come together, to see each other, for a few times, and under circumstances full of delusion, and then to vow eternal attachment. What is the consequence of this? In almost every instance they find themselves deceived. They are reduced to make the best of an irretrievable mistake. They are led to conceive it their wisest policy, to shut their eyes upon realities, happy, if, by any perversion of intellect, they can persuade themselves that they were right in their first crude opinion of each other. Thus the institution of marriage is made a system of fraud; and men who carefully mislead their judgments in the daily affair of their life, must be expected to have a crippled judgment in every other concern.

Add to this, that marriage, as now understood, is a monopoly, and the worst of monopolies. So long as two human beings are forbidden, by positive institution, to follow the dictates of their own mind, prejudice will be alive and vigorous. So long as I seek, by despotic and artificial means, to maintain my possession of a woman, I am guilty of the most odious selfishness. Over this imaginary prize, men watch with perpetual jealousy; and one man finds his desire, and his capacity to circumvent, as much excited, as the other is excited, to traverse his projects, and frustrate his hopes. As long as this state of society continues, philanthropy will be crossed and checked in a thousand ways, and the still augmenting stream of abuse will continue to flow....

Admitting these principles therefore as the basis of the sexual commerce, what opinion ought we to form respecting infidelity to this attachment? Certainly no ties ought to be imposed upon either party, preventing them from quitting the attachment, whenever their judgment directs them to quit it. With respect to such infidelities as are compatible with an intention to adhere to it, the point of principal importance is a determination to have recourse to no species of disguise. In ordinary cases, and where the periods of absence are of no long duration, it would seem, that any inconstancy would reflect some portion of discredit on the person that practised it. It would argue that the person's propensities were not under that kind of subordination, which virtue and self-government appear to prescribe. But inconstancy, like any other temporary dereliction, would not be found incompatible with a character of uncommon excellence. What, at present, renders it, in many instances, peculiarly loathsome, is its being practised in a clandestine manner. It leads to a train of falshood and a concerted hypocrisy, than which there is scarcely any thing that more eminently depraves and degrades the human mind.

The mutual kindness of persons of an opposite sex will, in such a state, fall under the same system as any other species of friendship. Exclusively of groundless and obstinate attachments, it will be impossible for me to live in the world, without finding in one man a worth superior to that of another. To this man I shall feel kindness, in exact proportion to my apprehension of his worth. The case will be the same with respect to the other sex. I shall assiduously cultivate the intercourse of that woman, whose moral and intellectual accomplishments strike me in the most powerful manner. But "it may happen, that other men will feel for her the same preference that I do." This will create no difficulty. We may all enjoy her conversation; and, her choice being declared, we shall all be wise enough to consider the sexual commerce as unessential to our regard. It is a mark of the extreme depravity of our present habits, that we are inclined to suppose the sexual commerce necessary to the advantages arising from the purest friendship. It is by no means indispensible, that the female to whom each man attaches himself in that matter, should appear to each the most deserving and excellent of her sex.

2. Selections from William Godwin, *The Enquirer: Reflections on Education, Manners and Literature in a Series of Essays* (1797).

i. From Part I, Essay VII, "Of Public and Private Education"

On the other hand, there is an advantage in public education similar in its tendency to that just described. Private education is almost necessarily deficient in excitements. Society is the true awakener of man; and there can be little true society, where the disparity of disposition is so great as between a boy and his preceptor. A kind of lethargy and languor creeps upon this species of studies. Why should he study? He has neither rival to surpass, nor companion with whom to associate his progress. Praise loses its greatest charm when given in solitude. It has not the pomp and enchantment, that under other circumstances would accompany it. It has the appearance of a cold and concerted stratagem, to entice him to industry by indirect considerations. A boy, educated apart from boys, is a sort of unripened hermit, with all the gloom and lazy-pacing blood incident to that profession....

The pupil of private education is commonly either awkward and silent, or pert, presumptuous and pedantical. In either case he is out of his element, embarrassed with himself, and chiefly anxious about how he shall appear. On the contrary, the pupil of public education usually knows himself, and rests upon his proper centre. He is easy and frank, neither eager to show himself, nor afraid of being observed. His spirits are gay and uniform. His imagination is playful, and his limbs are active. Not engrossed by a continual attention to himself, his generosity is ever ready to break out; he is eager to fly to the assistance of others, and intrepid and bold in the face of danger. He has been used to contend only upon a footing of equality; or to endure suffering with equanimity and courage. His spirit therefore is unbroken; while the man, who has been privately educated, too often continues for the remainder of his life timid, incapable of a ready self-possession, and ever prone to prognosticate ill of the contentions in which he may unavoidably be engaged.

ii. From Part I, Essay XII, "Of Deception and Frankness"

Rousseau, to whom the world is so deeply indebted for the irresistible energy of his writings, and the magnitude and originality of his speculations, has fallen into the common error in the point we are considering. His whole system of education is a series of tricks, a puppet-show exhibition, of which the master holds the wires, and the scholar is never to suspect in what manner they are moved. The scholar is never to imagine that his instructor is wiser than himself. They are to be companions; they are to enter upon their studies together; they are to make a familiar progress; if the instructor drop a remark which facilitates their progress, it is to seem the pure effect of accident. While he is conducting a process of the most uncommon philosophical research, and is watching every change and motion of the machine, he is to seem in the utmost degree frank, simple, ignorant and undesigning.

The treatise of Rousseau upon education is probably a work of the highest value. It contains a series of most important speculations upon the history and structure of the human mind; and many of his hints and remarks upon the direct topic of education, will be found of inestimable value. But in the article here referred to, whatever may be its merit as a vehicle of fundamental truths, as a guide of practice it will be found of the most pernicious tendency. The deception he prescribes would be in hourly danger of discovery, and could not fail of being in a confused and indistinct manner suspected by the pupil; and in all cases of this sort a plot discovered would be of incalculable mischief, while a plot rejected could have little tendency to harm.

iii. From Part I, Essay XIV, "Of the Obtaining of Confidence"

There is another reason beside that of the advantage to be derived from the assistance of superior age and experience, why the parent or preceptor should desire the confidence of the pupil. If I desire to do much towards cultivating the mind of another, it is necessary that there should exist between us a more than common portion of cordiality and affection. There is no power that has a more extensive operation in the history of the human mind, than sympathy. It is one of the characteristics of our nature, that we incline to weep with those that weep, and to rejoice with those that rejoice. But, if this be the case in our intercourse with an absolute stranger, it is unspeakably increased in proportion to the greatness of our esteem, and the strength of our attachment. Society in any undertaking, lightens all its difficulties, and beguiles us of all our weariness. When my friend accompanies me in my talk, and our souls mutually catch and emit animation, I can perform labours that are almost more than human with an undoubting spirit. Where sympathy is strong, imitation easily engrafts itself. Persons who are filled with kindness towards each other, understand each other without asking the aid of voice and words. There is, as it were, a magnetical virtue that fills the space between them: the communication is palpable, the means of communication too subtle and minute to be detected.

If any man desire to possess himself of the most powerful engine that can be applied to the purposes of education, if he would find the ground upon which he must stand to enable himself to move the whole substance of the mind, he will probably find it in sympathy. Great power is not necessarily a subject of abuse. A wise preceptor would probably desire to be in possession of great power over the mind of his pupil, though he would use it with economy and diffidence. He would therefore seek by all honest arts to be admitted into his confidence, that so the points of contact between them may be more extensively multiplied, that he may not be regarded by the pupil as a stranger of the outer court of the temple, but that his image may mix itself with his pleasures, and be made the companion of his recreations.

The road that a sound understanding would point out to us, as leading most directly to the confidence of another, is, that we should make ourselves as much as possible his equals, that our affection towards him should display itself in the most unambiguous colours, that we should discover a genuine sympathy in his joys and his sorrows, that we should not play the part of the harsh monitor and austere censor, that we should assume no artificial manners, that we should talk in no solemn, prolix and unfeeling jargon, that our words should be spontaneous, our actions simple, and our countenance the mirror to our hearts. Thus conducting ourselves, thus bland and insinuating with no treacherous design, we shall not probably meet a repulse in our well chosen endeavours to be admitted the confidents of youth. Habit will tend to establish us in the post we have obtained; our ascendancy will every day become confirmed; and it is not probable that we shall lose this most distinguishing badge of friendship, unless through our own misconduct and folly.

iv. From Part I, Essay XV, "Of Choice in Reading"

The moral of any work may be defined to be, that ethical sentence to the illustration of which the work may most aptly be applied. The tendency is the actual effect it is calculated to produce upon the reader, and cannot be completely ascertained but by the experiment. The selection of the one, and the character of the other, will in a great degree depend upon the previous state of mind of the reader.

Let the example be the tragedy of the Fair Penitent.[1] The moral deduced from this admirable poem by one set of readers will be, the mischievous tendency of unlawful love, and the duty incumbent upon the softer sex to devote themselves in all things to the will of their fathers and husbands. Other readers may perhaps regard it as a powerful satire upon the institutions at present existing in society to the female sex, and the wretched consequences of that mode of thinking, by means of which, in a woman "one false step damns her fame." They will regard Calista as a sublime example of a woman of the most glorious qualities, struggling against the injustice of mankind;—capable, by the greatness of her powers, and the heroism of her temper, of every thing that is excellent; contending with unconquerable fortitude against an accumulation of evils; conquered, yet not in spirit; hurried into the basest actions, yet with a soul congenial to the noblest. It is of no consequence whether the moral contemplated by the author, were different from both of these. The tendency again may be distinct from them all, and will be various according to the various tempers and habits of the persons by whom the work is considered.

From the distinctions here laid down it seems to follow, that the moral of a work is a point of very subordinate consideration, and that the only thing worthy of much attention is the tendency. It appears not unlikely that, in some cases, a work may be fairly susceptible of no moral inference, or none but a bad one, and yet may have a tendency in a high degree salutary and advantageous. The principal tendency of a work, to make use of a well known distinction, may be either intellectual or moral, to increase the powers of the understanding, or to mend the disposition of the heart. These considerations are probably calculated to moderate our censures, against many of the authors whose morality we are accustomed to arraign. A bad moral to a work, is a very equivocal proof of a bad tendency. To

---

1   A tragedy (1703) by Nicholas Rowe.

ascertain the tendency of any work is a point of great difficulty. The most that the most perfect wisdom can do, is to secure the benefit of the majority of readers. It is by no means impossible, that the books most pernicious in their effects that ever were produced, were written with intentions uncommonly elevated and pure.

The intellectual tendency of any book is perhaps a consideration of much greater importance, than its direct moral tendency. Gilblas is a book not very pure in its moral tendency; its subject is the successes and good fortune of a kind of sharper, at least, of a man not much fettered and burthened with the strictness of his principles; its scenes are a tissue of knavery and profligacy, touched with a light and exquisite pencil.[1] Shakespear is a writer by no means anxious about his moral. He seems almost indifferent concerning virtue and vice, and takes up with either as it falls in his way. It would be an instructive enquiry to consider what sort of devastation we should commit in our libraries, if we were to pronounce upon the volumes by their moral, or even by their direct moral tendency. Hundreds of those works that have been the adoration of ages, upon which the man of genius and taste feeds with an uncloyed appetite, from which he derives sense, and power, and discernment, and refinement, and activity, and vigour, would be consigned to the flames for their transgressions, or to the lumber-room for their neutrality. While our choicest favours and our first attention would often be bestowed upon authors, who have no other characteristic attribute but that of the torpedo, and the principal tendency of whose literature is to drive all literature and talent out of the world.

If we suffer our minds to dwell upon the comparative merit of authors, if we free ourselves from the prejudices of the nursery, and examine the question in the liberal spirit of scholars and philosophers, we shall not long hesitate where to bestow our loudest approbation. The principal praise is certainly due to those authors, who have a talent to "create a soul under the

---

1 Alain René Lesage, *L'histoire de Gil Blas de Santillane* (1715-35), one of the most widely read picaresque novels.

ribs of death;"[1] whose composition is fraught with irresistible enchantment; who pour their whole souls into mine, and raise me as it were to the seventh heaven; who furnish me with "food for contemplation even to madness;"[2] who raise my ambition, expand my faculties, invigorate my resolutions, and seem to double my existence. For authors of this sort I am provided with an ample licence; and, so they confer upon me benefits thus inestimable and divine, I will never contend with them about the choice of their vehicle, or the incidental accompaniments of their gift. I can guess very nearly what I should have been, if Epictetus had not bequeathed to us his Morals, or Seneca his Consolations.[3] But I cannot tell what I should have been, if Shakespear or Milton had not written. The poorest peasant in the remotest corner of England, is probably a different man from what he would have been but for these authors. Every man who is changed from what he was by the perusal of their works, communicates a portion of the inspiration all around him. It passes from man to man, till it influences the whole mass. I cannot tell that the wisest mandarin now living in China, is not indebted for part of his energy and sagacity to the writings of Milton and Shakespear, even though it should happen that he never heard of their names.

Books will perhaps be found, in a less degree than is commonly imagined, the corrupters of the morals of mankind. They form an effective subsidiary to events and the contagion of vicious society; but, taken by themselves, they rarely produce vice and profligacy where virtue existed before. Every thing depends upon the spirit in which they are read. He that would extract poison from them, must for the most part come to them with a mind already debauched. The power of books in generating virtue, is probably much greater than in generating vice. Virtue is an object that we contemplate with a mind at peace with itself. The more we contemplate it, the more we find our fortitude increase, enabling us to contend with obstacles, and even to encounter contempt. But vice is an object of a peculiarly unfavourable sort. The thought of entering into a

---

1 Milton. [Godwin's note; *Comus* ll. 560-61.]
2 Rowe. [Godwin's note; *The Fair Penitent*, V.i.211.]
3 Stoic philosophers of the first century AD.

vicious course, is attended with uneasiness, timidity and shame; it disarms, still more strongly than it excites us; and our reluctance to a life of profligacy can scarcely be overcome but by the stimulus of bold and impudent society.

v. From Part II, Essay IX, "Of Difference in Opinion"

One of the best practical rules of morality that ever was delivered, is that of putting ourselves in the place of another, before we act or decide any thing respecting him.

It is by this means only that we can form an adequate idea of his pleasures and pains. The nature of a being, the first principle of whose existence is sensation, necessarily obliges us to refer every thing to ourselves; and, but for the practice here recommended, we should be in danger of looking upon the concerns of others with inadvertence, consequently with indifference.

Nor is this voluntary transmigration less necessary, to enable us to do justice to other men's motives and opinions, than to their feelings.

We observe one mode of conduct to be that which, under certain given circumstances, as mere spectators, we should determine to be most consistent with our notions of propriety. The first impulse of every human being, is, to regard a different conduct with impatience and resentment, and to ascribe it, when pursued by our neighbour, to a wilful perverseness, choosing, with open eyes and an enlightened judgment, the proceeding least compatible with reason.

The most effectual method for avoiding this misinterpretation of our neighbour's conduct, is to put ourselves in his place, to recollect his former habits and prejudices, and to conjure up in our minds the allurements, the impulses and the difficulties to which he was subject.

Perhaps it is more easy for us to make due allowances for, or, more accurately speaking, to form a just notion of, our neighbour's motives and actions, than of his opinions.

In actions it is not difficult to understand, that a man may be hurried away by the pressure of circumstances. The passion may be strong; the temptation may be great; there may be no time for deliberation.

These considerations do not apply, or apply with a greatly diminished force, to the case of a man's forming his judgment upon a speculative question. Time for deliberation may, sooner or later, always be obtained. Passion indeed may incline him to one side rather than the other; but not with the impetuosity, with which from time to time it incites us to action. Temptation there may be; but of so sober and methodical a sort, that we do not easily believe, that its march can go undetected, or that the mind of the man who does not surmount it, can possess any considerable share of integrity or good faith.

No sentiment therefore is more prevalent, than that which leads men to ascribe the variations of opinion which subsist in the world, to dishonesty and perverseness....

Undoubtedly argument is in its own nature capable of effecting a change of opinion. But there are other causes which have a similar influence, and that unconsciously to the person in whom they operate.

Man has not only an understanding to reason, but a heart to feel. Interest, as has been already remarked, can do much; and there are many kinds of interest, beside that which is expressly pecuniary.

I was of one opinion in January, and am of another in June. If I gain a pension, or a rich church-living by the change, this circumstance may well be supposed to have some weight with me. If it recommend me to a wealthy relative or patron, this is not indifferent. It perhaps only tends to introduce me into good company. Perhaps I am influenced by an apprehension of something beautiful, generous and becoming in the sentiment to be embraced, instead of being under the mere influence of argument. Men are rarely inclined to stop short in a business of this sort; and, having detected one error in the party to which they formerly adhered, they are gradually propelled to go over completely to the opposite party. A candid mind will frequently feel itself impressed with the difficulties which bear upon its sentiments, especially if they are forcibly brought forward in argument; and will hastily discard its own system for another, when that other, if fairly considered, was liable to objections not less cogent than the former.

But, what is most material to the subject of which we are

treating, all these influences are liable, in a greater or less degree, to escape the man who is most rigid in scrutinising the motives by which he is influenced. Indeed we have spoken of them as changes of opinion; which implies a certain degree of sincerity. The vulgar indeed, where they suspect any sinister motive, regard the man as holding the same opinion still, and only pretending to have undergone a change. But this is a phenomenon much more rare than is commonly imagined. The human mind is exceedingly pliable in this respect; and he that earnestly wishes to entertain an opinion, will usually in no long time become its serious adherent. We even frequently are in this respect the dupes of our own devices. A man who habitually defends a sentiment, commonly ends with becoming a convert. Pride and shame fix him in his new faith. It is a circumstance by no means without a precedent, for a man to become the enthusiastic advocate of a paradox, which he at first defended by way of bravado, or as an affair of amusement.

3. Selections from Mary Wollstonecraft, *A Vindication of the Rights of Woman* (1792).

i. Thoughts on Marriage, from Chapter II, "The Prevailing Opinion Of A Sexual Character Discussed"

… Let me reason with the supporters of this opinion who have any knowledge of human nature, do they imagine that marriage can eradicate the habitude of life? The woman who has only been taught to please will soon find that her charms are oblique sunbeams, and that they cannot have much effect on her husband's heart when they are seen every day, when the summer is passed and gone. Will she then have sufficient native energy to look into herself for comfort, and cultivate her dormant faculties? or, is it not more rational to expect that she will try to please other men; and, in the emotions raised by the expectation of new conquests, endeavour to forget the mortification her love or pride has received? When the husband ceases to be a lover—and the time will inevitably come, her desire of pleasing will then grow languid, or become a spring of bitterness; and love, perhaps, the most evanescent of all passions, gives place to jealousy or vanity.

I now speak of women who are restrained by principle or prejudice; such women, though they would shrink from an intrigue with real abhorrence, yet, nevertheless, wish to be convinced by the homage of gallantry that they are cruelly neglected by their husbands; or, days and weeks are spent in dreaming of the happiness enjoyed by congenial souls till their health is undermined and their spirits broken by discontent. How then can the great art of pleasing be such a necessary study? it is only useful to a mistress; the chaste wife, and serious mother, should only consider her power to please as the polish of her virtues, and the affection of her husband as one of the comforts that render her task less difficult and her life happier.—But, whether she be loved or neglected, her first wish should be to make herself respectable, and not to rely for all her happiness on a being subject to like infirmities with herself.

… This is, must be, the course of nature.—Friendship or indifference inevitably succeeds love.—And this constitution seems perfectly to harmonize with the system of government which prevails in the moral world. Passions are spurs to action, and open the mind; but they sink into mere appetites, become a personal and momentary gratification, when the object is gained, and the satisfied mind rests in enjoyment. The man who had some virtue whilst he was struggling for a crown, often becomes a voluptuous tyrant when it graces his brow; and, when the lover is not lost in the husband, the dotard, a prey to childish caprices, and fond jealousies, neglects the serious duties of life, and the caresses which should excite confidence in his children are lavished on the overgrown child, his wife.

ii. On Friendship and Love, from Chapter IV, "Observations On The State Of Degradation To Which Woman Is Reduced By Various Causes"

… Personal attachment is a very happy foundation for friendship; yet, when even two virtuous young people marry, it would, perhaps, be happy if some circumstances checked their passion; if the recollection of some prior attachment, or disappointed affection, made it on one side, at least, rather a match founded on esteem. In that case they would look beyond the present moment, and try to render the whole of life respectable, by forming a plan to regulate a friendship which only death ought to dissolve.

Friendship is a serious affection; the most sublime of all affections, because it is founded on principle, and cemented by time. The very reverse may be said of love. In a great degree, love and friendship cannot subsist in the same bosom; even when inspired by different objects they weaken or destroy each other, and for the same object can only be felt in succession. The vain fears and fond jealousies, the winds which fan the flame of love, when judiciously or artfully tempered, are both incompatible with the tender confidence and sincere respect of friendship.

iii. On Rousseau's Treatment of Women and Marriage, from Chapter V, "Animadversions On Some Of The Writers Who Have Rendered Women Objects Of Pity, Bordering On Contempt"

THE opinions speciously supported, in some modern publications on the female character and education, which have given the tone to most of the observations made, in a more cursory manner, on the sex, remain now to be examined.

SECT. I

I SHALL begin with Rousseau, and give a sketch of his character of woman, in his own words, interspersing comments and reflections. My comments, it is true, will all spring from a few simple principles, and might have been deduced from what I have already said; but the artificial structure has been raised with so much ingenuity, that it seems necessary to attack it in a more circumstantial manner, and make the application myself.

Sophia, says Rousseau, should be as perfect a woman as

Emilius is a man, and to render her so, it is necessary to examine the character which nature has given to the sex.[1]

He then proceeds to prove that woman ought to be weak and passive, because she has less bodily strength than man; and hence infers, that she was formed to please and to be subject to him; and that it is her duty to render herself *agreeable* to her master—this being the grand end of her existence. Still, however, to give a little mock dignity to lust, he insists that man should not exert his strength, but depend on the will of the woman, when he seeks for pleasure with her.

[Wollstonecraft quotes from Rousseau's comments on the tractableness of women]

... "There results," he continues, "from this habitual restraint a tractableness which women have occasion for during their whole lives, as they constantly remain either under subjection to the men, or to the opinions of mankind; and are never permitted to set themselves above those opinions. The first and most important qualification in a woman is good-nature or sweetness of temper: formed to obey a being so imperfect as man, often full of vices, and always full of faults, she ought to learn betimes even to suffer injustice, and to bear the insults of a husband without complaint; it is not for his sake, but her own, that she should be of a mild disposition. The perverseness and ill-nature of the women only serve to aggravate their own misfortunes, and the misconduct of their husbands; they might plainly perceive that such are not the arms by which they gain the superiority."[2]

Formed to live with such an imperfect being as man, they ought to learn from the exercise of their faculties the necessity of forbearance; but all the sacred rights of humanity are violated by insisting on blind obedience; or, the most sacred rights belong only to man.

---

1 Wollstonecraft refers to characters in Rousseau's *Émile; or, on Education* (1762).

2 Rousseau, *Émile*. Trans. Allan Bloom (New York: Basic Books, 1979), 370, as noted by D.L. Macdonald and Kathleen Scherf, eds., Mary Wollstonecraft, *A Vindication of the Rights of Men and A Vindication of the Rights of Woman* (Peterborough, ON: Broadview Press, 1997) 205.

The being who patiently endures injustice, and silently bears insults, will soon become unjust, or unable to discern right from wrong. Besides, I deny the fact, this is not the true way to form or meliorate the temper; for, as a sex, men have better tempers than women, because they are occupied by pursuits that interest the head as well as the heart. People of sensibility have seldom good tempers. The formation of the temper is the cool work of reason, when, as life advances, she mixes with happy art, jarring elements. I never know a weak or ignorant person who had a good temper, though that constitutional good humour, and that docility, which fear stamps on the behaviour, often obtains the name. I say behaviour, for genuine meekness never reached the heart or mind, unless as the effect of reflection; and that simple restraint produces a number of peccant humours in domestic life, many sensible men will allow, who find some of these gentle irritable creatures, very troublesome companions.

"Each sex," he further argues, "should preserve its peculiar tone and manner; a meek husband may make a wife impertinent; but mildness of disposition on the woman's side will always bring a man back to reason, at least if he be not absolutely a brute, and will sooner or later triumph over him."[1] Perhaps the mildness of reason might sometimes have this effect; but abject fear always inspires contempt; and tears are only eloquent when they flow down fair cheeks.

Of what materials can that heart be composed, which can melt when insulted, and instead of revolting at injustice, kiss the rod? Is it unfair to infer that her virtue is built on narrow views and selfishness, who can caress a man, with true feminine soft-ness, the very moment when he treats her tyrannically? Nature never dictated such insincerity;—and, though prudence of this sort be termed a virtue, morality becomes vague when any part is supposed to rest on falsehood. These are mere expedients, and expedients are only useful for the moment.

[Wollstonecraft comments on Rousseau as a man of sensibility]

1 *Émile*, 370.

... But all Rousseau's errors in reasoning arose from sensibility, and sensibility to their charms women are very ready to forgive! When he should have reasoned he became impassioned, and reflection inflamed his imagination instead of enlightening his understanding. Even his virtues also led him farther astray; for, born with a warm constitution and lively fancy, nature carried him toward the other sex with such eager fondness, that he soon became lascivious. Had he given way to those desires, the fire would have extinguished itself in a natural manner; but virtue, and a romantic kind of delicacy, made him practise self-denial; yet, when a fear, delicacy, or virtue restrained him, he debauched his imagination, and reflecting on the sensations to which fancy gave force, he traced them in the most flowing colours, and sunk them deep into his soul.[1]

He then sought for solitude, not sleep with the man of nature; or calmly investigate the causes of things under the shade where Sir Isaac Newton indulged contemplation, but merely to indulge his feelings. And so warmly has he painted, what he forcibly felt, that, interesting the heart and inflaming the imagination of his readers; in proportion to the strength of their fancy, they imagine that their understanding is convinced when they only sympathize with a poetic writer, who skillfully exhibits the objects of sense, most voluptuously shadowed or gracefully veiled—And thus making us feel whilst dreaming that we reason, erroneous conclusions are left in the mind.

Why was Rousseau's life divided between ecstasy and misery? Can any other answer be given than this, that the effervescence of his imagination produced both; but, had his fancy been allowed to cool, it is possible that he might have acquired more strength of mind. Still, if the purpose of life be to educate the intellectual part of man, all with respect to him was right; yet, had not death led to a nobler scene of action, it is probable that he would have enjoyed more equal happiness on earth, and have felt the calm sensations of the man of nature instead of being prepared for another stage of existence by nourishing the passions which agitate the civilized man.

---

1 Wollstonecraft refers here to Rousseau's *Confessions* (1781-88).

But peace to his manes! I war not with his ashes, but his opinions. I war only with the sensibility that led him to degrade woman by making her the slave of love.

iv. On Choosing Good Husbands, from Chapter VI, "The Effect Which An Early Association Of Ideas Has Upon The Character"

... But one grand truth women have yet to learn, though much it imports them to act accordingly. In the choice of a husband, they should not be led astray by the qualities of a lover—for a lover the husband, even supposing him to be wise and virtuous, cannot long remain.

Were women more rationally educated, could they take a more comprehensive view of things, they would be contented to love but once in their lives; and after marriage calmly let passion subside into friendship—into that tender intimacy, which is the best refuge from care; yet is built on such pure, still affections, that idle jealousies would not be allowed to disturb the discharge of the sober duties of life, or to engross the thoughts that ought to be otherwise employed. This is a state in which many men live; but few, very few women. And the difference may easily be accounted for, without recurring to a sexual character. Men, for whom we are told women were made, have too much occupied the thoughts of women; and this association has so entangled love with all their motives of action; and, to harp a little on an old string, having been solely employed either to prepare themselves to excite love, or actually putting their lessons in practice, they cannot live without love. But, when a sense of duty, or fear of shame, obliges them to restrain this pampered desire of pleasing beyond certain lengths, too far for delicacy, it is true, though far from criminality, they obstinately determine to love, I speak of the passion, their husbands to the end of the chapter—and then acting the part which they foolishly exacted from their lovers, they become abject woers, and fond slaves.

Men of wit and fancy are often rakes; and fancy is the food of love. Such men will inspire passion. Half the sex, in its present infantine state, would pine for a Lovelace;[1] a man so witty, so graceful, and so valiant: and can they *deserve* blame for acting according to principles so constantly inculcated? They want a lover, and protector; and behold him kneeling before them— bravery prostrate to beauty! The virtues of a husband are thus thrown by love into the back ground, and gay hopes, or lively emotions, banish reflection till the day of reckoning come; and come it surely will, to turn the sprightly lover into a surly sus- picious tyrant, who contemptuously insults the very weakness he fostered. Or, supposing the rake reformed, he cannot quick- ly get rid of old habits. When a man of abilities is first carried away by his passions, it is necessary that sentiment and taste var- nish the enormities of vice, and give a zest to brutal indul- gences; but when the gloss of novelty is worn off, and pleasure palls upon the sense, lasciviousness becomes barefaced, and enjoyment only the desperate effort of weakness flying from reflection as from a legion of devils. Oh! virtue, thou art not an empty name! All that life can give—thou givest!

If much comfort cannot be expected from the friendship of a reformed rake of superiour abilities, what is the consequence when he lacketh sense, as well as principles? Verily misery, in its most hideous shape. When the habits of weak people are con- solidated by time, a reformation is barely possible; and actually makes the beings miserable who have not sufficient mind to be amused by innocent pleasure; like the tradesman who retires from the hurry of business, nature presents to them only a uni- versal blank; and the restless thoughts prey on the damped spir- its. Their reformation, as well as his retirement, actually makes them wretched because it deprives them of all employment, by quenching the hopes and fears that set in motion their sluggish minds.

If such be the force of habit; if such be the bondage of folly, how carefully ought we to guard the mind from storing up vicious associations; and equally careful should we be to culti- vate the understanding, to save the poor wight from the weak

---

1 The charming but dissolute rake of Samuel Richardson's novel *Clarissa* (1747-48), who seduces, rapes, and eventually brings about the death of the novel's innocent heroine.

dependent state of even harmless ignorance. For it is the right use of reason alone which makes us independent of every thing—excepting the unclouded Reason—"Whose service is perfect freedom."[1]

v. Thoughts on the need for reform in the education of women, from Chapter XII, "On National Education"

... A man has been termed a microcosm; and every family might also be called a state. States, it is true, have mostly been governed by arts that disgrace the character of man; and the want of a just constitution, and equal laws, have so perplexed the notions of the worldly wise, that they more than question the reasonableness of contending for the rights of humanity. Thus morality, polluted in the national reservoir, sends off streams of vice to corrupt the constituent parts of the body politic; but should more noble, or rather, more just principles regulate the laws, which ought to be the government of society, and not those who execute them, duty might become the rule of private conduct.

Besides, by the exercise of their bodies and minds women would acquire that mental activity so necessary in the maternal character, united with the fortitude that distinguishes steadiness of conduct from the obstinate perverseness of weakness. For it is dangerous to advise the indolent to be steady, because they instantly become rigorous, and to save themselves trouble, punish with severity faults that the patient fortitude of reason might have prevented.

But fortitude presupposes strength of mind; and is strength of mind to be acquired by indolent acquiescence? by asking advice instead of exerting the judgment? by obeying through fear, instead of practising the forbearance, which we all stand in need of ourselves?—The conclusion which I wish to draw, is obvious; make women rational creatures, and free citizens, and they will quickly become good wives, and mothers; that is—if men do not neglect the duties of husbands and fathers.

---

1   From "Morning Prayer, Second Collect, For Peace," *The Book of Common Prayer* (1549); as noted by Macdonald and Scherf, 251.

vi. On Affection between Husbands and Wives, from Chapter XIII, "Some Instances Of The Folly Which The Ignorance of Women Generates; With Concluding Reflections On The Moral Improvement That A Revolution In Female Manners Might Naturally Be Expected To Produce," Section VI

… The affection of husbands and wives cannot be pure when they have so few sentiments in common, and when so little confidence is established at home, as must be the case when their pursuits are so different. That intimacy from which tenderness should flow, will not, cannot subsist between the vicious.

Appendix B: The Writings of Jean-Jacques Rousseau

1. Selections from *Julie, ou La Nouvelle Héloïse* (1761). Translated by Gary Handwerk.

[Rousseau's epistolary novel chronicles the passionate attachment that develops between the young Julie and her tutor Saint-Preux, Julie's fall from virtue with her lover, and ultimately her return to respectability when she marries the Baron Wolmar and devotes herself to a virtuous life as a wife and mother. The emotional immediacy and lyricism of Julie's and Saint-Preux's letters to each other made *Julie* Rousseau's greatest popular success, and led to its vast influence on the genre of the novel of sensibility in England. Julie's choice demonstrates Rousseau's fundamental belief in the power of virtue as a human capacity that can control even intense passion in socially desirable ways. Godwin critiques this aspect of Rousseau's philosophy in Casimir Fleetwood's inability to control the force of his own sensibility.]

Part III, Letter XV, from Julie

It is too much, it is too much. Friend, you have conquered. I am not up to the trial of so much love; my resistance is exhausted. I have made use of all my forces; my conscience provides me with this consoling testimony. May heaven not ask from me more than it has given to me! This sad heart that you purchased so many times, and which cost yours so dearly, belongs to you without reserve; it was yours from the first moment when my eyes saw you, it will remain yours until my final sigh. You have deserved it too well to lose it, and I am tired of serving a chimerical virtue at the price of justice.

Yes, tender and generous lover, your Julie will be yours forever, she will love you forever; it is necessary, I wish it, I owe it. I turn over to you the power that love has given you; it will not be taken from you again. It is in vain that a deceitful voice murmurs in the depths of my soul, it will abuse me no more. What are the vain duties with which it confronts me compared to those of loving forever what heaven has made me love? Isn't my most sacred of all duties to you? Isn't it to you alone that I have promised everything? Wasn't the first vow of my heart never to forget you, and isn't your inviolable fidelity a new tie for mine? Ah! In the transport of love that makes me yours, my only regret is to have battled against such precious and such legitimate sentiments. Nature, o sweet nature, resume your rights; I abjure the barbaric virtues that annihilate you. Could the inclinations that you have given me be more deceptive than the reason that led me so often astray?

Respect these tender inclinations, my dear friend; you owe them too much to hate them; but accept the precious and sweet sharing of them; accept that the rights of blood and friendship not be extinguished by those of love. Do not think that I would ever abandon the paternal home in order to fol-low you. Do not hope that I would reject the ties that impose a sacred authority upon me. The cruel loss of one of the authors of my days [Julie's mother] has taught me too well to fear afflicting the other. No, the one from whom he [her father] henceforth expects all his consolation will not sadden his soul crushed by sorrows; I will not have caused death to everything that gave me life. No, no; I know my crime and cannot hate it. Duty, honor, virtue, all that says nothing to me any more; and yet I am not a monster; I am weak, but not unnatural. I have made my choice, I do not wish to cause desolation to any of those whom I love. May a father who is the slave of his word and jealous of a vain title dispose of my hand as he has promised; may love alone dispose of my heart; may my tears not cease to flow in the breast of a tender friend. May I be vile and unhappy; but may everything that is dear to me be as happy and content as possible. May the three of them form my entire existence, and may your happiness make me forget my misery and my despair.

We are reborn, my Julie; all the true sentiments of our souls have resumed their course. Nature has preserved our being, and love gives us life. Did you doubt it? Did you dare to believe you could take from me your heart? Ah, I know better than you this heart that heaven made to be mine. I feel them joined by a common existence that they can only lose upon death. Does it depend upon us to separate them or even to wish it? Are they held to one another by knots that human beings have formed and that they could break? No, no, Julie; if cruel fate refuses to us the sweet name of spouse, nothing can take from us that of faithful lovers; it will be the consolation of our sad days, and we will carry it to the grave.

Thus we begin living again to begin suffering again, and the feeling of our existence is for us only a feeling of sadness. Unfortunate as we are, what have we become? How have we ceased to be what we were? Where is that enchantment of supreme happiness? Where are the exquisite raptures whose virtues animated our fires? Our love is all that remains of us; love alone remains, and its charms have been eclipsed. Too submissive a daughter, lover without courage, all of our ills come from your errors. Alas! a heart less pure would have led you astray much less! Yes, we are lost because of its honesty, the upright sentiments that fill it have chased away wisdom. You wanted to reconcile filial tenderness with untamable love; in giving yourself over to all your inclinations at the same time, you confuse them rather than harmonizing them and become guilty out of virtue. O Julie, what inconceivable power you have! By what strange power do you fascinate my reason! Even in making me blush for our fires, you still make yourself esteemed for your faults; you force me to admire you in sharing your remorse.... Remorse! ... was it in you to feel that? ... you whom I loved ... you whom I cannot cease to adore.... Could crime approach your heart?... Cruel one! In giving over to me this heart that belongs to me, give it over to me as it was given to me before.

What did you tell me? ... what do you dare to make me hear?... You, to pass into the arms of another! ... some other to possess you!... No longer to be mine! ... yes, and for the height of horror, not to be mine alone? I, I would feel this frightful agony! I would see you outlive yourself!... No, I prefer to lose you than to share you.... May heaven give me a courage worthy of the transports that shake me!... Before your hand could be abased in a fatal bond abhorred by love and reproached by honor, I would go and with my own hand plunge a dagger into your breast; I would empty your chaste heart of a blood that would not have been sullied by infidelity. I would mingle with this pure blood that which burns in my veins with a fire that nothing can extinguish, I would fall into your arms; I would give forth a last sigh upon your lips.... I would receive yours.... Julie expiring!... These eyes so sweet extinguished by the horrors of death! ... this breast, this throne of love torn apart by my hand, pouring out its blood and life in great spurts!... No, live and suffer! bear the pain of my cowardice. No, I would wish that you were no more; but I cannot love you enough to stab you.

O, if you knew the state of this heart gripped tightly by distress! It has never burned with so sacred a fire; your innocence and your virtue have never been so precious to it. I am a lover, I am loved, I feel it; but I am only a man and it is beyond human capacity to renounce supreme felicity. One night, one single night has changed my entire soul forever. Take from me this dangerous memory and I am virtuous. But this fatal night reigns in the depths of my heart, and will cover with its shadow the rest of my life. Ah! Julie! adored object! if it is necessary to be miserable forever, let there be one more hour of happiness, and eternal regrets!

Listen to the one who loves you. Why would we wish ourselves alone to be more wise than the rest of men, and to follow with the simplicity of children the chimerical virtues of which the whole world speaks and that nobody practices? What! will we be better moralists than the crowds of wise men who populate London and Paris, all of whom mock conjugal fidelity and consider adultery as a game? The examples are not scandalous; it is not even permitted to find in them something worth repeating; and all the honest people here laugh at one who would resist the inclination of his heart out of respect for marriage. In effect, they say, isn't a wrong that exists only in opinion nothing at all when it is secret? What harm does a husband receive from an infidelity of which he is unaware? By what flatteries doesn't a woman compensate for her mistakes? What sweetness doesn't she employ for deflecting or curing his suspicions? Deprived of an imaginary good, he actually lives more happily; and this supposed crime about which people make so much noise is only one more tie within society.

God forbid, oh dear friend of my heart, that I would wish to reassure yours by these shameful maxims! I abhor them without knowing how to combat them; and my conscience answers them better than my reason. Not that I claim credit for a courage that I hate, nor that I would wish for so costly a virtue: but I believe myself less guilty in reproaching myself for my faults than in striving to justify them; and I consider it the height of crime to wish to remove its remorse.

I do not know what I am writing: I feel that my soul is in a frightful state, worse even than the one in which I was before having received your letter. The hope that you give me is somber and sad; it extinguishes the gleam of such pureness that guided us so many times; your attractions are tarnished and yet become only more touching; I see you tender and unhappy; my heart is inundated with the tears that flow from your eyes, and I reproach myself with bitterness for a happiness that I can no longer taste except at the cost of yours.

Yet I feel that a secret ardor still animates me and gives me the courage that remorse wants to take from me. Dear friend, ah! do you know how many losses a love like mine can make up to you? Do you know to what point a lover who breathes only for you can make you love life? Do you realize that it is for you alone that I wish henceforth to live, to act, to think, to feel? No, delicious source of my being, I will no longer have any soul except your soul, I will no longer be anything except a part of yourself, and you will find in the depths of my heart so sweet an existence that you will not be aware of whatever charms yours may have lost. Well then! we will be guilty, but we will not be unkind; we will be guilty, but we will always love virtue: far from daring to excuse our mistakes, we will groan over them, we will cry over them together, we will compensate for them if it is possible by virtue of being benevolent and good. Julie! oh Julie! what would you do! what can you do! You cannot escape from my heart; hasn't it married yours?

These vain projects of fortune that have crudely abused me have long since been forgotten. I am going to occupy myself solely with the care that I owe to my lord Edward; he wants to take me with him to England; he claims that I can serve him there. Well then! I will follow him there. But I will abscond every year; I will bring myself secretly near to you. If I cannot speak to you, at least I will have seen you; I will at least have kissed your steps; one look of your eyes will have given me ten months of life. Forced to depart again, in taking myself away from her whom I love, I will for consolation count the steps that would bring me back to her again. These frequent trips will cause a change in your unhappy lover; in leaving to go see you, he will think that he already enjoys the sight of you; the memory of his transports will enchant him during his return; despite cruel fate, his sad years will not be completely lost; there will be none that is not marked by pleasures, and the short moments that he will pass near you will multiply themselves across his entire life.

From Letter XVIII, from Julie

… Tied to the fate of a spouse, or rather, to the wishes of a father, by an indissoluble chain, I enter upon a new career that shall finish only with death. In beginning it, let us cast our eyes for a moment upon the one that I leave behind: it will not be painful for us to recall such a precious time. Perhaps I will find there lessons for making good use of the time that remains to me; perhaps you will find there lights for explaining what in my conduct has always been obscure to your eyes. At least, in considering what we were to one another, our hearts will feel the more what they owe one another until the end of our days.

It was about six years ago that I saw you for the first time; you were young, well-formed, amiable; other young people appeared to me more beautiful and better-formed than you, but none of them caused me the least emotion, and my heart was yours at first sight.

[What follows is a lengthy recapitulation by Julie of the stages of their relationship, up to the point where Saint-Preux's return from an enforced absence saved Julie from a serious illness brought on by her inability to reconcile her love for him and her parents' wishes.]

I saw you, I was cured, and I perished.

If I had not found happiness in my mistakes, I would never have hoped to find it there. I felt that my heart was made for virtue and that it could not be happy without it; I succumbed out of weakness and not by a mistake; I did not even have the excuse of blindness. There remained no hope for me; I could no longer be anything but unfortunate. Innocence and love were equally necessary for me; not being able to maintain both together, and seeing you go astray, I consulted only you in my choice and lost myself in order to save you.

But it is not as easy as one thinks to renounce virtue. It torments for a long time those who abandon it, and its charms, which produce the ecstasies of pure souls, cause the first agony of the villain, who still loves them but can no longer enjoy them. Guilty, but not depraved, I could not escape the remorse that awaited me; honesty was precious to me even after having lost it; my shame was not less bitter for being secret; and I would not have felt it more even if the whole universe had been its witness. I consoled myself in my sorrow like someone wounded who fears gangrene and in whom the feeling of his pain sustains the hope of being cured.

Nevertheless this state of opprobrium was odious to me. As a result of wanting to stifle the reproach without renouncing the crime, there happened to me what happens to every honest soul that goes astray and takes pleasure in its straying. A new illusion came to sweeten the bitterness of repentance; I hoped to extract from my mistake a means of repairing it, and I dared to form the project of forcing my father to unite us. The first fruit of our love was to seal this sweet tie. I asked it from heaven as the guarantee for my return to virtue and our shared happiness; I desired it as another in my place would have feared it; tender love, tempering by its prestige the murmur of conscience, consoled me for my weakness by the effect that I expected from it, and made so precious an expectation the charm and hope of my life.

I had resolved, as soon as I would have shown the visible marks of my condition, to make a public declaration of it to M. Perret [the local pastor] in the presence of my whole family. I am timid, it is true; I felt all that it would have cost me; but honor itself animated my courage and I preferred to bear for once the confusion that I had merited than to nourish an eternal shame in the depths of my heart. I knew that my father would give me either death or my lover; this alternative had nothing terrifying for me and, in one way or another, I envisaged in this step the end of my unhappiness.

This, my good friend, was the mystery that I wanted to conceal from you and that you sought to penetrate with such curious disquietude. A thousand reasons forced me into this reserve with a man as irascible as you, without considering that it was not necessary to arm your indiscreet importunity with a new pretext. It was especially appropriate to send you away during such a perilous scene, and I knew well that you would never have consented to abandon me in such danger if you had known of it.

Alas! I was deceived again in having so sweet a hope. Heaven rejected the projects conceived in crime; I did not merit the honor of becoming a mother; my wait remained ever in vain; and it was refused to me to expiate my mistake at the price of my reputation. In the despair that I conceived from this, the imprudent rendezvous that put your life in danger was recklessness that my insane love veiled in so sweet an excuse: I held the unsuccessfulness of my vows against myself, and my heart, deceived in its desires, saw in the ardor of contenting them only the concern to render them one day legitimate.

I believed for a moment that they had been accomplished; this error was the source of the most burning of my regrets, and the love with which nature had complied was only more cruelly betrayed by destiny. You have learned what accident destroyed, along with the seed that I carried in my breast, the last foundation of my hopes. This misfortune happened to me precisely at the time of our separation: as if heaven had wanted then to crush me with all the ills that I had merited and to cut all at once every tie that could unite us....

Virtue is so necessary for our hearts that, when we have once abandoned the true kind, we then make up another in our own fashion and hold on to it more strongly perhaps because it is our choice....

M. de Wolmar arrived and was not put off by the change in my appearance. My father gave me no time to breathe. The period of mourning for my mother was coming to an end and my sorrow was subject to the test of time. I could not allege one or the other in order to evade my promise; it was necessary to fulfill it. The day that was supposed to take me forever from you and from me appeared to me the last of my life. I would have seen the preparations for my burial with less terror than those of my marriage. The closer I drew to the fatal moment, the less I could uproot my first affections from my heart: they were irritated by my efforts to extinguish them. Finally I grew tired of fighting uselessly. In the very instant when I was ready to vow an eternal fidelity to another, my heart still vowed an eternal love to you, and I was led to the temple like an impure victim who soils the sacrifice where she is to be immolated.

Arrived at the church, I felt upon entering a sort of emotion that I had never felt before. I do not know what terror came to seize my soul in this simple and august place, wholly filled by the majesty of the one whom we serve there. A sudden fear made me shiver; trembling and ready to collapse, I had difficulty dragging myself to the foot of the pulpit. Far from recovering, I felt my distress increase during the ceremony, and if it allowed me to perceive objects, it was only in order to be frightened by them. The somber day of the edifice, the profound silence of the spectators, their modest and reflective demeanors, the procession of all my relatives, the imposing aspect of my venerable father, all that gave to what was going to take place an air of solemnity that aroused in my attention and respect, and which would have made me tremble at the mere idea of perjury. I believed I saw the agent of Providence and heard the voice of God in the minister gravely pronouncing the holy liturgy. The purity, the dignity, the sanctity of marriage, so vividly expressed in the words of the Bible, its chaste and sublime duties, so important for the happiness, order, peace, and continuance of the human species, so sweet to fulfill in themselves; all that made such an impression on me that I thought I felt a sudden revolution within me. An unknown power suddenly seemed to correct the disorder of my affections and to reestablish them according to the law of duty and of nature. The eternal eye that sees everything, I said to myself, is now reading in the depths of my heart; it compares my hidden wish with the response of my mouth: heaven and earth are witnesses of the sacred engagement that I am undertaking; they will do the same for my fidelity in keeping it. What right will anyone who dares to violate the first of all rights be able to respect among human beings?

A glance thrown by chance upon M. and Mme d'Orbe, whom I saw beside one another and fixing their tender eyes upon me, moved me even more powerfully than all the other objects had done. Amiable and virtuous couple, are you less united for knowing less of love? Duty and honesty tie you together: tender friends, faithful spouses, without burning from this devouring fire that consumes the soul, you love one another with a pure and sweet sentiment that nourishes it, that wisdom authorizes and that reason directs; you are only more solidly happy because of this. Ah! if I could only recover the same innocence in a similar tie and enjoy the same happiness! If I have not merited it as you have, I will render myself worthy of it by your example. These feelings awoke my hope and my courage. I envisaged the sacred bond that I was about to form as a new state that would purify my soul and convey it to all its duties. When the pastor asked me whether I promised obedience and perfect fidelity to the one whom I was accepting as spouse, my mouth and my heart promised it. I will keep it until death.

Returned home, I yearned for an hour of solitude and reflection. I obtained it, though not without difficulty; and whatever haste I may have had to take advantage of it, I only examined myself at first with repugnance, fearing that I had only felt a temporary fermentation in changing my condition and that I would find myself as little worthy as a spouse as I had been little wise as a daughter. The trial was certain, but dangerous. I began by thinking of you. I testified to myself that no tender memory had profaned the solemn engagement that I had just made. I could not conceive of the miracle by which your stubborn image had been able to leave me for so long in peace with so many subjects to recall it to me; I would have guarded myself against indifference and forgetting as a deceptive state that was too little natural to me to be durable. This illusion was hardly to be feared; I felt that I loved you as much and perhaps more than I ever had; but I felt it without blushing. I saw that I had no need to forget that I was the wife of another in order to think of you. In telling me how precious you were to me, my heart was moved, but my conscience and my senses were tranquil; and I knew from this moment on that I had really changed. What a torrent of pure joy then came to inundate my soul! What a feeling of peace, effaced for so long, came to reanimate this heart faded by ignominy and to spread a new serenity through my entire being! I thought I could feel myself being reborn; I thought I was beginning another life. Sweet and consoling virtue, I begin it again for you; it is you who will make it precious to me; it is you to whom I wish to consecrate it. Ah! I have learned too well what it costs to lose you, to abandon you a second time.

2. Selections from *Émile, or on Education* (1762). Translated by Grace Roosevelt and reprinted from her online edition, Institute for Learning Technologies of Teachers College, Columbia University (Available: http://projects.ilt.columbia.edu/pedagogies/Rousseau/).

[Rousseau's *Émile* was one of the most widely read and influential texts on education in the eighteenth and nineteenth centuries, and had a revolutionary impact on the way people in Europe and America thought about children. In this work, Rousseau advocates a new approach to education by guiding rather than coercing the child to develop an independent personality within a natural environment untainted by the injurious effects of civilization. In *Fleetwood* Godwin critiques both the methods and aims of Rousseau's model, especially its tendency to underestimate the pupil's rational capacities. Moreover, *Fleetwood*, and especially Mary Wollstonecraft's *A Vindication of the Rights of Woman* (1792), challenge Rousseau's stereotypical and essentializing views of women.]

a. [386] In the most elaborate educations the teacher issues his orders and thinks himself master, but it is the child who is really master. He uses the tasks you set him to obtain what he wants from you, and he can always make you pay for an hour's hard work by a week's compliance ...

[387] Take the opposite course with your pupil; let him always think he is master while you are really master. There is no subjection so perfect as that which keeps the appearance of liberty; one captures thus the will itself. Is not this poor child, without knowledge, strength, or wisdom, entirely at your mercy? Are you not in charge of his whole environment as far as it affects him? Cannot you make it affect him as you please? His work and play, his pleasures, his pains, are they not in your hands without him knowing it? Without doubt he ought only to do what he wants, but he ought to want to do only what you want him to do. He should never take a step you have not foreseen; he should never open his mouth without your knowing what he is going to say.

b. [587] For a long time my pupil and I have noticed that some substances such as amber, glass, and wax, when well rubbed, attracted straws, while others did not. We accidentally discover a substance which has a more unusual property, that of attracting filings or other small particles of iron from a distance and without rubbing. How much time do we devote to this game to the exclusion of everything else! At last we discover that this property is communicated to the iron itself, which becomes, so to speak, magnetized. One day we go to a fair. A magician has a wax duck floating in a basin of water, and he makes it follow a bit of bread. We are greatly surprised, but we do not call him a wizard because we do not know what a wizard is. Continually struck by effects whose causes are unknown to us, we are in no hurry to make judgments, and we remain peacefully in ignorance till we find an occasion to leave it.

[588] When we get home, as a result of discussing the duck at the fair, we try to imitate it. We take a needle thoroughly magnetised, we surround it in white wax which we fashion as best we can into the shape of a duck, with the needle running through the body and its head forming the beak. We put the duck in water and put the end of a key near its beak, and you will easily understand our delight when we find that our duck follows the key just as the duck at the fair followed the bit of bread. At another time we may note the direction assumed by the duck when left at rest; for the present we are wholly occupied with our work and we want nothing more.

[589] The same evening we return to the fair with some bread specially prepared in our pockets, and as soon as the magician has performed his trick, my little doctor, who can hardly restrain himself, tells him that the trick is not difficult and that he himself can do it as well. He is taken at his word. He at once takes the bread with a bit of iron hidden in it from his pocket. His heart throbs as he approaches the table and holds out the bread; his hand trembles with excitement. The duck approaches and follows his hand. The child cries out and jumps for joy. With the applause, the shouts of the crowd, the child becomes giddy and is beside himself. The magician, though disappointed, embraces him, congratulates him, begs

the honour of his company on the following day, and promises to collect a still greater crowd to applaud his skill. My young naturalist, full of pride, wants to stay and chatter, but I check him at once and take him home overwhelmed with praise.

[590] The child counts the minutes till the next day with laughable impatience. He invites every one he meets; he wants the whole human race to be witness to his glory; he can scarcely wait till the appointed hour. He hurries to the place. The hall is full already. As he enters his young heart swells with pride. Other tricks are to come first. The magician surpasses himself and does the most surprising things. The child sees none of these; he wriggles, perspires, and hardly breathes; he spends his time in fingering with a trembling hand the bit of bread in his pocket. His turn comes at last; the master announces it to the audience ceremoniously. He goes up looking somewhat shamefaced and takes out his bit of bread. The vicissitudes of human things! The duck, so tame yesterday, has become wild to-day; instead of offering its beak it turns tail and swims away; it avoids the bread and the hand that holds it as carefully as it followed them yesterday. After a thousand useless tries accompanied by hoots from the audience the child complains that he is being cheated, that is not the same duck, and he defies the magician to attract it.

[591] The magician, without further words, takes a bit of bread and offers it to the duck, which at once follows it and comes to the hand which holds it. The child takes the same bit of bread with no better success; the duck mocks his efforts and makes pirouettes around the basin. Overwhelmed with confusion the child abandons the attempt, ashamed to face the hoots any longer.

[592] Then the magician takes the bit of bread the child brought with him and uses it as successfully as his own. He takes out the bit of iron before the audience—another laugh at our expense—then with this same bread he attracts the duck as before. He repeats the experiment with a piece of bread cut by a third person in full view of the audience. He does it with his glove, with his finger-tip. Finally he goes into the middle of the room and in the emphatic tones used by such persons he

declares that his duck will obey his voice as readily as his hand. He speaks and the duck obeys; he bids him go to the right and he goes, to come back again and he comes. The movement is as ready as the command. The growing applause completes our discomfiture. We slip away unnoticed and shut ourselves up in our room, without relating our successes to everybody as we had expected.

[593] Next day there is a knock at the door. When I open it there is the magician, who makes a modest complaint with regard to our conduct. What had he done that we should try to discredit his tricks and deprive him of his livelihood? What is there so wonderful in attracting a duck that we should purchase this honour at the price of an honest man's living? "My word, gentlemen! had I any other trade by which I could earn a living I would not pride myself on this. You may well believe that a man who has spent his life at this miserable trade knows more about it than you who only give your spare time to it. If I did not show you my best tricks at first, it was because one must not be so foolish as to display all one knows at once. I always take care to keep my best tricks for emergencies; and I have plenty more to prevent young folks from meddling. However, I have come, gentlemen, in all kindness, to show you the trick that gave you so much trouble; I only beg you not to use it to harm me, and to be more discreet in future."

[594] He then shows us his apparatus, and we see with great surprise that it only consists of a strong and well armed magnet that a child, hidden under the table, was able to make move without anyone seeing him.

[595] The man puts up his things, and after we have offered our thanks and apologies, we try to give him something. He refuses it. "No, gentlemen," says he, "I owe you no gratitude and I will not accept your gift. I leave you in my debt in spite of all, and that is my only revenge. Generosity may be found among all sorts of people, and I earn my pay by doing my tricks, not by teaching them."

[596] As he is going he addresses a reprimand to me in particular. "I can make excuses for the child," he says, "he sinned in ignorance. But you, sir, should know better. Why did you let

him do it? As you are living together and you are older than he, you should look after him and give him good advice. Your experience should be his guide. When he is grown up he will reproach, not only himself, but you, for the faults of his youth."

[597] He goes out and leaves us very embarrassed. I blame myself for my easy-going ways. I promise the child that another time I will put his interests first and warn him against faults before he falls into them, for the time is coming when our relations will be changed, when the severity of the master must give way to the friendliness of the comrade. This change must come gradually; you must look ahead, and very far ahead.

[598] The next day we return to the fair to see the trick whose secret we have learned. We approach our Socrates, the magician, with profound respect; we scarcely dare to look him in the face. He overwhelms us with politeness and gives us the best places, which humiliates us even more. He goes through his tricks as usual, but he lingers affectionately over the duck, and often glances proudly in our direction. We are in on the secret, but we do not tell. If my pupil dared even open his mouth I'd want to squash him.

[599] There is more meaning than you suspect in this detailed illustration. How many lessons in one! How mortifying are the results of a first impulse towards vanity! Young tutor, watch this first impulse carefully. If you can use it to bring about shame and disgrace, you may be sure a second impulse will not appear for a long time. What long preparations! you will say. I agree; and all to provide a compass which will enable us to dispense with a meridian.

c. [1251] In all that does not relate to sex, woman is man. She has the same organs, the same needs, the same faculties. The machine is constructed in the same manner, the parts are the same, the workings of the one are the same as the other, and the appearance of the two is similar. From whatever aspect one considers them, they differ only by degree.

[1252] In all that does relate to sex, woman and man are in every way related and in every way different. The difficulty in comparing them comes from the difficulty of determining what in the constitution of both comes from sex and what does not. By comparative anatomy and even by mere inspection one can find general differences between them that seem to be unrelated to sex. However these differences do relate to sex through connections that we cannot perceive. How far such differences may extend we cannot tell. All we know for certain is that everything in common between men and women must come from their species and everything different must come from their sex. From this double point of view we find so many relations and so many oppositions that perhaps one of nature's greatest marvels is to have been able to make two beings so similar while constituting them so differently.

[1253] These relations and differences must influence morals. Such a deduction is both obvious and in accordance with experience, and it shows the vanity of the disputes concerning preferences or the equality of the sexes. As if each sex, pursuing the path marked out for it by nature, were not more perfect in that very divergence than if it more closely resembled the other! In those things which the sexes have in common they are equal; where they differ they are not comparable. A perfect woman and a perfect man should no more be alike in mind than in face, and perfection admits of neither less nor more.

[1254] In the union of the sexes, each alike contributes to the common end but not in the same way. From this diversity springs the first difference which may be observed in the moral relations between the one and the other. The one should be active and strong, the other passive and weak. It is necessary that the one have the power and the will; it is enough that the other should offer little resistance.

[1255] Once this principle is established it follows that woman is specially made to please man. If man ought to please her in turn, the necessity is less urgent. His merit is in his power; he pleases because he is strong. This is not the law of love, I admit, but it is the law of nature, which is older than love itself.

[1256] If woman is made to please and to be subjected, she ought to make herself pleasing to man instead of provoking him. Her strength is in her charms; by their means she should compel him to discover his strength and to use it. The surest way of arousing this strength is to make it necessary by resistance. Then amour-propre joins with desire, and the one triumphs from a victory that the other made him win. This is the origin of attack and defense, of the boldness of one sex and the timidity of the other, and even of the shame and modesty with which nature has armed the weak for the conquest of the strong.

d. [1266] The severity of the duties relative to the two sexes is not and cannot be the same. When a woman complains in this regard about the unjust inequality in which men are placed, she is wrong. This inequality is not at all a human institution, or at least it is not the work of prejudice but of reason. The one to whom nature has entrusted children must answer for them to the other. No doubt it is not permitted to anyone to violate his faith, and every unfaithful husband who deprives his wife of the sole reward of the austere duties of her sex is an unjust and cruel man. But the unfaithful wife does more; she dissolves the family and breaks the bonds of nature. By giving the man children that are not his own she betrays all of them; she adds treachery to infidelity. It is hard to imagine any disorder or crime which would not follow from that. If there is one terrible position to be in it is that of a miserable father who cannot trust his wife, dares not give in to the sweetest sentiments of his heart, and who wonders while embracing his child whether he may be embracing the child of someone else—a proof of his dishonor, a robber of his own children's inheritance. What is such a family if not a society of secret enemies armed against each other by a guilty wife who forces them to pretend to love each other?

[1267] It is thus not only important that the wife be faithful but that she be judged so by her husband, by those near him, by everyone. She must be modest, attentive, reserved, and she must have in others' eyes as in her own conscience the evidence of her virtue. If it is important that a father love his children, it is important that he respect their mother. Such are the reasons that put appearance on the list of the duties of women and make honor and reputation no less indispensable to them than chastity. Along with the moral differences between the sexes these principles give rise to a new motive for duty and convenience, one that prescribes especially for women the most scrupulous attention to their conduct, to their manners, to their behavior. To maintain vaguely that the two sexes are equal and that their duties are the same is to get lost in vain speeches. One hardly need to respond to all that.

e. [1271] I am quite aware that Plato in the Republic assigns the same gymnastics to women and men.[1] Having rid his government of private families and knowing not what to do with the women, he was forced to make them into men. That great genius has figured out everything and foreseen everything; he has even thought ahead to an objection that perhaps no one would ever have raised; but he has not succeeded in meeting the real difficulty. I am not speaking of the alleged community of wives, the oft-repeated reproach concerning which only shows that those who make it have never read his works. I refer to the civil promiscuity which everywhere brings the two sexes in the same occupations, the same work, and could not fail to engender the most intolerable abuses. I refer to that subversion of all the tenderest of our natural feelings, which are sacrificed to an artificial sentiment that can only exist by their aid. As if a natural bond were not required in order to form conventional ties; or that love for one's relations were not the basis for the love that one owes to the state; or that it is not through one's attachment to the small society of the family that the heart becomes attached to the larger society of one's nation; or that it is not the good son, the good husband, the good father who makes a good citizen!

f. [1297] Always justify the tasks you set your little girls, but keep them busy. Idleness and insubordination are two very dangerous faults, and very hard to cure when once established.

---

1   Plato (c. 427-348 BC), Greek philosopher whose dialogue, the *Republic*, provides a
     discussion of justice and a detailed description of the ideal city-state.

Girls should be vigilant and hardworking, but this is not enough by itself; they should be accustomed to annoyances early on. This misfortune, if such it be, is inherent in their sex, and they will never escape from it, unless to endure much more cruel sufferings. For their entire life they will have to submit to the most continual and most severe annoyances, those of proper decorum. They must be trained to bear constraint from the first, so that it costs them nothing, to master their own fantasies in order to submit to the will of others. If they are always eager to be at work, they should sometimes be forced to do nothing. Dissipation, frivolity, inconstancy are faults that can easily arise from their first corrupted and unchecked tastes. To guard against this, teach them above all to control themselves. Under our insane institutions, the life of a good woman is a perpetual struggle against her self. It is only fair that woman should bear her share of the ills she has brought upon man.

[1300] This habitual restraint produces a docility which woman requires all her life, for she will always be in subjection to a man, or to man's judgment, and she will never be free to set her own opinion above his. What is most wanted in a woman is gentleness. Formed to obey a creature so imperfect as man, a creature often vicious and always faulty, she should early learn to submit to injustice and to suffer the wrongs inflicted on her by her husband without complaint. She must be gentle for her own sake, not his. Bitterness and obstinacy only multiply the sufferings of the wife and the misdeeds of the husband; the man feels that these are not the weapons to be used against him. Heaven did not make women attractive and persuasive that they might degenerate into bitterness, or meek that they should desire the mastery; their soft voice was not meant for hard words, nor their delicate features for the frowns of anger. When they lose their temper they forget themselves. Often enough they have just cause of complaint; but when they scold they always put themselves in the wrong. Each should adopt the tone that befits his or her sex. A too gentle husband may make his wife impertinent, but unless a man is a monster, the gentleness of a woman will bring him around and sooner or later will win him over.

[1301] Daughters must always be obedient, but mothers need not always be harsh. To make a girl docile you need not make her miserable; to make her modest you need not terrify her. On the contrary, I should not be sorry to see her allowed occasionally to exercise a little ingenuity, not to escape punishment for her disobedience, but to evade the necessity for obedience. Her dependence need not be made unpleasant; it is enough that she should realise that she is dependent. Cunning is a natural gift of woman, and so convinced am I that all our natural inclinations are right, that I would cultivate this among others, only guarding against its abuse.

g. [1342] The reason which teaches a man his duties is not very complex; the reason which teaches a woman hers is even simpler. The obedience and fidelity which she owes to her husband, the tenderness and care due to her children, are such natural and self-evident consequences of her condition that she cannot honestly refuse her consent to the inner voice which is her guide, nor disregard her duty in her natural inclination.

[1343] I would not altogether blame those who would restrict a woman to the labours of her sex and would leave her in profound ignorance of everything else. But that would require either a very simple, very healthy public morality or a very isolated life style. In large cities, among immoral men, such a woman would be too easily seduced. Her virtue would too often be at the mercy of circumstances. In this philosophic century, virtue must be able to be put to the test. She must know in advance what people might say to her and what she should think of it.

[1344] Moreover, having to submit to men's judgment she should merit their esteem. Above all she should obtain the esteem of her spouse. She should not only make him love her person, she should make him approve her conduct. She should justify his choice before the world, and do honour to her husband through the honour given to the wife. But how can she set about this task if she is ignorant of our institutions, our customs, our notions of what is proper, if she knows nothing of the source of man's judgment, nor the passions by which it is swayed? Since she depends both on her own conscience and on public opinion, she must learn to know and reconcile these two laws, and to put her own conscience first only when the two are opposed to each other. She becomes the judge of her own judges, she decides when she should submit to them and when she should refuse her obedience. Before she accepts or rejects their prejudices she weighs them; she learns to trace them to their source, to foresee what they will be, and to turn them in her own favour. She is careful never to give cause for blame if duty allows her to avoid it. This cannot be properly done without cultivating her mind and her reason.

h. [1357] The search for abstract and speculative truths, for principles and axioms in science, for all that tends to wide generalisation, is beyond a woman's grasp; their studies should be thoroughly practical. It is their business to apply the principles discovered by men, it is their place to make the observations which lead men to discover those principles. A woman's thoughts, beyond the range of her immediate duties, should be directed to the study of men, or the acquirement of that agreeable learning whose sole end is the formation of taste. For the works of genius are beyond her reach, and she has neither the accuracy nor the attention for success in the exact sciences. As for the physical sciences, to decide the relations between living creatures and the laws of nature is the task of that sex which is more active and enterprising, which sees more things, that sex which is possessed of greater strength and is more accustomed to the exercise of that strength. Woman, weak as she is and limited in her range of observation, perceives and judges the forces at her disposal to supplement her weakness, and those forces are the passions of man. Her own mechanism is more powerful than ours; she has many levers which may set the human heart in motion. She must find a way to make us desire what she cannot achieve unaided and what she considers necessary or pleasing. Therefore she must have a thorough knowledge of man's mind—not an abstract knowledge of the mind of man in general, but the mind of those men who are about her, the mind of those men who have authority over her, either by law or custom. She must learn to intuit their feelings from speech and action, look and gesture. By her own speech and action, look and gesture, she must be able to inspire them with the feelings she desires, without seeming to have any such purpose. The men will have a better philosophy of the human heart, but she will read more accurately in the heart of men. Woman should discover, so to speak, an experimental morality; man should reduce it to a system. Woman has more wit, man more genius; woman observes, man reasons. Together they provide the clearest light and the profoundest knowledge which is possible to the unaided human mind—in a word, the surest knowledge of self and of others of which the human race is capable. In this way art may constantly tend to the perfection of the instrument which nature has given us.

Appendix C: The Novel of Sensibility

1. A Sentimental Journey through France and Italy, By Mr. Yorick (1768), by Laurence Sterne.

[Sterne's humorous and parodic travel narrative, in which appear several characters from his novel *Tristram Shandy* (1759-67), established conventions for sentimental fiction and for the depiction of the "man of feeling" that significantly influenced subsequent works in the genre. In the first passage below, the narrator, Yorick, has just learned that he may be imprisoned in France because he is traveling without a passport. While attempting to abate his anxieties concerning imprisonment, an encounter with a caged bird brings about his emotional realization of the value of his own liberty.]

from *The Passport: The Hotel at Paris*

... I had some occasion (I forget what) to step into the court-yard, as I settled this account; and remember I walk'd down stairs in no small triumph with the conceit of my reasoning—Beshrew the *sombre* pencil! said I vauntingly—for I envy not its powers, which paints the evils of life with so hard and deadly a colouring. The mind sits terrified at the objects she has magnified herself, and blackened: reduce them to their proper size and hue she overlooks them—'Tis true, said I, correcting the proposition—the Bastile is not an evil to be despised—but strip it of its towers—fill up the fossè—unbarricade the doors—call it simply a confinement, and suppose 'tis some tyrant of a distemper—and not of a man which holds you in it—the evil vanishes, and you bear the other half without complaint.[1]

I was interrupted in the hey-day of this soliloquy, with a voice which I took to be of a child, which complained "it could not get out."—I look'd up and down the passage, and

---

1   The Bastille was the infamous prison in Paris which the revolutionaries stormed on 14 July 1789, thereby initiating the French Revolution.

seeing neither man, woman, or child, I went out without further attention.

In my return back through the passage, I heard the same words repeated twice over; and looking up, I saw it was a starling hung in a little cage.—"I can't get out—I can't get out," said the starling.

I stood looking at the bird: and to every person who came through the passage it ran fluttering to the side towards which they approach'd it, with the same lamentation of its captivity— "I can't get out," said the starling—God help thee! Said I, but I'll let thee out, cost what it will; so I turn'd about the cage to get to the door; it was twisted and double twisted so fast with wire, there was no getting it open without pulling the cage to pieces—I took both hands to it.

The bird flew to the place where I was attempting his deliverance, and thrusting his head through the trellis, press'd his breast against it, as if impatient—I fear, poor creature! said I, I cannot set thee at liberty—"No," said the starling—"I can't get out—I can't get out," said the starling.

I vow, I never had my affections more tenderly awakened; nor do I remember an incident in my life, where the dissipated spirits, to which my reason had been a bubble, were so suddenly call'd home. Mechanical as the notes were, yet so true in tune to nature were they chanted, that in one moment they overthrew all my systematic reasonings upon the Bastile; and I heavily walk'd up stairs, unsaying every word I had said in going down them.

Disguise thouself as thou wilt, still slavery! said I—still thou art a bitter draught; and though thousands in all ages have been made to drink of thee, thou art no less bitter on that account.—'tis thou, thrice sweet and gracious goddess, addressing myself to LIBERTY, whom all in public or in private worship, whose taste is grateful, and ever wilt be so, till NATURE herself shall change—no *tint* of words can spot thy snowy mantle, or chymic power turn thy sceptre into iron— ...

from *The Passport: Versailles*

[In the passage below, Yorick's description of the pleasure he experiences in reading mirrors Fleetwood's effusions on the works of his favorite dramatic author, John Fletcher.]

... taking up *"Much Ado about Nothing,"* I transported myself instantly from the chair I sat in to Messina in Sicily, and got so busy with Don Pedro and Benedick and Beatrice, that I thought not of Versailles, the Count, or the Passport.

Sweet pliability of man's spirit, that can at once surrender itself to illusions, which cheat expectation and sorrow of their weary moments!—long—long since had ye number'd out my days, had I not trod so great a part of them upon this enchanted ground: when my way is too rough for my feet, or too steep for my strength, I get off it, to some smooth velvet path which fancy has scattered over with rose-buds of delights; and having taken a few turns in it, come back strengthen'd and refresh'd—When evils press sore upon me, and there is no retreat from them in this world, then I take a new course—I leave it—and as I have a clearer idea of the elysian fields than I have of heaven, I force myself, like Eneas, into them—I see him meet the pensive shade of his forsaken Dido—and wish to recognize it—I see the injured spirit wave her head, and turn off silent from the author of her miseries and dishonours—I lose the feelings for myself in hers—and in those affections which were wont to make me mourn for her when I was at school.[1]

Surely this is not walking in a vain shadow—nor does man disquiet himself in vain, *by it*—he oftener does so in trusting the issue of his commotions to reason only.—I can safely say for myself, I was never able to conquer any one single bad sensation in my heart so decisively, as by beating up as fast as I could for some kindly and gentle sensation, to fight it upon its own ground....

---

1 Here Yorick alludes to Book VI of Virgil's *Aeneid*, in which the Trojan hero Aeneas visits the Underworld and sees the shade of his former lover, Dido, who took her life when Aeneas abandoned her. The "Elysian fields" was the region of the Underworld believed by the ancient Greeks to be reserved for great heroes.

I NEVER felt what the distress of plenty was in any one shape till now—to travel it through the Bourbonnois, the sweetest part of France—in the hey-day of the vintage, when Nature is pouring her abundance into every one's lap, and every eye is lifted up—a journey through each step of which music beats time to *Labour*, and all her children are rejoicing as they carry in their clusters—to pass through this with my affections flying out, and kindling at every group before me—and every one of 'em was pregnant with adventures.

Just heaven!—it would fill up twenty volumes—and alas! I have but a few small pages left of this to croud it into—and half of these must be taken up with poor Maria my friend, Mr. Shandy, met with near Moulines.[1]

The story he had told of that disorder'd maid affect'd me not a little in the reading; but when I got within the neighbourhood where she lived, it returned so strong into my mind, that I could not resist an impulse which prompted me to go half a league out of the road to the village where her parents dwelt to enquire after her.

'Tis going, I own, like the Knight of the Woeful Countenance,[2] in quest of melancholy adventures—but I know not how it is, but I am never so perfectly conscious of the existence of a soul within me, as when I am entangled in them.

The old mother came to the door—She had lost her husband; he had died, she said, of anguish, for the loss of Maria's senses about a month before.—She had feared at first, she added, that it would have plunder'd her poor girl of what little understanding was left—but, on the contrary, it had brought her more to herself—still she could not rest—her poor daughter, she said, crying, was wandering somewhere about the road—

—Why does my pulse beat languid as I write this? And what made La Fleur,[3] whose heart seem'd only to be tuned to joy, to

---

1   See Sterne's novel *Tristram Shandy*, volume IX, chapter 24.
2   A reference to Don Quixote of Cervantes' Spanish novel *Don Quixote de la Mancha* (1605; 1615).
3   Yorick's valet.

pass the back of his hand twice across his eyes, as the woman stood and told it? I beckon'd to the postilion to turn back into the road.

When we had got within half a league of Moulines, at a little opening in the road leading to a thicket, I discovered poor Maria sitting under a poplar—she was sitting with her elbow in her lap, and her head leaning on one side within her hand—a small brook ran at the foot of the tree.

I bid the postilion go on with the chaise to Moulines—and La Fleur to bespeak my supper—and that I would walk after him.

She was dress'd in white, and much as my friend described her, except that her hair hung loose, which before was twisted within a silk net.—She had, superadded likewise her jacket, a pale green ribband which fell across her shoulder to the waist; at the end of which hung her pipe.—Her goat had been as faithless as her lover; and she had got a little dog in lieu of him, which she had kept tied by a string to her girdle; as I look'd at her dog, she drew him towards her with the string.—"Thou shalt not leave me, Sylvio," said she. I look'd in Maria's eyes, and saw she was thinking more of her father than of her lover or her little goat; for as she utter'd them the tears trickled down her cheeks.

I sat down close by her; and Maria let me wipe them away as they fell with my handkerchief.—I then steep'd it in my own—and then in hers—and then in mine—and then I wip'd hers again—and as I did it, I felt such undescribable emotions within me, as I am sure could not be accounted for from any combinations of matter and motion.

I am positive I have a soul; nor can all the books with which materialists have pester'd the world ever convince me of the contrary.

2. *The Man of Feeling* (1771), by **Henry Mackenzie**

[Henry Mackenzie's novel, to which Godwin alludes in the subtitle of *Fleetwood*, was a widely read and profoundly influential work in which the protagonist, Harley, is presented in a variety of situations that illustrate his unusually sensitive and emotional personality. Simple and naïve, Harley responds with great passion to a host of unfortunate characters with whom he comes into contact, and repeatedly performs whatever actions he can to help to improve their lots. The following passage illustrates Harley's reaction to learning that his beloved Miss Walton is to be married to another man, as well as Mackenzie's tongue-in-cheek manner of portraying his hero's high sensibilities.]

from Chapter XL
The Man of Feeling jealous.

The desire of communicating knowledge or intelligence, is an argument with those who hold that man is naturally a social animal. It is indeed one of the earliest propensities we discover; but it may be doubted whether the pleasure (for pleasure there certainly is) arising from it be not often more selfish than social: for we frequently observe the tidings of Ill communicated as eagerly as the annunciation of Good. Is it that we delight in observing the effect of the stronger passions? for we are all philosophers in this respect; and it is perhaps amongst the spectators at Tyburn that the most genuine are to be found.[1]

Was it from this motive that Peter came one morning into his master's room with a meaning face of recital? His master indeed did not at first observe it; for he was sitting, with one shoe buckled, busied in delineating portraits in the fire. "I have brushed these clothes, Sir, as you ordered me."——Harley nodded his head; but Peter observed that his hat wanted brushing too: his master nodded again. At last Peter bethought him, that the fire needed stirring; and, taking up the poker, demolished the turband-head of a Saracen, while his master was seeking out a body for it. "The morning is main cold, Sir," said Peter. "Is it?" said Harley. "Yes, Sir; I have been as far as Tom Dowson's to fetch some barberries he had picked for Mrs. Margery. There was a rare junketing last night at Thomas's among Sir Harry Benson's servants: he lay at Squire Walton's, but he

---

1   A London site of public execution through the late eighteenth century.

would not suffer his servants to trouble the family; so, to be sure, they were all at Tom's, and had a fiddle and a hot supper in the big room where the justices meet about the destroying of hares and partridges, and them things; and Tom's eyes looked so red and so bleared when I called him to get the barberries:—And I hear as how Sir Harry is going to be married to Miss Walton."—"How! Miss Walton married!" said Harley. "Why, it mayn't be true, Sir, for all that; but Tom's wife told it me, and to be sure the servants told her, and their master told them, as I guess, Sir; but it mayn't be true for all that, as I said before."—"Have done with your idle information," said Harley:—"Is my aunt come down into the parlour to breakfast?"—"Yes, Sir."—"Tell her I'll be with her immediately."—

When Peter was gone, he stood with his eyes fixed on the ground, and the last words of his intelligence vibrating in his ears. "Miss Walton married!" he sighed—and walked down stairs, with his shoe as it was, and the buckle in his hand....

[After breakfast with his aunt, Mrs. Margery, Harley goes into the garden]

He sat down on a little seat which commanded an extensive prospect round the house. He leaned on his hand, and scored the ground with his stick: "Miss Walton married!" said he; "but what is that to me? May she be happy! her virtures deserve it; to me her marriage is otherwise indifferent:—I had romantic dreams! they are fled!—it is perfectly indifferent."

Just at that moment he saw a servant, with a knot of ribbands in his hat, go into the house. His cheeks grew flushed at the sight! He kept his eye fixed for some time on the door by which he had entered, then starting to his feet hastily, followed him.

When he approached the door of the kitchen where he supposed the man had gone, his heart throbbed so violently, that when he would have called Peter, his voice failed in the attempt. He stood a moment listening in this breathless state of palpitation: Peter came out by chance. "Did your honour want any thing?"—"Where is the servant that came just now from

Mr. Walton's?"—"From Mr. Walton's, Sir! there is none of his servants here that I know of."—"Nor of Sir Harry Benson's?"—He did not wait for an answer; but having by this time observed the hat with its party-coloured ornament hanging on a peg near the door, he pressed forwards into the kitchen, and addressing himself to a stranger whom he saw there, asked him, with no small tremor in his voice, If he had any commands for him? The man looked silly, and said, That he had nothing to trouble his honour with. "Are you a servant of Sir Harry Benson's?" "No, Sir."—"You'll pardon me, young man; I judged by the favour in your hat."—"Sir, I'm his majesty's servant, God bless him! and these favours we always wear when we are recruiting."—"Recruiting!" his eyes glistened at the word: he seized the soldier's hand, and shaking it violently, ordered Peter to fetch a bottle of his aunt's best dram. The bottle was brought: "You shall drink the king's health," said Harley, "in a bumper."—"The king and your honour."—"Nay, you shall drink the king's health by itself; you may drink mine in another." Peter looked in his master's face, and filled with some little reluctance. "Now to your mistress," said Harley; "every soldier has a mistress." The man excused himself—"to your mistress! you cannot refuse it." 'Twas Mrs. Margery's best dram! Peter stood with the bottle a little inclined, but not so as to discharge a drop of its contents: "Fill it, Peter," said his master, "fill it to the brim." Peter filled it; and the soldier having named Sukey Simson, dispatched it in a twinkling. "Thou art an honest fellow," said Harley, "and I love thee;" and shaking his hand again, desired Peter to make him his guest at dinner, and walked up into his room with a pace much quicker and springy than usual.

This agreeable disappointment however he was not long suffered to felicitate himself upon. The curate happened that day to dine with him....

He had hardly said grace after dinner, when he told Mrs. Margery, that she might soon expect a pair of white gloves, as Sir Harry Benson, he was very well informed, was just going to be married to Miss Walton. Harley spilt the wine he was carrying to his mouth: he had time however to recollect himself before the curate had finished the different minutiae of his intelligence, and summoning up all the heroism he was master of, filled a bumper and drank to Miss Walton. "With all my heart," said the curate, "the bride that is to be." Harley would have said bride too; but the word Bride stuck in his throat. His confusion indeed was manifest: but the curate began to enter on some point of descent with Mrs. Margery, and Harley had very soon after an opportunity of leaving them, while they were deeply engaged in a question, whether the name of some great man in the time of Henry the Seventh was Richard or Humphrey.

He did not see his aunt again till supper; the time between he spent in walking, like some troubled ghost, round the place where his treasure lay. He went as far as a little gate, that led into a copse near Mr. Walton's house, to which that gentleman had been so obliging as to let him have a key. He had just begun to open it, when he saw, on a terrass below, Miss Walton walking with a gentleman in a riding-dress, whom he immediately guessed to be Sir Harry Benson. He stopped of a sudden; his hand shook so much that he could hardly turn the key; he opened the gate however, and advanced a few paces. The lady's lap-dog pricked up its ears, and barked: he stopped again.——

———"the little dogs and all
Tray, Blanch, and Sweetheart, see they
bark at me!"[1]

His resolution failed; he slunk back, and locking the gate as softly as he could, stood on tiptoe looking over the wall till they were gone. At that instant a shepherd blew his horn: the romantic melancholy of the sound quite overcame him!—it was the very note that wanted to be touched—he sighed! he dropped a tear!—and returned.

---

1 *King Lear*, III.vi.61-62.

3. *Julia de Roubigné* (1777), by Henry Mackenzie

[In this epistolary novel, Mackenzie's "man of feeling" is cast as Montaubon, a man whose irrational jealousy leads him to madness. Julia de Roubigné marries her father's friend Montauban when financial disasters preclude her father's continuing support of his family. Julia, however, has loved her childhood companion Savillon for many years. When Savillon returns to France after a long period in the West Indies, Montauban becomes convinced that he and Julia are planning to carry out a love affair. As Montauban's jealousy becomes ever more irrational, he begins to plan Julia's murder in retaliation. *Julia de Roubigné* draws heavily on the similar plot of Rousseau's *Julie, ou La Nouvelle Héloïse* (1761), and Mackenzie's characterization of the jealous Montauban had a profound influence on Godwin's conception of Casimir Fleetwood. In the following two chapters—letters in which Montauban writes to a friend, Segarva—the reader is given a first glimpse of Montauban's dissatisfaction with marriage and his tendency towards irrational jealousy.]

from LETTER XXXV.
Montauban to Segarva.

My wife (that word must often come across the narration of a married man) has been a good deal indisposed of late. You will not joke me on this intelligence, as such of my neighbours whom I have seen have done; it is not however what they say, or you may think; her spirits droop more than her body; she is thoughtful and melancholy when she thinks she is not observed, and, what pleases me worse, affects to appear otherwise, when she is. I like not this sadness which is conscious of itself. Yet, perhaps, I have seen her thus before our marriage, and have rather admired this turn of mind than disapproved of it; but I would not have her pensive—nor very gay neither—I would have nothing about her, methinks, to stir a question in me whence it arose. She should be contented with the affection she knows I bear for her. I do not expect her to be romantically happy, and she has no cause for uneasiness—I am not uneasy neither—yet I wish her to conquer this melancholy.

I was last night abroad at supper: Julia was a-bed before my return. I found her lute lying on the table, and a music-book open by it. I could perceive the marks of tears shed on the paper, and the air was such as might encourage their falling: sleep however had overcome her sadness, and she did not awake when I opened the curtains to look on her. When I had stood some moments, I heard her sigh strongly through her sleep, and presently she muttered some words, I know not of what import. I had sometimes heard her do so before, without regarding it much; but there was something that roused my attention now. I listened; she sighed again, and again spoke a few broken words; at last, I heard her plainly pronounce the name *Savillon*, two or three times over, and each time it was accompanied with sighs so deep, that her heart seemed bursting as it heaved them. I confess the thing struck me, and, after musing on it some time, I resolved to try a little experiment this day at dinner, to discover whether chance had made her pronounce this name, or if some previous cause had impressed it on her imagination. I knew a man of that name at Paris, when I first went thither, who had an office under the intendant of the marine. I introduced some conversation on the subject of the fleet, and said, in an indifferent manner, that I had heard so and so from my old acquaintance Savillon. She spilt some soup she was helping me to at the instant; and, stealing a glance at her, I saw her cheeks flushed into crimson.

I have been ever since going the round of conjecture on this incident. I think I can recollect once, and but once, her father speak of a person called Savillon residing abroad, from whom he had received a letter; but I never heard Julia mention him at all. I know not why I should have forborn asking her the reason of her being so affected at the sound; yet, at the moment I perceived it, the question stuck in my throat. I felt something like guilt hang over this incident altogether—it is none of mine then—nor of Julia's neither, I trust—and yet, Segarva, it has touched me nearer—much nearer than I should own to any one but you.

LETTER XXXIX.
Montauban to Segarva.

Segarva!—but it must be told—I blush even telling it to thee—
have I lived to this?—that thou shouldst hear the name of
Montauban coupled with dishonour!

I came into my wife's room yesterday morning, somewhat
unexpectedly. I observed she had been weeping, though she
put on her hat to conceal it, and spoke in a tone of voice affectedly indifferent. Presently she went out on pretence of walking; I staid behind, not without surprise at her tears, though, I
think, without suspicion; when turning over (in the careless
way one does in musing) some loose papers on her dressing-
table, I found the picture of a young man in miniature, the glass
of which was still wet with the tears she had shed on it. I have
but a confused remembrance of my feelings at the time; there
was a bewildered pause of thought, as if I had waked in another
world. My faithful Lonquillez happened to enter the room at
that moment; "look there!" said I, holding out the picture without knowing what I did; he held it in his hand, and turning it,
read on the back, "Savillon." I started at that sound, and
snatched the picture from him; I believe he spoke somewhat,
expressing his surprise at my emotion; I know not what it was,
nor what my answer: he was retiring from the chamber—I
called him back.—"I think, (said I) thou lovest thy master, and
would serve him if thou could'st?"—"With my life!" answered
Lonquillez—the warmth of his manner touched me: I think I
laid my hand on my sword. "Savillon!" I repeated the name; "I
have heard of him,". said Lonquillez.—"Heard of him!"—"I
heard Le Blanc talk of him a few days ago."—"And what did
he say of him?"—"And said he had heard of this gentleman's
arrival from the West-Indies, from his own nephew, who had
just come from Paris; that he remembered him formerly, when
he lived with his master at Belville, the sweetest young gentleman, and the handsomest in the province."—My situation
struck me at that instant.—I was unable to enquire further.—
After some little time, Lonquillez left the room; I knew not that
he was gone, till I heard him going down stairs. I called him

back a second time; he came: I could not speak.—"My dear master!" (said Lonquillez)—It was the accent of a friend, and it overcame me.

"Lonquillez, (said I) your master is most unhappy!—Canst thou think my wife is false to me?"—"Heaven forbid!" said he, and started back in amazement.—"It may be I wrong her; but to dream of Savillon, to keep his picture, to weep over it."—"What shall I do, Sir?" said Lonquillez.—"You see I am calm, I returned, and will do nothing rashly;—try to learn from Le Blanc every thing he knows about this Savillon. Lisette is silly, and talks much. I know your faith, and will trust your capacity; get me what intelligence you can, but beware of shewing the most distant suspicion."—We heard my wife below;—I threw down the picture where I had found it, and hastened to meet her. As I approached her, my heart throbbed so violently that I durst not venture the meeting. My dressing-room door stood a-jar; I slunk in there, I believe, unperceived, and heard her pass on to her chamber. I would have called Lonquillez to have spoken to him again; but I durst not then, and have not found an opportunity since.

I saw my wife soon after; I counterfeited as well as I could, and, I think, she was the most embarrassed of the two; she attempted once or twice to bring in some apology for her former appearance; complained of having been ill in the morning, that her head ached, and her eyes been hot and uneasy.

She came herself to call me to dinner. We dined alone, and I marked her closely; I saw (by Heaven! I did) a fawning solicitude to please me, an attempt at the good-humour of innocence, to cover the embarrassment of guilt. I should have observed it, I am sure I should, even without a key; as it was, I could read her soul to the bottom.—Julia de Roubigné! the wife of Montauban!—Is it not so?

I have had time to think.—You will recollect the circumstances of our marriage—her long unwillingness, her almost unconquerable reluctance.—Why did I marry her?

Let me remember—I durst not trust the honest decision of my friend, but stole into this engagement without his knowledge; I purchased her consent, I bribed, I bought her; bought her, the leavings of another!—I will trace this line of infamy no further: there is madness in it!

Segarva, I am afraid to hear from you; yet write to me, write to me freely. If you hold me justly punished—yet spare me, when you think on the severity of my punishment.

Appendix D: The English Jacobin Novel and the Lot of Women

1. *A Simple Story* (1791), by Elizabeth Inchbald

[In the first half of her influential Jacobin novel, Inchbald chronicles the romance and marriage of the young, coquettish Miss Milner and her guardian, the stern Lord Elmwood. The novel's second half picks up seventeen years later, when Lady Elmwood has been unfaithful to her husband during his multiple year absence from England on business. Lord Elmwood then angrily rejects both his wife and his innocent daughter Matilda. Ultimately Inchbald contrasts the vapid education that the foolish Miss Milner received in a ladies' finishing school to the more practical and "proper" education that Matilda receives from her father's mentor and chaplain, Mr. Sandford.]

from Volume III, Chapter 1

Lord Elmwood's love to his lady had been extravagant—the effect of his hate was extravagant likewise. Beholding himself separated from her by a barrier never to be removed, he vowed in the deep torments of his revenge, not to be reminded of her by one individual object; much less by one so nearly allied to her as her child. To bestow upon that child his affections, would be, he imagined, still in some sort, to divide them with the mother. Firm in his resolution, the beautiful Matilda was, at the age of six years, sent out of her father's house, and received by her mother with the tenderness, but with the anguish, of those parents, who behold their offspring visited with the punishment due only to their own offences.

During this transaction, which was performed by his lordship's agents at his command, he himself was engaged in an affair of still weightier importance—that of life or death:—he determined upon his own death, or the death of the man who had wounded his honour and his happiness. A duel with his old antagonist was the result of this determination; nor was the Duke of Avon (before the decease of his father and eldest brother, Lord Frederick Lawnly) backward to render all the satisfaction that was required.—For it was no other than he, whose love for Lady Elmwood had still subsisted, and whose art and industry left no means unessayed to perfect his designs;— No other than he, (who, next to Lord Elmwood, was ever of all her lovers most prevalent in her heart,) to whom Lady Elmwood yielded her own and her husband's future peace, and gave to his vanity a prouder triumph, than if she had never given her hand in preference to another. This triumph however was but short—a month only, after the return of Lord Elmwood, his Grace was called upon to answer for his conduct, and was left upon the spot where they met, so maimed, and defaced with scars, as never again to endanger the honour of a husband. As Lord Elmwood was inexorable to all accommodation, their engagement lasted for some space of time; nor any thing but the steadfast assurance his opponent was slain, could at last have torn his lordship from the field, though he himself was mortally wounded.

Yet even during that period of his danger, while for days he laid in the continual expectation of his own death, not all the entreaties of his dearest, most intimate, and most respected friends could prevail upon him to pronounce forgiveness to his wife, or suffer them to bring his daughter to him for his last blessing.

from Volume III, Chapter 3

Lord Elmwood was by nature, and more from education, of a serious, thinking, and philosophic turn of mind. His religious studies had completely taught him to consider this world but as a passage to another; to enjoy with gratitude what Heaven in its bounty should bestow, and to bear with submission, all which in its vengeance it might inflict—In a greater degree than most people he practised this doctrine; and as soon as the first shock he received from Lady Elmwood's conduct was abated, an entire calmness and resignation ensued; but still of that sensible and feeling kind, which could never force him to forget the happiness he had lost; and it was this sensibility, which urged him to fly from its more keen recollection as much as possible—this he alleged as the reason he would never suffer Lady Elmwood, or even her child, to be named in his hearing. But this injunction (which all his friends, and even the servants in the house who attended his person, had received) was, by many people, suspected rather to proceed from his resentment, than his tenderness; nor did he himself deny, that resentment mingled with his prudence; for prudence he called it not to remind himself of happiness he could never taste again, and of ingratitude that might impel him to hatred; and prudence he called it, not to form another attachment near to his heart; more especially so near as a parent's, which might a second time expose him to all the torments of ingratitude, from one whom he affectionately loved.

Upon these principles he formed the unshaken resolution, never to acknowledge Lady Matilda as his child—or acknowledging her as such—never to see, hear of, or take one concern whatever in her fate and fortune. The death of her mother appeared a favourable time, he had been so inclined, to have recalled this declaration which he had solemnly and repeatedly made—she was now destitute of the protection of her other parent, and it became his duty, at least to provide her a guardian, if he did not choose to take that tender title upon himself.—But to mention either the mother or child to Lord Elmwood was an equal offence, and prohibited in the strongest terms to all his friends and household: and as he was an excellent good master, a sincere friend, and a most generous patron; not one of his acquaintance or dependants, were hardy enough to draw upon themselves his certain displeasure, which was violent in the extreme, by even the official intelligence of Lady Elmwood's death.

Sandford himself, intimidated through age, or by austere, and even morose, manners Lord Elmwood had of late years adopted; Sandford wished, if possible, some other would undertake the dangerous task of recalling to his lordship's memory, there ever was such a person as his wife. He advised Miss Woodley to indite a proper letter to him on the subject; but she reminded him, such a step was still more perilous in her, than any other person, as she was the most destitute being on earth, without the benevolence of Lord Elmwood. The death of her aunt, Mrs. Horton, had left her sole reliance on Lady Elmwood; and now her death, had left her totally dependent upon the earl—for her ladyship, long before her decease, had declared it was not her intention, to leave a single sentence behind her in the form of a will—She had no will, she said, but what she would wholly submit to Lord Elmwood's; and, if it were even his will, her child should live in poverty, as well as banishment, it should be so.—But, perhaps, in this implicit submission to his lordship, there was a distant hope that the necessitous situation of his daughter might plead more forcibly than his parental love; and that knowing her abandoned of every support but through himself, that idea might form some little tie between them; and be at least a token of the relationship.

But as Lady Elmwood anxiously wished this principle upon which she acted, should be concealed from his lordship's suspicion, she included her friend, Miss Woodley, in the same fate; and thus, the only persons dear to her, she left, but at Lord Elmwood's pleasure, to be preserved from perishing in want.—Her child was too young to advise her on this subject, her friend too disinterested; and at this moment they were both without the smallest means of support, except through the justice or compassion of his lordship.—Sandford had, indeed, promised his protection to the daughter; but his liberality had no other source than from his patron, with whom he still lived as usual, except during the winter when his lordship resided in town, he then mostly stole a visit to Lady Elmwood—On this last visit, he stayed to see her buried.

After some mature deliberations, Sandford was now preparing to go to Lord Elmwood at his house in town, and there to deliver himself the news that must sooner or later be told; and he meant also to venture, at the same time, to keep the promise he had made to his dying lady—but the news reached Lord Elmwood before Sandford arrived; it was announced in the public papers, and by that means came first to his knowledge.

He was breakfasting by himself, when the newspaper that first gave the intelligence of Lady Elmwood's death, was laid before him—the paragraph contained these words:

"On Wednesday last died, at Dring Park, a village in Northumberland, the right honourable Countess Elmwood— This lady, who has not been heard of for many years in the fashionable world, was a rich heiress, and of extreme beauty; but although she received overtures from many men of the first rank, she preferred her guardian, the present Lord Elmwood (then the humble Mr. Dorriforth) to them all—and it is said, they enjoyed an uncommon share of felicity, till his lordship going abroad, and remaining there some time, the consequences (to a most captivating young woman left without a protector) were such, as to cause a separation on his return.— Her ladyship has left one child, a daughter, about fifteen."

Lord Elmwood had so much feeling upon reading this, as to lay down the paper, and not take it up again for several minutes—nor did he taste his chocolate during this interval, but leaned his elbow on the table and rested his head upon his hand.—He then rose up—walked two or three times across the room—sat down again—took up the paper—and read as usual.——Nor let the vociferous mourner, or the perpetual weeper, here complain—but let them remember Lord Elmwood was a man—a man of understanding—of courage—of fortitude—with all, a man of the nicest feelings—and who shall say, but that at the time he leaned his head upon his hand, and rose to walk away the sense of what he felt, he might not feel as much as Lady Elmwood did in her last moments.

Be this as it may, his lordship's susceptibility on the occasion was not suspected by any one—he passed that day the same as usual; the next day too, and the day after.—On the morning of the fourth day, he sent for his steward to his study, and after talking of other business, said to him,

"Is it true that Lady Elmwood is dead?"

"It is, my lord," replied the man.

His lordship looked unusually grave, and at this reply, fetched an involuntary sigh.

"Mr. Sandford, my lord," continued the steward, "sent me

word of the news, but left it to my own discretion, whether I made your lordship acquainted with it or not."

"Where is Sandford?" asked Lord Elmwood.

"He was with my lady," replied the steward.

"When she died?" asked his lordship.

"Yes, my lord."

"I am glad of it—he will see every thing she desired done.— Sandford is a good man, and would be a friend to every body."

"He is a very good man indeed, my lord."

There was now a silence.—Mr. Giffard then bowing, said, "Has your lordship any farther commands?"

"Write to Sandford," said Lord Elmwood, hesitating as he spoke, "and tell him to have every thing performed as she desired.—And whoever she may have selected for the guardian of her child, has my consent to act as such.—Nor in one instance, where I myself am not concerned, will I contradict her will."—The tears rushed to his eyes as he said this, and caused them to start in the steward's—observing which, he sternly resumed,

"Do not suppose from this conversation, that any of those resolutions I have long since taken are, or will be, changed— they are the same; and shall continue the same:—and your interdiction, sir, (as well as every other person's) remains just the same as formerly; never to mention this subject to me in future."

"My lord, I always obeyed you," replied Mr. Giffard, "and hope I always shall."

"I hope so too," replied his lordship, in a threatening accent.

2. *The Wrongs of Woman: or, Maria* (1798), by Mary Wollstonecraft

[Aiming to illustrate the powerlessness of women in the social and legal worlds of contemporary Britain in the context of a novel, Wollstonecraft worked on *The Wrongs of Woman* throughout the last year of her life, but left it unfinished when she died in September 1797. Godwin edited the work, assembled an ending out of Wollstonecraft's notes, and published the novel amongst Wollstonecraft's *Posthumous Works* the following year. In the excerpt that follows, the protagonist Maria addresses her young daughter in a memoir in which she describes her marriage to the wicked George Venables, and her kidnapping and imprisonment in a madhouse when she attempted to escape her husband's abuses.]

from Chapter IX

"I resume my pen to fly from thought. I was married; and we hastened to London. I had purposed taking one of my sisters with me; for a strong motive for marrying, was the desire of having a home at which I could receive them, now their own grew so uncomfortable, as not to deserve the cheering appellation. An objection was made to her accompanying me, that appeared plausible; and I reluctantly acquiesced. I was however willingly allowed to take with me Molly, poor Peggy's daughter. London and preferment, are ideas commonly associated in the country; and, as blooming as May, she bade adieu to Peggy with weeping eyes. I did not even feel hurt at the refusal in relation to my sister, till hearing what my uncle had done for me, I had the simplicity to request, speaking with warmth of their situation, that he would give them a thousand pounds a-piece, which seemed to me but justice.[1] He asked me, giving me a kiss, 'If I had lost my senses?' I started back, as if I had found a wasp in a rose-bush. I expostulated. He sneered, and the demon of discord entered our paradise, to poison with his pestiferous breath every opening joy.

"I had sometimes observed defects in my husband's understanding; but, led astray by a prevailing opinion, that goodness of disposition is of the first importance in the relative situations of life, in proportion as I perceived the narrowness of his understanding, fancy enlarged the boundary of his heart. Fatal error! How quickly is the so much vaunted milkiness of nature

---

1 Maria's uncle had provided her with a dowry of 5000 pounds; her husband, however, has no intention of sharing any of those funds with her sisters, who are being mistreated by the mistress of Maria's widowed father.

turned into gall, by an intercourse with the world, if more generous juices do not sustain the vital source of virtue!

"One trait in my character was extreme credulity; but, when my eyes were once opened, I saw but too clearly all I had before overlooked. My husband was sunk in my esteem; still there are youthful emotions, which, for a while, fill up the chasm of love and friendship. Besides, it required some time to enable me to see his whole character in a just light, or rather to allow it to become fixed. While circumstances were ripening my faculties, and cultivating my taste, commerce and gross relaxations were shutting his against any possibility of improvement, till, by stifling every spark of virtue in himself, he began to imagine that it no where existed.

"Do not let me lead you astray, my child, I do not mean to assert, that any human being is entirely incapable of feeling the generous emotions, which are the foundation of every true principle of virtue; but they are frequently, I fear, so feeble, that, like the inflammable quality which more or less lurks in all bodies, they often lie for ever dormant; the circumstances never occurring, necessary to call them into action.

"I discovered however by chance, that, in consequence of some losses in trade, the natural effect of his gambling desire to start suddenly into riches, the five thousand pounds given me by my uncle, had been paid very opportunely. This discovery, strange as you may think the assertion, gave me pleasure; my husband's embarrassments endeared him to me. I was glad to find an excuse for his conduct to my sisters, and my mind became calmer.

"My uncle introduced me to some literary society; and the theatres were a never-failing source of amusement to me. My delighted eye followed Mrs. Siddons, when, with dignified delicacy, she played Calista; and I voluntarily repeated after her, in the same tone, and with a long-drawn sigh,

'Hearts like our's were pair'd —— not match'd.'[1]

---

1 Wollstonecraft alludes to Nicholas Rowe's popular tragedy, *The Fair Penitent* (1703), II.i.99-100.

"These were, at first, spontaneous emotions, though, becoming acquainted with men of wit and polished manners, I could not sometimes help regretting my early marriage; and that, in my haste to escape from a temporary dependence, and expand my newly fledged wings, in an unknown sky, I had been caught in a trap, and caged for life. Still the novelty of London, and the attentive fondness of my husband, for he had some personal regard for me, made several months glide away. Yet, not forgetting the situation of my sisters who were still very young, I prevailed on my uncle to settle a thousand pounds on each; and to place them in a school near town, where I could frequently visit, as well as have them at home with me.

"I now tried to improve my husband's taste, but we have few subjects in common; indeed he soon appeared to have little relish for my society, unless he was hinting to me the use he could make of my uncle's wealth. When we had company, I was disgusted by an ostentatious display of riches, and I have often quitted the room, to avoid listening to exaggerated tales of money obtained by lucky hits.

"With all my attention and affectionate interest, I perceived that I could not become the friend or confident of my husband. Every thing I learned relative to his affairs I gathered up by accident; and I vainly endeavoured to establish, at our fireside, that social converse, which often renders people of different characters dear to each other. Returning from the theatre, or any amusing party, I frequently began to relate what I had seen and highly relished; but with sullen taciturnity he soon silenced me. I seemed therefore gradually to lose, in his society, the soul, the energies of which had just been in action. To such a degree, in fact, did his cold, reserved manner affect me, that, after spending some days with him alone, I have imagined myself the most stupid creature in the world, till the abilities of some casual visitor convinced me that I had some dormant animation, and sentiments above the dust in which I had been groveling. The very countenance of my husband changed; his complexion became sallow, and all the charms of youth were vanishing with its vivacity.

"I give you one view of the subject; but these experiments

and alterations took up the space of five years; during which period, I had most reluctantly extorted several sums from my uncle, to save my husband, to use his own words, from destruction. At first it was to prevent bills being noted, to the injury of his credit; then to bail him; and afterwards to prevent an execution from entering the house. I began at last to conclude, that he would have made more exertions of his own to extricate himself, had he not relied on mine, cruel as was the task he imposed on me; and I firmly determined that I would make use of no more pretexts.

"From the moment I pronounced this determination, indifference on his part was changed into rudeness, or something worse.

"He now seldom dined at home, and continually returned at a late hour, drunk, to bed. I retired to another apartment; I was glad, I own, to escape from his; for personal intimacy without affection, seemed, to me the most degrading, as well as the most painful state in which a woman of any taste, not to speak of the peculiar delicacy of fostered sensibility, could be placed. But my husband's fondess for women was of the grossest kind, and imagination was so wholly out of the question, as to render his indulgences of this sort entirely promiscuous, and of the most brutal nature. My health suffered, before my heart was entirely estranged by the loathsome information; could I then have returned to his sullied arms, but as a victim to the prejudices of mankind, who have made women the property of their husbands? I discovered even, by his conversation, when intoxicated, that his favourites were wantons of the lowest class, who could by their vulgar, indecent mirth, which he called nature, rouse his sluggish spirits. Meretricious ornaments and manners were necessary to attract his attention. He seldom looked twice at a modest woman, and sat silent in their company; and the charms of youth and beauty had not the slightest effect on his senses, unless the possessors were initiated in vice. His intimacy with profligate women, and his habits of thinking, gave him a contempt for female endowments; and he would repeat, when wine had loosed his tongue, most of the common-place sarcasms levelled at them, by men who do not allow them to have minds, because mind would be an impediment to gross enjoyment. Men who are inferior to their fellow men, are always most anxious to establish their superiority over women. But where are these reflections leading me?

"Women who have lost their husband's affection, are justly reproved for neglecting their persons, and not taking the same pains to keep, as to gain a heart; but who thinks of giving the same advice to men, though women are continually stigmatized for being attached to fops; and from the nature of their education, are more susceptible of disgust? Yet why a woman should be expected to endure a sloven, with more patience than a man, and magnanimously to govern herself, I cannot conceive; unless it be supposed arrogant in her to look for respect as well as a maintenance. It is not easy to be pleased, because, after promising to love, in different circumstances, we are told that it is our duty. I cannot, I am sure (though, when attending the sick, I never felt disgust) forget my own sensations, when rising with health and spirit, and after scenting the sweet morning, I have met my husband at the breakfast table. The active attention I had been giving to domestic regulations, which were generally settled before he rose, or a walk, gave a glow to my countenance, that contrasted with his squallid appearance. The squeamishness of stomach alone, produced by the last night's intemperance, which he took no pains to conceal, destroyed my appetite. I think I now see him lolling in an arm-chair, in a dirty powdering gown, soiled linen, ungartered stockings, and tangled hair, yawning and stretching himself. The newspaper was immediately called for, if not brought in on the tea-board, from which he would scarcely lift his eyes while I poured out the tea, excepting to ask for some brandy to put in it, or to declare that he could not eat. In answer to any question, in his best humour, it was a drawling, 'What do you say, child?' But if I demanded money for the house expences, which I put off till the last moment, his customary reply, often prefaced with an oath, was, 'Do you think me, madam, made of money?'—The butcher, the baker, must wait; and, what was worse, I was often obliged to witness his surly dismission of tradesmen, who were in want of their money, and whom I sometimes paid with the presents my uncle gave me for my own use."

3. *The Victim of Prejudice* (1799), by Mary Hays

[A devoted follower of Wollstonecraft, Mary Hays attempted a similar project of using fiction to illustrate the mistreatment of women in contemporary society. In *The Victim of Prejudice*, Mary Raymond is prevented from marrying her childhood sweetheart because her mother gave birth to her out of wedlock, and because she has no dowry to bring to a marriage. Despite her noble attempts to support herself after the death of her guardian, Mr. Raymond, Mary is tormented and ultimately raped by the evil Sir Peter Osborne. Moreover, despite her complete innocence, she finds herself a social outcast—a position that exactly parallels the experience of her mother. The following passage is excerpted from a letter to her daughter's guardian in which Mary's mother explains her "fall" from social respectability.]

from Volume I, Chapter XII

"'*To* MR. RAYMOND.

"'How far shall I go back? From what period shall I date the source of those calamities which have, at length, overwhelmed me?—Educated in the lap of indolence, enervated by pernicious indulgence, fostered in artificial refinements, misled by specious, but false, expectations, softened into imbecility, pampered in luxury, and dazzled by a frivolous ambition, at the age of eighteen, I rejected the manly address and honest ardour of the man whose reason would have enlightened, whose affection would have supported me; through whom I might have enjoyed the endearing relations, and fulfilled the respectable duties, of mistress, wife, and mother; and listened to the insidious flatteries of a being, raised by fashion and fortune to a rank seducing to my vain imagination, in the splendour of which my weak judgement was dazzled and my virtue overpowered.

"'He spoke of tenderness and honour, (prostituted names!) while his actions gave the lie to his pretentions. He affected concealment, and imposed on my understanding by sophistical pretences. Unaccustomed to reason, too weak for principle, credulous from inexperience, a stranger to the corrupt habits of society, I yielded to the mingled intoxication of my vanity and my senses, quitted the paternal roof, and resigned myself to my triumphant seducer.

"'Months revolved in a round of varied pleasures: reflection was stunned in the giddy whirl. I awoke not from my delirium, till, on an unfounded, affected, pretence of jealousy, under which satiety veiled itself, I found myself suddenly deserted, driven with opprobrium from the house of my *destroyer*, thrown friendless and destitute upon the world, branded with infamy, and a wretched outcast from social life. To fill up the measure of my distress, a little time convinced me that I was about to become a mother. The money which remained from my profuse habits was nearly exhausted. In the prospect of immediate distress, I addressed myself to the author of my woes. Relating my situation, I implored his justice and mercy. I sought in vain to awaken his tenderness, to touch his callous heart. To my humble supplications no answer was vouchsafed. Despair, for awhile, with its benumbing power, seized upon my heart!

"'Awakening to new anguish, and recalling my scattered faculties, I remembered the softness and the ease of my childhood, the doating fondness of my weak, but indulgent, parents. I resolved to address them, resolved to pour out before them the confession of my errors, of my griefs, and of my contrition. My lowly solicitations drew upon me bitter reproaches: I was treated as an abandoned wretch, whom it would be criminal to relieve and hopeless to attempt to reclaim.

"'At this crisis, I was sought out and discovered by a friend (if friendship can endure the bond of vice) of my destroyer; the man who, to gratify his sensuality, had entailed, on an unoffending being, *a being who loved him*, misery and certain perdition. My declining virtue, which yet struggled to retrieve itself, was now assailed by affected sympathy, by imprecations on the wretch who had deserted me, and an offer of asylum and protection.

"'My heart, though too weak for principle, was not yet wholly corrupted: the modest habits of female youth were still far from being obliterated; I suspected the views of the guileful deceiver, and contemned them with horror and just indignation. Changing his manners, this Proteus assumed a new form; prophaned the names of humanity, friendship, virtue; gradually inspiring me with confidence.[1] Unable to labour, ashamed to solicit charity, helpless, pennyless, feeble, delicate, thrown out with reproach from society, borne down with a consciousness of irretrievable error, exposed to insult, to want, to contumely, to every species of aggravated distress, in a situation requiring sympathy, tenderness, assistance,—From whence was I to draw fortitude to combat these accumulated evils? By what magical power or supernatural aid was a being, rendered, by all the previous habits of life and education, systematically weak and helpless, at once to assume a courage thus daring and heroic?

"'I received, as the tribute of humanity and friendship, that assistance, without which I had not the means of existence, and was delivered, in due time, of a lovely female infant. While bedewing it with my tears, (delicious tears! tears that shed a balm into my lacerated spirit!) I forgot for awhile its barbarous father, the world's scorn, and my blasted prospects: the sensations of the injured woman, of the insulted wife, were absorbed for a time in the stronger sympathies of the delighted mother.

"'My new friend, to whose tender cares I seemed indebted for the sweet emotions which now engrossed my heart, appeared entitled to my grateful esteem: my confidence in him became every hour more unbounded. It was long ere he stripped off the mask so successfully assumed; when, too late, I found myself betrayed, and became, a second time, the victim of my simplicity and the inhuman arts of a practised deceiver, who had concerted with the companion of his licentious revels,

---

1 In classical mythology, Proteus was a sea deity with the power to assume any shape or form.

wearied with his conquest, the snare into which I fell a too-credulous prey.

"'Evil communication, habits of voluptuous extravagance, despair of retrieving a blasted fame, gradually stifled the declining struggles of virtue; while the libertine manners of those, of whom I was now compelled to be the associate, rapidly advanced the corruption;

> "'Took off the rose
> "'from the fair forehead of an innocent love,
> "'And plac'd a blister there.[1]

"'In a mind unfortified by principle, modesty is a blossom fragile as lovely. Every hour, whirled in a giddy round of dissipation, sunk me deeper in shameless vice. The mother became stifled in my heart: my visits to my infant, which I had been reluctantly prevailed upon to place with a hireling, were less and less frequent. Its innocence contrasted my guilt, it revived too powerfully in my heart the remembrance of what I was, the reflection on what I might have been, and the terrible conviction, which I dared not dwell upon, of the fate which yet menaced me. I abstained from this soul-harrowing indulgence, and the ruin of my mind became complete.

"'Why should I dwell upon, why enter into, a disgusting detail of the gradations of thoughtless folly, guilt, and infamy? Why should I stain the youthful purity of my unfortunate offspring, into whose hands these sheets may hereafter fall, with the delineation of scenes remembered with soul-sickening abhorrence? Let it suffice to say, that, by enlarging the circle of my observation, though in the bosom of depravity, my understanding became enlightened: I perceived myself the victim of the injustice, of the prejudice, of society, which, by opposing to my return to virtue almost insuperable barriers, had plunged me into irremediable ruin. I grew sullen, desperate, hardened. I felt a malignant joy in retaliating upon mankind a part of the

---

1 *Hamlet* III.iv.42-44.

evils which I sustained. My mind became fiend-like, revelling in destruction, glorying in its shame. Abandoned to excessive and brutal licentiousness, I drowned returning reflection in inebriating potions. The injuries and insults to which my odious profession exposed me eradicated from my heart every remaining human feeling. I became a monster, cruel, relentless, ferocious; and contaminated alike, with a deadly poison, the health and the principles of those unfortunate victims whom, with practised allurements, I entangled in my snares. Man, however vicious, however cruel, reaches not the depravity of a shameless woman. *Despair* shuts not against him every avenue to repentance; *despair* drives him not from human sympathies; *despair* hurls him not from hope, from pity, from life's common charities, to plunge him into desperate, damned, guilt....

... "'Thou, also, it may be, art incapable of distinction; thou, too, probably, hast bartered the ingenuous virtues, the sensibility of youth, for the despotism, the arrogance, the voluptuousness of man, and the unfortunate daughter of an abandoned and wretched mother will spread to thee her innocent arms in vain. If, amidst the corruption of vaunted civilization, thy heart can yet throb responsive to the voice of nature, and yield to the claims of humanity, snatch from destruction the child of an illicit commerce, shelter her infant purity from contagion, guard her helpless youth from a pitiless world, cultivate her reason, make her feel her nature's worth, strengthen her faculties, inure her to suffer hardship, rouse her to independence, inspire her with fortitude, with energy, with self-respect, and teach her to contemn the tyranny that would impose fetters of sex upon her mind.

"'MARY.'"

Appendix E: The Resonance of Renaissance Drama

1. *A Wife for A Moneth* (1624), by John Fletcher

[In this play the evil King Frederick lusts for the beautiful
Evanthe, but Evanthe refuses his advances. Frederick vengefully
proclaims that Evanthe's lover, Valerio, may marry her, but only
for one month, at the end of which he must face execution. In
Volume III, Chapter 2 of Godwin's novel, Fleetwood and Mary
read the play together. Fleetwood describes Mary's reaction to
the passage below, in which King Frederick's wife, Queen
Maria, helps Evanthe to dress for her wedding, and prepares her
to handle the king's irrational wrath. Ironically, the situation
foreshadows the one that Mary Fleetwood will soon face with
her own husband.]

Act II.ii

Enter Queen [Maria] and Evanthe.
Maria.   You shall be merry, come, I'le have it so,
Can there be any nature so unnoble?
Or anger unhumane to pursue this?
Evanthe.   I feare there is.
Maria.   Your feares are poore and foolish;
Though he be hasty, and his anger death,
His will like torrents, not to be resisted,
Yet Law and Justice go along to guide him;
And what Law or what Justice can he finde
To justifie his will? what Act or Statute,
By Humane or Divine establishment,
Left to direct us, that makes marriage death?
Honest faire wedlock? 'twas given for increase,
For preservation of mankinde I take it;
He must be more then man then, that dare break it;
Come dresse ye handsomly, you shall have my Jewels,
And put a face on that contemnes base fortune,
'Twill make him more insult to see you fearfull,

Outlook his anger.

Evanthe.   O my Valerio!
Be witnesse my pure minde, 'tis thee I grieve for.

Maria.   But shew it not; I would so crucifie him
With an innocent neglect of what he can do,
A brave strong pious scorne, that I would shake him;
Put all the wanton Cupids in thine eyes,
And all the graces on that nature gave thee,
Make up thy beauty to that height of excellence,
I'le help thee, and forgive thee, as if Venus
Were now againe to catch the God of Warre,
In his most rugged anger; when thou hast him
(As 'tis impossible he should resist thee)
And kneeling at thy conquering feet for mercy,
Then shew thy vertue, then againe despise him
And all his power, then with a looke of honour,
Mingled with noble chastity, strike him dead.

Evanthe.   Good Madam dresse me,
You arme me bravely.

Maria.   Make him know his cruelty
Begins with him first, he must suffer for it,
And that thy sentence is so welcome to thee,
And to thy noble Lord, you long to meet it.
Stamp such a deep impression of thy beauty
Into his soule, and of thy worthinesse,
That when Valerio and Evanthe sleep
In one rich earth, hung round about with blessings,
He may run mad, and curse his act; be lusty,
I'le teach thee how to die too, if thou fear'st it.

Evanthe.   I thank your Grace, you have prepar'd me
strongly,
And my weak minde.

Maria.   Death is unwelcome never,
Unlesse it be to tortur'd mindes and sick soules,
That make their own Hells; 'tis such a benefit
When it comes crown'd with honour, shews so sweet too,
Though they paint it ugly, that's but to restraine us,
For every living thing would love it else,

Fly boldly to their peace, ere nature call'd 'em;
The rest we have from labour, and from trouble,
Is some incitement; every thing alike,
The poore slave that lies private has his liberty,
As amply as his Master, in that Tombe,
The earth as light upon him, and the flowers
That grow about him smell as sweet, and flourish;
But when we love with honour to our ends,
When memory and vertues are our mourners,
What pleasure's there? they are infinite Evanthe;
Onely, my vertuous wench, we want our sences,
That benefit we are barr'd, 'twould make us proud else,
And lazy to look up to happier life,
The blessings of the people would so swell us.
Evanthe.   Good Madam dresse me, you have drest my soul,
The merriest Bride I'le be for all this misery,
The proudest to some eyes too.
Maria.   'Twill do better; come shrink no more.
Evanthe.   I am too confident.   *Exeunt.*

2. *Don Carlos, Prince of Spain* (1676), by **Thomas Otway**

[Godwin's conception of Fleetwood as a jealous husband was
in part influenced by his reading of Otway's tragedy—a study
in the destructive effects of irrational jealousy that bears comparison to both Shakespeare's *Othello* and *The Winter's Tale*. In
this play, Philip II, King of Spain, has married the young Elizabeth of Valois, who had been intended to wed Philip's son,
Don Carlos. The king soon becomes easy prey to the evil Rui-
Gomez and his wife, the Duchess of Eboli, who fill his mind
with accusations of the Queen's infidelity with his son. In the
final act of the tragedy, the King learns of his wife's and his
son's innocence, but only after he has caused the Queen to be
poisoned, and after Don Carlos has taken his own life. The
other characters in the passage below include Don John of
Austria, the King's brother; a guard and servants.]

from Act III.i

King.   So Madam!——
Queen.   ——By the fury in your eyes,
I understand you come to tyrannize.
I hear you are already Jealous grown,
And dare suspect my Virtue with your Son.
King.   Oh Woman-kind! thy Myst'ries! who can scan
Too deep for easie weak believing man!
Hold! Let me look! indeed y'are wondrous fair,
So on the out-side *Sodoms* Apples were.
And yet within, when open'd to the view,
Not half so dang'rous, or so foul, as you.
Queen.   Unhappy Wretched Woman that I am,
And you unworthy of a Husband's name?
Do you not blush?——
King.   Yes Madam for your shame.
Blush too my Judgment e're should prove so faint,
To let me chuse a Devil for a Saint.
When first I saw, and lov'd, that tempting eye,
The Fiend within the flame I did not spy;
But still ran on and Cherish't my desires:
For heav'nly Beams mistook Infernal fires.
Such raging fires, as you have since thought fit
Alone my Son, my Son's hot Youth, should meet.
Oh Vengeance, Vengeance!——
Queen.   ——Poor Ungen'rous King!
How mean's the Soul from which such thoughts must spring!
Was it for this I did so late submit,
To let you whine and languish at my feet?
When with false Oaths you did my heart beguile,
And proffer'd all your Empire for a smile.
Then, then, my freedom 'twas I did resign,
Though you still swore you would preserve it mine.
And still it shall be so: For from this hour
I vow to hate, and never see you more.
Nay frown not *Philip*, for you soon shall know
I can resent and rage as well as you.

King.   By Hell her pride's as Raging as her lust:
A Guard there—Seize the Queen——[*Enter Guard.*

Enter Carlos *and Intercepts the Guard.*

D. Carl.   ——Hold Sir be Just.
First look on me whom once You call'd your Son.
A Title I was alwaies proud to own.
King.   Good Hea'vn to merit this what have I done?
That he too dares before my sight appear.
D. Carl.   Why Sir, where is the Cause that I should fear?
Bold in my Innocence, I come to know
The reason, why you use this Princess so.
King.   Sure I shall find some way to raise this siege:
He talks as if 'twere for his Priviledge.
Foul ravisher of all my Honour hence:
But stay: Guards with the Queen secure the Prince.
Wherefore in my Revenge should I be slow?
Now in my reach, I'l dash 'em at a Blow.

Enter D. John *of* Austria *and others.*

D.J.   I come Great Sir, with wonder here, to see
Your rage grown up to this Extremity
Against your beauteous Queen, and Loyal Son.
What is't that they merit Chains have done?
Or is't your own wild Jealousie alone?
King.   Oh *Austria* thy vain Enquiry Cease,
If thou hast any value for thy peace;
My mighty Wrongs so loud an accent bear;
'Twould make thee miserable but to hear.
D.Carl.   Father, if I may dare to call you so,
Since now I doubt if I'm your Son or no:
As you have seal'd my doom I may Complain.
King.   Will then that Monster dare to speak again?
D. Carl.   Yes: dying men should not their thoughts disguise;
And since You take such Joy in Cruelties;
E're of my death the new delight begin,

Be pleas'd to hear how cruel You have been.
Time was that we were smil'd on by our fate,
You not Unjust, nor I unfortunate.
Then, then, I was your Son, and you were glad
To hear my early praise was talk't abroad.
Then Loves dear sweets you to me would display,
Told me where this rich Beauteous Treasure lay,
And how to gain't instructed me the way.
I came, and saw, and lov'd, and blest you for't.
But then when Love had seal'd her to my heart,
You Violently tore her from my side:
And 'cause my Bleeding Wound I could not hide,
But still some pleasure to behold her took:
You now will have my life but for a look.
Wholly forgetting all the pains I bore,
Your heart with envious Jealousie boyles ore,
'Cause I can love no less, and you no more....

A Banquet then of blood since you design,
Yet you may satisfie your self with mine.
I love the Queen, I have confest 'tis true:
Proud too to think I love her more than you;
Though she by Heav'n is clear—but I indeed
Have been unjust, and do deserve to bleed.
There were no lawless thoughts that I did want,
Which Love had pow'r to ask, or Beauty grant.
Tho' I ne're yet found hopes to raise 'em on,
For she did still preserve her Honours Throne:
And dash'd the bold aspiring Devil's down.
If to her Cause you do not credit give
Fondly against your happiness you'l strive,
As some loose Heav'n because they won't believe.
Queen.   Whilst Prince, my preservation you design,
Blot not your Virtue to add more to mine.
The clearness of my truth I'd not have shown,
By any other light besides its Own,
No Sir, he through despair all this has said,
And owns Offenses which he never made.
Why should you think that I would do you wrong?

Must I needs be Unchast because I'm young?
King.   Unconstant Wav'ring heart why heav'st thou so?
I shiver all, and know not what I do.
I who e're now have Armies led to fight,
Thought War a Sport, and danger a delight:
Whole Winter nights stood under Heav'ns wide roof
Daring my foes: now am not Beauty proof.
Oh turn away those Basilisks thy Eyes,
Th'Infection's fatal, and who sees 'em, dyes.   [*Goes away.*

Appendix F: The Lure of Switzerland

1. **Travels in Switzerland, and in the Country of the Grisons: In A Series of Letters to William Melmoth, Esq.** (1778, 1789), by **William Coxe.**

[William Coxe's epistolary narrative of his travels in Switzerland was widely read in England, and was reprinted several times. His descriptions of Switzerland inspired William Wordsworth's *Descriptive Sketches* (1793), as well as Godwin, who occasionally borrowed whole phrases from Coxe in composing the description of Lake Uri in *Fleetwood*.]

from Letter 25. The Lake of Lucern—Gerisau—Schweitz—Origin of the Helvetic Confederacy—William Tell—Altdorf.

The Waldstætter See, or Lake of the Four cantons, is, from the sublimity as well as variety of scenery, perhaps the finest body of water in Switzerland. The upper branch, or the lake of Lucern, is in the form of a cross, the sides of which stretch from Kussnach to Dallenwal, a small village near Stantz. It is bounded towards the town of Lucern by cultivated hills sloping gradually to the water, contrasted on the opposite side by an enormous mass of barren and craggy rocks. Mount Pilate rises boldly from the lake, and is perhaps one of the highest mountains in Switzerland, if estimated from its base, and not from the level of the sea.

... Having re-imbarked at Brunnen, we soon entered the third branch, or the lake of Uri; the scenery of which is so grand, that its impression will never be erased from my mind. Imagine yourself a deep and narrow lake about nine miles in length, bordered on both sides with rocks uncommonly wild and romantic, and, for the most part, perpendicular; with forests of beech and pine growing down their sides to the very edge of the water. On the right hand, upon our first entrance, a detached piece of rock, at a small distance from the shore, engaged our attention: it is wholly composed of stones of the size and shape of bricks, so as to appear quite artificial. The same kind of natural masonry may be observed in the lofty cliffs which impend over this lake, not far from Brunnen. It rises to about sixty feet in height; is covered with underwood and shrubs, and reminded me of those crags that shoot up in the Fall of the Rhine near Schaffhausen: but here the lake was as smooth as crystal, and the silent solemn gloom which reigned in this place was not less awful and affecting than the tremendous roaring of the cataract. Somewhat further, upon the highest point of the Seelisberg, we observed a small chapel that seemed inaccessible; and below it, the little village of Gruti, near which the three heroes of Switzerland are said to have taken reciprocal oaths of fidelity, when they planned the famous revolution.

On the opposite side appears the chapel of William Tell, erected in honour of that hero, upon the very spot where he leaped from the boat in which he was conveying as a prisoner to Kussnach. It is built upon a rock projecting into the lake under a hanging wood: a situation amid scenes so strikingly awful, as must strongly affect even the most dull and torpid imagination! On the inside of this chapel, the several actions of William Tell are coarsely painted. While we were viewing them, we observed the countenances of our watermen glistening with exultation, as they related, with much spirit and sensibility, the cruelties of Gesler, governor of Uri, and the intrepid behaviour of their glorious deliverer. Indeed I have frequently remarked with pleasure the national enthusiasm which generally prevails in this country, and greatly admired the fire and animation with which the people discourse of those famous men among their ancestors, to whom they are indebted for that happy state of independence they now enjoy. This laudable spirit is continually supported and encouraged by the numerous statues, and other memorials, of the antient Swiss heroes, common in every town and village. Among these, Tell is the most distinguished, and seems to be the peculiar favourite of the common people: the reason is obvious; for his story partakes greatly of the marvellous.

2. *History of A Six Weeks' Tour* (1817), by Mary Wollstonecraft Shelley and Percy Bysshe Shelley.

[In the summer of 1814, Godwin's daughter Mary Wollstonecraft Godwin ran away from home on an "elopement" tour with the already-married poet Percy Bysshe Shelley. They were accompanied by Mary's step-sister, Claire Clairmont, and the three spent approximately six weeks travelling together through France, Switzerland, Germany, and Holland, before financial difficulties necessitated their return to England. Despite the fact that this situation created a deep breach in Godwin's relationship with his daughter and with Shelley, much of the young party's tour seems to have been planned in deference to Godwin's works. Their visit to Lake Uri, for example, seems to have been inspired by the importance of this highly picturesque location as a setting in *Fleetwood*.[1]]

… The money we had brought with us from Paris was nearly exhausted, but we obtained about £38. in silver upon discount from one of the bankers of the city, and with this we resolved to journey towards the lake of Uri, and seek in that romantic and interesting country some cottage where we might dwell in peace and solitude. Such were our dreams, which we should probably have realized, had it not been for the deficiency of that indispensible article money, which obliged us to return to England.

A Swiss, whom S*** met at the post-office, kindly interested himself in our affairs, and assisted us to hire a *voiture* to convey us to Lucerne, the principal town of the lake of that name, which is connected with the lake of Uri. The journey to this place occupied rather more than two days. The country was flat and dull, and, excepting that we now and then caught a glimpse of the divine Alps, there was nothing in it to interest us. Lucerne promised better things, and as soon as we arrived (August 23d) we hired a boat, with which we proposed to coast the lake until we should meet with some suitable habitation, or

---

1   See Jeanne Moskal, ed. *History of a Six Weeks' Tour, The Novels and Selected Works of Mary Shelley*, Nora Crook, gen. ed. (London: Pickering, 1996), vol. 8, 29n., 30n., 33n.

perhaps, even going to Altorf, cross Mont St. Gothard, and seek in the warm climate of the country to the south of the Alps an air more salubrious, and a temperature better fitted for the precarious state of S★★★'s health, than the bleak region to the north. The lake of Lucerne is encompassed on all sides by high mountains that rise abruptly from the water;—sometimes their bare fronts descend perpendicularly and cast a black shade upon the waves;—sometimes they are covered with thick wood, whose dark foliage is interspersed by the brown bare crags on which the trees have taken root. In every part where a glade shews itself in the forest it appears cultivated, and cottages peep from among the woods. The most luxuriant islands, rocky and covered with moss, and bending trees, are sprinkled over the lake. Most of these are decorated by the figure of a saint in wretched waxwork.

The direction of this lake extends at first from east to west, then turning a right angle, it lies from north to south; this latter part is distinguished in name from the other, and is called the lake of Uri. The former part is also nearly divided midway, where the jutting land almost meets, and its craggy sides cast a deep shadow on the little strait through which you pass. The summits of several of the mountains that enclose the lake to the south are covered by eternal glaciers; of one of these, opposite Brunen, they tell the story of a priest and his mistress, who, flying from persecution, inhabited a cottage at the foot of the snows. One winter night an avalanche overwhelmed them, but their plaintive voices are still heard in stormy nights, calling for succour from the peasants.

Brunen is situated on the northern side of the angle which the lake makes, forming the extremity of the lake of Lucerne. Here we rested for the night, and dismissed our boatmen. Nothing could be more magnificent than the view from this spot. The high mountains encompassed us, darkening the waters; at a distance on the shores of Uri we could perceive the chapel of Tell, and this was the village where he matured the conspiracy which was to overthrow the tyrant of his country; and indeed this lovely lake, these sublime mountains, and wild forests, seemed a fit cradle for a mind aspiring to high adventure and heroic deeds. Yet we saw no glimpse of his spirit in his present countrymen. The Swiss appeared to us then, and experience has confirmed our opinion, a people slow of comprehension and of action; but habit has made them unfit for slavery, and they would, I have little doubt, make a brave defence against any invader of their freedom.

Such were our reflections, and we remained until late in the evening on the shores of the lake conversing, enjoying the rising breeze, and contemplating with feelings of exquisite delight the divine objects that surrounded us.

Appendix G: Contemporary Reviews

1. From the *Critical Review,* Third Series, 4 (April 1805), 383–91.

WE opened, with a mixture of curiosity, doubt, and satisfaction, the book before us; curious to see the contents of a new novel from the extra-ordinary pen of Mr. Godwin; doubtful of its tendency; and satisfied that it would prove in some degree entertaining. But although upon perusal, our fears of what might be the nature of its principles were totally removed, we confess our curiosity was little gratified by the common incidents of the life of Fleetwood. Mr. Godwin certainly succeeds best in the description of astonishing and uncommon scenes. His mind is not of that playful cast, suited to detect and expose, with good-humoured ridicule, the absurd conduct of the characters in ordinary life. His heroes have ever stood alone in the world, beings of his own creative imagination, isolated by a dissimilarity of feeling and of passion from their fellow-men, and either on this account voluntary exiles, or excluded by unmerited odium from society. These are creatures who cannot move with dignity through the uninteresting routine of vulgar incidents; they must become, to excite our interest, the objects of persecution, or of awful wonder; hemmed in by a magic circle of their own, uninterrupted by trifling mortals, and solely occupied in the fulfilment of their great and peculiar destinies. With anxiety, kept up by a succession of undeserved misfortunes, we followed Caleb Williams to the catastrophe of Falkland; but we execrated the vile insinuations thrown out, in the course of the story, against our noble code of laws. We were fascinated, in spite of our judgment, with the miraculous inventions of St. Leon; and pleased with the *palinodia*[1] there published, of some obnoxious opinions before delivered to the world, we believe hastily, rather than with a foresight of the dangerous inferences that might be drawn from

---

1   A work in which an author recants something professed in an earlier work.

them.[1] But the tale of "the new Man of Feeling," as Mr. Godwin apprizes us in its preface, is almost devoid of any but the
most usual occurrences in the lives of those who rank in the
upper stations of the middle order of society. The hero is
brought up in seclusion by a worthy father; imbibes a fondness
for solitary rambles and reveries; and grows abstracted from the
consideration of common things by the daily sight of the stupendous phenomena of nature, among the mountains and
cataracts of Wales. This is a grand beginning; but alas! producing *fumum ex fulgore*.[2] The scene is then removed to Oxford.
Here our recluse degenerates into an idle gownsman, and mixes
in the stale unprofitable sports of his companions. One of their
"tricks upon freshmen" is recorded; the jest lies in making an
unhappy poet believe he is held in the highest admiration by
the society, and entrapping him into a public reading of his virgin tragedy upon the fifth labour of Hercules, the cleansing of
the Augean stables. This is told with much humour, which
pleased us the more as it was unexpected in the pages of Mr.
Godwin. It is possible that he has rather disdained attempts of
this kind, than felt unequal to them.—

The scene now changes to Paris, where Fleetwood is
involved in the debauchery of the latter years of the reign of
Louis XV. Here we have to mention a duty Mr. Godwin has
never violated; that of avoiding all occasions of indecent language in the choice of his scenes and incidents. Even where he
is attracted by the detail of his story towards danger, he slightly
passes over the subject, and may be allowed in its fullest extent,
the following honest boast. p. 126. "I write no book, that shall
tend to nourish the pruriency of the debauched, or shall excite
one painful emotion, one instant of debate, in the bosom of the
virtuous and the chaste." It were to be wished that this could be
said with equal truth of all the novelists of the present day. We
have, however, to object to some expressions of Mr. Godwin,
where he has trespassed even in more serious matters—talking

---

1   In his focus on his hero's relationship with his wife and children in his 1799 novel
     St. Leon, Godwin recanted some of the controversial remarks he had made on the
     institution of marriage in *Enquiry Concerning Political Justice*.
2   "Smoke from a flash of lightning."

of the education his father gave him, the *new Man of Feeling* says,

"He hired me a private tutor. I was perhaps sufficiently fortunate in the character of the person who was thus established in our house. He was not a clergyman. He did not shackle my mind with complex and unintelligible creeds, nor did he exhibit that monastic coldness and squareness of character which is too frequently the result of clerical celibacy. He was however a man of morals, and of religion. But religion was distinguished in his mind more by sentiments than opinions. Whatever related to his conduct toward God or man was regulated principally by a desire to satisfy his own conscience and obtain his own approbation, not to maintain a certain character and name in the world."

This is intolerably illiberal; both the attack and the manner of it. Gibbon has taught our writers this detestable mode of implication; this undermining of one character, by saying what another was not.

Mr. Godwin, without intending it, has described very nobly the arraignment of our blessed Lord at the tribunal of injustice:

"Innocence is nothing, if it is merely innocence. It is a guileless nature, when impleaded at a stern and inhuman bar, when dragged out to contumely and punishment, when lifting up its head in conscious honour, when heaven itself seems to interpose to confound the malice of men, and declares, This is the virtue that I approve! there, there is presented to us the most ravishing spectacle that earth can boast." Vol. III. p. 341.

But in page 12, vol. ii. there is a very improper passage upon this most sacred of all subjects:

"The offerings of gold, frankincense and myrrh, presented by the wise men of the East, were not more acceptable to the mother of Jesus, than this homely roll and butter were to me at this moment."

The levity of this comparison is unpardonable.

Our hero now joins the friend of his family in Switzerland, where this venerable old man endeavours to reclaim him from his vices. He does not adopt the old method of admonition; but, with (at first) some impenetrability of design, he chuses a beautiful evening for an excursion on the lake of Uri; he warms the mind of the young enthusiast (as Fleetwood suddenly becomes again, though not unnaturally, from being restored to scenes similar to those in which he spent his infancy) with the contemplation of the rocks, where was kindled the flame of liberty that spread over Switzerland; but we will extract the whole passage, and let Mr. Godwin speak for himself, for we think he never spoke with better purpose.

[A long passage is given from Volume I, Chapter 9, in which Fleetwood is told of his father's death.]

We have to except the above from what we said concerning the commonness of the scenes in which the character of Fleetwood is developed. The episode also of the early life of M. Ruffigny; where he sets out for Paris from Lyons, alone, and on foot, at nine years of age, is sufficiently improbable. In the last volume too there are some striking situations—particularly that in which the wife of Fleetwood is found (page 81) and the atrocious character Mr. Godwin has called "Gifford," is certainly as boldly drawn as the warmest admirer of the marvellous and horrible could desire. Of the softer scenes, the one at the conclusion of the second volume is very beautifully painted; it is upon the marriage of Fleetwood to a very amiable girl, the daughter of a deceased friend, bequeathed to the care of this *new* man of feeling, who uses her most cruelly from an unjust suspicion of her infidelity instilled into him by his perfidious kinsman Gifford, and is afterwards reconciled to her: but we have already made an extract of greater length, from a work of so small importance as a novel, than we should have done, had it not proceeded from the pen of so well-known an author as Mr. Godwin. We wish we could present our readers with two further extracts; one relating to the character of Rousseau, and the other strongly descriptive of Mr. Godwin's idea of the proper style of novel-writing; which is not to make us acquainted with his hero by a minute relation of the incidents of his life, as Fielding and others have done; but by favouring us with his soliloquies and reflections upon men and manners.[1] His chief characters are all metaphysicians; who are reasoning when they should be acting; but who reason in so extraordinary a manner, that they rivet our attention. In Vol. II. page 153-54, the reader will find what we think rather a tantalizing picture of what Mr. Godwin *might* have done, had he pleased, in this book.

Of Rousseau too we are told (vol. ii. p. 179) that our hero was in possession of several curious anecdotes, but they are withheld from us; for Mr. Godwin confines himself to *"generals"*—to drawing character, not by the exposure of its own traits, but by presuming that they exist, and animadverting upon them.

The story of Fleetwood is chiefly intended, we conclude, to inculcate "the folly of ill-sorted marriages, in point of age." The remarks upon the force of habits, unalterably fixed by the peculiarity of an early education in solitude, and working upon a naturally selfish disposition during a long single life, are forcible and judicious—old things well repeated. But we are at a loss to conceive why a man, who turns misanthrope from disappointment, who is most savage in jealousy without caring to ascertain the cause of it, can be called the *New Man of Feeling*, unless in absolute contradistinction to the old.

Upon the whole, we think the present publication likely to add much to Mr. Godwin's literary character, from the entertainment its story will, we are confident, afford to a numerous class of readers, and from the improved purity of the author's style. Nor will there be wanting those, we hope, in a candid public, who will, in justice, welcome "Fleetwood" the more

---

1   Henry Fielding (1707-54), English novelist known mainly for *Tom Jones* (1749).

warmly, as it is a perfectly harmless book, coming from the pen of an individual, upon whose more early writings that justice has pronounced the severest censure.

2. From the *Edinburgh Review* 6 (April 1805), 182–93, by Walter Scott.

WHOEVER has read Caleb Williams, and there are probably few, even amongst those addicted to graver studies, who have not perused that celebrated work, must necessarily be eager to see another romance form the hand of the same author. Of this anxiety we acknowledge we partook to a considerable degree; not, indeed, that we had any great pleasure in recollecting the conduct and nature of the story; for murders, and chains, and dungeons, and indictments, trial and execution, have no particular charms for us, either in fiction or in reality. Neither is it on account of the moral proposed by the author, which, in direct opposition to that of the worthy chaplain of Newgate, seems to be, not that a man guilty of theft or murder is in some danger of being hanged; but that, by a strange concurrence of circumstances, he may be regularly conducted to the gallows for theft or murder which he has never committed. There is nothing instructive or consolatory in this proposition, when taken by itself; and if intended as a reproach upon the laws of this country, it is equally applicable to all human judicatures, whose judges can only decide according to evidence, since the Supreme Being has reserved to himself the prerogative of searching the heart and of trying the reins. But, although the story of Caleb Williams be unpleasing, and the moral sufficiently mischievous, we acknowledge we have met with few novels which excited a more powerful interest. Several scenes are painted with the savage force of Salvator Rosa;[1] and, while the author pauses to reason upon the feelings and motives of the actors, our sense of the fallacy of his arguments, of the improbability of his facts, and of the frequent inconsistency of his characters, is lost in the solemnity and suspense with which we expect the evolution of the tale of mystery. After Caleb

---

1 Salvator Rosa (1615-73), Italian painter known for his wild, savage landscapes.

Williams, it would be injustice to Mr. Godwin to mention St. Leon, where the marvellous is employed too frequently to excite wonder, and the terrible is introduced till we have become familiar with terror. The description of Bethlem Gabor, however, recalled to our mind the author of Caleb Williams; nor, upon the whole, was the romance such as could have been written by quite an ordinary pen. These preliminary remarks are not entirely misplaced, as will appear from the following quotation from the preface to Fleetwood.

> "One caution I have particularly sought to exercise: 'not to repeat myself.' Caleb Williams was a story of very surprising and uncommon events, but which were supposed to be entirely within the laws and established course of nature, as he operates in the planet we inhabit. The story of St. Leon is of the miraculous class; and its design, to 'mix human feelings and passions with incredible situations, and thus render them impressive and interesting.'"[1]
>
> "Some of those fastidious readers—they may be classed among the best friends an author has, if their admonitions are judiciously considered—who are willing to discover those faults which do not offer themselves to every eye, have remarked, that both these tales are in a vicious style of writing; that Horace has long ago decided, that the story we cannot believe, we are, by all the laws of criticism, called upon to hate; and that even the adventures of the honest secretary, who was first heard of ten years ago, are so much out of the usual road, that not one reader in a million can ever fear they will happen to himself." Vol. I. Pref.

Moved by these considerations, Mr Godwin has chosen a tale of domestic life, consisting of such incidents as usually occur in the present state of society, diversified only by ingenuity of selection, and novelty of detail. How far he has been successful, will best appear from a sketch of the story.

---

1   The subject of *St. Leon* concerns the narrator's involvement with two supernatural phenomena: the philosopher's stone and the elixir of life.

[Scott provides a lengthy and detailed summary of the novel's plot through Fleetwood's marriage to Mary Macneil.]

... Fleetwood and Mary are at length married; and from this marriage, as we have already noticed, commences any interest which we take in the history of the former. Indeed it can hardly be called a history, which has neither incident nor novelty of remark to recommend it, consisting entirely of idle and inflated declamations upon the most common occurrences of human life. The union of Mary and Fleetwood, considering the youth and variable spirits of the former, and the age and confirmed prejudices of the latter, promises a more interesting subject of speculation. Upon their arrival in Wales, the reader is soon made sensible that a man of feeling, upon Mr Godwin's system, is the most selfish animal in the universe. We appeal to our fair readers if this is not a just conclusion, from the following account of the matrimonial disputes of this ill-matched pair.

[Scott describes Fleetwood's irrational anger in response to Mary's taking over his favorite closet, and quotes from the novel concerning Mary's sleepwalking.]

... This kind of partial derangement of the intellect is very strikingly described. It has not, however, the merit of novelty, as the same idea occurs in the licentious novel of Faublas, written by the famous Louvet.[1] At the conclusion of that work the hero tells us, that still when the south wind whistled, or the thunder rolled, his disordered imagination presented to him the scene which had passed at the death of his mistress; he again heard the sound of the midnight bell, and the voice of the centinel who pointed to the river, and coldly said, "She is there." We quote, from memory, a work which, for many reasons, we would not choose to read again; but we think that this is the import of the passage, and it considerably resembles that in Fleetwood, though the idea in the latter is more prolonged and brought out.

---

1   Jean Baptiste Louvet de Couvray, *The Life and Adventures of the Chevalier de Faublas* (1789-90; translated into English 1793).

[Scott concludes his plot summary and quotes a lengthy passage from the account of the mock wedding that Fleetwood arranges for the wax effigies of Mary and Kenrick.]

... Having occupied so much room in detailing the story, we have but little left for animadversion. The incidents during the two first volumes, are chiefly those of the common life of a man of fashion; and all that is remarkable in the tale is the laboured extravagance of sentiment which is attached to these ordinary occurrences. There is no attempt to describe the minuter and finer shades of feeling; none of that high finishing of description, by which the most ordinary incidents are rendered interesting: on the contrary, the effect is always sought to be brought out by the application of the inflated language of high passion. It is no doubt true, that a man of sensibility will be deeply affected by what appears trifling to the rest of mankind; a scene of distress or of pleasure will make a deeper impression upon him than upon another; and it is precisely in this respect that he differs from the rest of mankind. But a man who is transported with rage, with despair, with anger, and all the furious impulses of passion, upon the most common occurrences of life, is not a man of sentiment, but a madman; and, far from sympathising with his feelings, we are only surprised at his having the liberty of indulging them beyond the precincts of Bedlam.

In the third volume, something of a regular story commences, and the attention of the reader becomes fixed by the narrative. But the unnatural atrocity of Gifford, and the inadequate means by which he is so nearly successful, render this part of the tale rather improbable. The credulity of Fleetwood is unnecessarily excessive, and might have been avoided by a more artful management of incident.

But we have another and a more heavy objection to him, considered as a man of feeling. We have been accustomed to associate with our ideas of this character the amiable virtues of a Harley,[1] feeling deeply the distresses of others, and patient,

---

1 The highly sentimental hero of Henry Mackenzie's *The Man of Feeling* (1771).

though not insensible of his own. But Fleetwood, through the whole three volumes which bear his name, feels absolutely and exclusively for one individual, and that individual is Fleetwood himself. Indeed he is at great pains, in various places, to tell us that he had been uncontrouled in his youth, was little accustomed to contradiction, and could not brook any thing which interfered either with his established habits, or the dispositions of the moment. Accordingly his despair for the loss of his two French mistresses, is the despair of a man who loses something which he thinks necessary to his happiness, and in a way not very soothing to his feelings: But as we understand him, he can no more be properly said to be in love with either of these fair ladies, than a hungry man, according to Fielding's comparison, can be said to be in love with a shoulder of Welsh mutton. In like manner, his pursuit after happiness, through various scenes, is uniformly directed by the narrow principle of self-gratification; there is no aspiration towards promoting the public advantage, or the happiness of individuals; Mr Fleetwood moves calmly forward in quest of what may make Mr Fleetwood happy; and, like all other egotists of this class, he providentially misses his aim. But it is chiefly in the wedded state that his irritable and selfish habits are most completely depicted. With every tie, moral and divine, which can bind a man to the object of his choice, or which could withhold him from acts of unkindness or cruelty, he commences and carries on a regular system for subjecting all her pleasures to the controul of his own, and every attempt on her part to free herself from this constraint, produces such scenes of furious tyranny, as at the beginning nearly urge her to distraction, and finally drive her an outcast from society. In short, the new Man of Feeling, in his calm moments a determined egotist, is, in his state of irritation, a frantic madman, who plays on a barrel-organ at a puppet-shew, till he and the wooden dramatis personæ are all possessed by the foul fiend Hibbertigibbet, who presides over *mopping* and *mowing*. We close the book with the painful reflection, that Mary is once more subjected to his tyranny; and our only hope is, that a certain Mr Scarborough, a very peremptory and overbearing person, who assists at the denouement, may, in case of need, be a good hand at putting on a strait waistcoat.

3. From *The Anti-Jacobin Review and Magazine* 21 (August 1805), 337-58.

WE were sorry to find Mr. Godwin descending from the higher and more dignified walks of literature, to engage again in the manufacture of novels. This line of composition, is, at present, so degraded by the dulness or stupidity of the scribblers who deal in it, that men of talents and sense regard it as disreputable. To this charge, we are sensible, there are many exceptions; and, by those who have read Mr. Godwin's former works, it will readily be supposed, that no production can come from his pen, without exhibiting unequivocal marks of a strong and vigorous mind; yet, this novel, we must say, greatly disappointed us. It contains, undoubtedly, many splendid passages, which, in point of conception, as well as of expression, bespeak the hand of a master, but, as a whole, it hardly rises to mediocrity. "One caution," says the author, "I have particularly sought to exercise: not to repeat myself." It is possible, we think, that this very caution may have fettered his powers, and obstructed his success. It is certain, that the present work will bear no comparison with Caleb Williams; for, though the tendency and design of that publication were mischievous in the extreme, it yet displayed abilities of very high consideration.

The "New Man of Feeling" can scarcely be said to have any plot; and no interest whatever is excited by the story till we arrive at the last volume. The two first are filled with strained declamation on a variety of subjects, and the general tone is strongly indicative of a gloomy imagination, which loves to dwell on the disagreeable occurrences of life. The conclusion is absurd to the last degree. The author, indeed, confesses in his preface, "the inability [which] he found to weave a catastrophe such as he desired, out of the ordinary incidents" to which he confined himself. If this was really the case, Mr. Godwin must be possessed of less ingenuity than the world gives him credit for. The difficulty, we think, might have been easily surmounted, and the absurdity avoided. But to the catastrophe we have a more serious objection than even that of absurdity. We object to it in a moral view, as will be fully stated in the proper place; at present, we proceed, in general, to observe, that Mr. Godwin seems to have formed a most erroneous opinion of his own performance. "Multitudes," he says, "of readers have themselves passed through the very incidents [which] I relate; but, for the most part, no work has hitherto recorded them. If I have told them truly," he continues, "I have added somewhat to the stock of books, which should enable a recluse, shut up in his closet, to form an idea of what is passing in the world." (Pref. ix. x.) "The following story," he says, in another place, "consists of such adventures, as, for the most part have occurred to at least one half of the Englishmen now existing, who are of the same rank of life as my hero." (P. vii.) Now, we are decidedly of another mind, for some of these adventures are such, we are persuaded, as never occurred to a human being; and the work, instead of teaching the recluse to form an idea of the world, will tend only to mislead him. It is, indeed, itself, at least in appearance, the work of a recluse, who has studied the world in his own reveries, and not in the busy haunts of men. The truth is, that the views of life and manners exhibited in these volumes, are, in various instances, unnatural and false; while the sentiments and actions ascribed to the principal character, are, in many cases, not only extravagant, but ridiculous. Our author, however, seems fully convinced that his sketches are copied from real life, in proof of which, he observes, as follows:— "Most Englishmen of the same rank of life as my hero have been at college, and shared in college excesses; most of them have afterwards run a certain gauntlet of dissipation; most of them have married; and, I am afraid, there are a few of the married tribe, who have not, at some time or other, had certain small understandings with their wives." (P. viii.) This is all very true, undoubtedly, yet, it does not by any means, therefore follow, that these gentlemen have had the same adventures with Fleetwood. In cases of this kind the colouring is every thing, and our author's pictures are greatly overcharged; they are, besides, not unfrequently, so distorted, as to be absolute caricatures. With regard to the language, though it is often energetic, and sometimes sublime, it is occasionally mean, now and then ungrammatical, and, in places almost innumerable, disgraced by a kind of slovenly carelessness, which we, certainly, should not have looked for from a writer of Mr. Godwin's education and taste.

Mr. Godwin may think the observation hypercritical, but we cannot help objecting to the *title* of his book. We conceive it, indeed, to be a capital misnomer. By "A Man of Feeling," is generally understood a man of warm and active benevolence, whose heart is exquisitely sensible to the distresses of every being around him, and whose hand is ever ready, as far as his influence extends, to alleviate or relieve them. This, we think, is the common acceptation of the terms; and to those who have read (as almost every person has) Mackenzie's little work, that acceptation has been rendered little less than sacred, by the force of strong association; but, if the reader expects to find any resemblance between Fleetwood and Harley, he will soon discover his mistake, for these gentlemen are of families totally distinct, and are as unlike as two human creatures can well be. The former, it is true, has a superabundance of feeling, but it is feeling of a very contracted kind, and confined to very few objects. "This man of feeling feels but *for himself.*" In short, Fleetwood is a most disgusting egotist, and one of the most selfish characters which it is possible to conceive. To every thing which concerns himself, he is, indeed, all alive; the most trifling inconvenience disconcerts and irritates him, but he bears, with the utmost composure and philosophy, such unpleasant circumstances in the lot of others, as do not touch his own comforts.

[After quoting the concluding paragraph from Godwin's preface, regarding his stance on marriage, the reviewer continues.]

… Among those who are thus magisterially admonished for having made Mr. Godwin's "supposed inconsistencies the favourite object of their research," it is not at all impossible, we think, that we ourselves may have the honour of being comprehended. In his Life of Chaucer, we certainly thought that we perceived good symptoms of amendment in Mr. Godwin's sentiments with regard to marriage, and we took the liberty to congratulate him on the change. Our remarks, however, on that occasion, proceeded from no impertinent delight which we took in hunting for Mr. Godwin's inconsistencies, but from the unaffected gratification which we felt on observing, as we supposed, a man, whose talents we respect, recovering from the pernicious influence of prejudice and paradox. It seems, indeed, that we were greatly deceived, and that Mr. Godwin does not thank us for our praise. The obvious intention of the foregoing paragraph is, to inform his friends, that he has, in no respect, abjured his original principles, and that those have wronged him who have hinted at such an alteration in his creed. He is afraid, it would appear, of losing, in consequence of such an imputation, his "*claim to public distinction and favour.*" Mr. Godwin may, like many other men of genius, have indulged the bewitching dreams of ambition; he may have aspired to the glorious destiny of founding a sect, and of so establishing a wide and permanent dominion over the minds of men. Of all the objects of ambition, this, perhaps, is the most fascinating; and we well remember to have heard, some years ago, a very warm admirer of Mr. Godwin assert, that his incomparable writings must infallibly, in time, have such an effect; but if either he or his admirers expect that this distinguished honour is to be derived from the "Enquiry concerning Political Justice," we are convinced that their hopes are rather too sanguine. The principles of that work have become unfashionable, and they are not likely, we conceive, to be soon revived. They were not, in truth, calculated for taking a lasting hold on the grave good sense of Britons, and, accordingly, the book has sunk into oblivion, from which all its acuteness and ingenuity have been unable to preserve it. Mr. Godwin, notwithstanding, we really think, has talents which qualify him both to merit and to obtain "public favour and distinction;" but, if these be his aim, he must renounce the maxims which he formerly maintained in his Political Justice; he must exert himself to strengthen, instead of dissolving, the obligations which hold society together.

With respect to his former notions of marriage, we should, certainly, never have thought of recalling them to the minds of our readers, if he had not himself, in this curious passage, taken pains to inform us, that he still considers them as just and correct. He inquired, he says, whether marriage, "as it stands described and supported in the *laws of England*," might not be modified to advantage. Mr. Godwin, we understand, was bred a divine. From an author of *that* character, when treating of a subject which occupies so conspicuous a place in the writings of the New Testament, some regard, we think, was due to the *laws of Christ*. We shall not, however, press this consideration; but, certainly, Mr. Godwin must be jesting, when he pretends that, in his proposed modifications of marriage, he had any regard to the laws, we do not say of England, but of any civilized society. "So long," says the author of Political Justice, "as I seek to engross one woman to myself, and to prohibit my neighbour from proving his *superior desert*, I am guilty of the most odious of all monopolies." What species of desert the author wished to establish as the criterion of victory in this interesting dispute, we attempt not to conjecture, but how he conceived such an intercourse between the sexes, as is here contended for, to be, in any sense, *a modification of marriage*, is a problem which we are wholly unable to solve. Such an intercourse, however, it is very clear, is one of those "grand and comprehensive improvements," which were the objects of our author's "discussions and reasonings," and by which he endeavoured, on a great and extensive scale, "to renovate the face of society."

Mr. Godwin, indeed, is for no piddling work, he will either have a general renovation or none. Common moralists consider it as a great point gained, when they are able to reclaim even a few individuals, but our author flies at higher game; he is far from proposing that "each man, for himself, should supersede and trample upon the institutions of the country in which he lives." Were this assertion to be literally and strictly taken, we, for our part, should only be tempted to say, that our ingenuous author was the better entitled to the execration of the public. For nothing, surely, can be more deserving of execration, than the efforts of him who labours, on systematic principles, to introduce universal profligacy. But the truth is, that Mr. Godwin has here thought proper to take the benefit of a little jesuitical evasion, and to indulge himself in language which he has not the best title in the world to use. He has told us himself, in another of his works, called, "Memoirs of the Author of a Vindication of the Rights of Woman," that, at one time, he condescended to act on less elevated views, and to recommend, *by his own example*, (the most powerful, they say, of all recommendations) the very conduct which he here affirms, that he would be "the last man in the world to recommend." He was fortunate enough to meet with a kindred soul, as zealous as himself for *renovating the face of society*, and they were naturally attracted to one another. But "we did not" says Mr. Godwin, with dignified brevity—"WE DID NOT MARRY." We shall be very careful not to speak of this conduct, as "*a pitiful attempt;*" for, when two distinguished philosophers of different sexes, the one an enthusiast for the "Rights of Man," and the other an enthusiast for the "Rights of Woman," come together on any terms, it is, *a priori*, abundantly plain, that there can be nothing *pitiful* about them. Most persons, we believe, indeed, will be ready to allow that this illustrious pair most notoriously "superseded and trampled upon the institutions of the country in which they lived," and to one of them, at least, the practice was not new. But it is not chiefly for the sake of commenting on past transactions, that the circumstance is brought to the reader's recollection; the flimsy and unsubstantial defence, which Mr. Godwin has advanced of his consistency on the subject of marriage, has indeed, unavoidably, suggested them to our remembrance, and we may be permitted to express our regret, that even philosophers are not always superior to the common weaknesses of humanity; their practice, it would seem, is not always exactly in harmony with their principles, and Mr. Godwin, with most other men, may say,

——————"Video meliora proboque,
"Deteriora sequor."[1]

We are now, however, sufficiently convinced of our former egregious want of penetration. We are convinced, that Mr. Godwin entertains as little respect for marriage, as ever he did, at any time of his life; but it may, perhaps, be admitted as some excuse for our mistake, that his late language on the subject

---

1   "What I see and approve of as superior, I later see as inferior."

tended to mislead us, and we have the melancholy satisfaction to know that we have not been the only dupes to that language. "Godwin, once," says a late ingenious author, "talked and wrote loosely of marriage, but even Godwin has recanted." This preface will prove to the learned writer, the danger of trusting implicitly appearances, even the most fair. There is, indeed, in the Memoirs of Mary Wollestonecraft, a passage which may satisfy every reader, that a mind so spiritual as that of Mr. Godwin can never be reconciled to the vulgar and shocking ceremony of marriage. The passage is remarkable, and therefore we insert it:—

"It is difficult to recommend any thing to indiscriminate adoption, contrary to the established rules and prejudices of mankind; but certainly nothing can be so ridiculous upon the face of it, or so contrary to *the genuine march of sentiment*, as to require *the overflowing of the soul to wait upon* a ceremony, and that which, wherever delicacy and imagination exists, is of all things most sacredly private, *to blow a trumpet before it, and to record the moment when it has arrived at its climax*."

In the same publication Mr. Godwin favours us with some information which shews marriage to be no less disgraceful, than it is indelicate. The position will make some of our readers stare, but Mr. Godwin has clearly established the truth of it. After living some time under no other laws, but those "which love has made," he and his sweet partner thought it right to comply with the "institutions of the country in which they lived." "Mary and myself," he says, "supposed that our marriage would place her upon a sure footing *in the calendar of polished society*." But, wonderful to tell! It had a contrary effect. "While she was, and constantly professed to be, *an unmarried mother*, she was fit society for the squeamish and the formal. The moment she acknowledged herself a wife, *and that by a marriage perhaps unexceptionable*, the case was altered." The lady, though, to use her husband's language, "the firmest champion, and, as I strongly suspect, the *greatest ornament* her sex ever had to boast," was avoided; he consoled himself, however, by observing, that "it was only the supporters and the subjects of the unprincipled manners of a court that she lost." With all due deference to Mr. Godwin, we suspect that this contempt is mere pitiful affectation; he was evidently hurt that a marriage with a person so important as himself was not sufficient to wipe off every former stain from the object of his choice, and he modestly seeks to evacuate his spleen at the expence of the most exemplary, as well as most exalted, couple in the kingdom. In this, we conceive, there is not much wisdom; the morals of the great are not, indeed, so correct as they ought to be. But the treatment which Mrs. Godwin received is a proof that they are not yet totally corrupt. The ladies, of whom Mr. Godwin complains, admitted the society of Mary Wollestonecraft, so long as they thought her the wife of Mr. Imlay, but when, by her marriage with another man, it was evident that she had lived with that gentleman in the capacity of *a mistress*, they withdrew their countenance, and their conduct does them honour. From Mr. Godwin's own representation of this woman, it is plain that she was *an abandoned libertine*—A LIBERTINE SYSTEMATICALLY AND ON PRINCIPLE, with whom no modest woman could reputably associate. No wonder, therefore, that even her *unexceptionable marriage* could not wash her clean.

On the whole we shall give Mr. Godwin credit for his present professions with regard to marriage, unless he shall think fit, publicly, to retract them. His expressions of respect for that sacred institution we shall consider as so many involuntary sacrifices, on his part, to the prejudices of his country; as so many vile fetters tyrannically imposed by the unnatural and distempered state of society, which compels an enlightened and ingenuous mind, to speak, with reverence, of that which it abhors. His real opinion seems to be, that marriage is necessarily destructive of happiness; and to inculcate this notion appears to be the direct design of the strange catastrophe which concludes his performance. [Here the reviewer provides a brief synopsis of the events of Volume III.] ... When the parties meet at the end of the work, the "Man of Feeling" exclaims, "I never till now was sensible of half the merits of my wife!" He forgot that she was no longer his *wife*, and that his child was *a bastard*. Yet in this situation, which was so easily avoided, our author leaves them; for no other purpose that we can conceive, except that of suggesting that the happiness which Fleetwood never found in the state of marriage, he cannot miss, though living with the very same woman, when delivered from its oppressive yoke.

[After a thirteen-page plot synopsis, the critic concludes his review by quoting at length from the passage in which Fleetwood destroys the wax effigies of Mary and Kenrick, which he introduces as follows: "We conclude our account of Mr. Godwin's performance, with a pretty long quotation, descriptive of a scene, so perfectly extravagant, that the author, when he wrote it, was, in our opinion, as completely deranged as the madman who is supposed to have acted it."]

4. From the *British Critic* 26 (August 1805), 189–94.

THIS author, in his Preface, says, with reference to his former novels, that, in Fleetwood, he has been careful "not to repeat himself." He has not indeed condemned a man, upon legal evidence, for a crime of which he was not guilty; nor has he, in this domestic tale, introduced supernatural agency; but he has, on more occasions than one, repeated his former profaneness, and mixed with human feelings events which, though not miraculous, are utterly incredible.

[The reviewer summarizes the plot of the novel through the incident in which Mary takes over Fleetwood's favorite closet. Fleetwood's sexual affairs in Paris are said to be "depicted in all those glaring colours which were so generally offensive in the romance of the Monk."[1]]

... We are told, in the title page of the book, that he was a man of feeling; but it is well added, the *new* man of feeling, for the feelings of Fleetwood had no resemblance to those of

---

1 *The Monk* (1796), by Matthew G. Lewis, was a widely read Gothic novel known for its wildly fantastic and salacious incidents.

Harley ... A husband of such feelings was, at the age of forty-five, prepared to become jealous, within reason, of a wife young, beautiful, and lively.

It must be confessed, however, that the conduct of Mary, as here depicted, was not what it ought to have been. Though blameless in itself, and such as a husband of her own age would perhaps have approved, it was not calculated to sooth the heart of such a man as she *knew her husband* to be. Yet, for the jealousy and selfishness of Fleetwood, no apology can be devised; and for the honour of human nature, it is to be hoped that few men exist such slaves to caprice and suspicion as he is represented.

[The plot summary continues.]

Such are the outlines of this novel, which are filled up in many places with great skill. The conclusion is indeed absurd; and the absurdity might have been easily prevented, merely by throwing such obstacles in the way of Gifford's proceedings, as should have delayed the passing of the bill by parliament till the truth had been brought to light. The reader is disappointed likewise at the *abruptness* of the conclusion, before the suborned witnesses were convicted and punished, and Mrs. Fleetwood's innocence made as public as had been her infamy; and it is impossible not to wish that Gifford, before his execution, had in a letter to Fleetwood confessed all his crimes. The novel seems to have been constructed, like Johnson's Rasselas,[1] merely to be a vehicle of moral and prudential reflections; and the reflections which it contains are in general just, though frequently polluted by profane allusions to subjects too sacred to be lightly introduced into works of mere entertainment. The language is occasionally elegant and vigorous; but it is often slovenly, and sometimes ungrammatical; whilst the author, forgetting his own just reflections on the purity of English style,[2] introduces on every occasion French words and phrases which can never

---

1   *The History of Rasselas, Prince of Abyssinia* (1759), a didactic romance by Samuel Johnson.

2   See his Enquiries, part 2, Essay 12. [Reviewer's note]

be assimilated to the idioms of our tongue. Fleetwood is certainly less exceptionable with respect to moral tendency, than either of Mr. Godwin's former novels; but it will add nothing to his fame, and very little to the stock "of books which enable a recluse to form an idea of what is passing in the world;" it is a work which we dare not wholly recommend, nor can severely censure.

5. From the *Monthly Review* 49 (January 1806), 102.

We have here another instance of Mr. Godwin's ability in sketching situations and characters with a peculiar boldness of design, and in eliciting those reflections which assist us in dissecting and analysing the human heart. Fleetwood and Ruffigny are personages evidently drawn to exhibit the author's philosophy, and so far they are both worth of notice: but the former, though laboured with most care, is not so happily delineated as the latter; nor, in the whole fable, is any part so interesting as the Episode which gives the history of Ruffigny. Though the novel professes to be a series of natural incidents, it is far from being of this character towards the conclusion; where the author seems to be embarrassed, and to have surrendered himself to the genius of romance and stage effect. In several instances, he represents Fleetwood, who in general appears to be a man of sound judgment, as acting like a perfect simpleton. It might be the author's object to shew by this character in what various ways man, even in his best state, "disquiets himself in vain," and how, by the leven which insinuates itself into our mental composition, and by our intercourse with society, life becomes disturbed and acidulated. The moral tendency of this detail is unexceptionable; since it shews that, however vice may assume the attire of enjoyment, and the dissipation of the world may mislead us, innocence is the soul of pleasure, and goodness the corner stone of true excellence.

If the state of youth were not a state of natural drunkenness, to which the precepts of wisdom and the admonitions of experience are delivered in vain, we might expect that the delineation of the vicious part of Fleetwood's life would operate as a caution: but passion and madness will despise the lessons of reason; and though author follows author in proclaiming the depressing truth that "vanity of vanities, all is vanity," the rising generation will open their eyes on the world with the gayest visions of hope, and like their predecessors will insist on trying and judging for themselves.

6. From the *European Magazine and London Review* **49 (April 1806), 259-61.** *Strictures on "Fleetwood: or, The New Man of Feeling, by William Godwin."*

MR. GODWIN has distinguished himself as the author of various productions; but he first appeared as a *political inquirer,* and in that character attracted very general attention; but while he obtained the approbation of *some,* the principles he endeavoured to maintain and diffuse were severely, and we think very properly, censured by those who were well affected to the established order of things, and reprobated every attempt to introduce new systems of governments, morals, and manners. We apprehend, however, these political disquisitions have had but little influence over those who prefer the dictates of experience to the innovations of speculation, and who revert with joy and exultation to that period when, with swords in their hands and power at their disposal, the assembled Barons declared their *fixed* determination to preserve *Magna Charta* inviolate, and uttered those memorable words, "*Nolumus leges Angliæ mutari.*"[1] We, who respect their *valour* and admire their *wisdom* more than the sagacity of our modern reformers, cheerfully acquiesce in their decisions, and enjoy with gratitude the invaluable privileges they have bequeathed us. The novel of *Caleb Williams* is another production of Mr. Godwin, and was apparently intended to enforce and exemplify some of those favourite *doctrines* he had endeavoured to inculcate in his Political Justice. But the Life and Age of Geoffrey Chaucer will convey his name safe into the harbour of immortality, *when, on account of the rottenness of the materials* with which they were constructed,

---

1   "Let us refuse to change the laws of England."

his Novels and Political Justice shall have perished in the *Gulf of Oblivion*. The last work that has issued from the *ingenious* pen of Mr. Godwin is "Fleetwood; or, The *New Man of Feeling*:" and on this performance we shall beg leave to offer a few observations. Mr. G. is no *servile imitator*: indeed so truly *original* are the characters he has drawn, that they appear to be actuated by passions, prejudices, and opinions, very different from those which influence the generality of men. It was, however, the boast of Fielding, Smollett,[1] and many other eminent Novelists, that as *they copied* human nature, and painted life in its various and complicated scenes, we might recognise the pictures of many of our friends, and look on their foibles with a smile, and view their virtues with admiration, without injury to their feelings or gratification to their pride. Though we do not pretend to deny that a character similar to Fleetwood may exist, yet we sincerely hope none of our readers are infested with so *troublesome* an acquaintance.

As he is entitled a *Man of Feeling*, we shall now proceed to examine how he sustains by his *actions* the character he has assumed.—The father of Fleetwood is a gentleman who, having amassed a considerable fortune by the honourable occupation of a merchant, retires to an estate in Merionethshire, there to pass the remainder of his days in ease, tranquillity, and peace. Fleetwood, his only son, accompanies him to this retreat, and early imbibes a predilection for the beauty of the place and the romantic scenery with which it is surrounded. The father, anxious that the education of his son should not be neglected, engages a tutor to superintend his studies, who, we are informed, is tolerably acquainted with the Greek and Latin languages, besides being conversant with mathematics, history, &c., and of a character altogether unexceptionable. Here, then, we might naturally expect the *Man of Feeling* would display *innate benevolence*, and evince the sensibility of his *feeling*, by behaving with kindness, gratitude, and respect, to that tutor who appears to have been sincerely desirous of promoting his

---

1   Henry Fielding, cf. note on page 517; Tobias Smollett (1721-71), English novelist who wrote *The Adventures of Roderick Random* (1748) and *The Expedition of Humphry Clinker* (1771), among other works.

welfare.—But no! because Fleetwood, forsooth, (a complete boy,) is sufficiently conceited and presumptuous to imagine, that, in comparison with *his* own *transcendant abilities*, those of his tutor are exceedingly moderate; he conceives the utmost contempt for the man, and treats him with supercilious and haughty disdain. How this is to be reconciled with the conduct of one who pretends to be susceptible of feeling, we are at a loss to determine.

After some time spent in preparation, Mr. Fleetwood resolves to send his son to Oxford. And in accompanying him to that seminary of learning, we might expect to find the Man of Feeling assiduously employed in cultivating his mind, and pursuing his studies with ardour and success. But instead of being thus engaged, he is wasting his time *in riot and dissipation*; instead of devoting the superfluity of his fortune to acts of *beneficence and charity*, in relieving the poor and succoring the oppressed, he supports those of his fellow-collegiates, whose funds do not keep pace with the demands of their *situation*. Of what nature these demands were we are left unacquainted. A college life, in reality, admits of few embarrassments, because the student who is sedulously attentive to improve the opportunities afforded him by the place, has little time to gratify vicious propensities and to satiate imaginary wants. It is natural, therefore, to imagine the gratuitous *offerings of* Fleetwood, were intended to enable his fellow students to participate in all those dissolute enjoyments to which he himself, was addicted. But what shall we think of the understanding, as well as *feeling* of Fleetwood, when we find him thus justifying his excesses: "I was contented to associate with those whose characters I *judged to be finished* already, and whom I persuaded myself, *my* encouragement could not make *worse*; and thus with stretched sophistry, I worked my mind into the belief, that while I yielded to a vicious course, I was doing no harm." Instead of mitigating, does not this increase our indignation at his conduct? We pity the errors of ignorance, but his audacity is insufferable, who at the time of yielding to "a vicious course," expatiates upon its enormity—'tis execrable in one who calls himself a *Man of Feeling*.

[The reviewer discusses the anecdotes of the mocking of Fleetwood's school-fellow, Withers, and of Fleetwood's sexual affairs in France.]

... And what right has Fleetwood to the appellation of a *Man of Feeling*, when he thus blindly follows every impulse of *passion*, and transgresses, without reluctance, the most obvious *principles of religion and morality?*...

[The reviewer describes the scene in which Fleetwood learns of his father's death from Ruffigny, and then closes the review with the signature "T.T.," promising that the review will be concluded in a future Number of the magazine, which has not been located.]

7. From the *Examiner* (16 December 1832), 803-04.

We are indebted to the judgment of the publisher of the "Standard Novels" for the gratification we have received from a revived acquaintance with *Fleetwood*. Of Mr. Godwin's works of fiction, this stands next to *Caleb Williams*, though at a considerable interval. There are faults in the story: after it reaches the climax of distress it becomes improbable, and the author, as he is apt to do, tears a passion to tatters. *Fleetwood* is a prosaic *Othello*. When advanced in manhood and of formed habits, he marries a young and beautiful woman, and desires the impossibility of assimilating her tastes and pursuits to his own, and at the same time, of allowing her youth its customary pleasures. *Fleetwood* is prone to jealousy, and an *Iago* (Gifford) finds no difficulty in exciting his suspicions of his innocent wife, and working him up to a conviction of her guilt. He quits her, directs that she may be turned out of his house, and roams about, wretched or raging, but finally discovers her innocence by the detection of the villainy of *Gifford*, who, impatient for the possession of a legacy, attempts to murder his betrayed benefactor.

Fleetwood is made so easily and bitterly jealous, that the reader is more disposed to anger at his folly than to sympathise with his distress. He is too dull a dupe; and his extravagances even exceed those which are natural to the excitement of cold meditative characters. *Mary*, his wife, is a beautiful design, exquisitely preserved throughout. The great merit of *Fleetwood*, however, is not in the fable, the incidents, or the characters, but in the truth and originality of the observations on men and things with which it abounds.

[The reviewer provides Fleetwood's comments on literary men from Volume II, Chapter 8, as an example of such observations.]

The subjoined remarks on infant labour in a French silk mill are of melancholy interest, and the truth of the picture and the spirit of the reflections will be felt in full force, now that the attention of humanity is earnestly turned to the subject:—

[The review concludes with the quotation of a lengthy passage from Ruffigny's descriptions of his life as a child laborer in the silk mill at Lyon.]

Select Bibliography

Editions

Godwin, William. *Fleetwood: or, The New Man of Feeling*. 3 vols. London: R. Phillips, 1805.

———. *Fleetwood: or, The New Man of Feeling*. London: R. Bentley, 1832.

———. *Fleetwood*. Ed. Pamela Clemit. *Collected Novels and Memoirs of William Godwin*. Mark Philp, gen. ed. 8 vols. London: Pickering & Chatto, 1992.

Critical and Related Works:

Bass, Robert D. *The Green Dragoon: The Lives of Banastre Tarleton and Mary Robinson*. New York: Henry Holt, 1957. 397-98.

Blum, Carol. *Rousseau and the Republic of Virtue*. Ithaca: Cornell UP, 1986.

Boulton, James T. "William Godwin, Philosopher and Novelist." *The Language of Politics in the Age of Wilkes and Burke*. London: Routledge and Kegan Paul, 1963.

Bruhm, Steven. "William Godwin's *Fleetwood*: The Epistemology of the Tortured Body." *Eighteenth-Century Life* 16 (1992): 25-43.

Clemit, Pamela. *The Godwinian Novel: The Rational Fictions of Godwin, Brockden Brown, Mary Shelley*. Oxford: Oxford UP, 1993.

Cobb, Joann P. "Godwin's Novels and *Political Justice*." *Enlightenment Essays* 4 (1973): 15-28.

Dart, Gregory. *Rousseau, Robespierre and Romanticism*. Cambridge: Cambridge UP, 1999.

Furbank, P.N. "Godwin's Novels." *Essays in Criticism* 5 (1955): 214-28.

Handwerk, Gary. "Historical Trauma: Political Theory and Novelistic Practice in William Godwin's Fiction." *Comparative Criticism* 16 (1994): 71-92.

Kelly, Gary. "Convention and Criticism in William Godwin's Early Novels." *Keats-Shelley Journal* 33 (1984): 52-69.

———. *English Fiction of the Romantic Period, 1789-1830*. London: Longman, 1988.

———. *The English Jacobin Novel, 1780-1805*. Oxford: Oxford UP, 1976.

Kiely, Robert. *The Romantic Novel in England*. Cambridge, MA: Harvard UP, 1972.

Kovačević, Ivanka. *Fact into Fiction: English Literature and the Industrial Scene, 1750-1850*. Leicester: Leicester UP; Atlantic Highlands, NJ: Humanities Press, 1975.

———. "William Godwin, The Factory Children and Dickens's *David Copperfield.*" *Filoloski pregled*, III-IV (Beograd, 1970): 29-43.

Locke, Don. *Fantasy of Reason: The Life and Thought of William Godwin*. London: Routledge and Kegan Paul, 1980.

Marshall, Peter H. *William Godwin*. New Haven: Yale UP, 1984.

Palacio, Jean De. *William Godwin et son monde intérieur*. Lille, 1980.

Pollin, Burton R. *Education and Enlightenment in the Works of William Godwin*. New York: Las Americas Publishing Co., 1962.

———. *Godwin Criticism, A Synoptic Bibliography*. Toronto: U of Toronto P, 1967.

———. "The Significance of Names in the Fiction of William Godwin." *Revue des Langues Vivantes* 37 (1971): 388-99.

Rajan, Tilottama. "Mary Shelley's *Mathilda*: Melancholy and the Political Economy of Romanticism." *Studies in the Novel* 26. 2 (1994): 43-68.

Scheuermann, Mona. "The Study of Mind: The Later Novels of William Godwin." *Forum for Modern Language Studies* 1 (1983): 16-30.

Shore, Elizabeth M. "Godwin's *Fleetwood* and the Hero of Meredith's *The Amazing Marriage.*" *English Studies in Canada* 8 (1982): 38-48.

St. Clair, William. *The Godwins and the Shelleys: A Biography of a Family*. New York: W.W. Norton, 1989; Baltimore: Johns Hopkins UP, 1991.

Thorslev, Peter L., Jr. *The Byronic Hero: Types and Prototypes*. Minneapolis: U of Minnesota P, 1962.

Tysdahl, B. J. *William Godwin as Novelist*. London: Athlone Press, 1981.